AT WAR'S END
A Mystery Guild Omnibus

By Anne Perry

FEATURING WILLIAM MONK

The Face of a Stranger
A Dangerous Mourning
Defend and Betray
A Sudden, Fearful Death
The Sins of the Wolf
Cain His Brother
Weighed in the Balance

The Silent Cry
A Breach of Promise
The Twisted Root
Slaves of Obsession
Funeral in Blue
Death of a Stranger
The Shifting Tide

FEATURING THOMAS AND CHARLOTTE PITT

The Cater Street Hangman
Callander Square
Paragon Walk
Resurrection Row
Bluegate Fields
Rutland Place
Death in the Devil's Acre
Cardington Crescent
Silence in Hanover Close
Bethlehem Road
Highgate Rise
Belgrave Square

Farriers' Lane
The Hyde Park Headsman
Traitors Gate
Pentecost Alley
Ashworth Hall
Brunswick Gardens
Bedford Square
Half Moon Street
The Whitechapel Conspiracy
Southampton Row
Seven Dials
Long Spoon Lane

THE WORLD WAR I NOVELS

No Graves As Yet
Angels in the Gloom
Shoulder the Sky

At Some Disputed Barricade
We Shall Not Sleep

THE CHRISTMAS NOVELS

A Christmas Journey
A Christmas Guest

A Christmas Visitor
A Christmas Secret

At War's End

AT SOME DISPUTED BARRICADE

WE SHALL NOT SLEEP

by
ANNE PERRY

BALLANTINE BOOKS · NEW YORK

AT SOME DISPUTED BARRICADE
Copyright © 2007 by Anne Perry

WE SHALL NOT SLEEP
Copyright © 2007 by Anne Perry

All rights reserved.

ISBN 978-0-7394-8041-0

Manufactured in the United States of America

At Some Disputed Barricade

To my brother, Jonathan,

army surgeon

ONE

*T*he sun was sinking low over the waste of no-man's-land when Barshey Gee staggered up the trench, his arms flying, his boots clattering on the duckboards. His face was ashen and streaked with mud and sweat.

"Chaplain! Snowy's gone!" he cried, bumping into the earthen wall and stopping in front of Joseph. "Oi think he's gone over the top!" His voice was hoarse with helplessness and despair.

That morning Snowy Nunn had seen his elder brother sawn in half by machine-gun fire in yet another pointless attack. It was now late July 1917, and this mid-Cambridgeshire regiment had been bogged down on this same stretch of ruined land between Ypres and Passchendaele since the beginning, those far-off days of courage and hope when they had imagined it would all be over by Christmas.

Now mutilation and death were everyday occurrences. The earth stank of three years' worth of latrines, poison gas, and corpses. But it was still different to see the brother you had grown up with reduced to bleeding jelly in front of your eyes. At first Snowy had been too stunned to do anything, as if the sheer horror of it had paralyzed him.

"I think he's gone over," Barshey repeated. "He's lost it. He's gone to kill the whole German army himself. They'll just wipe him out." He gulped.

"We'll get him back," Joseph said with far more certainty than he felt. "He might have been taken back to the first aid post. Have you—"

"Oi looked," Barshey interrupted him. "And in the cookhouse, and Oi looked in all the dugouts and the holes big enough for anyone to crawl in. He's gone over the top, Captain Reavley."

Joseph's stomach clenched. It was pointless to cling to hope they both knew was futile. "You go north, I'll go south," he said briefly. "But be careful! Don't get yourself killed for nothing!"

Barshey gave a bark of laughter so harsh it was almost a sob, and turned away. Joseph started in the opposite direction, south and west toward the place where a man could most easily go over the parapet and find the shelter of what was left of the trees—shell-torn, blackened, and mostly leafless, even now in full summer.

" 'Evenin', Chaplain," the sentry said quietly from his position on the fire step, peering forward into the gathering gloom. The German guns were rumbling sullenly, starting the night's barrage, flashes from their muzzles red. The British answered. There were Canadian and Australian regiments up in this section, too.

"Evening," Joseph answered. "Seen Snowy Nunn?" He had too little time left to afford discretion. Grief had shattered all sense of self-preservation. Of course Snowy had seen men killed before: burned, drowned, gassed, frozen, or blown to pieces, some caught on the wire and riddled with bullets. But when it was your own brother, there was something that tore you in an inner way that nothing else could reach. Tucky had been his childhood friend and protector, the companion in his first adventures, the one who first told him daring jokes, the one who had stood up for him in the school playground. It was as if half his own life had been destroyed obscenely right in front of him.

Joseph had seen Snowy's face, and known that when the first numbing shock wore off his emotion would turn to rage. He had just expected it to take longer.

"Have you seen him?" he asked the sentry again, this time more sharply.

"Don't know, Captain Reavley," the sentry answered. "Oi bin watching forward."

"He hasn't done anything," Joseph said, clenching his teeth to keep control of the helplessness rising inside him. "I want to get to him before he does!" He knew what the man was protecting. Joseph was an officer and a priest, tied to the command by both rank and conviction. There were whispers that men in the French army had already mutinied, said they would hold their positions but would not launch any attack. They had demanded improved rations and whatever humanity of treatment was possible in this universal misery. Thousands had been charged, and over four hundred had been sentenced to death, but so far apparently very few had actually faced the firing squad.

In the British Army the losses had been equally appalling. Men were exhausted and morale was low, but as yet no mutiny. Now there was talk of another push forward against the German lines and there was no heart left for it. Everyone had seen too many friends dead or crippled to gain a few yards of clay, and nothing had changed, except the numbers of the dead. The sentry's sympathies were with the men, and he was afraid.

"Please!" Joseph said urgently. "His brother was killed and he's in a bad way. I need to find him."

"And tell him what?" the sentry said raspingly, turning at last to face Joseph. "That there's a God up there who loves us and it'll turn out all right in the end?" His voice was raw with misery.

Joseph had not expressed that sentiment in a long time. Certainly such words were no help. Young men of nineteen or twenty who had been sent out to die, in a hell those at home could not even imagine, did not want to be told by a priest almost twice their age, who had at least had a chance at life, that God loved them in spite of every evidence to the contrary.

"I just want to prevent him from doing something stupid before he's had time to think," he said aloud. "I know his mother. I'd like to get one son back to her."

The sentry did not answer. He turned back to face over the parapet again. The sky was fading into a soft, bright peach trailed across by a wisp of scarlet cloud, still burning in the sun. There were a few naked trees in Railway Wood to the west, silhouetted black against the hot color, more ahead over the German lines beyond Glencorse and Polygon Woods. That was the direction toward which they'd mount the attack.

"Oi don't know," the sentry said at last. "But you could troy Zoave Wood." He jerked his hand to the right. "There's one or two decent places over there you could sit boi yourself. If that was what you wanted."

"Thank you." Joseph moved on quickly. Ahead of him he heard rats' feet scraping along the boards. The trenches were full of them, millions scavenging among the unburied dead. Men went out at night, Joseph often among them, and brought back the bodies, the living first, then what dead they could.

He passed the dugouts off to the side where stretchers and extra first aid supplies were kept, although each man was supposed to carry with him at least the basics to stanch a wound. It was getting dark and occasionally star shells burst above, briefly lighting the mud with a yellow-white glare, leaving men in momentary blindness afterward.

He still did not know what he was going to say to Snowy when he found him. Perhaps there was nothing more he could do than be there, sit with him in the long agonized silence. Snowy probably would not ask him the impossible questions. He had ceased to imagine there were any answers, and certainly none that Joseph knew. Snowy was over twenty, a veteran. Most of these boys coming out now had been taken from the schoolroom.

When they were broken and dying, it was their mothers they called for, not God. Out here what was there to say to God? Joseph was not sure how many people believed in such a being anymore, or thought that if He was there, then He was just as helpless as everyone else.

The trench walls were deep here, the sides firmly riveted with wood.

He passed a couple of men squatting on their heels over a Dixie can of tea.

"Seen Snowy Nunn?" he asked, stopping beside them.

One lifted a pale face, smeared with mud, a long scar across his cheek. Joseph recognized him as Nobby. "Sorry, Cap'n, not lately, poor sod. Tucky were a good chap." There was no horror in his voice and his eyes stared beyond Joseph into a distance no one else could see.

"Thanks, Nobby," Joseph acknowledged, and moved on quickly. There were more sentries, a group of men telling tall stories to each other and laughing. Somebody was singing a music hall song with risqué alterations to the words.

Joseph passed an officers' dugout, its entrance down steep steps. It was narrow as a tomb, but at least it was safe from sniper fire, and in the winter as warm as anyone could be in the frozen earth. He emerged from the confining walls of the trench into Zoave Wood. Most of the trees here were blasted or burned, but a few still had leaves. Beneath them the earth that normally was covered with undergrowth was trampled flat. The front line passed right through what was left of the wood.

He stood close to the trunk of the nearest tree and felt its rough bark against his back. If Snowy was here in these few acres behind the line it was just a matter of walking quietly, crisscrossing it like a gamekeeper looking for a poacher. Except that Snowy would probably be motionless in his grief, alone, growing cold even in this summer night because he was exhausted not in body but in heart. Perhaps he was consumed by that terrible, inexplicable guilt that survivors feel when for no reason at all they live on after those they loved have died.

Joseph started to walk, placing his feet softly on the bare ground. The wind stirred in the few remaining leaves, and shadows flickered, but he could hear nothing else above the noise of the guns. It was a warm night and the stench of the dead mixed with that of the latrines was thick in his throat, although these days he hardly noticed it. It was there all the time. You had to get right away from the lines, into one of the towns, perhaps in an estaminet, and smell cheese and wine and sweat before you lost it. Fortunately there was opportunity for this in places like Poperinghe or Armentières and the small villages within a few miles.

Something moved to his right. It must be a soldier. There were no animals left, and even birds would not come this close to the lines. He turned toward the figure and walked zigzag from tree to tree. It was a while before he saw the movement again. It was not Snowy. The man was too tall.

The sky was completely dark now, the only light emanating from gun flashes and star flares. They made the trees black and filled the spaces between with jagged shadows as the rising wind swayed them to and fro. The summer heat could not last. Soon there would be rain, maybe a thunderstorm. It would clear the air.

He almost stumbled on them: five men sitting in a slight hollow, facing each other and talking, all of them dragging on cigarettes, the brief glow marking their positions and momentarily showing a cheek or the outline of a nose and brow. At first he could not hear the words, but at least one of the low, emotion-charged voices was familiar: It was Edgar Morel, one of his own students from Cambridge days.

Joseph dropped down to his hands and knees to be less obvious, and crept forward soundlessly, keeping his movement steady so he didn't catch anyone's eye.

Morel drew on his cigarette again. The burning tobacco glowed red, showing his gaunt features and wide, dark eyes. He was speaking urgently and the anger in him was clear in the rigid lines of his shoulders and chest as he leaned forward. His captain's insignia gleamed for a moment, then the darkness returned and the smoke he blew out was almost invisible. Joseph could smell it more than see it.

"They're going to send us over the top again, toward Passchendaele," Morel said harshly. "Thousands of us—not just us but Canadians, French, and Aussies, too. It's all just as bloody hopeless as it's always been. Jerry'll pick us off by the hundreds. It'll wipe us out. There's almost nothing left of us already."

"They're all barking mad!" Geddes said bitterly. He was a lance corporal with a long, thin face. The hand holding his cigarette was shaking. It could have been nerves, or shell shock.

Somebody else lit another and passed it across. The man who took it thanked him and took a long drag, then coughed. Joseph stiffened, his stomach knotting. It was Snowy Nunn. He could not see the white blond hair under his helmet, but he recognized his voice.

"They've bin saying all summer that we're going," the fourth man said wearily. "Can't make up their bloody minds. But when did they ever know their arse from their elbow anyhow?"

"The twenty-first of March, loike clockwork," Snowy said quietly. "First day of spring, an' over we go. They must think Jerry doesn't have a calendar or something." He took in a deep, rasping breath, his eyes filled with tears. "What for? What's the point?" He stopped, his voice choking off.

The man next to him reached out and put a hand on his shoulder. "The question is, what are we going to do about it?" Morel looked from one to the other of them, his expression unreadable in the darkness, except for his mouth, an angry line in the glow of his cigarette. "Are you willing to be driven over the top to get slaughtered for no bloody reason? The French aren't, God help them."

There was a bark of laughter. "You reckon it's better to be tried and shot by your own? You're just as dead, and your family's got to live with the shame."

"It's show," Morel argued. "The French aren't going to shoot more than a dozen or two. But that isn't the point." He leaned forward, his body no more than a deeper shadow in the gloom. He spoke with intense earnestness. "Jerry's a hell of a lot better prepared for us than we thought."

"How d'you know that?" Geddes demanded. "What makes you God Almighty? Not that I've got any time for generals, or anybody else who thinks he's better than his neighbor 'cos he was born with a silver spoon in his mouth."

"Because I was questioning a prisoner a couple of days ago," Morel answered sharply. "The Germans know we're coming."

"I forgot you speak bloody kraut," Geddes said angrily. "Is that what you went to Cambridge for?"

A voice in the darkness told him to shut up.

"The point is, I do," Morel answered.

"The point is, did you tell anyone?" one of the others asked. "Like Penhaligon, for example."

"Of course I did!" Morel spat. "And he passed it on up. But they don't want to know. Most of us are going to die anyway," he went on urgently. "I'd rather go for a cause I believe in than be sent over the top because some damn fool general can't think of anything except the same futile slaughter, year after year, no matter what the intelligence tells him. We're no closer to winning than we were in 1914. I'm not sure that the Germans are our real enemies. Are you? You've fought opposite them for the last three years, captured some of them. I'm not the only one who's talked to them. Our sappers have been in tunnels so close under their lines they can hear them talking at night. What about? Killing us? No, they aren't! Ask any of the sappers, they'll tell you they talk about their homes, their families, what they want to do after the war, if they live through it. They talk about friends, who's been killed or wounded, how hungry they are, how cold, how damn wet! They make rotten jokes just like ours. And they sing, mostly sad songs."

No one argued.

"I don't hate them," Morel went on. "If I had the choice, I'd let them all go back to the towns and villages where they belong. I hate the bastards that sent them. What if we copied the French, and told the generals to fight their own bloody war!"

There was a stunned silence.

"You can't do that," Snowy said at last. "It's mutiny."

"Afraid of being shot?" Geddes asked sarcastically. "Then you're in the wrong place, son. An' you know that as well as I do."

Snowy did not answer. He sat without moving, his head bent.

"I'll fight for what I believe in," Morel went on. "It isn't this senseless death. The land stinks of it! The best men of our generation are sacrificed for nothing! The generals commanding this farce haven't any more idea of what they're doing than their poor bloody horses have! Somebody's got to stop it while there's still anyone alive to care."

Joseph was sick at heart, and his legs were cramped where he was crouching to the earth. He had felt the anger in the men for months, the growing helplessness since last summer, but still he had not expected anything so overt, not from a man like Morel. He had known him since 1913 when Joseph had first come back home to Cambridge after his wife's death. The loss of Eleanor had left him too crippled in faith to lead a parish anymore. He had retreated into teaching. The theory in academic study of biblical languages was so much easier than trying to face the crises of love and faith, doubt, loss and disillusion that were part of the practice of religion.

He moved his leg, kneading the muscle to get rid of the pain. He should have realized that if anyone finally rebelled against the slaughter it would be Morel. Joseph's job had been to try to teach eager, intelligent young men such as he to think for themselves! University was only partly about acquiring knowledge. Mostly it was about learning how to use the mind, refine the processes of thought.

He felt the steel against his cheek, cold as ice. He froze. Somehow the Germans had gotten a raiding party through the lines. Then he realized that if that were true, the men smoking a few yards from him would have been the first to be seen. He relaxed and tried to turn and see who it was, but the pressure increased.

Morel stood up and came toward him. He stopped about five feet away and struck a match. It flared for only a moment before the breeze blew it out, but long enough for him to recognize Joseph.

"What are you doing here, Captain Reavley?" he said coldly.

The rifle barrel moved away from his cheek, now that the man holding it knew who he was, and Joseph rose to his feet also, easing his aching muscles. It was strange how in the broken woods, earth bare even in high summer, they faced each other like strangers. All memory of being master and pupil had vanished.

There was no corresponding ease in Morel's stance. His face was almost invisible. It raced through Joseph's mind to behave as if he had heard nothing of their talk of mutiny, but he knew Morel would not believe him. Even were it true, he could not afford to take the risk.

"Captain Reavley?" Morel repeated, his voice harder.

"I was looking for Snowy Nunn," Joseph replied. He outranked Morel and he was several years older, but he was a noncombatant, a chaplain rather than a fighting soldier. And perhaps out here in the woods, without a gun, that was irrelevant anyway. If Morel was really thinking about mutiny then all discipline and respect for rank were already gone. Would he shoot a chaplain, a man he had known for years?

Death was all around them, hundreds of men, sometimes even thousands every day. What did one more matter? Unless it was your brother— like Tucky Nunn? Then it ate inside you with a grief almost like madness, as if your own life were being torn apart. Friendship was the only sanity left.

"I know he came out this way," Joseph went on.

"Come to say a prayer?" Morel asked sarcastically, his voice shaking a little now. "Don't waste your time, Captain. God's gone home; the Devil is master here. Don't bother telling Snowy that. He knows."

"Don't decide for me what I am going to say, Morel," Joseph responded curtly. "That is arrogant and offensive."

A star shell went up and burst with a brief flare, showing the slight surprise on Morel's face, and then the anger. "And you were just—" The rest of whatever Morel said was lost in the roar of gunfire less than fifty yards away. The light died and they were in darkness again.

Joseph made up his mind quickly. "Are you planning mutiny, Morel?"

"So you heard!" Morel said bitterly. "I think you'd have left me some doubt. That wasn't very clever, Chaplain. I should have realized that when it came to it, you were just as stupid as the rest. I used to admire you so much." There was a regret in him now, a loss so deep it was as if all the world he had loved had finally slipped from his grasp, the very last vestige gone in this ultimate disillusion.

"You called me *chaplain*," Joseph reminded him. "Had you forgotten I am a priest? What you tell me in confidence I cannot repeat to anyone at all." He breathed in and out quickly. "Let's see how stupid you are, Morel."

Snowy had stood up as well, but he did not move. He was facing toward them although it was impossible to tell how clearly he could see them.

"Not stupid enough to trust one chaplain with a loyal conscience and not enough brains to see that this is just a futile slaughter now." Morel's voice was sharp with emotion. "We won't win, we'll die for nothing. Well, I won't! I care, Chaplain, whether you do or not! I won't see these men sacrificed on the altar of some idiot general's vanity. I don't believe in God. If He existed, He would put a stop to this. It's obscene!" He spat the word as if it were filth on his lips. "But I care about my men, not just the Cambridgeshires, but all of them. We've already lost Lanty and Bibby Nunn, Plugger Arnold, Doughy Ward, Chicken Hagger, Charlie Gee, Reg, and Arthur." His voice dropped. "And Nigel. The only good I know of is to be sane, not to kill and not to be killed."

"That would be best," Joseph agreed, struggling to keep himself steady. Morel had named all the men from his own village deliberately. "But that's not on offer right now," he said. "Your choice is whether to trust me and let me walk away, or shoot me, and then shoot all the others who saw you do it. Is that what you want for them?"

"I won't shoot them!" Morel said derisively. "They're in it just as much as I am."

"Oi in't," Snowy said from close to Morel's back. "Not if you shoot Captain Reavley, Oi'm not. That's murder."

Joseph waited. There was a lull in the gunfire and he could hear the wind sighing in the branches. Then the crackle of machine guns burst out again and the deeper roar of the heavier shells from far behind the lines. One exploded five hundred yards away, sending the earth flying forty feet into the air.

"Some poor bastard's got it," Morel said quietly. "Aussies along that way. I like the Aussies. They don't take damn stupid orders from anybody. Did you hear about them striking up their band every time the sergeant told our boys to drill in the sun, just to keep them busy? The Aussies couldn't play 'God Save the King' to save themselves, but they made such a row banging and squealing on every instrument there is that the sergeant had to give up. I hope that's true."

"Yes, I heard," Joseph answered. He smiled with a bitter grief in the darkness, but no one saw him.

"Is it true?" Morel asked.

"Yes." He had no idea, but he wanted it to be, not only for himself but for all of them. He looked at Snowy, who had moved a step closer.

Morel was still hesitating. Should Joseph take the risk of moving to ease his limbs? One of the other men, indistinguishable in the dark, had his rifle in his hands, pointed loosely toward Joseph.

Snowy turned to him. "Goin' to shoot me, too, are you? What for? Going over, or not going over? Or you just want to shoot someone, an'

Oi'm an easy target what won't shoot back? 'Cos I won't. Not at me own mates."

"Get out!" Morel said sharply. "Get out, Reavley, and take Nunn with you."

Joseph grabbed Snowy by the arm and, almost pulling him off his feet, set out as fast as he could over the rough ground, snarled with tree roots, back toward the trench again and the cover of its walls.

"Thank you," he said when they were finally safe below the parapet.

There was no life in Snowy's voice. "Couldn't let 'em shoot you," he said flatly. "Moi fault you were out there."

"Just came to see if you wanted company."

"Oi know," Snowy replied. "Oi seen you do it for hundreds of other men. There in't nothing you can say. Tucky's gone. Reckon we'll all be gone in another month or two anyway. Good night, Chaplain." And without waiting to see what Joseph might say, he turned and walked down the connecting trench toward the supply lines, keeping his balance on the duckboards with the ease of long practice.

It was a fairly quiet night, just the usual sporadic shelling and occasional machine-gun fire. Joseph never forgot the snipers and as the summer dawn came early, he kept his head well below the parapet in the forward trenches.

Fresh water and rations came up and the men stood to. There were all the usual drills, inspections, cleaning of kit, patching up of walls breached during the night. It was still hot and the lice were making men scratch their skins raw.

The mail came, and those with letters sat in the sun with their backs to the clay walls and read. For a few moments they were in another world. Fred Arnold, the blacksmith's son from St. Giles, roared with laughter at a joke and turned to Barshey Gee next to him to pass it on. They were friends. Both had lost their brothers here, in this regiment.

There were other brothers as well, Cully and Whoopy Teversham. At home their family had a long and bitter feud with the Nunns over a piece of land. Out here it was all absurdly irrelevant.

Tiddly Wop Andrews, good looking but painfully shy, was reading a letter for the third time, blue eyes misty. It must be a love letter at last. Perhaps he could write what he could not say aloud. Joseph had tried many times to help him put his feelings into words, but of course he would not say so now. The men teased each other mercilessly, perhaps to break the tension of waiting for the next burst of violence.

Punch Fuller was sitting with his back to the clay wall and his face up to the sun. He would get his large nose burned if he was not careful. Joseph told him so.

"Yes, sir, Captain," Punch said, and took no notice at all. He had long learned to ignore remarks about his most prominent feature. He closed his eyes and continued to make up even bawdier verses for "Mademoiselle from Armentières" than the classic ones, trying them out to himself in a surprisingly musical voice.

Joseph came to the end of the connecting trench and walked toward his dugout. Officers had a little privacy, cramped but comparatively safe under the ground. Gas was the worst threat because it was heavy and sank into any crater or hole. But it was unlikely to land this far back.

Just before he reached his dugout he met Major Penhaligon, his immediate commander. Penhaligon was about thirty, eight years younger than Joseph, but today he looked harassed and hollow-eyed. He had cut his cheek shaving and not had time to deal with it. A smear of dried blood marked his skin.

"Ah, Reavley," he said, stepping in front of Joseph. "How's Snowy Nunn? Did you see him? That was too bad. Tucky was one of the best."

Tucky's cheerful face was as clear in Joseph's mind as it must have been in Snowy's. They were alike, with blunt features and fair hair, but Tucky had had the confidence, the brash good humor, always ready to seize a chance for anything. He had been wiser than some men thought him, steadier in a crisis. He had helped Joseph more than once with a word of advice, a well-timed joke, an earthy sanity that reminded men of home, laughter, the things that were worth loving.

"Yes, sir," Joseph replied. Death was death. It should not be harder for one than another, but it was. "Snowy's taking it badly."

Penhaligon had no idea what to say, and it showed in his eyes. He felt it his duty to try; both brothers were his men. He struggled through the weariness and the knowledge of the campaign ahead of them for something to say that would help.

It was Joseph's job to break the news of loss to people, and think of a way to make it endurable when they would never really get over it, without unintentionally sounding as if he neither understood nor cared. It was his job to steady the panic, create courage out of terror, help men believe there was a purpose to all of this when none of them had any idea if there really was. He had no right to leave it to Penhaligon.

"I talked to him," he said. "He'll be all right. Give him a little while, but . . . keep him busy." Should he say more, ask Penhaligon to give Snowy some duty that would guard him from Morel's path?

"We'll all be busy soon enough," Penhaligon said with a twist of his mouth. "There's going to be a pretty big push forward, starting in a day or so."

"They've been saying that ever since the spring," Joseph replied truthfully.

"Mean it this time," Penhaligon told him, his eyes steady, trying to see if Joseph understood him beyond the mere words. "Afraid you'll have a lot to do."

The morning sun was hot already, but Joseph was chilled inside. He wanted to tell Penhaligon that the men were not ready, some of them not even willing anymore. He had no idea how many others there were like Morel.

Joseph became aware that Penhaligon was watching him, expecting him to speak. He wanted to warn him about Morel, but he had given his word that it ranked as a confession and was sacred. But Penhaligon was commanding a unit with an officer in it who was trying to subvert the entire campaign. Did what Joseph had overheard amount to mutiny? Or was it still only an exaggerated example of the kind of grumbling that was everywhere? The men were exhausted, emotionally and physically—and casualties were almost uncountable. What man of any spirit at all would not question the sanity of this, and think of rebelling against a useless death?

"Chaplain?" Penhaligon prompted him. "Is there something else?"

"No, sir," Joseph said decisively. Morel had not spoken of any specific intent, simply complained of the violent senselessness of it all. Men had to be free to do that. Even if he thought of anything like refusing to obey an order, he was a Lancashire man born and bred, the Cambridgeshires would never follow him against other Englishmen. "Just thinking about what lies ahead, that's all."

Penhaligon smiled bleakly. "It'll cost us a bit, but apparently it'll be a real strategic advantage if we take Passchendaele. Damned if I know why. Just one more wretched hell, as far as I can see."

Joseph did not answer.

The advance began the next morning, July 31. Judith Reavley stood with the men eating their last hot breakfast before the ration parties returned. Her stomach, like theirs, burned with hot tea and the fire of a tot of rum. At ten minutes to four, half an hour before the summer sunrise, the whistles blew and she watched in awe and misery as almost a million men moved forward over the plowed and torn-up fields, slick with mud after the occasional drizzle of the last few days. They threw up pontoons over the canals and poured across the water and up the other side. They moved on through the few still-standing copses of trees and small woods. The noise of guns was deafening and murderous fire mowed down whole platoons, tearing them apart, gouging up the earth.

By midmorning it began to rain in earnest, and a mist descended so that even four or five hundred yards away she could see that the outline of Kitchener's Wood was no more than a smudge in the gloom.

Two hours later she was struggling to drive her ambulance over the sodden, rutted land to get it as close as she could to the makeshift first aid post to which the wounded were being carried. The road was bombed out and there was nothing but a track left. The shelling was very heavy and in the rain the mud was getting worse. The heavy clouds made it gray in spite of it being close to midday. She was afraid of being bogged down, or even tipping sideways into a crater and breaking an axle. It took all the strength she had to wrestle with the wheel and to peer through the murk to see where she was going.

Beside her was Wil Sloan, the young American who had volunteered at the beginning of the war, long before his country had joined only a matter of months ago. He had left his hometown in the Midwest and hitched a ride on the railroad to the East Coast. From there he had worked to earn his passage across the Atlantic. Once in England he had offered his time—his life, if need be—to help the troops in any way he could. He was not the only one. Judith had met several American drivers and medical orderlies like Wil, and nurses like Marie O'Day, doctors, even soldiers who had enlisted in the British Army, simply because they believed it was right.

Since January America itself had joined the Allies, but there were no American forces in this stretch of the line.

She knew there were shadows in Wil's life. His blazing temper had run out of control more than once before, and had finally forced him to leave his home. He had never told her how serious the breach had been, but he had hinted at it. Perhaps because they were close enough friends that honesty compelled him, he could not pose to her as an unblemished hero.

Now he was sitting beside her, calling out warning and encouragement alternately as they bucked and slewed over the rough ground, trying to discern through the mist and rain where to stop for the wounded.

"There!" he shouted, pointing to what looked like a level spot slightly below a rise in the slope. There was a mound of some sort, and a man standing near it, waving his arms.

"Right!" she answered, but her voice was drowned by a shell exploding fifty yards away, sending mud and earth up like a gout of water. The debris fell on them, battering the roof and sides of the ambulance and flying in, striking both of them through the open part of the front above the windshield and the door.

She kept on with her hand on the accelerator. There was nothing to gain, or lose, by stopping before they reached the post. Finally she slithered to a halt, a few yards short of the level she had been aiming for. Almost immediately a soldier was beside her, shouting something she could barely hear, and gesticulating behind him.

Wil leaped out and splashed through the mud and rain to start helping the first wounded into the back. He would take only those too badly injured to walk. They could carry five, maybe six at the most. God only knew how many there were. He could do something to stanch bleeding—pack a wound, put on a tourniquet—but that was about all. If an artery was lacerated very often a man bled to death and there was little anyone could do about it. But if a limb was torn off completely, the artery constricted and the blood loss was far less. If they could prevent him dying of shock, there was a good chance of saving him.

Now Judith kept the engine running while Wil and several other men loaded in the wounded. As soon as they gave the signal, she could turn and begin the difficult journey back to the nearest clearing station. She had already made two trips, and she would go on as long as she could, all day and all night if necessary. She did not think that far ahead. One ambulance had been blown to pieces already today, killing everyone in it, and a crater had broken both axles of another.

Wil shouted and she felt the jolt as the door was slammed shut. She moved her hand and accelerated. The wheels spun, sending mud flying. She tried again, and again, then reversed before she could get them to grip.

The journey back was a nightmare. Twice, shells exploded close enough to them to batter them with debris. Once they got stuck, and Wil and the two injured who could stand had to get out to lighten the weight. By the time they reached the clearing station, one of the wounded men was dead. Wil had done everything he could, but it was not enough.

"Shock," Wil said briefly, his face drawn under the smears of earth and blood. He shrugged. "Should be used to it," he added, as if it were self-criticism, but his voice wavered.

She smiled at him, and said nothing. They knew each other well enough that he would understand, remember the words from the countless times they had done it all before.

They went back again and again all day, breaking only long enough to eat a little bread and a tin of Maconachie's stew and hot tea out of a Dixie tin. It all tasted of oil and stale water, but they barely noticed.

By dusk, they were unloading wounded and helping to carry them into a makeshift operating theater in a tent somewhere in an open field. Everything was shrouded in rain. She could see a copse of trees about fifty yards away, but she had no idea which of the many woods it was. All that mattered was to get the men to some kind of help.

Inside the tent, medical orderlies were looking at the newcomers, trying to assess who to treat first, whose wounds could wait, and who was beyond saving anyway. The injured half-sat, half-lay, ashen faced, waiting with the terrible, hopeless patience of those who have looked at horror so often they can no longer struggle against it. They were trying to absorb the reality that their arms or legs were gone or their intestines spilling out into their blood-soaked hands.

Judith was half-carrying a man whose left leg was ripped open by shrapnel which they had bandaged as well as they could. His more important wound was his left arm, which was gone from the elbow down.

The surgeon came over to her. His coat was soaked with blood, his fair hair plastered back. His eyes were sunken and dark-ringed with exhaustion. She had worked with him countless times before.

"We've done what we can, Captain Cavan, but he was injured several hours ago," she said. "He's pretty cold and shaken up." It was a magnificent understatement, but everyone dealt in understatement; it was a matter of honor. Ask any man how he was, and he would say, "Not too bad. Be all right in a while," even if an hour later he was dead.

"Right." Cavan acknowledged her with a brief smile, a momentary warmth to the eyes, then he moved to the other side of the man and supported him over to the corner inside the tent where he could lie until they could take him onto the table. "Come on, old son," he said gently. The man was perhaps seventeen, his beard hardly grown. "We'll have you sorted in a minute or two."

"Don't worry, sir," the man responded hoarsely. "It's not too bad. Actually I can't feel it much. Leg hurts a bit." He tried to smile. "Suppose I won't be playing the violin now."

Cavan's face registered a sudden pity.

"Sorry, sir," the man apologized. "I never played it anyway. Don't like the piano much, either, but my mam made me practice."

Cavan relaxed. "I expect she'll let you off now," he said drily. "Wait there and I'll be with you in a minute." He eased the man down gently, then turned back to Judith.

She read in his eyes the struggle to conquer the emotions that wrenched at him. There was no time, and they served no purpose. The only help was practical, always practical: clean, scrub, stitch, pack a wound, find something to take the edge off the pain, ease the fear, move to the next man. There was always a next man, and the one after, and a hundred after him.

Judith turned and went back to help Wil with the next casualty.

Ten minutes later a VAD nurse with a plain, sallow face handed her a mug of tea. It was sour and oily, but it was hot and someone had been thoughtful enough to lace it with about half a shot of rum. It loosened some of the knots inside her.

Another ambulance arrived and she helped them unload it. The men were badly wounded and the driver had caught a piece of shrapnel in the shoulder.

"You can't go out there again," he said, wincing as he tried to lift his arm. "Jerry's putting up a hell of a barrage and we're too close to the front here. They'll probably have to evacuate this as it is. They'll need us for that, after they've patched up the worst. It's a bloody shambles. Thousands are dead, and God knows how many wounded."

Judith walked back into the tent and over to the table where Cavan was stitching up a lacerated arm on a soldier with dark hair.

"Another lot, sir," she said quietly. "Looks to be three bad ones, and the driver's got a shrapnel tear in his right shoulder. He says it's pretty grim out there, and Jerry's coming this way, so we'll probably get told to retreat. Do you want us to stay here and help if we have to go suddenly?"

"I've got men I can't move," he replied without looking up at her. His voice was very quiet. "We'd better see what we can do to defend ourselves. If it's only the odd raiding party we'll be all right." He tied off the last knot. "Right, soldier. That'll do. You'd better start making it back. That bandage'll hold till you get to the hospital."

The man eased himself off the table and Cavan put out his arm to steady him. "Go with MacFie over there. You can hold each other up. You'll just about make a good man between the two of you."

"Yes, sir. Thank you, sir." The man swayed, gritted his teeth and went gray-white. Then he steadied himself and, swaying a little again, made his way over to MacFie.

Cavan started with the next man. The one after that was beyond his help. Judith brought him a mug of tea. "If you survive it, it'll make a new man of you," she said wryly.

"Then you'd better get a river of it." He took the mug out of her hands gently, his fingers over hers for an instant. "We're going to need a whole new bloody army after this. God Almighty! Whose idea was this attack?"

"Haig's, I imagine," she replied.

"I'd like to get a scalpel to him sometime," he responded, pulling his mouth into an expression of disgust as he swallowed the tea. "This really is vile! What the hell do they put in it? No, don't tell me."

"I could do it with a bayonet," she replied bitterly.

"Make the tea?" he asked in surprise.

"No, sir, perform a little surgery on General Haig."

He smiled and it softened his eyes. She could glimpse the man he would have been in peacetime, at home in the green fields and quiet hills of Hertfordshire. "Good with bayonets, are you, Miss Reavley?" he asked.

"I thought all you had to do was charge, shoulders down and your weight behind it," she replied. "Isn't it enthusiasm that counts rather than accuracy?"

This time he laughed and his fingers rested gently on her arm. It was just a brief contact, almost as if he had changed his mind before he completed the movement. Only his eyes betrayed the warmth within him. "Those guns sound closer. Perhaps you'd better start getting the wounded out of here and back to the first aid posts."

"They're no closer than before, sir," she told him. She was as used to the sound of them as he was.

"That's an order, Miss Reavley."

She hesitated, wondering whether she dared defy him, or if she even wanted to. It had been the worst day's casualties she had experienced so far, even worse than the first gassings two years ago, but leaving now would look so much like running away.

"Take those men back." He still spoke sufficiently quietly that only she could hear. "Get them to the hospital now, while you can."

"Yes, sir." Reluctantly she turned, still feeling as if she were somehow deserting her duty, being less brave, less honorable than he was. She had gone only as far as the entrance flap of the tent when she heard the shots. This time there was no question that they were rifle fire and much closer than the German line. The next moment she saw them: a dozen German soldiers running toward her out of the gloom, rifles in front of them, bayonets fixed.

Wil Sloan dropped to the ground and she felt almost as if she had been hit herself. She stood frozen. A bullet tore into the canvas and she dived forward and ran to Wil, falling almost on top of him. It was idiotic to try to save him—they would all be dead in minutes—but still she grasped his shoulders to turn him over, needing to see where he was hit.

"Get off me, you fool!" he growled. "I need to get the gun up!"

She wanted to slap him out of sheer relief. "What gun?" she demanded furiously. "If you've got a gun, don't bloody lie there, shoot someone!"

"I'm trying to! Let go of me!"

She obeyed immediately and he hunched up onto his elbows and knees. There was far more gunfire now. The other ambulance driver was firing back and there were more shots from the far side beyond the tent.

"Get the ambulance started," Wil told her. "We'll get everyone out that we can. It'll be a hell of a crush, but we'll get most of them, with two vehicles. Hurry. Don't know how long we can hold them. This could be just the first of bloody thousands!"

She obeyed and, bending low, ran back to the tent. Half the wounded were gone already. All those who could stand had rifles. Cavan was at the operating table, still working. A man lay on it bleeding heavily, his belly ripped open. The anesthetist held the ether, but he was shaking so badly the mask seemed to jiggle in his hand.

"You've got to get out!" Judith shouted at them. "We've got two ambulances. We'll get everyone in. Just hurry! There are at least a dozen Germans broken through and only five or six of us with guns. We can't hold them off much longer."

Cavan did not look up from his work of stitching. "We can't go yet, Miss Reavley," he said steadily. "If I leave this man, he'll die. So will the others who have just been operated on. The journey under fire will tear their sutures open. Tell the men to stand fast. Then come back and help me. I'm afraid my orderly is dead."

It was only then that Judith noticed the body on the floor. When she had turned to go outside five minutes ago he had been assisting Cavan. The bullets that had torn through the canvas had struck him in the chest.

"Be quick," Cavan added. "I need you back here. I can't keep on much longer without help."

"Yes, sir." She swiveled and went out, almost bumping into a lance corporal with a heavily bandaged leg. He was kneeling against a packing case firing round after round at the raiding party. One moment they were visible through the drifting rain only by the flicker of their rifle fire, then suddenly the wind gusted and they could see them clearly, more than a dozen of them pressing forward.

"Captain Cavan says to stand fast," she said loudly. "Tell the ambulance drivers we've got to fight."

He looked at her incredulously, his face slack with disbelief.

"You heard me, Corporal," she replied. "We've got wounded men to defend."

He swore under his breath, but he did not argue. "You'll 'ave ter tell 'em yerself, miss. Oi can't move. Oi don't mean Oi won't. Oi can't!"

"Sorry," she apologized, and bending low again she scrambled over to Wil and repeated Cavan's order to him.

"*Stand fast?*" he repeated incredulously. "You English!" He aimed the rifle again. "Remember the Alamo!" he shouted, and fired. In the distance someone fell.

She gave him a pat on the shoulder and went back to the tent to help Cavan. She knew enough about field surgery to pass him the implements he asked for, even though she could not keep her hands steady. When she tried to thread the needle for him it was hopeless.

"Hold this," he ordered, indicating the surgical clamp in his hand buried deep in the abdominal wound.

She took it and it slipped off the flesh, blood spurting up hot, catching her across the face. She had never been more ashamed of her inadequacy.

Cavan took the clamp from her and grasped the flesh again.

"Swab it," he commanded.

She prayed under her breath and cursed herself. She tried to still her breathing, control her muscles. She must not be so stupid, so ineffectual. This was a man's life she was holding. Her fingers steadied at last. She mopped up the blood, then threaded the needle and passed it to him.

He glanced upward and met her eyes. His look was warm for an instant, then he took the needle. She reached for the clamp.

The gunfire started again, louder and more rapid than before, volley after volley. It sounded as if it was just outside the tent flap. Cavan did not hesitate in his slow, steady work. "Keep swabbing," he told her. "I need to see what I'm doing."

A spray of bullets shredded the tent wall and the anesthetist collapsed silently, buckling to his knees, then sliding forward, his back scarlet. Through the ragged tear stepped a German soldier, rifle pointing at Cavan. Behind him were two more, their weapons pointing at Judith also.

"Stop!" the leader said clearly in almost unaccented English.

"If I do, he'll bleed to death," Cavan replied without looking up, his hands still working. "Swab, please, Miss Reavley."

Imagining the bullets crashing into her, bringing instant white-hot death, Judith obeyed, soaking up the blood within the wound.

"Stop!" the German repeated, speaking to Cavan, not Judith.

"I have two more men to operate on," Cavan replied. "Then we will withdraw."

There was more rifle fire outside. Someone cried out. The German turned away.

Cavan went on stitching. He was almost finished. The bleeding was contained.

The German looked back. "Now you stop."

The tent flap opened and one of the wounded men stood there. He was swaying slightly, blood streaming down his tunic where his left arm should be, a revolver in his right hand. He raised it and shot the first German soldier through the head. The other two fired at him at the same moment, hurling him back against the canvas. He was dead before he touched the tent wall, and slithered to the floor.

Cavan swung round and dived toward him, hands outstretched.

"It's useless!" Judith shouted at him. One of the other soldiers raised his gun to aim at Cavan. She reached for the instrument tray, picked up a scalpel and drove it into the man's neck. His bullet went through the ceiling.

Cavan was half on top of the dead soldier on the floor. He knew he could do nothing for him. It was his gun he was after. He rolled over, covered in blood, and shot the third soldier through the head.

The second one, gasping and spewing blood from his neck wound, staggered back through the tent the way he had come.

The gunfire outside never ceased.

"We have two more wounded we might save." Cavan clambered to his feet, shaking, his face white.

"Only one now," Judith corrected him. "Can...can we hold them off?"

"Of course we can," he replied, his breath ragged, swaying a little. "But we've lost a scalpel."

Joseph heard about it in the morning, standing in the wreckage of the forward trench, the parapet collapsed, mud up to their knees.

"It's about the only good thing, Captain Reavley," Barshey Gee said to him grimly as they stopped working on rebuilding the trench walls for a moment. "He's some doc, eh, Cavan? There he was, cool as a cucumber, stitching away like there were nothing going on! An' your sister with him. An' that Yank ambulance driver, too." Barshey was a tall man with thick hair. Before the war he had been slender; now he was gaunt and looked years older than twenty-four. "Got 'em out, they did. Didn't leave a single live one behind."

Joseph felt a wave of gratitude that Judith was still alive. It was so powerful he smiled fatuously in spite of his effort not to. He forced himself not to think about her most of the time. Everyone had friends, brothers, someone to lose. It would cripple one to think of it too much.

"I'm afraid Major Penhaligon's dead, sir," Barshey went on. "Pretty well half the brigade dead or wounded. The Canadians and the Aussies got it hard, too. Word is we could have lost around fifty thousand men...." His voice choked, words useless.

"This summer?" Joseph said. It was worse than he had thought.

"No, sir," Barshey said hoarsely, the tears running down his cheeks. "Yesterday, sir."

Joseph was numb. It could not be. He drew in his breath to say "Oh God," but it died on his lips.

The battle of Passchendaele raged on and the rain continued, soaking the ground until it oozed mud and slime and the men staggered and sank in it.

On August 2, Major Howard Northrup arrived to replace Penhaligon. He was a slight man, stiffly upright with wide blue eyes and a precise manner.

"We've a hard job ahead of us, Captain Reavley," he said when Joseph reported to him in his dugout. He did not invite Joseph to sit, even though he was obliged to bend because of the low ceiling.

"It's your job to keep up morale," Northrup went on. He appeared to be about twenty-five and wore his authority heavily. "Keep the men busy. Obedience must be absolute. Loyalty and obedience are the measure of a good soldier."

"Our losses have been very heavy, sir," Joseph pointed out. "Every man out there has lost friends. . . ."

"That is what war is about, Captain," Northrup cut across him. "This is a good brigade. Don't let the standard down, Chaplain."

Joseph's temper flared. He had difficulty not shouting at the man. "I know it is a good brigade, sir," he said between his teeth. "I've been with them since 1914."

Northrup flushed. "You are a chaplain, Captain Reavley, a noncombatant officer. Morale is your job, not tactics. I don't wish to have to remind you of that again, or in front of the men, but I will do so if you make it necessary by questioning my orders. Thank you for your report. You are dismissed."

Joseph saluted, then turned and went out, blind with fury.

TWO

"*M*r. Corracher, sir," Woodrow said, opening the door to Matthew Reavley's office and showing in a man in his early forties who was dressed formally in a dark suit. His hair was smooth and sleek, off his brow. Normally he would have been distinguished looking, but today his features were marred by anxiety.

Matthew stood up and offered his hand.

Corracher took it so briefly it was barely a touch.

"Thank you, Woodrow." Matthew excused the clerk. "Sit down, Mr. Corracher. How can I help you?" That was a euphemism. Matthew was a major in the Secret Intelligence Service and Tom Corracher a junior cabinet minister of great promise. However, now he was sweating, in spite of the fact that the room was not overly warm. He had asked for an urgent appointment with someone in charge of counterespionage in London, and since America's entry into the war in January Matthew's duties were more general than previously, when America had been neutral, and German diplomacy across the Atlantic and sabotage of American munitions supplies a more immediate concern.

Did Corracher really have anything to say, or was he one of those who jumped at shadows? Many people were. The news was bad almost everywhere. Naval losses were mounting all the time and there was no end in sight. It seemed as if every day ships were going down somewhere. Britain was blockaded and in some places rations were so short the old, the weak, and the poorest actually died of hunger.

The news from the Western Front was devastating, and only moderately better in Italy, the Balkans, the Middle East, and Egypt. In Russia the tsar's government had fallen and been taken over by the revolutionaries under Kerensky. Perhaps Corracher was merely reflecting the nation's grief? He had a reputation for courage and a degree of candor. To Matthew it looked as if he might have been overrated in both.

"What can I do for you, Mr. Corracher?" he repeated.

Corracher drew in a long breath and let it out slowly. He had the air of a man about to be sent over the top to face enemy fire. Considering the real loss of life in Passchendaele, Matthew's patience was fast dwindling.

Perhaps Corracher saw it. "I have been in Hungary recently," he began. "I am not sure if you are aware of it, but the political situation there is very volatile. Losses in the Italian Front have been critical and it looks as if there may even be revolution there also—as well as in Russia, I mean." He took a deep breath and steadied himself with an obvious effort. "I'm sorry. I am not making a great deal of sense."

Matthew did not argue.

Corracher began again. "There is more unrest in Hungary than many people are aware of. A very strong element wishes to break away from the German- and Hungarian-dominated rule by Austria and become independent. If they did so, that would radically alter the balance of power in Southeastern Europe. The whole Balkan peninsula might be persuaded to ally with Italy and strengthen it against Austrian oppression." Corracher smiled bleakly. "I see from your face that you appreciate at least some of what I am saying."

"I do," Matthew conceded. "Unfortunately that is not my area of expertise. I have been—"

"I know," Corracher cut in. "America. But if my information is correct, you have also done some subtler and more dangerous, shall I say politically complicated, work here in England." The nervousness had returned even more markedly. His body was rigid, his hands locked around each other, stiff fingered, and the sweat glistened on his face.

Matthew was aware of the silence in the room and the faint sound of footsteps beyond. Corracher was a cabinet minister, but he could still tell him nothing.

Corracher licked his lips. "There are men in this country, highly placed, who did not wish us to go to war against Germany, and do not now wish us to win. They do not wish us to lose, of course, but would rather we made an even-handed peace." He was watching Matthew intently.

Matthew knew that far better than Corracher possibly could have. His own parents had been murdered in 1914 in order to regain a copy of the proposed treaty between King George and the Kaiser that his father had found and taken. It would have allied Britain with Germany in an empire that would have dominated the western world. But he had hidden it too well, and Matthew and Joseph had found it on the eve of the outbreak of war. But John Reavley had warned them that the conspiracy ran so high that they had not dared to trust anyone. Since then the man behind it— they referred to him among themselves as the Peacemaker—had maneuvered ruthlessly to end the war, even at the cost of Britain's surrender. He had been willing to kill to achieve it, a lesser sacrifice for a greater cause. But Corracher could not know any of this.

"Indeed," Matthew said as noncommittally as he could. It was hard to keep the emotion out of his voice. The memory could be pushed to the back of his mind, but the pain was always there: his parents crushed to death in a car wreck, then Cullingford murdered in the street; last year Blaine—and all the other men sacrificed to that terrible cause.

But Matthew had identified the Peacemaker, and the Peacemaker was dead now. It was a nightmare that came back to him waking or sleeping, heavy with the knowledge of betrayal and counterbetrayal. None of it had anything to do with Corracher.

"If you have come to tell me that, Mr. Corracher, it is unnecessary," he said aloud. "We are aware of it. The most powerful man behind such a sentiment is dead. He was killed at sea, in the Battle of Jutland, last year."

None of the fear left Corracher's face; if anything, it increased. "Possibly." His voice was flat.

"I was there. There can be no doubt." Matthew remembered the German destroyer looming out of the darkness, the earsplitting sound as the huge twelve-inch naval guns on the deck of the *Cormorant* exploded, the searing fire belowdecks, magazines on fire, the stench of burning corticine, shattered glass, and smoke. Most of all he remembered Patrick Hannassey's face as he stood with the prototype of the missile guidance system in his arms and hurled it down. He had turned to leap to the German ship that had rammed them and been carried away and back again by the sea, crashing into them over and over. Matthew had lunged after Hannassey. He could not afford to let him go with the knowledge he had of their scientific failure. He had locked with him, struggled, and won. He could still see Hannassey going over the side, whirling for an instant in the air, lit by the flames of the burning ship, arms and legs flailing. Then the German destroyer had heaved up on the wave and smashed into them *Cormorant* again, crushing Hannassey like a fly.

Corracher was staring at him, eyes wide. "Oh . . ." he gulped. "Then he . . . he can't have been alone in the cause."

Matthew's emotions were too raw with the memory for him to argue. Hannassey was the only man he had ever killed with his own hands, but it was the knowledge of what happened to Detta that wounded him. She was the Peacemaker's daughter. Of course long before he knew that, he had known she was an Irish Nationalist, just as she had known he was in British Intelligence. They had used each other. That did not stop him from loving her, or feeling the pain twist in his gut because he had beaten her at the game of betrayal. Her own people had crippled her in punishment for losing. Beautiful Detta—who had walked with such dark and subtle grace.

"Exactly what is it you want to tell me, Mr. Corracher?" Pain was jagged in his voice. "There have always been traitors and profiteers. Unless you come about someone of whose acts you have proof, there is nothing I can do. Perhaps it is a police matter rather than intelligence?"

Corracher appeared to come to some decision. The embarrassment in his face was acute, but this time he did not hesitate.

"I have worked hard and had some success in persuading the independent elements in Hungary to swing to the allied side. But they are my contacts, my mother's family, and others they knew among the Hungarian aristocracy, who trust me. But I have been a voice within the cabinet against any kind of softening or appeasement," he went on. "One of the few left." He swallowed with difficulty, as if his throat was tight. "I am about to be charged with a crime I did not commit, but the evidence against me is overwhelming. Mr. Lloyd George will have no choice but to dismiss me from office, and leave the criminal prosecution to take what course it will." His voice cracked. "It is unlikely that I will escape prison. But even with the best legal defense I can find, if I am cleared it will not remove the slur from my name, or the suspicion that I was guilty."

Matthew felt the anger grow within him. If the man really was innocent, it was appalling. "I'm sorry," he said sincerely. "How can Intelligence help you? Do you know who is behind it?"

Corracher's eyes reflected an emotional exhaustion that was crippling. "If you mean names, I have no idea," he replied. "I don't believe there is anything you can do. I'm not seeking your help, Major Reavley, I am giving you information. I am not the only person to whom this has happened. Other men with views inconvenient to some have left office for one reason or another. Kemp was killed in a zeppelin raid last autumn. Newell resigned, no real reason given. And Wheatcroft is threatened with a scandal which will destroy his life."

Suddenly Matthew's attention was total. A coldness settled inside him. In the instance of Wheatcroft, he knew exactly what Corracher was referring to; word of it had crossed Matthew's desk. Alan Wheatcroft had been accused of acts of gross indecency with another man much younger than himself. It had not been proved, and he had protested his innocence, but whether anyone believed him was almost irrelevant. When the accusation became widely disseminated, as inevitably it would, his career would be finished.

"What views did the other three have?" he asked. The belief that he knew was not sufficient.

Corracher smiled bitterly. "Kemp's sister married a Belgian. All her family was killed in the first German advance. He wants crippling reparations. Newell was something of an expert in Russian affairs. Wheatcroft is different." A flicker of puzzlement lit his eyes for a moment. "I'm not sure what interest he would be to anyone else. Maybe there's something about him I don't know."

Matthew's mind was racing. Had the Peacemaker been alive he would have seen a pattern in it, but Hannassey was dead. Matthew had seen his body crushed beyond recognition. Nothing could have survived that impact.

"Do you understand me, Major Reavley?" Corracher said quietly, leaning forward across the desk a little, his hands clenched white.

"Yes," Matthew answered, drawing his attention back. "Yes, I do, Mr. Corracher. I can look into the other cases, but tell me about yours." He was aware that it would be difficult for Corracher, and embarrassing, but he could not investigate without the facts.

Corracher was very pale and his hands were locked till the knuckles were white.

"It is extremely sordid," he said huskily. "I am actually being charged with blackmail."

Matthew was startled. "You mean someone is saying that *you* are a blackmailer? Not that you are being blackmailed . . ."

"That's right." Two spots of color stained Corracher's cheeks.

"Who is saying this?"

Corracher bit his lip. "Mrs. Wheatcroft."

"Mrs. Wheatcroft?" Matthew was incredulous. "Alan Wheatcroft's wife? For God's sake, why? Hasn't she got more than enough trouble already?"

"That's it." Corracher all but swallowed his words. "She is saying that I blackmailed Alan after creating the situation with which he was charged. He claims it never existed in reality. I set it up in order to take money from him." He stared at Matthew with desperation. "I can see how his wife would wish that that were true, but it is not. I knew nothing at all about it until the police accused me! I was as shocked as anyone."

"Do you imagine that Wheatcroft told her that?" Matthew asked. His pity for Corracher was intense, but far greater than for any one man was the threat he implied to the integrity of government and the country in general. The only way to fight it was to find the truth.

Corracher frowned, struggling with his own emotions. "I could understand his wanting to find any way of escaping the charge. He must have been desperate. Anyone would be. But why say it was me? Why not one of his closer friends, somebody more likely?"

"For example?" Matthew pressed. He loathed doing this—it was personal in the most distasteful way—but to evade it now out of squeamishness would make it worse.

Corracher looked embarrassed. "Well there are people with . . . connections to that sort of thing. I mean . . . men . . ." He tailed off miserably, as if the air in the room oppressed him.

Matthew was less delicate. "Who prefer other men rather than women," he finished for him. "But presumably are discreet about it. Yes, of course there are. You think one of them may have set up the scene, or possibly was himself blackmailed into it?"

"It seems probable," Corracher conceded.

"Any idea who?"

"No. I . . . I could give you a list of names of those whose nature I am aware of, but it seems a despicable thing to do." His face registered his disgust at the manipulation of a shared vulnerability in such a way.

"I'm only interested in finding who set up the Wheatcroft scandal and blamed you," Matthew said vehemently. "If you are right, then someone is effectively ruining both of you. They are robbing the government of the men most likely to fight for a lasting peace. One that will prevent enemy alliance with future elements in Germany which would allow the same thing to happen again. God knows, we need a just peace, but not a weak one."

"That is why I came to you, Captain Reavley," Corracher said, his eyes meeting Matthew's again. "I don't believe it is coincidental. Whoever has created the evidence that makes me look guilty has been very clever. There's no way I can fight against it without betraying other good men and raising doubts about other men's personal lives."

Matthew saw it very clearly. It was simple and supremely effective. Like a slip noose, every movement against it pulled it even tighter. "Tell me about Wheatcroft," he asked. "Exactly what is he accused of doing? Where? Who else was involved, and what part are you supposed to have played? What evidence is there, written or witnessed? Is any of it true, even the bits that merely support or contribute?"

Corracher was deeply unhappy. He began slowly, hesitating as he searched for words, too embarrassed to look up. "Wheatcroft is accused of having solicited a sexual act with a young man in a public lavatory near Hampstead Heath. He lives not far from the heath and was walking his dog, which he does regularly. He had been seen talking to the same young man at least twice within two or three hundred yards of the place a week or two earlier. He says that this man simply asked him directions and he gave them."

"Both times?" Matthew interrupted.

"Yes. It was quite late, at dusk, and he was apparently lost."

"What does the young man say?"

Corracher's face tightened. He looked up quickly, then away again. "That's the thing. He's a friend of mine, at least his father is. I've known him in a casual way most of his life. He's a bit wild. He's run up a degree of debt that he can't pay, and it would be difficult for his father to come up with that much."

"I take it he says Wheatcroft approached him?" Matthew concluded.

"Yes."

"And it couldn't be true?"

"He says I told him to say it!" Corracher's face was scarlet now, but the anger in him was painfully real.

"Give me times, dates, and names," Matthew said gently.

"There's more." Corracher's voice was husky. "Wheatcroft says I asked him for money to keep it quiet, and he paid me a hundred pounds, but when I came back for more he told me to go to hell. And that was when I told Davy Pollock—the young man in question—to report it to the police. There is a hundred pounds in my bank that I can't account for. Wheatcroft said he put it there the day after I demanded it, and he has the paying-in receipt."

"How are you supposed to have asked for it?" Matthew asked.

"In a typewritten note."

"Which I imagine he gave to the police?"

"Yes."

"Write down everything you can think of, Mr. Corracher, including where I can reach you at any time, and I'll do everything I can to expose the truth," Matthew promised.

"Thank you." Corracher seemed relieved that at last someone appeared to believe him. He rose to his feet a little unsteadily and offered his hand, then withdrew it and turned to the door. Was he afraid Matthew would decline to shake it? It was a mark of how deeply he already felt tainted by the charge.

After he had gone, Matthew read all the information, made the briefest of notes himself, then left his office to begin his inquiries.

Outside the air was close and heavy, as if waiting for thunder. The streets were quiet compared with peacetime. Petrol was scarce and expensive, and the army had first call on good horses. There was something heartbreakingly drab about the quiet women waiting in queues or patiently walking along the pavements. The omnibuses had women conductors. One passed Matthew as he waited on the curb to cross. The driver was a woman also, her hair drawn back off her face and tied behind her neck. The girls who worked in munitions factories had actually cut theirs short. It was too easy to get it caught in the machinery and literally have one's scalp torn off.

No one seemed to wear red or pink anymore, as if it were somehow indecent in the face of so much loss.

Matthew crossed the street and reached the other side, stepping up onto the pavement past a group of white-faced women, silent, each lost in her own world. There were such groups in every town and village all over Europe, waiting for the casualty lists. In some places where a whole brigade had been wiped out, every house in street after street would have the blinds half drawn and stunned, white-faced women would sit in the August heat and wonder how they were going to face tomorrow, and all the tomorrows after that.

Too much had been paid to allow this ever to happen again, anywhere, for any reason. To appease now would be to make this terrible sacrifice meaningless. That thought was not bearable.

He walked past them to the top end, caught an omnibus to Hampstead Heath, and climbed the steps to the upper deck. He sat alone, his mind turned inward.

He barely glanced at the streets he passed through. They were gray and dusty, the city trees in full leaf between the occasional stretch of fire-scarred rubble where a zeppelin had bombed.

Was it possible that Hannassey had left some legacy behind him? Matthew had never imagined that the Peacemaker worked alone, but he had believed that the Peacemaker was not only the brain of the conspiracy, but the heart and the will of it also. Was he wrong? Was there still someone with the skill to concoct a plan like this and carry it through? Had the Peacemaker designed it and left the instructions before his death?

He dismounted at Hampstead Heath and walked to the police station. With his credentials, it was not difficult to find a senior officer willing to tell him about the alleged incident, the young man involved, and his debts.

"Miserable business," Inspector Stevens said unhappily, sitting behind a desk piled with paperwork. He stirred a tin mug of tea to dissolve the sugar in it.

Matthew had declined the offer of tea.

"Could it have been a misunderstanding on Wheatcroft's part?" he asked. "Unwise, perhaps, and young Pollock jumped the gun a bit?"

"Of course it could," Stevens answered. "Pollock withdrew the complaint anyway. Said he was put up to it when he was drunk and only half knew what he was saying." His bland face registered a weariness and unutterable contempt. "Young waster should be in the army, like everyone else!" He could not disguise the bitterness and the grief in his face. For a moment it was embarrassingly naked. Matthew did not need to ask where his own son was, or if he was still all right. The answer was stifling, like the hot air in the closed room.

"Why isn't he in the army?" he asked, because he needed to know more about the boy.

Stevens shot him a look of disdain. "If someone propositioned him, it'd be the first time he bloody complained about it!" he said hoarsely.

"Obvious he was willing?" Matthew asked.

Stevens raised his eyebrows. "You mean should Wheatcroft have known what he was and kept clear? Not necessarily. He wasn't refused by the army for that. Flat feet! That's what it says on the forms. But that isn't the point. Wheatcroft said the whole incident never happened, and Pollock changed his story. Said Corracher put him up to it."

"Could that be true?"

"God knows!" Stevens replied. "I doubt it. Wheatcroft denied that Corracher tried to blackmail him at first, and then he refused to say anything at all. Seemed in a blue funk to me. Sweating like a pig and white as paper." He ran his hand over his face, rubbing it hard. "He wanted to withdraw the whole thing, let it go, but his wife was furious, determined to charge Corracher, in case it ever came up again. Prove once and for all that he was a vicious liar."

"Professional rivalry between the two men?" Matthew asked.

Stevens looked genuinely surprised. "Political? You mean for office? Never thought of that, but I don't think so."

"What do you think?"

Stevens rubbed his face again and moved his eyes to meet Matthew's. "Honestly? Ever met Mrs. Wheatcroft? Formidable woman. Beautiful as cut glass, and about as comfortable. My guess would be that Wheatcroft behaved like a fool, refused to do the honorable thing and own up to it. Took the way out by blaming Corracher, until the alternative became facing his wife over it, and her public embarrassment if it became known. If he denied it to her—and maybe quite honestly—it might have been no more than an indiscretion. Then she insisted on taking the way out offered by blaming Corracher. Or at least he didn't have the courage to deny that it was him. Poor devil!"

"Corracher?"

Stevens looked at him bleakly.

"Both of them. But it's only my guess. Could be wrong. I don't know Corracher, except by repute. And I've long ago learned that damn near anyone can surprise you—for better *or* worse."

Matthew did not press him any further. He thanked him, asked him for David Pollock's address, and went to see him. He was a handsome, rather effeminate young man. However on looking at him more closely, Matthew realized that that effect had been achieved more by allowing his hair to grow longer and wearing a loose shirt like an artist's smock than by the basic cast of his features. At first he affected a slight lisp, but as soon as he became angry he forgot it.

"Of course I didn't!" he said furiously. "It's all lies! That damn politician put me up to it. Scared me silly. Thought I was going to be accused of . . . of being a . . ." He did not finish the sentence, as though the thought were too repellent for him to speak it. "The army refused me because I have flat feet! I couldn't march if my life depended on it."

Matthew did not bother to respond. He did not know the truth of his fitness, or his honesty. Nor did he care. It was not his job to chase cowards. It was Corracher who mattered, and the possibility of the Peacemaker's plans still alive, still working their slow poison.

He did not believe Pollock, but neither could he prove him a liar. All he had achieved was to substantiate what Corracher had told him.

He left and walked back across Hampstead Heath in the late, thundery dusk. The leaves seemed to shiver in the heavy air and the breeze smelled of rain.

He turned it over in his mind. Was this plot a legacy of the Peacemaker? Or was it possible that Hannassey had been the tool, not the principal of the conspiracy? It was now a year since the Battle of Jutland, and Matthew had basked in a certain kind of peace. He had heard about the punishment of Detta and it had hollowed out a new place of pain inside him, but he had known it would come, even if not in so savage a form. He had found a degree of calm inside himself knowing that the man who had caused the death of John and Alys Reavley had finally met his own death. He was both horrified and satisfied that Hannassey's end, too, had been violent, even that Matthew himself had caused it. He had had no moral alternative but to kill him, and when he had woken in the night, sick and sweating at the memory, that knowledge had enabled him to sleep again.

And there was the infinitely larger issue of the Anglo-German alliance, which the Peacemaker had so nearly brought about, with its monstrous dishonor. Now that, too, was laid to rest.

Except that perhaps it was not. The removal from office of four junior but highly effective members of the government was exactly the sort of thing the Peacemaker would do, and the skill and subtlety of the method suited his style. It was only by chance that the plot had come to Matthew's notice. Now he realized with a chill that there may have been other plots during the year since Jutland, successful ones that he had not recognized because his assumption that the Peacemaker was dead had blinded him to even considering such a thing. He would have to rectify that fault urgently.

The next day he began inquiries about the death of Kemp in the zeppelin raid. No one had considered it suspicious at the time. There had been many deaths in such raids; his was simply more notable because of his position. Where he had lived was a matter of public record.

"Could it have been murder?" Matthew asked the fire warden who had been first on the scene.

"Murder?" the man looked startled, as if Matthew had said something in bad taste. "Call it that if you like, sir, but it's better just to say it's the war. Murder's sort o' personal. It's this way for everybody at the moment."

"What I mean, Mr. Barker, is could he have been killed by some other means and left with the casualties, to hide the fact that in his case it was murder?" Matthew explained.

Barker was taken aback. "Oo'd want ter do a thing like that?"

"Most people who have power also have enemies," Matthew said evasively. "Is it possible?"

Barker still looked confused. " 'Ow would I know, sir?"

"Where was he found? Inside the house? Under rubble? With other people or alone?" Matthew elaborated.

"Alone. In the street just outside the 'ouse," Barker replied thoughtfully. "You sayin' as 'e were put there, an' we reckoned as it were the bombs wot killed 'im, but it weren't? Yer never goin' ter prove nothin' now!"

"I daresay not. I'd just like to know."

"Then 'e could a' bin. Or not."

"Thank you."

About Newell he could learn nothing. Reasons of health were given for his resignation, but no one had any knowledge of what illness it might be. Newell himself refused to see or speak to Matthew, claiming that he was not well enough, and had nothing relevant to say.

Blackmail again? Possibly. Its particular nature did not matter. Matthew was now certain in his own mind that there was a concerted plan to get rid of ministers who were individually able to affect the course of war, through diplomatic skill or connections, whether it was the Peacemaker who was behind it or not. The nation was exhausted with the loss of men, with shortages of food, fuel, and luxuries of all sorts, with the drabness and ever-present fear of bombing. They dreaded even greater hunger, and ultimately invasion and conquest. Perhaps after that might come civil war, Briton against Briton as some surrendered, believing it the lesser evil, and others fought on until the slaughter and defeat were total.

But Matthew still found he was striding out even more rapidly, with his anger against the Peacemaker, alive or dead, so hard inside him it hurt his chest to breathe.

Now he had enough information to report his findings to Calder Shearing, the head of his branch of Intelligence.

"Morning, Reavley," Shearing said as Matthew came into his office. "Anything on the sabotage in the factory in Bury St. Edmunds yet?" He looked up from his desk. He was a man of barely average height. His black hair was receding severely, but his face was so dominated by his dark eyes and powerful, expressive brows that one did not notice the expanse of his forehead. His nose was aquiline, his lips delicate and unusually sensitive.

"Yes, sir," Matthew replied, still standing at attention. One did not relax until Shearing gave his permission to. "I have sufficient evidence for the police to deal with it now."

"Then give it to them," Shearing ordered. "There's plenty more to be getting on with. There's an unusually high number of accidents at the munitions factory in Derby—Johnson Heathman and Company. I—"

"I'll give it to Bell," Matthew interrupted him almost without realizing that he did so. "Tom Corracher came to see me two days ago with something far more urgent."

Shearing's brows rose and his eyes were bright and cold. "More urgent than sabotage of our munitions factories, and yet you left it for two days to come and tell me?"

Matthew remained at attention. He had worked with Shearing since before the war, and at times their tacit understanding of each other was like the best sort of friendship. They did not speak of emotions. Even last week when they had sat up all night together over merchant shipping losses, bruised at heart over the deaths of hundreds of men, no words had been necessary. To Matthew these losses were infinitely more vivid since his experiences during the Battle of Jutland. Now he knew the slow, crawling fear of night patrol when the enemy could be anywhere under the dark water and fire, explosion, and drowning came without any warning at all. He knew the head-splitting noise of the great guns, the smell of blood and fire.

And he knew what it was like to sink an enemy ship and watch it go down, with a thousand men just like yourself, to be buried in the darkness of the ocean forever.

What he did not know was anything of the nature or the passions, the background, the home or family of the man sitting behind the desk now, waiting for his explanation. He did not even know if Shearing had ever personally seen anyone die. Perhaps for him it was numbers, something all in the mind, like a chess game.

There was one picture in Shearing's office, a painting of the London docks at twilight, and nothing else that betrayed his taste, his feelings, his own inner life. There were no books except those of a professional nature; no novels, no poetry. There were no photographs on the desk or the walls. He never mentioned his family, if he had any, or where he lived or had grown up, his school or university—nothing.

There had been many times when Matthew had wondered if Shearing himself could be the Peacemaker, before he knew it was Hannassey. It was a fear that had gripped him with an acute sadness. He had wanted to like Shearing. He found it easy to admire him. The suppleness of his mind, his occasional dry wit, the self-mastery and the dedication which kept him at his desk all day and half the night. It was the ability to trust him that had eluded Matthew, until Jutland had proved that the Peacemaker was Hannassey. Then suddenly relief, sweeter than he had expected, swept away suspicion. Now the trust was eroded again. Still he had no choice but to tell Shearing what he was doing; to attempt it secretly would betray his doubt, and he could not afford that.

"Reavley!" Shearing's voice cut across Matthew's thoughts impatiently.

"Yes, sir!" Matthew snapped his attention back. "It was a story I needed to investigate before I brought it to you. I couldn't judge the importance of it without making some careful inquiries."

"And you found it true." That was a statement.

"It seems to be."

"Then sit down, man, and tell me!" Shearing snapped. "Don't stand there like a damn lamppost!"

"Yes, sir." Matthew pulled up the chair and sat down. He recounted everything that Corracher had said, and how much of it he had been able to verify.

"And you believe that the removals of these four men are connected?" Shearing asked when Matthew finished. "Who do you consider responsible? Hannassey is dead."

"Yes, sir," Matthew responded, knowing the words were meaningless.

There was a wry amusement in Shearing's eyes. "One of his disciples taken his mantle of power?"

"I don't know, sir. That is first among the many things I would like to find out. But whoever it is, his purpose seems to be broadly the same, and his skill is obviously formidable. And I'd like to save Corracher, if possible."

Shearing's mouth pulled tight. "Not likely," he said bitterly. "If the man behind this is as clever as you think, he'll have made provision for

Corracher fighting the charge. Wheatcroft's wife has powerful family connections. They'll all want to believe her, and take the blame off Wheatcroft, true or false. Think carefully before you act, Reavley—and keep me informed. You might end by making it even worse."

It was a dismissal, but Matthew refused to stand up. "Are you telling me not to do anything, sir?" he said between his teeth.

"No, I'm telling you to use your brain, not your emotions!" Shearing said tartly. "Be as angry as you like. Go home and smash the china, swear at the neighbors, punch the furniture. Then grow up and do your job."

Matthew sat motionless.

"Now!" Shearing shouted suddenly. "It's a filthy thing to do! It's deceit and betrayal and it soils everything it touches. Don't sit there like a grave ornament! Do something!"

"Yes, sir." Matthew stood up. Quite unreasonably, it made him feel better to see Shearing's temper snap, too, and to know that under his tightly controlled surface he was just as furious and offended as Matthew himself.

That evening the man whom Matthew had referred to as the Peacemaker stood at the window of an upstairs room in his house on Marchmont Street, only a few miles away from Matthew's flat. He was waiting for a visitor and uncertain when he would arrive. It was no longer possible to rely on steamers or trains. The German Grand Fleet had not left harbor since the Battle of Jutland, but U-boats still patrolled the seas, necessitating that British warships guard troop carriers bringing back the wounded from France and Flanders.

It grew darker. The soft colors of the sky were fading, light reflected on windows opposite. The fire watch would be out soon, looking for zeppelins, waiting for the explosion of bombs. The streetlamps would make the city an easy target from the air.

His hands clenched and unclenched, his nails digging into his palms when he saw a taxi slow as it passed his house, then speed up again. He had known it would not be Richard Mason; he would not be foolish enough to get out right at the door. However, he would be tired after the long, dangerous, and heartbreaking journey. He might be careless. He had been once before.

The Peacemaker drew the curtains closed and turned away from the window, impatient with himself and the emotion raging inside him, which locked the muscles of his arms and chest, making them ache. Mason, the man he was waiting for, was possibly the best of all the war correspondents. He had sent dispatches from all the places where the fighting was fiercest: France, Flanders, Northern Italy, Bulgaria, Palestine, and Mesopotamia. He did not quote figures of men dead or wounded, or yards of mud-soaked land gained. He wrote with passion of individual experience, one act of heroism, one victory, one death. He described the weariness, the disgust, the hunger he himself felt, or the laughter, the letters from home, the silly jokes and terrible food. He hid nothing. Through the human suffering and tragedy of a few he painted the whole. In his words the destruction of Europe, now spreading across the Near East, North Africa, India, and America as well, was brought to life.

The Peacemaker had always known that the human cost of war was beyond measuring. As young men during the Boer War, he and Mason had both seen the concentration camps, the brutality, the degradation of the spirit. They had not known each other then, but the experience had given them a common goal. Both were consumed by an ideal that war should never be allowed to happen again, but the Peacemaker was willing to go to any lengths. One man, ten men, a hundred were a price not worth the counting if it could prevent the slaughter of ten million and the ruin of nations.

The Peacemaker had conceived a plan, and but for a collision of events no one could have prepared for, he would have succeeded. The treaty that would have bound Britain and Germany in an alliance unbeatable by any other axis of nations had been found by John Reavley, and seeing its potential with short-sighted patriotism rather than a world vision, he had stolen one of the copies to expose it. There was no time to write it out again, and have the kaiser sign it. The assassination in Sarajevo had altered everything. Even killing Reavley had not retrieved the document, and the buildup to war had become unstoppable.

Of course he had tried to find ways to bring about peace since then— he had never stopped trying. It had become a passion that devoured everything else in him, overtook his life and cost him every other wish or dream, every principle or ideal he had treasured, certainly all personal happiness. But what was that when balanced against the ruin of Europe and its centuries of beauty, its magnificence of thought, its philosophy and dreams, not to mention the loss of human life?

Every attempt had been foiled either by tides of circumstance or the intervention of an individual. In at least three instances that he knew of he had been frustrated by the sons of John Reavley, who were still bent on avenging his death, and still held his foolish idealism.

After the first poison gas attack in the trenches at Ypres in 1915, and the slaughter on the beaches of Gallipoli, Mason had written a brilliant article exposing the arrogance and extreme incompetence of the command in the second instance. Joseph Reavley had been briefly at Gallipoli also.

He had pursued Mason back toward England and finally caught up with him in an open boat in the English Channel when they had survived the sinking of the ship they had been in.

What conceivable part of Reavley's shortsighted philosophy could have changed Mason's mind and persuaded him to abandon not only his article but also the entire cause? It had taken the Peacemaker more than a year to win him back and make him see the greater cause again.

It was Matthew Reavley who had caused the death of Patrick Hannassey, but this had not been unwelcome. Hannassey had been extremely useful, but by the summer of 1917 he was becoming a liability—greedy and unreliable. Corcoran had been one of the Peacemaker's successes. Other plans were almost ripe as well.

So he paced the floor of his room trying to compose his mind as he waited for Richard Mason and the report he would bring from Russia, and even more important, from Germany itself. The Peacemaker had seen a year ago that the key might lie in the deluge that was about to break over the tsar's government and bring it to an end. Now it had happened. Kerensky was in control now. He was a man of vision and humanity, a man of compromise. Lenin was there now, too, and Trotsky—but they were extremists. In time they would take Russia out of the war. There would be no more Eastern Front to bleed away German strength and crush its men with the deadly cold and hunger, and the useless marches and sieges that had ruined every army that had tried to conquer that vast country. Dear God, even Napoleon had learned that at crippling cost. Did the kaiser really delude himself he could do better?

God knew Germany tried hard enough to keep the United States out of the war, knowing how their strength would renew the almost beaten forces of Britain and France. Until January of this year, 1917, they had succeeded. But Zimmerman, the German foreign secretary, had sent that idiotic directive to Mexico to attack the United States. The telegram had somehow found its way to President Woodrow Wilson. America had had no choice but to declare war on Germany and join the Allies.

Tens of thousands more lives would be lost as the war dragged on for another year, and another. The blind, insensate stupidity of the leaders who sacrificed men for nothing but their own arrogance, their petty "little England" mentality, brought the hot rage to his mind. The sweat stood out on his body and he could feel his heart pounding. Britain and Germany were natural allies. Together they could have brought peace and safety to half the world, prosperity and civilized government, and the highest culture mankind had ever seen.

Instead Britain in its imperial conceit had loosed a storm of destruction that threatened to bring back the Dark Ages, and leave Europe all but uninhabited, except by the old, the crippled, and the lonely women whose men were buried in the blood-soaked earth.

He steadied himself with difficulty, breathing in slowly and out again, counting the seconds. There was still hope. He must be in total control when Mason arrived.

He heard another car go past and whirled around to stare at the door, then was furious with himself for giving in to such impulse.

And it was meaningless. Mason would not drive past this house. He would stop at least a hundred yards away.

Then there was the knock on the door.

"Come," he said quietly.

The manservant came in. "Mr. Mason is here, sir," he said respectfully. "Would you like tea, or perhaps a glass of whisky? There is Glenmorangie in the decanter, sir."

"Bring tea and then leave us," the Peacemaker replied. Mason would be tired and cold. There might be something to celebrate later, but not yet. It depended very much on what news he also brought from Germany.

"Yes, sir."

Mason's footsteps sounded on the stairs, and a moment later he came into the room. He was thinner than when the Peacemaker had last seen him, but he still moved with a certain grace in spite of the fact that he must have been exhausted. It was an energy of mind rather than of body that kept him going. It burned in his dark eyes now, and the power of his emotion was suggested in the lines of his face, the broad cheekbones and wide mouth.

"Have a seat, Mason," the Peacemaker said calmly, as if it were only days since they had last seen each other, and not months. "I've sent for tea, but if you'd rather have whisky, it's here."

"Tea, thank you." Mason sat down in the armchair opposite him, and only as he eased himself into it did his tiredness show. There was clearly a stiffness in his back, and the light of the lamp above the mantel accentuated for an instant the hollows around his eyes.

"Bad journey?" the Peacemaker asked, also sitting.

Mason did not hide his feelings; perhaps he couldn't. "Trains are full of wounded," he replied, his voice quiet and precise as always, but the pain in it undisguised. "Mostly from Passchendaele. Hundreds of them, gray-faced, staring into space. Some are straight from the schoolroom—fifteen, sixteen, slaughtered before they've tasted life." He stopped abruptly, his breathing ragged as he tried to block the memory from his mind and think of the present: the Peacemaker and the quiet rooms where at least for a few hours he was comfortable and safe.

There seemed nothing to add, and trivialities would have been offensive to both of them. They waited a few moments with no sound but an occasional car in the street and the steady ticking of the clock on the mantel. It was now completely dark outside. The manservant brought tea and sandwiches, apologizing for the liberty.

"Fish paste, sir, and cucumber. I hope it is acceptable?"

Mason gave him a bleak smile. "After the rations I've had, it's food for the gods. Thank you."

"You're most welcome, sir." He inclined his head, then withdrew, closing the door.

The Peacemaker passed the tea and pushed the plate of sandwiches toward Mason. His stomach was tense and his mouth dry, but he sat calmly, as if there were all the time in the world. He would not ask for the article yet, with its encoded message from Berlin. He forced himself to wait until Mason had eaten, before he spoke again.

"What is the news from Russia?" he said when finally Mason put down his cup. "Has the revolution progressed since you were there before?" He made it sound as if he were no more than interested, not that the fate of the war might depend upon it.

Mason's face was motionless, looking within himself, as he answered. "Yes, it has progressed, not as I had hoped. Kerensky is an intelligent man, a visionary, a moderate who wants to build the new without destroying the old."

"The tsar will not give in," the Peacemaker said with some distaste. He had little respect for Nicholas II, or for his tsarina Alexandra and her absurd dependence upon the filthy monk Rasputin. "What is Kerensky doing to hasten his complete control? He cannot wait forever!" His voice was sharper than he had meant it to be. With an effort he steadied it. "Russia is bleeding away in this senseless war, just as we are. And God knows their people deserve freedom from the centuries of oppression they have suffered. Don't tell me about the hunger and the deaths on the Eastern Front, or the poverty across the land. Any dispatch can tell me that. What is the mood in St. Petersburg? Moscow? Or Kiev? What of Lenin, or Trotsky, or any of the men of real vision? When will they move to take over the leadership?

Mason was somber. He met the Peacemaker's eyes at last. "I wish I didn't have to say this," he answered quietly, "but Kerensky is out of his depth. He is in many ways a man of both vision and morality, but history has overtaken him. He has neither the fire nor the obsession to match the mood of the people now, or their needs. It has passed beyond his kind of moderation."

The Peacemaker sat still. Suddenly the restlessness was gone inside him, replaced by something like a solitary fire. If Mason was right about the mood in Russia, then his hope would be realized, perhaps soon. With the Eastern Front no longer a threat, Germany could turn all its men and forces toward the west. The German plan to ship Lenin into Russia in a sealed train had worked. They were on the brink of harvesting its fruits.

"I see," he said aloud. He had never intended to tell Mason anything of the secret diplomacy that had brought some of this about. Mason hated war with a passion and a horror equal to anyone's, but he was an Englishman, and the thought of England beaten would reach his emotions with unpredictable effect. It was prudent that he know only what was necessary. "You look tired," the Peacemaker went on. "Have you an article for me?"

Since the American entry into the war in January he could no longer route his communications with Berlin through Washington. Now he relied on Mason to meet secretly with Manfred von Schenckendorff in any of the neutral territories Mason visited. He encoded his information within his articles, so nothing could ever be betrayed, and gave them to the Peacemaker on his return. The Peacemaker altered them slightly to remove the information and gave them back. It worked in reverse with copies of notes as if for an article yet to be written.

Mason pulled half a dozen slips of paper out of his pocket and passed them across.

"Thank you." The Peacemaker accepted them. He had difficulty keeping his fingers from shaking, but he forced himself to leave the papers closed. He would read them later, alone.

"I wish I could say there is nothing urgent to discuss, and allow you to rest," he said quietly. "But Passchendaele is a disaster." He had no need to act to thicken his voice deliberately with pain; it was real enough, gouging into him, bringing back memory of Africa and a wave of nausea at sight of the dead, obscene and helpless. "It looks as if it is going to be worse even than the Somme," he went on hoarsely.

Mason must have caught the sudden, ungoverned pain in him. "I know," he answered softly.

The Peacemaker straightened a little in his chair, needing to mask the nakedness of his momentary lapse.

"Of course you do—at least from the figures, and the trainloads of wounded you'll have seen. But that is not all. It is not widely known, at least to the public, but part of the French army mutinied. . . ."

Mason jerked his head up, his eyes hot and angry. "The poor devils had just cause," he said, as if the Peacemaker had leveled an accusation.

The Peacemaker nodded slowly. "I know that. They are brave and patriotic men, like ours, but their conditions are intolerable, and now they are being driven onto the enemy guns in pointless suicide. And it's happening again all along the Flanders Front. We need an honest voice to tell us what is happening to our own men. This is no longer a war of the people, Mason, it's become a senseless destruction the leaders are too blind or too incompetent to put a stop to. Get a good night's sleep. See me in the morning and I will give you back your article. Then go to Ypres again. Forget the propaganda and the figures, and what the commanders say. Find the truth of what the men who are fighting and dying really think. We have to know!" Without realizing it he leaned forward. "We have the moral need to know, and they have the moral right that we should. If you won't speak for them, who will?"

Mason did not argue. "I'll go tomorrow night, after I've reported to my paper," he said simply. His face hardened as he smothered the weakness within himself, the momentary faltering, the longing to turn away. "There's no reason to delay."

"Good," the Peacemaker said simply. He looked at the empty tea tray, sandwiches all eaten. "Would you like a Glenmorangie?"

"Yes," Mason accepted. "Yes, I would."

Richard Mason was not the last visitor to the house in Marchmont Street that evening. At close to midnight, after he had read the article and deleted Schenckendorff's message the Peacemaker stood in the dark before the uncurtained window, his mind racing with new ideas. Hope had rekindled in him for an end to the madness of the battlefield. It might even be that the ordinary soldier himself at last could take control of his destiny. Most men who were actually commanded to kill the enemy, to fire the bullets, to let off the gas, who charged with the bayonets fixed, had no personal enmity toward the German soldiers in the lines opposite them. They knew they were just ordinary men like themselves. If the French could mutiny, then surely so could the British. Mason would bring him back the truth of morale in Flanders. Then perhaps there would be an end to it.

There was a knock on the door again, tentative at this late hour.

The Peacemaker swung around angrily. "What is it?" he demanded. He was inwardly exhausted by the unceasing emotional soar and plunge between despair and the blindness and the folly of those with whom he had to work. Time and time again he had been on the brink of success, the beginning of the end, only to have it dashed from his hand. "What is it?" he said again.

The manservant opened the door, looking apologetic. "It is a gentleman to see you, sir. He won't give his name, but he says it is to do with a certain event on Hampstead Heath. Shall I ask him to leave, sir?"

"No. Tell him to come in," the Peacemaker said quickly. "Do not disturb us. We shall require no refreshment. You may retire. I shall show him out."

"Yes, sir. I'll send the gentleman up."

The man who arrived a moment later was thin, with a dark mustache and large, red-knuckled hands. He closed the door behind him. He met the Peacemaker's eyes without flinching, as if they were equals. The Peacemaker did not like him. They were on the same side by force, not idealism. There was no passion for humanity in this man, only for himself and his own profit, but he was useful. "Yes?" he said curtly.

"Corracher's been talking to someone in the Secret Intelligence Service," the man told him. "He's seen the pattern, and it looks as if he could make a fight of it."

"Rubbish!" the Peacemaker snapped. "He'll only dig himself in deeper. No one's going to believe him."

"This man did," his visitor replied. "Started asking a lot of questions, getting police records—times and places. He was very thorough."

The Peacemaker felt a tiny flash of anxiety, nothing more than a cold touch inside, there and then gone again. "Any idea who it is?"

"The man from Intelligence? His name is Matthew Reavley." The man said it without expression, as if it meant nothing to him.

"Thank you." The Peacemaker's voice was little more than a whisper, and he stood perfectly still in the room. Reavley again. The name was like a curse. He cleared his throat. "I doubt he will do anything, but I will attend to it. I am obliged to you that you had the foresight to tell me. Good night." He led the way down toward the front door, holding it open for the man to leave, then he locked and barred it behind him.

He returned to the upstairs room with an inexplicable sense of loss. It disturbed him. Of course Matthew Reavley would have to be killed. There was now no choice. Getting rid of ministers like Corracher was vital to the peace negotiations when they came. His Hungarian connection had proved far better than the Peacemaker had foreseen. He was striving for unity! A single state, led by Britain and Germany. A renegade Hungarian leadership waiting to break up the old Austro-Hungarian Empire was the last thing needed.

It was also vital that the right men guided the peace. After the defeat of the generals on both sides, the ordinary men might still ally and lay the foundations of an empire that would begin to rebuild with justice, bring order and finally prosperity again and beauty out of the present chaos.

Why should he grieve that it cost the life of Matthew Reavley? That was a sentimental weakness he must not allow himself. He was bone weary, but far deeper than that he was heartsick. What on earth was one life more? Passchendaele was costing thousands a day! Every day!

But London was still outwardly civilized, so it must be done with care. He would set the act in motion tomorrow, speak to the right man for the task. If he allowed personal regret of any kind to hold him back he was despicable, not fit to lead. The best men in the country had lost sons and brothers.

He sat down at his desk and encoded a short letter to Manfred for Mason to take tomorrow. Manfred von Schenckendorff had been the Peacemaker's ally from the beginning, when it had still seemed possible that they might have won peace with honor, and avoided this whole misguided tragedy of war between two nations who should have been brothers—together. Manfred would understand the pervading sense of loss he felt that he had to destroy a good but stubborn man, as he had had to destroy Reavley's father before him. He would so much rather have won him to the cause.

This new turn of events with Corracher had left him no choice. Manfred would appreciate that; they had always understood each other in the subtler ways of honor and logic and the wounds of unnecessary tragedy.

He walked over to the gramophone, wound it up, and placed a record on it: Beethoven, the last quartets, composed after he was deaf—complex, subtle, marvelously beautiful, and full of pain.

THREE

*R*ichard Mason walked along the rutted and cratered road in the steady rain. The sky was leaden and the rumble and crack of gunfire was mixed with occasional thunder. The few trees still left standing had branches torn from them, lying rotting on the ground. His clothes were sodden and sticking to him and his feet were covered in the thick Flanders mud. It seemed to be everywhere. The unhedged fields swam with it, the ditches were awash, and it lay thick and churned up across the way ahead.

He had passed more troops going forward, more wagonloads of ammunitions and supplies. And of course there were columns of the walking wounded, moving slowly, awkward with pain, their eyes unfocused in that strange, blank stare of those who have seen hell and carry it within them. Some had their eyes bandaged, and stumbled forward, arms outstretched and hands on the shoulder of the man in front of them. Mason turned away, choked with grief.

He was less than two miles from the trenches now. He could smell the familiar stench of death.

What could he write that would be new about any of this? Were there really rumors of mutiny, or just the usual complaining that was part of any life? Possibly it was little more than a good-natured sympathy for the French.

An ambulance passed him, loaded with wounded, and he glanced at the driver. Every time he saw the high, square outline of an ambulance he thought of Judith Reavley and finding her before on a stretch of road just like this. It was knotting his muscles and making his chest ache, as memory of her always did, quickening the blood and stirring him with a deep, unsettling hunger. Then, she had been slumped over the wheel of her ambulance, motionless at the side of the road.

At first he had been terrified she was actually dead. His relief when she opened her eyes and looked at him had been like warmth on freezing limbs. Then she had spoken and he realized the vibrancy was gone from her voice, the passion. Even the anger was snuffed out. Something beautiful was broken. He had never hated the war as savagely as he had at that moment. All the injured men and riddled corpses he had seen had not moved him any more deeply. She had symbolized all that was precious in living: the laughter, the courage, and the strength.

He had managed to see her twice since then, once in Paris, very briefly and almost by accident. The second time, in London, was a great deal more by design.

It seemed a long time ago now, and unconsciously he quickened his step, almost unaware of the soaking rain.

Half an hour later, he reached the dressing station behind the supply trenches. It was on the third line back from the forward trenches on the edge of no-man's-land. The large tent was half supported by wooden walls at one side, and like everything else, was awash with mud. Through the gray air of late afternoon it was easy to imagine the dusk settling, although at this time of the year it would be hours yet before sunset.

Mason walked across the duckboards at the entrance and into the yellowish light of the lamps over the operating tables. He could smell blood and disinfectant. There were half a dozen men sitting on the floor, backs against packing cases. Two or three were drinking hot tea from tin mugs, their faces white. The others simply stared ahead of them into the distance as if they could see farther than the canvas wall or the darkening, rain-soaked air outside.

Another man lay on the table, the scarlet stump of his right leg making his injury hideously apparent. The surgeon working on him did not even look up as Mason came in. The anesthetist glanced at him, saw he was standing upright, and returned his attention to the patient.

A middle-aged medical orderly came over to him, his face lined with exhaustion. "Where are you hurt?" he said with little sympathy. His time was too precious to waste on the able-bodied.

"I'm not," Mason replied, understanding his feelings. "Richard Mason, war correspondent."

The orderly's face softened. "Oh. Come to see Captain Cavan? Up for the V.C., he is." There was pride in his voice and his head lifted, the weariness gone for a moment.

Mason changed his mind instantly about what he had been going to say, so that when he answered it had become the truth. "When he's got time. Are those men waiting for the ambulance?" He realized with a sudden grip like iron in his stomach that he did not know for certain if Judith was still alive. Ambulances were shelled like everything else. Drivers could be killed or injured. Just because someone was unhurt a week ago did not mean they were safe now.

"Yes," the orderly replied. "Shouldn't be long."

"Still got the American driver, Wil Sloan?" Mason pursued. It sounded as if he was looking for a story, even though his voice cracked a little. "Or did he go over to the American forces now they're in it, too?"

"They're not along this stretch," the orderly told him, his lips thinning for a moment. "We're all men who've been here from the beginning: English, Welsh, Canadians, French. Quite a few Aussies and New Zealanders, too. But Sloan's still here. At least he was this morning."

Mason did not ask what he meant. He had seen the casualty figures. His mouth was dry. "And Judith Reavley?" His heart pounded so he could hardly draw his breath as he waited the long seconds till the orderly answered. He realized how stupid the question was. Would the man even know one V.A.D. driver from another, or care, in this hell?

The orderly smiled, perhaps seeing Mason's emotion raw in his face, unguarded until too late. "Must have been a demon on the roads in Cambridgeshire, that one! She certainly is here."

Mason smiled back. He thought of saying something about his intention of writing an article on women in the battlefield, and then stopped himself in time. It would be absurd, and certainly wouldn't fool the orderly. "Thanks," he said simply. He accepted a hot cup of tea, which tasted of oil and dirt, and sat down to wait for a chance to speak to Cavan, and with the knowledge that in the next few hours Judith would come to this station.

The shelling grew heavier, but was still falling some distance from them. More wounded came in, but most of the injuries were superficial. Cavan acknowledged Mason briefly. He finished his operation on the man who had lost his leg, but could not leave him until the ambulance came. The rain never ceased its steady downpour, drumming on the canvas roof and adding to the already swimming craters outside. The wounded men's hair was plastered to their heads, their faces shone wet, their uniforms stained dark. Some were covered in mud up to their armpits and must have been manually hauled out of the shell craters before they could drown.

It was nearly an hour before the ambulance arrived. They did not hear it in the noise of guns and the beat of rain. Mason noticed the movement at the entrance and looked up to see Wil Sloan. He looked tired, pale-skinned, and filthy, but had the same cheerful smile on his face that Mason remembered from a year ago. "Hi, Doc," he said casually, looking across at Cavan. "Anyone for us?" His eyes went to the man on the table, who was still mercifully unconscious.

"Have you got a driver?" Cavan asked. "Someone'll have to sit with him. He's in a bad way."

Sloan's face tightened and he nodded. "Sure. If anyone can get us through this bloody bog, it's Judith . . . Miss Reavley."

Mason's heart lurched.

The ghost of a smile touched Cavan's face. "You're picking up our bad language, Wil? You'll shock them at home. I'll help you carry him out." He turned back to the table, his shoulders bent a little, a long smear of blood down his arm.

Mason stood up quickly. "I'll give you a hand," he offered. "I'm doing nothing. I'll get the stretcher."

Wil followed Cavan inside to help the other men who would take up the rest of the space in the ambulance. It would be only those who could not walk.

The minute Mason was outside the shelter of the tent the rain drenched him again. He could hardly discern the square outline of the ambulance through the gloom. His feet slipped in the mud and he found himself floundering. God knew what it must be like trying to struggle through it with ninety pounds of equipment and ammunition on your back and a rifle, knowing the bullets and shrapnel could tear into you any moment.

He saw Judith step out of the driver's seat of the ambulance and come forward to help him, mistaking him for a wounded soldier. He straightened up, feeling foolish. He wanted to think of something engaging to say, but his mind was racing futilely.

"There's an amputee coming out on a stretcher," he said instead. "Still unconscious. We're bringing him now. Wil Sloan's going to have to ride in the back—" The rest was cut off by the roar and crash of a shell landing five hundred yards away. It sent a tower of earth and mud high into the air, which rained down on the roof of the tent behind them, and onto the ambulance with the dull thud of metal.

Judith took no notice at all. Her face showed surprise and an instant of pleasure as she recognized him, then she went straight around to the back of the ambulance and opened the doors. She pulled out the stretcher without waiting for his help. She was swift, efficient, even oddly graceful.

Next moment Wil Sloan was there as well and all their thoughts were overtaken by the need to load the unconscious man. They carried him as carefully as possible in the wind and rain, and then had to decide which of the others were most in need of riding along with him, bearing in mind that there had to be room for Wil also.

"How's the road, Miss Reavley?" Cavan asked Judith when they were ready to go. The rain had eased a little but the heavy, overcast sky had brought darkness early and they were no more than outlines in the gloom.

"Bad," she answered, her voice strained with anxiety. "But there's no choice." She knew the amputee had to reach a hospital soon if he was to live.

"Wil can't leave him," Cavan warned her. "I'm sorry." They stood a yard away from each other and neither made a move or a gesture, but there was an intense gentleness in Cavan's face in the headlights, and Judith's eyes did not once waver from his. Mason saw it and was stung by a surge of jealousy so powerful it clenched his whole body. He was astonished at himself.

"Can I help?" he said immediately. "I can speak to you another time . . . sir."

"Yes," Cavan said. "Ride in the front with Miss Reavley. If there's a wheel to be changed, or debris to move from the road, she'll need another pair of hands." He did not ask Judith; it was an order.

"Yes, sir." Mason was pleased to obey. He splashed around to the other side and climbed in.

Cavan bent and cranked the engine, and it fired easily. Judith slipped in the clutch. There was a violent spurt of mud and they were jerked backward. Mason was startled, thinking she had forgotten which gear she was in.

She laughed. "On a slope," she explained. "Going uphill the tank drains backward and we get no power. Drive in reverse and we're fine. I'll turn here." She stopped and slewed around as she spoke, her hands strong on the wheel, muscles taut, then she drove forward along the dim, cratered road.

Every now and then star shells went up, lighting the landscape with its jagged tree stumps and erratic gouges out of the clay now filled with mud and water. There were wrecked vehicles by the side of the road and here and there carcasses of horses, even sometimes helmets to mark where men had died. Broken gun carriages and burned-out tanks showed up in the glare, and once the barrel of a great cannon projecting from a crater angled at the sky. Then the shell would fall and the darkness seemed more intense, in spite of the headlights, which showed little more than the slanting rain and the wilderness.

"How on earth do you know where you're going?" he asked her incredulously.

"Habit," she said frankly. "Believe me, I know this stretch of road better than I know my own village. Only trouble is we can't get Jerry to put the craters in the same place each time. He's a damn awful shot. All over the place like a drunken sailor."

He forced himself to smile, although he knew she could not see him, and the lunacy of the whole thing almost choked him. Didn't she see it, too? Was she deliberately blinding herself to it in order to survive? How could anyone tolerate being imprisoned in this, knowing the rest of the world was clean and sane? Somewhere beyond the endless violence, dirt, and incessant noise there were cities and villages where the sun shone, women wore pretty dresses, and people picked flowers, talked about crops and church fêtes, and gossiped. They ate around tables, washed in clean water, and slept in beds.

Another ambulance passed, lurching over the ruts, going toward the front line. For a moment its headlights lit Judith's face as she raised her hand in salute. He saw her high cheekbones and beautiful, vulnerable mouth. She looked older, more finely honed by horror and exhaustion, but the spirit was back as he had first known her.

He was amazed. How did she do that? Did she simply refuse to think? Had she no idea what was going on everywhere else, the suffering and monumental loss, the crushing futility of it all?

They barged over a rut and came down hard. Mason felt the bones of his spine jar. What must it be like for the injured men in the back, especially the one he had seen operated on?

He could not see Judith's face anymore as they lurched forward. He could just make out her shoulders as she clung on to the wheel, struggling to keep the vehicle on the road. The rain was harder again.

It was she who broke the silence.

"Did you come here to interview Captain Cavan?"

"Not particularly," he replied. "It seemed like a good opportunity. Does he deserve the V.C.?"

"Oh, yes." She could not keep the lift of excitement out of her voice as if there were new hope, and new life because of it. "His courage was extraordinary."

He had known she would say that and it frightened him. It was so easy! One man's heroism changed nothing, it was just a candle lit against the night. It would be quenched by the next gust of wind, and then the darkness would seem even worse. She was still just as naïve as ever. How many other men and women were there here just like her, believing the impossible, giving their lives pointlessly to defend a mirage?

"Did he really hold off a German attack practically single-handedly, and save his patients?"

"Not single-handedly," she corrected him. "We all fought. But he commanded. He was the one who defied them and refused to leave."

"We?" His voice was hoarse. "Are you speaking figuratively? You weren't there?" he insisted. He did not want it to be true because of the danger to her, but as much as the knowledge of how close she had come to death, he did not want her to have been part of Cavan's heroism.

"Yes, I was there," she replied as if it still surprised her. "We were caught off guard. We didn't expect the attack. It was well behind the lines."

He was stunned. A shell exploded to their left, flinging mud up against the side of the ambulance and across the windshield. They lurched badly. Judith swore and wrenched the wheel over, trying to right them again. He leaned across and put his weight against it, his hands touching hers.

"Thank you," she said matter-of-factly.

He did not reply, moving his hands away again and straightening himself in his seat. Suddenly he was acutely conscious of her, the mud and bloodstains on her gray dress, the curve of her cheek, the startling strength in her arms.

Ten minutes later they reached better roads which were still water-logged, but without the shell holes, and they picked up speed. The rain eased until it was no more than a fine mist like a veil across the headlights, forever shifting and parting to show trees black against the sky. When they moved through villages, they found that a few buildings were burned out but most still stood, windows curtained against showing light. No one was in the streets.

"Have you been in France?" she asked him.

"Not lately," he replied. "I was on the Eastern Front, up in Russia."

"Is it as bad as they say?"

"Probably. Kerensky's trying hard, but he's changing too little. The time for moderation is gone. They want extreme now, someone more like Lenin or Trotsky. The hunger's appalling." He told her of individuals he had seen—the poverty, the hollow faces, the emaciated bodies. He said far more than he meant to, needing her to feel what he had, both the anger and the pity. He glanced sideways at her face, trying to read the emotions in it as she listened to him, seeing her expression fleetingly as they passed the lights of other vehicles. "Everybody's sick of the war," he finished.

"Only a madman wouldn't be," she replied, leaning forward to peer through the gloom. "But some things are necessary. Fighting is terrible. The only thing worse is not fighting." There was no doubt in her voice, no wavering.

"Is it really better to fight?" he challenged her. "Always? Even at this cost?" His voice was harsher than he had meant it to be because his own certainties had been torn away, leaving him naked, and he hated it. "And do you really know enough about the French to judge?" The instant the words were out he regretted them. He wanted her as she had been the first time he had met her, ignorant and brave, luminous with her own belief, even if it was absurd, and wrong. It was what made her beautiful. "I'm sorry...." he started.

"Don't apologize. Not to me. At least you have the courage to say what you believe."

Should he answer her with the truth? He had seen the conditions in France, the unimaginable losses, the destruction, and it lacerated him with pity.

He did not want a division between them. He wanted her to care for him, to love him, but what use was that if he hated himself? What could he win with lies?

"It isn't always the enemy you have to fight," he said, weighing his words. "The French had reason for what they did. Enemies can be behind you as well as in front. The soldiers were mostly peasants, not revolutionaries at all. They objected to unfair rations and curtailed leave. New recruits were treated with favor while long-serving men were sent back to almost certain death, knowing their families at home were left to go hungry. Those who were excused from military service profiteered at their expense. Leave for agricultural purposes was based on political favoritism. They were willing to fight, and to die, but they wanted justice. I don't see that as cowardice, or disloyalty."

She remained silent, accelerating the ambulance over the smoother road. The rain had stopped and there were rents in the clouds. The moonlight showed the summer trees, heavy boughed and glistening as the headlights caught the wet leaves.

"I didn't know that," she said at last. "Poor devils. Do you think they'll be executed?"

He heard the pity in her voice, but no anger that he had shattered her illusion. He reached out his hand to touch her, lay his fingers on her arm, then changed his mind and withdrew it. He did not want to risk being rebuffed. He knew how it would hurt.

"Only a few," he answered her question. "Enough to make an example."

She said nothing. A few minutes later they pulled in at the hospital. From then on everyone was busy helping to unload the wounded. The amputee was still alive, but very much weaker, and in great pain. The only thing that Judith or Mason could think about was getting him out of the ambulance and into a bed as easily as possible.

After the men were all unloaded, Judith was standing with Mason when Wil Sloan emerged from the side door of the hospital ward into the cobbled yard. He looked almost ghostly in the lamplight.

Judith went over to him and locked her arm in his, leading him across the yard to the ambulance. "Let's see if there's somewhere open for a glass of wine and a sandwich," she said.

"It's half past one in the morning," he pointed out with a tiny smile.

She gave a shrug. "So we'll find someone who'll let us use their kitchen to make our own. We've got to sleep somewhere. Can't go back to the trenches until I've cleaned the ambulance and got some more petrol anyway." Mason had followed her. "Do you want to go back?" she asked him.

"Better than walking," he replied. "Unless, of course, you'll be shot for giving a civilian a ride?"

She gave him a quick smile. "We can always poke you with a bayonet, and put you in the back," she offered. "Then you'll be genuinely wounded!"

He was too tired to think of an answer.

Mason woke at five to find Wil Sloan's hand on his shoulder, shaking him gently. It was already daylight and the ambulance was clean and refueled. There was time for bread and tea, and then they were in the yard beside the ambulance and ready to go again.

Judith looked tired. In the morning light, which was harder and colder than the dusk of yesterday, he saw the fine lines in her face and the shadows around her eyes. She was twenty-six, but she could have been ten years older. Her dress was plain gray and completely without adornment. The hem was still crusted with mud, but now he could see that the bloodstains were old and had already been washed many times. They were too soaked into the fiber ever to be removed.

She saw him watching her and gave him a tiny, self-conscious smile.

He remembered their first meeting with a catch in his throat that was as sharp as pain. It had been in 1915, in the Savoy Hotel. She had been dressed in a blue satin gown that had hugged her body and she had walked with a grace that had forced him to look at her. She had been angry, mistaken about almost everything, and utterly beautiful, enough to charm any man and stir forgotten hungers inside him.

Now the feeling was quite different. It was nothing to do with laughter or conquest, but a need within himself for something tender and clean, and immensely vulnerable, still capable of pain, and hope.

"Not quite the Savoy, is it?" she said drily, as if she had read his thoughts.

He felt the heat in his face. He wanted to look away from her, and could not. She would be gone too soon!

She was embarrassed also. "Come on!" she said quickly. "Get in!"

They spoke of general things. She asked him more about other battle-fronts he had seen and he found it easy to tell her. He felt no more need to hide his feelings or his knowledge of casualties. He tried to describe the ravaged beauty of northern Italy with its exquisite skies over Venice and Trieste; the courage of partisan fighters in the mountains of Albania, particularly some of the women he had seen, struggling to get medical supplies to the wounded.

He even found himself explaining some of the moral dilemmas he faced as to how much or little he should tell the truth of certain events in his articles.

She listened with interest—and understood enough to offer no solutions.

It was a windy day with only a light rain. When they were two or three miles from the front, they saw a gun carriage on its side and a soldier standing beside it waving his arms in desperation. There were three others behind him near the gun and two horses harnessed to the gun carriage.

Judith pulled the ambulance to a halt as close as she could and the soldier was at her side immediately.

"Can you 'elp me, miss? Private 'Oskins is 'urt pretty bad. That bloody gun just pitched back into the mud and none of us could shift it, even with the 'orses. 'E's gonna die if we don't 'elp 'im. Both 'is legs is bust an' 'is back's gorn. I dunno 'ow ter move the thing wi'out makin' it even worse. Please . . ."

Judith turned off the engine. "Yes, of course we will," she said, climbing out without hesitation. "Come on." She gestured to Mason, then hurried around to the back just as Wil Sloan opened the door and looked out. "We need help, Wil," she told him. "Man trapped under a field gun. You'd better get tourniquets, and splints, and a stretcher." She turned to Mason. "You come with me." It was an order. Without seeing if he would obey, she picked up her skirts and waded through the ditch, in water up to her thighs. With a hand from the soldier she climbed out, then floundered across the thick, plowed clay to the crater. There, the other soldiers were trying to hold the gun from sliding even deeper, keeping the weary, patient horses leaning against the harness.

The injured man was almost submerged in the filthy water. Another man, who looked to be no more than sixteen or seventeen, held his head up, his eyes wide with terror. He was losing. He could feel the weight of the man slipping out of his grasp, slimy with mud and blood, and he was helpless to prevent it.

Mason dropped in beside him without even thinking about it, and grasped them both. They were freezing. The shock of it took his own breath away. A moment later Wil Sloan appeared with the stretcher. Judith was giving orders. "Hitch it tighter, move forward, slowly! Steady!"

There was a great squelch of mud and running water. Someone shouted, and the gun reared up. Mason put all his strength to pulling the wounded man, lost his footing, and fell back deeper into the crater himself. He thrashed around, suddenly terrified of drowning also. The clay held him. Water was in his eyes, in his mouth, over his head. It was vile, stinking of death. Someone caught hold of him and he was in the air again, gasping, filling his lungs. His hands still held the blouse of the wounded soldier. Wil Sloan was heaving on them both and one of the other soldiers as well.

They scrambled up onto the bank. Without even examining the wounds, Wil was binding tourniquets. Judith still held the horses.

"Hurry!" she shouted. "This gun's going to slide backward any minute. I'll have to cut the horses loose or they'll go, too!"

"Stretcher!" Wil bellowed. Mason staggered to his feet and grasped it. Together they rolled the wounded man onto it, and then raised it up. They were a couple of yards clear when Judith cut the harness. The gun and carriage both fell back into the crater, sending up a wave of mud and water that drenched them, even at that distance.

"What the bloody hell are you doing?" a voice shouted furiously.

Mason looked at the captain who stood on the side of the road glaring at them. He was a slender man, his wide, dark eyes seeming overlarge in his haggard face.

"Whose damn fool idea was it to take a gun across a field full of mud?" he demanded.

The corporal snapped to attention as well as he could, standing in the gouged-up clay and over his knees in mud. "Orders of Major Northrup, Captain Morel. I told 'im we'd get stuck, but 'e wouldn't listen."

Morel turned to Judith. "Get that man to the nearest field station. Cavan's only about a mile forward. Be quick."

"Yes, sir." Judith waved at Wil to go on, then climbed into the ambulance, her sodden skirts slapping mud everywhere, and took her place behind the wheel. "Will you have one of the men turn the crank for me?" she requested.

Wil slammed the door shut from inside with the wounded man. Morel himself turned the crank and the engine fired.

Judith looked quickly at Mason and he shook his head. There was a story here he had to find, and perhaps to tell. He hoped she understood. There was no chance to tell her.

She nodded briefly, then gave all her attention to driving.

Mason stood in the road and watched them go. He would speak to Cavan another time.

Captain Morel was tight with fury. His features were pinched and white except for two spots of color on his cheeks. His movements were jerky, his muscles locked hard.

"Leave it, Corporal!" he shouted at the man with the gun. "Save the horses and get them out of there."

"But, sir, Major Northrup told us—"

"To hell with Major Northrup!" Morel snapped back, his voice shaking. "The man's a bloody idiot! I'm telling you to get the horses out and rejoin your platoon."

The corporal stood where he was, torn with indecision. Mason could see that he was terrified of what Northrup, who outranked Morel, would do to him for disobeying his order.

Morel saw it, too. He made an intense effort to control his fury. His face softened into pity so naked Mason felt almost indecent to have seen it. He wanted to look away, yet his own emotion held him. He was involved whether he wanted to be or not. Equally, he was helpless. This was one tiny instance of idiocy in a hundred thousand times as much.

"Corporal," Morel said quietly, ignoring the rain running down his face. "I outrank you and I am giving you a direct order. You have no choice but to obey me, unless you want to be court-martialed. If Northrup questions you, tell him that. I'll answer for it; you have my word."

The corporal's face flooded with relief. He was no more than eighteen or nineteen. "Thank you, sir." He gulped.

Morel nodded. "Do it." He turned away, then, realizing Mason was still there, he faced him. His eyes were hard and belligerent, ready to attack if Mason criticized him.

Mason looked at him more closely. Everything about him spoke of a terrible weariness. He was probably in his mid-twenties, a public school boy, and later, judging by his accent, a student at Cambridge. A wounded idealist, betrayed by circumstances and blind stupidity that no sane man could have conceived of.

Mason thought of all the Frenchmen, also betrayed and slaughtered. Would the man in front of him mutiny, too? There was a rage in him too fragile, too close to snapping.

"Who are you and what do you want?" Morel demanded.

"Richard Mason, war correspondent," Mason replied. "Who is Northrup?"

Morel let out his breath slowly. "Major Penhaligon was killed on the first day of Passchendaele. Northrup's his replacement."

"I see."

"I doubt it." Morel glanced up the road the way the ambulance had gone. "You'll have to walk. Follow the stench. You can't get lost. Although it doesn't matter a damn if you do. It's all the same."

"I know."

Morel hesitated, then shrugged and turned away back to his own men and the staff car still parked on the edge of the road. After the driver cranked it up, Morel climbed in and they drove off.

Mason started to walk.

How should he write up this incident? Should he record it at all? It was a classic example of the idiocy of some of the officers now in command and, as always, it was the ordinary men who paid the price. Thanks to Judith's intervention, this one would only have two smashed legs. He might even walk again, if it hadn't caught his back as well. Others would be less fortunate.

He could see Judith in his mind's eye, ordering the soldiers to lift, stand, hold. Her voice had been perfectly calm, but he had seen the tension in her. She knew what she was doing, and the risks. If one of the horses had slipped or she had lost control of it, the gun carriage would have rolled back into the crater and crushed the soldier to death.

She had not seemed to give reason even a passing thought. Morel's fury had had no visible effect on her. She could have been a good nanny watching a small child throw a tantrum, simply waiting for it to pass before she told him to pull himself together and behave properly. It had not entered her head to rebel against the madness.

Why not? Did she lack the imagination? Was she conditioned to obedience, unquestioning loyalty no matter how idiotic the cause? Perhaps. John Reavley had stolen the treaty, and she was his daughter. Joseph Reavley was her brother. Maybe sticking to ideals regardless of pain or futility, in defiance of the evidence, was considered an evidence of faith, or some other virtue, in the family? She had been taught it when she was too young to question, and now to do so would feel like a betrayal of those she loved.

Mason's feet hurt in the wet boots, and he was growing cold in spite of the exertion of walking. Two years ago Joseph Reavley had followed him from the shores of Turkey right to Gibraltar, then out into the English Channel. After the U-boat had sunk the steamer, they had ended in the same open boat in the rising storm, trying to make for England.

Would Joseph really have let them both drown rather than surrender his ideals to fight to the end? That one article, had Mason written it, might have ended the recruitment of hundreds of thousands of men, God knows how many of them dead in the two years since.

Yes, Judith was probably just like Joseph.

Mason remembered with surprise how he had believed Joseph then. For a brief time he too had understood the reasons for fighting. They seemed to embody the values that made all life sweet and infinitely precious. Indeed, was life worth anything at all, worth clinging to without them?

How many more had given their lives, blindly, heroically, since then? For what?

What would happen if he wrote that honestly, put quixotic sacrifice in its place? It was meaningless in the long run, no comfort to the hundreds of thousands left all over Europe, whose sons and husbands would never return, lonely women whose hearts were wounded beyond healing. Judith would think him a traitor—not to the cause, but to the dead, and to the bereaved who had paid so much.

He realized only now, in the wind and rain of this Flanders road where the stench of death was already knotting his stomach, that her disillusion in time would be a pain he would never afterward be free from. It would be one more light gone out forever and the darkness would be closer around him than he could bear.

Joseph came out of his dugout at the sound of Barshey Gee shouting almost incoherently. Gee swung around as he saw Joseph. His face was red, his thick hair sodden in the rain.

"Chaplain, you've got to do something! The major's told us to go back out there and get the bodies, roight now!" He waved his arm toward the front parapet and no-man's-land beyond. "We can't, not in that mud! In the loight. Doesn't he know we'd do it if we could?" His voice was hoarse and half choked with tears. "Jesus! Fred Arnold's out there! Oi've known him all moi loife! Oi got stuck up a tree—scrumping apples in old Gabby Moyle's orchard. It was Fred who got me down before Oi were caught." He drew his breath in in a gasp. "Oi'd go if there were any chance at all, but that mud's deep as the hoight of a man, an if yer get stuck in it you've no chance. Jerry'll pick us off like bottles on a wall. Just lose more men for nothin'."

"I know that, Barshey," Joseph said grimly.

Barshey was shaking his head.

"Oi refused an order, Chaplain. We all did. He can have us court-martialed, but Oi won't send men out there." His voice was thick with tears.

"I'll talk to him." Joseph felt the same anger and grief hot inside him. He had known Fred Arnold, too, and his brother Plugger Arnold who had died of his wounds last year. "Wait here." He turned and strode back toward the officers' dugouts where he knew Northrup would be at this time of day.

All dugouts were pretty similar: narrow and earth-floored. There was room enough for a cot bed, a chair, and a makeshift desk. Most officers made them individual with odd bits of carpet, pictures of home or family, a few favorite books, perhaps a wind-up gramophone and several recordings.

Entrance was gained down steep steps and doorways were hung with sacking to keep out the rain.

"Yes, Chaplain?" Northrup said as Joseph answered the summons to come in. Northrup looked harassed and impatient. He was sitting in the hard-backed chair in front of the desk. There were half a dozen books on it, which were too worn for Joseph to read the titles. There was also a picture of a woman with a bland, pleasant face. Judging by the age of her and the resemblance about the set of eyes and the high brow, it was his mother.

Joseph disliked intensely having to speak, but he had no choice.

"Sir, I understand you ordered Corporal Gee to lead a rescue party to find the dead or wounded in no-man's-land."

"Of course I did, Captain Reavley." His voice was faintly patronizing, even if he did not intend it. "We can't leave them to die out there. Or fail to bring back the bodies of those who have. I regret that the corporal refused a direct order. I've given him half an hour to get his courage back, but if he doesn't, I'll have to put him on a charge. This is the British Army, and we obey orders. Do you understand me?"

Joseph wanted to tell him that the French command had driven its own men to mutiny, but he knew it would be disastrous to do that now. Northrup was thin-skinned enough to regard it as a personal insult and react accordingly.

He kept his temper under control with difficulty. "Sir, I've known Barshey Gee most of my life, and served beside him since 1914. He's one of the bravest men in this regiment, and if he could have gone out there without sacrificing his men pointlessly, then he would have. One of his closest friends was lost last night...."

Northrup's face was hard, his pale blue eyes hot with anger. "Then why doesn't he get out there and look for him, Chaplain?"

Joseph had to struggle to keep his voice level. It was hard to breathe without gasping. "Because it's been raining for a week, Major Northrup," he said with elaborate patience that grated in spite of his effort to be civil. "The men are being sucked down into the mud and drowned! The craters are ten or twelve feet deep and no one can keep their footing for more than a few minutes. A soldier with full equipment hasn't got a chance. He'd be stuck fast, a sitting target. He's not willing to sacrifice more men pointlessly."

"Recovering the wounded is not *pointless*, as you put it, Captain Reavley." Northrup's face was white, his hand on the desk pale-knuckled and trembling. "I would have thought that, as a chaplain, you of all people would have known that! Think of morale, man. That's your job. I shouldn't have to do it for you!"

"I am thinking of morale, sir." Joseph's words came between clenched teeth. "Court-martialing one of our best soldiers because he won't lead his men on a suicidal mission is going to do infinitely more harm than the losses overnight."

Northrup glared at him. His certainty had evaporated, and he was doubly angry because he knew Joseph could see it.

"Sir!" Joseph started again, unable to hide his emotion. "These men have been here for three years. They've endured hell. Every one of them has lost friends, many of them have lost brothers, cousins. Their villages have been decimated. You know nothing of what they've seen, and if you want their respect, then you must also show them the respect they deserve."

Northrup remained silent for several minutes. Joseph could see the struggle in his face, the anger at being challenged and the fear of weakness. "Other men have gone out," he said finally. "That puts paid to your argument, Reavley."

"And have they come back?" Joseph asked. He sounded challenging and he had not intended to be. He sensed Northrup's need to prove himself right and that he might dig himself in if he felt threatened, and yet he had gone too far to stop.

"Not yet," Northrup said defiantly. "But Eardslie's a good man, an officer. He didn't refuse to go."

Nigel Eardslie was another of Joseph's students from St. John's, before the war: a sensitive, intelligent young man, a good scholar, and a close friend of Morel's. Suddenly the argument with Northrup was pointless. What did it matter who won it or who lost it? All he could think of was Eardslie and his men out in no-man's-land in the mud.

"It's not raining now," Northrup added, as if that vindicated him.

"It's not the rain that matters, it's the mud!" Joseph snapped. "If you'll excuse me, sir, I'll see if I can help." He did not bother to explain any further. Northrup was out of his depth and afraid to show it. Joseph saluted and left, pushing the sacking aside and climbing the steep steps up to the air again.

It took him nearly half an hour to make his way to the forward trench.

The duckboards were awash, some floating knee-high in the filthy water. Others were almost waist-high, clogged with the bodies of dead rats, garbage, and old tins. The leg of a dead soldier stuck out from the gray clay of the wall. There were patches of blue sky overhead, but Joseph was cold because he was wet to the skin.

Going uphill slightly, he came to a relatively dry stretch and several groups of men cleaning equipment, telling bad jokes and laughing. One had his shirt off and had scratched his flesh raw where the lice had bitten him. Another had coaxed a flame inside a tin and was boiling water. Some were reading letters from home. Five of them could not have been over seventeen. Their bodies were slight, smooth-skinned, although their faces were hollow and there was a tight, brittle tension in their voices.

A hundred yards farther on he came to a connecting trench. Huddled along it, their backs to the walls, were a dozen men. He recognized Morel. He was standing a little apart from the others, bracing himself against the earth, his head back in a blind stare upward. The angles of his body were stiff, almost as if he were waiting to move, yet afraid to.

Joseph felt his chest tighten and his breath grew heavy in his lungs. He tried to go faster but the duckboards had rolled and were broken, and his feet could get little purchase in the mud.

No one took any notice of him when he stopped. He knew most of them. Bert Collins was there, caked in mud, his right arm blood-soaked. Cully Teversham and Snowy Nunn stood together with Alf Culshaw, who was smaller, narrow-chested, dapper when he had the chance. He always managed to scrounge whatever you wanted from rations—for a consideration, of course. He looked grim and tired, and there was a bandage wrapped tightly around his left arm. Stan Tidyman for once was not talking about his favorite food. He was shoulder to shoulder with George Atherton, who could mend anything if you gave him pliers, a bit of wire, and the time. The last one was Jim Bullen.

It was Cully who saw Joseph first, but there was no smile on his face. He did not even speak. No one saluted or came to attention.

Morel turned slowly but it was several seconds before his eyes focused and he recognized Joseph. His expression did not change. Snowy Nunn also stared unblinkingly.

They were covered in mud, wet to the waist, or—in the cases of Cully Teversham and Stan Tidyman—up to the armpits; all except Morel. In a blinding moment, Joseph understood: Barshey Gee had refused to take a party into no-man's-land to look for survivors and bring back what dead they could find, but these were the men Nigel Eardslie had led.

"Eardslie?" Joseph's voice was hoarse, almost unintelligible, except that they all knew what he was asking. He gulped air. "Wounded?"

"Dead," Morel said huskily. "There wasn't enough of him left to bring back. You want to bury one arm, a foot, Chaplain? Couldn't even tell if it was left or right." He could not control the tears running down his face.

Joseph was furious, raging against believing it, as if to refuse to acknowledge the fact could stop it being true.

"You went?" he said incredulously. "For God's sake, what's the matter with you?" He flung his arms out toward the sea of stinking, gas-soaked mud beyond the hastily thrown-up line. Then words choked him and failed.

"No, of course I bloody didn't!" Morel shouted back at him, his voice so high-pitched it was almost a scream. His chest was heaving and he seemed hardly able to breathe. "That idiot Northrup ordered them and told them it was mutiny if they refused, and he'd charge them. And the stupid bastard would have, too!"

Joseph was overwhelmed. Grief and a terrible sense of helplessness stunned him. He had nothing left to say, no answers anymore. He stared at Morel and saw at the same time the young man he had first met at St. John's: careless, hot-tempered, quick to laugh, and possessed of a hard, supple intelligence. The idealist in him was bruised to the bone, scorched with pain at the loss, and at the monstrous stupidity of it. Everything in Morel's nature and his education told him it was his responsibility to stop it. He was bred to lead, to answer for actions and pay the price of them. It was naked in his face now, and he was teetering on the edge of mutiny. He would take Snowy with him—that was clear, too—and possibly several of the others.

How could Joseph tell them there was a God who cared? He felt his own belief slipping out of his grasp. He closed his eyes, his mind crying out, "Father, if You are there, if You still remember us, do something! We're dying! Not just smashed and bleeding bodies, we're dying inside. There's no light left."

"What do you say now, Reverend Reavley?" Morel's voice cut across his mind like a knife edge.

Joseph opened his eyes and wiped a muddy hand across his face. "Barshey Gee refused to go," he answered. "Northrup'll have to back down. Did you find any wounded still alive?"

"Of course we bloody didn't!" The tears streamed down Morel's face. "Those that weren't blown apart are drowned! And Northrup won't back down. He'll crucify the lot of us, if we don't get to him first. There's no point in waiting for God—Chaplain! How long does it take you to realize that there's no God there? No God that gives a damn, anyway." He turned and walked down the trench, blundering into the walls, bruising himself without knowing or caring.

Joseph had nothing to say. It even stole into his mind that perhaps Morel was right.

FOUR

*F*our nights after Eardslie's death, Northrup led a major assault. The rain had eased a little, but the water did not soak away through the thick clay of Passchendaele. It lay coating the paths and filling the craters and trenches.

Gradually they inched forward. The guns roared all night, and star shells lit up the sky. The landscape looked like the surface of the moon. It was hard to believe anything had ever lived on it, or would again.

They were long past midsummer and the days were shortening. The dawn was heavy and dull, a drifting mist and occasional rain obscuring most of the newly gained land. The woods ahead, beyond no-man's-land, were not even a darkening of the gray. It was ideal for going out to search for wounded.

"Bloody Jerry won't see anyone in this," Barshey Gee said cheerfully, swinging his rifle over his shoulder. "Ready, lads?"

"Roight," Cully Teversham agreed. Behind him Stan Tidyman, John Geddes, George Atherton, and Treffy Johnson nodded.

"Captain?" Barshey looked at Joseph.

"Of course." Joseph led the way up the fire step, across the parapet and down onto the slimy mud on the other side. They had to be careful because the winding path through the craters and bogs changed with every bombardment. Bodies floated beside it, grotesquely swollen, and the stench of rotting flesh and effluent flooding over from the latrines was hanging in the almost motionless air.

They went in twos, one man to help the other if either lost his footing. They spread out to cover as much ground as possible. No one spoke.

The misty rain would probably deaden sound, but it was not worth the risk.

Cully Teversham went with Joseph. He was a big man with ginger hair that even the army barber couldn't tame and hands that dwarfed everything he held. He moved calmly, picking his way, testing the ground under his feet, always looking ahead and then to the sides.

A long spike of barbed wire caught around Cully's leg and he stopped, bending slowly to cut himself free. Joseph helped, and they moved forward again.

Ahead and to the left they saw Geddes and George Atherton. They were no more than shapes in the gloom, identifiable only by Geddes's stiff shoulders and the swing of his arms.

It was half an hour before they found the first wounded man. His side was torn open by shrapnel and one leg was broken, but he was definitely still alive. Awkwardly, slipping and floundering in the mud, they got him back across the parapet and to the dressing station behind. Then they went back to look for more. The mist was clearing, and in another hour their camouflage could be gone.

This time they were more certain of the path, and the urgency was greater. Joseph moved ahead, his feet sucking and squelching, tripping over occasional broken equipment, spent shells, and now and then part of a corpse. He was sweating. It was warmer and there were patches of blue sky above.

He saw the body before Cully did. It was lying on its side, looking as if it were asleep rather than dead. There was no apparent injury. Joseph quickened his step, slithered the last few feet, and bent over him. It was then he saw the crown on one shoulder. It was a major! He turned the man gently, trying to see who it was, and where he was wounded. It was Major Northrup.

Cully was at his shoulder. "In't no good, Captain. Look." There was no emotion in his voice. He was pointing at the man's head.

Joseph saw. There was a small blue bullet hole in his skull, just above the bridge of his nose, exactly in the middle.

"Sniper," Cully remarked. "Damn good shots, some o' those Jerrys. Mind, I suppose he were pretty far forward. Clean way to go, if you've got to, eh?"

"Yes," Joseph agreed. It was. Far better than being gassed, coughing your lungs up, drowning in your own body's fluids, or being caught on the wire, riddled with bullets, and hanging there perhaps for days till you bled or froze to death. But that was not what was in his mind. Why had none of his own men brought Northrup back? Surely they had seen him fall? But no one had even reported him missing.

"Let's get him back," he said grimly.

"Yes, sir," Cully said obediently.

It was an awkward journey and as the sky cleared and the heat burned through, the ground steamed gently. But the cover it offered was too little. Shots began to ring out, shells and sniper fire starting to miss them too narrowly.

They reached the forward lines, then the parapet, and rolled over into the shelter and filth of the front trench. Hands reached out to help them.

"He's dead," Cully said matter-of-factly. "Can't do nothing for him, not now."

"The major!" Stan Tidyman said in surprise. "Well Oi never!"

"Now we'll have to get another one," Tiddly Wop Andrews remarked. "Can't be worse than this, though, can he?"

Barshey Gee fished a sixpence out of his pocket and slapped it on the fire step. "Sixpence says it can," he said with a smile. "Oi'll be happy to lose."

The others laughed.

It was Joseph's duty to report the death to Colonel Hook at the regimental command. Northrup would have to be replaced. Headquarters might send someone, or it might be a field promotion of someone already with them, but he had no time to think about it. Please heaven it would not be Morel. Joseph still did not know what to do about him, how to help or where his first obligation lay. Morel was angry at Northrup's incompetence and his arrogance at refusing to be helped by a man from the ranks, even when he was right. But he was far from the only experienced man to feel that. And he was grieved at Eardslie's death. They had been friends for years.

Geddes and Bill Harrison helped Joseph carry Northrup to the table in the first aid post. He would be buried close by, probably tonight. Precious transport had to be kept for the wounded.

He thanked them and Harrison remained behind. "Can I help you, sir? Tidy him up a bit?"

"Thank you," Joseph said. It was a grim task, but he had done it so often it was almost mechanical now. Such decencies really were for those left alive who would know, a rather pointless exercise in humanity, as if it could make any difference. Northrup was beyond help, and no one else cared. It was a pretense that in the seas of blood each death was somehow important. The whole of the Western Front was strewn with broken bodies; many of them would never be found. He had presided at burials where there was little more to identify than a handful of dog tags.

Still he accepted the offer, and together they straightened his uniform, took off the worst of the mud and washed his face. Northrup looked frightened. There was no resolution or peace in his pinched features.

"Reckon as he saw it coming, don't you, sir?" Harrison asked with a touch of pity. Perhaps now that Northrup could do no more harm he felt free to treat his weaknesses with humanity.

Joseph looked down at the corpse. He closed the staring eyes. "Yes," he agreed. "It looks like it."

"Poor devil," Harrison said bleakly. "Is there anything else I can do, sir?"

Joseph found his throat dry, his hand trembling a little. "No, thank you. This is just routine. I'll have to go and tell Colonel Hook, but I'll make Northrup look a bit better first."

"Yes, sir." Harrison saluted and left.

When Joseph was certain he had gone he looked again at Northrup's face. Even with his eyes closed, the fear was still there, ugly and painfully naked. How long would it be before Harrison realized that Northrup could not possibly have seen the sniper? Any German must have been at least five hundred yards away from where they had found Northrup's body. Had Northrup simply panicked under fire? Please God that was it!

Please God? Did he think God was listening after all? Joseph had wanted Northrup removed before he killed any more men with his arrogant stupidity, but not this way!

He slid his hand under Northrup's head and felt the exit wound. The bone was splintered, hair matted with blood and brain. There was no point in trying to wash it off. Simpler to bandage it briefly, decently. Make him look whole.

He took off the tin helmet and washed that clean. He stared at it. There was no scar, no mark on the metal where the bullet had exited. Where was the bullet? Fallen out onto the ground, or inside his clothes?

The answer was obvious but he still resisted it. There must be another explanation.

Deliberately, methodically, he examined the rest of the body. There were no other injuries on him, except for a chafing at the wrists. It was not much more than red marks and a little broken skin, as if he had been firmly tied, but not harshly.

Joseph knew it before he forced himself to accept it. Old memories flooded into his mind of finding another body and bringing it back, and then realizing it was not a casualty of war but murder. That time he had at first assumed a German soldier had held the dead man's head below the water. This time he knew straightaway it was his own men who had killed

Howard Northrup. But now, two years and thousands of deaths later, Joseph would be a great deal more careful what he did about it. The grief of that time, and the guilt of his own part in it, still haunted him. Before he reported this to anyone, he would learn more about Northrup's incompetence, how serious it was, how many lives it had cost, or had appeared to cost, and whose. He would look further than an instant judgment of what seemed to be justice. He was wiser now, more aware of the complexity behind an apparently simple act. These men lived in circumstances unimaginable to those who had originally written the rules. How could any sane man have conceived of this horror, let alone framed laws to meet its needs?

He reached for a wet rag and was making sure the crowns on Northrup's epaulettes were clean, when he saw Richard Mason standing in the doorway. His dark face which concealed so much emotion was set in lines of tense expectancy.

"Hello, Mason," Joseph said with slight surprise. The last article of Mason's he had read had been sent from Russia. "There's nothing new here. You could copy what you put last time, just change the casualty figures."

Mason's mouth tightened in the barest of smiles. He came farther into the room. "Was he alive when you found him?" he asked.

"No." Joseph knew in that moment that he would give Mason no information he did not have to. He needed time. He liked Mason personally; they had struggled through the nightmare of Gallipoli together, and then the storm in the English Channel, but Mason was a war correspondent. He would publish the truth of a situation, no matter how hideous, if he believed it served a greater good. Perhaps that was right, but Joseph had already learned how hard it was to judge where a path might lead, and that it was too late to be sorry afterward. Very little was simple.

Mason was looking at him, eyes unwavering. "Sniper?"

"Looks like it," Joseph said. He knew it was a lie, but he needed to learn more before he committed himself. "Why? Are you going to write an obituary for him?"

Mason smiled this time, but there was no light in it, no humor. "Do you think I should, Reverend? What should I say? Killed in the line of duty, Passchendaele, the eighth of August, 1917. Not exactly individual, is it! I could write that for tens of thousands of men. They're all unique to those who loved them, someone's only son, only brother, husband, fiancé, friend." His eyes widened and his voice became harsher. "What should I say about Northrup? That he was an arrogant fool and his men hated him? His death may save the lives of a few poor devils he'd have sent over the top uselessly?"

"If you set yourself up to judge one man, then you need to judge them all," Joseph replied, this time facing him without flinching. "Do you feel you have the right or the ability to do that, Mason?"

Mason's mouth turned down in a wry wince. He leaned against the upright of the tent flap and put his hands in his pockets.

"Of course I don't. That wasn't really my point. I notice that you question my right to say so, but not that it is true."

"I question your right to come to that conclusion," Joseph corrected him. "But I don't really care what you think, only what you say."

"And you don't want me to say that Northrup was an incompetent officer and it's a blessing for his men that he's dead?" Mason raised his eyebrows. "His men are saying it themselves."

"Possibly," Joseph agreed. "To each other, but they wouldn't write it down, or repeat it where his family will hear."

"Perhaps that's the problem?" Mason suggested. "We cover the errors, however disastrous, if it's going to hurt someone's feelings, especially if that someone is an officer."

"We do it for the dead, whoever they are," Joseph corrected him again.

"Ah." Mason smiled. "That's the point, isn't it? Now he's dead, his mistakes die with him. He's no more danger, so why cause unnecessary pain?"

Joseph was beginning to feel cold in spite of the August sun burning outside and the close, overwarm air. "What is it you want, Mason? As you said, the man was arrogant and a fool, but he's dead. Do you feel some moral obligation to soil his name and make his family's grief the greater, just because it's true? What about the families of the men who died because of his ignorance or bad judgment? Do you think knowing that will help their pain?"

"That's what it's about, isn't it, Chaplain? Pain to other people?"

Joseph stared at him. The fierce intelligence in Mason's eyes did not allow him to delude himself any longer. "Part of it, yes."

"And is covering their sins the part you've taken on yourself?"

"Northrup's sins are not my business, Mason," Joseph told him. "Neither are they yours. He can't do any more harm now."

Mason straightened up. "It won't work, Reavley. I'm not referring to Northrup's sins, and you know that. I'm talking about how he died. I saw you look at the helmet. The bullet wasn't there, was it?"

"Probably fell out." Joseph still tried to evade the issue.

Mason walked over to the table and looked down at Northrup's face. "He was shot by his own men, or at least by one of them. And the others are covering for him. You know that. Are you going to lie, by implication, so they escape with murder?" Now he was looking at Joseph, his eyes searching Joseph's, probing for honesty. "Does war really change things so much, Chaplain?"

"I don't know what happened yet," Joseph answered him. "I want to find out before I jump to conclusions."

"Liar," Mason said quietly. "You want to find out if it was one of the men from your own village who killed him, so if it was, you can protect him."

Perhaps a year ago Joseph would have lost his temper. Now he kept it tightly governed. "I want to find out what happened before I set in motion a chain of events I can't stop or control," he said gravely. "Perhaps moral issues are all black and white to you, although I doubt it. I know you've been prepared to sacrifice one goal to attain another." He was referring to their argument in the Channel two years ago, and the implicit fact that Mason would allow some of his own countrymen to be killed in order to save the vast majority. Or was he naïve enough not to know decisions like that faced military commanders every week?

Mason smiled. The expression softened his face, changing him. "But we are not the same, Reavley. I'm a war correspondent. I can observe, tell stories, ask questions. You're a chaplain, supposedly a man of God. People think you know the difference between right and wrong. They look to you to tell them, especially now when the world is falling apart. If you won't stand, Reverend, who will?" There was mockery in his face, but a wry, self-conscious sort of hope as well. He wanted Joseph to have the certainty and the faith he did not. He might have denied it—Joseph believed he would have, because it was too precious to put to any test. Fragile as it was, ephemeral, he would be lost without it.

"I did more than that before," Joseph answered him. "And I'm not sure whether I was right or not."

"Northrup was murdered." Mason bit his lip. "If he hadn't been, you wouldn't argue the issue now, you'd just deny it."

"I've only just seen the helmet." Joseph told the truth, but it was still a prevarication, and the moment he had said it he was sorry. He should have known what to do, if right and wrong were as clear to him as Mason seemed to imagine. And not only Mason. Many of the men thought he should not be confused, as they were. They wanted answers, and felt let down if he could not give them. Priests were God's authority on earth. For a priest to say he did not know was about the same as admitting that God Himself did not know; that He had somehow become confused and lost control. Life and death themselves became meaningless.

Mason was waiting.

"You are not naïve," Joseph told him. "Your faith doesn't rest on me. Don't blackmail me with it. I don't know what happened to Northrup. Of course his own men might have killed him. It happens. I'd like to know more of the circumstances before I report it to Colonel Hook."

Mason's eyes were steady, unblinking.

"Why? In case the man who did it is someone you like, whose father and brothers you know? Or are you afraid the morale of the whole brigade will crumble if you tell the truth?"

"Aren't you?" Joseph continued. "Or is that what you want? Truth at all cost? Whoever pays?"

"Who pays if the chaplain condones men murdering one of their officers because they don't agree with his orders?" Mason asked.

"Is that how you see it?" Joseph said tensely. "If it's as simple as that to you, maybe you should be the chaplain. You seem to have right and wrong very clearly labeled. You know far more about it than I do?"

Mason shrugged. "No. But I know what the men will say, and so do you. If you let Northrup's death go, who's next? I haven't any faith that what we're fighting for is worth the price. I think the whole bloody nightmare is madness. If I believed in the devil, I'd say he's taken over." He spread his strong, supple hands. "This has to be as close to hell as it gets. But you believe in something. You don't have to be here. You could have stayed at home and looked after a nice quiet parish in the countryside, comforted the bereaved, and kept spirits up on the home front. But you're here. Why? Just going down with the ship because you don't know what else to do? Can't find a way to admit you were wrong, or can't face telling the men that?"

He had touched a nerve. How many nights had Joseph wrestled in prayer to find some sense, some light of hope in the endless loss? If God really had any power or cared for mankind at all, why did He do nothing?

Was Northrup's murder just one more ugly and senseless tragedy for him, for his family, and most of all for the man who had pulled the trigger? Or would it be the catalyst for a general mutiny against the senseless daily slaughter?

Joseph could divert the attack against himself by attacking Mason in return, but it answered nothing, and Mason would know it, just as he knew it himself.

"You seem to think I should be the judge of what to do," he said slowly. "And yet you have decided for me, before either of us knew what happened, or what result will come from pursuing it."

"I know what result will come from not pursuing it," Mason told him. "And so do you. Either you tell Hook, or I do."

Joseph did not put him to the choice. If Hook had to be told, it would be his way.

"You're quite sure, Captain Reavley?" Hook said unhappily. He was a lean man who had been spare to begin with and was now almost gaunt. He had been twice wounded, and the way he stood betrayed every so often that his shoulder still ached.

Joseph had said only what he had found, without drawing conclusions. "Yes, sir."

"Any idea who is responsible?"

"No, sir. I'm afraid Major Northrup angered quite a few of the men."

Hook gave him a dour glance. "He angered the whole bloody lot, Reavley. That isn't what I asked."

"I have no idea which of the men is responsible."

Hook stared at him. His eyes were shadowed. He had seen too many of his men die, and he was helpless to do anything but go on ordering them forward in endless attack after attack. He wanted to avoid this one further pointless grief. He sighed. "See what you can find out when you have the chance." He waited, trying to gauge if Joseph understood him.

"Yes, sir." Joseph came to attention. "As soon as I have the opportunity."

Hook relaxed a little. "I'll write to his father. I should do it myself. Thank you, Reavley. You can go."

Two days later, on the tenth of August, the rain burst like a monsoon over Ypres and Passchendaele, running in rivers down the slopes of the slight hills, filling the trenches till men were waist-deep in it. The fields became quagmires, latrines flooded, stores were ruined and swept away. In every direction one looked was water and more water.

Men made jokes about collecting animals.

"Anybody give me two cows for two rats?" Cully Teversham asked hopefully.

"Two cows for twenty rats?" George Atherton improved the offer, then laughed with the odd, jerky sound he always made.

"Oi'd give you all the sodding rats in Belgium for two cows," Tiddly Wop Andrews retorted.

"I've already got all the sodding rats in Belgium!" Geddes said bitterly.

Into this morass came General Colin Northrup to mourn the loss of his son. He arrived in the middle of the afternoon, climbed out of his car, and stood in the torrential rain as if completely unaware of it, his back ramrod stiff, his face ashen.

It was Joseph's task to meet him. Apart from his obvious grief, and his rank, the general was instantly recognizable because of his physical resemblance to his son. His coloring, the angle of nose and jaw, the steady blue eyes were all the same. Only his mouth was different. There was none of his son's indecision in it, none of the hesitation or lack of fire.

Joseph saluted him and received a smart salute in return.

"If I can be of any service to you, General Northrup, I am at your command. May I extend the condolences of the whole brigade, sir. We all feel his loss."

"I'm sure you do," Northrup said quietly, his voice raw with hurt. "I understand he is the second commanding officer you have lost in a short space of time."

"Yes, sir." It seemed ridiculous to equate Northrup with Penhaligon, but only to Joseph who knew them both and had liked and admired Penhaligon. He struggled to find anything to say that would be even decent, let alone helpful. He understood grief. He had lost his wife, Eleanor, in childbirth in 1913, and his son as well, then both his parents had been murdered by the Peacemaker's agent the year after. God knew how many of his friends had also died since then. There was not a man here who could not name a dozen they had lost. He knew no one could ease this man's grief, but he could at least not insult him with dishonesty. "It always hits the men very hard. I'm sure you know that they often cover their feelings with jokes. It's the only way to hold on to sanity."

"Yes." Northrup swallowed. "Yes, I know that, Chaplain. I don't expect to see the loss I feel in anyone else, nor will I mistake levity for lack of respect. They did not have time to know him as I did, or what a fine man he was."

"No, sir. We have a dugout for you, if you'd like to stay, but I daresay you would prefer to see his grave, and then decide for yourself what to do next. When you are ready, I'll show you. It's . . . it's quite a decent place. We have very good men there."

Northrup's face was set so hard the muscles in his jaw quivered and a nerve ticked in his temple. "Show me my son's grave, Captain Reavley."

Joseph obeyed. It was over a mile's walk through the drenching rain, but Northrup was too lost in his grief to be aware of physical discomfort. When they reached the place, which was filled with makeshift crosses, its earth newly turned, they stood in silence. Joseph already knew where Major Northrup's grave was among the thousands. He took the general to it, then left him alone with his thoughts. Joseph, too, had agonizing memories that made him appreciate solitude. Half the men who had left England with him lay covered in this earth.

He waited until the general moved at last, stiffly, as if all his body ached and his joints pained him. Northrup could not have been more than in his early fifties, but he seemed an old man.

"Thank you, Captain," he said courteously. "He was my only child."

There was no answer to give that had any meaning. Joseph treated it with the dignity of silence.

The battle continued unabated. Joseph sat in his dugout, the endless rain beating unheard on the roof above him. It was difficult to keep the water from running down the steps and inside.

He had already written the day's letters of condolence, five of them to the same small village half a dozen miles from St. Giles where he lived. He did it now almost as if in his sleep. He could no longer think of anything individual to say, even though he had known each of the men.

Now it was time to answer his own mail, the first chance he had had in several days. He picked Matthew's letter off the top of the pile. It was general news, gossip about people they both knew, what was on in the theater or the cinema, a book he had wanted to read but could not find, an art exhibition everyone was talking about. It was not the facts that mattered but the pleasure of hearing from him, the familiarity of the phrases he used; as for everyone, it was the contact with home and people he loved.

He wrote back with all the harmless news he could think of, the bad jokes and the opinions, the rivalries and the generosity.

He replied similarly to his sister Hannah at home in St. Giles. She, of course, had written to him about the village and the people they both knew, but mostly of her children and the odd scraps of news about her husband, Archie, at sea in command of a destroyer.

She described the late summer trees, the gold of the fields, how untidy the garden was, and regretted that she could think of no way to send him raspberries, which were now ripe.

He smiled as he thanked her. Then he told her about Tucky Nunn, and asked her particularly to do what she could for his mother. Not that there was anything, but one had to try.

He wrote also to Hallam Kerr, the vicar in St. Giles who had been so utterly useless last year when Joseph had been home recuperating from injury. Then Kerr had sputtered platitudes, out of touch with any kind of real emotion. By the time Joseph left, Kerr had begun to grasp reality and find the courage to face it. Since then he had matured into a man who was usually adequate, and sometimes superb, but good or bad, he no longer ran away or hid in meaningless ritual answers.

He could not offer Kerr advice, nor did he need it; he simply re-affirmed friendship.

The most difficult letter to answer was the last he had received from Isobel Hughes. In 1915 her husband had been killed and Joseph had sent his condolences along with the official notice of bereavement. She had written back to thank him, and a warm and honest friendship had developed between them. Often he had found he could tell her of his feelings more openly than he could anyone else. Her answers, her faith in him and her easy, natural stories of her own life, hill-farming in Wales, had been a balm to him on many long and bitter nights.

Her last letter had woken in him almost a sense of betrayal. He was aware how ridiculous that was, and yet it was taking time for the smart to go away. He had never met her, and yet he had been taking some part of her affection for granted.

Now she had told him, perhaps a little awkwardly, maybe not soon enough, that she had met a young man, invalided out of the army, and was falling in love with him, and he with her.

Joseph sat in his rickety chair, holding the notepaper in his hands and reading her words again. What was he losing, exactly? More than a corre-spondent? He knew Isobel Hughes's ideas, nothing more. That was not how love worked, not really. Did he want comfort, or did he also want the urgency, magic, the beating heart?

Could he fall in love again, after Eleanor?

Yes, if he was honest, he could. Was that a betrayal, too? Was that what he was afraid of? He wanted someone safe, so he would never risk that sort of pain again.

There it was, in the open. Fear. He was looking for safety.

He took out the pen again and wrote: *Dear Isobel,* and then quite eas-ily the words came to wish her happiness, and rejoice with her.

Then he wrote to Lizzie Blaine, the widow of the young scientist who had been murdered in St. Giles last summer. It was she who had told him how Hallam Kerr had grown more than Hannah had, or anything Kerr himself had written. But then Lizzie was blazingly honest, even when she was the one most hurt by it. And she was brave. Her husband's death had been appalling, but she had never flinched from seeking the facts, facing them wherever they led. It was not that she was not afraid, he had seen it in her eyes, her hands gripped on the steering wheel of her car as she had driven him on his quest both of pastoral care and of investigation, his in-juries having prevented him from driving himself. She was deeply afraid.

But she had a wry, self-mocking humor and a courage that forced her forward, whatever the price.

He could not remember that time with its horror and its burning disillusion without thinking of her also, and the companionship they had shared in such quiet adversity was a balm to the pain of it, a bright thread woven through the darkness, a loyalty amid the betrayal.

He wished he could tell her of Northrup's death and the things he was afraid of now, but military censorship would only cut it out. He knew better than to try. Instead he told her how much he missed the richness of summer at home, the quiet lanes, the smell of growing things, the sight of horses leaning into the plow, men laughing over pints of ale after the work was done, faces burned by the sun.

He missed the silence. His ears ached for it. He missed dew on the grass, and the smell of clean earth. He told her all of that, more clearly than he ever had before, and setting the words down almost brought it within his grasp again.

There was a sharp rap on the wood by the sacking curtain, jerking him back to the present. The moment he answered, General Northrup came in. Joseph was startled, having assumed that he had left. Now his face was as pale as before, and his body as stiff, but his eyes were hot with anger. He did not attempt to conceal it, but stood swaying very slightly on the damp earth floor, his hands locked behind his back. He spoke before Joseph could rise to his feet.

"Captain Reavley, I have to tell you that I find morale among your men so low that they have descended to the grossest disloyalty toward their officers. There is a laxity that I cannot and will not tolerate." He spoke very clearly, enunciating each word. "I have even heard oblique suggestions that my son was less than competent in his command. It is a slur on the name of a fine man who gave his life in the service of his country, and it is . . . obscene." He took a deep breath. "In the name of decency it must cease. The men responsible for such traitorous talk must be identified and punished." He drew his shoulders back even further. "I am disappointed in you, sir, that you did not take action sooner than this to stop such infamy."

Joseph was standing now. He felt the heat burn up his cheeks, not for shame that he had not defended Major Northrup, but because he had allowed himself to hope that the general would leave without hearing it.

"Perhaps you believed that you were being loyal to Colonel Hook," Northrup went on. "You are mistaken. The ultimate loyalty is to the truth. You do the army no service by keeping silent while slander and betrayal go on. As a man of God your duty is to the highest principles of honor. Your own convenience is nothing." He sliced his hand in the air, then put it back stiffly to his side again. "You have let down your cloth, sir. I will not permit you, or any man, to dishonor my son. Do you hear me?"

"Yes, sir." Joseph's mind raced. How could he respond to this man who was so deeply outraged by what was essentially the truth? If only right were as clear as General Northrup imagined. Did one place ideals of truth before compassion for men? This was a hell where just to survive took all a man could dredge up out of his soul. Hope and sanity were lights on a hill the other side of the abyss.

Northrup was waiting for an answer. His son was dead and his grief was insupportable. What good was forcing him to see the truth?

"Well?" Northrup's temper broke. "Don't just stand there, man! Account for yourself!"

How many explanations were there that would not wound irrevocably? They would sound to Northrup like lies and excuses anyway.

"I'm sorry, sir," Joseph began. "Major Northrup replaced a man deeply respected. It was after that that we suffered a great many losses, both wounded and dead. Some of the men blamed Major Northrup for giving orders that cost many of those lives."

"Rubbish!" Northrup snapped. "To blame an officer for necessary orders is close to mutiny, sir. Which you must know as well as I do! You may be a man of the cloth, but you are in the army. How long have you been out here?" His eyes narrowed and he looked Joseph up and down critically.

"Since September 1914, sir," Joseph answered him equally curtly.

Northrup swallowed. It was far longer than he had been there himself. In that instant Joseph knew it, and Northrup saw that he did.

"With these same men?" Northrup asked more quietly.

"Yes, sir, those that are still alive. A lot of them are replacements, recently recruited. Half the old regiment's gone."

Northrup sighed, his face ashen. He swallowed convulsively. "They are still at fault, Captain. They have no right to question an officer's order in the field. That is not the worst of it. I have . . . I have even heard suggestions that his own men are glad he is dead." He did not add the last fearful thought to that, but it was in the air unsaid.

Joseph had to face it. "If you are asking what I think you are, sir, then that is nonsense. There is always some degree of loose talk. The men are facing death. Most of them will not come back, and they know it. They have two or three weeks to live, at most. Some will die easily, by one bullet through the head, like Major Northrup. For others it will be far harder. I think we should ignore the more foolish things that are said."

General Northrup's voice was hoarse. "Do you? Do you indeed? Well, I do not. Stupidity I can allow. They are, as you say, ordinary men facing a grim death. But I will not have my son's name slandered. And if you will not stop it, then I will speak to Colonel Hook."

"General Northrup!" Joseph knew the man was going to provoke the very disaster he most feared. Of course he could not bear to think his son was a fool, or that his men had hated him, but by forbidding them to say so, he would force the truth into the open. Someone's temper would snap, and he would say it simply to defend himself or, more probably, to defend someone else.

"What is it, Captain?" Northrup said tersely.

"Sir, you can command men to obey you, and shoot them if they don't. You cannot command them to respect you. That you have to earn, especially after you have given orders that have cost lives and achieved nothing."

Northrup's face mottled dull red. "Are you saying that my son gave such orders, Captain Reavley?"

"I'm saying that no one can govern what the men think, sir. When people speak foolishly, because they are exhausted, beaten, and afraid, it is better to overlook—and forget."

"That is the coward's way, sir," Northrup replied. "If you will do nothing, then I shall speak to Colonel Hook. Good day, Captain Reavley." He turned and went out without a salute, leaving Joseph standing alone.

That night the bombardment was heavy. The rain never ceased. It looked like it would be the wettest August anyone had ever known. By morning the casualties were heavy, some of them from drowning.

By midday Joseph was so bone weary his body ached, his head throbbed, and his eyes felt as if they had burning grit in them. His clothes were stiff with blood and his skin was rubbed raw.

He had worked with Cavan in the field hospital most of the night, helping in every way that he could. The man seemed never to cease working. His eyes were bloodshot, his face ashen, but he moved from one broken body to the next like a man in some terrible dream.

That afternoon Joseph was standing in the supply trench, eating a heel of bread and trying to keep it out of the rain, when Barshey Gee came up to him.

"Sorry, sir," Barshey said, screwing his face up. "Colonel Hook would like to see you, sir. Right away." He looked unhappy. There was a scar down his cheek oozing blood which was washed away instantly. His right arm moved awkwardly because of the thickness of the bandage beneath his tunic.

Joseph put the rest of the bread in his mouth. "Right," he acknowledged.

"Sir . . ." Barshey began, then stopped.

"Yes?"

"General Northrup's with him, Chaplain." He said no more, but Joseph understood. There was no avoiding it now.

"I'll do what I can," Joseph promised. He knew Barshey would understand what he meant.

Hook was waiting for him in the command dugout. General Northrup was sitting on the other decent chair, which left an old ammunition box for Joseph to sit on, after he had saluted and been told to be at ease. It was hot and airless inside the confined space, but it was relatively dry.

Northrup looked like a man who had won a bitter victory, exhausted but justified.

"Captain Reavley," Hook began miserably, "General Northrup informs me that there is considerable talk among the men that his son, Major Howard Northrup, did not die as a result of enemy fire."

Northrup shifted his weight in the chair impatiently, but he did not yet interrupt.

Hook was aware of it. "If that is so, of course," he went on, "then it is an extremely grave matter. . . ."

Northrup could not contain himself any longer. "It is more than grave, Colonel Hook," he cut across him. "It is murder, plain and simple. It means you have men who under ordinary law are guilty of the most terrible of all crimes, and under military law are also guilty of mutiny, and must face a firing squad."

Hook kept his courtesy with a very obvious effort. He remained looking at Joseph, as if desperate for his help. "If that is so," he continued, "then it is, as General Northrup says, a capital crime. I can't imagine why any of our men would do such a thing." He spoke carefully, enunciating every word. "Major Northrup had been here only a matter of a week or two. I can't think how he could have made an enemy of that depth in so short a time."

"Of course he didn't!" Northrup snapped. "Your men are out of control! On the verge of mutiny. Major Northrup exerted some discipline, perhaps for the first time, and they resented it. Or possibly there was mutiny planned, and he discovered it, and would naturally have had them arrested and shot. Have you considered that? It is a perfectly obvious motive. A child could understand it." His eyes were watery and he blinked several times.

"Even a child would require that you prove such a thing before exacting punishment," Hook told him, then turned back to Joseph. "Captain, I regret the necessity for this, most particularly now in the middle of one of the hardest offensives we've ever experienced, but I have no alternative other than to investigate the possibility of a crime, even though I do not believe it to be so."

Joseph understood exactly what Hook was saying. Everything about it was bad. Even the suggestion of such a crime would damage morale irreparably. It was already fragile with the appalling losses, the failure to make any significant gain of land, the disastrous weather, the whispers of mutiny among the French troops—even if there was very little real evidence. Even though at least outwardly the men condemned the idea of mutiny, inwardly they had a profound natural sympathy.

And the additional tragedy was that in Northrup's efforts to avenge his son's death and protect his reputation, he was actually going to expose him far more. Now only his own immediate men knew he was incompetent. Soon his name would go down in history as having provoked a murder among the very men he led, murder in order to save their own lives from his stupidity. Joseph knew there was a pity in Hook that wanted to rescue Northrup from himself.

"Yes, sir," he said aloud. "I can see that such rumors, however untrue, must be investigated and silenced, one way or the other."

"One way or the other?" Northrup challenged him sharply, swiveling in his chair to face him. "There is only one way, Captain Reavley, and that is with the truth, and the justice that comes from it."

"I meant, sir, whether there is any charge resulting from what we find, or if it is no more than careless talk," Joseph corrected him. "I've heard nothing more than the usual grumbling and bad jokes. The men always complain, usually about petty things. It's a way of making it bearable."

"I am perfectly acquainted with front line humor, Captain," Northrup said bitterly. "It does not extend to blackening the name of a dead officer."

Hook drew in his breath, but Joseph preempted him. He looked at the general. "What are they saying of Major Northrup that is more than the usual complaints that fly around of any officer, sir?"

Northrup's face was bright pink, his cheeks burning. "That he was an incompetent officer and gave orders that cost lives unnecessarily," he said between his teeth, his voice trembling. "It is to cover their own cowardice."

"My men are not cowards!" Hook said furiously, his thin body stiff, the color rising in his haggard face. "And deeply as I regret the death of your son, sir, I will not tolerate any man, of any rank, saying that they are. That is inexcusable, even in grief."

Northrup glared back at him. "If they murdered my son in cold blood, then they are worse than cowards, sir. They are traitors!" His voice trembled. "And I will see every last one of them shot. Do you defy me, Colonel Hook?"

Hook was shaking. "No, sir, I charge you to make your accusations after they are proved, and to treat my men with the honor they deserve unless and until that time."

"Then prove it!" Northrup's voice was close to a shout. "Don't hide behind your chaplain's protection. Institute a proper inquiry."

"By whom?" Hook could not keep the sarcasm from his tone. "I have no fighting men to spare . . . sir! Captain Reavley is the best man to do it. He is both liked and trusted, and he has known most of these men since they joined up. If anyone can find the truth and prove it, he can!"

"I want military police," Northrup replied, gulping. "The chaplain is not qualified to investigate murder, and his profession makes it impossible either to be practical and insist that men speak to him and answer his questions, or that he should repeat what they say if they do. He might very well learn the exact truth, with a confession, and be unable to act on it."

"That's my answer, General Northrup," Hook told him. "If you want to take it to the general in command of the Ypres Salient, then you must do so. I think it extremely unlikely he will spare men at the moment to investigate any front line soldiers on the possibility that there may, or may not, have been a crime, when there is no evidence beyond some ugly talk."

"We'll see," Northrup retorted, rising to his feet. His face was ashen but for the flaming spots of color in his cheeks.

"Sir!" Joseph stood up, turning toward Northrup and barring his way out. "Major Northrup was very new to this section of the front. He made some bad decisions, specifically sending men out across no-man's-land to look for wounded or dead when the weather and visibility made it recklessly dangerous. No one was rescued, and Lieutenant Eardslie, a well-liked and decorated officer, was killed. I would rather not have told you that. All men make mistakes, but this was a particularly foolish one, and he was told by the experienced men here that it was wrong, but he wouldn't listen."

Northrup was shaking; his whole body trembled. He stared wordlessly at Joseph, grief and incredulity naked in his face.

Joseph was furious with him and pitied him at the same time. It was a uniquely painful conflict within him.

"If I investigate his death, sir," he continued, "I shall bring my findings to Colonel Hook, and any stories that are unnecessary to repeat, I shall make no written record of, and repeat them to no one. I think it would be wiser, and fairer, if we were to learn all we can before we make any decisions at all."

Northrup stood silently for so long that Joseph thought he was not going to answer, then finally he spoke. His voice was hoarse, little above a whisper.

"Do so. But I will see my son's name cleared, and if any man in the British Army, whatever his rank or his record, had a part in his death, I will see that man shot, and alongside him anyone who defends him or lies for him." He snapped to attention, then before anyone else could speak, he strode the three steps to the entrance and went out.

"Thank you, Reavley," Hook said with intense feeling. "For God's sake, be careful what you find. We're losing thousands of men a day to the Germans, or to the bloody rain. The men are on their last legs. Most of them will be killed anyway. The French weren't cowards; they were just driven beyond human endurance. But Northrup looks readier to face a firing squad himself than see the truth, God forgive him."

"Yes, sir. I'll be very careful," Joseph promised. He gave a very faint smile. "I've done this before."

Hook looked up at him. "Oh, yes, the murder of that bloody awful correspondent, Prentice, or whatever his name was, in 'fifteen. I heard about it. You didn't ever find out who killed him though, did you?"

Joseph did not answer him.

Hook put both his hands over his face and let his breath out slowly. "I see."

Joseph knew it would be difficult even to find a place where he could make himself heard, never mind to frame the questions. He was acutely conscious of disturbing men in their few moments' peace to ask pointless questions. And if he was honest, he was not sure he wanted the answers. He had been just as appalled by Northrup's stupidity as they were. He had prayed for some kind of release from it—but not this.

He began with Tiddly Wop Andrews. He found him standing on the fire step up to his knees in water, drinking tea out of a Dixie can. It was early evening.

"Hello, Chaplain," Tiddly Wop said between the bursts of artillery fire. He always spoke quietly. He was a handsome man but profoundly shy. "Looking for someone?"

Joseph was on the trench floor. The duckboards had been swept away and he found it difficult keeping his balance in the mud. Because he was lower than the fire step, he was up to his thighs in it.

"Anyone who might know exactly what happened to Major Northrup," he replied.

Tiddly Wop grinned. "He got shot," he replied cheerfully. "That's one

Jerry whose hand Oi'd loike to shake. Moight even give 'im a cup o' moi tea!" He pulled a face. " 'Cepting Oi' wouldn't want ter poison the poor bleeder."

"Don't pretend you don't know." Joseph kept his own face straight with an effort. "The general thinks he was shot by one of our men. Colonel Hook has asked me to make inquiries."

Tiddly Wop's blue eyes opened wide. "You going to, then?"

"If he was murdered, don't you think I should?" Joseph countered.

Tiddly Wop thought about it. "You know, Chaplain, Oi used to think Oi knew pretty good what was roight and what wasn't. But nothing much looks the same as it used to. Oi'm not so certain anymore." He frowned. "Oi hated Major Northrup 'cos of the men who died 'cos he wouldn't listen. Oi didn't shoot him, but if Oi knew who did, Oi'm not saying Oi'd tell you. Oi 'spect Oi'll be facing whatever judgment there is in a few days, an' most of moi mates with me. Oi'd rather answer to them than to General Northrup."

So would Joseph, but he could not admit it. He did not know what to say.

"If Oi knew, and Oi told you, what'd you think of me?" Tiddly Wop asked gravely.

"Maybe it's just as well you don't know," Joseph answered him. He would never be sure if that was the truth or not, nor did he wish to be.

"Chaplain," Tiddly Wop started as Joseph turned to leave.

"Yes?"

"It's koind of hard at the moment. Oi'd be careful if Oi was you . . . about asking, Oi mean."

"Yes, I know what you mean. Thank you." Joseph waded away, sliding and squelching through the mud.

He sat in his dugout the second evening, tired and cold to the bone because he was wet. He had spent two days asking questions and heard more stories of Northrup's ignorance. There was little sympathy for him, sometimes even open hostility without any disguise that Joseph was wasting his concern on the dead instead of doing what he could for those still alive. He had no argument to rebut it: simply that Colonel Hook had ordered it, and better he than the military police.

Night had come, violent and full of pain. The next day had been the same. A few yards were gained, and they were closer to Passchendaele than before. But another thousand men were dead, with twice as many injured.

He had been told stories of Northrup's last leadership of the men into no-man's-land. No one had seen him fall. No one had been there at the time. Everyone accounted for everyone else. Friendship and its loyalties were the beacons that towered above the darkness. Joseph knew they were lying because in several instances they actually contradicted each other in their eagerness to protect everyone. He realized with surprise that he would have accepted it all and relayed it to Colonel Hook exactly if he had thought there was the slightest chance of his believing it.

He shivered and stared around him. He had lived in this hole in the ground for more than a year, like some hibernating animal. Half a dozen of his favorite books were here, his picture of Dante, the writer of *The Divine Comedy*. Could his vision of hell have been as bad as this reality?

What of Dante's beliefs, his searing portraits of good and evil? Would he be so certain of it if he had seen this welter of terror, heroism, loyalty, and death? Joseph wasn't. He ought to be unequivocally for the law, sure of the few absolutes of justice and the perceived order that had sustained them for more than a thousand years.

Surely there was a constant morality, values beyond any questions, no matter what? Were the truths that spanned the abyss not the surest evidence of God's existence, and His continuing governance of the world? Sometimes in darkness such as this they were the only evidence.

He was lying to himself. The sure theories of the past broke before the need to save lives now, to understand whatever it was that had happened to Howard Northrup, and to the men who had brought it about. The answers did not obey rules. Compassion, loyalty to the living who trusted him to understand, swept away the old faith in rules.

Or was it just a simple and very human matter of who you liked, and who you didn't, who belonged to your pack, the old bonds of loyalty again? He had prayed for understanding, some answers to make the slaughter comprehensible, so men at least knew what they were dying for, and he had received this, which only made it worse.

There was a parcel from Hannah with cake, raspberry jam, a bundle of books, and new socks. There was a note with it where briefly, almost self-consciously, she described the familiar, heart-stopping beauty of the countryside, the harvest-gold fields, the soaring poplars, leaves fluttering in the sunset breeze, the heavy elms, skirts down to the ripe corn heads, the starling whirling across the evening sky.

He pulled out paper to answer her, and wrote possibly too much. Sharing his confusion with her only made him see more clearly how uncertain he was, and his reasons sounded like excuses. In the end he tore it up. It sounded too much as if he were expecting her to find a solution for him. He would thank her properly later.

Instead he wrote to Lizzie Blaine again. He smiled as he remembered how quick she had been to understand last year, how she had had the wisdom not to offer false comfort when he had at last found the awful answer, and had to accept it, and his deep and bitter disillusionment.

The physical pain of his shattered arm and ripped-open leg had almost gone; only now and then did it ache and remind him. But the wound to his faith in people and in his own judgment, the destruction of old loves and old certainties would not ever be forgotten. The truth about Shanley Corcoran had broken something in him.

Lizzie knew that things were never solved, only a little better understood, the doubts faced, courage gripped a little more tightly. It was easier to admit to her than to Hannah that he was troubled by his own sympathy with the men more than the law, that he could conceal the truth, turn away from it, in the needs of mercy.

Perhaps he cared less what she thought of him than he did about Hannah. Or it could be that Hannah was his sister, and might need to believe that he knew more of the answers than he did. He had been there all Hannah's life, when so much else had been ripped away. She had found the loss of her mother particularly hard. And the war had taken all the old certainties she had loved, the way of life she had grown up believing would last forever. She was not like Judith, hungering for adventure. She loved the sweetness of what she had, village life, her home and family, giving the quiet service of a good neighbor—food for the hungry, time with the lonely, a quiet hand for the sick or afraid. She did not want glory; she wanted peace and the assurance of a tomorrow.

There was none, especially for a woman whose husband was at sea, whose eldest son was fast approaching the age when he could join the navy also—not to speak of both a brother and a sister on the Western Front.

To Lizzie he would not matter so much, and he could write honestly, without fear of hurting her. Her friendship seemed a clean and precious thing. He wrote with ease.

FIVE

*M*atthew spent a wretched afternoon at the police station with the officers in charge of prosecuting Alan Wheatcroft, and now of prosecuting Tom Corracher as well. He had hoped they would have some information to indicate who had set the scandal in motion, and that it would eventually lead back toward the Peacemaker. Matthew was more and more convinced it was he behind the dismissal of all four ministers.

"Sorry, sir," the young policeman said with extreme discomfort. "We'd 'ave 'eld off if we could. Fine man, Mr. Wheatcroft. Rather not know these things, as long as no one's 'urt. But we 'ad no choice."

"Really? Someone important, Constable?" Matthew had asked hopefully. "I thought it was the boy himself who complained. And you believed him?"

"It was, sir. That's the thing of it." He looked apologetic. "You see, it wasn't the first time we had a complaint about Mr. Wheatcroft. First time the boy was younger, and we thought as possibly 'e'd got 'old o' the wrong idea, so to speak. It was all dealt with very quietly. We couldn't do it a second time."

"Oh!" Matthew was startled. It was not something he had foreseen at all. "Who knew of this original claim?"

"No one, sir. For the boy's sake, we said nothing."

"But possibly his parents knew."

"His father, sir. We didn't want to distress his mother with it."

"What was his name?"

"I can't tell you that, sir. Discretion, confidence, you understand?"

Matthew had not argued. It would be easy enough to get to know from Wheatcroft himself tomorrow. There was now no way of avoiding seeing him.

However, before he did that, there was one last man he would see who had known Wheatcroft as a student in Cambridge, fifteen years ago: Aidan Thyer, Master of St. John's. It was a calculated risk. Matthew had once believed Thyer himself might be the Peacemaker. He certainly had both the intelligence and the influence. He had been a brilliant scholar in his youth, and now as master he had the position and the charisma to mold generations of students who would be the future teachers, philosophers, scientists, and governors of the nation. He might even have access to members of the Royal Family and friends in power throughout Europe and the Empire. And of course he was a Cambridge man whom John Reavley would have known. He was fluent in several languages, an idealist with a vision quite broad enough to have conceived the Anglo-German Empire the Peacemaker envisioned.

Was he also ruthless enough to commit murder to bring it about? In the name of peace, in the cause of saving the millions of lives already lost, and the bleeding away of thousands more every day across the Channel, would he have destroyed a few, a handful?

Somebody had!

Matthew left the police station and walked quietly up the street. The August afternoon was still and damp, the road surface glistened in the late sun, and after the downpour the gutters were running deep. There was little traffic. People either took the underground trains or walked where possible.

He wished he could go to the cinema and escape for a couple of hours. He would sit in the dark with strangers and laugh animatedly at Charlie Chaplin, with his absurd walk, his cane, his courage, his defiance, and the individuality that would not be crushed. Or at Fatty Arbuckle and his fights with custard pies that were so brilliantly choreographed they were almost like ballet.

Or perhaps it would be fun to see a real melodrama. Someone had told him that Theda Bara would soon be appearing in *Camille*. That would be something to see.

He crossed the road, oblivious to a speeding motorcar. The vehicle passed him by mere inches, and he staggered, lost his balance, and tripped. There was a screech of tires and brakes as he sprawled into the street, wrenching himself so hard his shoulder was twisted in its socket.

An engine accelerated and tires squealed again.

Struggling to catch his breath, he started to clamber to his feet, feeling more than a little ridiculous. Anger boiled up inside him.

Someone offered him a hand and pulled him up. It was an elderly gentleman with a white mustache and military bearing.

"That was a close shave, sir," he said with a shake of his head. "Damn fool driver! Must have been drunk as a newt. Are you all right? You look a trifle shaken."

Matthew was damp from the pavement and there were smears of mud on his elbows and knees. His left foot was wet where he had stepped in the gutter, but other than the wrench to his shoulder and a few bruises, he was unhurt.

"Yes, sir, thank you. I didn't see him coming at all." He felt extremely foolish.

"You wouldn't, sir," the other man said crisply. "Come round the corner driving like a Jehu! Straight for the pavement. If it weren't ridiculous, I'd say he was aiming straight for you. I'd thank your stars, sir, and go home and have a hot bath, if there is such a thing available to you, and a large whisky."

"Thank you," Matthew said sincerely. "I think that's exactly what I will do."

But when he was back in his flat, sitting in the armchair with a single lamp shedding a soft light over the familiar room, and a glass of whisky in his hand, he was still cold, and his mind was racing. Was it possible that the incident in the street was not an accident?

Surely not? It was just somebody drunk, or even distracted perhaps with bad news. There was certainly enough of it about. Matthew was angry because he had been frightened, for a moment, and made to look vulnerable and ridiculous.

He telephoned Aidan Thyer and made an appointment to see him the next day. There was no point in wasting time going all the way to Cambridge, and then finding that Thyer was too busy to see anyone, or even not there at all. But telephoning did mean he was warned. If he was the Peacemaker, then he might already know what Matthew was doing, and the reason he was coming.

If it proved to be Thyer it would hurt Joseph. He had liked the man and trusted him. It would be a double betrayal because of Sebastian Allard's death as well, and the manner of it, as well as the murder of John and Alys Reavley.

Matthew went over in his mind yet again the course he had followed in seeking the Peacemaker. It had to be someone with connections to the Royal Families of both Britain and Germany. Although since the king and the kaiser were first cousins, with Queen Victoria as a common grandmother, a connection with one might well open doors to connections with the other. He had also to be a man of extraordinary intelligence, boundless ambition, an understanding of world politics, and an idealism he could follow with ruthless dedication regardless of all cost.

Because John Reavley had found a copy of the treaty that proposed this monstrous alliance, and been murdered in the attempt to expose it, the Peacemaker had to be someone who knew him sufficiently well to predict his actions, even his daily routine.

But Matthew and Joseph had considered Aidan Thyer, Master of St. Giles; Dermot Sandwell, senior government minister and confidant of royalty; and Ivor Chetwin, Secret Intelligence agent and longtime friend of John Reavley, until an ethical difference over the morality involved in spying had divided them. Matthew had once dreaded that it might be Shanley Corcoran, brilliant scientist and lifetime friend of John Reavley. He had not even dared suggest that to Joseph. It would have wounded him desperately. But then Corcoran's betrayal last summer had wounded him even more deeply. And he was dead now, hanged for treason.

Matthew sipped the whisky again, and did not taste it. He barely felt its fire slip down his throat. He himself had been sure it was Patrick Hannassey who had been the Peacemaker, and he had seen him die. Even up to a couple of weeks ago he had believed it was he. But this new conspiracy was too like the Peacemaker's work to cling on to that false comfort anymore.

And of course there was always his own superior, Calder Shearing. Matthew liked Shearing. He understood his sudden explosions of temper when stupidity caused unnecessary loss. He admired both his intelligence and his emotional energy, the strength of will that drove him to work until he was exhausted, the patience to pursue every chain of reasoning, to wait, to watch and go over and over details meticulously. He was honest enough to admit his errors, and he never took credit for another man's work. But more than any of these things, Matthew liked his dry wit, the laughter he saw in Shearing's eyes even when the appreciation was wordless.

None of these things altered the fact that even after five years working with him, he did not know anything about Shearing beyond those boundaries. He seemed to have no personal life. He never spoke of family either past or present. He was widely knowledgeable but he never spoke of a school or university. Nothing seemed to be known of him but the present.

Could he be the Peacemaker? Yes, of course it was possible. The thought was both frightening and painful, like so much else.

"Matthew! How good to see you." Aidan Thyer came into the Master's Lodge sitting room, his hand outstretched. He was a slender man with flaxen-pale hair, which flopped forward onto his brow, and a sensitive, highly intelligent face. Matthew remembered now with sudden regret that Thyer's beautiful wife, Connie, had loved another man. It was honor and probably affection that kept her loyal. But it was not love, and Thyer knew it.

"How are you, sir?" he asked aloud, taking Thyer's offered hand. The courtesy title came to him naturally. Matthew had not studied at St. John's, but the respect for a master of college was innate.

"Well, thank you," Thyer replied. "Although the casualty lists are worse than any nightmare. I heard just the other day that Nigel Eardslie was lost in Passchendaele. He was one of Joseph's students, you know."

"I'm sorry." There was nothing more to say.

"Sit down." Thyer waved to a chair, and took the one opposite. "I'm sure you must have lost friends as well. There's no one in England who hasn't. Europe has become an abattoir. But no doubt you didn't come here to discuss that. What can I do for you?"

"Alan Wheatcroft was a student of yours some time ago," Matthew began. Thyer knew he was in intelligence; there was no purpose whatever in being overdiscreet.

Thyer sighed. "Unfortunate," he said quietly. "Yes, I heard about it, of course. Very foolish. End of a fine career."

"You think he was guilty?" Matthew asked.

"Probably of nothing more than indiscretion," Thyer replied. "And a startling naïveté. What did he imagine a good-looking boy was doing hanging around in a public toilet? He should have given the boy a wide berth and not even spoken to him, let alone indulged in a conversation."

"And Corracher?"

"Corracher? Tom Corracher?" Thyer's fair eyebrows rose. "How is he involved?"

"Wheatcroft's defense is that the whole episode was set up to blackmail him, by Tom Corracher," Matthew replied.

Thyer was incredulous. "For God's sake, what for? Money?"

"Yes, to begin with. Once you've paid money to keep quiet over something, then you establish a precedent. It's as good as an admission. After that, other things can be asked for: favors in office, information, the right vote. The list is endless."

"What a damnable mess." Thyer's face was filled with distaste but his eyes never left Matthew's. "What is it you imagine I can do that would be of service to intelligence?"

"Wheatcroft is going to take Corracher down with him," Matthew began.

"You don't think Wheatcroft will survive this?" Thyer asked. "No, probably not. That sort of mud sticks once it's public." He pulled his mouth down at the corners. "Still, if he was ill-advised enough to get caught out in such behavior and leave himself open to blackmail, then guilty or innocent of the charge of approaching the boy, he's guilty of unforgivable stupidity."

"Apparently his wife is very handsome, and an heiress, and he has two sons," Matthew pointed out.

"Yes, of course," Thyer said guardedly, a shadow of pain crossing his face. "If he loves her, or his sons, he may be far more concerned with their feelings, and belief in him, than any continuance in high office. Blaming Corracher might seem the obvious escape."

Matthew looked at him. If he were in truth the Peacemaker, and had engineered this whole tragedy, knowing each man's weaknesses, then he was a superb actor. But the Peacemaker was superb. Time and again that had been only too evident.

"Do you think he's deliberately lying in order to save himself?" Matthew asked. "It's a pretty filthy thing to do."

Thyer stood up, walked over to the French windows and looked out. The lavender was buzzing with bees; the scent of flowers and crushed herbs filled the air. Beyond the hedges, the mellow walls of St. John's rose into a blue sky. It had looked like this in 1914, and probably in 1614.

"If you don't know that men lie and betray when they are frightened of losing what they most want, Matthew, then you are unfit for intelligence work—or much else," Thyer said softly. "The average priest or schoolteacher would tell you as much."

"It doesn't occur to you that Corracher could be guilty of blackmail?" Matthew asked.

"Frankly, it doesn't. I know Wheatcroft. He is . . . susceptible," Thyer said regretfully. "Can you help Corracher? Is that why you are interested?"

"Partly." Should he tell Thyer the truth, and see what his reaction was? Saving Corracher was important. Finding the Peacemaker might be vital. Or was he allowing his own vendetta to blind his judgment? Had he lost perspective?

Thyer did not prompt him, but waited quietly, his fingers propped in a steeple, the sunlight shining on his pale hair.

Matthew plunged in. Caution had gained him nothing. "The rest is to see if you consider it likely that there could be someone else behind it, pulling the strings, as it were."

Thyer looked startled. "I have no idea. To what end? Do you imagine Wheatcroft is sufficiently important that someone would do all this in order to get rid of him? Why, for heaven's sake?"

"Both Wheatcroft and Corracher," Matthew pointed out. "I think possibly Corracher is the more important."

Thyer was suddenly motionless. Matthew could hear the birds singing outside.

"Do you mean a German, or at least a German sympathizer?" Thyer said slowly.

"They were two of the strongest standing in the way of a settlement of peace before total obliteration of one side or the other," Matthew pointed out.

Thyer sighed. "Do you really think that is realistic, Matthew, after all we have lost? Is there not too large a section of the country who have paid in blood for victory, and will feel betrayed by any government that settles for less?"

"Does that make them right?" Matthew parried.

Thyer was watching him almost unblinkingly, his pale eyes brilliant. "It makes them the voice of the majority," he said. "And whether that is correct or not, it is moral, since we are a democracy."

"Is government to follow rather than to lead?" Matthew asked.

Thyer thought for several moments. "In matters where it is the people who have fought and died, yes, I think perhaps it is. Government may argue a case for something different, or lay before them arguments, facts, and reasons, but in the end we must abide by their decision. And before you argue that point, consider the nature of leading without reference to public wish. Would that not be dictatorship? I imagine most dictators believe themselves to have superior wishes to those of the people, and certainly superior information. That may even be true in the beginning, but eventually it leads to government by oppression rather than consent, and finally to tyranny."

He flexed his fingers as if they were stiff. "And it is also supremely impractical," he added with an oddly gentle smile, "unless you have a very great force at your command. And believe me, we have all had enough of bloodshed. We do not need civil war after this . . . if there is an afterward? From what I read, a German victory is far from impossible. We seem no closer to defeating the kaiser than we were in 1914, and half of an entire generation is mutilated or dead. What man who has seen this war in its hideousness will ever return from it whole in mind, even if his body seems preserved?"

Matthew did not answer. Either Thyer was far from the Peacemaker in his philosophy, or his mask was impenetrable. Matthew was driven back again to consider Dermot Sandwell, or Shearing. He had excluded Sandwell once, because evidence had made it seem impossible, but everything within him recoiled from believing it was Shearing.

And yet in his own way the Peacemaker had begun as an idealist. It was not his ultimate aim—peace—that was intolerable, it was the means he was prepared to use, even from the beginning, to obtain it: a betrayal of France and eventually of America, and dominion, in the cause of an enforced peace, that would extend across half the world. Was that better or worse than war?

"Could there be someone behind Wheatcroft's accusation against Corracher?" he asked aloud.

"Of course there could," Thyer replied. "But I have no idea who. I can make some highly discreet inquiries, if you wish?"

How much was there to gain, or to lose? Matthew had committed himself already. "Thank you," he said. "Yes. But be careful, they will think nothing of killing you, should they feel you threaten them."

Thyer gave the ghost of a smile. "War is full of death," he said very softly. "It is an occupational hazard."

Since he was already close, Matthew took the local train to Selbourne St. Giles and spent the night in the old family home with Hannah. It was her husband Archie MacAllister, who had commanded the *Cormorant* at the Battle of Jutland, where Matthew had killed Patrick Hannassey, just before the burning ship had gone down. Several times he had drifted in and out of consciousness before being picked up. He still woke in the night fighting for breath, beating his way out of a darkness that threatened to crush his lungs, his face, everything in him that longed for life.

It had given him a new closeness to Archie and an understanding of both the horror and the comradeship of the men who faced the real violence of the war, not just the crushing fear of defeat that came from knowing the casualty figures better than most people. He saw reports that the public did not, and knew the shortages, the ever-shifting political alliances and the new threats internationally. He read the reports from agents in Europe and the rest of the Empire.

Before the Battle of Jutland he had only imagined the numbing horror that Joseph saw every day in the trenches. He had had no experience of the exhilaration and the horror of battle, no idea what it did to the mind and body to watch another human being—a man with whom you had shared jokes, food, the long tension of waiting—broken to a bleeding, unrecognizable pulp at your feet. He had never even imagined physical pain of that degree, the indescribable noise, the smell of blood and burning flesh.

After supper he sat quietly with Hannah in the soft summer dusk and watched the last light fade beyond the elms. The fields lay wide and quiet.

The garden was overgrown. She had not had time to pull weeds, or to prune, and there were no young men to hire. They were either dead or in France, or like Archie, at sea. There were no delivery boys anymore, hardly any men in shops or banks or even on the land, only those too old to fight, or too ill. Women did the work now, in hospitals, factories, and farms, and they had no time for private gardens. They drove buses, cycled all over the place delivering things. He saw dozens of them on the country roads or out in the fields.

Hannah knew that Matthew's visit was not simply for pleasure. "The Peacemaker again?" she asked with a twisted little smile. She knitted automatically as she sat, the needles almost soundless in her hands.

He had not told her about Hannassey, at least not all. He still found it hard to talk about. Part of the pain he felt was because of the price Detta had paid. She had been spying for her cause, just as he was for his. One of them had had to lose. If it had been he, and he had done so deliberately, then he would have betrayed both himself and his country.

"I thought he was dead," he replied to Hannah's question.

"I know you did," she said with a tight little smile. She was looking more like her mother as she reached her mid-thirties. Something of Alys Reavley's inner calm was there in her features in repose. Matthew liked it, but it tugged at memories, reminding him of an old safety that could never return.

"Then why do you ask?" he said aloud.

"There's an excitement inside you, an edginess," she told him. "And what else would bring you back here now?"

"Any number of things," he said.

She looked up from her work. "You mentioned St. John's. Is that to do with Aidan Thyer? Do you still think it could be him?"

He was startled. Had he been so transparent?

She continued knitting, the faint click of her needles an intensely comfortable sound in the quiet room. All three children were upstairs, either in bed or doing homework.

He thought of denying it.

"It doesn't matter." She dismissed it. "I expect you can't tell me. Just don't lie."

"I don't know whether he is or not," he admitted. "I thought I knew who it was last year, and that he was dead—after Jutland. Now things have happened that make it look as if I was wrong, and he's still alive."

She looked up quickly. "Be careful, Matthew!" There was fear in her voice, and in her dark eyes so like Alys's.

He did not think of her words again until two days later. He had returned to London the morning after and pursued all the further information he could. It was distasteful, the sort of investigation into who had been seen offering or accepting illicit sexual activity that was one of the sadder and grubbier sides of police work. But he needed to know if Wheatcroft was guilty of seeking an escape from scandal by trying to blame Corracher, saying that he had deliberately set a trap for him in order to blackmail him, and he was entirely a victim. There seemed no doubt he had behaved extremely foolishly, at the kindest judgment. But was his blaming of Corracher a ploy he had thought up for himself? Or had the idea been planted in his mind, directly or indirectly, by someone else?

The only way to answer that was to see Wheatcroft himself, in spite of all his excuses that he was ill and had nothing to say. Matthew used the power of his Intelligence authority to force the issue. Even when he arrived at Wheatcroft's house, the servant at the door, an elderly, obviously infirm man, refused to admit him.

"No, sir," he said resolutely. "Mr. Wheatcroft is unwell, sir. He is not receiving visitors. Doctor's orders."

"I am from the Intelligence Service, and my orders supersede the doctor's," Matthew answered. "I can return with the police, if you oblige me to resort to such extremes. But I am sure that since you are as patriotic as the next man, you would wish Mr. Wheatcroft to assist the country's forces as much as he would wish to himself."

"Well . . ." the man said, confusion filling his face. "I . . . I'm sure I would, but I have my orders, sir. I can't just let anybody in here because they say so!" But he backed away several steps to allow Matthew to enter the hallway, and closed the front door behind him. It was a larger house than average, graciously furnished. Even in these restricted times, the marks of elegance were easy to see: the paintings, the gilt-framed mirrors, the crystal vase of roses on the table near the bottom of the stairs below the carved newel post.

"Sir!" The manservant's voice rose a little in protest as Matthew came farther in.

A door opened and a slender woman in a fashionable blue dress stood in the entrance. She was handsome in a fair, brittle way, but Matthew did not mistake the delicacy of her coloring for any fragility of mind or will.

"Mrs. Wheatcroft?" he asked, stepping around the manservant.

"Of course," she said coldly. "Oh, do be quiet, Dobson," she said to the manservant. "I can see what has happened." She waved her hand in dismissal without looking at him. "Who are you?" She regarded Matthew's uniform with distaste. "What are you doing forcing your way into my home?"

"Captain Matthew Reavley of the Secret Intelligence Service, Mrs.

Wheatcroft," he replied. "I am sorry for disturbing you, but matters have arisen about which I need to speak to Mr. Wheatcroft."

"I'm afraid whatever you have to ask him will have to wait!" she replied. "My husband is unwell, as I believe Dobson has already told you."

"It is a matter of information necessary to the Intelligence Service, Mrs. Wheatcroft," he insisted. "It cannot wait."

She looked at him icily. "My husband has served his country all his adult life, and been repaid for it by vile accusations which are distressing to him and to all his family. Now you come here and push your way into his home demanding he answer your questions? You are brutal, Captain . . . I forget your name. The answer is no. You will have to wait for a more fortunate time."

"Reavley," he said again. "Undoubtedly your husband has served his country. So have we all. Some of us are fortunate that it has cost us no more than a little discomfort. I have a brother in the trenches at Passchendaele, and a sister out there driving ambulances for the few wounded they have some chance of saving. Now go and find Mr. Wheatcroft in his bedroom, and tell him I need to see him immediately. He may come down, or I shall go up."

She glared at him, her body trembling, searching wildly for an answer to hold him at bay, and finding none. She wheeled around, her skirt swinging, and marched away.

Five minutes later she returned. Without speaking she led Matthew up the stairs and across a spacious landing whose long windows gave a view of a sunlit lawn. Then, after a brief knock, she opened the master bedroom door. She stared at Matthew, leaving him to go in unannounced.

"Thank you," he said pointedly. He closed the door behind him, but he did not know if she waited outside it.

Alan Wheatcroft was sitting in a chair by the window, not in a dressing gown as Matthew expected, but fully dressed. He was ash pale and his skin shone with sweat. For a minute Matthew wondered if perhaps he really was ill, then he saw the hands clenched, white-knuckled, and decided it was more probably fear that made the man look so wretched.

"I'm sorry to disturb you, Mr. Wheatcroft, but the matter cannot wait." He spoke very quietly, only sufficiently to be heard, aware that Mrs. Wheatcroft might be only just beyond the door.

"My wife said so." Wheatcroft also kept his voice low. "Although I can't imagine what I might know that would be of interest to the Intelligence Service. I haven't been in my office for . . . for several weeks." His hands clenched even more tightly on the rug over his knees.

Matthew sat on the edge of the bed, more to avoid towering over him than for comfort. "It is nothing to do with your office," he replied. "It is a matter of possible treason."

"Treason!" Wheatcroft was stunned. There was no comprehension in his eyes, not even fear, simply total bewilderment. "I know nothing about anything remotely treasonous. I haven't been out of my house since . . ." He drew in his breath sharply and then let it out without finishing his sentence.

"Since you were accused of approaching a young man for homosexual favors at the men's convenience on Hampstead Heath," Matthew completed it for him.

A tide of color washed up Wheatcroft's neck and face. He started to speak, and stopped again.

"I'm sure the charge is profoundly embarrassing," Matthew said with some sympathy. "Any man would find it so. Whose idea was it to save your reputation by saying that Tom Corracher set up the whole scene in order to blackmail you?"

Wheatcroft stared at him in horror, as if Matthew had physically struck him.

"Presumably not only to salvage something of your career, but to save your wife's feelings," Matthew added. "Whether you actually approached the boy or were merely naïve is not my concern. I don't wish to know."

"You . . . you are assuming . . ." Wheatcroft began.

"That it was not your idea? Yes, I am," Matthew agreed. "Your record up to this suggests you are a man of honor."

"I did not approach that boy," Wheatcroft said in a whisper. "I . . . I may have been foolish, but that's all! It is . . . inadvisable. Perhaps I deserve to lose my government position for such stupidity. That I can accept. But I have committed no crime!"

"No," Matthew agreed. "But blackmail is very definitely a crime, and you are accusing Corracher of that. If he is found guilty then he will not only lose his position, he will go to prison."

Wheatcroft looked so wretched, it was hard to believe he was not physically ill. "What has that to do with Intelligence? What is it you think I know? For God's sake, don't you think I've done enough to him? I don't believe he's a traitor. I've nothing more to say about it."

"I don't believe so, either," Matthew responded. "I don't know who it is behind the charge, but I believe you can help me find out."

Wheatcroft did not look up. "If I knew of any treason, I'd have reported it! I haven't sunk so low as that."

Matthew felt brutal, but there was no alternative. Neither affection nor pity were excuses to add to injustice. "What made you think of accusing him of blackmail?"

"I . . ." He stopped.

"Didn't," Matthew finished for him. "Someone else suggested it to you?"

"It wasn't that . . . simple!" Wheatcroft's face was ashen and glistening with sweat. "Corracher came to see me a couple of days after . . . after the . . . event. We quarreled over something else, stupid. They were putting a man called Jamieson to take over my work temporarily. Eunice, my wife, seemed to . . . she . . . assumed the quarrel was about the incident. She leaped to conclusions. I . . . I allowed her to. It . . ." He gave up helplessly. His eyes beseeched Matthew to understand without forcing him to put it into words.

Matthew felt both disgust and pity. Wheatcroft was trapped. It was his cowardice in allowing himself to be used in turn to trap Corracher that Matthew despised.

"Withdraw the charge," Matthew told him. "I doubt you can restore his career. People don't forget. But you can save yourself some honor out of it."

"I can't!" Wheatcroft protested. "It would be as good as saying that I was guilty! And before God, I wasn't!"

"And it is unjust to be punished for something you didn't do?" Matthew had asked.

"Yes! And my family ruined!"

"I imagine Tom Corracher feels the same way."

Wheatcroft stared at him as if he stood on the edge of an abyss.

Matthew opened his mouth to apologize, then said nothing. He could not withdraw his words. They were true. There was some agony within Wheatcroft that he could not share—a guilt, a fear for himself or for others—but Matthew could not let him escape it at the price it would cost.

Did Wheatcroft know who had manipulated his wife? Probably not. Certainly he would not tell Matthew. He remembered her icy face, the fear in her and the immediacy to attack. She would tell him nothing, maybe even warn the Peacemaker, knowingly or not.

He left the Wheatcroft house with a feeling of oppression and went back to his office.

He worked late to learn all he could about Eunice Wheatcroft, searching for a connection to anyone who might be the Peacemaker, dreading the link that would tie them, however tenuously, to Shearing. But if it was there, whatever it cost him, he could not look away.

By the time he left he was tired. His neck and shoulders ached with tension and his mouth was dry. He walked outside in the dark to get a bus home. He alighted two or three streets away and took a shortcut through an alley to save himself a hundred yards.

He heard the noise behind him. It was no more than a loose pebble kicked, but he swung around, losing his balance a little. A figure fell hard against him and metal clanged on the brick.

Some deep memory of those last minutes on the *Cormorant* awoke in him the feel of Hannassey's relentless strength as they struggled at the railing with the German destroyer looming out of the darkness. He lashed out hard and straight with his left fist, all his weight behind it. It connected with the man's face and he felt bone break. Still he followed it with a lunging kick to the groin and the man went down, letting out a scream that was almost instantly choked with blood.

Matthew hesitated. He must have broken the man's nose. Should he stay and see if the injury was worse than that? What if he couldn't breathe—if he died?

He looked down. He could see little more than movement, a writhing on the pavement. Perhaps the man was reaching for whatever had fallen and clanged against the brick. A knife? Matthew turned and ran, feet echoing on the alley cobbles until he emerged into his own street.

Even upstairs in his flat, with the door locked, he found he was shaking uncontrollably. The memory of the violence washed over him until he was gulping for breath. It was as if he could feel the strength of Hannassey again, the struggle, then the sudden victory. In his mind he saw Hannassey falling, spinning, arms and legs wide, until he hit the dark water, and a moment later the German destroyer squashed him like a fly.

Matthew poured himself a whisky, spilling a little, and tossed it down his throat so its fire could calm his stomach. He had not killed the man in the alley; he had seen him still moving frantically, arms groping. If Matthew had not hit back, then it would be he who was lying on the cobbles, possibly bleeding to death.

Was that what it was? An attempt to murder him? Was that really why he was shaking like this, because he knew it was not a robbery? Thieves might knock you over the head; more likely they would simply lift your wallet without you knowing it. The car driver the other day was not an accident, either.

Did this mean that at last he was enough of a nuisance to be worth killing? Even too close to the truth to be left alive? That made his heart race with excitement.

Was the Peacemaker Aidan Thyer after all? Or Calder Shearing? That was an ugly and viciously painful thought—one that made nausea grip his stomach and the sweat break out on his body. It was a strange friendship, almost tacit, and yet its depth was uniquely precious. There was a wealth of understanding between them that needed no words, and the comfort of that was immeasurable, the betrayal would be infinite. He remembered Joseph and Corcoran, and then pushed the thought from his mind.

Or could it be Dermot Sandwell, in spite of Matthew having ruled him out before? That would be far more bearable. Or someone he had not even thought of yet, but somehow had come close to without realizing it?

In Marchmont Street, the Peacemaker was woken in the small hours of the morning by his manservant. He dressed because he would not receive any visitor at the disadvantage of not being properly clothed.

He knew as soon as his guest entered the upstairs sitting room with its graceful proportions and lean, elegant furniture that the news was bad. The man who stood in the center of the floor reeked of failure.

The Peacemaker waited for him to speak.

"He got away," the man said simply. "I thought my fellow was good, but he said Reavley fought like a tiger. Broke his nose and ruptured his spleen. He's lucky to be alive."

The Peacemaker was astonished. "Are you sure he had the right man? Reavley's a thinker, not a doer."

"I'm perfectly certain," the man replied. "He's been followed on and off for weeks. Discreetly—he was never aware."

The Peacemaker raised his eyebrows skeptically.

"He wouldn't have gone alone down an alley at night if he'd been aware he was followed, . . . sir," the man replied.

The Peacemaker was annoyed with himself. He had allowed the failure to kill Reavley to rattle him, and now he had displayed a weakness in reasoning in front of this man, a rat of a creature who must be kept under tight control. He loathed having to use such people, and the necessity that drove him to it.

"You have failed twice," he pointed out. "I cannot afford a third error. Leave him alone. I shall think of a way of dealing with him that does not depend upon your very dubious skills. I'll send for you if I need you again."

The man opened his mouth to argue, then met the Peacemaker's eyes, and changed his mind. He left without speaking further.

The Peacemaker returned to his bed, but sleep eluded him. It required all his concentration and discipline of mind not to allow the Reavleys to dominate his thoughts and become an obsession. They were a nuisance, but peripheral to his main activities. The great cause was peace: first with Germany, then with the world. Never again would there be pointless slaughter like that going on at this moment at Passchendaele. The thought of it was enough to make humanity tremble and weep.

It was the night after that, with the air close and damp, and promising thunder, when Richard Mason returned from the Western Front and reported in the upstairs room. His face was gray with exhaustion. He had obviously shaved hastily and cut his chin. But it was the emotional tension in him, the grief in his eyes, the nervous tic at his temple that moved the Peacemaker to pity and a sense of the enormity of the horror. Mason had seen almost every battlefield of the war, not only in Europe but in Russia and the Middle East. He had never looked as haunted as he did now.

"Sit down," the Peacemaker said quietly. "Whisky? Tea? Have you eaten? What can I get you?"

Mason smiled bleakly. It was no more than a bare curving of the lips, hardly noticeable. "Tea would be nice. I can't afford to be light-headed. And a sandwich. Bread that isn't moldy. And a clean cup to drink out of."

The Peacemaker rang for the manservant. They spoke of trivialities until the food and drink came and they could close the door and be assured of privacy. He allowed Mason time to eat and drink before he approached the subject of his report.

"Thank you," Mason said. He met the Peacemaker's eyes. "It's beyond description. It's beyond human suffering. It is hell itself."

"But you have come with something to tell me." The Peacemaker had seen it in Mason's patience, his assurance. He had watched the man report on one atrocity after another over years, and he knew every mood of his mind and read its reflection in his face. Mason had brooding, sensitive features, powerful and yet more expressive than perhaps he himself realized. The depth of his emotion was mirrored too easily.

Now he answered slowly, measuring his words. He described Howard Northrup and his appointment to replace the much-respected Penhaligon. With no more than a trace of anger, he told of his stubborn incompetence. Watching him intently, the Peacemaker saw in Mason not only fury but pity as well for a man placed beyond his depth both of experience and of character.

Then, still slumped in the armchair, Mason told of Northrup's body being found with a single bullet through the brain, fired from right in front of him, and Joseph Reavley's unsuccessful attempt to learn from the men exactly what had happened.

"Reavley, the chaplain?" The Peacemaker kept his voice devoid of emotion with the greatest effort. He had not forgotten how Mason had thrown away his article on the nightmare of Gallipoli, with all its propaganda value, because of Reavley's sense of futile, narrow patriotism. "And what did Reavley find?"

Mason laughed. It was a jerky, painful sound that said more vividly than words how lacerated he was inside. "Nothing! Which I imagine was what he wanted, and intended. He's learned since Prentice's death. He's investigating because he has to. Neither he nor the Colonel wants anyone charged. The whole army in that section is facing slaughter. It will take both genius and lunacy to keep them facing forward and over the top, God help them! And God forgive us!" He left the words brittle and sharp in the air, unsaid between them, that they could have prevented it all, if any of their plans had succeeded.

"There's open talk of mutiny, and it won't take much to bring it about," he went on. "Then they'll have to fire on their own men. They'll have no choice." There was absolute certainty in his eyes. "Reavley will have more sense of right and wrong, and of survival, than to find anything."

"Write your article," the Peacemaker said earnestly. "Write up the action in which the surgeon saved his men. In the men's own words: all their comradeship, loyalty to each other, their courage, and how they were betrayed by arrogant and incompetent leadership. For readers far away from the battle you must write the tragedy of it, and the sacrifice. Paint the loss as you saw it."

Mason stared at him, eyes shadowed and uncertain. "The noise, the mud, and the slaughter are unimaginable."

"But of course," the Peacemaker said grimly. "If we here at home knew what it was like, without the poetic words of sacrifice and honor to gild it for us, we would never allow it to go on. We would be sick with shame that we had ever tolerated it in the beginning. We sit in clean withdrawing rooms of quiet houses and weep into our handkerchiefs, and we talk to each other about glory. Write it as it is, Mason! For the love of God, write the truth!"

Mason sat still, the trouble still heavy in his face.

The Peacemaker leaned forward. "I know the figures, Mason. I know we have barely gained a few yards of mud at the price of a hundred thousand lives. It has to stop. The government won't do it; they've staked too much on victory to settle for less than that now. They're old men, dedicated to war. We need new men, with a vision of peace and the courage to pay what it costs in pride." For an instant he thought of Wheatcroft and Corracher standing in the way, young men with old men's vision. But they had been dealt with! Eunice Wheatcroft's pride would see to that. "But they can't do it without the truth," he went on, intent upon Mason again. "Doesn't the vast mass of our suffering people deserve to decide on truth, not lies? If not for them, then for the men you've seen paying the price of their folly. Is their enemy really the German soldier opposite, suffering the same hunger, the same horror and pain? Or is it the blind cowards behind them driving them forward?"

The argument died in Mason's eyes. The Peacemaker saw it and knew he had won.

Matthew reached a decision. Detection of facts had achieved very little. All his inquiries into Eunice Wheatcroft's connections had gained him nothing. He still had no proof who the Peacemaker was. He would carry the battle to Sandwell, and perhaps spur him to action, which would show him innocent or guilty.

He contrived to have himself invited to a dinner party Sandwell was giving at his home in order to discuss intelligence matters. As a senior minister, it was part of his responsibility. This was an elegant occasion with all the glamour and discreet good taste of the years before the war. The meal was abstemious, as became men who led a country where some of the poor actually starved. The talk was somber. There was no pretense made that victory was certain, only that surrender was unthinkable. The dead had paid too much for the living to betray them.

After the coffee and brandy had been served, Sandwell rose to his feet. He was slender, almost gaunt now, his fair hair gleaming in the subdued light from the lamps. He asked the others to excuse him, and gestured to Matthew to follow him into one of the smaller side offices.

It was tidy, gracious, and sparsely furnished. Sandwell sat down in one of the armchairs and invited Matthew to the other. He crossed his legs, his polished shoes shining for an instant as he moved. His eyes were almost electric blue, curious, amused. He waited for Matthew to speak.

Matthew began his well-rehearsed discourse. "Thank you, sir. I'll not waste time with prevarication. I imagine you are aware of the original prosecution against Alan Wheatcroft, and now that against Tom Corracher as well?"

"Naturally," Sandwell agreed. "Is that of interest to the intelligence service?"

"I believe so. Corracher is not guilty of any attempt to blackmail Wheatcroft. The accusation is Wheatcroft's way of escaping the consequences of either a very naïve action, or possibly a minor offense, but one with major effects upon his career, and probably more important to him, his marriage."

Sandwell was watching Matthew intently. Matthew tried to read the emotion in the brilliant eyes, and could discern nothing. It was like looking into a mirror.

"You mean Wheatcroft laid the charge of blackmail falsely, as a way of becoming victim rather than offender?" Sandwell grasped it immediately. "I'm surprised. It shows rather more nimbleness of mind than I thought he possessed."

Matthew smiled in spite of himself, and saw the answer in Sandwell's face.

"Yes, sir, I think it does, which is why I believe the idea may not have originated with him."

"I assume you asked him?"

"Yes. He told me it was his wife's suggestion."

"Ah. The redoubtable Eunice."

"You know her?" Suddenly the air was electric. Had Sandwell stiffened? Was Matthew at last facing the Peacemaker in a ridiculously civilized, lethal fencing match with words? Or wasting time talking in riddles to an innocent man?

The Peacemaker was an idealist: passionate, ruthless, believing utterly in his cause. He would crush Matthew as he had his father, with regret, but without hesitation.

"Do you know Mrs. Wheatcroft, sir?" Matthew reiterated.

"I have met her," Sandwell replied. "But I was speaking of her reputation. Elegant but chillingly cold."

"My impression exactly," Matthew agreed. "I think if I were Wheatcroft I would not wish to incur her displeasure, let alone her contempt."

"Sufficiently to accuse a friend of blackmail, falsely?" Sandwell asked with a lift of surprise. "That is a particularly squalid thing to do."

"It is a particularly squalid charge," Matthew pointed out.

"I don't see how it concerns Intelligence, even so. Or what I could do to be of assistance."

Matthew had hoped the question would arise and he had prepared for it. "Tom Corracher is an able man, with unique connections in Hungary. We can't afford to lose him so easily. Apart from the damage to morale of such a sordid scandal just now when the army is taking the most hideous losses. We need strength and honor at home."

"I see." Sandwell sat silently for some time. Footsteps sounded in the corridor outside, and a burst of laughter came from the dining room where the men were still passing the port and brandy.

Somewhere a clock chimed and then struck eleven.

"You wish me to intervene on Corracher's behalf. I assume you believe him innocent? Although perhaps that is not the major issue. You are right, a scandal would damage morale when we are too vulnerable to bear it easily. Thank you for bringing it to my attention, Reavley. I shall do what I can. Your argument is persuasive." He smiled and rose to his feet, holding out his strong, narrow hand with its long fingers.

Matthew took it, still not certain what he had learned. "Thank you, sir."

They stood for a moment, neither moving. Then Sandwell let go and turned to the door. Was his smile a shade less certain? Or was it only a change in the light and Matthew's imagination?

Matthew was a little late the next morning and was still eating a slice of toast when the telephone rang. He picked it up to hear Shearing's voice. It sounded tense and very formal, as if he might have been aware of being overheard.

"Morning, Reavley. Will you go to Wheatcroft's house, please. Immediately. Take full identification with you."

Matthew drew in his breath to ask why, and then let it out again. "Yes, sir."

He took his car this time. A taxi would have had to fight traffic just the same, and he knew London almost as well as any cab driver. It took him half an hour, even though he had to break the speed limit in several places and cut a dozen red lights too fine.

He was met at Wheatcroft's door by an elderly policeman who was well past the age at which he would usually retire. He looked distressed, which was sufficient to warn Matthew that whatever had happened was very grave.

"Yes, sir?" the sergeant said stiffly.

"Captain Reavley, Intelligence Service," Matthew identified himself.

"Yes, sir. Sergeant Roberts. I was expecting you. Mr. Wheatcroft's in the bedroom, sir. But there's no question how it happened."

"How . . . ?" Matthew began.

"Suicide, Captain." Roberts swallowed. "There's a letter. Wife said it's his handwriting, and we compared it with other papers we know were his. There's no doubt."

Matthew felt a wave of guilt rise up and choke him, tightening his chest till he could hardly breathe. He was gasping, his lungs struggling for air.

"You all right, sir?" Roberts's voice came from a distance.

"Yes, thank you. What did the note say?"

"That he was innocent, but he couldn't face the shame of the prosecution. That he'd been haunted over a piece of foolishness, his career was finished and there was no use or happiness left for him. For his family's sake he wasn't going to begin on a downward path which had no end."

Matthew cleared his throat awkwardly. "Those words?"

"Yes, sir. The note's up there beside him. Room's locked. Doctor's with the wife. Very strong woman, taking it with great courage, no hysterics, but looks like she should be buried alongside him, right enough, poor thing."

"Thank you." Matthew held out his hand for the key, then turned and walked up the stairs, leaving the sergeant at the bottom. He knew where the bedroom was. It seemed only hours since he had been there.

He opened the door, fumbling for a moment before he could turn the lock, then went in and closed it behind him. The curtains were drawn to a twilight gloom, but rather than pull them back he switched on the electric light.

Wheatcroft was lying on top of the bed. He had either not undressed last night or he had risen and dressed this morning. He had apparently shaved also. Matthew touched the bloodless face. It was cool. Had he died hours ago? He looked ravaged now, wasted as if by disease, his flesh sunken.

Was it despair that had driven him to this? And how would it reflect on Corracher? Was that another blow waiting to fall? This certainly would not stop the prosecution.

He picked up the note. It was quite long, and not addressed to anyone in particular—not even to his wife, as might have been expected. It mentioned his work and how he had believed in it, and that his successor, Marlowe, lacked the connections in Hungary to carry it through.

After that, it was pretty much as Roberts had said. He proclaimed his innocence and said he could not face the humiliation and would not publicly fight a battle he could not win, but significantly, he did not blame Corracher.

Matthew folded the note and put it in his pocket. He searched the papers, letters, notes of meetings, diaries, but there was nothing else there to help or hurt Corracher's cause.

Finally he left to go back and report to Shearing. He felt miserable, guilt-dogged, and yet confused as to what he could or should have done differently. Perhaps Wheatcroft was guilty after all, and the whole thing was a catalogue of small errors and profound tragedies, and the Peacemaker had simply seized the opportunity to use his weakness and destroy Corracher with it.

Was this suicide now a result of Wheatcroft's guilt over accusing

Corracher? He had not openly admitted the lie; perhaps that was too much to ask, for his family's sake. But the prosecution against Corracher would have to be dropped.

Another victim of the Peacemaker, intentionally or not.

Had Matthew's conversation with him provoked the guilt? Or had it been brought about subtly, ruthlessly, by Sandwell, after Matthew's discussion with him last night? Probably he would never know.

SIX

By now Joseph had concluded his fruitless questioning about Northrup's death. He had gone through the motions so that Hook could tell General Northrup honestly that they had done everything they could to ascertain the truth of his son's death. But if anyone had known it and was willing to speak, they must have been among the casualties, which increased by the thousands every day.

After seventy-two hours Joseph went to see Hook in his dugout. It was yet another gray morning, with a weeping pall of cloud across the sky. The rain seemed to have soaked into everything. There was no dry ground, no food or equipment untouched. Everything dripped and was clammy to the touch. Bread was moldy before it arrived at the forward trenches, battle tunics never dried out, socks and boots were permanently sodden. Men's hair was plastered to their heads, and their pale skins shiny wet, streaked with mud and blood.

Joseph slipped on the step and jarred himself against the wooden lintel on the way down to the dugout. Hook looked up as he heard him and called out to come in.

"Morning, Reavley," he said a little huskily. His face was colorless and lined with exhaustion.

Joseph let the sacking fall back over the entrance and stood to attention.

"Morning, sir." He gave the casualty figures as he knew them, and mentioned the names of those men he was aware Hook had known personally. Then he moved on to close the issue of Northrup's death. "I've made all the inquiries I can, sir. If it was the sort of thing we feared, no one is saying anything. Of course it shouldn't have happened, but in the face of the circumstances, I strongly recommend that we close the issue. There seems to me to be two possible answers: either the whole thing is no more than loose talk by men angry and demoralized, speaking out of turn. This could be the best answer for all of us, especially Major Northrup himself. Or there was a piece of very regrettable indiscipline, but those concerned are themselves dead now. We can't now determine what it was, and in respect to Major Northrup, who can't defend himself, we should mention it no further."

Hook regarded him with a bitter humor in his eyes. "You did actually ask?"

"Yes, sir." That was the truth, although he had neither expected nor wanted an answer.

"Thank you, Reavley. I'll inform General Northrup. I don't imagine he'll be pleased, but he'll have to accept it."

But Northrup did not accept it. He sent for Joseph personally and demanded a more detailed explanation, and there was nothing Hook could do to protect him from it. It was in Hook's dugout again, in the early afternoon. Joseph had spent almost twenty hours helping wounded and dying, endlessly carrying stretchers. He had struggled through the mud and round the awkward corners of the few trenches that were still negotiable in the ever-deepening water. He had watched young men he knew and cared for die in indescribable pain.

He had managed to snatch a couple of hours' sleep, his body bruised, wet to the skin and shivering. Now he fumbled to straighten his clothes, splash his face with moderately clean water, and report back to Hook again. There was no time to shave, none even to try to light a flame and heat water for a cup of tea.

Outside, the earth smelled of death. The light was gray and the air close and warm.

Inside the dugout one oil lamp was burning, the light red and green on the backs of a pile of books. He saw General Northrup immediately. He looked thin, a little stooped; his face was tight with anger.

Joseph drew himself to attention, pulling his shoulders back with an effort. The muscles in his body shot through with pain and he could not fill his lungs with air.

Hook's voice was rough-edged. "I gave your report to General Northrup, Captain. However, he has made certain inquiries himself and he is not satisfied that we have exhausted all possibilities."

"I know of no others, sir," Joseph said doggedly. He knew that Hook was prepared to back him, and the men.

Northrup did not wait for Hook to reply but cut across him looking straight at Joseph. There was both pain and contempt in his voice. "I can understand your desire to shield your men, Chaplain. I even have some sympathy with your reluctance to believe any of them capable of such a crime. But if we have any right to claim that we fight for civilized values, a way of life acceptable to man and God, then we do not look away from the truth because it is not what we wish it to be or find comfortable to deal with."

Joseph was speechless with fury. The word *comfortable* was a blasphemy in this blood-soaked gateway of hell. He croaked the word, almost unintelligibly, like an animal sound in the back of his throat.

Hook heard the warning in it, the self-control fraying and coming apart. He intervened. "Chaplain, General Northrup has been speaking to the men also, and he believes that Corporal Fuller may have been involved and knows what happened. He insists that we ask him, under pressure if necessary."

"Punch Fuller?" Joseph was startled. "I haven't seen him for days. He must be ..." he blinked, trying to hold back his emotion. "Among the dead." He had liked Punch with his pleasantly ugly face and his inexhaustible memory for the words of every song, orthodox and otherwise.

A nerve twitched in Northrup's cheek. "He is not dead, Chaplain! Not even wounded. Corporal Fuller is on leave in Paris, and no doubt enjoying himself. If we fight for anything, it must be for honor. If we have lost that, then there is nothing else left worth winning—or losing." His voice thickened. "I will not bury my son the victim of a cowardly murder and keep silent about it. I do not know if you would—that is not my concern—but if you would, then I pity you, and those who love or trust you I pity even more. What use are you to your men, sir, if you have neither the courage nor the strength to uphold the truth or the honor of the God you chose to serve?"

"General ..." Hook began to protest, leaning forward a little, his skin yellow now in the lamplight.

Joseph could not allow Hook to fight in a defense he was not prepared to make for himself. "General Northrup." He turned to face him. "If Corporal Fuller knows something of Major Northrup's death, then with Colonel Hook's permission, I will go to Paris, find him, and learn what it is. Supposing you believe *that* is of more service to my men than remaining here to help them." He stared at Northrup's tired, wounded eyes without wavering.

Northrup blinked.

It was Hook who answered. "I think you had better try, Reavley. You could get a little sleep on the train, some dry clothes, maybe hot food. Give it a couple of days anyway."

"Yes, sir. Immediately?"

"Might as well," Hook replied. "If Fuller comes back and you miss him, you might not get another chance." He gave Northrup a sidelong glance, but Northrup was impervious. He could see only justice; the near certainty of death in battle seemed not to touch him.

"Yes, sir." Joseph saluted and left.

He was tired enough to sleep most of the journey from Ypres to Paris, jammed into a seat between other soldiers going on leave, a few staff officers, and several silent and uncomfortable civilians in cars rattling and jolting over the tracks. He was barely aware of them. Exhaustion lent him a few hours of oblivion, and when he finally disembarked at the station and pulled his thoughts together it was to consider at which of the many places the men on leave stayed in Paris he should begin to look for Punch Fuller.

He had heard many of the men joke about the music halls that were still open, the nightclubs, the cafés, and the brothels.

He stood on the platform outside the railway station looking at the street, hearing the clip of horses' hooves and the hiss of tires on the wet cobbles, the blare of motor horns and someone singing loudly and off-key, miserably drunk. A boy with a cap too large for him was selling newspapers, black headlines counting more losses at Passchendaele, Verdun, the Somme, and right along the front. A group of sailors swung by, with trouser legs flapping around their ankles. An ambulance passed, driven by a woman.

Joseph felt an overwhelming sense of being lost, even though he had been to Paris many times, both before the war and then on leave. He had spoken French passably since school. It was not that he did not care about France, or appreciate the country's wit, history, and culture; he just ached for the familiar, the idioms of his own people. He longed for things he did not need to think about, places his feet would find unguided. He was too tired to begin a search for one man in all this weary, grieving city that had lived the last three years with the enemy on its doorstep, trying to keep a brave face while smiling at disaster, pretending it wouldn't really happen. God knew how many of its sons would never return. Did they hear the guns in their sleep?

It would be dusk soon. He must find a billet of some kind for the night, maybe three nights. He did not really want to find Punch Fuller, but he had to try. Damn Major Northrup for his stupidity, a father too blind to let his son lie buried in peace.

He found a room; it was small and expensive, but quite clean. The

landlady made him an omelette with herbs and charged for it extortion-
ately. But it was the best meal he had eaten since the early spring and he
told her so with gratitude. There was no tea, and the coffee was bitter, but
at least it was served in a cup, not a Dixie can, and there was no taste of
oil to it.

He slept late, vaguely discomforted by the physical ease of a bed, and
the silence compared with the guns he was used to. It should have wrapped
him round in peace, but it didn't.

He went out again, asking first at the half dozen or so small hotels he
knew the men used when in Paris. He kept his chaplain's collar showing to
allay suspicion that his search had any ill intent, but it didn't help. He
spoke of Punch Fuller by name, and described him fairly closely: his long
nose and sharp chin, his slightly rolling walk, his ready wit. They all stared
at him with blank faces, many openly hostile.

Then he tried the cafés, bars, and other drinking places—all without
success. By near midnight again he was nursing a glass of rough red wine
in a nightclub in the cellar of one of the older hotels. There were several
other British soldiers there. They seemed determined to stay awake for
every precious hour of leave, savor it to the last breath of smoky, wine-
filled atmosphere, hear every aching note of the music from the three-piece
band. A middle-aged woman with a thin body sang in a languorous voice
filled with heartbreak.

Suddenly Joseph could no longer keep from his mind the awareness of
how everything had changed since he was last here on leave himself, too
short a time to go home. It was only three months ago, but now it was all
just a little shabbier; a few more chairs were broken and not mended, and
the tables more deeply scarred. Windows were cracked, lamps missing
pieces of colored glass. It was this room he could see as he sat, but in his
mind it was everywhere. Coffee was thin and bitter. Women's faces were
bleak, numbed with loss. Clothes were patched and repaired, the few shreds
of style left a little more desperate. Outside there was uncollected rubbish
blowing in the gutters, and windows were boarded up where there was no
glass to mend them.

The comradeship was still there, the anger and the pain, and a shred
of the old ironic wit. But the shell was thin, and too near to breaking.

Joseph sipped his wine again and watched the group of Tommies at
the bar. None of them looked more than twenty, several far younger,
maybe sixteen or seventeen. They were laughing too loudly. They thought
they were pretending to be brave, knowing that tomorrow or the next
day they were going back to be killed. Joseph knew the courage was real—
but behind the stupid jokes, white faces were slicked with the sweat of

uncertainty and fear. Finally, Joseph realized, each man was desperately alone.

The three-piece band started a Cole Porter song. Porter himself was somewhere here in Paris, so Joseph had heard, but he would be in a better place than this, more sophisticated.

He should start looking for Punch Fuller again. He had to tell General Northrup that he had tried. Stupid man. The truth would hurt everyone, himself most of all.

And yet Joseph knew that some Englishman had shot Major Northrup on purpose, to save him from bringing on them even more destruction, and more of his friends sacrificed for nothing. Did duty require you to die pointlessly? If Punch were to ask him that, what would he say?

He had no idea. Too many of the old certainties were gone. Once he would have known exactly what to say to Morel about honor and leadership. Now he understood Morel's belief that his duty was toward the men whose lives were in his charge, to save them from incompetents who would take their loyalty and sacrifice it hideously and for nothing, unaware even of what they were asking.

He had tried again to argue with Morel. He could hear the words in his mind—"You can't lead them to mutiny! Think what it means. They'll be shot."

"How terrible," Morel had said sarcastically. "Good men shot."

Joseph had floundered, seeking something to say, a core of belief within himself to cling to and give him fire and conviction. He had found nothing sure enough, and Morel knew it as much as he did. He had failed.

He felt a hand on his shoulder and looked up to see a man smiling at him. He was tall and dark with a long nose and a mercurial, ironic laughter in his eyes. Just now there was a strange gentleness in him, an instant of naked emotion.

"Sam?" Joseph's voice was hoarse. Amazement and joy welled up inside him. It was Sam, wasn't it? Sam Wetherall, whose grave he had wept over, even though he knew it was not his friend's body in it, but someone else's wearing his tags. They had arranged it. It had been the only answer to Prentice's death and the knowledge afterward.

Sam grinned. "You look like hell, Joe. But it's still good to see you. Don't make a fuss."

Joseph's heart raced with fear, hope, intense, pounding relief. There was no question anymore. Sam was alive. "What are you doing here?" He managed the words although his lips were dry and his throat tight. Sam was not in uniform. "Are you on leave?" Surely he could not have left the army, even in his new identity, not deserted? It wasn't possible, not the Sam he knew. He realized he was shaking with fear. His belief in Sam was one of the few certainties he relied on. He did not want it tested.

Sam eased himself into the stool beside him. "Took a leaf out of your brother's book," he said very quietly.

Joseph stared at him, struggling to understand. Intelligence? But Sam was a sapper, one of those who dug under the enemy lines, listened, set mines, blew up defenses. Perhaps the tight spaces and the claustrophobia had gotten to him at last. It got to most men, sooner or later. Too many were buried alive in collapses, drowned in the mud and debris, crushed by falls.

He found himself smiling simply because Sam was alive. Memories poured back of conversations they had had on the line in 1915, when it had all been so new. They had thought then that the war wouldn't last a year. It had been talk of glory, of heroism and sacrifice. Now it was just death, endlessly and pointlessly ever more death. The soldiers were even younger.

"Here in Paris?" he asked aloud, his voice almost level.

"Mostly." Sam's eyes were far away for a moment. "How's the regiment?" He did not ask for anyone by name, but Joseph thought of the men Sam had known who were dead now. There was no need to tell him.

Sam interrupted his efforts to concoct a good answer. "You were never a good liar, Joe. Who's gone? Everyone?"

"No!" Joseph denied too quickly, thinking of those whose comradeship had been so precious. "Only a few: Tucky Nunn, Eardslie, Chicken Hagger, Lanty and Bibby Nunn both, Doughy Ward, both the Arnold brothers."

Sam's hand tightened on his arm. He said nothing. He had never wasted words.

The barman poured him some absinthe and he ignored it.

"I'm looking for Punch Fuller," Joseph said quietly.

"Deserted?" Sam said with slight surprise. "Poor sod. Is that really the best use they can find for you, to send you to Paris after the poor devils that reached the end of the line?" He frowned. "If he's really cut and run, Joe, there's no point in finding him. He's a casualty of war. You can't save him."

"No, he's not a deserter," Joseph said slowly. Perhaps he should not tell Sam about it, but he knew he was going to. He had no idea what Sam had done in the dreadful years since they had parted, just before Sam went over the top that day in spring of 1915. But he was the same man with whom he had shared the chocolate biscuits, sitting in the dugout, and told stories of the laughter and the memories that mattered, of the

England they loved and the past that was slipping a little further away each day.

Sam was waiting, watching him. His face was leaner than before, more deeply lined. Joseph could barely even guess at the pain losing his identity must have caused him, hollowing out places of loneliness, character, and grief he could not imagine. He could never return to England, the familiar hills and fields, the villages, the rhythm and music of speech, the common history that framed even the simplest things.

Had Joseph been wrong to offer that way out? He had so desperately wanted Sam to live, and the decision had seemed right at the time, the only thing possible.

"We had an incompetent officer shot," he said aloud, looking at Sam again. "It might have passed off without any fuss, considering the overall losses, but another damn war correspondent saw it and left me no way out. The man's father is a general, and he's determined to see justice done and his son's good name reinstated, and of course whoever murdered him tried for it, and face the firing squad."

"What has Punch Fuller got to do with it? Don't say you're playing detective again, Joe!"

"Not willingly," Joseph answered, more memories almost drowning him. If he had been wiser last time, Sam would still be in the British Army, under his own name, and if he survived the war, free to go home to his brother.

Sam saw it in his eyes. He smiled. "Don't blame yourself for being who you are, Joe. I don't. I never wanted you to betray yourself, and that's what it would have been."

"I don't want to know who killed Northrup," Joseph retorted. "And I already know why. The man was a fool, and dangerous."

"All this old question of loyalty," Sam said softly. "Do you violate the old standards to save your friends? Or do you keep your conscience, and let them die?"

"I used to think I was sure of lots of things," Joseph answered ruefully. "Now I'm only sure of the values of humanity, of courage and honor and pity. Keep your word whatever it costs. Face forward, even if you're so terrified your guts turn to water. Help someone if you can, anyone, doesn't matter who they are or what you think they've done. Don't think, just help the pain. Stay with them, don't let go. Don't judge."

Sam's eyes were very gentle.

"And what happens if you go back without finding Punch Fuller?" he asked.

"General Northrup will go on looking for whoever killed his son, and trying to prove it was murder, until one day he finds out his son was an ass and the men hated him. Then he'll pin the blame on someone and his vengeance will be satisfied."

"You mean he'll settle for lies as long as he extracts the solution he wants?"

"Something like that."

"I assume you've already considered blaming someone who's dead?" Sam asked. "God knows, there must be enough of them."

Joseph smiled, aware of the irony. "Yes, I thought of it. But I wouldn't have much chance of getting away with it if I don't have any idea what actually happened. Punch Fuller might be able to tell me that."

Sam rolled his eyes very slightly. "Come on, Joe! If he does, it'll be in the nature of a confession! You won't be able to use it. For God's sake, have a little sense!"

"I won't be able to use it to prove anything," Joseph agreed with a pained smile. "But then I really don't want to!"

Sam's eyebrows rose.

"Don't you? You'll let them get away with murdering an officer because they think he's incompetent! God, you have changed!"

Joseph realized with a sense of amazement that in spite of the mockery, the chaffing, and the laughter, Sam wanted Joseph to cling to his belief. That he didn't share it, or professed not to, was irrelevant. Perhaps as long as Joseph did, Sam felt there was something certain. As a last resort, something to trust. When everything else was destroyed, then perhaps it would stand.

Maybe that was what a chaplain's job really was—not to teach others to believe, but to be seen to believe oneself. To stand not so much for a specific faith, but for the endurance of faith, for its power to outlast everything else. He must do it now, a gift for Sam, after all he had taken away from him.

"It's a matter of weighing one loyalty against another," he began delicately. "It's a matter of the men's loyalty to each other, after three years in the trenches living together, and before this is over, dying together. Weigh that against Northrup's answering for the truth of his incompetence, and I'm not so certain whoever did it was wrong that I'd be willing to force the issue and see them hang for it. Especially now. You may not know it here in Paris, but the whole of the British line is too close to mutiny to stomach a glaring injustice like that. I don't know if I'm right, Sam. There are a lot of things I don't feel so sure of that I'd ask another man to pay the price of it. I'll pay it myself. I want to know what happened. When I do, I'll go back and tell Colonel Hook—and General Northrup, if he wants to know."

"Are you sure the dead officer was an idiot, more than most?" Sam asked thoughtfully.

"I am. I saw some of his handiwork myself. Nigel Eardslie died as a result of it. Edgar Morel is ready to lead a mutiny, I think."

Sam smiled and his eyes were surprisingly bright. "I apologize. You haven't changed. Just a little more complex, that's all. You'll make a regular Jesuit, if you survive the war."

"Jesuits are Catholic," Joseph pointed out, but a tiny flicker of warmth was back inside him. "Can you help me find Punch Fuller? You must know Paris a hell of a lot better than I do. Have you got people I can ask? I haven't much longer to look."

Sam sat still for several moments before he answered. "Yes, there's someone I can ask," he said at last. "If I tell her you need to know for a good reason, she'll help. But you'll have to trust me, Joe. No questions, nothing reported to anyone, not to prove a point, not even to save a man's life. There are far more lives hanging on it. Your word?"

"My word," Joseph agreed, holding Sam's gaze.

Sam considered the absinthe for a moment, and decided against it. He put a few coins on the counter, then stood up, and Joseph followed him out of the club and up the narrow steps into the street. It was dark and still raining very slightly, a sort of drifting mist that covered everything with a sheen that gleamed bright and wet in the few lights that were still on.

"You all right to walk?" Sam asked quietly. "It's mostly alleys. We need to cross the river."

"Of course I'm all right to walk!" Joseph said tartly, but without ill temper. "Carry you, if you need it!"

"We have some problems," Sam said cheerfully, his voice on the edge of laughter in the dark. "Don't always know who our friends are. Keep up, and say nothing."

They went together through the old part of the city, along alleys and byways that predated Napoleon's grand redesign—places that echoed to the footsteps of revolutionaries, and had run with blood then. Now they held the furtive whispers of different secrets, fears, and griefs.

They crossed the river to the Île de la Cité. The rain had eased, and the water glistened in the faint moonlight. A string of barges was black on its shining surface. Everything was wet. A thin strain of a saxophone drifted and was lost. Someone laughed.

Sam spoke to someone, their voice murmuring, and a few minutes later they crossed the river at the far side onto the left bank. There were more whispered exchanges with people, sometimes no more than a few words.

It must have been after two in the morning when at last Sam led the way down steep flagged steps into a cellar. One flame burned in a glass lamp, leaving most of the room in shadows.

"Monique?" he said in little more than a whisper.

She answered him in French, only one word to acknowledge that she was there. Joseph, straining his eyes to discern through the shadows, was certain there was at least one more person there.

"We need to find a British soldier," Sam told the woman and whoever it was beside her. "This is Chaplain Joseph Reavley. I've known him since 'fifteen. You can trust him."

"Deserter?" Monique asked. "If so, I'm surprised you came. I can't do that, and you know it. Not when he has information about German plans. Sapper, is he?"

Joseph drew in his breath to speak, then remembered he had promised Sam to remain silent.

"Knows the truth of an execution," Sam replied. "Wants to avoid the wrong man going to the firing squad. Better right now if no one does. Man from a Cambridgeshire regiment—name of Punch Fuller. On leave in Paris right now."

The woman turned to look very carefully at Joseph, moving the light closer, studying his face. He did not avert his gaze but looked back at her. She was beautiful, in a soft, intense way, with a strong nose, wide, gentle mouth. Her cloud of dark hair accentuated the pallor of her skin and the shadows around her eyes.

She turned back to Sam. "You swear for him?"

Sam did not hesitate. "Yes."

Monique turned to the man beside her and for a moment the light swayed a little toward him. Joseph had a glimpse of wide, light gray eyes and a thin face of extraordinary intelligence; then Monique moved the light away and everything became indistinct again.

"If he is still in Paris, we'll find him," Monique answered. "Have lunch in the Café Parnasse at one o'clock."

Sam thanked her and took Joseph by the elbow, leading him back up the steps into the street again. "Where are you staying?" he asked.

Joseph told him.

"I'll take you back close enough for you to find your way. The Café Parnasse is in the Rue Mazarin, near the river. Be there. That's the best I can do for you."

"Thank you."

Sam did not ask him what he would do if he discovered Punch Fuller was involved with the murder of Northrup. It was a delicate balance between them, understood that even if he were, Joseph would not instigate any court-martial that involved him. The success of the intelligence network for which Sam worked depended upon freedom of information, and trust that it was never used for police work, for private gain, or for vengeance.

From the very little Sam had said, Joseph assumed that what they dealt in was information about German troop movements. Sam had made a laughing reference to carrier pigeons, and Joseph knew their use in war. He could only imagine the courage and patience of scores of men and women posted all over Europe watching, listening, making notes, and risking their lives to report everything to one source, here in Paris, where it could be collated to form a picture.

They walked together speaking little. There was too much to say, and too little time even to begin. Perhaps most of it they already understood, and the rest did not matter tonight. Facts, details were irrelevant. They had the same understanding of the enormity of the change since the comparative innocence of the time when they had fought in the same trench, side by side.

Joseph asked a few questions about Paris, although nothing that could be secret; he simply wanted to picture Sam's life.

"Do you get reasonable food?"

Sam shrugged. "Most of the time. Better than you do! I'd back any Frenchman alive against an army cook, any day of my life!"

Joseph smiled, but he heard the moment of hollowness in Sam's voice. He remembered the chocolate biscuits Sam's brother had sent, and the rotten, scalding hot tea.

"It's important work," he said, then wondered if it sounded condescending. "And dangerous. It must be hard to know who you can trust. At least I know which way the enemy is." Then he wished he had not said that, either. The old comradeship was so precious that the memory of it now seemed almost like golden days, and yet those days had frequently been nightmare awful.

"It's which way he's going next we're working on," Sam said drily. "It's a sort of mental puzzle putting the pieces together. There are some decent chaps, and women, too. Different kind of courage. Paris isn't home, but it has charm, like a beautiful woman who falls ill. It's worth fighting to see her recover, get back the color and the wit again, to see her dress with style."

"See you in the Café Parnasse, after the war!" Joseph said impulsively.

Sam slapped Joseph on the shoulder, gently. "Done!" he agreed. "First anniversary."

They came within sight of Joseph's lodging. Sam gave a small salute, a smile, and without any more words he was gone into the shadows. The night was empty again, the warmth and the safety of it gone.

Joseph went to his room. The chill in his flesh—into the bones—had nothing to do with the weather, or even his tiredness: It was a knowledge of loss.

Punch Fuller was in the Café Parnasse at one o'clock. He was flirting shamelessly with a French girl who was perhaps no more than fourteen, a beautiful, self-possessed child-woman with a magnificent head of curly hair. She was very patient with him, brushing him off with easy skill.

"Hello, Punch," Joseph said when he was almost beside him. "May I have soup and bread, please, mademoiselle?" He sat down on the seat next to Punch.

Punch was startled. "Hello, Chaplain! You come to keep me out of the paths of sin? That's downright unsporting of you." He looked at Joseph narrowly to see if he understood that it was a politely worded request to go away.

Joseph smiled. "I didn't find you by accident, Punch. Colonel Hook sent me."

Punch froze, not even turning his head toward Joseph. He was twenty-three, plain with his hooked nose and sharp chin, but quick-witted and an easy, loyal friend. "Whoi's that then?" he said guardedly.

Joseph had intended to be direct; he needed Punch to believe him. "Because Major Northrup's father, General Northrup, is tearing the regiment apart determined to find out who shot his son," he replied.

"Oi got no oidea who that'd be, sir," Punch said immediately.

"No, of course not," Joseph agreed. "Nor have I. Not sure that I really want to. The man was an ass. But the thing is, the general isn't going to go away until he has an answer, even if it's a wrong one, and some innocent man ends up before a firing squad."

Punch turned to look at him, his blue eyes troubled. "So what is it you reckon Oi can do about that then, sir?" The suspicion was sharp in his face that Joseph was trying to manipulate him into giving someone away.

Joseph had his answer planned. "He won't leave until he gets an answer. I want to find one he'll accept, and stop looking."

"Loike wot, Chaplain? If it weren't a Jerry, it had to be one of us."

"True," Joseph conceded. "With our casualty rate, probably someone who's dead, too, by now."

"Roight." Punch nodded. "But still won't be very good for his family, though, will it? An' d'yer think the general'll believe it? Sort of convenient, don't you think? An' apart from that, Chaplain, who's going to tell him a loi? You aren't!"

Joseph was both pleased and frustrated by Punch's faith in him. The next part of his plan was very carefully judged. "I realize you don't know exactly what really happened, Punch," he began. "But let's create a sort of working model, for something that's close enough people would believe it. The major was a liability. He didn't know what he was doing, and he wouldn't be told. It cost several good men's lives, plus a smashed leg here and there, the odd amputation."

"That's roight," Punch agreed guardedly. "We all know that."

"So far General Northrup doesn't," Joseph corrected him. "He's still denying all such accusations."

"So whoi does he think we shot him, then?" Punch said reasonably.

"That's a good point," Joseph said vehemently. "I can find chapter and verse of that easily enough. And when I do, the people who suffered most, or those whose friends did, are going to be suspect. That's the reason I haven't made a point of looking very hard so far. I hoped he'd realize it's going to be ugly. Do as much damage to his son's reputation as anyone's. But he isn't listening."

"Don't necessarily follow!" Punch protested. "You can't say as it was this man or that just because of who got killed!"

"I know that."

"Could've been lots of people!" Punch emphasized.

An idea was crystallizing in Joseph's mind. "Do you mean lots of people together, Punch, or just any one of lots of people?"

Punch was thinking hard.

Joseph waited.

"How would it be . . ." Punch said very slowly, "if you was to tell him that it was lots of men, dozen or more. Not one man gone mad who wanted to murder him, but a dozen who'd all had enough, and could see that more an' more men were going to get killed if the major didn't stop and listen to someone with experience? And it was only meant to scare some sense into him."

"How was shooting him going to scare sense into him?" Joseph said dubiously.

"Not shoot him, Chaplain. Set up a trial, loike. Make him sit an' listen to what a fool he was, evidence. Foind him guilty of incompetence, causing other men's deaths, an' pretend to shoot him. Scare the hell out of him." He studied Joseph's face earnestly, searching for understanding.

It was beginning to be very clear. "You mean a kangaroo court-martial?" Joseph said very softly.

"I'm only suggesting it!" Punch protested. "D'you think the general moight believe that?"

"Private soldiers court-martialing an officer?"

"Not just privates, nor corporals neither."

"Officers?" Joseph was not really surprised. "Captain Morel?"

"An' Captain Cavan. He were the one who had to amputate poor Matheson's leg, just 'cos that idiot sent him to cart a bloody great field gun through the mud. Everyone told him it was dangerous!" He stared at Joseph, challenging him to argue.

Joseph sat numbly, no longer even aware of his surroundings. It was worse than he had thought. They were speaking theoretically, but both knew that what Punch was really saying was the truth. If Cavan had been involved and Northrup ever found out, it would be a court-martial that would tear apart more than just the regiment. Cavan was one of the best surgeons on the Ypres Salient, and one of the bravest men. His recommendation for the V.C. had heartened every man who knew him. If he were now court-martialed for Northrup's murder, it might be the final grief and absurdity that would break the spirit of some, and ignite others to the mutiny that had lain just beneath the surface in men like Morel. There wouldn't be a serving soldier on the front who wouldn't think Cavan was worth ten of Northrup, whatever the law said.

"Captain Reavley?" Punch said anxiously.

"Yes. Yes, I see. It was designed to frighten Major Northrup. What went wrong?"

"Oi don't know, sir. Oi swear."

"Thank you."

"You aren't going to go an' tell Colonel Hook what Oi said, are you? Oi'll deny it, sir." His eyes were angry and frightened.

"No, I'm not," Joseph said sharply. "I told you I wasn't. But I can't find a story the general will believe if I don't know what the truth is. This way none of the facts anyone can discover will prove it false."

"Roight. Yes, I see. Thank you, Chaplain."

It was dusk as Joseph left in a staff car returning to the front. The air was motionless, wet and close to the skin. The sky leached the last tones of warmth out of the waterlogged land. Thin vapors of mist provided a curious softness but hid none of the desolation: the broken trees; the bare, scorched wreckage of houses and farms; the litter of broken guns and vehicles on the roads.

The car was on a cratered road now, and he smelled the familiar stench long before they reached even the outpost farthest back. The first star shells were bursting, and gradually the sound of the heavy guns blurred one raid into another. A stray eighteen-pound shell exploded fifty yards away, jarring the earth and sending eruptions of heavy Flanders clay high and dark into the air. Most of it was far in front of the car, over the woods toward Passchendaele itself.

As he alighted, he thanked the driver who had given him a lift, glad of a few hundred yards to walk. He felt battered by the noise, as if it were a physical assault, but he needed the time for a last arrangement of thoughts in his mind.

He found Hook in his dugout. He was looking at maps, although he must have known the whole of the Ypres Salient better than he knew his own garden. The photograph of his wife had been moved to the top of the gramophone, as if both had to be forgotten for the moment.

"Ah, come in, Reavley," he said, looking up as if relieved to forget the advances and retreats for a while. "Did you learn anything?"

"Yes, sir," Joseph replied, letting the sacking fall closed over the doorway and standing to attention as well as he could. It was raining again outside and his boots were heavy with mud, his legs soaked almost up to the knee. "I found Punch Fuller, and he told me a good deal of what happened."

There was no light in Hook's face. "As a confession?" Clearly he hoped it was; then Joseph could not tell him.

"No, sir—more or less theoretically, the sort of thing that could have happened," Joseph answered unhappily. He stood to attention, refusing to sit. "I really think, sir, that General Northrup would prefer not to know this," he said very clearly. "And it would serve no purpose at all to tell him. The major was an arrogant and inexperienced officer who inadvertently caused the deaths of several good men, and the serious injuries of others. It provoked intense ill feeling among almost all the men, not just an odd one here or there. Any action you take is going to have to involve at least a dozen men, sir. And I have reason to think that his actual death was not intended but was an accident."

Hook looked weary. He gestured to Joseph to be seated on an upturned ammunition box.

"You can't have it all ways, Reavley," he said. "Either a dozen men were involved because he had angered them beyond their control, or his death was an accident. Which was it? And if you're going to say it was an accident, then you are going to have to produce the man who fired the shot, and prove its accidental nature. What the hell was he doing pointing a loaded weapon at an officer anyway?"

"I don't know who did it, sir," Joseph said honestly. It was the one part of the story he had no need to blur.

"Don't play games with me, Reavley!" Hook snapped. His uniform was crumpled and bloodstained. His face was haggard with exhaustion.

"I've got men dying out there by the hundreds every day!" His hands were trembling. "I need to get Northrup off my back and out of the way! Either you know what happened or you don't! What did Fuller tell you? You said a dozen men. Do you mean a kangaroo court-martial?"

There was no point in denying it. Hook obviously knew. Joseph felt the net of circumstance tightening around him, but he was determined to give Hook a way out. "Yes, sir, but only with the intention of frightening him into taking advice in the future. Not to kill him."

Hook's face was pale, his mouth pulled down with grief. "Who was involved, Reavley?" His voice dropped. "I have to know."

Joseph looked straight back at him. He would not make the same mistake this time. He was prepared to lie, evade, whatever was necessary, and live with his conscience. "I don't know, sir. Fuller told me what happened, not who was concerned. And I promised him I'd not betray him. I think the men may know, sir, but no one will say. You can't blame them if their loyalty to each other is greater than to some military principle of obedience to an incompetent officer who, out of sheer stupidity, is going to cost the lives of their friends." He chose his words deliberately. "We owe them more than that."

Hook passed his hand across his face. Joseph could hear the faint rasping of dry skin over the stubble of his beard. "I don't have the luxury of choosing my own morality, Reavley. I can tell Northrup this, but he won't believe me. He can't afford to, because it makes his son a disgrace to him. And it would set a precedent that would be impossible to live with. Truth or lie, the army can't afford to grant that it is just."

"Then tell him it was an accident," Joseph demanded. "Let Major Northrup be buried with some semblance of honor. That would serve everyone."

Hook gave a sharp bark, supposed to be laughter. "I'll try!"

Joseph spent the night working with Cavan at the dressing station as casualties poured in. He snatched a few hours of sleep, then went to sit with the wounded or dying and do what he could for them. Mostly it was simply not leaving them to die alone.

At ten o'clock, Barshey Gee came and told him the colonel wanted to see him, and ten minutes later Joseph was back in Hook's dugout facing General Northrup, white-faced and standing so ramrod-stiff it seemed as if his back was arched.

"Are you saying, Captain Reavley, that my son was murdered by the common consent of a dozen or more of his own men?" His voice rasped in his throat as if he could not gulp the air into his lungs. "What in God's name has this army come to? Are we a crowd of barbarians, beyond the law? I will not surrender humanity and decency, sir, to a bunch of hooligans so demoralized by drink and terror that they turn on their own officers! Is there no morality left? How dare you stand there in the uniform of a man of God, and condone such . . . such evil!" His body trembled and he was obviously having difficulty controlling his voice.

"Sir, I did not say he was murdered," Joseph replied as calmly as he could.

"What do you call it, then?" Northrup demanded passionately. "A dozen men with guns against one unarmed officer? Pray, what does that pass for in your terminology?"

"You obviously know more about it than I do, sir," Joseph said stiffly. "What I heard was that the men pleaded with Major Northrup to listen to the evidence of more experienced soldiers, even though they were junior in rank. When he would not do so, and it was costing lives unnecessarily, they used force to make him listen, to save their own lives and those of their comrades. He was killed by accident, not intentionally. I don't know how that happened, or who was involved."

"The records of killed and injured should make that plain enough," Northrup replied. "These men all come from the same villages, played in the same football teams or brass bands, or whatever. Even a half-wit could find out who conspired together for this, if they wanted to. Whatever it began as, it ended as murder! And I shall see justice."

"Sir . . ." Hook began, but it was obvious in his face that he had already tried remonstrating with every argument he knew and had failed.

"It ended as tragedy," Joseph corrected him. "Most things do out here, sir. I believe profoundly that it would be better for everyone if we allow it to remain an honorable tragedy. Major Northrup was an officer respected by his men, who mourn their loss. Does it serve anyone to say that he was so incompetent that his men feared for their lives, and shot him in what they believed to be self-defense?"

Northrup winced as if Joseph had struck him, but he did not retreat. "I daresay that is what you would prefer, sir, but it is not the truth," he said hoarsely. "He was murdered by men who panicked and lost their discipline. I will find out who they are! If you will not assist me, I shall do it alone! And Headquarters will know that you endeavored to cover it up, to your eternal disgrace."

He gulped.

"I am forced to believe it is because the surgeon, Captain Cavan, was involved, and you are jealous of your regiment's chance of gaining a V.C. Captain Morel, who is a renegade if ever a man was, used to be your student in Cambridge, and you are deliberately shielding him. It will not be difficult to find the others, and when I do, you will have no choice but to arrest them! Sir!" He snapped to attention, saluted Hook, then pushed past Joseph and went up the steps and out into the mud.

Hook sat down and buried his head in his hands.

Joseph said nothing. He knew Cavan and Morel at least would be arrested by morning, probably all the others within another twenty-four hours. He had done everything he knew—and he had failed.

SEVEN

*J*udith jolted abruptly into wakefulness. She was lying on an ambulance blanket on the floor of the tent where she had fallen asleep. She had no idea how long ago that was. Day and night had blurred into one long cacophony of guns and engines, rain-soaked darkness split by star shells and the flash of explosions.

Now it seemed to be murky daylight, and comparatively quiet, just a distant rumble. She shivered because her clothes were wet and her bones ached from the hard floor.

"Is it time?" she said automatically, blinking and trying to clear her head.

Wil Sloan was bending over her, his grip still hard on her shoulder. His face was pale and slicked with rain, his hair dripping. There were bruises of exhaustion around his eyes.

"Something terrible's happened," he said huskily.

Fear boiled up in her like a wave of nausea. Was he going to tell her that Joseph had been killed? It was the thing she dreaded most of all. She found her throat was closed and the words wouldn't escape her lips.

"They've arrested twelve men for killing Major Northrup," Wil said. "Harrison came and told me."

"Twelve!" She was both relieved and appalled. "Twelve?" She propped herself on one elbow. "That's ridiculous. How could twelve . . . all of them?"

"Kangaroo court-martial," he replied, just as she realized it herself.

"And shot him?" she whispered.

"That's what they're saying. But the thing is . . . Cavan was one of them."

Now she understood his horror. "Cavan?" It was too awful to grasp. "But they can't take our doctor away! What about the wounded? That's . . . monstrous! They . . . they can't!"

"They have," he said. "And Captain Morel."

She sat up straight, pain shooting through her muscles. "Why? How do they know it was them?"

His face was bleak. "I'm sorry, Judith. The chaplain went to Paris and found one of the men who knew, and got it out of him somehow."

"I don't believe it!" She refused to. Joseph would not do that. "You must be wrong," she insisted. "Anyway, if the man confessed to a priest, you can't use it! Joseph would never repeat a confession. He couldn't!"

"He didn't say who it was." Wil shook his head. "Just that it was twelve. Northrup worked out who was angriest with the major and took it from there."

Judith struggled to her feet. "We've got to do something about it. This is terrible."

Wil stood also. "Right now we're on duty. And we'll have to take the wounded all the way back to the field hospital because there'll be no one able to do much in the dressing station."

"What a bloody nightmare." She sighed. "We'll have to do something about it! We can't let this go on, Wil. The men'll mutiny! To lock up our best surgeon over some idiot like Northrup! Are we trying to lose this war?"

"Keep your shirt on, Judith," he said anxiously. "Don't do anything rash. We can't afford to get ourselves locked up, too. That won't help. I'll get a cup of tea. It's going to be another bad night."

It was. Judith drove in a daze, fighting to keep the ambulance on the shell-pocked road and not get mired in the mud on either side or break an axle in one of the craters. It took all her strength to hold the wheel, and twice she had to get out and crank the engine to life again after a particularly violent stop.

All the time her mind was wrestling with the thought of Cavan in military prison awaiting trial. She could picture him as clearly as if she were looking at him. She could hear his voice in her mind. If they found them guilty of having mutinied and shot Northrup, they would all face a firing squad. There was no possible alternative. The worst thing was that she knew that he could have done it. He cared for the wounded above all things; he would put them before anything else. He had the anger and the courage.

How could Joseph have let it happen? He must have known General

Northrup was rabid for revenge. Why had he not simply said he couldn't find out who was responsible? Even General Northrup couldn't arrest the entire regiment.

She peered through the windshield, trying to discern what the dark shapes ahead were. The shellfire was getting heavier. The last one had landed only fifty yards away, and the debris had fallen heavily on the roof.

Maybe if she found out every stupid and dangerous thing Major Northrup had done she could widen the field of men likely to want him dead so far that they couldn't possibly arrest all of them. There couldn't be exactly twelve who had lost someone. How did they know they had the right twelve? Wasn't there some legal principle about it being better to let ten guilty men go free than punish one innocent one?

Surely the general would not want his son's name to go down in history as an officer so incompetent his men had had to kill him to save their own lives? He was refusing to believe that now, but if there was proof, he would have to. Or at least he would know that others would believe it, and that was what mattered.

They were near the front line. She slewed to a stop as a couple of soldiers ran toward her, their Red Cross armbands catching the headlights. Wil leaped out and threw the ambulance doors open. Someone was scrambling through the mud, sliding and floundering, waving his arms at stretcher bearers. Someone else was staggering across the lights, bandaged around the head and eyes, blood on his hands.

She tried to keep the engine running as she felt the weight go into the back and the balance alter. A shell exploded so close that the metal of flying shrapnel clanged on the ambulance sides. A gout of mud slapped against the window and spurted into her face.

More figures drifted across the headlights, blurred by mud and rain, and the weight jolted again.

Then Wil appeared at the door. "We're full! You'll have to back out, there's water everywhere! Don't lose the engine, you might never get it going again in this. I'll get in when you've turned." He disappeared.

It took her ten minutes, with considerable help, before she was back on the road facing in the opposite direction. She heard the door slam, and opened the throttle to push the engine as hard as she could. They lurched forward, splashing up sprays of water, hesitated a moment, then caught a purchase on the mud and gravel and moved forward.

She drove as hard as she could, knowing that because Cavan was locked up in some French farmhouse far behind the lines, they would have miles more to go before they could find help.

It was dark except for the occasional flares, and the rain became worse. They hit a deep crater in the mud, which was masked by water until it was too late. She was fortunate not to break the axle. There was no help for it but to turn off the engine and get out.

Wil came around from the back. He could see at a glance what was wrong, even if the violent lurch had not told him.

"It's too deep," she said desperately, wiping the rain out of her eyes. "You'll have to get at least some of them out. We'll have to lift it. I'll see if there's a piece of wood or something we can use as a lever, get it up, if someone else pushes." She looked around to see if there was any other light or sign of movement.

Wil pushed his hand through his sodden hair and left a smear of blood on his face. "Alf Culshaw's blinded, but he's still got both legs and arms. If we point his hands in the right place he can lift. The others are too far gone. One poor devil will be lucky if we get him there alive." His voice caught. "Jesus wept! This is so bloody senseless!" He turned and plowed back through the mud to the back of the ambulance and pulled the door open.

Judith started after him. It would take both of them to help the injured men out to lighten it enough to lift. They were heavy, awkward, and in desperate pain. Her hands slipped on the wet stretcher handles and her back ached unbearably as she tried to keep her balance and carry the heavy bodies to the side of the road.

"I'm sorry," she said to them over and over. "Got to lighten it so we can lift it out."

The first man was peacefully unconscious, blood soaking through his bandages in the rain.

"It's not too bad," the second said, trying to smile. "Don't worry, miss."

She felt the hot tears on her face as she bent to touch his hand. "Won't be long. Just got to lift a little, then we'll get you back."

Together with Wil she lifted two more out, leaving only the worst injured behind. Alf Culshaw she led slowly, warning of the puddles and ruts, until he and Wil were on either side of the stuck wheel. She placed Culshaw's hands under the edge of the frame. "Are you sure you're all right?" she asked him. "I wouldn't ask you if I didn't have to."

"I know," he said quietly. "Just don't ask me to guide you where we are going." He gave a dry, hacking laugh.

"You lift. I'll drive," she replied. "Better that way. I can't lift for toffee! Thanks." She had the wood ready—broken pieces from a dead tree and a couple of lengths of old sacking.

"Go on then," Wil directed. "One, two, three!"

The ambulance rocked and heaved level. Judith threw the wood and sacking in and it settled down again. She ran to the driver's seat and scrambled in. Wil moved Culshaw out of the way, then cranked the handle and they moved forward at last.

"Right!" Wil yelled, jumping backward. "Let's get them in again!"

She left the engine on, brake tight, and scrambled back to lift the stretchers in again to a cheer, and then to help Culshaw back into the seat.

She drove without incident the rest of the way. It seemed to take hours—but it was probably not more than forty-five minutes longer. A strange doctor, white-faced and obviously harassed, took the wounded in. The last man was already dead. Judith and Wil got back into the ambulance and started for the front again, this time with Wil in the front.

"We'll get Cavan back," he said when they were half a mile from the dressing station. "We'll find a way. He can't have been the one who shot Northrup. He must be covering for someone. It'll come out."

"Do you think so?" she asked, glancing sideways at him, although she could see nothing more than his outline in the dark.

"We've got to make it!" he said grimly. "If General Northrup could find out who the twelve most likely are, then we have to be able to find out why, as well. They'd never have done it without a hell of a good reason. We've got to find the people who'll swear to it."

"And take it to Northrup?" she asked. Her stomach knotted up with fear at the thought of it.

"You game?" Wil said, touching her arm for a moment.

She swallowed and felt her heart beating in her throat. "Of course."

On the final trip of the night she found Joseph at the field dressing station. He helped her with the last stretcher. The man was already dead from his wounds. Defeat overwhelmed her, and a sense that everything was slipping out of the last trace of control that she had.

"If we could have taken him to Cavan's dressing station he'd have been alive!" she said furiously, tears choking her. "But those men are bleeding to death because he's locked up in some damn farmhouse waiting to go on trial and be shot over that idiot Northrup!" She stared at him defiantly. "Why couldn't you leave your stupid conscience out of it and just keep your mouth shut? You didn't have to tell Colonel Hook it was a kangaroo trial! You could just have said you didn't know! Why can't you ever leave well enough alone?"

Joseph looked so tired his skin was gray in the early daylight, the stubble dark on his chin. There was no light in his eyes at all.

"I had to tell him something close to the truth, or he could too easily find out I was lying," he answered her.

"Don't tell him anything at all!" she shouted back. "Why didn't you just say you didn't know? He can't force you!"

Joseph looked down at the muddy boards they were standing on. "I thought if General Northrup knew it was at least a dozen men, a court-martial, not a private murder, he'd be so ashamed he'd let it drop rather than leave his son so disgraced. It would have been better for everyone. Otherwise he could just have found the worst enmity, the man he thought unjust, and blamed him. He isn't going to let it go."

"He isn't *now!*" she retorted. "He's charged Cavan, and we've got to take wounded men twice as far to get them treated—and they're dying, Joseph! They're dying, when they don't have to!"

"I know. . . ."

She felt guilty for attacking him when he was so obviously blaming himself anyway, but she was too angry and too frightened to stop. "We've got to save Cavan. What are we going to do?" She tried to moderate her voice a little, hearing the shrill edge to it. "Does Northrup really want it to come out that his son caused all those people's deaths? If we can prove it, find all the evidence of what a fool he was, who's dead because of him, and why there were twelve men willing to risk their own lives in order to get rid of him, wouldn't he want that silenced?"

They could both hear the sounds of movement inside, voices giving orders, stifled murmurs of pain.

"He wasn't meant to be killed, only frightened," Joseph explained.

"So who shot him?" she demanded.

"I don't know."

"Then they won't believe it. It sounds like an excuse. Were they really going to let him go again, after they'd put him on a mock trial?"

"I don't know, Judith. That's all I could get out of the man who told me."

Another ambulance pulled up outside. They saw the lights and heard the squelching in the mud, and voices shouting. Joseph moved aside and she followed him.

"Was he there? Is he in prison now?" she urged. "Why should anyone believe him? And if he told you in confession, why did you report it? He betrayed all his fellows!"

"He wasn't one of them," Joseph corrected her. "He knows because I think lots of the men do. Consider, Judith—if there were twelve men as a jury, surely others kept watch for them and covered what they were doing. There are a lot more than twelve men involved."

She saw a glimmer of hope, just a thread. "Then that's better. Everyone agreed Major Northrup was a disaster! Can't we take that to the general, and show him what it'll do to his son's reputation? Even to his own, for that matter?" Men started carrying stretchers into the dressing station. She stepped closer to Joseph. "Joe, in the general's place wouldn't you forgo revenge rather than have the name of someone you loved publicly vilified and all their mistakes proved?"

"Of course I would. Revenge is worth nothing anyway. But General Northrup doesn't feel that way."

"Then we'll have to make him!"

He looked at her blankly, anxiety puckering his brow, but he did not argue. It was only then that she realized he had intended to do it anyway; he merely needed time to gather the evidence. Perhaps her pain had made her too quick to judge.

"Hurry!" she urged. "The general could leave, and then it'll be too late. I'll help. I know Wil Sloan will, too, and others."

He drew in his breath to argue and—realizing the futility of it—let it out again without speaking.

Judith knew there was no time to wait for Joseph to speak to General Northrup. Northrup was somewhere far behind the lines. She and Wil knew who was involved and they had transport. It was not difficult to arrange to be the drivers who took several patients back to the hospital at Lille, and then divert on the way back and find Northrup's headquarters. Certainly they would be away longer than they should be, and they would have to commandeer petrol for the extra miles, but no one would have to be asked to cover for them or tell the necessary lies. A score of men were only too eager, vying for the privilege.

It required a little more bravado and finesse to find herself actually standing in the general's presence in the small French farmhouse in which he was currently headquartered. It was a comfortable place, gently domestic, once somebody's home. He was immaculately smart: boots polished, face pale and shaved to a perfect smoothness.

"You say you have further information on the death of my son, Miss . . . Miss Reavley?" he said stiffly. "Are you in a position to testify to this at the court-martial? It will not be easy for you. The whole regiment is of a sullen and mutinous nature. Discipline has been allowed to fall into laxity. Your fellow V.A.D. volunteers may make it difficult for you. Are you prepared for that?"

She had already weighed her answers. She stood to attention. "I am prepared to tell the truth, sir, because it is the truth, whoever likes me or dislikes me for it." Her gaze did not waver from his. She saw a tired and grieved man, the skin around his eyes paper thin, his shoulders held square by little more than pride.

She felt a wave of pity for him, for his arrogance and blindness, for the fragility that had stopped him seeing his son as he was, and his need to believe a lie and cling on to it even at the cost of other men's lives. But if she did not break him, then he would break Cavan, and all the others. Worst of all, he would have broken all the men's belief in justice and the bonds of loyalty here and now. And here and now those were almost the only things left that were good.

Northrup's voice was hoarse with emotion when he spoke. "You are a fine woman, Miss Reavley. You have more courage and honor than your regiment's chaplain. Is he related to you?"

"Captain Reavley is my older brother, sir." His insulting Joseph made it easier. She was angry with him herself, but that was quite different. She would have defended him to the death against anyone else. With one sentence Northrup had taken away the impediment to striking the blow.

"What is it you know, Miss Reavley?" he asked.

She replied without hesitating.

"Well, sir, in order to prove beyond question why these twelve men in particular should do such a . . . dangerous and terrible thing, the court will have to show something very special. All the hardship and loss the men have faced over the last three years has never made them . . . mutiny. And I suppose that's what it is?"

"That is what it is, Miss Reavley," he agreed. "Make no mistake."

It was time to tell him the truth, before someone interrupted them.

"Well, sir, in the case of Captain Morel, it was the order Major Northrup gave to move a field gun from one position to another across half a mile of plowed clay. The men argued that it would get stuck. They might lose the gun itself, and the wagons and the horses, possibly even some of the men, if it slipped." She watched his face and saw the muscles tighten in his neck. He knew it was a stupid order, born of inexperience and too much pride to listen to lesser ranks.

"They argued, perhaps insolently," she went on. "Major Northrup insisted. They obeyed and got stuck. They saved the horses, but two men were injured, one man's leg was broken so badly Captain Cavan had to amputate it." She hated continuing, but it was like a gangrenous limb: It must all come off or it was pointless having begun. "And Captain Morel was very upset about sending out a rescue party into no-man's-land on a day when the German snipers could simply pick them off. Some refused to go, but others did. Several men were injured. Captain Eardslie was killed. He was one of my brother's students in Cambridge, and he and Morel were great friends."

Northrup's face was ashen. She felt as if she were killing a man already wounded fatally. Still she drove it home. "I have details for all of them, sir, and men prepared to swear to every incident sufficiently to prove a motive for each one of the twelve, especially Captain Cavan. It took a great deal to break him, but I can—"

"Yes!" he interrupted her. "I see you have taken a great deal of care to have every point documented, Miss Reavley. It will not be necessary." His voice was shaking and the muscles in his neck and jaw were so tight he could not control the tic in his cheek.

Her stomach was knotted until she felt nauseous. "Don't you want to prove the guilt of all of them?" she asked quietly. "Not just the one who pulled the trigger? He may simply have panicked. Aren't they all equally to blame? The whole twelve?"

His voice was barely audible. "What is it you want, Miss Reavley? You are not a fool! Are you trying to have my son's name dishonored, to have revenge for your . . . your mutinous friends?"

She swallowed.

"No, sir. As I said in the beginning—and you praised me for it—I want the whole truth to be told, to be fair to everyone. Nobody is going to believe that good soldiers—especially exceptional ones like Captain Cavan—mutinied unless we can show what reason they had . . . or imagined they had."

He stared at her, knowing he was being manipulated. He was certain in his own mind that it was Cavan she was trying to save, and yet he could see no way out, nothing with which he could accuse her. "They are already charged," he pointed out. "Are you so bent on revenge?"

She hesitated. Was it necessary to strike the last blow? Yes it was. She dared not stop in case she was just short of victory. "Not revenge, sir, surely? Is it not justice?"

His voice dropped to a whisper.

"My son does not deserve to be buried with dishonor. Is it not enough for them that he is dead?"

"It is terrible that he is dead, sir. And Captain Eardslie, and all the others. Over half a million of them, I believe. Not counting the French, and of course the Austrians and Germans, and the Italians, and Russians. And I suppose we have to start counting the Americans, too, now."

"I will speak with the prosecutor. Perhaps the charge can be lessened."

She smiled very slightly, afraid to say anything in case she spoiled it. "Permission to return to my ambulance, sir?"

"Granted, Miss Reavley."

Mason arrived back at Passchendaele to find it worse than before. It had rained almost without ceasing, the wettest August in human memory. Men lived and died in a hell past sanity to imagine. It went on day after day, night after night, with no victory and no end in sight except the possibility that there would be no life remaining—human, animal, or plant—and finally the mud would claim everything.

He thought of his beloved Yorkshire with its wild fells, shining tarns beneath wind-ragged skies, and steep villages with cobbled streets. But the memory was too all-consuming: It robbed him of words powerful enough to capture the passion and tenderness of a love so deep. Instead he began writing of England in general.

"It doesn't seem possible." He started a rough draft. "At home the trees tower green like clouds over the gold of the harvest fields. Horses bend to the plow and the fruit ripens in the orchards. Poppies burn scarlet grazing the corn with hot color. The men are gone. Women now get ready to reap and bind, laughing with each other, growing used to their new tasks.

"Here there are no trees, only a few shattered trunks and the scarlet is blood as men are crushed and trodden back to the all-consuming clay from which we are told we were fashioned by a deity who has grown tired of us and turned away. These few terrible miles hold so much human flesh you cannot set foot without standing on some man's rotting body."

Then he tore it up and wondered how to start again. Words needed to be simple for this, clear of all sentimentality. But what was there for anyone to say? For the first time in his life, words seemed pointless, his own too small, too shallow for the burden.

"We died in hell—they called it Passchendaele." He could only quote others. "Oh, Jesus, make it stop!"

But it seemed no God was listening.

He heard the news of the arrests of Cavan, Morel, and the other ten before he reached the section where it had happened. He wanted to speak to Colonel Hook when he had the chance and to Joseph Reavley. He needed the whole story to write up, all the information he could find before the court-martial began. And of course he wanted to see Judith as well. That was at the forefront of his mind, as it had been lately, too often for his emotional comfort.

He found the ambulance parked outside a first aid station, just behind the supply trenches. It was covered with mud; he saw several scars and dents on it, and a few bullet holes. The air was soft and muggy, full of flies and the ever-present stench. The occasional fine rain did nothing to help.

He asked for Judith and was told that she and Wil Sloan were both inside the makeshift tent. There were several other men with them, all with apparently minor injuries, and they were clustered around Judith, looking at her and laughing. Most of them had mugs of tea, held up as if in a toast.

Mason's shadow across the door made one then another turn, and they froze.

He walked in. He could not help looking first at Judith. She was very slender, as if under the gray V.A.D. uniform with its long skirt she were thin enough to be fragile. She had been at the front for three years. She must be so weary of dirt and pain, and never having time for laughter, never dressing in pretty clothes, being admired, playing games and falling in love. There was something fierce and uniquely beautiful about her, a waiting passion that war had robbed her of living yet.

She was flushed and her eyes were bright. The men had been looking at her as they raised their mugs. Why? Had something happened, and he knew nothing of it?

They recognized him. Wil Sloan came forward, still smiling a little, but guarded now. "Hello, Mr. Mason. You looking for someone?" he asked.

Mason made up his mind immediately. "I was going to do a piece on your surgeon, Captain Cavan. I meant to last time I was here, but he was too busy. If he still is, I thought I'd ask other people about him. You must all have stories you could tell. It would be especially good for morale." He would have to keep up the lie to Judith, and hope she never knew he had heard about the arrests.

They stared at him, the laughter dying out of their faces. Wil turned to Judith, as if seeking her permission to answer.

"I think that's an excellent idea," she said vigorously, looking at Mason with a bright challenge. "Captain Cavan is one of the best men in the whole Army Medical Corps, and they're all good. We should tell you in detail about his holding off the German attack, which is why he's up for the V.C. But there are lots of other stories as well." Her voice was warm, vibrant with enthusiasm, her eyes shining. There was even a faint flush in her cheeks.

Mason felt an acute sensation of dismay, and then of inexplicable anger. Damn it, even after he was arrested for mutiny and murder, there was a fire in her when she spoke of Cavan that was there for no one else. Judith

Reavley, the idealist, the unquestioning patriot, was going against all her convictions for this man! What was the matter with her?

Cavan was in his early thirties, and a good-looking man, fair-haired, strong, with an intelligent face. He remembered seeing him working with Judith, easily, as if understanding were there without the need for words. Should he have seen it then?

He felt shut out, cold to the core of his belly. He had been thinking of her far too often, allowing her to matter. He realized how much of the hope, the peace inside, the warmth that was worth having, had rested in the thought of her.

They were waiting for him to answer. He must control himself—hide the awful vulnerability inside him. "Thank you," he said. "That would work very well. Then a few words with him will be enough." He was not going to let them dupe him entirely. Apart from pride, he could not afford to appear a complete fool, which he would do if he wrote a piece about Cavan, apparently not knowing he was charged with mutiny and murder. When the court-martial began, that would be the biggest story of the entire British Army on the Western Front. The only thing that could overwhelm that would be for the army to break through and advance considerably. And at the moment they were paying in blood for every yard.

Judith began to organize it immediately. She directed one man to recount his memory of helping Cavan carry wounded men to shelter and set broken limbs right there in the forward trench with mortar fire all around them. Another she told to repeat his tales of good humor through long hours operating in the field hospital, patience teaching new men now to assist. And for good measure a good few long and rambling jokes were added.

Mason sat through them, making notes, watching thin, strained faces and hearing the laughter and the pain in their voices. He hated being an onlooker. There was something vaguely indecent about drawing such memories from men whose passion and nakedness of heart could be extinguished by blood and shellfire in the next week or two, while he went safely home.

And yet those who read his work were the families of those men, and countless more like them. They deserved to know.

He was very aware of their enthusiasm to keep him there, and he knew the reason. Judith might be directing the situation, but the men understood and were more than willing. The murder of Major Northrup was already known. Did they really imagine they could keep the arrest of twelve men secret? Why even attempt it? It must be only a matter of days until the court-martial. Since it was a capital charge, and twelve men accused, including two officers, the army would send a militarily appointed prosecutor from London. Even so, like every other sentence of death, it would still be referred right up to Field Marshal Haig himself before it was carried out. That rule applied to the newest private, let alone to an officer nominated for the V.C.

What a bloody horrible, senseless tragedy! Why on earth had they done such a thing? Had they really imagined for a moment that they would get away with it? Or were they driven by a power far beyond the capacity for thought?

He refused to decide at the moment exactly what story he would write, but possibilities crowded his mind. The one he knew the Peacemaker would want was to make Cavan the hero, betrayed by an incompetent and cowardly command. A bad officer had been put in charge, and a surgeon had had to get rid of him in order to stop even more pointless slaughter of his men. All the stories about Cavan that he was now hearing would help with that: the laughter and comradeship, the heroism in the face of madness.

He took it all down carefully, noting the name and rank of those who told him. Judith went outside and did some work on her ambulance, then returned an hour later. There was still the same suppressed excitement about her, and he began to realize that she was following a very definite plan of some sort. For a wild moment the thought flashed to him that it was the same as his and the Peacemaker's. She had finally seen too much slaughter and was prepared to take a small step toward ending it. She was watching him now as he finished the last notes from the men. She came over toward him. She walked with grace, the weariness under such rigid control was completely hidden. He wondered when she had last slept properly in any kind of bed, or eaten a meal that wasn't cooked in a Dixie can. She must be so tired of dirt, endless chores, and desperate jokes one hardly dared laugh at. And yet laughter and that all-consuming comradeship of those who share life and death were the only shreds of human sanity left.

"Did you get some good stories?" she asked Mason, sitting down at the other side of the small table.

"Yes, thank you. But I'd still like to hear about his stand against the German raiding party for which they've put him up for the V.C. You were there, weren't you?"

She looked at him wryly.

"You know I was. Would you like me to tell you now? I'm not back on duty for an hour." She pushed a strand of hair off her brow. "I can do it."

"What about a chance to sleep?"

"Are you telling me I look tired?"

He studied her face. He was surprised at the strength in her, and the defensive challenge in her eyes in that question. How different she was from the girl who had worn the blue satin gown at the Savoy with such infinite femininity. She must know that, too, with a different kind of regret from his.

"Actually you look beautiful." He said it deliberately, and yet it was totally sincere. "But reason says that, like everybody else, you must need to sleep."

There was a moment's confusion in her eyes, uncertainty whether to believe him or not. Then she flushed very slightly and he knew in that instant how much it mattered to her. It was a belief that if there were ever peace again she could still be the woman she was inside, before the war.

"I'll sleep next break," she answered. "You might have gone by then, and you need to get the story." Without waiting for him to reply, she told him in vivid and dramatic detail exactly what the raid had been like and how Cavan's remarkable courage had saved all their lives. He could simply take it down and rewrite it using her words, there was such a force of life in them. Never once did she hesitate or repeat herself.

As he wrote it, he began to understand at last what it was she was doing. She was re-creating in the readers' minds the situation that had brought about Major Northrup's death, and showing Cavan as a man who had had no moral choice but to act as he had. She was paralleling his courage and decision in the trenches with his decision to frighten Northrup into acting with some sense.

Did she really believe that all they had meant to do was frighten him? Or did she not care?

When she had finished, he asked the question that had waited at the back of his mind since the beginning. "Can you arrange for me to see Cavan himself, even if only for a few moments? I have to have a quote from him." He watched her, wondering what she would do.

"You can't." She looked back quizzically, trying to judge whether he was testing her, or if he really did not know.

"Can't I?" he said aloud.

"No one can," she replied, her eyes unwavering. "General Northrup found the twelve men with the best cause to kill his son, and had them all arrested, including Captain Cavan. No one confessed, and no one denied it. We don't know whether they're guilty or not. General Northrup said he would try and get the charge reduced from mutiny and murder down to insolence, disobeying an order, and accident. But it hasn't happened yet. It's bloody chaos. He was our best surgeon, and men are dying he could have saved." The misery in her voice was savage. He flinched at the sound of it.

"Why would General Northrup try to get the charge reduced?" he asked, puzzled.

She looked at him with a twist of defiance, even pride. "Because in order to prove deliberate murder he'll have to show motive, of course! Why on earth would twelve loyal soldiers without a blemish on their records get together and murder an officer?"

"Because he's a dangerously arrogant and incompetent idiot!" he responded.

"Exactly. Which I can prove. But General Northrup is not so keen to have that demonstrated. When he realized just how—"

"Yes, I see," he said quickly. "Was it you who pointed out to him how unfortunate that would be?" He knew the answer. That was the source of the fire in her eyes, and why the men were toasting her in Dixie cans of tea. No doubt it was also why she was keen that Mason should write a piece just now extolling Cavan. Was it because she cared for Cavan with more than friendship, or simply that she was brave and driven by the same passionate loyalty to her friends that bound all the fighting men together? She had charged in blindly to the rescue, without thinking of the cost or the chances of success. That is who she was, like Joseph: all pointless idealism, and dreams that were fragile and idiotic, and desperately beautiful.

The lock of hair had fallen forward again across her brow. Without thinking, he reached across and pushed it into place, only afterward realizing how intimate the gesture was.

"I'm sorry," he apologized, feeling self-conscious.

She colored as well, suddenly aware of his physical nearness.

"You're still going to write about him!" she said urgently. "Nothing that Northrup says changes that. And Cavan might have had nothing to do with it. They've just arrested the most likely twelve."

Mason reflected that, in a different age, she would have been married to some nice local doctor or landowner by now, probably with a couple of children. Her days would have been spent in a little socially admirable work, probably connected with the church, and the occasional society party, or hunts ball. Instead she was watching the carnage of a generation. It was not happiness but a kind of sublime lunacy that kept her going. It was all pointless, and it would break her in the end, and that was something he dreaded. It would be like the very last lights going out as the darkness consumed everything.

He loved her for it with a kind of hunger he dared not face. It was precious beyond his reach and like the reflection of a distant fire, a warmth he could not touch or hold. It was an illusion, what she believed in was not real, and yet the beauty of it haunted him too fiercely to let it go.

"I'll write the best I can," he promised. "But it won't change anything, Judith. I wish I could say it would. I expect it's out of Northrup's hands by now."

Her mouth tightened; she bit her lower lip. "Are you warning me to give up?" she said a little huskily.

"Never," he whispered. "Just be prepared to be beaten, at least this time." He put his hand over hers where it lay on the tabletop. Her hands were very slender, stiff now in resistance. "Cavan won't escape, unless he can prove he wasn't part of it."

"And leave the others?" she said indignantly. "He'd never do that."

Of course not. Cavan was just like her! Quixotic . . . absurd.

"Oh, Judith! Can't you . . ." He stopped. He would be asking her to deny her very nature. "No, of course you can't." He rose to his feet and leaned across the table, kissing her softly on the mouth. For a long moment of infinite warmth, as if a new fire melted every aching shard of ice inside him, he clung on to her. Then slowly he pulled away, leaving her behind, but never the memory. He turned and walked out into the incessant, clinging, suffocating rain.

Judith was right, of course; he had no opportunity to speak to Captain Cavan, or any of the other imprisoned men. He did not tip his hand to the authorities by asking for it when he knew it was an impossibility. Instead he went forward to the front line and gathered all the factual information he could. He saw how they were struggling to manage without Cavan, as Judith had told him—and for that matter, without Morel, who had been a good officer.

He asked men about Morel, and gained perhaps a slightly biased picture. But even accounting for that, he emerged as a brave and widely experienced man, which was unusual in these times of sweeping casualties. A front-line officer with three years' service was rare. He was joked about because it was the easiest way of defusing the emotion, although the men knew he was burning with anger and emotionally unreliable. However, neither his courage nor his judgment of a military situation were ever doubted. They felt his loss keenly.

Still Mason could not stand by and simply make notes of it all, like some recording demon—angels were beyond the power of his imagination. Useless or not, he went out with the stretcher parties as he had done in Gallipoli, or the Italian Front facing Austria where men also died in the tens of thousands, and on the bitter Russian Front in the east, and the sands of Egypt and Mesopotamia. The weather was different, and the terrain; death was the same.

He saw Joseph on the third day. They had both returned from no-man's-land, up to the armpits in mud from digging men out of the craters and attempting to carry them back. Off balance with the weight of the unconscious wounded, they had floundered and fallen. They had helped each other up again awkwardly, picked up their burdens again and finally reached the front-line trench. It was filled with water like a stagnant canal, with broken pieces of duckboard, and corpses of rats and men.

Still helping each other, they made it at last to a drier stretch and passed the wounded over to an ambulance crew. Then they sat shivering with exhaustion in one of the dressing station tents. Someone put blankets around them and passed the Dixie cans of hot tea laced with rum.

Joseph looked at Mason and smiled.

"Still think all this is a good idea, Chaplain?" Mason asked, waving his hand to indicate everything around them.

Joseph could see in Mason's face a darkness that would not now be won over by any word or act as it had been in the small boat back in 1915. "I think it's hell," he answered the question.

Mason looked at him curiously, an urgency behind his probing.

"I was talking to Judith," he began; his eyes flickered away, self-consciously, then back again. "She still believes there's some point to all this, some moral purpose that makes it worthwhile. Do you?"

Joseph hesitated a moment, not only as to the truth of any answer, but even to how honest he should be to Mason. "There can't be a heaven if there's no hell. But I admit, I hadn't envisioned having to spend so much time in hell."

Mason's mouth twisted a little but his eyes remained steady. "I wasn't looking for a metaphysical answer, Reavley—something a little more from the heart and the belly. Not what you want to believe, or what you think you ought to believe! What is there inside you, really?"

"When? Now? Just bewilderment and exhaustion," Joseph replied. "Tomorrow morning, or next time I see someone I love, or an act of total unselfishness, or courage more than I could manage myself? Then yes, I believe there's something wiser and better than I am, and infinitely greater. Do I know where I'm going? No. Do you?"

"I'm not sure if anywhere I wish to go exists," Mason replied.

"Then build it," Joseph replied. "If you survive, of course," he added with a smile.

"Is that what you tell your men when they're dying?" Mason would not give up.

"If it's what's needed. Usually it isn't. Just being there, talking about anything, so they're not alone."

"Saying what they need to hear." Mason turned the words over, still looking at Joseph steadily. "Because you've nothing else to say? Charging the guns, obediently, like the Light Brigade at Balaclava, because you don't know what else to do? Following orders, Chaplain? Aren't you supposed to be leading?"

Joseph saw the rage and pain in him, the knowledge of darkness closing in, not just at Passchendaele, but everywhere.

"I think the most I can do is keep going," Joseph told him.

Mason was silent for a long time. "Thank you at least for honesty," he said at last. "I don't know how you can survive on that—it isn't enough."

"As long as there's somebody you can touch in the darkness, it has to be enough," Joseph told him.

Mason did not answer. Slowly he drank the rest of his tea.

Joseph finished his also. He meant what he had said. The fact that he too needed more, just a glimmer of hope that one day there would be an answer he could understand, was none of Mason's business.

"Yes?" the Peacemaker said urgently as Mason sat in the chair opposite him in the upstairs room in Marchmont Street. "I know all about the losses. It's the epitome of all we sought so desperately to prevent. I would have given everything I've ever had, my own life if it would have helped, to prevent this. Even you don't have words to describe the horror or the futility of it. What about this trial for mutiny and murder? They have twelve men arrested, you say?"

"Yes." Mason looked up. He was haggard. His heavy black hair made his skin look even more pallid, almost bloodless, and there was a consuming grief in his eyes as if no passion would ever burn them alive again. The Peacemaker was concerned for him. Could a war correspondent suffer battle fatigue?

"The twelve men with the best motives, apparently, for wanting Major Northrup dead," Mason answered. "Or—I should say more accurately—removed from command. And since those above him either didn't know how incompetent he was, or didn't care, death seems to have been the only way. I imagine, since he was a general's son, it was beyond the power of Colonel Hook to remove him. The thing is, Captain Cavan, the surgeon up for the V.C., is one of them."

"Perfect." The Peacemaker breathed the word like a sigh. "It is so absolutely farcical we couldn't have created anything more likely to make even the sanest and most blindly loyal of men rebel against this suicidal injustice." He felt he was on the brink of something that could be used to turn the tide at last.

"There's word that General Northrup will try to get the charge lessened to one of insubordination, and that Northrup's death was more of an accident than intentional murder," Mason warned.

"Really!" The Peacemaker felt a sudden chill. "Why?"

Mason sighed. "Because to prove intent they must prove motive. Doing that will automatically expose Major Northrup's disastrous incompetence. His father does not want that. And believe me, the men are all loyal to the mutineers. If the charge is kept at murder, they'll make damned certain Major Northrup is exposed."

"And does the general know this?" The Peacemaker was fascinated. It opened up possibilities of further mutiny he had hardly dared hope for.

"Yes, of course he does," Mason replied.

"This is very good," the Peacemaker said decisively. "I shall make certain that the prosecutor appointed is a hard-liner. I have just the man in mind. He will make certain the full charge is retained, and prosecuted to the full. We need have no doubt of a capital sentence. Captain Cavan, V.C., will be put before the firing squad. It will be the spark that finally sets the tinder afire."

He smiled slightly, an unexpected regret tugging at him. "The British troops will never stand for an injustice of such obscenity. And I think the country may even be behind them, if we handle it the right way. There comes a point when people will no longer be herded to slaughter like sheep. Believe me, Mason, the Russians are very close to that point now. If the tsar does not make peace with Germany, withdraw her troops from the battle front altogether, and institute radical social reform, the Russian people will rise up in a way we have not seen since the High Terror in Paris in 1793 when the gutters ran red with blood."

"The tsar won't change—not that much!" Mason looked stunned, almost buried by the enormity of the idea.

"I doubt it," the Peacemaker agreed. "I think by next month, or the month after, we will see riot in the streets of St. Petersburg, and blood." He felt the exultation surge up inside him, catching his breath and his throat. "We are at the beginning of the end, Mason! There will be peace by Christmas! Peace! Dear God, peace!"

EIGHT

"Sir?" Joseph stood in Colonel Hook's dugout, assuming from the message that had summoned him that the news was dire.

Hook looked up from the paper he had been reading. His skin was gray and an uneven stubble shadowed his jaw.

"Ah, Reavley. I've just been informed that London is sending a prosecutor for the court-martial. I was hoping we could have someone from one of the regiments near here. At least they'd understand the . . . the pressures. But they're sending a man called Faulkner. I've heard of him." He looked up at Joseph, frowning. "He has something of a reputation, very rigid, believes in the ultimate deterrent. I don't think the bastard's ever seen action." He rubbed his hand over his head. "Sorry. I shouldn't speak of him like that. I suppose he might be able to . . ." His voice tailed off. He sounded utterly without hope.

Joseph sat down without being asked. He cleared his throat. "What are the chances of General Northrup getting the charges reduced?"

Hook was surprised. "From Faulkner? None at all. He'll make an example of Cavan and Morel. Reavley, I'm afraid of what the men will do when they hear. We've got just over three days; then it'll be too late."

Joseph did not need to ask him what he meant. Once the twelve men were charged with mutiny and murder—unless they were found not guilty, which was virtually impossible—there could be no other sentence but death. The chances were high that there really could be mutiny. With the resultant loss of morale, the lines would be smashed and the forces that survived would be driven back behind the last defenses. The Germans would simply carry on straight through to Paris, and France would fall.

After that there was nothing between the German Army and the beaches of England except twenty miles of flat summer sea. Defeat would be only weeks away.

Joseph looked up at Hook and saw understanding of exactly the same thing in his eyes.

"Is it worth telling Faulkner what it would be likely to do to the men?" he asked.

"It would if he believed it," Hook replied. "Men like that usually have an excellent escape from situations they don't want to be responsible for: They simply refuse to believe it. He would say the British Army never mutinies and never surrenders. It is only the occasional soldier who does, and that sort of man has to be weeded out . . . severely. He would consider this an excellent opportunity to make an example."

"It won't make an example of anything except ignorance and brutality," Joseph said, hearing his own voice crack with emotion and something close to despair. "No matter how good men are, or how brave, there's a point beyond which they break. There's no point afterward in excusing yourself by saying you were too damned stupid to see it!"

"I know." Hook looked down at the paper again. "I'll try appealing to London, but I don't know what good it'll do."

It was dismissal. Joseph stood, excused himself from the claustrophobic safety of the mud and earth, and the few familiar objects of Hook's personal life, and went out into the faint, misty sunlight. He felt acutely guilty. At some point there must have been a time when he could have acted differently, hidden something, even lied outright so it would never have reached this stage.

He walked slowly along the track, his boots squelching in the thick mud. At this slightly higher level it was shallower, the water puddling rather than running along. Out in the craters of no-man's-land either it would be steaming a little in the August heat, or there would be low-lying mustard gas again. It wasn't always easy to tell.

If Mason had not seen Northrup's body and known he had been shot by a British gun, there would have been no need for anyone to be aware that it wasn't just another casualty. God knew there were enough of them!

He stepped and banged into a piece of broken riveting where the earth wall had collapsed.

It was Mason again. This was playing straight into the Peacemaker's hands. Was he behind it? Or was Joseph just indulging his delusions? The last letter from Matthew had said he was chasing down the old enemy at last. There was no other way to interpret that. Now it looked as if thanks to a catalogue of stupid mistakes, the Peacemaker was going to win after all. Britain would be in mutiny and defeat, with the best part of a million men dead, countless more wounded in body and crushed in mind and spirit. It was a defeat he could not even have imagined when they first left for France three years ago, thinking they would be home for Christmas. It had been all heroism and honor then, dreams of glory. Now there was only despair.

It would have been better to have turned a blind eye to Northrup's murder, better even to have shot the man himself, than have it come to this. What was the point at which he had made the wrong judgment? Perhaps that was the secret of life, knowing when was the precise moment at which you decide to do something irrevocable, rather than being a coward, a man always thinking, poised on the edge of decision, and never making it.

Joseph went to bed in his own dugout a little after midnight and slept more deeply than he had expected. However, just before dawn he woke with a jolt, his heart pounding, the sweat pouring off his body. Everything was familiar—the books, the picture of Dante, his chair and desk—but there was rifle fire close at hand and men's voices, high-pitched, shouting.

He rolled off the bunk and stood up, his body shaking. There were more shouts, and bursts of fire rather than controlled aiming.

There was a noise immediately outside on the steps, then the sacking curtain was yanked aside and a figure blocked out the shred of light.

Joseph half expected to see the spike-crested helmet of a German officer. He made a supreme effort to calm himself and look, and realized it was a British Tommy, but bareheaded.

"Capt'n Reavley! You there, sir?"

"Yes, I am." Joseph swallowed. "What is it, Tiddly Wop?"

"They're gone, Captain. All of 'em, 'cepting Captain Cavan. Gawd knows how it happened, but they're gone!" Andrews replied.

Joseph struggled to grasp what the words meant. It could not possibly be true. "Gone?" he repeated foolishly. "You mean they've been taken somewhere else? They're going to have the court-martial at another regiment?"

"Oi don't mean been took, sir. Oi mean gone themselves! Nobody knows where they are. They escaped. Could 'ave gone anywhere."

Now Joseph was cold, as if his hands and feet hardly belonged to him. "They couldn't have got out of the farmhouse. What happened to the guard? How could they get out?"

"Guards are all tied up like turkeys for dinner, but not a hair of their head broke."

"You said Captain Cavan is still there?" Joseph was bitterly disappointed. For a moment he had believed the impossible, and now reality plunged him back even deeper. "That doesn't make sense, Tiddly Wop."

"Since when did anything in this bleeding war make sense, Chaplain? If it does to you then, whoi in't you telling anyone else?"

"The other eleven have gone? How did they get out?"

"No idea," Tiddly Wop said with a shadow of anger. "An' if Oi did, Oi wouldn't be telling. Oi just thought you'd loike to know."

"I do! I . . . I just wish Captain Cavan had gone, too."

A faint glimmer of light caught Tiddly Wop's teeth gleaming as he grinned. "Sorry. Oi shouldn't have said that, Chaplain. Course you do."

There was more shouting outside but the rifle fire had stopped. Tiddly Wop turned around and made his way out, Joseph on his heels. It was relatively quiet, the heavy guns only sporadic. Joseph stared around at the figures sprinting across the open ground, and others standing almost idly. There was a military car parked on the driest piece of ground. A man in officer's uniform stood beside it, waving his arms, apparently giving directions to the others.

"Got to look loike we want to find them," Tiddly Wop said sententiously.

"How long ago did they go?" Joseph asked.

Tiddly Wop shrugged. "How do Oi know? They could be on their way to Paris by now. Only more likely they'll go to Switzerland. Oi would."

"The Swiss border's hundreds of miles away," Joseph retorted.

"Then Oi hope they get a lift. Not that they would, of course!" he added hastily, taking a nervous glance at Joseph.

"They might have gone the other way altogether." Joseph entered the conspiracy without hesitation. "Maybe making for the sea."

"Back to Blighty?"

"No, more likely Sweden." Joseph found himself smiling. He knew it was stupid to be amused. They would be found and brought back. Cavan was probably showing more sense in staying. And it might buy more time. It could take several days to catch them all, if they ever did. Some might get killed, in the ordinary course of the war. "I wonder if we can help," he added aloud.

"Roight!" Tiddly Wop agreed. "Oi'll go an' see if Lieutenant Moore wants a hand. He don't know north from south, that one. If someone don't give him a hand he'll end up in Switzerland himself!"

Joseph offered to look for the escapees, and he spent the next hour pretending to search. Like the rest of the men, he generally made sure that all signs of which way they might have gone were thoroughly obliterated.

He shared a Dixie can of tea with Colonel Hook, sitting in the back of the supply trench on a couple of sandbags.

"Find any trace?" Hook asked, eyebrows raised.

"None at all," Joseph said immediately. He met Hook's eyes with complete candor.

"No," Hook replied. "Didn't think you would."

By midday it was a very different matter. General Northrup had returned, and word had come up the line that Lieutenant Colonel Faulkner would arrive before sunset. Northrup was furious.

"How can you be so totally incompetent?" he shouted at Hook. His face was pinched and two blotches of color stained his cheeks. "Don't you mount some kind of guard? For God's sake, your command is falling to pieces around you! Pull yourself together, man!"

They were in the small command post. It was little more than a room in a farm outbuilding, furnished with a table and half a dozen chairs. Northrup was pacing the floor, his boots scratching on the wooden boards. He swung his arms and jabbed the air.

The accusation was grossly unjust, and both tragic and absurd. Joseph intervened, although both of them outranked him.

"The men are exhausted, sir," he said to Northrup. "No one is getting more than a few hours' sleep any night. The wounded are pouring back from the battlefront and we are finding it more than we can do to get them to hospital, keep any sort of supplies coming forward of either food or ammunition. The only men we've got to spare for guarding prisoners are those who are wounded already. We don't know what happened, and blaming them is premature and deeply unfair. In any other circumstances they'd be invalided out and taken care of in a decent hospital."

"I know the conditions are hard, Captain Reavley," Northrup said with a tight little grimace. "This is not the only part of the line battered almost to breaking—although I grant you it is the worst. But it's all the more important we keep up our standards, for the sake of morale."

"If somebody is found to be culpable, it will be attended to." Hook broke his long silence, rising to his feet and picking up a pile of dispatches. "Now, sir, if you will excuse me, I must go and see to some of these things."

As soon as he had left, Northrup stared at Joseph. "This is a preposterous situation, Captain. I realize that your sympathies are with your men, and perhaps that is how you see your calling, but this cannot be ignored as if it were not a capital offense." He stared at Joseph accusingly. "You must realize that? Now, of all times, we must stand fast to those principles we believe in, when there is the greatest temptation to give in, or to cut and run. Officers must set an example. It is what we are here for."

Joseph drew in breath to argue, to tell him forcefully how absurd and cruel and utterly pointless he was, that he had lost all touch with reality. Any day now they would lose the battle of Passchendaele, and the whole Western Front could buckle and break apart. The last thing on earth the army needed was an idiotic prosecution of one of its few heroes still alive.

Then suddenly he saw General Northrup as an old man, perhaps in years not more than fifty, but worn out in heart and mind, trying to keep up a belief in his son that he knew was false. He might deceive others, or they might concede to his view out of fear or respect—or more than that, pity—but in the end he would be left alone with the truth. He faced forward and he spoke of duty because it was the only road he had left in a world that was slipping away from him and taking with it all that he had believed in.

"Yes, sir," Joseph said gently. "I think all the men are trying to do what they think is right. When you are facing death it becomes terribly important. There isn't going to be time to try again."

Northrup stared at him, blinking rapidly several times. "What are you saying, Captain Reavley? That there is some kind of justice other than a court-martial?"

"I am saying that the men are afraid that finding Captain Cavan and the other men guilty of murder, and having them shot, will damage morale more seriously than we can survive, sir, and may even give the Germans the chance to break through and run for Paris. We have fought too long and too hard, and lost too many of our friends, for that."

"Take an easy way," Northrup retorted, his eyes never leaving Joseph's. "A wrong way, because we cannot face the enemy and stand for what we believe, for justice, and the rule of law, and each man to account for his own sins? Is that what you are saying?"

"No way is easy, sir," Joseph answered him. "And who judges what is a sin, and who is responsible for it? It is seldom only one of us at fault over anything."

Northrup shifted his weight slightly, his eyes hard and troubled. He seemed about to challenge what Joseph had said as soon as he found the words for it.

"War strips a man naked of all the ideas his brain was taught, but didn't really believe," Joseph went on. He was compelled to argue, just in case there was still a chance Northrup could plead for Cavan, and the other men if they were caught. It might be hopeless, but he could not stop trying. "These men, ultimately, were loyal to each other, and to the will to win rather than to blind obedience."

Northrup's lips were pressed tight. His eyes reflected his racing mind, and emotion filled his face, the confusion and pressure of anger and doubt inside him. Still he could not find the words.

"Legally, Major Northrup was in the right," Joseph began again. "He was the senior officer, and that gave him the power to command, whether his orders were brilliant or suicidal. But it did not make him militarily right. The men who obeyed were legally correct, and then obedience caused some of them to be killed or mutilated. Those who disobeyed are alive, but it looks as if we ourselves will kill them. And in doing so we will destroy the trust and the morale of those who look to us to lead, because they have no other choice."

Northrup was shivering very slightly; it was just a tic in his right temple, a tremor in his hands.

"With being an officer comes the duty to be right," Joseph added, knowing what he was doing to the man in front of him. "To put your men's lives before your own vanity. In peacetime you can order obedience, regardless of your own qualities, but in war you have to earn respect. Moral courage is required as well as physical—the more so of officers."

Northrup lowered his eyes. "You have no need to labor the point, Captain. I have been obliged to accept that my son's qualities fell short of the command he held, and that the army offered his men no recourse but to obey or rebel." He stood almost motionless. "And I am accountable to God for whatever part of his character made him refuse to be guided by junior men who knew better from experience. If he was weak, that was my failure—perhaps more than it was his. Perhaps I allowed him to believe that being in command is a matter of rank, not of knowing your job, or that honor is what other men say of you, not what is true even when you stand alone. If that is so, then I will answer to God, and to my son, but I will not answer to you, sir." He blinked rapidly, his face flushed and his eyes bright with tears.

Joseph ached, almost physically, to find anything to say that could comfort him. The only way to ease the pain would be to deny the truth of his part in the private tragedy of a son who had proved unequal to the final test.

"In the end it is only God's judgment that matters for any of us," Joseph said. "And it looks as if the end could be rather soon."

Northrup drew in his breath sharply as if to deny it, then let it out in a sigh and said nothing. He seemed drained of everything inside himself, as if only a shell were left which kept up the façade as an act of will. If he had been wrong and, without realizing it at the time, destroyed the son he had loved, in his own way, then at least he would not now lose the only virtue of which he was certain: courage.

"I am sure you have duties, Captain. Thank you for your time."
Joseph accepted the dismissal, saluted, and turned to leave.

Lieutenant Colonel Faulkner arrived before sunset, as he had said he
would. Joseph did not see him, but he heard the comments of the men.

"Looks loike one o' them guard dogs who can't find his dinner," Alf
Culshaw said sourly. "Reckon we're it!"

Barshey Gee shook his head and winced. He had a heavy bandage on
his right arm, but the wound was not serious enough to send him off the
front line. "Why is it they send the decent blokes up here with the guns to
shoot at Jerry, poor sod, and keep the real bastards back o' the lines to
shoot at us? Who thought that up, d'you suppose?"

"Some bloke as thought up hard rations an' Sunday drills and . . ."
Snowy offered.

"An' his Ma must've knitted moi socks!" George Atherton added with
his characteristic jerky laugh. "Got more lumps in 'em than Lofty's porridge."

"That's what Oi'd loike," Barshey said longingly, his eyes dreamy. "A
noice hot bowl o' porridge, with sugar an' the top o' the milk on it."

George threw a dollop of mud at him.

Bert Collins arrived to tell Joseph that Colonel Hook wanted to see
him. He pulled his face into an expression of disgust. "An' the new man,
sir, Lieutenant Colonel Faulkner. You'll know which one he is, sir, 'cos he
looked like he just ate a wasp, 'cept it's too wet for wasps. If it don't stop
soddin' rainin' soon we'll all drown. What I want to know, Chaplain, is why
aren't you buildin' an ark, eh?"

"No wood," Joseph said with a tight smile. "And no animals to put
in it."

"An' no women," Barshey added. "Koind of more loike no point!"
Several of them laughed.

Joseph followed Bert Collins back to the command post, and went
into the small room with its bare floor and sparse furniture. It smelled of
damp, like everything else. He stood to attention and waited.

Hook was freshly shaved, a nick on his cheek still oozing a little blood.
His uniform was comparatively clean, no more than a couple of bloodstains on the arms and mud splattered up to the thigh. He had probably
worn it no more than a day.

Beside him was Faulkner. He had very short, fair hair and a thin, powerful face that seemed all brow and bone. And yet it was not a face without imagination or a degree of emotion. His uniform was immaculate, tai-
lored to fit his square shoulders and lean body.

"Captain Reavley," Hook began, his voice formal, a warning in his eyes. "This is Lieutenant Colonel Faulkner, who is going to be prosecuting the case against the men accused of shooting Major Northrup."

"Yes, sir," Joseph acknowledged.

"As you are aware, we presently have in custody only one of those men."

Faulkner made a noise in the back of his throat. It was wordless, but his disgust was as plain as if he had spoken.

"Unless we can find those who have escaped within the next two days, we are going to have to delay the court-martial—" Hook began.

"We can try Captain Cavan," Faulkner interrupted. "And we can try the others in absentia for desertion. There can be no question as to their guilt of that."

"No, we will not try Captain Cavan separately," Hook said curtly. "And we will not try the other men for anything in their absence. Every man has the right to face his accusers and defend himself. . . ."

"They chose not to do that," Faulkner pointed out. "They gave it up; it was not denied them."

"Nevertheless, we will not try them in their absence," Hook repeated. "You are appointed prosecutor, not judge. Captain Reavley will do all that he can to trace the men's whereabouts, and—"

"For God's sake, man!" Faulkner snapped. "They've deserted! They are probably halfway to Switzerland by now."

"They may be," Hook agreed. "Or not. All we know is that they are not here, except Cavan." He looked at Joseph.

"Yes, sir," Joseph said quickly. "I will do all I can to determine exactly what happened, and if possible find the men and return them. Apart from anything else"—he studiously avoided Faulkner's eye—"it will be extremely difficult to try Captain Cavan if none of the other men are here who could testify in the matter. There will be no one to give evidence or be questioned. I believe he has not confessed to anything . . . has he?"

"No," Hook said instantly. "Quite right, Captain Reavley. Begin immediately. If there is any help you require, I'll see that you are given it."

"Report back in twenty-four hours, Captain," Faulkner said stiffly. "Although I can't imagine what you think you will find. They have deserted, apart from Cavan. And he may well also be guilty of conniving at and concealing the escape of the others. Certainly he has refused to tell us anything."

"Or he may be innocent," Joseph said sharply, a raw edge of anger to his voice. "And feel that he will get a fair hearing, and be able to prove it."

"You are excused, Captain," Faulkner told him. "The sooner you begin your inquiries, the sooner we may proceed."

Joseph saluted, then turned on his heel and left. He had no intention whatever of finding out where the men had gone, even if there had been the remotest chance of succeeding. Privately he thought Faulkner was right and they would almost certainly have made for the Swiss border. However, he was afraid that the regiment in general might suffer, especially anyone who had either positively assisted them, or negatively turned a blind eye. And profoundly he did not wish Cavan to be tried at all, but if it was inevitable, then it should be on a lesser charge, simply of having been aware that some of the men were unhappy with Major Northrup and not reporting it. The general might still succeed in getting the charge reduced.

He was also sure that Hook felt as he did, and had asked him to make the inquiries precisely because he knew he would appear to be busy, but actually do nothing at all.

Some of the men were suspicious at first, resentful that he should appear to be cooperating with Faulkner, but a couple of sharp words from people like Barshey Gee and Bill Harrison and goodwill was restored. Some even joined in a little play-acting, as if determined to help.

But of course it deceived no one. Joseph reported to Faulkner twenty-four hours later.

"I'm sorry, sir," he said, investing his voice with as much apology as he could. "None of the men appear to know anything useful. I daresay those accused were very careful to keep it all secret."

Faulkner listened to him with open disbelief, but he could prove nothing.

At noon the day after that, on Faulkner's orders, Joseph was arrested for failure to obey a direct order of a superior, and locked up in the same farmhouse from which the eleven men had escaped.

This time there were regular military police on guard, not wounded men, and in order to preserve their own liberty, they were determined that there should be no further breakouts.

They were embarrassed to lock up a chaplain and apologized awkwardly. They treated him with the greatest respect. He did not want to assault their consciences by obliging them to be other than courteous.

By two o'clock he was sitting on the floor in what had once been one of the smaller bedrooms of a farmhouse. The only window gave onto the roof, but from there it was a sheer drop to the ground, where a soldier stood on duty, his rifle at the ready. Not that Joseph had considered escaping. It would only make a desperate situation even worse.

There was nothing to do. Time crept by. Joseph stood up and paced back and forward again. Where were the men? Had they gone east, making for Switzerland? Perhaps they believed the Germans would break the line and the war was lost anyway. It was painful to accept that Morel would desert now. Joseph would have imagined him doing something more dramatic, more imaginative, truer to his roots and his nature than flight. Possibly he would have gone over the top in a grand gesture, giving his life in a way none of his fellows would ever forget.

This escape was tragic, tired and grubby, and the pain of it cut deep.

Food was brought to him at about six o'clock. It was hard rations, much the same as if he were still free. The young soldier looked embarrassed as he put it on the floor just inside, then backed away.

"I'm not going to hurt you," Joseph said wearily. "You don't need to look like that."

"No, sir, but I got to be careful. Can't afford to have anyone else go, or I'll be the one shot."

"Why? Was it your fault?"

"No!" He looked indignant.

"How did they get out?"

The soldier shook his head. "You won't be able to copy 'em, sir. Please don't try. I really don't want to shoot you. We're on the same side, sir. We all are."

Joseph looked up quickly.

"Who else is in here?"

"Just you an' Treffy Johnson, an' the doc, of course."

"Treffy? What is he here for?" Joseph was startled.

"Insubordination. Nothing much. Probably let him out tomorrow."

"And send him back up to the line?"

"Yes, of course. Poor little sod."

Joseph waited.

The soldier pulled his mouth down in a grimace. "He's only fifteen. Scared stiff, and can't hardly bring himself to shoot another man, Jerry or not."

A dozen ideas flashed through Joseph's mind: to keep Treffy Johnson in here on some other charge, to find a medical reason why he should be invalided out, even as a last resort to put him beside someone who would care for and protect him. They were all pointless. He was one of thousands. He might survive. Even if he did, he would never be the boy he was before. No one would.

"Eat it." The soldier indicated the tray of food on the floor. "It's rotten, but it's probably better than you'd get up the line. And at least it isn't raining in here." He went out and closed the door. The moment after, the lock turned and the tumblers fell home.

Joseph walked back to the window out of curiosity. How had the eleven men gotten out, then tied up the guards, and left? The more he thought of it the more obstacles there seemed to be.

He stared over the roof. A man with a good head for heights could probably manage it quite easily and reach a place where there was a down pipe. Except that the whole place was in such disrepair after three years of neglect, and the occasional bombardment extremely close by, that he could not see any down pipes left fully attached. The weight of a man, let alone eleven one after the other, would rip them off altogether. The yard below was paved. Anyone landing on it would be likely to break an ankle at the very least.

He tried to remember the other walls as he had seen them when he came in. There had been nothing to give a firm enough hold to climb down: no outhouses attached, no woodshed or apple house or milking shed. Nothing of half the height to form a safer landing. Certainly there were no trees left within half a mile. And that meant there was also no cover to hide anyone fleeing. But then they had gone at night. Still, the distant artillery lit the sky and would have made any figure on the barren landscape as obvious as a fly on a whitewashed wall.

There had been twelve men imprisoned here, and Treffy Johnson. How had they been separated? There were not thirteen rooms in the house, so at least some had been together. There were no blankets in his room, only a straw palliasse. But then one had no blankets in trenches. And it was August. Could they have used their own clothes to make a rope to descend from the window? All of them? At the same time? Were they even in communication with one another?

The light faded outside and it began to rain again. He could hear it on the window.

He sat on the palliasse in the dark. The more he considered and weighed what he knew, the more it seemed impossible that the men had all gotten out at the same time and tied up the guards. Without help, how had they escaped over the barren land and gone sufficient distance that, by the time their absence was known, they were untraceable? The escape must have been carefully planned—and it must have been effected with a vehicle large enough to take all eleven men.

Such as an ambulance! That was the thought Joseph wanted to push out of his mind altogether, but the harder he tried the more firmly it became fixed.

He lay down at last. He was cold in spite of the warmth of the air. It was probably because he was tired and miserable, and—no matter how hard he tried to quell the thought—afraid for Judith.

If the court-martial of Cavan went ahead, and they found him guilty, there would be only one sentence: the firing squad. It would be referred right up to Field Marshal Haig.

Joseph realized that in the morning he must find a way of persuading the guard to let him see Cavan. Cavan was a doctor and Joseph was a priest! There must be some argument for one of them needing the other!

When his breakfast came, the tea was at least hot. He was grateful for that.

He disliked lying to the guard, but he could think of no better alternative. He sat hunched forward, looking wretched, trying to make one shoulder lower than the other.

"Something wrong, Chaplain?" the soldier asked.

"Think I've pulled a muscle," he replied. "Thought it would be all right yesterday, but it kept me awake all night." He gave a bleak smile. "First time I've had the chance to lie down for more than a couple of hours. Could you let me see Cavan? Lock us in. Room with no window. I don't care. He might be able to put it right for me."

The guard hesitated.

"I'm not dangerous," Joseph went on. "For heaven's sake, he and I aren't going to attack anyone. And the fact that Cavan's still here should prove he's not trying to escape. I'm not charged with anything except not looking hard enough for the men who did escape."

"Yeah, all right. The doc in't no harm." The guard shrugged. "I reckon as the whole damn thing's a farce anyway! Lock up the doc an' the priest, and let the lunatics run the army! Come on. Can you stand up? I'll take you to him. Want to finish your tea first?"

"Please." Joseph remembered to drink using his left hand, and put the mug down so he could still use his left hand to eat the bread. "Thank you," he said when he was finished. He stood up awkwardly, careful again not to use his right arm at all.

Cavan was sitting on the floor when the soldier opened his door and pushed Joseph in ahead of him.

Cavan looked up in surprise, and—when he recognized Joseph—rose to his feet. He noticed Joseph holding his right arm awkwardly.

"Hurt your shoulder, Chaplain?" he said curiously, his eyes flicking to the guard and then back to Joseph.

"Yes. I was wondering if you could ease it back or something?" Joseph replied.

"No doctors on the outside?" Cavan said with a wry smile that barely reached his eyes. He looked tired and strained, deep lines scored into his face and a hollowness around his eyes. He must know that death was no longer a probability for him, but a certainty.

Joseph felt a sudden, blinding rage at the injustice of it. "I expect they're good enough," he replied, his voice trembling and sounding more strained than he had intended. "But since I'm in here and can't get out, I hoped you would help."

Cavan was nonplussed. "In here? You? For God's sake, what for?"

"I was ordered to look for the escaped men," Joseph replied. "Lieutenant Colonel Faulkner believed I was being dilatory in my duty, or even possibly intentionally obstructive."

"That's absurd!" Cavan said, shaking his head.

"Actually it's perfectly fair," Joseph told him. "If I'd fallen over them I wouldn't have told him. Not that I did! I imagine they are miles away from here. I hope so."

The guard cleared his throat. "I'll leave the chaplain 'ere with you, Captain Cavan, if I may, sir? See if you can fix 'is shoulder for 'im." He went out and closed the door. Again the heavy sound of the lock reminded them he had no intention of being held to blame for their escape.

Joseph straightened his shoulder. It was becoming painful holding it at a unnatural angle.

Cavan noticed.

"Thank you for healing it so quickly," Joseph said with a tight smile. He walked over and sat down on the floor a few feet away from where Cavan had been sitting. "He may be back soon," he went on. "I hope not, but you can't rely on him. At least, I assume you can't?"

Cavan looked confused. He sat down also, but said nothing.

"I've been thinking about how to escape," Joseph went on conversationally. "The more I consider it, the less I can see any way at all, without pretty brave and well-thought-out help from at least one person outside. More likely two."

Cavan's face was expressionless, carefully so. "Your escaping seems pretty pointless. They haven't got a charge against you that will stick. Faulkner's done this in a fit of temper, that's all."

"Yes, I know that," Joseph agreed. "I'm hoping they might even release me later today. That's why I need to speak to you now."

Cavan's face darkened.

"If you think I'm going to try and buy some kind of leniency by telling you how the others escaped, or who helped them, then you're a far bigger fool than I thought you. And a bigger knave as well. What kind of a traitor to my friends do you think I am?"

"I think you are a man too exhausted to think clearly," Joseph answered. "And actually I didn't ask you who helped them. I would very much prefer not to know. Although I have an idea, and, if I am right, then it is the last person on earth I would betray."

Cavan blinked quickly, aware that he had given himself away. He tried to hide it by lowering his eyes. "If you don't want to know that, what do you want?" he asked softly. "I wouldn't tell you where the men were if I knew! And I don't."

"I want to know what happened at Northrup's mock trial," Joseph answered. "I was told that you didn't mean to kill him. General Northrup is reasonably inclined toward having the charge reduced to insubordination and accidental death."

"Rubbish!" Cavan lifted his head, his eyes wide. "His son is dead. Apart from wanting revenge, he's a military martinet. Discipline is his catechism."

"He's a proud man," Joseph said thoughtfully. "And limited. He has little imagination, but he is not essentially dishonest. And certainly he does not lack courage. He knows his only son was incompetent and a danger to his men, which is a very hard fact for a military father to face."

"Why would he face it?" Cavan asked.

"He has no choice," Joseph explained. "If this charge goes ahead as it is, then the prosecutor will need to prove a very powerful motive for twelve men to conspire to murder an officer."

"We had one," Cavan argued, a little impatiently. "He was getting men killed and maimed unnecessarily. He was grossly incompetent, and too proud or too stupid to be guided by the men who'd been out here for months, or even years, and knew how to avoid most of the losses."

"Exactly." Joseph nodded, watching Cavan to see if he understood. "Do you imagine that is something his father wishes proved beyond reasonable doubt in a court-martial?"

A flash of comprehension lit in Cavan's eyes. "Someone has pointed that out to him? Are you sure?"

"Absolutely positive."

Cavan bit his lip.

"I see. Why do you want to know? Do you really believe it will make any difference? I like optimism, but not unreality. Shouldn't you be helping me to face the truth, perhaps make my peace with God? Isn't that what you call it?"

"It's a little early for that," Joseph said drily. "Unless that's an oblique way of telling me that you personally shot Northrup, intentionally and avoidably?"

"I've no idea who shot Northrup!" Cavan said tartly. "Except that it had to be one of the twelve of us, and it wasn't me."

Joseph asked the question to which he dreaded the answer.

"Were you loaded with blanks, or did you deliberately shoot wide?"

Cavan stared at him. "I suppose you want the truth?"

"Yes."

"Where would we get blanks?" There was the faintest smile in Cavan's eyes. "The army supplies only live ammunition."

"You wouldn't get it from supplies," Joseph pointed out. "You'd use a pair of pliers to take the heads off live bullets, then crimp the casing closed again."

"Make our own blanks. Yes, I suppose we would."

"It would be a bit rash to leave anyone to simply shoot wide," Joseph said, not taking his eyes from Cavan's. "It would be so easy for someone to make a mistake and shoot the man accidentally. You'd be lucky if you ever found out who it was—or unlucky."

"Yes, it would be rash," Cavan agreed. "Neither I nor Morel are rash. The two of us blanked the bullets ourselves."

"So someone changed theirs for a live one." It was the unavoidable answer: deliberate murder.

"Must have."

"But you have no idea who?"

"No. Honestly, I haven't. I don't believe it was Morel, but I don't know. I'm sure I didn't, and ten of the others didn't."

Joseph believed him. He had never thought him guilty of anything but wanting to frighten Northrup into taking advice in order to cut down on the useless deaths. And now, of course, of refusing to betray whoever had rescued the others.

"Why didn't you escape, when you could?" he asked curiously, shifting position a little on the hard floor.

"I couldn't," Cavan said with the very slightest shrug. "I'd given my word."

Joseph understood. An officer's word was binding. "And the others?"

"I didn't give my word not to help anyone else escape." Cavan smiled.

Joseph had to ask. "Morel?" He was an officer, too.

"Refused," Cavan answered. "They put him in with the men. Six in one room, five in the other. That left me alone in here."

"So you helped them, and stayed behind?"

"Yes." Cavan's face was suddenly filled with emotion, as if a crippling restraint on him had momentarily broken. "Speak for them, Captain Reavley. Northrup was a dangerous man, weak and arrogant. Even when he knew he was wrong, he wouldn't listen. The men were at the end of their endurance. Someone had to act." His voice was urgent, pleading. "It was only meant to frighten him into listening. They weren't bad men, just desperate to save their friends."

"I know," Joseph said softly. "I come from the same village. I've known a lot of those men all their lives. Morel was one of my students in Cambridge." He took a deep breath. "Judith is my sister."

Cavan closed his eyes for a moment. When he opened them, they were bright and sad, but he said nothing.

A moment later the guard opened the door again. When he saw that Joseph's shoulder was apparently mended, he took him back to his own room.

In the middle of the afternoon Joseph was released and escorted to Colonel Hook in his dugout.

"Sit down!" Hook said impatiently. He looked as if he had slept little since the last time they had been here. "Don't stand at attention like a fool! Faulkner's gone, at least for the moment."

Joseph obeyed, sitting on an old ammunition box. "Is he still insisting on court-martialing Captain Cavan alone?"

"I've managed to prevent that, at least for a week or two," Hook replied. "He thinks we can find out how they escaped."

Joseph's stomach clenched. Did he already suspect someone? "Really?" he said huskily. "How?"

Hook gave a little jerk upward with his hands. It was angry, a denial. "He doesn't know the men. No one is going to tell him anything. Did you see Cavan in the farmhouse?"

"Yes. I don't know whether he knows or not, but if he does, he certainly isn't going to say."

"I don't imagine you asked him, did you?"

"No, of course not."

"Could you have escaped?" Hook regarded him curiously.

"No . . . but I didn't try."

"I'm asking you, officially, to try now."

"Officially?" Joseph wanted to be quite clear.

"Yes." Hook gave a very slight smile, so small it could even have been an illusion of the light.

"Yes, sir. Of course." Joseph stood up from the ammunition box. "I'll let you know as soon as I hear anything."

"Oh, don't wait that long, Reavley. Tell me in a couple of days. I'll tell Faulkner."

"Yes, sir." Joseph went to the step, then with one hand on the sacking he turned back. "Only one of them is guilty, you know. There were eleven blanks and one live round."

"We don't have blanks," Hook pointed out.

"They made their own. It's simple enough. The others are innocent."

"Not innocent," Hook said with a grimace. "Guilty of insubordination, not murder. But I'm glad to hear that."

"It makes a difference, sir. If they were tried and found guilty of insubordination, it might be a matter you could deal with. No need to take it higher. All inside the regiment?"

"That isn't going to help whoever sprang them out of custody, Reavley. Faulkner will still want them court-martialed. And probably shot."

Joseph felt the cold hurt tighten in his stomach again. "I realize that, sir. I imagine it will be very difficult indeed to find out who they are. Practically impossible."

"Still, we must oblige Lieutenant Colonel Faulkner. Attend to it, Reavley. Good luck."

"Thank you, sir." Joseph went out, praying that the good luck he would have would be a complete and total failure to find any proof whatsoever.

It was difficult even to find a man he could decently ask about the escape. It was not merely that no one wished to help find the men themselves; they were even less eager to add to the general misery by exposing whoever had been clever enough, and above all brave enough, to free them. Everyone was overwhelmed by the continuing battle for Passchendaele. The losses mounted, not in twos or threes but in dozens, too often scores. Sometimes the rain eased, but it always came back again until the trenches were like canals; shell craters were deep enough to drown a man and often did; and running water gouged out channels down every incline so savage they would sweep a man off his feet.

Joseph carried stretchers, when there were any, men on his back when that was all there was. As always, he did what he could for the dying and the dead. There was little enough time to think of anything else.

Still, as discreetly as he could, he began to find out where different people had been on the night of the escape. He did not begin with Judith, aware that Faulkner might follow his steps. What he could learn, so could others.

He hoped he could find that she had been miles away, with a dozen witnesses—perhaps other officers new to the area and who had no personal stake in the escape. He sensed the anger as he asked, the suspicious looks, the reluctance to answer. Men stopped talking when he approached; shaggy-dog jokes died halfway through. They did not offer him the usual tea—or Woodbines, even though they knew he did not smoke.

Most men simply said they had no idea of Judith's whereabouts. Others had observed her in at least half a dozen different places at the time of the escape, all miles from the farmhouse. She and Wil Sloan were the only ones about whom such a variety of lies were sworn to. All other V.A.D. staff were in one place only.

These men were not very sophisticated liars. If Joseph could follow that trail so easily, so could Faulkner, once he thought where to look. Then there was only one possible end: Wil and Judith would be arrested and charged. All the lies in the world would not help, because the truth was obvious. He had thought only a little while ago that it was someone extremely clever; now he thought perhaps only supremely brave, and trusting in the loyalty of the men. The guards might even have been party to it.

He walked in the late afternoon mist, his boots sodden and sloshing in the mud. He moved slowly because he had no wish to arrive. The gunfire sounded far away, over the rise and beyond the woods toward Passchendaele itself—or what was left of it. All along the Ypres Salient there were miles of mud and blasted tree stumps, craters with corpses floating in the stagnant water, some still wreathed in the heavy poison gas.

He could imagine the scene at night: Judith and Wil Sloan arriving in the ambulance, possibly even two ambulances. They would stop. One would get out, probably Judith, tired, tense, her face pale in the headlights, skirts heavy and dark with mud. She would have gone up to the guard and asked for something—perhaps fresh water or another blanket.

Wil might have waited until they were occupied helping her, and crept up. Or had they simply been honest and said what they wanted, and asked for help? Joseph might never know, and it did not matter. Without thinking about it at all, he knew if they were ever facing trial, they would say they had done it by violence and deceit. They would see that no one else was blamed.

Joseph reached Colonel Hook's dugout. He pulled back the sacking and saw the light burning inside. He knocked on the lintel.

Hook looked up and waved Joseph in. Fear was in his eyes for an instant, then he mastered it. "Yes, Captain Reavley? Have you found out anything about the escape?"

"Nothing at all, sir," Joseph said instantly. "It could have been anyone at all. The only answer is to see if we can find the escaped men. I am quite certain that only one of them is guilty of murder. The others did no more than . . . than behave insubordinately, provoked by extraordinary circumstances. Then we could have a court-martial that would be fair and reasonable . . . sir."

"We have no chance of finding the men, Reavley. They could be anywhere. Unless—" Hook stopped. "Do you believe you can?" His face puckered, gaunt with weariness. He did not daresay it, but he was begging Joseph not to tell him what he did not want and could not afford to know.

"I believe so, sir." Joseph stayed standing to attention. "If I have your permission, I would like to try. Immediately."

"They have several days' start on you," Hook pointed out.

"I know. But I think the Royal Flying Corps might give me a little help if I explain. And if you give me orders . . . sir?"

"Try," Hook said quietly. "And God help you!"

NINE

*T*he day after Wheatcroft's death, Matthew received an urgent summons from Dermot Sandwell. He had asked for Sandwell's help, but he had not expected to hear from him so soon. He went eagerly, even with a sharp flutter of excitement. He found his heart beating hard as he strode along the pavement, bumping into people unintentionally, having to apologize. He had spent three years seeking the identity of the Peacemaker, moving from one fear to another, hoping and yet also dreading the moment when he could no longer deny that it was someone he knew and liked. It had to be someone his father had once trusted, and that trust had cost his father his life.

It was a close, heavy day in late August. The air seemed to clog his throat. The sky was hazy and there were heavy clouds gathering to the west. There would be a thunderstorm by midafternoon. The armies along the Western Front would be drenched once again.

Matthew walked because it was ridiculous to try to find a taxi for the mile or so to Sandwell's office. He kept to the main thoroughfares and moved briskly.

Everything was scarce at the moment: petrol as much as food and clothes. Naval losses had severely limited all imports; nevertheless in London, if you had money, you could get almost anything, while in some areas in the country there was actual starvation.

He reached Whitehall and went in, giving his name and telling the official on duty that Mr. Sandwell was expecting him.

He was received immediately. Sandwell stood up from behind his desk and came forward, extending his hand. He looked tired. The lines were etched more deeply in his face, both across his brow and around his mouth. His fair hair had paled to silver at the temples, but his eyes were as deeply blue as ever and the grip of his long, thin hand was firm.

"Thank you for coming so promptly, Reavley." He waved to a chair and peered at Matthew intently as they both sat down. "Miserable business about Wheatcroft's suicide. Did you learn anything of value from him?"

"No, sir." Instinctively Matthew guarded the threads of impression he had of someone else behind Wheatcroft's accusation of Corracher. "I'm afraid not." It sounded too bare. "He still protested his innocence, but felt no one would believe him."

"The reason for his suicide, do you think?" Sandwell asked.

In that instant, Matthew knew what he *did* think. "Possibly. That's certainly what his note implied."

"Implied?" Sandwell picked up the word.

"Said," Matthew corrected.

"And Corracher's betrayal of him," Sandwell added quietly. "Poor man."

Matthew said nothing. It was Wheatcroft's betrayal of Corracher that lodged in his mind, and something else that eluded him, a memory of something that did not fit where it should.

Sandwell leaned forward, his blue eyes studying Matthew's face. "I'm afraid I have come to some deeply disturbing conclusions. I must swear you to secrecy before I share them with you. You will understand why as soon as I do."

"Secret from whom, sir?" Matthew asked, puzzled by such a request—in fact it seemed to be a condition. He had imagined he was being told in order to refer them to Shearing.

"From everyone, at least for the time being," Sandwell answered. "What I have discovered is more dangerous than I can begin to tell you, and I have no idea yet how far it extends. A word or a whisper in the wrong ear, and we could both be killed for it, if I am correct." He leaned forward. "Do I have your attention now?"

Matthew stiffened. "Yes, sir."

"I imagined I would." Sandwell smiled openly. "Apart from your loyalty to your country, a man such as you could never resist the sheer curiosity of it. If you could have stood up and walked away from here without knowing, I should have recommended your removal from the Intelligence Service."

"Why me?" Matthew asked. It was a bold question and to one of Sandwell's seniority perhaps impertinent, but it was not irrelevant.

Sandwell's eyes widened slightly, appreciating the perception. "You are ideally placed" was all he said. "I think you will understand when I have told you what I know and what I fear."

"Yes, sir."

Sandwell touched his fingertips lightly together in a steeple and looked at Matthew.

"You said that in the beginning you believed Corracher was not guilty of attempting to blackmail Wheatcroft, although Wheatcroft might indeed have behaved indiscreetly. I considered the possibility that you were right. If that were so, then there is only one conclusion that makes sense, and that is that there is a conspiracy behind it, formed and carried out by someone else."

He continued to regard Matthew steadily. "I weighed the likelihood of it being purely personal, driven either by ambition or revenge. I could find nothing to suggest it, and it seemed less likely than the desire to get rid of them both from their positions of political power. They are of similar beliefs in many issues, especially regarding the kind of peace we may make with Germany."

The muscles of his face tightened as if for an instant the reality of the deaths and the rage of destruction overwhelmed his mind, and the quiet room overlooking Horse Guards Parade on a great August morning was only an island, a temporary haven in the midst of ruin.

Matthew waited.

Sandwell composed himself again, but he did not apologize for his emotion. "I have noticed that two other rising politicians of similar mind have also been lost to us recently. Do you begin to understand me, Reavley?"

Matthew drew a deep breath, as if standing on the edge of an abyss and having looked down.

"Yes, sir. Someone is . . . planning ahead, maneuvering so that when the time comes they will have control over whoever is in power to agree to the terms of peace." At last he was not alone in his knowledge, but Sandwell had glimpsed only a fraction of the Peacemaker's design, just this last few months' work. Should Matthew say any more? Not yet. Be careful. Listen, only listen. And there was still the frayed end he could not place that lingered at the edge of his mind.

"Precisely," Sandwell agreed. "And doing it with very great skill. Which leads me to wonder why he is doing this *now*."

Matthew was about to point out the obvious, that now there was the greatest hope of the end to the war. But that was not true. They had hoped for it as early as the autumn of 1914. He bit back the words. Then with a catch of his breath, he realized what Sandwell really meant! If someone had these hopes and designs now, where had he been during the last three years?

Sandwell read him perfectly. "Exactly," he said in little more than a whisper. "What else? What has there been all through the years since the beginning that we have not seen?"

Matthew's mind raced. Had he found an ally at last? Then suddenly he heard his father's voice in his mind again, that last day on the telephone, warning him that the conspiracy went as high as the Royal Family. He knew now that that had been a reference to the treaty that the Peacemaker had wanted the king to sign.

"Reavley?" Sandwell's voice interrupted the sense of loss as sharp as the day of John Reavley's death. It jerked Matthew back to the present. "Yes, sir. The thought is . . . overwhelming. It is possible this is his first act . . . but . . ."

"His?" Sandwell questioned him. "Whose? Do you think it is one man?"

Matthew spoke slowly. Without having reached a decision consciously, he could not bring himself to trust Sandwell. He must weigh every word. He was acutely aware of Sandwell's extraordinary intelligence. "No, certainly not acting alone," he answered. "But it might be one man leading and others following. It seems to have a coherence about it. Forgive me, sir, if I am a little slow. The thought is enormous, and incredibly ugly."

"But not new to you," Sandwell pointed out.

Should he admit it? He saw the knowledge reflected in Sandwell's eyes. He knew at least something of Matthew's earlier convictions of conspiracy, but how much and from whom? Shearing? Someone else in the Intelligence Service?

"We're always looking for conspiracies," he said aloud, trying to make his voice sound rueful. "It's still a surprise when you find them. I did suspect that Corracher might be innocent, and if he was, then Wheatcroft is implicated, even if just another victim with less honor than Corracher, willing to ruin another man in order to escape himself. It is the other thought, of what else might have been done, or yet planned by the man behind this, that stuns me."

"As well it might." Sandwell leaned back in his chair, his eyes still on Matthew's face. "And it is that which we must address, Reavley. Saving Tom Corracher is a relatively small matter. Finding this . . . this archtraitor is the main thing. As long as he remains hidden, with the power he has—and we have no idea how much it is—then we are desperately, perhaps even fatally vulnerable."

"And have always been," Matthew added.

Sandwell let out his breath in a slow sigh. "Tell me, Reavley, you have been in intelligence since the beginning of the war. You must have as good an idea as anyone how our enemies work. Where are we most vulnerable? If you were this . . . this man, where would you have struck already? And where would you strike next?"

Matthew saw the depth of the question and the power. If he did not answer, he would betray the fact that he did not trust Sandwell. And if he did answer, he would show that he did trust him, completely, perhaps more than an intelligence officer should trust anyone at all, especially anyone outside the service, even if he were of cabinet rank in the government. It was a position of ironic delicacy. Did Sandwell know that? He dared not assume that he didn't. He was forced to tell the truth, or something extremely close to it.

"In the past," he began carefully, "I would have struck with propaganda aimed at morale, especially within the forces. I would have aimed it particularly at recruitment points. Next I would have struck against the navy. Without sea power we'll lose in weeks. Being an island is both our strength and our weakness."

Sandwell nodded.

"And now?" he said very softly, almost as if he feared being overheard, even though there was no one else in the room.

"I would try to neutralize the effectiveness of some of our ministers who have strong diplomatic contacts abroad, particularly in countries that might be persuaded to turn against Germany and its allies, such as Hungary. Or to hasten the withdrawal of Russia."

"Yes." Sandwell's eyes were the clearest, most brilliant blue. "That would be the natural thing."

"And of course if possible weaken the Western Front." Matthew heard his own voice loud in the utter silence. "Passchendaele is proving the most terrible battle we have ever fought. At this rate there will be a quarter of a million more dead before it's over."

Sandwell's face was white; the misery bit so deep it drove the blood from his veins. "I know . . ."

"Morale is almost at breaking point," Matthew added. "One really disastrous injustice, even a fatal mistake, and the men might even mutiny. Then the line might not hold." Instantly he wondered if he had gone too far. Sandwell looked as if he was in emotional pain so intense it had become physical. He was short of breath and his muscles were locked as if in a spasm. His face was ashen.

Matthew waited. He could hear the clock ticking on the mantel over the ornate fireplace and the first heavy spots of rain that fell against the window.

"I was right to trust you." Sandwell let out his breath in a sigh, his shoulders relaxing. "You understand perfectly. There has been an incident. An incompetent officer was shot by his own men. They know who it was, and they are up for court-martial." His voice was quite light. "Unfortunately two of these are officers; both have served the full duration of the war with distinction. In fact, one is up for the V.C. If he is found guilty and faces the firing squad for what was essentially saving his own men's lives by getting rid of a disastrous officer, then there is your incident of injustice. It could even be seen as a betrayal, if you believe sending brave men into battle led by an idiot to be a betrayal of their trust. And God knows, they deserve better than that!"

Matthew stared at him. Was it possible that at last he really did have an ally? One with power! He remembered Cullingford with a grief so sharp it brought a wave of nausea. "Be careful!" he said with sudden urgency, unable to help himself from the warning.

"Oh, I am, Reavley. Believe me, since I have become aware of this possibility, even probability, I have been extremely careful." He frowned. "But what makes you say that? Have you felt yourself in danger, personally, I mean?"

Matthew hesitated for a fraction of a moment. Again, he could not afford to be caught in a lie. But could Sandwell possibly know the truth? No, but that was not the point. Matthew had given the warning. He had to justify it.

"Yes, twice," he answered. "Once might have been an accident; the second time it was definitely an attempt to kill me."

Sandwell blinked. "You are certain? Or am I foolish to ask?"

Matthew gave a half smile. "If this man would betray his country and cause the deaths of thousands, tens of thousands, why on earth not a single one, if that one was a danger to him?"

Sandwell blinked. "Cause the deaths of . . . I was thinking rather more of someone who wants peace, even if it is the peace of defeat, rather than a continuing of this . . . slaughter. . . ." The word came out with a burst of passion which he controlled only with an intense effort of will. He bit his lip. "I'm sorry. I suppose I have no evidence for that. I just have . . ." He took a deep breath. "I have intense fear as to who this man may be, how highly placed in order to have done what he has. I had not considered his motives. I admit, Reavley, I find the whole thing shattering."

"You have some idea who it is?" Matthew asked, unable to stop his voice from trembling.

Sandwell looked away. "I would rather not say anything yet. It . . . it is so appalling. But I will give you all the information I have, as well, of course, as placing copies in my safe where they will be available to the prime minister if anything happens to me. But it is your safety I am concerned about, Reavley, because it is your skills that will unmask the man, if anyone can do it."

"But why not reveal your suspicions now?" Matthew insisted.

Sandwell met Matthew's eyes unflinchingly. "I would prefer you reach your own conclusions. You may see the same facts as I do, and place some different interpretation on them. But I am correct regarding the catastrophe about to happen on the Western Front when this court-martial takes place. Begin by looking at the record of the military prosecutor they have appointed to the case."

"Yes, sir," Matthew said very slowly, his mind grasping at sudden reality, a course to pursue. "I'll begin immediately." He rose to his feet.

"Reavley!" Sandwell stood up also. "Be careful! No one must know what you are doing, even in your own office. In fact"—he sighed—"especially in your own office."

Now there was a chill in the room, in spite of the August closeness of the air. "I understand, sir."

"Do you?" Sandwell questioned. "I hope for your sake, for your life's sake, that you do."

Matthew did precisely as Sandwell had warned him, and told no one that he was going back to see Mrs. Wheatcroft again. As before, he found himself obliged to use the weight of Sandwell's name in order to be received.

He stood uncomfortably in the withdrawing room. The bay windows overlooked the immaculately groomed late summer garden.

Mrs. Wheatcroft entered with only the briefest acknowledgment of him. She stood pale and graceful in a long muslin dress.

"I don't know how I can further assist you, Captain Reavley," she said coldly. "If it were not that apparently you have some connection with Mr. Sandwell, I should not have seen you at all."

"So much you made clear, Mrs. Wheatcroft," he replied. "However, I assume that if there is a conspiracy to ruin your husband—and Mr. Corracher—in the interests of German victory, then you will be as keen as Mr. Sandwell and I are to uncover it."

She bit her lip, momentarily confused. "Do you think it is such a thing? I had assumed it was simply Mr. Corracher's greed, both for money and personal advancement."

"Mr. Sandwell does," Matthew answered. "If you doubt that, call him and ask. I understand you are acquainted with him?"

"Socially," she said, the chill returning. "I would like to believe that I could trust an officer of our Intelligence Services, but if you wait here, I shall place a call to Mr. Sandwell. Then I shall consider what he advises."

"An excellent idea." He sat down in the armchair before she left the room. She saw his ease and her face tensed with disapproval at the liberty.

It was half an hour before she returned, looking considerably chastened. Now the hinted aggression was gone, replaced by fear, and for the first time she met his eyes candidly.

He had risen as she came in, but she waved him to sit down again, and sank into the chair opposite him, barely bothering to straighten her skirts.

"I apologize," she said briefly. "Mr. Sandwell has advised me to tell you the absolute truth, so that is what I shall do." She took a deep breath. "My husband had a weakness. I did not know it when I married him, but I learned it within the first few years. If you repeat this, I shall say you are a liar." For an instant the defiance was back in her eyes.

"It is not in my interest to repeat it, Mrs. Wheatcroft," he told her. "Nor to make judgments of him. I am happy to accept the story that he was no more than naïve and unfortunate. What I do not accept is that Tom Corracher tried to extort money from him in exchange for silence on the matter. Nor do I believe that it was his own idea to put up that defense." He was watching her closely, and saw the flicker in her eyes.

"His letter—" she began, then stopped abruptly.

Then he remembered the element that did not fit. It was a matter of timing. He was cold as the confusion fell apart, leaving the beginning of a picture even uglier.

"I read it," he agreed. "He had obviously written something—the pen and ink were there, freshly spilled and blotted. But the letter I found was written days ago, before he knew about Marlowe being transferred."

She looked confused. "Who's Marlowe? What has that to do with Alan's death?"

"Nothing. Marlowe was the man he thought would take over from him, but by the day before he died, when I saw him, he knew it was Jamieson."

She stared at him, frightened and unable to hide it now.

"You destroyed his real letter, didn't you?" he said grimly. "Because he admitted that Corracher was innocent, and he had accused him to save himself . . . and of course you. But he couldn't live with the lie, and couldn't face you if he told the truth."

She drew her breath in sharply to protest, but the guilt was hot in her face and she saw no escape. There was something else in her eyes as well, an acid, corrosive hate.

He was glad to see it. It made it easier to crush her.

Something must have relaxed in him and looked to her like retreat.

"You can't prove that," she pointed out. "I burned his second letter, and he did write the first, just not then. He wrote several. It wasn't hard to put one together. He always used the same ink and the same paper. There's nothing you can do."

"Whose idea was it, Mrs. Wheatcroft?"

"Mine!" she said quietly.

"If you had said it was his, I would not have believed you," he told her. "You had to force him into it, if not for your sake personally, then for your sons."

"If you like!" She had regained her composure. "But when Alan realized what his disgrace would do to them, he was willing."

"I doubt it," he said drily. "But it's irrelevant now. It was the guilt of lying that killed him."

"It was the guilt of being so unbelievably stupid!" she snapped.

"How did you know to blame Tom Corracher rather than anyone else?" He remembered Sandwell's words about political ideology, and the Peacemaker's plan behind the ruin of all four men.

For an instant she hesitated, then grasped after an answer. "That was Alan's idea. I just said to think of someone."

"Someone with the same political beliefs about the terms of any possible peace treaty with the Germans," he elaborated.

Again there was confusion in her eyes, then a sudden new understanding. "They worked together. It made sense."

She was guessing. Actually they had not worked together, simply held the same opinions. Someone else had suggested the idea of blaming Corracher to her. Perhaps she knew who it was and why. More probably she was simply a willing tool, caring only to save herself and her sons. Anyone would do as a sacrifice, and the larger cause was irrelevant.

"Was anyone else aware of this, Mrs. Wheatcroft?" he asked casually, as if it were no more than a passing thought.

Again the half-second's hesitation, then she denied it. "No, of course not."

He looked at her chiseled face. It was beautiful in a hard, brittle way, but without yielding, without forgiveness. Perhaps she was a knowing tool after all. In protecting her own, she was not open to the vulnerability of mercy or conscience.

"Thank you, Mrs. Wheatcroft." He rose to his feet. "You have been most civil. I shan't need to trouble you again."

A faint smile touched her lips. "It would be courteous to say I regret that, Captain Reavley, but I do not. Good day."

He also took Sandwell's other piece of advice and made inquiries about the man who had been sent to prosecute the twelve soldiers accused of murdering Major Northrup. The answer that came back was exactly what Sandwell had warned. Faulkner was known to be a stickler for the law in every detail. He believed justice, and therefore society, was best served by following procedure to the letter. The innocent were protected by the unfailing punishment of the guilty, and there was no room for personal interpretation of the law.

Matthew arranged to meet an old friend, Errol Lashwood, for luncheon at the Ivy Restaurant in Covent Garden. They received excellent food, and the atmosphere was easy and charming. The restaurant was highly popular with all manner of people, especially the theatrical community. Matthew had on occasion seen Bernard Shaw there, and Ellen Terry and Gladys Cooper last year when they had been playing in J. M. Barrie's *The Admirable Crichton* at Wyndham's Theatre.

This time Lashwood smiled and pointed out the amazing profile of Ivor Novello, who was sitting only a couple of tables away.

"Faulkner." Matthew returned him to the subject.

"Not a bad man," Lashwood said wryly. "Just highly unimaginative, and very little sense of joy in the absurd. I think, personally, that he is rather afraid of change, and therefore feels threatened by anything he does not understand." He shrugged. "Or perhaps I am thinking beyond the mark. The man infuriates me. He could be so much better than he is. I believe he once fell in love with a highly unsuitable woman, and the whole experience soured him for life. His father was the same." He smiled. "But his mother is as different as could be. Delightful woman, charming and eccentric and full of life. Still wears rather old-fashioned clothes, almost prewar, very feminine. Has a famous collection of gorgeous parasols and hats with flowers on them. Loves the horse races . . . and a good champagne."

"What on earth does she make of her son?" Matthew said in amazement. "I presume he is scandalized by her?"

"On the contrary," Lashwood assured him with a smile. "She is his only redeeming feature. He adores her."

"But she has never managed to imbue him with her own joy in life?"

"Never." He speared a succulent morsel of meat from his plate and put it into his mouth. "He considers it his duty, and his privilege, to look after her, and indulge her, which she accepts with the utmost grace."

Matthew's heart sank. It was far too little information to be of any use. "How the hell did we get lumbered with having him prosecute the men accused of killing Northrup? And how do we get him changed for someone with a little more compassion and imagination, possibly amenable to considering the larger picture?"

Lashwood pulled his mouth into a grim line. "Difficult, old fellow. He's a friend of your boss. Sorry, but for all I know, it could have been he who picked him out."

Matthew was suddenly cold. "Picked him out? You mean for this prosecution?" Was this at last what Sandwell had been wanting him to find out? It was the fear that had rested like poison at the back of his mind almost from the beginning—the Peacemaker was Shearing himself. He had hated the Peacemaker for killing John and Alys Reavley, and all those since then: good people, men who had trusted him.

But how many more had died fearful deaths on battlefields all over the world? How many were shot, frozen, gassed, drowned in mud, or carried to the bottom of the sea in the millions of tons of shipping lost? How many starved to death, even here at home? How many more were maimed in mind and body or crippled by grief? How much of the whole world was ruined in blood and fire and grief?

The Peacemaker had wanted to prevent it and, when that was too late, to stop it, at any cost! He was an idealist who had lost his balance. He had worked to save lives, but had taken to himself the power to decide what cost was to be paid.

He could hate such a man, but he could also understand him.

"Reavley!" Lashwood's voice cut across his thoughts.

Matthew jerked himself back to the present. "Yes. You are quite sure? No possibility of a mistake?"

Lashwood frowned. "I've known Faulkner for years, and his mother." He leaned forward across the table. "You look a bit green, old boy."

Matthew struggled to compose his face and respond noncommittally. "So you think there's no chance of getting him changed?"

"Not really. Bad show. Wish I could think of something helpful. But from what I hear, he actually requested the case."

"No point in going over it. Spoil what's left of a good meal," Matthew said, trying to smile. He left the thoughts raging in his mind until he could escape and find privacy to think.

That opportunity came as he walked back across the park. It took him a mile and a half longer than necessary, but he could not yet bear to face Shearing. Lashwood would not have lied, nor could he have been mistaken. Shearing knew the man, knew his rigidity, and had allowed this, possibly even contrived it. Was that something Sandwell had also known Matthew would find, and be driven to the inevitable, hideous conclusion?

He found himself taking the other path across the grass, not in the direction of his own office, but back toward Sandwell's.

He had to wait most of the afternoon to see him, but at four Sandwell returned from a Cabinet meeting in Downing Street, and admitted Matthew immediately.

"I see by your face that you have followed the trail to its bitter conclusion," he said quietly. He walked over to the table at the far side of his office and picked up the crystal decanter from the tantalus, pouring two glasses of brandy and offering one to Matthew. "I'm sorry. It's the worst of all answers."

"Why would he do such a thing?" Matthew asked, taking the brandy. "Who is he? What is he? There's nothing in his office—no pictures, no mementos, nothing from the past at all! He never mentions family, or even friends, where he went to school or university, or any other place that matters to him."

Sandwell's face was bleak. "He wouldn't," he answered, motioning Matthew to sit down and sitting opposite him. "He sounds like an Englishman because he's taught himself to, and he's nothing if not thorough. Actually he's an Austrian Jew. Settled here thirty years ago. No idea what happened to his family. None of them are here in Britain, or ever were." He sipped his brandy. "Unless they came in under forged papers, but I'm as certain as I can be that they didn't. His name was originally Caleb Schering." He spelled it out, in the German way.

Matthew drank a mouthful of his brandy. It was a waste of a fine spirit, but he needed its fire more than its savor. "How in God's name did we come to have him in the Secret Intelligence Service at all, let alone as head of it?"

"Because he started when we had no cause to fear Germany, let alone the Austro-Hungarian Empire," Sandwell said simply. "And there's no proof of a single error or slip of any kind against him. English sense of fair play, I suppose!" He shrugged slightly. "Added to which, I daresay he knows where a few bodies are buried. No one will want to be the first to suggest anything. He's an agreeable man. People like him. One doesn't want to seem paranoid, seeing ghosts where there are none."

"God Almighty!" Matthew swore. "How . . . how bloody amateur!"

Sandwell smiled, his expression suddenly warm and extraordinarily charming. "The English disease," he said ruefully. "And at times our genius."

Matthew closed his eyes. "Not this time."

"What are you going to do?" Sandwell asked after a moment or two.

"Collect evidence," Matthew replied. "There's nothing else I can do."

"Where will you take it?" Sandwell's face darkened. "Be careful, Reavley. There have been murders already. I don't know how many, but he is playing for empires, even millions of lives. Yours would be nothing to pay for victory."

Matthew grimaced. "I'll remember."

Matthew spent a wretched night. Unable to sleep, he sought every kind of escape from the only conclusion now possible.

He lay staring at the ceiling. He was safe and comfortable in his own bed. The silence surrounded him, cocooning him from the world. He began to think about his brother.

Joseph, if he was sleeping at all, would be in a hole dug in the sodden earth of Flanders. There would be no silence there. The guns never entirely stopped, least of all now with the battle for Passchendaele raging on. Now and then phosgene or mustard gas would be pervasive. Death and decay would be everywhere—the smell of it, the taste of it. Those Joseph shared tea and bad jokes with tonight might be torn apart by shrapnel tomorrow, and he would bury what was left of them.

And here was Matthew in silence and clean sheets, tossing and turning because tomorrow he would begin proving that Calder Shearing was the Peacemaker, the idealist turned betrayer who had killed John and Alys Reavley.

He finally gave up trying to sleep and made himself a cup of tea. Then he sat in his armchair noting all he knew already, and what he needed to learn from a reputable source who would not take the inquiry back to Shearing.

The second was the more difficult. He remembered Sandwell's warning that Shearing would not hesitate to kill if he was threatened. Matthew already knew that. He had never forgotten Cullingford, and his loss still hurt. Looking back now he was certain that the attack in the alley when he had so nearly been knifed himself was not an attempted robbery but a murder foiled more by luck than skill.

Why? He had not suspected Shearing then. In fact it was barely twenty-four hours since they had eaten a hasty supper together of ham sandwiches and coffee, set up over maps of safe houses and escape routes for saboteurs. He could see it exactly in his mind's eye: the lamplight on the table, Shearing's dark head bent over the diagrams, his sudden smile when he had seen the solution, and then the eagerness in his voice. It had been one of the rare betrayals of emotion in him. Matthew had felt an intense companionship at that moment. They had even joked afterward; Shearing had told some long-winded story about a dog and a newspaper. They had laughed, mostly from relief.

There was really only one person he could speak to, and that was Admiral "Blinker" Hall, the head of naval intelligence. He had gone to him before when he had had knowledge that was sensitive and painful. He was used to harboring secrets that would make or break nations, and that could never be revealed.

It was still a little after one the following afternoon when Matthew was shown into Admiral Hall's office. Hall was sitting behind the desk, papers spread in front of him. He was a stocky man with an eaglelike face and thick white hair. His narrowed blue eyes blinked rapidly every now and then, as if he could not help himself.

"Well, Reavley, no preamble. No time. What is it that you must tell me that cannot wait?"

"Not tell you, sir," Matthew corrected him. "*Ask* you."

"You had better know a good reason for this. Sit down, man. I'm not spending my time straining my neck looking up at you! Spit it out."

Matthew sat obediently.

"Information has come to me, sir, from a source high in the government that casts doubt on some of Colonel Shearing's actions and decisions." He felt like a traitor saying it aloud.

"For example?" Hall asked, blinking several times.

"His explicit approval of Lieutenant Colonel Faulkner as prosecutor in the court-martial against Captain Cavan, and the other men, if they are caught," Matthew answered. "Faulkner is an absolute hard-liner, and if Cavan is found guilty and shot, it will be a disaster to morale, possibly beyond our ability to cope with. It could even become a full-scale mutiny." He had no need to elaborate for Hall what would follow that disaster.

"Have you asked him?" Hall raised his eyebrows.

"No, sir. I realize I know nothing about Colonel Shearing except that he is an Austrian-Jewish immigrant. He arrived some thirty years ago, and none of his family is in this country, as far as we know."

"No, they aren't," Hall agreed, leaning back a little and making a steeple of his fingers on the desk. He regarded Matthew over the top of them. "All his family are dead. Both his parents were killed by the Austrian police. The woman he loved—Ingrid, I believe her name was—was raped and killed in a particularly brutal incident on the Serbian border. He and his brother, Baruch Schering, escaped to England, but Baruch went back, working for British Intelligence, to see what information he could gain about political alliances in the Balkans at the time. He was especially concerned about Austrian treaties with Russia which might affect us in the future."

His eyes were steady, the blink forgotten. "He was caught and tortured, but he died without giving away any of our other men, although he knew the names of at least a dozen of them. It is because of Baruch and our debt to him that we trusted Caleb . . . Calder Shearing. He has never let us down. I am prepared to stake Captain Cavan's life, and the outcome of the court-martial in Passchendaele, on his honor in this, if not his judgment. If, indeed, he really did propose Faulkner."

Matthew sat still, his face burning, his brain trying to accommodate all he had heard, and decide what he believed. He had come in accepting at last that Shearing was the Peacemaker. Deeply as that hurt, he no longer fought the idea. Now all was confusion again.

Hall must have seen it in his face. "I understand your concern, Reavley. On the face of it, to send Faulkner seems the worst possible choice. He may have reasons we are unaware of. Find out, and bring me the answer."

"I have no authority with which to question him, sir," Matthew began.

"I said find out, Reavley, not ask him," Hall snapped. "Learn what you can about any friendship between them. Is it possible Shearing is so burdened with other issues he has been misled, careless, or used by someone else? And do it quickly. We have no time to spare. Report to me in forty-eight hours. Or less, if you find a satisfactory answer."

Matthew stood up. "Yes, sir." His head was swimming. He heard every tick of the clock on the desk as if it were consuming the seconds until Cavan should be shot, and the whole Western Front collapse.

Judith also had very little sleep, and even in those brief hours snatched here and there she was troubled by memories and fears. She was accustomed to physical exhaustion and the discomfort of being bruised by the constant jolting of the ambulance over rough ground, her muscles aching from floundering in mud and trying to lift stretchers awkwardly. She was also, like everyone else, accustomed to being wet most of the time, having her feet hurt as her rough shoes scraped where the leather had become twisted and hard from being soaked and caked with mud. She felt permanently filthy. Like everything along the entire Western Front, she almost certainly smelled stale and dirty. She felt about as feminine as a road navvy or railway stoker . . . or a soldier.

Over the last year, that had not mattered. Seeing the wounded, thinking about the war in general and this Salient in particular was all that anyone had time for; helping friends, and friends were whoever was near you. But Mason had looked at her with that tender, aching intensity, the softness in his eyes so naked it tore through her like a fire, destroying complacency and balance.

Before the war she had been beautiful. She knew it from the reflection in men's eyes. Now they looked on her as one of the chaps, something of a mascot even: a good driver, a good sport, brave, reliable, someone to trust. And yet still not really one of them.

As she lay curled up in the back of the ambulance, she could dimly see the outline of Wil Sloan a few feet away. He was breathing evenly, almost certainly asleep. She had never admired anyone more. Wil was brave with a casual air as if it were ordinary, and he made off-beat silly jokes, told long stories about the American West that no one else understood. But he laughed at the English tales that must have been equally obscure to him. He shared his food and blankets, when there were any, and he never complained. She would have trusted him with anything except the vulnerability of her emotional need and confusion at the moment.

He had helped her free the accused men from the farmhouse, and that could have cost him his life. It still might, for that matter. Colonel Hook had asked Joseph to find out how the escape had been effected, and he had been so obviously dilatory that Faulkner had insisted he be imprisoned for his collusion.

She turned over in bed carefully as her muscles tweaked with pain. Poor Joseph. He had been so wretched over realizing that Northrup had been shot by his own men, even though this time there was no way he could have avoided it. Mason knew, and that was the end of his chance to conceal it.

The last time she had seen Mason there had been a bitterness in his words, an anger that was not at the Germans just beyond the ridge, or at circumstances that had brought them all here. It was as if he had expected incompetence and futility, and hoped for nothing better. His faith in the world was gone.

She huddled a little tighter, remembering their conversation.

"Do you know *Through the Looking Glass?*" he had asked wryly.

"Yes, of course I do," she had answered. She had loved it, possibly even more than *Alice in Wonderland.* There was an extra absurdity to the logic, and the poetry stayed in her mind, especially the White Knight. " '. . . fingers in a pocket full of glue. Or madly pushing my left-hand foot into my right-hand shoe.' " Aloud she had said "Why?"

" 'Walrus and the Carpenter,' " he had replied. "Walking along the beach, 'wept like anything to see such quantities of sand.' "

She picked it up. " 'If seven maids with seven mops swept it for half a year. Do you suppose, the walrus said, that they could get it clear?' "

" 'I doubt it, said the carpenter, and shed a bitter tear,' " he finished. "How many women, in how many factories, their backs aching, feet sore, labor all day and all night, to make the shells that are shattering this land and sending mud into new piles, for someone else to blast all over a slightly different place tomorrow, and tear apart a few more human bodies in the process? That's real absurdity. A world that makes no sense."

She had longed for something to say that would explain to him the will to fight, the love of all the remembered sweetness of life: small things like a walk in the woods at bluebell time; lark song early in the morning; sunlight on shaven fields in autumn when the air is gold; and big things like laughter with friends, and faith in tomorrow. But she did not want him to damage her faith with his disbelief, and paint gray over her dreams. They were too precious to risk. Without them she might not survive.

Now there was a darkness in Mason that saw no point in their efforts, almost as if he derided them in his own way. She remembered his words as they had stood together in the dark, talking in between the crashes of mortar fire and the heavy shells exploding less than a mile away. Even in the clouded night they could see the great gouts of earth and mud flying into the air. Judith perceived his anger—not only what he said, it was the edge of despair in his voice.

It was at that moment that she had realized how small a part of his life she was. Yes, he could laugh and need and give like anyone else. But how much courage had he to hope when it was almost impossibly difficult? To lay the soul bare to the darkness, with the knowledge that it might not end? All the intelligence, the imagination, and pity, the moments of tenderness, were not enough without hope as well.

She sank into a kind of sleep at last, and by five o'clock she was awake again in the gray light. A splash of cold water on her face brought her to attention. Wil gave her a large mug of hot tea. She picked a bedbug out of it, then drank. It was so strong she could barely taste the strange mixture of things that had been in the Dixie can before it.

She was doing a little maintenance on the ambulance when she heard footsteps across the cobbled farmyard. At first she assumed it was Wil again, returned from his errand, but when he spoke she swung around in amazement to see Joseph. He looked tired, as always, the shadows around his eyes making them look even darker.

"Sorry," he apologized. "Didn't mean to startle you."

She saw an intensity in him that sent a wave of fear through her. In spite of all his care not to, had he found undeniable evidence that it was she who had organized the escape of the prisoners? Would he lie to protect her—tell a deliberate, outright lie? Maybe he couldn't. Maybe he had some kind of priestly oath, or a covenant with God. Perhaps he would not break that oath for her, or anyone.

"Hello, Joseph." Her voice croaked a little.

"I know I'm interrupting, but I need to speak to you," he said. "It's important."

She put down the rag with which she had been cleaning the carburetor.

"About the escape," he went on.

She tried to look as if she had no idea why he was asking her, and knew that she failed.

He smiled bleakly, his face tight, his eyes gentle. "Be careful what you tell me," he continued. "So far I have ideas of who was involved, but I don't know for certain, and without proof I wouldn't say anything."

"Oh." She let out her breath in a sigh. "I see. What is it you do not want to ask me?" She was puzzled. "I wouldn't tell you who it was, even presuming I knew."

"Of course you wouldn't," he agreed hastily. "I imagine you have an intense admiration for them. It was clever, simple, and took great courage, and of course a loyalty as deep as that of any of the soldiers on the line." He was still looking at her intently, eyes so shadowed with weariness she could not read them. "They are willing to die for one another. And that is what it would come to. If that person, or two people probably, were to be caught, it would be a firing—" His voice cracked, too. "A firing squad matter. I wouldn't ask you to tell me . . . if you know. That kind of betrayal is unthinkable."

Her mouth was dry, her heart pounding. He was playing a game, but what? And what for? "Joseph—"

"But I want you to use your imagination," he cut across her. "I've just spent a little time in the farmhouse where they were kept. And I spoke with Cavan. I know more about what actually happened now. I think only one of them is guilty of murder, the rest of . . . let's say 'conduct unbecoming.' "

She cleared her throat. "Does it make any difference?"

"I think so. I'm going to go after them and try to persuade them to return and face court-martial."

"They won't!" She was appalled at his naïveté. "For heaven's sake, Joseph, they'd be shot! Guilty or innocent, the army's after blood! You know that."

"Not if they come back willingly," he argued. "If they stay away then they're deserters and fugitives. Worse than deserters, actually: mutineers and murderers."

"Then they'll just stay in Switzerland! Or—" She stopped abruptly, realizing she had told him which direction they were going. But they had at least three days' advantage on him. "Or wherever they go," she added lamely.

"Yes. Or South America, or wherever we have no treaties of extradition for murder," he said grimly. "They can never come back to England. Never have careers, never stop looking over their shoulders, never be honest with anyone. That's a heavy burden to carry all your life."

She almost said that there might not be an England to come back to, but that was a terrible possibility she refused to harbor. Then the enormity of their situation began to sink in: the endless state of not belonging; the loneliness for anything deeper than passing acquaintance; the knowledge that you were forever a stranger.

"Think of their families," Joseph said quietly. "They're not cowards, not ruthless or without honor. I think they would rather try to prove their reasons for acting as they did, their innocence of murder, than run for the rest of their lives."

"Maybe. But it would take almost impossible courage."

"If anyone on earth has it, it's the men here," he said simply. "All I want to do is give them the chance, Judith," he said. "Where were they making for? Were they going to travel alone, in separate groups, or all together?"

She did not bother to pretend anymore. "Switzerland," she answered. "Pretty well all together, although if anyone got hurt or wanted to drop out, the rest would go on. They went on foot, so as to look as much like ordinary soldiers as possible. There was no way of making them look like civilians. Also, only Morel really speaks French, and anyway they're all of military age and obviously perfectly fit enough to fight, so there wouldn't be any explanation for their being out of uniform anywhere but a neutral country."

He gave her a sudden hard embrace and held her for several moments. "Thank you," he said gently. "Thank you very much."

"Be careful, Joseph," she said, clinging onto him. They were always in danger, but this mission was particularly unsettling. This time he was going away from Passchendaele and into country neither of them knew. He would be among strangers, and no one would bring word of him. "Be careful!" she said again, more urgently.

"I will," he promised. Then he broke free and gave her a quick salute. "You, too," he said huskily. He turned and walked across the cobbled yard without looking back.

TEN

*J*oseph realized that his only chance of finding the escapees before they crossed into Switzerland would be with the help of one of the reconnaissance planes from the Royal Flying Corps. They were fast enough to cover the distance in hours, and skilled enough to spot a group of men moving eastward instead of with the rest of the troops.

For this, of course, he had a letter of authority from Colonel Hook. Other than that, he took only a shaving kit, toothbrush, the minimum of clean underwear, an extra pair of socks, a pocket copy of the New Testament, and the regulation soldier's first aid equipment and hard rations.

When the staff car dropped him off at the Royal Flying Corps airfield, the sun was breaking through the mist and it looked like a good day for air reconnaissance. He felt a sudden lift of optimism as he thanked the driver and started walking toward the huts that served as headquarters.

Joseph spoke to the first officer he met, a good-looking young man with dark hair brushed back off his brow, deep-set eyes, and a shy smile. At the moment he had a pipe clamped between his teeth.

"Lost, Padre?" he said, looking at Joseph's dog collar and squinting a little in the sun. "Or are you an answer to someone's prayer?"

"I doubt it!" Joseph answered drily. "At the moment, I'm looking to receive help rather than give it."

The man extended his hand. "Captain Jones-Williams."

"Captain Reavley." Joseph shook the offered hand.

"What can we do for you, Captain Reavley? Looking for a trip up to find God?" Jones-Williams gestured into the milky blue of the sky.

"Actually I'd settle for eleven escaped prisoners," Joseph replied with a rueful shrug. "Sounds a little disrespectful, but I've got a few things to do before I meet God. Not really ready for that yet."

Jones-Williams laughed outright. "A priest who'd rather find eleven escaped prisoners than find God is worth getting to know. Will any eleven do, or do you have a particular set in mind?"

"Sorry, I have a very particular set in mind," Joseph replied. "They were held in a farmhouse just this side of Passchendaele, and—"

Jones-Williams's face was suddenly desperately grave. "From that poor bloody regiment that's being slaughtered? Can't you let 'em go? Turn a blind eye? Wouldn't your faith allow you that much mercy?"

"They've been accused of mutiny and the murder of an officer, Captain."

"Sorry, old fellow," Jones-Williams said with a brief smile. "We're pretty shorthanded ourselves. Lost quite a few lately. Got to keep what we have for taking a look at Jerry and what he's up to. Can see troop movements quite well from up there. I'd give it up, if I were you."

Joseph knew exactly why the captain was refusing, and he understood the pity and the revulsion behind it. He liked the man the more for it. "That's not the whole picture," he said, meeting his companion's eyes. "They would be fugitives for the rest of their lives. Never go home again. And I think all but one of them are innocent. I want to give them the chance to come back and clear their names."

"Of murder and mutiny?" Jones-Williams's eyebrows rose in disbelief. "They'll shoot them. They'll have no choice."

"I think the officer's father, who is a general, might push pretty hard to get the charge withdrawn."

"Really?" Jones-Williams still looked skeptical.

"A capital charge has to be pretty thoroughly proved," Joseph pointed out, "and the defendants given every opportunity to put their case."

The drone of an airplane broke the silence above, sounding like an angry insect. Automatically Joseph glanced upward as it made its way lower and sank toward the airfield, sputtering now and then.

Jones-Williams chewed his pipe stem a moment. "I'd have thought in this instance those two were rather the same. Their defense that the man was an ass, and a dangerous one at that, gives the prosecution their motive on a plate. Doesn't excuse shooting him, though, even to save their own lives. On that score they could get rid of half the officers we've got!"

"Thing is," Joseph went on thoughtfully, "General Northrup won't enjoy having the court-martial drag out and prove each point of his son's incompetence, and exactly how many men were maimed or killed because of it. Even the surgeon, Captain Cavan, soon to be V.C., felt no alternative but to put him on trial."

The plane landed at last, and Joseph felt his shoulders ease with relief that it was safe.

Jones-Williams took the pipe out of his mouth. "So what do you want from us? A lift as far as possible along the line to look for them?"

"That's exactly what I'd like. I realize it's only a chance I'll find them, but it's worth a try. You'd better see my authority." He fished in his pocket for the paper.

"What?"

Joseph smiled. "Well, I could be a deserter looking for a damn good start eastward myself!"

"No point. Your dog collar could be real or not, but at your age you could reasonably beg out anyway."

Joseph winced. "Depends how desperate we are. You won't have them in the R.F.C., but we have fourteen-year-olds in the army. Lied about their age, of course, but we know. Sooner or later they say something that gives them away." He stopped abruptly.

"That was a bit tactless of me," Jones-Williams said by way of apology. "Come on and I'll find you someone to take you up for a look, and drop you off as near to the Swiss border as you think you want." He turned and sauntered over toward the line of hangars beyond the smaller buildings of offices and control tower.

Joseph followed him, catching up quickly. He glanced once at the three planes drawn up on the strip, including the one just landed.

"Take you in something much bigger than those," Jones-Williams said cheerfully. "Two-seater. One of the observation planes. Keep low much of the time. Hedgehopping, we call it. D'you know how these fellows of yours went? Got a car or anything?"

"On foot, at least to begin with," Joseph replied.

"Won't have got far, then. Hey, Vine!" he called to a slender young man in R.F.C. uniform, goggles and scarf around his neck, flying jacket slung over his shoulder and helmet swinging from his hand.

"Yes, sir?" Vine paused a few yards away from them, more or less to attention.

"Chaplain here is from the army," Jones-Williams explained. "He's looking for a hand to find a few fellows gone AWOL. He thinks if they come back they'll have a chance of doing better than if they keep on running. Wouldn't like to take him along the lines a bit, would you?"

"Of course," Vine agreed obligingly, turning to look at Joseph curiously. "How far, Chaplain?"

"Until you find them. Or Switzerland," Jones-Williams said cheerfully. "Good. All set then." He turned to Joseph. "Come and have a cup of tea. Officers' mess is over there. We'll find you some decent goggles and a jacket. Chilly up there. Vine will come for you when he's all ready."

"Thank you." Joseph found himself off balance with the speed of the decision, but he could not afford to question it. He thanked Vine again, and followed Jones-Williams over to the low, rather rambling buildings at the side. He felt grateful now for time to prepare himself for the flight.

But all the imagination of his life was futile compared with the reality. First there was climbing up onto the wing and into the small seat and fastening the harness to hold him in. The engine was started with a tremendous roar, then a moment later the tiny, frail craft went racing over the grass, bumping on every tussock, before lifting off jerkily. The plane bucked slightly, catching the light wind and clearing the neighboring stand of trees by what felt like no more than a few feet.

It was an appalling sensation, being out of touch with the earth—and apparently completely out of control. Joseph felt he was a prisoner.

He was sitting behind the pilot. A lightweight machine gun—a Lewis gun, to be precise—was mounted beside him. He had been told cheerfully that it was just in case they should meet any opposition.

They seemed to veer around quite badly as they gained height. Joseph had the very alarming feeling that he could be pitched out any moment and find himself falling through the air. Was he high enough up that it would kill him outright? Or might he be left broken but alive? Why on earth could he not have left well enough alone and stayed on the ground?

Then there was the question of keeping his stomach in place.

They were a few hundred feet up now and steadying. He could see nothing but trees slightly below him. The airfield and control tower were somewhere over to the left.

He steeled himself to look down, afraid of an overpowering sense of vertigo, but below him and stretching into the distance he saw a landscape that took his breath away. There was a strip of desolation a few miles wide, ruined, it would seem, beyond recall. It was cratered with shell holes that steamed in the August warmth—or perhaps it was poison gas that curled yellow-white in the hollows.

Blasted tree trunks poked up here and there. The wreckage of vehicles and guns was easy to see by outline rather than any difference in color. Everything was gray-brown, leached of life. Shape also distinguished the corpses of men and horses, too many to count. From up here the sheer enormity of it was overwhelming. So many dead, enough men to populate cities, and all destroyed.

Faint sunlight gleamed on the watery surfaces of trenches in recognizably straight lines, zigzagged to block the lines of fire. Two long stretches were waterlogged, like some gray mire, dotted with corpses.

He could see men moving around, foreshortened, dun-colored like the clay. Up here it was ridiculous how anonymous they seemed, and yet he probably knew all of them. He understood what they were doing only because he knew; he had done it all himself: shoring up walls, carrying supplies, cleaning weapons. A few cars chugged slowly on pockmarked roads, sending little puffs of exhaust out behind them. Judith might be in one of them, seeming to crawl along compared with the crazy speed of the plane. Ambulances were easy to spot. Columns of men moved on foot, reinforcements going forward, wounded going back. It was also easy to see the field guns, the huts and tents, the dressing stations, and the first aid posts. Some of the humps in the ground he knew were dugouts.

The plane gained more altitude, and Joseph could see the German lines as well. He knew their trenches were deeper, their dugouts better organized—and better furnished, so he had heard. But the land was the same: shattered and poisoned. The men, such as he could see, were engaged in the same activities. They, too, when motionless, catching an hour or two of sleep, blended into the earth and became almost invisible.

The terrain was becoming less distinct as they climbed higher. Beyond, the green was visible again, in both directions: Trees had leaves; there were patches of grass. On toward the horizon to the south and west there were the dark scars of roads and railways, but they lay across cornfields and meadows, and soft, blurred patches of woodland. Here and there Joseph saw the silver curl of a river.

It was like looking at the track of a wound across the land, or the scorched path of shrapnel through flesh, leaving the rest oddly whole.

For three long, terrible years they had faced each other over those few thousand yards of ground, and killed—and killed—repeatedly. It was madness! In the silence up here with nothing but wind and sun and the shattering roar of the engine, it was so obvious he wanted to lean over and shout invectives at them. But of course no one could hear him. He might as well scream at an anthill.

They were moving east and south. He saw railway tracks and marshaling yards. He thought he recognized some of the features of the land, the curve of hill and river. He saw what he thought was Lille, but he was not sure how far they had come.

Half an hour passed in silence. He searched the sky nervously, but there were no other aircraft visible. The French lines below them looked the same as the British or Canadian: just gray mud, wreckage, what one could make out of men moving about the same midday duties.

When was Vine going to go low enough for him to have any idea if there were men moving eastward? So far they had followed the battle line southeast as it curved away from the advancing German army.

Had they not gone far enough yet? He had lost any sense of where they were. The ground was so far below he could barely make out the roads, let alone who was moving on them. Perhaps this was an idiotic cause anyway, and Jones-Williams had let him come only because he had no imaginable chance of succeeding.

He leaned forward and shouted at Vine, and as he turned for a moment, Joseph pointed downward.

Vine held out his hand, thumb up, and obediently swooped the plane low, hedgehopping, as Jones-Williams had called it. Details became sharper—roads, the colors of men, horses, and artillery—but Joseph saw nothing to indicate the presence of his eleven men. He thought they would have moved much farther eastward by now. They could have covered twenty or thirty miles a day with a little help—a lift here or there. They were all fairly fit and used to marching.

Suddenly and with absolutely no warning, the aircraft pitched and yawed like a tub in high seas. One minute the sky was above them, the next they rolled so the earth swung around, over their heads, then right and left wildly. Finally it fell away as they reared up and climbed steeply, racing toward the faint shreds of cloud, which were still far above.

Joseph thought he was going to fall out. Only the harness jerking violently on his body held him in. Bruised and shocked, he was sick over the side. They were still climbing. He clung onto the cockpit, knuckles white. Even yesterday, it had never occurred to him that he would die this way.

They swiveled around and dived, then climbed again. That was when Joseph saw them, black outlines against the sky like dragonflies, swooping and diving. They seemed angry, turning on each other, always going back again into the heart of the swarm. It was a great aerial dogfight, high above them, up almost to the thin layer of cloud.

Vine was keeping their plane lower, probably hoping that against the darker background of the fields and interlacing support trenches they would be almost invisible. The pilots in the dogfight would be concentrating on each other, looking for who was in their sights and who was on their tails.

The seconds seemed to stretch forever. They climbed a little. Joseph did not know why, but he assumed it would be to give them space to dive and evade if they were seen.

Joseph touched the Lewis gun experimentally. He was a noncombatant, a man who served the fighting soldiers, but did not possess a weapon himself. But if they were attacked now, not only Joseph's life but Vine's as well would depend upon Joseph shooting and doing it effectively. He did not even think of trying to find an escape from it.

The dogfight was still above them and only a short distance behind.

Vine put the aircraft into a climb again, trying to gain height in case they needed the speed of a dive to make a run for it.

From the whirling dance of the dogfight one plane exploded, red fire and black smoke staining the sky. The pieces of it plummeted downward. Another blossomed a long trail of smoke, smearing across the blue. Then it cartwheeled over and over, hideously slowly.

They were climbing again, then without warning another plane roared above them. It was probably fifty feet away, but seemed barely to miss them. It was so close Joseph could see the pilot's face for an instant—his head bent forward, his muscles tense. Then it was gone, swinging away and up again. On its tail was a red-winged triplane, guns blazing.

Vine suddenly swung wide also, and for a moment—there and then gone again—Joseph had the red-winged plane in his sights. Too quickly it was away and there was nothing there but blue sky.

He was dizzy as they soared up, and he realized there had been another plane above and behind them. Bullets ripped through the very edge of the wing as they slithered sideways, around, and then up even higher.

Now there were planes all around them. The maelstrom had descended. More bullets streamed overhead and struck the tail of a plane above them.

Joseph was galvanized into movement at last and gripped the gun. Next time he saw anything in his sights, if it was German he would fire. If he had long enough to be sure.

The need came before he expected. Vine swung the plane around, over in a roll too close to a somersault, pitching Joseph almost over the side. He straightened up, bruised, heart pounding, and raised the barrel of the gun. It turned easily. He found he could follow the course of a plane for seconds. Long enough to hit it.

Except that Vine never kept them still. They surged and slithered across the sky. One minute Joseph was staring at fields, the next at gray trenches, then the sky. Other planes crossed his vision and by the time he was certain they were German, they were gone.

Then bullets tore the wing again, and the red triplane was there.

Joseph squeezed the trigger and bullets exploded out of the muzzle. They just caught the very edge of the red tail. An instant later it was gone.

Joseph sat hugging the gun, his heart pounding. It was the first time he had ever fired a gun at a human being, intending to kill. It was an extraordinary feeling, decisive, shameful, exhilarating. He had passed a certain barrier. How much did it matter that he had not hit the man? The wind rushed past him as the plane banked.

They were in the middle of a swarm, like angry hornets, engines roaring, bullets stuttering. Another plane whirled and cartwheeled, spiraling down with a black plume of smoke trailing behind it. He saw it strike the ground and explode in flames. He realized only then that he had not noticed whether it was British or German, only that the pilot would die.

There was another rattle of bullets. Several struck so close to him that he flung himself backward with a jolt, mouth dry, gasping to regain his breath. Then he grabbed the gun savagely. When the next German plane came into his sights, he let off a stream of fire in return and was elated to see the tracer bullets strike the back part of the fuselage. It tipped the balance wildly, the plane yawing like a sailboat in a bad sea.

Vine raced after the damaged plane, turning wide to give Joseph another shot. He hesitated, almost lost aim, then at the last second shot at the engine. It was a senseless distinction from shooting at the man. If the plane went down the pilot would be killed anyway. The difference was a sophistry.

On it went, almost like a three-dimensional dance. Up here it was noise, engines, bullets, wind ice-cold on the skin. They wheeled and climbed, juddered on the top of the ascent, careened sideways, swooped, guns chattering. Then they increased speed until the wind was screaming in their ears and the ground seemed to race up toward them. They struggled to break out of the dive and bank around again, caught the enemy in the gunsights and shot.

He lost all count of time. He shot in short, rapid bursts at other planes with no idea if he hit them or not. He was hardly even aware of it at first when the bullets struck them. It was even a moment or two before he realized with mind-numbing clarity that the smoke was their own. This long dive was not going to end in the swift turn and banking up into a climb again.

The ground came closer and closer. He could see trees clearly and a farmyard. Then he realized Vine was making for the fields beyond. He was going to try to land.

The seconds were endless. Joseph had no doubt that he was going to die in seconds now. He had expected to die in Ypres, certainly, but this was France now, a summer cornfield ready for harvest. Almost like Cambridgeshire. Almost as good as home.

Now he had no more time to do better, try harder. Soon he would know the truth, whatever it was. He ached with a blinding pain for what he left behind.

They leveled out, lower than the trees. There was nothing but fields ahead. Something tore at the wheels, pitching him forward so violently for a moment he could think of nothing but the weight of the blow. He felt bruised in every part of his body. They were still moving, tearing through the corn, ripping a path in it toward the little copse of trees.

Then everything was still, eerily silent after the noise.

He heard Vine's voice shouting: "Get out! Run! Reavley, get out!" There was fear in it—high, sharp-pitched fear.

He was jerked out of his stupor. Awkwardly, oblivious of the pain, he scrambled to release himself and get out of the cockpit. He clambered over the edge and dropped into the corn. The black smoke was still pouring out of the engine.

He staggered to his feet. He must get as far away as possible. Then after a couple of steps he turned. Vine was still in his seat.

"Come on!" Joseph yelled at him. "Get out!"

"Can't!" Vine called back. "Got a bust leg, old boy. Get going while you can. This thing could go up any moment. Good luck."

Whatever it cost, Joseph knew he must try to get Vine out. He could not run for his own safety and leave the pilot to be burned to death. Vine was only here because of him. He stumbled back the few steps, climbed up onto the wing and over to the cockpit.

"Get out!" Vine said sharply. "Don't you understand? I can't stand anyway. My whole right leg is shot up. Go on!"

"I'm used to carrying wounded men," Joseph told him. "It's mostly what I do. Get that harness off and grab hold of me. This is not that much different from a mud crater, and God knows how many men I've pulled out of those."

Vine hesitated.

"Come on, damn it!" Joseph shouted suddenly. "Don't be a bloody hero. You'll get us both killed! Hold on to me!"

Vine unfastened his harness and gripped Joseph. His face was white under the smears from the smoke, and there was a sheen of sweat on it.

Joseph looked down to see the blood-soaked leg, wanting to cause as little extra pain as possible. He was hideously aware that any moment the engine could catch fire and the fuel tanks explode, killing them both. He took hold of Vine and tried to heave him up. It was far more difficult than he had supposed. He knew he was hurting Vine, but the only alternative was to run and let him die. He could feel his own muscles tearing with the strain, and the sweat of fear running down his body.

Vine rose a little. The seconds were ticking by. Smoke billowed out, sharp, hot, and acrid.

Joseph pulled again, putting all his strength and weight behind it. Please God he could do it! He must!

With a bitten-off scream of pain, Vine came out of the cockpit. Joseph collapsed backward onto the wing and slid down it to land on his back in the corn, Vine on top of him.

Then he felt hands pulling him and heard voices. For a moment he did not understand. Then with blessed relief he realized people had come from the farmhouse and he was being lifted up. He and Vine were half-dragged, half-carried across the ripe ears of corn, their stalks catching and poking at them.

They were seventy yards away when the plane exploded. The blast knocked all of them off their feet, scorching them with its heat.

Joseph sat up slowly, at first his vision obscured by the tops of the corn. Then he saw the flames and the black column of smoke going up.

"Thanks," Vine said hoarsely from beside him. "Thanks, old fellow. Wouldn't have liked to be in that. Bit of a mess, eh?" His face revealed a pain so intense he could barely keep consciousness.

A couple of yards away an elderly man rose to his feet, muttering expletives in French. He was gray-haired, his shoulders sagging, and the stubble of a beard darkened his chin. He shook his head and looked regretfully at the scorched and trampled field, then he turned to Vine and apologized in broken English.

Vine was lying on his back. He looked crumpled, smaller. His eyes were closed, and it seemed as if the agony of his leg had finally overtaken him.

A broad-shouldered, handsome woman—possibly the old man's daughter—staggered to her feet, yanking her skirt out of her way impatiently. She was clicking with her tongue, her face anxious.

Joseph spoke to her in French. "We need to stop the bleeding, and see if we can splint where the bone is broken," he said urgently. "I expect there'll be an army hospital not far away, but he'll die if we don't do that much immediately."

"Yes, yes," she agreed. "It looks bad. Poor man. And you, are you all right?"

"Fine. Only a few bruises," Joseph replied. "He made a good job of landing. Sorry about your field."

She waved her hand, as if dismissing the subject. Then she looked up in the sky where they could just make out the tangle of planes wheeling around each other. "Circus of the Red Baron!" she said disgustedly. "I suppose you are lucky to get out alive."

Joseph remembered the red triplane. He had actually taken a shot at it himself! Even hit a piece off the tail. Manfred von Richthofen—but he would have time to think about that later. Now they must look after Vine.

It was an arduous job, but one at least that Joseph was accustomed to. With the help of the French farmer and his daughter—as she proved to be—they splinted Vine's leg and then stopped the worst of the bleeding, at least for the moment. Then they put him in the one decent wagon left and hitched up the ancient horse.

It took them two hours of driving along mud-rutted lanes to get Vine to the French military field hospital behind the lines, but he was still alive—and conscious again—by then. The surgeon looked at the leg and said he thought he could save it.

"Thanks," Vine said when he was alone with Joseph, after the farmer and his wife had gone. He was lying in a hospital cot, a sheet up to his neck. "Good luck in finding your fellows. Tell them from me they'd better come home and face the music. They owe you that."

"They owe *you* that," Joseph corrected him. "I'll be sure to tell them so. Good luck."

Vine's face tightened in momentary pain, then relaxed again into a smile. "I expected you to say 'God be with you, my son,' or something of that sort."

"God be with you," Joseph replied wryly. "I trust God. It's the luck I'm a bit dubious about!"

He went to the commanding officer of the section, no more than half a mile from the hospital.

"We'll find someone to give you a lift back to your regiment, Captain," he said in excellent English. He was a slender man with a dark, intelligent face. He had an air of weary resignation, but he was unfailingly courteous.

"Thank you, sir," Joseph replied, also in English. "But I was making my way to Switzerland, or at least in that direction." And he explained his errand, showing him Colonel Hook's letter as proof. Without it he could hardly expect anyone to think him other than a deserter himself. He said that the men were wanted for the murder of Major Northrup, a grossly incompetent officer, but it was his belief that only one of them was actually guilty. He skirted around the issue of mutiny, aware that it might be a sensitive subject for a French officer, especially if introduced by an Englishman. He had no idea what this particular man's sympathies were. He was aware of sounding rather stilted. Then he saw the smile on the Frenchman's face and appreciated that he had understood Joseph rather better than he had intended. But to apologize would make it worse. Instead he simply smiled back.

"So you are going east after the eleven men?" the Frenchman asked.

"Yes, sir."

"Let me give you a good dinner and a night's rest first," he offered. "Then if you wish to proceed, may I suggest that you change your attire? You appear to speak French at least adequately." He pulled a slight face. "Not enough to pass for French, unless you claim to come from some other region—Marseille, perhaps?" His tone suggested that to him Marseille was barbaric, barely French at all. "Have you any other language? German, perhaps?"

"Yes. And rather better," Joseph admitted. "But I don't think passing for German would be very clever."

The Frenchman gave a particularly Gallic shrug.

"Of course not. I was thinking German-speaking Swiss," he said. "That would account for your accent. A Protestant priest, Swiss, and therefore neutral."

The idea was very appealing, except that if he were captured out of uniform he could be shot as a spy rather than held as a prisoner of war. He pointed that out.

"Indeed," the Frenchman conceded. "I was considering your chances of success in traveling unnoticed, and finding your eleven men. We can get you some suitable clothes. Stay as far back as the supply trenches, or even farther, and you are unlikely to be taken by Germans. Do what you think best."

When Joseph set out in the French staff car the following morning he was well fed, by trench catering standards, and well rested.

It was not raining and the late summer air was soft and bright. He was so accustomed to the smells of overcrowding, open latrines, and too many dead to bury that he barely noticed them. He thought instead of the sun on his face and—at least to the south—a land that held some echo of its prewar glory. Farms were ruined, villages bombed and burned as every-where else, but on the horizon there were trees and the hills rolled away green in the distance. He could even see cattle grazing here and there when he veered farther away from the trenches and the incessant sound of guns.

Just as in his own lines on the Ypres Salient, there were men returning to battle after brief leave, often because of injury. There were columns of wounded making their painful way back to field dressing stations, and there were supply trucks, munitions, and ambulances on the crowded roads.

The car took him another thirty miles. After that he had to walk.

He stopped only to ask directions or seek information of anyone who might have seen a group of men together who were going along the lines rather than back or forward to fight. He was appalled how easily it came to him to invent lies to explain his errand. The only part that did not vary was his physical descriptions of the most noticeable of the men, particularly Morel, the one he was sure could speak French fluently and would be the natural leader.

He slept where he could. Men were unfailingly willing to share the meager rations they had. Any thanks he offered were inadequate, but gratitude was all he had.

When he finally found someone who seemed to have seen them the day before, he was dubious. The description he received in return could have been almost any soldier.

That evening the sighting was much more positive. Crouching in one of the rear support trenches, Joseph listened to a group of French soldiers describe someone lost and badly frightened. Apparently the man had admitted considering mutiny, which they sympathized with wholeheartedly. The man had divulged that he had an idiot for an officer, that he had rebelled against his orders. As a result he was now a fugitive, cut off from his friends and all his connections with home. Worst of all, even if they won the war, he could probably never go back. He had stuck with it for three years, gone through hell, and one stupid useless officer had ruined it all.

Since Joseph was pretending to be Swiss, they did not think he had any serious interest in the issue, so they were prepared to talk about it to him, and he did not disabuse them. He set out again with quickened hope and moved more rapidly than before, believing the escaped men were not far ahead of him.

Directly to the east was the German border. He was past the field of Verdun, where 350,000 Frenchmen had been killed or wounded the previous year, and still the battle raged on. Joseph had no idea how many Austrians and Germans had been killed there, but he knew it must be at least as many. The Russian Front he had only heard about, and the Italian, and the Turkish fronts, and the arenas of war in Africa, Egypt, Palestine, and Mesopotamia. He refused to think about them. All he could do was this one tiny contribution: give Morel and the other fugitives a chance to come back. Even that might be beyond him, but trying had become almost as important for his own sanity as for their survival. It would mean that in this endless destruction there was something within his control.

In the end, he found them in the ruins of a bombed village, so little of which was left that even its name was obliterated. He had followed a rumor: a joke about someone's French being notoriously bad. Some young men, worn out and with several days' beard, had asked for directions to a farm where he and his friends could sleep. Only he had mispronounced it as *une femme*—a woman. He had met with much bawdy laughter, and remarks about all ten of them.

The joke was told with pity for their desperation but then everyone was desperate. It was not that they were unwilling to share what they had, but they too had nothing. They were gaunt-faced, exhausted young men with eyes that stared beyond the mark, seeing a hell they would never forget. The images lay inside the eyelids, waking or sleeping, and coiled into the brain, pounding in the blood. The sound of guns never stopped; even in the rare silences it was still there in the head.

The escapees saw Joseph at the same moment he saw them. He knew Morel instantly, even in silhouette against the sunlight on a stretch of wall still standing. He was thin, and his uniform was filthy—perhaps on purpose to disguise its markings. But the way he stood was characteristic. Even now the grace had not left him, the natural elegance he had always had. Trotter and Snowy Nunn were sitting on piles of rubble. Snowy was drinking from a tin can. The others were out of sight, perhaps asleep somewhere.

Morel saw Joseph and froze, his hand on his revolver.

Joseph stood motionless. He did not have a weapon, but even if he had he would not have used it. He took a step forward experimentally.

Morel raised the revolver.

"That would change everything," Joseph said quietly.

Morel stiffened, recognizing him now, even though Joseph was wearing borrowed French civilian clothes, and Morel was facing the sun.

"Would it?" he asked. "Who would know?"

Joseph stood still. "You would," he answered. "You might forget shooting me, although I doubt it. In hot blood now, it might be all right, but peace will come eventually, of one sort or another. . . ."

"I can't count the number of men I've killed," Morel told him wearily. "Most of them were perfectly decent Germans doing no more than I'm doing, fighting for their country. What choice do they have, any more than I?"

"None," Joseph said honestly. "I expect it hurts them just as it does most of us. But you know me. I'm part of your peacetime as well as your war. But even if you can live with it, can Snowy? Can he ever go back to St. Giles, to his family and his land, if you kill me?"

Morel gave a sharp burst of laughter. "What the hell is so special about you? You're ridiculous!" There was deep, wounding pain in his face. "A million Englishmen are dead. God alone knows how many French and German. Why should it make any difference if you're dead, too?"

"Not *because* it's me," Joseph corrected him. "As you say, that's nothing.

It's the circumstance. To shoot an armed soldier is one thing, albeit he's a mirror image of yourself. To shoot your priest is different. Ask Snowy."

Snowy rose to his feet slowly, the sun catching his pale hair. He looked older, his young face etched with tragedy.

"Stand still," Morel ordered him.

"Or what?" Snowy asked, lifting his shoulders and letting them drop. "You'll shoot me, too?"

"Because I damn well ordered you to!" Morel snapped.

"What's the matter, Captain?" Snowy said quite casually, although his voice shook a little. "Don't you approve of men thinking for themselves when it's a moral issue? What's that, then—mutiny?" He took a step forward, then another.

Morel raised the gun a little higher. "Don't be stupid!" he warned. "Whatever he's come for, he hasn't deserted. He's here to get us to go back, and you know as well as I that if we do, we'll be court-martialed and shot. There's no way on earth they'll let us get away with killing Northrup."

"Did you kill him?" Joseph asked, doubt in his voice.

"No, I didn't!" Morel said with sudden anger. "But it's academic. I arranged the mock trial and I was in charge. It's my responsibility. That's how the army works. It's how life works. You want to lead, then you take the glory—*and* the blame."

"True," Joseph conceded. "To do less is without honor. Did Snowy shoot Northrup? Did Trotter?"

Trotter was still sitting in the rubble, staring from one to the other of them. There was a bandage on his arm, but it had bled through.

"No," Morel replied.

"Are you sure?"

"Yes, I'm bloody well sure!"

"How can you be?" Joseph persisted.

"Don't be idiotic!" Morel's patience was shadow thin. "You know Snowy. He fires high at the bloody Germans. He couldn't kill anyone except by accident."

"And Trotter?" Joseph's voice wobbled a little with fear of failure, now that success might be so close. It was hot here in the sun, and quiet. They were miles from the guns; they could hear them only in the distance. "Are you sure about him?"

"Yes, I am! It was Geddes who killed Northrup."

"Why?" He had to say something, and he wanted to know, to be certain.

"I've no idea, and I don't care," Morel replied, still holding the gun steady. "And the court-martial won't care, either. Don't soil your dog collar by lying, Captain. I'd rather take my chances in Switzerland than come back and be shot by my own. Can't go home anyway, so it's all point-less."

Snowy took another step toward Joseph.

"Stand still!" Morel snapped at him, jerking the gun toward him. "Think, Snowy! It might be all very heroic and honest to go back, but if they shoot us, what do you think that's going to do to morale, eh? Do you want a real mutiny? All along the line?" His voice caught and there were tears on his face. "The Germans would make mincemeat of us—those of us that are left of the Cambridgeshires. Is that what you want?"

Snowy froze.

"They'll shoot Cavan anyway," Joseph pointed out.

It was so quiet now that they could hear birds singing in the summer sky.

Snowy Nunn walked slowly over to Joseph. Not once did he turn to look at Morel. "I want to go home," he said simply.

Joseph waited.

Morel put the revolver away. "They'll shoot all of us," he said again, but there was an exhaustion in his voice so intense that pity gripped Joseph like a vise.

"General Northrup wants to reduce the charge," Joseph told him, his own voice gravelly, slipping out of control. He explained what the general had said.

Morel shrugged. "It won't make any difference. What a bloody fiasco. We must be the stupidest people on earth. You won't get Geddes back so easily, supposing you ever find him."

"Where are the rest of you?" Joseph asked.

"I'll tell them what you said," Morel smiled bleakly. "They can make up their own minds. You go for Geddes; he's the one you want."

"Did he go on to Switzerland?"

"That was his intention." Morel hesitated. "Look, Reavley, you're a decent man, but you haven't a ghost of a chance of bringing Geddes back. You aren't even armed, for God's sake! He'll shoot you if he has to, to get you off his trail. I'll come with you. That way you've a chance."

"No—" Joseph began.

"Snowy and Trotter can put your arguments to the others," Morel cut across him bluntly, all the old respect and acknowledgment of seniority gone. "They'll get back. You'll give your word, won't you?" He turned to Snowy, Nunn, then to Trotter.

"Yes, sir," Snowy said immediately. Trotter agreed also, rising stiffly to his feet at last. Only then did Joseph notice that his left leg was hurt as well.

"I'd give you my gun," Morel went on, looking at Joseph. "But I don't suppose you would know which end to fire."

"Actually I nicked the tail of the plane of the Red Baron," Joseph said with some dignity.

Morel stared at him.

"From another plane, with a Lewis gun," Joseph added. "How do you suppose I got here so quickly?"

Morel began to laugh. It was a wild, hysterical sound, very nearly out of control.

Joseph came to a decision immediately, although possibly not a sensible one. He stuck out his arm, pointing.

"Right. Snowy, you and Trotter go and find the others, or as many of them as you can. Get them back to the regiment. Make sure you give yourself up and aren't taken!" He looked at Snowy closely, his eyes hard. "Do you understand? It could all rest on that!"

" 'Course Oi understand, sir," Snowy said gravely. "It shouldn't be too bad. Nobody'll be looking for us going the other way. Good luck, Chaplain. But you watch for Geddes, sir. He's a hard one, an' he's got nothing to lose now."

Joseph and Morel turned south and made the best time they could. Joseph managed to persuade Morel to change clothes with a middle-aged man invalided out of the army and now mending shoes in a small shop. They continued with Morel looking less like a British officer on the run. Joseph also convinced him to speak German, and say that he too was Swiss, heading back home. No one was interested enough to challenge them seriously. They all had their own troubles.

Joseph and Morel were tired and hungry. They were within thirty miles of the Swiss border when the trail they had been following petered out. The village they arrived at had not suffered as much as many, and they were treated with courtesy, although less than the profound kindness that Joseph had received earlier when he was still in uniform. The people were war-weary, robbed by circumstance of almost everything they had. Still, they faced the possibility of invasion and occupation, and the loss of the only thing they still possessed: the physical freedom to be themselves— Frenchmen who owned their own land, blasted and burned as it was. Joseph did not blame them if they were less than wholehearted friends to men going back to a land that chose to fight on neither side.

"Can't find any trace of him," Morel said despondently.

Joseph's feet hurt and his back ached. The late August sun was hot, and he was thirsty enough to have been grateful for even rainwater in a clean ditch. "No," he said honestly. "I think we've lost him."

Morel sat down on the grass, waiting silently for Joseph to make a decision. The sunlight on Morel's face showed not only the ravages of emotion but the physical exhaustion that had almost depleted him. He was so thin his bones looked sharp beneath his skin.

Joseph, too tired to remain standing, sat down in the dust. He felt empty. He had not allowed himself to plan against the eventuality of losing Geddes. Consequently, he had no reserve strategy now to fall back on. If he had been alone he would have prayed, but it would be awkward in front of Morel, who had no faith left in God.

Was Joseph any better? What did faith mean? That everything would turn out right in the end? What was the end? Could any overriding plan one day make sense of it all?

"I don't think he's gone to Switzerland after all," Morel said, interrupting Joseph's thoughts. "If he were just a deserter, it would be one thing; but he's wanted for murdering an officer, and that's quite different. Any Englishman there, and maybe even many of the Swiss, would turn him in anyway."

"Well, the French certainly would," Joseph agreed. "No question."

"Yes, but the Germans wouldn't," Morel pointed out.

For a moment Joseph barely breathed. "Through the lines?" he said softly, understanding at last.

"Why not?" Morel looked back at him, his dark eyes steady. "The ultimate escape."

Joseph climbed to his feet slowly and dug his hands into his pockets. He stared beyond the lines in the distance, at the German trenches beyond. "Perhaps," he murmured. "You speak German. So do I."

Morel rose to his feet also, his eyes wide. "Really?"

Joseph knew what he was asking. "I want him back, to get the rest of you off. Especially Cavan. Are you game to try?"

"Of course," Morel responded. He gave an abrupt little laugh. "What use would you be by yourself?"

ELEVEN

*A*s darkness came, Joseph grew more and more apprehensive. Crossing the lines was likely to get them killed. Maybe Geddes was already dead and they would never know why he put live ammunition in his gun and deliberately betrayed his fellows by executing Northrup instead of merely frightening him.

The only plan they could form was to lie low until the first attack, then join with the French soldiers going over the top, keeping as far from the lights as possible. Become separated from the group as if by the fighting, and in the general turmoil press farther and farther forward. At least no one would be likely to suspect anyone coming up from behind and going on over.

The more Joseph thought of it, the more suicidal it seemed. But was it worse cowardice still to back out now and simply go home with Morel and hope he was believed.

"We should go now." Morel's voice came out of the darkness. "We might need all night to work our way into the French force and join them. We don't know when they'll go over. I don't suppose they know, poor sods."

That was the decision made. To argue now would look like fear. At the very least it would leave Morel to go alone, and that was unthinkable.

"Right," he said as if Morel were in charge. Perhaps he should be. Joseph had been into no-man's-land more often than he could count, but as a chaplain, in order to pick up whatever bodies he could find and help the wounded. After the worst night's fighting he had been as far as twenty yards from the German trenches, but he had never faced an enemy soldier in anger, never fired a gun at a man.

"Are you all right, Chaplain?" Morel asked, the use of his occupational title betraying the uncertainty he felt of Joseph's mettle.

"Yes, I'm right behind you," Joseph said. "If we go over just behind the first attack, we can look like stretcher bearers. Attract less attention, and go as far forward as possible."

"Won't fool anyone for long," Morel replied over his shoulder. "But maybe by the time they realize it we'll be through. Just hope they don't take us for deserters."

"Deserters usually go the other way," Joseph pointed out. "That's what makes Geddes clever."

"He's a clever bastard, all right," Morel agreed dourly, his voice low in the darkness in spite of the guns in the distance. He did not add anything more, and they went the rest of the way in silence, dropping down the slight slope toward the field dressing station a thousand yards away.

They curved around it, keeping as far away from the light as possible. Joseph, with his priest's collar, did not need to account for his presence. For Morel it was harder. He had no rifle, only the revolver.

All around them were French soldiers, their outlines in the near dark little different from the men of the Cambridgeshires: helmets smooth, the occasional peaked cap, rifles stark. Their voices were muted, a little harsh with tension. Many smoked and the smell of Gauloises was different from Woodbine, but the long, slightly sour jokes were similar: self-mocking, the laughter quick.

There was coffee in their own version of a Dixie can. It was offered generously and both Joseph and Morel took it. It was bitter as gall.

A little over an hour later the order was given to advance, and without guns they rose with the other men and charged forward. Like the Ypres Salient with which Joseph was familiar, no-man's-land was desolate, but drier than the thick Flanders clay. There was the same greasy film of chemical residue from shelling. The earth was strewn with the wreckage of guns and half-sunken vehicles. The same stench of decaying corpses filled the nose and mouth. Drowned men, bloated and inhuman, rose to the surface of water-filled craters when they were disturbed.

They moved forward as fast as possible, struggling in the mud, crouching low to avoid the return fire of the enemy. Star shells lit the sky, rose high and bright, then faded away again. The noise of guns was everywhere, and now and then the dull *whoomph* as a shell sent earth and mud flying up only to fall, crushing and burying everything it landed on.

There was a surge forward again. There were men running all around Joseph, bent forward, flailing in the mud. Every now and then one would stumble and fall. Sometimes they got up again, sometimes not. Instinct and long habit made him want to go back and see if he could help. Once he stopped and Morel lunged at him, half dragging him forward, all but wrenching his arm out of its socket.

They were far closer to the Germans now. When the flares went up they were clearly visible running and firing. Joseph realized with sudden, stomach-jarring horror that in a few moments he would be fighting for his life. He would have to kill or be killed, and he had no idea how to do it. He was not a soldier, he was only playing at it—wearing the uniform, eating the food, sharing the grief and the hardship, but never doing the fighting, never seeing the purpose for which a soldier lived and died.

Ahead of him a figure stumbled and fell forward into the mud. Automatically Joseph stopped and knelt beside him, almost tripping Morel in the process.

"Are you hurt?" Joseph shouted in French at the man on the ground. He tried to turn the man to see, and realized his chest was torn away.

"Come on!" Morel lunged at him to pull him up.

Joseph tore the rifle out of the dead man's hands. *"Merci, mon brave!"* he said briefly. He took the ammunition belt as well, putting it on with clumsy fingers as he stood up again. *"Pardon,"* he added.

"Get on with it!" Morel yelled at him. "We've got more pressing things to do than get shot or bayoneted here. We've got to get that son of a bitch back and clear the rest of us!"

Joseph moved forward, following on Morel's heels. He had grown up in the country. He had no pleasure in shooting, but he knew how. He could understand overwhelmingly the ordinary young soldier's desire to aim wide rather than at a living man.

The next moment they were almost at the German trenches. The noise was indescribable: gunfire, the scream of shells and the roar of explosions, shrapnel flying—all alternating between darkness and glare.

Suddenly there was a man in front of Joseph. He saw the light on the blade of bayonet and in trying to avoid it he slipped in the mud and staggered forward. It was all that saved him from having his stomach ripped open. Immediately there was someone else in front of him. He saw the high point in the center of the helmet, and lifted his rifle to fire. The man fell, but he did not know if it was he who had shot him, or someone else. There seemed to be gunfire everywhere.

He plowed forward, sliding into the trench and running along it toward the supply line leading backward. He shouted in German at Morel to follow him.

The trench was deeper than he had expected, and drier. It startled him and he felt both ashamed and resentful. It was several minutes before he realized that he needed to change identity. Now he must be German. Being covered in mud was an advantage. He threw the gun away and looked around for a wounded man, any wounded man, to make it look as if he were helping.

Where the devil was Morel? There was no time to go back and look for him. What if in those last few seconds he had been shot? What if he was lying wounded, maybe bleeding to death just beyond the parapet, while Joseph was pretending to be a German soldier and running for the supply trench?

He turned back just in time to see Morel fall over the parapet and raise his gun to fire at him.

He froze. It was the final absurdity. They had made it, and were going to shoot each other! He started to laugh, crazily, idiotically.

Morel lowered the gun and came toward him. "Chaplain, are you all right?" he asked sharply.

"In German!" Joseph snapped back at him, using that language for the command. "Are you badly hurt?" he went on.

"I'm not . . ." Morel began, then as a German corporal came around the corner of the trench he doubled over and all but collapsed in Joseph's arms.

Joseph took his weight with difficulty. "It's all right, I've got you," he said in German. "I'll take you back to the dressing station. Here!" He half-lifted Morel over his shoulder and, ignoring the corporal, set out along the supply trench.

"Can you manage?" the corporal called after him.

"Yes, thank you," Joseph answered. "I'll carry him to the surgeon, then I'll be back."

Morel muttered something into his ear, but he did not catch enough of it to make sense.

Joseph kept his head down, easing Morel's weight higher—both because it was easier to walk, and because it allowed him to hide most of his face without arousing suspicion. He hurried, as if Morel were bleeding to death and he had to get him out of the range of fire and then attend to him.

He passed other people: stretcher bearers, medical aides, even another priest. There was enough noise from gunfire to make conversation difficult and everyone had their own duties. Even so, there were more offers of help, which he refused.

It was eerily like a mirror image of the British trenches he was so used to where he knew every yard, every bend and turn, every rise to stumble over or pothole to turn your ankle in. He knew every ledge and shallow dugout where a man could curl up and snatch an hour of sleep.

These trenches were deeper, drier. He passed a dugout with electric lights. It was harder going out into the darkness again. Morel was growing very heavy.

Suddenly there were two figures black in the gloom ahead of him, talking softly in German. Cigarette ends burned brightly for an instant, then disappeared.

Suddenly panic seized him and he slithered to a stop. Morel dropped over his shoulders to land in the mud, cursing roundly, but having remembered to do it in German.

"Bless you," Joseph replied. "Are you hurt?"

"Bruised to hell." Morel stood up slowly, wincing. "You might have warned me."

"Geddes," Joseph whispered, pulling Morel away from the men. "Which way?"

Morel looked around carefully. "There." He pointed forward. "He's getting away from the lines as fast as possible."

"Does he speak any German? He must, or he wouldn't dare come through."

"Picked up some, but he won't want to put it to the test this close to the firing line." Morel started along the trench again and Joseph caught up with him, moving swiftly now.

They kept out of sight as much as possible, but always as if priests ministering to the wounded. Reluctantly, Morel had gotten rid of his gun also. It was too dangerous to keep if he wanted to maintain his disguise.

By dawn they were two or three miles behind the lines. The light came early in a clear sky, which held only a few shreds of gray cloud, lit from beneath with pale brilliance. It showed a land shattered by war. Trees were splintered, their naked trunks leafless, some scarred black by fire. Farmhouses were roofless, walls fallen away. Fields were scoured up, crops ruined.

Joseph glanced at Morel but did not speak. It was time he thought more clearly. Now they were through the German lines they needed to plan, and first to deduce what Geddes would have done.

"Change clothes," Joseph said slowly, thinking aloud. "Eat. More important, drink. Water would do, anything clean. Need strength." He imagined Geddes giddy with freedom, but so tired he could barely stand, and knowing he was a fugitive who did not even speak the language and understood very little of it. "Might have to fight later," he went on. "Need a safe place to rest first. Exhausted now, and need to plan."

Morel was staring at him, frowning. "We have to find Geddes," he said awkwardly, his face twisted with sudden and startling pity, so deep it gave him pain.

Joseph saw it and it took him by surprise. Morel had misunderstood, thinking he was speaking of himself. The pity was for him, and perhaps for what he had once been, in another age, in Cambridge. He realized something would be broken between them if he said the wrong thing now. The emotion must be acknowledged, then put away as if it had never happened. He looked over toward the fields and the road, away from Morel's eyes. "You know him better than I do," he went on, as if considering deeply. "What do you think would be his first priority?"

Morel answered after only a moment's hesitation, and he kept his voice very nearly expressionless, as if he had known what Joseph meant from the beginning. "As far from the lines as possible," he said, relief making his voice a little high. "He's not a coward, but he wouldn't look for trouble. He's strong. He grew up in the country. If any man knows how to survive on the land, he does."

Joseph turned to look at him for a moment, then at the fields again.

"I know." Morel lowered his voice, almost as if in the presence of the dead. "It looks pretty bad, doesn't it? I should think if there's anything to eat in that, the locals will have had it. Turnips, wild berries, even roots, nettles. God! What a . . ." His voice caught. "I don't know. I haven't got a word for it. *Tragedy* doesn't seem big enough." He pushed his hands into his pockets. "If one man with the potential to be great is brought to his knees by a single weakness, we call it tragedy. We haven't got a word for an entire continent committing suicide."

"It's mutilation, not death yet," Joseph said softly, willing himself to believe it.

"Isn't it?" There was little hope in Morel's face.

Joseph started forward. "Let's see if anyone's encountered Geddes."

They walked in silence for more than a mile. They passed only one person: an ancient man leading a plow horse, a dog at his heels.

Then Joseph picked up the conversation. "What are we going to say? I should be able to make them believe I'm a priest. And that I'm nearly forty. They'll believe I'm that old."

Morel gave him a wry look. He was in his mid-twenties, but he looked gaunt and there were deep lines in his face. "Or more," he said drily. "But so are plenty of fighting men. I'd better think of something, and before we reach that farm." He gestured toward a group of buildings perhaps half a mile away. One side was black from fire.

"The simplest is best," Joseph answered, having already given the matter some consideration. "You are a priest also."

"What happened to my collar?" Morel asked the obvious. "German priests wear them, too."

"Swiss," Joseph corrected him. "Your accent isn't good enough for a native. You were helping someone and got blood all over it. You could wash yourself, but your collar and tunic were ruined. Don't forget the tunic, nobody gets blood only on their collar. They'll know you're lying. Another tunic is no problem from a dead man, but he wouldn't have a priest's collar. You know enough from your prewar studies of biblical languages to pass as long as you don't try to conduct a service."

Morel smiled. "You lie better than I expected."

"Thank you!" Joseph said sarcastically. "Geddes won't get away with that. So what would you do in his place?"

The farm was only a hundred yards away now. It was dilapidated, mended with old boards and clearly whatever had come to hand. There obviously had been no glass to replace the shattered windows, and perhaps no putty either. It must take either courage or desperation for the inhabitants to have remained here.

"He doesn't have more than a few words of German," Morel said dubiously. "But he's a fly bastard. He'll have thought of something."

"If you don't understand, best to pretend you can't hear," Joseph observed. "Maybe he'll pretend to be shell-shocked and deaf."

Morel looked at him with a flash of respect, but he said nothing. They were at the entrance to the farmyard. An elderly woman was putting out kitchen scraps for a few scrawny chickens. She was raw-boned and thin, her face seamed with grief. She looked up at them with alarm.

Joseph smiled at her. "Bless you, mother," he said quietly in German. "Can you spare us a little clean water to drink?"

She saw his collar, and the fear melted out of her eyes. Joseph was ashamed at the ease of the deception. "Of course," she answered him, only glancing at Morel. "And food? Are you hungry?" That was a gracious formality. Of course they were hungry. Everyone was hungry.

Joseph hesitated. Which was worse—to take her food or to insult her by implying that she had too little to give away?

"Come," she directed, and led them into the farmhouse kitchen. It was stone-floored, with heavy wooden rafters across the ceiling from which in better times there would have been a flitch of bacon and strings of onions, as well as the few dried herbs there were now. Being late August there was no need to heat the room, and she had allowed all but the embers to go out in the big black range. She had probably been going to eat whatever she had cold. Now she opened up the door of the range and prepared to put a small piece of wood inside.

"It is hot walking," Joseph said quickly. "Pastor Morel and I would both be grateful for cold water, if that is possible? My name is Josef . . ."—he picked the first name that came into his head—". . . Bauer."

She introduced herself shyly and then turned her attention to cutting dark rye bread into slices and finding a small portion of cheese and half an onion. She served it carefully on polished plates, and with glasses of cold water, presumably from the well. They were far enough back from the battle line for the water to be unpolluted.

Joseph began the conversation by explaining their presence. He said they were looking for a young man, a parishioner in peacetime, who was badly shell-shocked and who had run away, terrified. They were afraid if they did not find him he might be shot as a deserter, but since the incident he had been deaf and would not understand. Had she seen such a young man pass this way?

She said she had not seen him herself, but her neighbor three miles to the south had mentioned just such a man to her only yesterday. They thanked her profusely and took their leave. She had given them directions to the nearest village, and then to the small town beyond. She felt certain that anyone in the young man's position would head in that direction, hoping to hide and find shelter and possibly food before making his way home.

They thanked her and left.

They passed munitions and supply columns going toward the front, men on foot going back from leave and brief recovery after minor injuries, and raw recruits going to join the front. Most of these last were painfully young and their faces soft with the last remnants of childhood. Now they were struggling to mask fear and honor their commitment, and their families' faith in them. Many would already have lost fathers and older brothers.

"Jesus wept!" Morel said under his breath. "That blind boy on the right looked just like Snowy Nunn! What the hell are we doing here, Chaplain? What are we doing anywhere except at home?"

Joseph did not bother answering. Platitudes were no use anyway, and there was nothing else to offer but words that had all been said before.

They found shelter for the night in someone's byre. Even though it was dry, clean, and perfectly comfortable, the owner apologized, quite unnecessarily. The next morning they were offered a kind of gruel for breakfast. They ate it gratefully and without asking what was in it. Everyone they saw was hungry, frightened, trying hard to hang on to some dignity and a shred of hope.

Morel knew nothing of the Peacemaker, and for a few moments Joseph was overcome with the longing to talk to Matthew, to try to explain why looking at this land, these people, he could understand the dreams and the pain that had driven a man to want peace at any price. The world in which right and wrong had seemed so obvious was gone like a bubble grasped at by a hand, disappeared in an instant.

But he could not say as much to Morel. Morel needed him to be certain of at least something—therefore he must seem so.

Finally it was Morel who broke the silence. "Will you go back to St. John's?" he asked, staring straight ahead, avoiding Joseph's eyes.

Joseph was appalled. Is that what Morel thought of him, that he would go back to the same old escape, exactly as if nothing had happened? Build himself another cocoon!

"I don't imagine there'll be much to go back to," he said a little sharply. "I can't see many people wanting to learn biblical languages in the aftermath of this, can you?"

"They have their uses," Morel said with a frown. "Perhaps if we'd studied the past a little more diligently we'd have seen further into the future."

"That's a leisure pursuit," Joseph said. "I don't think we'll have much leisure in the years after the war. It isn't going to be the same."

"*Nothing's* going to be the same," Morel agreed with intense earnestness. "Women are doing half the jobs men used to. A woman's life isn't defined by who she marries anymore. It won't go back to that, not now. Think of your sister."

Joseph knew he meant Judith, but even Hannah was changed. All over Europe there were women who had learned to manage alone, to find courage and learn skills that had not been imagined before the war.

"You can't turn time backward," he said aloud.

"Good God, no!" Morel was suddenly savage. "Not in anything! I've fought beside men who used to wait on me at table or clean my boots. We can't and mustn't go back to that."

"We won't." Perhaps because Joseph had been home on leave so little, and then only to St. Giles, where social barriers were as old as the land and who owned and worked it, most of the change had made little impression on him. He had always known men like Barshey Gee, Snowy Nunn, and the others. He had played with men like them in the village school, knowing they would go on to work with their hands, and he would go up to university.

"There'll be a new government," Morel said thoughtfully. "If they don't care for the sick and disabled, then we'll force them to. There'll be legislation so it's every man's right to work, or if there's no work, then to be cared for, to have medicine, food, a roof over his head regardless, and over his children's. And the right to be taught because he has the brains to learn."

He was walking with his shoulders hunched, muscles tight. "Not out of charity, but because it's every man's right. We're quick enough to call him up to fight in the blood and filth of the trenches and to die for his country. And he came in the millions, without a question or a complaint. We owe, Chaplain! And by God, if I live through this, I'm going to do what I can. Not just for them, but for ourselves. What are we worth if we don't?"

It was a challenge. Joseph knew he meant it. It was for the men he led that he had been willing to mutiny against Northrup, and that was blazingly clear now. It was not one isolated anger or a personal rebellion. It was his nature, and he would be as true to it in civilian life as he was now. Joseph could imagine him in the future, a firebrand politician fighting for social justice, with a decency man to man that owed nothing to charity. The loyalty in the face of horror would not fade just because the guns were silent.

Nor would the suffering. Only a fool could imagine that. The dead would never return, nor would most of the crippled or blinded ever be whole again.

Was Morel waiting for him to say what he would do? The silence within his own head demanded it. There was only one decent answer: to go back into an active ministry, if there was one that would have him. What faith would there be after this? Millions would be desperate for help, comfort, and hope in the future, a belief that there was meaning to the ruin of so much. But would they look to God for it? Or would the Church seem as much an anachronism swallowed in the past as the golden afternoons of cricket and tea on the lawn in that last gilded summer of 1914?

And could he do it alone, without a wife to encourage him, explain the village gossip, the relationships he did not even see, to pick up his mistakes and oversights, simply to believe in him?

Joseph had no answer for himself, never mind for Morel. "In any event I'll not go back to St. John's."

"Didn't think you would." Morel smiled.

It was the second night, after a gaudy sunset painted across the southwestern sky, that they arrived at the bombed-out part of a small town where they hoped to find Geddes. They were moving carefully, aware that he was a fugitive and although he would not expect them, he would be wary. He spoke little German and knew he was in enemy territory, and a hunted man.

For their own safety they had long ago discarded their French rifles, and even Morel's British Army revolver. As priests they had no justification for carrying them, much less for using them. Geddes, on the other hand, would certainly have armed himself with a German pistol to go with his masquerade as a German soldier.

There was little light in the sky and it was several moments before

Morel was even certain that the man they had spotted was Geddes. He waited, watching as the man looked one way then the other, preparing to settle himself for a brief rest. His face was haggard, stubble growth on his cheeks. He could easily have been what he pretended: shell-shocked, exhausted, terrified because he could not hear.

Deliberately Morel tapped his boot on the stone lintel of what was left of the house. The man spun around, facing the last of the light from the fading west. He saw only Morel's outline in the archless doorway. There was a second when he was uncertain what to do. His movement had betrayed that he could hear. That ruse was lost to him. He could not recognize Morel, who was deliberately standing with his back to the light, and one hand near his hip where a gun would have been—had he still had one.

Joseph was at the far side, closer to Geddes. When he saw Morel nod, he moved to stand close enough to Geddes that he could push a small piece of wood into his side, like the barrel of a gun. "Don't move, Geddes," he said quietly. "I'd rather deal with you alive, but if need be, dead will serve."

Geddes froze. He might not have known Joseph's voice, but the fact that he had spoken to him in English was sufficient.

Morel strode forward and took the piece of wood. "Thank you," he said easily. "Now I think we should all start off home while it's still dark. It's a long hike. But as long as we make the lines before dawn, we have as good a chance as we'll get."

"I'm not going anywhere," Geddes said flatly. "Shoot me if you want to."

Morel was not in the least perturbed. "Actually I do rather want to," he said quite lightly. "If you hadn't shot and killed Northrup, we wouldn't all have this present spot of bother. What the hell did you do that for? We could have made our point without hurting him."

"Maybe you could," Geddes said sullenly. "What about the poor bloody soldiers he was going to order into the next stupid piece of action? Wouldn't be you, would it, Major! Your skin's safe."

"Not now, it isn't," Morel answered. "But a little testimony from you would help."

Geddes sat down deliberately. "Too bad." His sneer was visible in the half-light. "Because I'm staying here. Shoot me, if that's what you want. It won't get you anything—no testimony, no defense. Please yourself."

"I wasn't thinking of shooting you to death," Morel told him. "Something rather more painful, but not fatal—at least not yet."

Geddes was motionless. When he spoke, his voice wobbled a little. "You wouldn't . . ."

"The Chaplain might not," Morel admitted. "But I would. The way I see it, Geddes, it's your life or mine. And not only mine, but Cavan's and all the others'. Put like that, and you bloody bet I would!"

"If you get me back, what makes you think I'll tell the truth?" Geddes stayed where he was, but there was no ease in his body now. His back was stiff and the muscles were corded in his neck. "I could say it was you! More than that, I could tell them how we got out of that farmhouse." His smile widened a little. "I could tell them all about that nice V.A.D. driver who rescued us and her Yank friend. Do you want to see them shot, too? And make no mistake, they would be. Can't have V.A.D.s deciding who faces court-martial and who doesn't!" He turned slowly to peer at Joseph in the near dark. "Isn't that right, Chaplain? You'd better go while you can. You're in enemy territory!"

Did he know Judith was Joseph's sister? Probably. The enormity of the situation washed over Joseph like a cold tide. What had he been thinking to imagine they could get Geddes home and that he would simply confess rather than take as many people down with him as he could? He was desperate—a murderer, a mutineer, and now a deserter as well. He had nothing to lose. If he were to survive at all, it would have to be this side of the lines.

"Maybe you can't see it in this light," Joseph said quietly, hating doing it. "But we are dressed as Swiss priests. We both speak German. You don't, and you are in German uniform. Who do you think the Germans will believe if we're caught?"

Morel did not move. Geddes sat still on the floor.

Outside, a car engine rumbled in the distance. They were not far from the road.

Geddes cleared his throat. "You wouldn't do that, Chaplain. Isn't that against your oath or something?"

"You're planning to let Cavan be shot for your crime if we don't get back, and to betray the V.A.D. who helped you if we do. What do you think, Geddes?" he asked.

"You tell the Germans who I am, I'll tell them who you are," Geddes replied, sitting a little more upright.

The red in the wash was fading to pink and the shadows were impenetrable.

Joseph changed direction. "Why did you kill Northrup, anyway? You've made it very clear you don't give a damn about the lives of your fellows, so it can't be that, which is almost the only thing that would be understandable. What is it? Money? Hate? Stupidity?"

"Because he deserved it!" Geddes snarled. "He was an arrogant, incompetent fool as an officer, and he wouldn't listen to anyone. Always had to do it his way, even if it cost other men's lives." He was facing Joseph now, ignoring Morel. "But I know more about him than you do. Scare the hell out of him, he still wouldn't have learned." He jerked his arm toward Morel. "They all thought you could talk sense into him. I know better. He was born that way. His father thought the sun shone out of his ass, indulged him rotten, let him do any damn thing he wanted. Lorded it over the rest of the village, ran up debts, then when he hadn't the guts to admit it to his father, lied in his teeth."

Joseph did not interrupt. Geddes's voice had the bitter ring of truth— at least the truth as he saw it and felt it burning like acid inside him.

"He ruined my father that way," Geddes went on. "My father trusted him, the more fool he. I could've told him Northrup was a liar and a coward, but he wouldn't hear ill of the old general's son. Cost him his house. Our house!"

"So Northrup dies a hero, shot by mutineers, and Cavan goes to the firing squad for it," Joseph said with equal bitterness. "Who was it you said was the fool?"

Geddes was silent.

"You'll not make it here," Joseph went on. "You'll starve, if they don't shoot you as a spy first. Nobody likes spies. They might question you a bit first, to see what you can tell them about our positions. Or is that what you're going to bargain with, betraying your regiment?"

Geddes swore viciously.

"Then they'll shoot you," Joseph went on. "They don't regard traitors any more highly than we do. You can come back to Passchendaele and at least tell your story."

"If you come back you'll get revenge," Morel added. "If you stay here, you'll get nothing at all. Although actually I'm not going to let you stay here anyway." Without warning he walked forward and raised his arm. He gave Geddes a hard clip on the side of the head with the butt of the gun, and Geddes crumpled over without a sound. "Do you really want to take him back?" Morel asked quietly. "On the chance that he could still betray the V.A.D. who let us out? It was your sister, you know? Maybe you didn't realize that?"

"Yes, I know," Joseph replied. It would be ridiculous to deny it now. "Anyone looking into it could prove it pretty easily. But we're not going to shoot Geddes. We're going to get him back to the lines, and then through them."

"How?" Morel asked. "He's out cold now. Who knows what he'll say when he comes around again, but whatever it is, it'll be in English, because that's all he knows."

"Then we'll have to see that he doesn't say anything," Joseph replied.

"We'll take him as a wounded man. We're priests. That's reasonable. We'll be heroes. Who knows—they might even help us. We'll tie his head and face up, with a gag underneath the bandages, so he can't speak. Cut him a little so there's blood. Just hope to hell that whoever helps us isn't a surgeon!"

"We can't carry him that far," Morel pointed out reasonably. "We've come four or five miles at least!"

"If we go back on the road we'll find some debris. With luck, something with wheels. We can cannibalize it and make a carriage for him."

"I realize how little I knew you at Cambridge," Morel said drily. "I was a child!"

"We all were," Joseph replied. "Let's tie him up first. We don't know how soon he'll come around."

They used Geddes's own shirt to bind him for lack of anything better. They slit it with the knife he had and tore it into strips. It would be enough to hold him until they found better. Then they took turns carrying him as far as the road. He was a young man, heavy-boned and well muscled although any surplus flesh had long since gone, and he was dead weight. In fact, twice Joseph was anxious enough about him to stop and make sure he was still breathing. He was not certain how hard Morel had hit him.

They had to carry him another laborious half mile along the road before they came to a car that had been blown to bits. But no matter how they tried to imagine it, there seemed no way to take any of it apart. Reluctantly they abandoned it and again began the arduous task of carrying him.

They were still three or four miles from the nearest trenches when they were passed by a couple of soldiers who had apparently become separated from a relief column. It was a summer night, cloudless with a three-quarter moon, and light enough for Joseph to see how gaunt they were. He judged them to be veterans who had been wounded, and sent back too soon out of desperation. He had seen the same in the British ranks. In so many ways this was a mirror image of home. It tore at him with a familiarity, an acute understanding he would rather not have had.

The two men stopped. Neither looked strong enough to help carry Geddes, for which Joseph was grateful. Geddes was going home to face trial. He would never fight again, but still it would be one deceit too far.

"Looking for the nearest field station?" the taller one asked.

"Yes," Joseph replied. "Not sure how bad he is."

Geddes must have been conscious. He started to wriggle and become extremely awkward to hold. Had they been alone Joseph would have threatened to drop him, and done it. Geddes was trying to shout.

"He's in a lot of pain," Morel offered. "We're looking for something to wheel him on, if we can find anything."

"There's bound to be something with wheels," the shorter man said hopefully. "Even something broken might do. We could fix it to take the weight. He's nothing like as heavy as field artillery."

"Nothing like as useful, either," Morel said under his breath.

They walked together, alternating Geddes's body from one to another. The Germans insisted on taking their turn, and there was no way to refuse them without offense.

They had gone another half mile when they came to a pony cart at the side of the road. One wheel was blown to bits and what was left of the pony's carcass was still between the shafts. They put Geddes down, Joseph adjusting the gag to make sure it was not working loose, and also retightening the binding around his body so it was less obviously a restraint and rather more like a bandage.

The other three undid the harness and lifted the broken trap off, then hauled it up onto the road. It sat sideways because of the missing wheel.

"Got to find another wheel for it," Morel said thoughtfully. "Even one a different size would be better than nothing. Pity we have no tools. It won't be so easy. Have to make do with lashing things together. Still, not far to go."

The Germans had introduced themselves as Kretschmer and Wolff. Wolff and Morel now wandered off to see what they could find. Joseph and Kretschmer set about getting the three good wheels clean from the rubbish and making sure they could turn as freely as possible.

Wolff reappeared with a small wheel from a barrow of some sort, and Morel had a length of rope and a short piece of chain. Using everything, and considerable ingenuity, they lashed together a fourth leg for the cart, with the wheel on the end. It still did not make the height exactly, but it was a great help. Pleased with themselves, they laid Geddes on it as comfortably as possible, and set off on the road, taking turns, two at a time, carrying the shafts. The wheels squeaked appallingly.

"Here," Kretschmer said cheerfully, digging into his pocket and bringing out a small bottle. "Have some schnapps." He offered it to Joseph.

Joseph thanked him and took a mouthful. It felt as if a fire had exploded in his stomach. He was sure he could belch flame. Coughing hard, he thanked Kretschmer and passed it on to Morel, who took it rather more easily, then offered it to Wolff.

A mile later, after a couple more changes of shift as to who was pulling, they passed the schnapps around again. Joseph realized with a smile that they were marching in time to the squeaking of the wheels. The last shreds of cloud had gone and the moonlight shone pale on the cratered road, making black skeletons of the few shattered vehicles and broken trees. In the distance they could make out the standing walls of a burned house.

Wolff began to sing a drinking song. His voice was light and pleasant. Joseph remembered a little of the tune from his visits before the war, and he joined in.

An ambulance passed them going back, and a munitions supply convoy passed going forward to the lines.

They found a second song, and a third. There were still at least two miles farther to go. Joseph started to worry about how they were going to explain leaving these two men who in some absurd way had become friends. The last drop of schnapps was gone and none of them had any food. The squeaking of the wheels was incessant, and they were all unquestionably a little drunk.

Wolff began to sing again, this time in English, and they all joined in.

"There's a long, long trail a-winding, into the land of my dreams,

"Where the nightingales are singing and a white moon beams . . ."

They went through all the verses, then began again. The three-quarter moon lit the road, but the only sound apart from their voices was the squeaking of the wheels, and the guns roaring a couple of miles ahead. The odors of bodily waste and putrefying flesh were already strong, and in the distance there was the flash of red and yellow mortar fire.

Joseph had no idea how they would get through the lines, other than the same way as they had come. Additionally, they would have to untie Geddes so he could run. But first they would have to find a way of parting from Kretschmer and Wolff, who with luck, would have a specific place to report.

But for this moment, his feet hurt, and his hands were blistered from holding the cart. His back and his legs ached and he was so hungry he could have eaten a raw turnip with pleasure, if he could have found one. But he was light-headed with schnapps, singing in the moonlight, and there was a kind of happiness in it that was desperately, passionately real.

CHAPTER

TWELVE

*M*ason returned to London with a heavy sense of oppression. His mind should have been crowded with thoughts of the slaughter at Passchendaele and the impending farce of the court-martial of Cavan, the only one of the twelve men who was actually in custody.

But all the way across the Channel, and then standing crowded in the troop train from Dover to London, jostled and jolted, kept upright largely by the press of other men's bodies around him, he felt a deep and abiding misery that was almost paralyzing. There seemed no light in his inner landscape at all. Had he really imagined the court-martial would solve anything?

Rationally, perhaps the idiocy of it all, the casualty toll climbing toward a quarter million men for the gaining of one shattered town, would have been enough to make sane men call a halt to it, at whatever cost, on whatever terms. But was there any sanity left? No one looked at the whole monumental disaster. They all looked at their own little patch of it.

Perhaps it was too big for anyone to comprehend the ruin that stretched right from the Atlantic waves that swallowed men and ships off the battered shores of Britain right to the blood-soaked sands of Mesopotamia, to the snowbound graves of Russia. Europe was a charnel house. No one could count the millions of dead, let alone those maimed forever.

And yet Judith Reavley was prepared to risk her life to help eleven mutineers escape and flee to Switzerland, and Joseph was equally willing to risk his life to bring them back! In the scheme of things both actions were equally pointless, and just as likely to end in death.

Perhaps that was what hurt? Joseph had hardly any chance of succeeding, which—if he were a logical man—he would have known; but he wasn't logical! He was an idealist, a dreamer, seeing the world he wanted more clearly than the real one.

Mason wished he did not like him so much. He had wit and imagination, courage to the point of stupidity—no, actually beyond it. And compassion, again beyond sense. You could not argue about honor with him because he did not listen. He followed his own star, even though it was an illusion; beautiful, better than the truth, but a mirage. And when he reached the place where he thought it was, he was going to discover that there was nothing there. That was what Mason hated: the disillusion he knew had to come. No one would be able to help them. What does a man do when he climbs the vast heights, struggles his way upward to heaven, and when bleeding and exhausted he gets there and finds it empty?

He was furious with Joseph for being so vulnerable, and leaving people like Mason to be wounded by his pain.

The train jolted and threw him against the man beside him, knocking him off balance. He apologized. They stopped somewhere in a siding, crowded together, hot and exhausted, legs aching.

The minutes dragged by. He was impatient, although it made little difference when he reached London. He was going to see the Peacemaker, and he would be admitted whatever time he got there. He was going to report on the court-martial and the mood of the men. The Peacemaker would not be pleased. The court-martial was not only going to be absurd, it was going to appear so. Might someone step in and prevent it even now? Was there anyone who could? If so, it would be obvious they had, and that would be absurd also.

The train started to move, lurching with a clang of couplings, then stopped again. Someone swore under his breath. There was another lurch and bang, and another. Then slowly they picked up speed.

Mason was lying to himself: It was not really the thought of Joseph that weighed him down, it was Judith. He could remember the touch of her lips, and her eyes as she looked at him when he drew away at last. He wanted to hold that forever, and he knew he was losing it already. Even if no one ever betrayed the fact that it was she and the American volunteer driver who had rescued the mutineers, she had been willing to do it. That was the division between them that was uncrossable. She was impulsive, quixotic, rushing in like a fool to do something noble without thinking of the inevitable result.

He should force himself not to care. He would only be hurt. She was not going to change. Possibly she was not even going to live through the war! That had always been a risk. Ambulance drivers did get killed, of course they did! Anyone on the battlefront ran that risk.

Why did that thought all but make him sick with despair? She was not part of his life. They had no commitment to each other. They had met only a few times, shared intense emotions of terror and hope and pity, laughed too much, to the edge of weeping, and kissed just once.

He was lying to himself again. She was part of his dreams, of the quiet places inside him that fed his strength, the things for which he struggled and climbed to his feet when he fell, the thing that gave the journey a purpose, a distinction, a place to belong.

The train was moving swiftly now, swaying with a kind of rhythm, everyone so close they held each other up, and all lost in their own thoughts.

How had he allowed himself to do something so stupid? Why could he not have chosen any of a dozen pretty, intelligent, and reasonable girls he had known? Because to persuade himself that he cared for any of them was one lie he could not get away with. There are parts of a man that will accept only the truth.

The train slowed going over the bridge, and finally pulled into Waterloo. They spilled out onto the platform—stiff, dirty, their bodies aching and so tired no one spoke. Mason pushed his way to the entrance to find a taxi, but there was a queue so long it would take hours, and many of the men standing there had injuries far worse than the few cuts and bruises he had. He went instead to the underground train, and an hour later was walking along Marchmont Street in the warm evening air. He passed a newspaper seller and ignored him. Their chief correspondent on the Western Front was a man he knew well. He could imagine what he would make of the court-martial story, and he would be bound to get it. He would make Morel look like a traitor, and Joseph Reavley like a fool.

He reached the Peacemaker's home and was let in by the same manservant as always, and received in the upstairs sitting room. A moment later he was joined by the Peacemaker. He was wearing a smoking jacket, as if possibly he had been reading a little while, having a last cup of tea, or whisky and soda, before going to bed.

"You look tired," he said sympathetically. "Rough crossing?" He gestured to Mason to sit down. He had already asked the manservant for sandwiches and fresh tea.

Mason sank into the familiar chair. "No. Calm as a millpond," he replied. "But no room to sit on the train. Stood all the way from Dover. Hardly room to lift your elbows." He was not looking forward to reporting on the state of the court-martial. He did so briefly, almost tersely, to get it over with.

"What a mess," the Peacemaker said with little expression, surprising Mason by his control. "I assume someone helped the mutineers escape? Any idea who?"

"None at all," Mason lied without compunction. "Could have been any of a thousand people. Nobody wants this court-martial to go ahead."

"Any chance of capturing the escaped men?"

"One in a thousand, maybe," Mason said, leaning back in his chair. "But I can't see that it would improve matters. Just increase the chances of someone saying who helped them." He spoke honestly, then felt the pain grip his heart and knot in his belly as he thought of Judith in the dock beside Cavan. It was a sense of loneliness as if the lights had gone out in the world, or in his part of it. But it was also jealousy. Judith admired Cavan, and surely he must admire her, too. They would stand side by side, ready to be crucified for loyalty to the men they served. Everyone else was shut out, especially someone like Mason who thought the whole thing was a pointless sacrifice.

He looked across at the Peacemaker, expecting his reaction to be one of fury, perhaps most of all for the waste of good men of just the kind of nobility, courage, and loyalty he himself so valued. But the Peacemaker was smiling bleakly, his eyes bright. He saw what Mason was describing, understood the words if not the heart of it, and was ready to move on to the thoughts that obviously took precedence with him. It was as if he were not really even surprised.

"Thank you," he said aloud, crossing his legs comfortably. "It is exactly as you say: a final piece of idiocy. I wish we could prevent it, but I know of no way. I believe they are sending Faulkner to prosecute, and he will carry it to the last degree. A narrow man full of fears. He worships the letter of the law, because he has neither the courage nor the imagination to see the spirit behind it."

Mason remained silent, not trusting himself to speak. His mind raced, skittering around, crashing into ideas in his search to think of anything at all he could say or do that could save Judith, or even save Cavan! Would he save Cavan, for her, knowing that it would exclude him forever?

That was a stupid and crassly sentimental thought. There was no *forever*. The darkness had begun in August 1914, and now, three years later, it was almost complete.

"I have more news from Russia," the Peacemaker was saying. He was leaning forward again in his chair, fixing Mason with the intensity of his eyes. "They are on the brink of a real revolution! Not the halfhearted affair of Kerensky and his Mensheviks, but one that will change everything, sweep away all trace of the old regime. They will get rid of the tsar and all his family forever." He made a short, jerky movement with his long hand. "Lenin is back, and he and Trotsky will lead it. It will be violent at first; there is no alternative." His face pinched for a moment. "There will be many deaths, because the old guard is strong—they have been there for centuries and the corruption runs deep. No one gives up power unless they are forced to." The light came back into his face. "But think of the future, Mason! Think of all that the Bolsheviks can do with their passion and ideals. A new order, started from the beginning! Unity, equality, an end to war."

"It will drown Russia in blood." Mason was appalled. He should have guarded his speech. He knew his protest was pointless, or—worse than that—dangerous, but the words were out in spite of himself.

"No, it won't!" the Peacemaker argued, too excited to be angry. "It will be violent to begin with, of course it will. The tsar had warning after warning but he took no notice. What else can they do, Mason? As long as the Romanovs are alive there will always be the old nobility, the property owners, the oppressors who will try to return. They are of the old aristocracy of privilege and violence who know no social justice. They use the ordinary man as cannon fodder in a war the people of Russia have no interest in. It must stop! It is not the tsar or his supporters who are dying out there in the bitter snows of the Eastern Front—it is the ordinary man! It is the family of the ordinary man that is starving at home."

He leaned farther forward. "Well, no more. The people will rise. They will refuse to fight. Mason, we are at the beginning of the end. By Christmas there will be peace in Europe. We can begin to rebuild, not just materially but socially as well." His face was alight, his eyes burning.

It was a dream again. Mason had a sudden terror that he was being swept along in a fantasy in which everyone else believed, and only he could see the bitter truth. Individual ambitions would always play their part; men would build on towering visions and subsequently forget the details that would undo them.

The Peacemaker had lost sight of the individual in his sweeping plan, as if one man's ideas could command the loyalty of millions, and their obedience.

For the first time Mason began to wonder if the Peacemaker was mad. No man had the power to do what he dreamed, and no man should.

Perhaps he had seen too many dead and become tired, his own passion exhausted. Judith would hate everything the Peacemaker had said. She would tell him it had nothing to do with reality, the way people actually were.

The Peacemaker would say her sight was too small, too ordinary.

She would say that his was too far from the human heart to see into it: too overweening, exercising not leadership but dominion.

"Mason!" the Peacemaker said sharply. "It is the beginning of the end! Can't you see that? Peace! There need never be this abomination of war again!"

"Yes, sir," Mason said a little flatly. "Well, not here anyway."

The Peacemaker was not to have his spirits damped. "You're tired. Go home and sleep. Write your article. Then go back to Passchendaele. Attend the court-martial and write the truth about it. The men deserve that. Cavan deserves it."

Joseph and Morel, with Geddes in tow, made the crossing back through the German lines, over no-man's-land and then through the French lines. They had great difficulty but achieved it in the same manner as they had crossed the other way: running, crawling, scrambling the moment it was dark enough between the star shells. Perhaps they had been a little less frightened, thanks to the schnapps, and for the same reason also a little clumsier.

They had found parting from Kretschmer and Wolff had occurred naturally because the German soldiers had had to report to their units. In the darkness and the tension before an attack, other people's minds had been more preoccupied with what was to come than identifying individuals. Like the British and French armies, their regiments had also been decimated. The losses were staggering, and men were assigned anywhere just to fill in the numbers and make up a platoon or a brigade. There were more strangers than friends left. No one questioned Joseph or Morel closely, and the clerical disguise did the rest.

Getting through the French lines was more difficult. They were taken prisoner at the point of a rifle—in fact several rifles.

"We've got a German prisoner," Morel said immediately, in French, indicating Geddes, whose mouth and lower face were still bound. He was still in his stolen German uniform, so there was nothing to make the statement appear untrue.

The French lieutenant in command looked dubious, but he accepted the story, at least on the surface. Joseph was so covered in mud that his dog collar was all but invisible.

When they had been taken farther back to a dry dugout suitable for interrogation, they told the truth, more or less.

The French lieutenant shook his head. "I suppose you want to take him back to Ypres now?"

Joseph smiled. "Yes, please. If you can help it would be enormously appreciated."

The lieutenant shrugged. "Well, you can barely walk! And I don't suppose your prisoner is very keen. We'd better have somebody drive you." He rolled his eyes. *"Entente cordiale,"* he observed, making an elegant gesture of despair with his hands, but he was smiling. He might never admit it, but he obviously found it secretly rather entertaining. It was something different, and a story to tell.

He must know, just as Joseph did, and any other soldier anywhere would, that war is frequent terror, occasional hideous violence, sometimes terrible pain, a lot of exhaustion and discomfort and hunger, but it is mostly boredom. It is the comradeship, the laughter, the stories and bad jokes that make it bearable, the sharing of the glorious and the absurd, the dreams and memories, and the letters from home through which one clings to sanity.

Thus it was with the help of the French lieutenant, after a meager but well-cooked meal, and armed with a new stock of tall stories, they were driven the long way back to Passchendaele. They arrived the following day, with Geddes still bound but no longer gagged since there was no necessity for it.

They thanked the French driver profusely and offered him a tin of Maconachie's and a bar of decent chocolate, which he accepted reluctantly but with grace.

Before reporting to Colonel Hook, Joseph had a brief moment alone with Morel. There was a military police sergeant in the doorway; there would be no second chance to escape. He wanted to ask Morel what he intended to say about his original escape. Faulkner would ask, and if Morel refused to answer he would add to the original charge that of concealing the identity of his helpers who had committed a criminal act in aiding him.

It was a crime Joseph was guilty of as well.

Far more urgent, however, was the matter of what Geddes would say. It would have been pointless trying to persuade him not to betray Judith and Wil. He was already facing the firing squad. There was nothing they could offer him or threaten him with. It would depend upon what the other men said. There was a faint glimmer of hope that if they all stuck to the same story, it would be believed over Geddes's testimony. It would be suggested that he named Judith as accomplice out of revenge, because it was Joseph who had brought him back.

But he could say none of that now. He and Morel had traveled together, shared laughter and pain. Each man's survival had depended upon the other; but now Joseph was going to resume his duties, and Morel was facing court-martial and perhaps dishonor and death. Nothing was equal between them anymore.

"Thank you" was all Joseph could think of to say that was not condescending, false, and completely pointless. He offered his hand.

Morel took it, held it hard for a moment, then turned and walked over to the sergeant. Without looking back, he went out of the door.

Admiral Hall had given Matthew forty-eight hours before reporting back on Faulkner, and Matthew knew that they could afford no more. He toyed with the idea of simply asking Shearing why he had chosen him, but in spite of what Hall had told him of Shearing and his family, he still could not silence that last whisper of doubt. Sandwell's words stayed with him. Whatever he learned, it must be from his own investigation, his own sources. And it must be discreet.

But all the searching he was able to do swiftly and discreetly only confirmed that Faulkner was an extreme disciplinarian, rigid in his interpretation of the law, a man who seemed unfailingly to have pushed for the letter of the law above mercy. He had served all his career in England and had, so far as was known, never seen the battlefield or had the slightest knowledge of life in the trenches, let alone death in no-man's-land.

He seemed the worst possible choice to prosecute Cavan, Morel, and the others. If Faulkner was single and he had any weakness, or even any redeeming factors, whatever it was, Dermot Sandwell had not known of it. He believed Faulkner was invulnerable, and Shearing had agreed to him for precisely that reason.

Matthew had no time left, and now no alternative but to face Shearing.

As they sat facing each other in Shearing's office, Matthew began without apology or preamble. "Sir, I recently had a matter which I took directly to Admiral Hall. He gave me instruction to investigate it and report to him within forty-eight hours. That time is up today, and I have no satisfactory answer. I need to know if you have any knowledge on the subject."

Shearing put down his pen carefully and sat back, staring at Matthew. "I assume this is about your vast conspiracy again," he said slowly, his face tight and wary.

Matthew evaded the answer. "It is about Lieutenant Colonel Faulkner, sir," he said. "He is going to prosecute Cavan. And any of the other men, if they are found."

Shearing's eyes were cold. "I told you, Reavley, that matter is in hand. You are not to interfere with it. That is a direct order. If you disobey me, I shall have you transferred to the front—immediately. Do you understand me?"

Matthew felt the chill as if a window had been opened onto an ice storm. "Yes, sir. But I have been studying his past record..."

Shearing sat upright sharply. "Who gave you permission to do that? You could have jeopardized the whole court-martial! You—"

"Admiral Hall, sir," Matthew cut across him.

Shearing's eyes were like black stones. "Do you think me incompetent, Reavley? Or that I am involved in this conspiracy of yours?"

Matthew stared at him and felt guilty for the spark of pain he saw in Shearing's face. It took him by surprise and he found himself speechless.

Shearing breathed a faint sigh. "There is no good solution, Reavley. Faulkner is simply the best we have—"

"I don't see how," Matthew interrupted him bitterly. "He's—"

"I know what he is!" Shearing snapped. "If you think about it a little harder, use your brain rather than your emotions, you might see it yourself."

"He'll insist on the charge of mutiny and murder," Matthew said wretchedly. "General Northrup might have moderated it, to save his son's reputation, but from what everyone says of Faulkner, there isn't a cat in hell's chance he'll go for anything less than the full thing, and a firing squad—no matter what a rank injustice it is, who gets executed, or even what it does to the regiment, or even the whole damn Western Front! He's an obsessive, single-vision martinet." His anger and helplessness made him louder than he had intended.

"That is precisely what he is, and it is the single weakness that may, with great skill and luck, be turned against him." Shearing's voice was elaborately patient as he held up his hand, fingers stiff. "There are three possible verdicts: guilty of mutiny and murder, guilty of mutiny and manslaughter, or guilty of gross insubordination and accidental death— for all except the man who deliberately front-loaded the live round. He alone is guilty of murder."

"Faulkner will insist on mutiny and murder," Matthew interrupted him. "Even mutiny and manslaughter will get the firing squad. They might be able to delay it a while on appeal, but what use is that? The end is just as inevitable, and everyone knows it."

"Which is why there is no use finding a prosecution who will go for the middle charge," Shearing said grimly.

Matthew still saw no hope. "There's no way Faulkner will accept gross insubordination!"

Shearing's lips were drawn into a tight line. "Of course there isn't! He will insist on murder, and if we can get the right man to defend Cavan and the other men, he will force Faulkner to prove it, to the very last act and word, even thought, beyond any doubt at all, reasonable or unreasonable. He will hang on like a bulldog, until the arena is swimming in blood, but he won't let go."

Matthew was stunned.

Shearing's voice was very low. "It will destroy Howard Northrup's reputation, but for his father it will be like seeing him killed again. It will show the court exactly why Cavan and Morel and the others felt they had no choice whatever, no morally acceptable choice, but to take an action which they believed would save the lives of at least some of the men they led, and who trusted them, for whom the army had made them responsible."

At last Matthew understood. He breathed out very slowly. "It's a hell of a risk, sir."

"Can you think of something better?"

"No," Matthew admitted. "Have you got a military lawyer with the nerve to do that? And the knowledge of the front line?"

Shearing smiled with a bitter irony. "No. It's customary for an officer from the regiment to defend on lesser charges. I think the very best they can do is pick one of them this time. . . ."

Matthew was appalled. "Against Faulkner? His opponent will be crucified!"

There was a bright, hard light in Shearing's eyes. "It doesn't need a brilliant student of the law, Reavley. It needs a man of passion, courage, and undeviating loyalty, a man who knows the accused and what they have endured, and why. A man who will be prepared to sacrifice himself before he will stand by and allow an injustice to be done. A man whom the court will respect as one of their own."

Matthew could feel his heart pounding in the oppressive room with its still, hot air. "And you have such a man?"

"Naturally! He knows the case better than anyone else, and he believes in their moral innocence. Also, he does not know when he is beaten, so he will not give up."

"Joseph . . ."

"Precisely," Shearing agreed. "I have an excellent man there to brief him. Let's hope he does not get himself killed in the meantime!"

In Passchendaele the fighting wore on. A sense of foreboding filled the air they breathed, the clothes they wore, the food they ate, and darkened the vision, like the rain, everywhere. It was all hopeless, as if the final insanity had seized the world. Rescue was pointless. Whoever did not die today would die tomorrow, or the day after.

Colonel Hook sent for Joseph. It was late. As August moved into September, the nights were drawing in. Summer was fading.

"The court-martial is going ahead," Hook said gravely. "The preliminaries are tomorrow, the real stuff the day after."

Joseph had expected it. It was unrealistic to hope for anything different. All the arguments and pleas had been made and rejected. The desperate state of the battle had been argued, as had the morale of the army, the possible effect of such a trial and the verdict on the entire Western Front, and therefore on the war as a whole.

"Rubbish!" Faulkner had dismissed it. "We are winning the battle of Passchendaele," he had insisted. "The discipline of the entire army depends upon never, in any circumstances, being seen to allow mutiny and murder. If disgruntled men who think they know better than their officers can take the law into their own hands and commit murder and get away with it, then no officer will be safe from now on. It is impossible that you can be so stupid as not to see that. If we do not serve justice both when we wish to, and when we do not, then we serve nothing. The essence of justice is that personal feelings do not enter into it. Either it is impartial, or it is meaningless."

Alone with Hook, he was at a loss to know why he had called him to tell him no more than they already knew.

The briefest of smiles touched Hook's face. "I know you are already aware of that, Reavley. What you don't know is that it has been requested from London that you represent the accused men."

"Of course I shall be there," Joseph said quickly. "But it would be far better if their defense did not call me. Much of what I know I cannot testify to. Let Morel tell them about finding Geddes and bringing him back, and anything he said about Northrup and his father. He knows it all as well as I do."

Hook pushed his hand through his hair. "I have no intention of letting you testify, Reavley. I know perfectly well that you know who helped them escape. I have a damn good idea myself. I am not calling you as a witness. You are to defend them."

"What?" Joseph was horrified.

"You are to defend them," Hook repeated.

"Me? I have no experience—and no natural ability," Joseph protested. "I don't know the first thing about military law. They need an expert. In fact they need the best there is."

"No," Hook said wearily. "They need a man who believes in them, and doesn't know when to give up. They need a man who knows what it is to fight, and what our losses have been." The briefest flicker of amusement touched his eyes. "I would also prefer it if you were not called to testify. I'm sure you'd lie in your teeth rather than implicate . . . whoever it was who helped them escape." His gaze did not waver. "Even if it was a civilian, such as the V.A.D., for example, and not subject to military law, only ordinary imprisonment. They were not worried about betrayal of anyone.

Morel in particular thought you would lie, possibly hating doing it, but lie nevertheless."

"I must remember to thank him," Joseph said drily. "That doesn't alter the fact that I have no experience. Faulkner would make mincemeat of me."

"I don't think so," Hook told him. "But regardless of that, it is you they have chosen, and I agree with them. And London is satisfied."

"That's hardly enough!" Joseph exclaimed, desperation rising inside him, and a hard, stomach-twisting fear. He would fail! He would let them all down!

Hook did not flinch. "They're facing the firing squad, Reavley. They've a right to ask for whomever they wish. I'm assigning you, so you'd better go and prepare. You've got tonight and probably most of tomorrow. You've seen courts-martial before. You know the drill. There'll be people there to keep you straight on the law. If you're still on speaking terms with God, you'd better ask Him for a little help. You'll need it."

"Yes, sir." Joseph saluted a little clumsily, and walked out into the darkness wondering if he was actually still on speaking terms with God. He had once believed that he knew the truth of doctrine, and morality, and that he could argue it with conviction.

But that was a long time ago. Now he was confused, torn by emotion, and above all afraid. He stood in the mud and looked up at the enormity of the September sky, for once glittering with stars.

"Please help me" was all that came to his lips. "Father, please help me."

THIRTEEN

*J*oseph's mind was racing, and yet the words poured over his head uselessly. He was sitting in his own dugout with an army legal officer trying to help him understand the legal niceties of what he could do, or not do, in order to defend the twelve men. Outside in the distance the gunfire was sporadic, mostly sniper fire, but it was growing dark and the rain was starting again. In an hour or two some poor devils would be going over the top.

The air was heavy and close; it seemed to cling to the skin. The oil lamp on the table burned steadily with a small, yellow flame, casting highlights and shadows on the familiar objects, the few books, the picture of Dante, a tin of biscuits, the pen and paper.

They had been through the procedure three times. Joseph was feeling as if the whole trial and verdict were as inevitable as the tides of the sea, and anything he did would make as little difference as he would to them.

"Remember the difference between civilian and military law," Major Ward said urgently, leaning forward, elbows on his knees. "Civilian law has the right of the individual at the front, the first concern. Military law is at least as much about the good of the unit. You'll have soldiers in active service on the panel. The president will be a major general from a division just like this one, who's fought along the Ypres Salient since 1914, just as you have. Give him half a chance and he'll be on your side. Never forget that, Reavley, and you could save them."

Joseph rubbed his hand across his brow, pushing his hair back so hard it hurt. "Why on earth did they choose me? You know the law. You'd do a far better job. I'm a priest, an ordinary soldier!"

"Haven't you been listening?" Ward demanded, frustration and weariness sharpening his voice. "That is exactly why you might succeed! You don't need to know the law, man! You need to know the army, the trenches, the reality of death and loyalty and what it means to be part of a regiment."

Joseph wanted to believe him but he had no faith in his ability to overcome the unarguable facts of the law. The men were placing a trust in him that was born of faith and desperation, and possibly some hope he had given them falsely, and beyond his ability to live up to. He would have betrayed them as deeply as the whole war had. In his own way, he was as incompetent as Northrup, another man put into a job for which he had not the skills.

"Nobody wins them all," Ward said to him drily. "But you damn well fight them all!"

An ugly suspicion flashed into Joseph's mind that they had put him onto this case because they did not want one of their own to be seen to defend mutineers, and of course to fail.

"Yes, sir," he answered.

Joseph got little sleep. By the following day, when the court-martial proceedings were under way with the usual declarations, and the accused men's right to challenge all the officers was in progress, time had assumed the character of an infinitely slow nightmare.

There was a farcical element to sitting in this airless room in what was now September heat, and hearing all the prescribed questions put to each man as if somehow it were going to make any difference. As Ward had said, the president was major general Hardesty from a nearby section of the line, and the other officers were Colonel Apsted from the regiment immediately to the west, and Major Simmons from a regiment to the east. It would have been pointless to object to any of them, but the protocol had to be followed.

Throughout, Lieutenant Colonel Faulkner sat behind his table, backbone like a poker. His face was tense, only a tiny muscle twitching in his cheek betrayed the looseness of his hands in front of him as a calculated pose.

The twelve accused stood together. It was an unusual circumstance for there to be so many, but the prosecution had chosen deliberately not to divide them. To present one accusing another might allow an intimidated or overcompassionate president to say he could not choose between them. He could excuse all on the argument that it would be better for the army to let guilty men go free than to be seen to punish the innocent. But *innocent* was a word Joseph already knew Faulkner did not allow easily. He believed that the authorities hardly ever accused innocent men, and in this particular case the evidence was overwhelming.

Joseph felt the sweat trickle down his sides and soak into his tunic, and yet he was cold. He looked around the room. He must not avoid their eyes. Morel and Cavan were easy to distinguish at a glance because they were officers. The rest of the men were noncommissioned. Most of them had been in the army since late 1914 or early 1915. That alone made them worthy of some respect, especially from a man like Faulkner, who had never seen a shot fired in anger. He had never gone over the top at night, into the mud and darkness, knowing that the men facing you had guns as well, and the murderous shrapnel could tear a man's body in half and leave his head and chest a yard away from his legs, and his guts streaming across the ground.

Joseph forced his mind back to the present. These men had asked him for help, not pity. Anger only clouded his thinking.

The charges were being read out: mutiny and murder. He had known it would be, but it was still a crushing of ridiculous hope to hear them.

He looked around to see General Northrup. Had he really tried to get the charge reduced? Or had his grief and anger at the death of his son overridden everything else, and he had dismissed the ruin of his reputation?

Despite Joseph's sympathy for General Northrup, it was the sight of Morel that bit most deeply into his emotions. He could remember the youthful Morel arriving at Cambridge his first year. The man he was now—honed hard by mental and physical suffering, the isolation of leadership, the rigor of living with his own decisions—was not even foreshadowed in him then. That had been only five years ago, but when the world was still young.

Morel should have been graduating this year, and wondering what to do with his life! Instead he was standing in a farmhouse near Ypres expecting to face a firing squad of his own countrymen, because he had rebelled against what he believed passionately to be wrong. Was there any way on earth Joseph could make that argument in his defense?

Morel stood straight now, at attention as the charges were repeated.

The farmhouse room was full of men, and a few women from among the nurses and V.A.D. corps. The three officers were seated behind the wooden table. Joseph and Faulkner were at separate tables immediately in front.

Joseph still had only the barest idea what he was going to say. He was reluctant to think of departing from the truth on moral grounds, and in practical terms that course was far too dangerous. To be caught in even an evasion would destroy the only advantage he had, which was the hope of understanding. If they had any defense at all, then it was that their act had been driven by a moral necessity.

The preliminary formalities were over. Faulkner rose to his feet, but did not move from behind his table. He had a curious quality of stiffness that was apparent from the very beginning. He made no gestures with his hands nor did he even seem to alter the weight of his body from one foot to the other.

He called his first witness: the medical orderly who had initially examined Howard Northrup's body. The man was manifestly unhappy, but the facts were not contestable. Northrup had died as the result of a rifle bullet to the head. It had struck him through the brow. He had to have been facing forward at the time.

"Let me understand you clearly, Corporal Tredway," Faulkner said heavily. "Whoever fired the shot was standing in front of Major Northrup, looking straight at him?"

"Yes, sir." Tredway gulped. He had no room for evasion, although he would clearly like to have had.

"Head up?" Faulkner persisted. "Head down? Turning, ducking?"

"No, sir," Tredway said wretchedly.

"And you know this how?"

"Path of the bullet, sir. Straight through and out at the back, sir."

"And the distance the man with the gun stood from Major Northrup when he fired the shot?"

General Hardesty looked inquiringly at Joseph, but Joseph made no objection.

"The distance?" Faulkner repeated.

"Hard to say, sir," Tredway answered.

"Touching him? Fifty feet? Half a mile?" Faulkner raised his eyebrows.

"Most like fifty feet, sir."

"How do you know this, Corporal?"

" 'Cos o' the wound, sir. An' how far the bullet went through."

"And can you tell the kind of gun it was fired from? At least whether it was a handgun or a rifle? A British gun or a German one? Or French, perhaps?"

"We've got no French 'ere, sir," Tredway said tartly. "They're up farther to the east." There was clear contempt in his voice for Faulkner's ignorance. He was a man who shuffled papers, not one who fought.

"I was thinking of the gun itself, Corporal," Faulkner corrected him. "Not the nationality of the man who fired it."

There was a rustling in the room. Someone coughed.

Tredway flushed. "A rifle, sir."

"British?"

"Couldn't say, sir." His jaw set hard.

"A rifle, possibly British, fired at apparently fifty feet," Faulkner summarized. "Thank you, Corporal." He gestured to invite Joseph to ask his questions.

Joseph stood up. Now that the moment had come he felt a sort of calm hopelessness. "Corporal Tredway, your knowledge is impressive, although I imagine after three years' active service you have seen a great many wounds of all sorts? Rifle, revolver, pistol, shrapnel, shell splinters, even injuries caused by explosions, overturning gun carriages, panicking horses . . ."

Faulkner stared at him with mounting irritation.

Hardesty winced but did not interrupt. His expression suggested pity more than anger.

"Yes, Chaplain . . . I mean . . . Captain Reavley," Tredway said, frowning.

"Any way to tell if they are caused by accident or by malice, Corporal?" Joseph asked.

"No, sir," Tredway said, meeting Joseph's eyes squarely. There was a flicker in them, as if he might have thought of smiling. " 'Cept for horses panicking, like. That's almost always accident. They don't often do it maliciously. They're better than people, that way."

There was a slight ripple of laughter in the room.

Faulkner's face tightened.

"And gun carriages," Tredway added. "That's more likely accident, down to stupidity . . . sir. They don't have no malice neither."

Joseph preempted Faulkner. "But gunshots would be most likely intended, I assume. Is there any way you can tell, from the injury itself?"

"No, sir. None at all, sir."

"Thank you."

Faulkner declined to pursue the issue. General Hardesty also did not take up his right to question the witness. He looked around slowly, gauging the emotion of the court, and perhaps judged correctly that almost to a man they were in sympathy with the accused. They would have to be forced or tricked into giving any evidence against them if it could be withheld, misinterpreted, or simply denied.

But Joseph knew it was a shallow victory. In the end it was the officers who would decide, not the men who crowded the benches or stood at the back waiting, their hands clenched, faces tense. There was no jury, no public opinion. Those who attended were either witnesses called or men who were off the front line due to injury.

The next witness took the stand. He recounted who he had seen—and where—on the day of Northrup's death. He was neatly tricked by Faulkner into stating that most of the men charged, and Cavan in particular, had not been at their usual posts in the early evening. In fact, Cavan had not been in any of the places he usually was at that hour. The man's testimony, intended to help, went to indicate that Cavan behaved out of character, and that no one knew where he was.

Joseph knew he would not improve the situation by questioning the man; more likely it would make it more obvious that he was lying in an attempt to save Cavan.

Hardesty looked as if he was aware that emotion was having a far larger effect than the facts, but he did not intervene.

Faulkner called more men and elicited similar responses, building a picture of curious and unexplained behavior that night. Each piece was minute, but placed carefully together, as Faulkner did, they were like the fractions of a mosaic, and the picture was chillingly clear. Twelve men were unable to find a single witness as to where they were. The conclusion was only implicit, but it sank with deeper and deeper weight on everyone in the hot and overcrowded room.

There was a brief recess. Joseph saw Judith come in. Actually what he saw was the crowded men move to make space for her, and then the light on the fair streaks of her hair, bleached from when the summer had been bright, before the battle at Passchendaele, and the rain. Their eyes met. She was frightened, but had he not known her so well he would not have seen it in her pale face.

The court resumed.

Faulkner began calling his other witnesses. This was the most difficult part for him, far worse than any defense Joseph might mount. He must prove some kind of motive for such a terrible and self-destructive act as mutiny, and by officers, in particular, who had until that time shown exemplary service. There cannot have been a man in the room, or beyond it in the regiment, who was not burningly aware that Cavan had been put up for the Victoria Cross. Compared with him Howard Northrup was both a moral coward and a military fool.

At the same time Faulkner must not allow anyone to suggest that Northrup had deserved his fate, or even that he was seriously incompetent. It must seem that every other man faced with the same situations might have given the same orders, with the same results. There must be motive, but no justification. It was a delicate balance, but he stood on the balls of his feet, weight slightly forward, voice confident.

Joseph looked over to where General Northrup sat, his face so pale the shadows under his eyes looked like old bruises. His lips were tight, his nose pinched as if he had long carried an inner pain which had finally come to a crisis.

Joseph turned away. To stare at a man in such distress was intrusive, the more so because Joseph would only add to it when circumstance allowed him. There was little room for compassion here, perhaps none at all. It was deeply against his instinct to strike at a man whose grief he had seen so openly, who had possibly even trusted him. But gentleness toward one now might yield the death of the others, and his loyalties could not be divided. Everyone else in the court might be evenhanded, but his duty could be only to the men whose champion he was.

Faulkner was careful in his questioning, almost to a fault. He called men as witnesses who had been on the edge of incidents, and were not caught up emotionally. By presenting such a bland view he showed that he was not ignoring the incidents. He conceded that they had occurred, robbing Joseph of the need to and if Joseph were to then call men who gave very different accounts, they would be seen as biased.

Their closeness would in itself color their views and they could easily be suspected of leaning too far in the opposite direction, of seeing fault in Northrup simply to justify the actions of their friends who now faced judgment. Joseph saw the trap, and yet he still feared overbalancing into it.

His hands clammy and his chest tight, he rose to cross-examine the third witness, a young soldier who had been at the front only a matter of three months. He came from the Derbyshire Peak District and had no ties with Cambridgeshire.

"Private Black," Joseph began. "You have given us a clear account of this unfortunate accident with the gun carriage, which you say some of the men felt was Major Northrup's fault. You saw nothing to suggest that it was?"

"No, sir," Black replied. He looked uncomfortable and confused. He was very young, perhaps sixteen.

"But you say they were extremely angry?"

"Yes, sir. At least, they were cussing a lot, and swore he was . . . well . . . not up to much as a soldier."

"Did anyone suggest that he should take advice in the matter from some of the more experienced men?"

"I dunno, sir."

"Are you quite sure about that, Private Black?"

Black glanced at Faulkner, then back at Joseph. It seemed to occur to him for the first time that he was out of his depth, and that whatever Faulkner promised him, it was the men of his own regiment whom he would have to live with, and very possibly die with. He stood fidgeting slightly, clenching and unclenching his hands.

Joseph could not afford to be sorry for him. Everyone in the room—and especially the officers who would have to make the judgment—must surely have seen that look.

"Do you know why you in particular were asked to give evidence to-day?" Joseph pressed his advantage.

"No, sir."

"You did not have a particularly good view of the accident?"

"No, sir." Black was now visibly unhappy.

"Nor much knowledge of field guns, horses, mud, bad weather?" Black was sweating. "No, sir. I only just got here, sir."

"Did you volunteer to testify?"

"No, sir!" That was from the heart.

"I see. Perhaps you simply represent a certain point of view, a very impartial one?" Joseph suggested.

"I think impartiality is what we are seeking, is it not?" Faulkner interrupted coldly. "It is the indulgence of emotion and personal opinion over obedience, discipline, and loyalty which has brought us to this place."

"Impartiality perhaps," Joseph said, knowing his voice was rough-edged with the power of his own feelings. "But not apathy, indifference, or, above all, total ignorance." He stopped himself from continuing only with an intense effort. In spite of himself, of seeing it open in front of him and knowing its exact nature, he was still overbalancing into the trap.

Faulkner smiled. "I have nothing further to ask Private Black," he said.

Hardesty turned to Black.

"Did you hear talk of mutiny, Private?"

"No, sir!"

"Simply distress at an accident?"

"Yes, sir!"

He was excused, and Faulkner proceeded with perhaps a little less assuredness. He called more witnesses of military misjudgment, lack of knowledge or foresight, but always making it seem like no more than the misfortunes of combat that happened all the time, and to other men as well as Northrup. He built up a careful picture of resentful men who were desperate to escape the battle line, to blame someone else for their pain and fear, and their helplessness to alter the terrible fate ahead of them.

The case closed for the day.

Joseph left the farmhouse and walked alone back toward his dugout. It was more than four miles, but he wanted the time alone to think. If there was to be justice then eleven of the twelve men would be found guilty of no more than insubordination, and that even with understanding; but Howard Northrup would not be exposed to the whole army as an arrogant and incompetent man, a failure. He had been placed by circumstances into a position he was not suited to fill. Possibly an ambitious father who saw what he wished to was additionally responsible. But was there any justice served by forcing him, publicly, to see every bitter moment of his own mistakes, and what they had cost?

Joseph would like to have saved them all.

He trudged through the mud in the dying sun, refusing to accept that it was impossible. Was he capable of virtually crucifying General Northrup?

If he did not, then his evasion, his cowardice, would condemn Cavan and Morel and the others. And it could also betray the rest of the regiment who trusted him to fight for them all. And they did see the fate of them all in whatever happened to the twelve, he had seen that in their eyes, the tension in their movements, the questions they did not ask. They believed they knew him.

Perhaps that was the decision made. He could strip the defenses for Howard Northrup, and those from his father, as far as he had to. He would be careful to say nothing but the truth. That was bitter!

No, it wasn't! The fact that in one man's opinion something was true, or part of a truth, did not rob him of judgment whether to speak it or not. The responsibility was still his. It was the ultimate hypocrisy to shelter behind morality instead of standing before it.

He reached the lines, ate a brief meal of stew and hard bread already beginning to mold, then walked through the mud to his dugout. He read for a little while, and finally fell asleep after three in the morning, with the words crying out in his mind "Father, help me!" but no idea of what that help could be.

The next day began with Faulkner once again calling witnesses from among the men who had been at the front only a short time and had no personal loyalty to Morel or to Cavan, and no friendship with the other men of the Cambridgeshire regiments.

Within the first half hour, his questions turned in the direction Joseph had dreaded from the beginning. "Why," Faulkner asked, "if the accused men were not guilty as charged, did they escape custody and flee the battlefield, and try to reach neutral Switzerland? And what is more interesting—how did that escape occur?"

Joseph was cold to the pit of his stomach. Had he underestimated Faulkner in thinking he did not know that Judith and Wil Sloan had helped them? Was he looking for someone to betray that? Was he trying to apply pressure on Joseph that would force him to lie to protect them both, and thus expose himself as a passionately interested party doing everything he could to conceal a crime out of personal motives?

Was that why they had chosen Joseph to defend the men? Because he had the ultimate weakness and they had known it all along? How blindly,

arrogantly stupid he had been! Yet again he had walked, open-eyed, into total betrayal! And not only Cavan, Morel, and the other men, but Judith and
Wil Sloan would pay for it with their lives.

Now he was angry, deeply and passionately angry. He was sweating.
The room seemed to roar in his ears as if he were underwater. Surely the
Germans had not advanced far enough to make the room ring and tremble
like this?

Faulkner was questioning one of the guards who had kept the prisoners in the farmhouse rooms. The man stared back stolidly, answering exactly as required.

"Yes, sir, Captain Morel refused to give his word, sir, so we had no
choice but to lock him up."

"But separately, not with the other ranks?" Faulkner clarified.

"That's right, sir."

"And he escaped?"

"Looks that way, sir."

Faulkner's eyebrows shot up. "You have some doubt, Corporal
Teague?"

"Only know he was there in the evening, an' gone the next morning,
sir," Teague replied blankly. "Don't seem likely he was abducted."

There was a snigger of laughter around the room.

Faulkner flushed. "You find this amusing, Corporal?" he said icily.
"We are investigating a man's death!"

"Holy God!" Teague exploded, his face suddenly white. He swung his
arm out in a generally northeast direction. "We got a thousand men out
there dying every single bloody day!" he shouted. "One idiot officer gets a
clean bullet in his brain, or what passes for one in his case, and you become
righteously indignant, as if it never happened before? I got no bloody idea
what happened to him, and I don't sodding care!"

His voice was growing more strident. "Good men got crippled or
killed because he was too stiff-necked to let anyone tell him what he didn't
know. And God 'elp 'em if they tried! If someone bust them out, I don't
know who it was. They give me a clip on the back of the head, an' I don't
blame them one bit, but I never saw their faces." He flung his arm out to
point at the accused men, but still stared defiantly at Faulkner. "Haven't
you got something better to do than stand here arguing the toss over those
poor sods? We're going to lose the war 'cos you lot shot us from behind!"

Faulkner's face was burning with rage, but General Hardesty stepped
in before he could speak.

"Corporal Teague, one of the reasons we fight this war is because we
believe in the rule of law, not of barbarism. We appreciate that you have

been tested to the extreme by seeing the deaths of your comrades, some of them perhaps unnecessary deaths, but you will apologize to the court for your disrespect, and then answer Captain Reavley's questions, should he have any for you."

Teague controlled himself with an effort. "Sorry, sir." His voice was strangled. He turned attentively to Joseph, his expression changing to one of utmost respect.

Joseph stood up, an overwhelming sense of belonging surging through him, and a passionate will to succeed.

The tension in the room was teetering, willing Joseph to defeat Faulkner, but the law was even more tightly around the accused men now than before Teague had spoken. But Joseph's mind was racing with fear for Judith. Did everyone know it was she who had rescued the prisoners, just as surely as they all knew Northrup was a fool?

They would not execute Judith, but they'd send her to prison. Even after all she had done here, the years of hardship and danger, pushing herself to exhaustion, living in hunger and filth. Would prison finally destroy her? Would bitterness at the injustice of it break her spirit?

"Corporal Teague," he began. What could he ask this man who so fiercely wanted to help?

"Yes, sir." Teague stood smartly to attention.

"You guarded these men during their imprisonment?"

"Yes, sir." There was disappointment in Teague's face. He had been hoping for something brilliant.

An idea flashed in Joseph's mind, partial, a hope only. "Did you hear them talking to one another at all?"

Teague hesitated. "Yes, sir." His eyes were wide, tentative. He wanted to be led.

It must be done with exquisite care. Joseph breathed in and out slowly, steadying himself. "Were they always aware of you overhearing them?"

"Er . . . no, sir."

Good. He dared not smile, not give the slightest encouragement. "Did you ever hear them say that they had intended to kill Major Northrup?"

"No, sir." The disappointment was back again in Teague's face, deeper.

Faulkner gave an exaggerated sigh of exasperation.

The silence prickled in the room.

Joseph plunged on. "Did you ever hear them say that they had wished he would listen to advice from men who were familiar with the battlefield? With horses, for example? Or the peculiar nature of the clay mud here?" Faulkner objected, but Joseph ignored him. "Or when it was more dangerous," he said clearly, "or *less*, to go over into no-man's-land to try to recover wounded or dead? Or even the lie of poison gas. Or sniper fire, visibility, any of the things the rest of us have learned by experience over the years."

Teague was following him now. "Yes, sir," he said cautiously. "Yes, I did hear them say as it would've been better if he would've listened, but no one could make him. 'E were dead stubborn...." He blushed. "Sorry, sir. But 'e were a very proud, unbending sort of man. The ignorant ones often are."

There were several gasps in the room, followed by a moment's silence.

"Why did they want him to take advice, Corporal?" Joseph needed him to nail it home.

Teague blinked. " 'Cos we were getting hurt bad, or killed," he said with incomprehension at Joseph's stupidity. "No man sees his mates getting killed for nothing an' stands by with his fingers up his arse . . . sir."

"You mean the army is built on loyalty to the men beside you, whose lives depend upon you and yours upon them, even more than upon obedience to discipline?" Joseph made it doubly clear.

"Yes, sir, I do mean that," Teague agreed. "Being obedient isn't enough. When you're out there with Jerry firing everything he's got at you, you got to be right as well."

"Yes," Joseph agreed. "Yes, I know. I've carried the bodies home."

"Yes, sir. I know you have. And a lot o' the ones still alive."

Joseph thanked Teague and resumed his seat at the defense table.

Faulkner knew well enough to remain silent. His face was pale, the freckles standing out.

Hardesty asked Teague again if he was certain that he did not know who had let the prisoners go. Teague repeated that he had no idea.

Faulkner called upon the testimony of other men, particularly those who had searched for the escapees afterward, asking about how the escape could have been effected, and drew from them the answers he wanted. It required a vehicle large enough to transport all eleven men, and of course a driver. No vehicle had been reported lost or abandoned. The conclusion was obvious: An ambulance had carried away the prisoners.

The room seemed to be hotter, smaller, the walls crowding inward.

Joseph accepted the possibility that he would have to lie under oath to defend Judith. Could he? Could he swear on the Bible that he knew so well, not only in the poetic glory of the King James version but in the Hebrew and Greek and Aramaic as well?

Yes, he could. Words were strong and beautiful, but it was the reality they spoke of that mattered. What were all the scriptures in the world worth if he placed his own emotional comfort first and let Judith suffer, even be broken, for doing what she believed was essentially the right thing?

And the fact that all the men of the regiment whom he knew, whose lives and dreams he shared, thought so too eased the decision. Yes, he would look Faulkner in the face, and lie to him. If he had to.

Judith was wondering the same thing, and yet it did not frighten her as much as it should have. She had known the risk when she took it, and would have done it again. It was Cavan and Morel she was afraid for, and the other ten, not herself. She had known Teague would lie about knowing who was behind the escape.

She looked at General Northrup's face and saw the pain in it. He must be realizing now that every rank and file man in the room, every man who actually went out into the mud and death of battle, would risk his own freedom, perhaps his life, to lie for the men accused of Major Howard Northrup's death. Could there be a loneliness, a failure more bitter?

There was a stir in the crowd to her left and automatically she turned to look. It was Richard Mason. As if he felt her gaze, he turned toward her. He must be here to report on the court-martial. He looked tired, more than physically exhausted, as if there were a weariness inside him. The ridiculous thought flashed into her mind that he had been wounded and what she saw was the debilitation of pain. But she knew that was not so. She had seen him too recently for such a wound to have been sustained and then healed enough for him to be here now.

As soon as there was a break in the proceedings she looked for him, to find him also looking for her. When they met outside the farmhouse only a few yards from other war correspondents, drivers, and witnesses, she could think of nothing to say. She knew from the fine lines in Mason's face dragging downward, and the tiredness of his eyes, that he had lost something. Immediately her mind went back to what Joseph had said about a darkness in Mason that would prevent him from making her happy, and the coldness of that thought touched her now. Since she had seen him last, a fire had gone out of him, as if some hope or trust had been betrayed.

She was suddenly angry. All hope might be betrayed, all trust soiled, used and thrown away. It did not alter the value of all the things that were loved, or the need to go on fighting for them. What was the alternative? To deny that they were infinitely precious, whatever the cost proved to be? There was no second best, no fallback position worth having.

"Hello, Judith," he said quietly. "Joseph is putting up a better battle than I thought he would."

"What did you think he was going to do?" she said with unexpected bitterness. "Fold up like a deck of cards? You should know him better than that."

"Not fight a battle he can't win," he replied, but he said it softly, as if it caused him pain.

She searched his face and saw not triumph or any vindication of his earlier views but a sense of loss that startled her. It seemed so immediate, as if the erosion were happening as she watched.

"Sometimes you don't win battles," she answered quietly, but with unwavering certainty. "But your side wins the war. People get lost, soldiers get killed. Do you only fight if you know you'll win? That sounds like a coward to me."

He winced. "I choose my battles," he answered. "There are not many of us fighting my war. Every loss counts."

"What is your war?" It was a challenge and she meant it as such. She looked at his dark face with its powerful lines—the shadowed eyes, the emotions within—and she remembered the joy and compassion they had shared. And she remembered how he had kissed her, as if she could smell the warmth of his skin now, and taste him. She had given him more of herself than she had realized.

"What is your war?" she repeated. "What is it you're fighting for? Or have you given up?"

"Sanity," he replied, the hurt in his eyes deep. "And yes, I probably have given up. I ought to. Joseph can't get these men off, and if he isn't careful they'll take you down with them as well."

She felt a sharp grip of fear, like a cramp in the stomach. Would Mason betray her, thinking the truth worth more than individual loss? Exactly what did he believe in? Had she ever known, really? She found herself staring at him, searching, trying to dig deeper than she had any right to, tear off the protecting mask and understand the dreams and the pain underneath.

"Judith!" he said desperately.

What did he want? Trust? She could not give that to him. There was a dark, unknown void inside him that could swallow the things she loved: Joseph, Wil Sloan, Cavan, the men she had known as friends all these years, the men who trusted her. If she let them down there would be nothing left of herself, either.

She turned away from Mason, tears stinging her eyes. There was not anything to say, nothing words could capture or enfold. Either he understood already, or it was too late.

He watched her go with a sense of a door having been closed against him, shutting him out. The blow was not unexpected. He had known she helped the prisoners escape, and he was exasperated with her but not surprised. It was the sort of insane, thoughtless, idealistic thing she would do. She still had the same heroic ideals that the young men had had who went to war three years ago, believing it was glorious. Most of them were dead now, or crippled, shell-shocked, disillusioned. Rupert Brooke, the epitome of them all, the golden poet, had died of blood poisoning before the battle of Gallipoli. The poetry now was of realism, of destruction, of anger and loss. Only dreamers like Judith refused to grow up, clinging to a paper-thin mirage.

And Joseph, of course, trying to defend the morally just and legally indefensible! He would go down with it, like the captain of a sinking ship.

So why did Mason, standing in the sun watching Judith's gaunt, square shoulders and the light on her hair, feel as if he had been shut out of Paradise? The pain of it caught him by surprise, taking his breath away, taking his hopes, and he was naked without them.

Early in the afternoon Faulkner closed his case for the prosecution. It was legally perfect, and he knew it. There was no doubt that the twelve men accused had mutinied, regardless of their motives, and that as a result of their act Major Howard Northrup had been shot by one of them, and it could not have been accidental. Which one had fired the bullet that killed him was immaterial to the charge. He turned to Joseph, inviting him to attempt a defense.

Joseph stood up, forcing himself to keep calm, to try to look as if he knew what he was doing. This was his last chance.

Hardesty asked him the usual questions. Did the accused wish to testify in their own behalf? Did they wish to call any witnesses?

"Two of the accused will testify on behalf of them all, sir," Joseph replied. "And we have two witnesses." Please God this was the right decision.

He had racked his brain, considered every possibility both likely and unlikely. He had prayed about it, but no sense of ease came to still the gnawing doubts in his mind or comfort any of the fear. If that was a sign the decision was wrong, that left him with no answer at all. Every other alternative was worse.

Hardesty nodded grimly. "Very well. Proceed, Captain Reavley."

"Thank you, sir." He called Cavan first.

Cavan swore to his name and rank and exactly where he served and for how long. Joseph had considered listing some of Cavan's achievements, but decided it would give the impression that he was desperate. He was, and probably Faulkner knew it, but bluff was all he had to play.

Carefully, and in sparse, verifiable detail, he drew from Cavan a list of men he had treated and what their injuries had been. Every time he asked if Cavan knew whether the men had survived or not, and if so, if he had lost limbs or eyes.

The court listened in silence. Every man Cavan named was known to them, a friend, possibly even a cousin or brother. If Faulkner could be unaware of the feeling around him then he was truly anesthetized to life. He was at least wise enough not to challenge Cavan.

"Thank you," Joseph said gravely. He turned to General Hardesty. "Sir, it is a matter of record which I will be happy to have Colonel Hook verify that each of these men was injured while obeying the direct orders of Major Northrup. I shall call other witnesses to confirm that the orders were given against the advice of more experienced but junior men."

"That will be necessary, if you wish to make this evidence of any value in these proceedings, Captain Reavley," Hardesty replied. "So far all you have achieved is to illustrate for us the tragedy of war, of which we are all wretchedly aware."

"All except Colonel Faulkner, sir," Joseph replied. "I believe he has not seen action."

"It is irrelevant!" Faulkner snapped, his face pale except for two spots of pink in his cheeks. "This court-martial is to address the crimes of mutiny and murder, not to praise or blame the war record of the officers concerned, or to comment on the tragedy of young men's deaths."

"It is to exercise the circumstances, Colonel Faulkner," Hardesty responded coldly. "You will have your opportunity to contest any of Captain Cavan's testimony, if you wish." He turned to Joseph. "Continue, Captain Reavley. You have a long way to go before you have made this relevant to the charge." There was warning in his face and sadness. Was it for the dead and injured, or because he believed Joseph could not succeed?

Joseph reached the moment of decision. He turned to Cavan again. "When you realized that Major Northrup was not going to take the advice of the men familiar with the conditions and the dangers, Captain Cavan, what did you do?"

"I knew there were many other men who felt as I did," Cavan answered quietly. "Particularly Captain Morel. We decided to use force to make Major Northrup listen. We decided to frighten him badly enough he would feel he had no choice. Morel devised a plan that we hoped would make him see that it was both wisdom and his duty to act on advice, and I agreed immediately."

"What was that plan, Captain?"

"To take him by force to a place where we could hold a mock drumhead court-martial and charge him with the mutilation and deaths of the men who suffered because of his arrogance," Cavan replied. "If we proved to him that it was his fault, we believed he would be willing to change. He was a stupid man, arrogant and out of his depth, but he was also frightened, and I believed he wanted to succeed; he simply didn't know how. He wasn't actually cut out to be a soldier, but then most of the men here wouldn't be if they had a choice." His voice was quiet and clear, the anger in it almost hidden. "We thought it was a way out for all of us."

"And why wasn't it, Captain Cavan?" Joseph asked.

There was complete silence in the room. No one even shifted position.

Cavan's face was white, but he stood stiffly to attention, his eyes fixed on Joseph's. "He was terrified. We found him guilty of gross negligence, and followed it through with a mock execution. We thought it was necessary at the time, in case once he was free again he reneged. We all loaded with blanks—"

"Blanks?" Joseph interrupted sharply. "The army doesn't issue blanks. Where did you get them?"

"We didn't," Cavan said. "We made them. It's easy enough."

"Is it safe?" Joseph pressed. "How did you know they wouldn't still fire bullets? It looks as if one did."

"No sir, it's not possible. The bullet that fired was a live round." Cavan again explained carefully exactly how a blank was made.

"Then one of the men replaced his blank after you had seen him load it?" Joseph deduced.

"Yes, sir."

"Did you know that at the time?"

"Of course not!" Cavan clenched his fists, and his voice shook. "Do you think we wanted this?"

"No, I don't think so," Joseph replied. "But we need to demonstrate it to the court. Who shot the live round?"

"I have no idea, sir, except I don't believe it was I."

"Why not?"

"The kick from a live round is different. I'd have felt it. From a blank there is no recoil."

"You are a surgeon," Joseph pointed out. "How do you know what firing a live round feels like?"

Cavan blushed faintly. "I've fought as well, sir. I have fired a rifle many times."

There was a murmur around the room. Many knew of his V.C.

"Thank you, Captain Cavan."

Faulkner rose to his feet.

Joseph swallowed, his mouth dry. He sat down.

"Yes, thank you, Captain Cavan," Faulkner said. "I'm not sure how much of your story I believe, but I can think of only one thing further to ask you. Regarding these various men and their injuries, I imagine you will only repeat what you have already told us." He smiled bleakly. "However, I am interested in the fact that when your eleven coconspirators in this . . . disciplinary action of yours chose to escape and run for a neutral country, leaving the battle front altogether, you did not. Why was that, Captain?"

"I had given my word not to, sir," Cavan answered.

"And you are a man of the utmost honor?" Faulkner gave the question only the barest lift of interrogation. "So much so that you will remain to face a firing squad rather than break your given word?"

"Yes, sir. I would have imagined that as an officer yourself you would have understood that," Cavan replied, the faintest edge of contempt in his expression.

Cavan had not seen the trap, but Joseph did. He felt the sweat break out on his skin and his stomach clench.

Faulkner smiled. "I do, Captain, I do. Who organized the escape of the other eleven men held prisoners with you?"

The heat in the room prickled. Someone shifted their weight and a board creaked.

"As you observed, sir," Cavan replied. "I am an officer and I gave my word. I was not imprisoned with the men. I did not see them go, nor did I see who assisted them."

"That was not exactly what I asked, Captain Cavan," Faulkner pointed out. "I asked you if you knew who it was, not if you saw them. But as a matter of fact, Captain Morel went, and he is of the same rank as yourself, an officer! Were you not billeted together?"

"No, sir. Captain Morel was with the men."

"Indeed? Why was that?"

"You must ask him, sir."

"I will. You have not answered me as to who effected this . . . rescue. I accept that you did not see them. I asked you if you know who it was!"

Joseph rose to his feet, his legs stiff. "Sir!" he said to Hardesty, far too loudly. "If Captain Cavan did not see who it was, then he cannot know. Anything else would be no more than an educated guess, or what somebody else had said, and not evidence." He had phrased it badly, forgotten his legal terminology.

"Quite," Hardesty agreed. He looked at Faulkner. "You may consider the action reprehensible, Colonel, but hearsay evidence will not stand up. Captain Cavan has told you that he was imprisoned separately and did not see anyone. That is the answer to your question. Proceed."

"I have nothing else," Faulkner said curtly. "For this witness."

Now it was Morel's turn. He stood as stiff as Cavan had, but he was far leaner, almost haggard, all taut muscle and bone, his face thin, dark eyes hollow.

Joseph found his throat too tight to swallow. He had to clear it to speak. "Do you wish to amend anything in what Captain Cavan has said, Captain Morel?"

"No, sir." Morel's voice was hoarse. He straightened his back even more.

Joseph knew he must address the escape first. The knowledge and the fear of betrayal was in the room like an unexploded bomb.

"When you were arrested and imprisoned in the farmhouse you refused to give your word that you would not escape. Did you expect to be rescued?" he asked.

"No, sir."

"Do you know who rescued you?"

Morel hesitated. He was so tense he was swaying a little with the concentration of keeping control. He knew he must be believed. Joseph had told him everything rested on that.

"Yes, sir."

Joseph could hear his own breath in the silence of the room. The walls seemed to swell and then recede, as if they were the chest of some sleeping monster. "Who was it?"

"I refuse to say, sir. They risked their lives for us. We do not betray our own men."

"Just so." Joseph felt his heart pounding. "Did you fire the shot that killed Major Northrup?"

"No, sir."

"Do you know who did?"

"Yes, sir."

"And will you refuse to tell us that also?"

"No, sir. He did not act for the good of the regiment or to save the lives of his men. It was a private vengeance for a civilian matter and had no place here."

"Who was it?"

"Lance Corporal John Geddes, sir."

There was a rustle of movement, indistinguishable voices.

Hardesty looked startled.

Faulkner was taken aback, angry.

"And how do you know this, Captain Morel?" Joseph asked loudly.

"I heard him tell the whole story when we were returning from our escape," Morel replied. "It would be easily verifiable. I expect General Northrup, who is here in court, would testify to most of it, since it happened in the village where he and his family live, and so also does Geddes's family. I daresay General Northrup would find it painful, but I believe he would not lie."

A score of men in the room turned to look at Northrup who sat ramrod straight and ashen-faced.

"The motive might be easy enough to check," Joseph agreed, his voice husky. He loathed doing this, but he was aware that he must raise all the objections before Faulkner did—bite first and draw the poison. "That does not prove Geddes's guilt. Why would he tell you this? And if he was indeed guilty, why would he return to stand trial rather than simply continue in his escape? Was he not already far beyond British jurisdiction when he made that decision?"

"Yes, sir." There was not a flicker in Morel's face. Now everyone had turned toward him. "He was in German territory, sir," Morel continued. "Hurt, alone, starving, and unable to speak the language. If the Germans had caught him, I think it possible he would have been treated as a spy. He might not have been shot cleanly, and we can do at least that for him."

"How do you know this, Captain Morel?"

"I was there, sir."

"Do we have anyone's word for this, apart from yours?"

"Yes, sir." Again there was not a flicker in Morel's face. "There are a number of French officers who could testify to various points of our journey. And you yourself could testify to all of it."

There was a rustle around the room, a murmur of voices, one or two gasps. Then Hardesty leaned forward. "Is this true, Captain Reavley?" he demanded.

"Yes, sir."

"And are you willing to testify? If you do so, you will, of course, be subject to cross-examination by the prosecution."

Joseph cleared his throat. He had no choice. He had struggled to avoid it from the beginning, but there was no way around it that did not make him look like a liar. "Yes, sir," he said hoarsely.

"Very well. After Lieutenant Colonel Faulkner has questioned Captain Morel, we shall have you testify."

Faulkner obtained nothing further from Morel that was of any use and Hardesty adjourned the court for the long, miserable night. Joseph spent most of it awake, trying to think of a safer way to introduce the evidence he needed. It all depended on the understanding of morale, of the loyalties that bound the men together, their trust in Morel and his knowledge of it, the obligations he felt. His own testimony of that was useless.

Faulkner would judge it self-serving and dismiss it. Only men like Morel could know what he believed and why.

A jury of his peers. The phrase flashed into his mind in burning clarity. It was still only a chance. Faulkner might still trip someone and catch them out over Judith, and of course Wil Sloan. Although since Wil was American, the consequences might be less severe for him.

Finally, almost as the sky was paling in the east, he fell asleep.

FOURTEEN

*T*he next morning Joseph called his first witness. Snowy Nunn stood scrubbed and stiff, answering with surprise to his given name, almost as if he did not recognize it. He had been called "Snowy" since before he could talk.

"Private Nunn," Joseph began, addressing him formally.

"Yes, sir." Snowy was so rigid Joseph could see where the fabric of his uniform was strained by the unnatural posture.

"How long have you been in the army?"

"Since the autumn o' 'fourteen, sir. Oi soigned up immediate."

"Why?"

Snowy looked startled. "Roight thing to do, sir. Same loike everyone, you know that, sir. You did the same thing. And your sister, to droive ambulances."

"Yes, I do know," Joseph agreed. "But perhaps General Hardesty and the other officers on the panel did not. And of course Colonel Faulkner. Does that mean you have known most of the accused men for all that time?"

"Yes, sir, most of them. Known the rest since summer of 'fifteen, just after the gas attacks started. Came to replace . . ." He swallowed. "Some o' those we lost."

"How long have you known Captain Morel, for example?"

Faulkner rose to his feet, addressing General Hardesty rather than Joseph. "Sir, the prosecution is happy to concede that Private Nunn, and indeed the majority of the men in the Cambridgeshires, all know each other and have a loyalty greater to the men of their own villages than to their king and country, or to the laws thereof. It is wasting the court's time for witness after witness to attest to it."

Hardesty looked deeply unhappy. Beside him Apsted grimaced.

"Sir," Joseph responded. "I object profoundly to Colonel Faulkner stating that any man in the Cambridgeshire regiment has a greater loyalty to his fellow soldiers than to His Majesty, or to England. On the battlefield a soldier's loyalty is to the men who fight beside him, and to those for whom he is responsible. We fight for king and country, give our lives if necessary, endure injury, hardship, and sometimes appalling pain, but we do it here. These are the men whose backs we defend, whose lives we save, or who save ours, whose rations we share, with whom we laugh, and weep, and face the evening, and whose wounds we will try to stanch if we can, or who will carry us back from no-man's-land—dead or alive. Loyalty is not an idea here, sir, it is the price of life."

There was a murmur of approval from the body of the court. One man raised his hand and shouted out his agreement.

"For God's sake!" Faulkner snapped. "This is not the place for a sermon. We are dealing with facts, and the law—not emotionalism. We are only too well aware that the chaplain is partisan; I may say, highly partisan. He comes from the same village and has known these men all their lives. I do not question his honesty, but I do most profoundly question his ability to separate the law from his personal loyalties."

"Thank you for not questioning my honesty," Joseph said with considerable sarcasm. "The fact that you raise it at all suggests that you might."

"If you give me cause to, I shall, sir," Faulkner retorted. "I believe Captain Morel was a student of yours in your Bible teaching days in Cambridge? And one of the better-known women ambulance drivers is your sister? Your personal loyalties are deep enough to make questions not unnatural, Captain Reavley."

The attack on Judith had come at last, and not to answer it would be to signal his vulnerability. Joseph dared not ignore it. The challenge had been very cleverly made, discreet, oblique enough not to seem deliberate, and yet of course it was. He had walked into the trap. Had there ever been a way of avoiding it?

"My sister is one of the ambulance drivers," he agreed. "And yes, Captain Morel was one of my students, of Biblical languages, actually, not of the Bible itself. And certainly I have known most of the men in the regiment all their lives, or if not them, then men exactly like them, from villages like my own. That makes me better able to understand them than you are."

"I understand the law, sir, which it seems increasingly apparent you do not!"

Hardesty drew in his breath, as if to speak. There was a sharp snap as Apsted broke a pencil, accidentally twisting and turning it too hard.

It was time for Joseph to play his only card. He looked unblinkingly at Faulkner. "One of the few things I know about the law, and have admired the most, is that a man is entitled to be tried by a jury of his peers. Not men who are higher or lower than he is, or who are of a different nature or class, or who have never walked a step along his path and know nothing of his faith, the trials he has faced, or the burden he has carried. We cannot be judged fairly by the arrogant or the ignorant. I hope to demonstrate that I am not too partisan to see the truth, but partisan enough to understand it, and the men who have lived for it, or died for it."

He steadied himself. It must be done. "And that includes the grief of General Northrup, his desire for justice, and perhaps for revenge, his guilt that he pushed his son into a rank and a position for which he was not equipped, and which ultimately destroyed him. And for Major Northrup who was sent to a miserable death by men who did not understand him, and circumstances that are beyond the control of any of us."

Faulkner was furious. "Sir, you exceed your own position! You are a captain. You are a priest in uniform, because the army must offer what spiritual comfort it can to men who face death. You have no right and no remit to judge your superior officers, or the military ability or record of any man at all. To insult General Northrup from the safety of your appointment to this court is a despicable act. I hope the court will see fit to admonish you."

Hardesty was pale, his face tight with anger. "Colonel Faulkner, I will exercise my own discipline, without suggestion from you, sir."

He waited, but Faulkner did not apologize. He inclined his head and then straightened his shoulders as if he would have taken a step backward, but the room was so crowded men stood pressed against each other; there was nowhere for him to go.

Hardesty turned to Joseph. "For goodness' sake, Captain Reavley, ask your questions and get on with it! Does Private Nunn have anything to contribute or not?"

"Yes, sir," Joseph replied. He looked at Snowy, doing his best to hide the helplessness he felt. He was not sure now if calling him was wise—in fact if the entire strategy, which had seemed in the night to be possible, was not a disastrous idea. "Private Nunn, do you know all the men who are here accused of mutiny and murder?"

Snowy's face was almost as pale as his hair. He stared at Joseph, desperately seeking guidance. Joseph dared not give him any, and was too transparently honest—it would show instantly.

"Do you?" Joseph repeated. "Just answer truthfully."

Snowy relaxed a fraction. "Yes, sir."

"Including Captain Morel?"

"Yes, sir."

"You are a private. He is a captain. How do you know him, other than to take orders?"

Snowy hesitated, unsure how much Joseph wished him to say.

"Your brother Tucky was recently killed," Joseph prompted him.

Snowy swayed, struggling to get his breath.

Joseph waited. He felt brutal, but he knew even worse could be ahead.

"Yes, sir. He was shot going over the top," Snowy answered. He took another shuddering breath. "Oi suppose that was when Oi got to know Captain Morel a bit more. He was . . . he was very good to me. Knew how Oi felt. Tucky an' me . . ." He stopped again, unable to go on.

Joseph had to rescue him. "Were very close. I know. I think we all know a great deal about loss, comforting one another . . . the responsibility."

Faulkner rose to his feet.

"Yes, sir!" Snowy said loudly, before Faulkner could speak. "Captain Morel took it very hard when any of his men got killed . . . or injured, either. He's a good man, sir. Oi hope—" He stopped abruptly, aware that he had nearly said too much. He blushed scarlet.

Hardesty had the briefest of smiles, little more than a softening of the eyes.

"I hope so, too," Joseph said softly. "It is my responsibility to look after my men, and I will do everything I can to fulfill that duty. In your judgment and experience serving under him, did Captain Morel feel that same sense of duty to his men, Private Nunn?"

"For heaven's sake!" Faulkner said furiously. "That's an idiotic, self-serving question. The man's a private! He's hardly going to say *no*. He's talking about his officer! And one who showed him some compassion when his brother was killed. Sir!" He appealed to Hardesty.

Joseph cut across them both. "It's also an excellent opportunity to earn credit with his new commanders, and at the same time get a certain revenge, if he felt Captain Morel had been less than the leader he wanted. Private Nunn risks far more speaking for him than he would against him, sir."

"You have an excellent point, Captain Reavley," Hardesty conceded. He looked at Snowy. "Private Nunn, will you please tell me, in your own words, not Captain Reavley's, what was your experience of Captain Morel as an officer."

"Yes, sir." Snowy stood very straight. "He was a hard soldier and he didn't like any lip, but he could see a joke like anybody else. He expected you to be obedient, jump to it instant, loike, no slacking, no hesitating once you'd gone over the top. Always look after your own, help the wounded, bring everyone back if you could. Always looked out for his men. Be loyal to him, an' he'll be loyal to you, even to his life. Sir."

"Thank you, Private Nunn." Hardesty looked at Joseph.

For a moment Joseph hesitated. Was it better to reinforce what Snowy had said, or leave it as if Hardesty had done enough? Leave it. The deference to Hardesty was wiser.

"Thank you," Joseph said aloud. "That was my point precisely, sir." Awkwardly, still not quite sure, he sat down.

Faulkner stood up. He looked at Snowy with weary disgust.

"Do you believe mutiny is wrong, Private Nunn? Or let me put it this way, is your loyalty to your country, or to the Cambridgeshire regiment?"

"Oi reckon as they're the same, sir," Snowy answered.

"Well, Cambridgeshire may be your whole world, Private Nunn, but I assure you there is a great deal more of England than that!"

"Oi expect there is," Snowy agreed steadily. "But all Oi know is Cambridgeshire and here, and maybe it's all Oi'm like to know. Cambridgeshire'll do me."

There was a rumble of approval from the men in the room.

"So your loyalty is to a Cambridgeshire captain before the king!" Faulkner challenged, his face pink.

"Oi don't know the king, sir," Snowy told him unblinkingly. "An' Captain Morel's from up Lancashire somewhere."

Faulkner stood motionless, unable to decide whether it was worth pursuing what seemed to be a fruitless course.

Joseph waited also, terrified Faulkner would go on and try to provoke Snowy into a mistake, or worse, into losing his temper. He had tied himself irrevocably to Morel, and through him to all the accused men. It would be disastrous. He stared across at Snowy, trying to will him to stay calm.

"Private Nunn," Faulkner said again. "I ask you, do you condone mutiny? A simple *yes* or *no* will do."

"Oi never thought of it, sir," Snowy answered. "Oi trust Captain Morel. Oi know him. Oi'd go over the top if he told me to, any day. Oi have done. He wouldn't order it if it weren't necessary. He knows what he's doing, and he respects his men, sir. Loike they do him."

"That wasn't what . . ." Faulkner began.

"You have the best answer you are going to get, Colonel Faulkner," Hardesty told him. "If you have any further questions for Private Nunn, ask them."

"No, sir. It seems pointless to ask. Except one thing." He turned again to Snowy. "Private Nunn, do you have any idea why Corporal Geddes, alone among the accused men, should have wished to kill Major Northrup? You seem to know all your comrades so well, surely you know that?"

"No, sir, Oi don't know," Snowy answered. "But Oi don't think Corporal Geddes is stupid. If he had a good reason in his own mind for thinking of something like that, he isn't daft enough to tell me about it. He'd know Oi wouldn't go along with it, sir." It almost amounted to insolence, but not quite.

Faulkner gave up. "That's all, Private Nunn." He looked at General Hardesty. "Sir, since this defense claims that only Corporal Geddes was guilty of murder, perhaps Captain Reavley will provide a credible witness as to what possible motive he could have had. I have questioned him myself, and he denied it. I do not find Captain Morel credible, since his interest in the issue is that his own life depends upon it. Captain Reavley would testify, since he was apparently present when Geddes allegedly admitted to the crime. Then in the interests of both law and justice, I may cross-examine him on his testimony."

The trap was sprung, tidily and completely. Joseph could not refuse him or he would appear to be denying what Morel had said, and the whole defense would collapse. And once Joseph was cross-examined, Faulkner would find a way of raising the escape again. Could Joseph lie? And if he did, would that jeopardize everything in the defense so far?

He had no choice. He was sworn, and briefly told them all that Geddes had said on the long journey back. No one interrupted him.

"A most interesting tale," Faulkner said finally. "Did you believe him, Captain Reavley? Or is it Chaplain, in this case?"

"If you mean, am I breaking the sanctity of confession, no, I am not. If you remember, Colonel, Captain Morel was also present."

"Oh, yes, of course, your onetime student, Captain Morel. You have a great loyalty, Captain Reavley. How does your loyalty to your calling, to the truth and honor you have spoken about so eloquently, compare with your loyalty to the ambulance driver who helped the mutineers to escape, and of course the murderer Geddes, as well?"

All movement in the room ceased. Everyone looked at Joseph.

He stared back at Faulkner, terrified that he might accidentally look at Judith.

The slightest misstep now, even a word, and Faulkner would have him. "I do not know who helped them escape, Colonel," he said.

"Come now," Faulkner said tartly. "Is being disingenuous to this degree not morally the same as a lie? You may have taken great care not to have anyone repeat news to you, but are you telling this court that you really do not know who it was? Be very careful precisely where your loyalties lie, Chaplain!"

"You are quite right," Joseph admitted. He could feel the sweat trickle down his face. Deliberately he relaxed his hands. Was Judith afraid he would betray her, even accidentally? "I have taken very great care indeed not to know who it was. And I have been successful," he said levelly. "I can guess, but as you yourself have pointed out, most information comes to me in the way of confession, and I cannot repeat it. Not that anyone *has* confessed to that."

"And you do not consider it your duty as an officer to report such a crime?" Faulkner said in amazement.

"No, sir. I consider it my duty as an officer to go after the men who escaped, and bring them back to face trial. Which I did. It redressed the situation, without betrayal of any trust."

"Bringing them back for trial, and possible execution, was not a betrayal of their trust? You amaze me." Faulkner's voice was heavy with sarcasm.

"I persuaded them to come back freely," Joseph corrected him, feeling the heat burn up his face. "For trial. I believe them to be innocent of mutiny or murder, and I hope this court will find them so."

"Except Geddes! He didn't come willingly!"

"He admitted to murder. That is different."

"Not one of your village men, Chaplain?"

"No." Joseph knew what was coming next. But at least they had left the subject of the escape, for a moment.

"Could that be why he is guilty?"

"If you are suggesting all Gloucestershire men are murderers, that is ridiculous," Joseph retorted.

"I am suggesting, sir, that your loyalty to your own men supersedes all honor or balance or judgment on your part. Fighting together in these appalling circumstances, and your fearful losses, have warped your judgment and upset the balance of your thinking. We have no one's word for it but yours and Captain Morel's that any of these events in Major Northrup's home village ever took place."

"Are those your last questions to me?" Joseph found his voice was trembling and there were pins and needles tingling in his fingers. The last chance, the one he had been hoping to avoid since the beginning, was now facing him.

"They are," Faulkner replied with a gleam of satisfaction.

Joseph turned to Hardesty. "Sir, I need to call one last witness who can substantiate the greater part of what I have said."

"Who is it, Captain Reavley?"

"General Northrup, sir."

Hardesty stared at him, eyes wide, questioning.

Joseph stared back. The fact that he had made the decision did not lessen his revulsion at it.

"Very well," Hardesty agreed. "General Northrup, sir. Will you take the stand." It was an order, not a request. There was no choice for either of them.

Slowly, as if his whole body ached, Northrup rose to his feet and walked forward, back straight, shoulders angular and rigid. He was sworn in and turned to face Joseph. There was nothing gentle in his face, no silent plea for mercy. He looked like a man facing his execution. It seemed Faulkner had convinced him that Joseph was utterly partisan, a man without justice, only blind loyalty to his own, regardless of innocence or guilt.

Joseph wavered. He longed to be able to prove him wrong. He had mercy, honor, a sense of justice being for all, as it was for none. But his calling here was to fight for his own men, and that did not allow him space to cover Major Howard Northrup's weaknesses with mercy. He wanted General Northrup to know that, to understand. He realized in the same moment that to do the right thing was necessary, to need to be seen to do it was a luxury, even a self-indulgence, and completely irrelevant.

"General Northrup," he began, his voice firmer than he had expected. "Would you confirm for the court that you live at Wood End Manor in Gloucestershire, and that your son Major Howard Northrup grew up there, and lived there until the outbreak of war in 1914?"

"That is correct," Northrup replied coldly.

"Did Corporal Geddes's family live in the same village at that time?"

"Yes."

"Did Corporal John Geddes's father become involved in a business venture with Major Northrup?"

General Northrup stiffened, his face pink. "I did not concern myself in my son's financial affairs," he replied quietly.

Joseph loathed doing it, but his voice was perfectly steady. "Every man in this court would understand your desire to protect your son's name, sir, but you are under oath, and other men's lives depend upon your honesty— good men, soldiers like yourself. Are you swearing on your word as an officer that you at no time involved yourself, financially or otherwise, in your son's business affairs?"

Northrup's face burned scarlet. "I...I lent him money when it was...necessary. Once or twice. Not...not as a habit, sir."

"Would it be truthful to say that you indulged many of his desires, and that when he overspent, you paid his debts?" Joseph pressed. "Or did you never do that?"

"I did it.... It was a matter of honor," Northrup said savagely. His eyes blazed in sockets so shadowed as to seem hollows in the bones of his head. He had aged bitterly in the weeks since his son's body had been found.

"Did the Geddes family lose their home?"

Northrup's hand jerked up. He drew his breath in as if to deny it, then remained silent.

"Is the Geddes family still in the home in which Corporal Geddes grew up?" Joseph insisted. "If necessary we can find out, but it will delay proceedings, surely pointlessly. The answer will be the same. Is it something you wish to hide?"

Faulkner rose to his feet, and Hardesty waved him sharply down again.

"No, sir," Northrup said very quietly. "I believe they were evicted."

Joseph chose his question very carefully. "Did your son's business succeed or fail?"

"It failed."

Joseph was aware of Faulkner tense in his seat, ready to spring to his feet any moment. He would need only a shred of a chance.

"Might it be possible that Corporal Geddes could believe that was Major Northrup's fault, whether it was or not?"

"It...." Northrup swallowed, a flash of gratitude in his eyes, there and then gone again instantly. "He might have believed it, yes."

"Thank you, General Northrup. That is all I have to ask you, sir."

Faulkner shot to his feet, stared at Northrup's ashen face, then very slowly sat down again. "I have nothing to add to this...this fiasco," he said angrily.

Hardesty looked at Northrup. "Thank you, sir," he said quietly. "The court has nothing further to say, either."

In a room electric with hostility, Faulkner made a closing speech demanding justice against one man who had committed murder, and eleven others whose act of mutiny had condoned it and made them accessories both before and after the fact. He requested that the court sentence them all to death, for the sake of law, justice, and the values the army and the country stood for. He demanded that they not allow sentimentality or fear of the enemy to dissuade them from doing their duty.

He sat down again, still with the court in utter silence.

Joseph stood up.

"The circumstances of this war are unlike anything we have ever known before," he began. "A man who has not floundered in the mud of no-man's-land, faced every fire, and seen his friends and his brothers torn apart by shellfire, riddled with bullets, or gassed to death, cannot even imagine what courage it takes to face it not just day after day, but year after year. Many of us will never leave here. We know that, and we accept it. Almost all of us came here because we wished to, we came to fight for the land and the people we love, our own people."

He took a deep breath. He realized with surprise how passionately he believed what he was saying. "But in order to walk into hell, we need the loyalty of our brothers, whether of blood and kin, or of common cause. We have to trust them without question, trust that they will share with us their last piece of bread, the warmth of their bodies in the ice of winter, and that they will never sacrifice our lives uselessly, on the altars of their own pride, or expect us to pay the price of their ignorance. If you will follow a man into the darkness and the mouth of the guns, then you have to know beyond question that he will do the same for you, that he will give all he has to be the leader you believe him to be."

He was speaking to Hardesty and the two men beside him, in whose hands judgment rested, but he faced the body of the court.

"Captain Morel and Captain Cavan, and nine of the other ten men here, took the action of trying to curb Major Northrup in order to fulfill the duty of trust they know their men placed in them.

"They were guilty of gross insubordination. It was the price they were willing to pay to save the lives of their fellows. They will accept judgment for that at the hands of their peers, of men who know what it is to be a soldier at Passchendaele, and they will serve whatever punishment those men decide is just, because they have walked the same path."

He sat down again, the sweat prickling on his skin, his heart pounding.

"Thank you, Captain," Hardesty said quietly. He looked at the men on either side of him. "Gentlemen, we shall return to the farmhouse kitchen in case there are any points of law you wish to consider." He rose to his feet and Apsted and Simmons went out after him.

Not a man or woman left the court. No one even spoke. Minutes ticked by.

Hardesty, Apsted, and Simmons returned.

Joseph found his heart beating so violently he gagged on his own breath.

As the junior officer, Simmons gave his verdict first.

"I find Corporal John Geddes guilty of murder," he said quietly. Then he listed the names of all the others, which seemed interminable. No one moved a muscle. "I find them guilty of gross insubordination, sir."

Hardesty thanked him and turned to Apsted.

The tension was almost unendurable. It was like the minutes before men go over the top into the enemy guns.

"I find Corporal John Geddes guilty of murder." Apsted swallowed hard. "And all the other accused, guilty of mutiny."

Joseph felt the sweat run down his body and his hands clench till his nails drew blood. The room swayed around him.

Hardesty spoke last. "I also find Corporal John Geddes guilty of murder." He listed all the other men. "I find them guilty of gross insubordination. By a majority decision, that is the verdict of this court. Sentence of death on Corporal Geddes will be referred up through the usual channels. The others accused will be dealt with at regimental level."

Then at last the cheering erupted. Men shot to their feet, shouting, holding hands high, gasping, laughing, with tears in their eyes and on their cheeks. Morel and Cavan were saluted, the others grasped by the hand, hugged rapturously by friends.

Mason waved his notebook in the air, his eyes bright, although he knew that in London the Peacemaker would be white with rage, uncomprehending that somehow, yet again, the Reavleys had beaten him. Judith wept openly with relief and overwhelming joy.

Joseph was hoisted up and carried out on the shoulders of Snowy Nunn, Barshey Gee, and he knew not who else. He had found a decision within himself and been prepared to pay the price of it, bitter as it was. He had not flinched. He had repaid the trust. Now he was dizzy with hope and a searing promise of faith, a belief in the possibility of the impossible, even out of utter darkness.

And to the north, toward Passchendaele, the big guns continued their relentless pounding of the lines.

About the Author

ANNE PERRY is the *New York Times* bestselling author of the World War I novels *No Graves As Yet* and *Shoulder the Sky*, as well as four holiday novels: *A Christmas Journey, A Christmas Visitor, A Christmas Guest,* and *A Christmas Secret.* She is also the creator of two acclaimed series set in Victorian England. Her William Monk novels include *Death of a Stranger, Funeral in Blue,* and *Slaves of Obsession.* The popular novels featuring Thomas and Charlotte Pitt include *Long Spoon Lane, Seven Dials,* and *Southampton Row.* Her short story "Heroes" won an Edgar Award. Anne Perry lives in Scotland. Visit her website at www.anneperry.net.

About the Type

This book was set in Centaur, a typeface designed by the American typographer Bruce Rogers in 1929. Rogers adapted Centaur from the fifteenth-century type of Nicholas Jenson and modified it in 1948 for a cutting by the Monotype Corporation.

We Shall Not Sleep

Take up our quarrel with the foe:
To you from failing hands we throw
The torch; be yours to hold it high.
If ye break faith with us who die
We shall not sleep, though poppies grow
In Flanders fields.

—John McCrae

ONE

*H*ome for Christmas this year, Chaplain?" Barshey Gee said with a wry smile. He turned his back to the wind and lit a Woodbine, then flicked the match into the mud at his feet. A couple of miles away in the gathering dusk the German guns fired desultorily. In a little while the shelling would probably get heavier. Nights were the worst.

"Maybe." Joseph would not commit himself. In October 1914 they had all imagined that the war would be over in months. Now, four years later, the situation was dramatically different. Half the men he had known then were dead; the German army was in retreat from the ground it had taken, and Joseph's Cambridgeshire regiment had advanced nearly as far as Ypres again. They might even make it tonight, so every man was needed.

They were waiting now, all around him in the gathering darkness, fidgeting a little, adjusting the weight of rifles and packs on their shoulders. They knew this land well. Before the Germans had driven them back they had lived in these trenches and dugouts. Friends and brothers were buried in the thick Flanders clay around them.

Barshey shifted his weight, his feet squelching in the mud. His brother Charlie had been mutilated and bled to death here shortly after the first gas attacks in the spring of 1915. Tucky Nunn was buried here somewhere, and Plugger Arnold, and dozens more from the small villages around St. Giles.

There was movement to his left, and to his right. They were waiting for the order to go over the top. Joseph would stay behind, as he always did, ready to tend the wounded, carry them back to the Casualty Clearing Station, sit with those whose pain was unbearable, and wait with the dying.

His days were too often spent writing the letters home that told women they were widows. Lately the soldiers were younger, some no more than fifteen or sixteen, and he was telling their mothers how they died, trying to offer some kind of comfort: that they had been brave, liked, and not alone, that it had been quick.

In his pocket Joseph's hand tightened over the letter he had received that morning from his sister Hannah at home in Cambridgeshire, but he refused to open it yet. Memories could confuse him, taking him miles from the present and scattering the concentration he needed to stay alive. He could not think of evening wind in the poplar leaves beyond the orchard, or across the fields the elms motionless against a sunset sky, starlings wheeling up and out, black fragments against the light. He could not allow himself to breathe in the silence and the smell of earth, or watch the slow tread of the plow horses returning along the lanes after the day's work.

There were weeks to go yet, perhaps months, before it was over and those who were left could go back to a land that would never again be as they had left it.

More men were passing through the shadows. Allied trenches were dug more shallowly than the German ones. You had to keep your head down or risk being caught by sniper fire. The earthen floor was always muddy, though not as bad now as times he could remember when the ooze had been deep enough to drown a man, and so cold some actually froze to death. Many of the duckboards were rotted now, but the rats were still there, millions of them, some as big as cats, and the stench was always the same—death and latrines. You could smell the line miles before you actually reached it. It varied from one place to another, depending on the nationality of the men who fought there. Corpses smelled differently according to the food the men had eaten.

Barshey threw away the last of his cigarette. "Reckon we'll make Passchendaele again within the week," he said, looking at Joseph and squinting slightly in the last of the light.

Joseph said nothing, knowing no answer was expected. Memory held them together in wordless pain. He nodded, looked at Barshey for a moment, then turned to pick his way over the old duckboards and around the dogleg corner into the next stretch. All the trenches were built in a zigzag so that if the enemy did storm them, they could not take out a whole platoon with one burst. The wooden revetting that held back the crumbling walls was sagged and bulging.

Joseph reached Tiddly Wop Andrews just below the fire step. The young soldier's handsome profile with its quiff of dark hair was clear for a moment against the pale sky; then he ducked down again.

" 'Evenin', Reverend," Andrews said quietly. He started to say some-thing else, but the increasing noise drowned it out as a hundred yards to the left the machine guns started to chatter.

It was time for Joseph to go back to the Casualty Clearing Station, where he could be of use to the wounded as they were brought in. He passed other men he knew and spoke a word or two to them: Snowy Nunn, his white-blond hair hidden by his helmet; Stan Tidyman, grinning and whistling through his teeth; Punch Fuller, instantly recognizable by his nose; and Cully Teversham, standing motionless.

Like every regiment, the Cambridgeshires had originally been drawn from a small area: These men had played together in childhood and gone to the same schools. But with so many dead or wounded, remnants of many regiments had been scrambled together to make any kind of force. More than half the soldiers now going up and over the parapet into the roar of gunfire were almost strangers to him.

Joseph came to the end of the dogleg and turned into the connecting trench back toward the support line and the station beyond. It was dark by the time he reached it. Normally the station would not have been busy. The wounded were evacuated to the hospital as soon as they were fit to move, and the surgeons, nurses, and orderlies would be waiting for new casualties to be brought in. But with so many German prisoners pouring through the lines, exhausted, defeated, and many of them injured, there were still nearly twenty patients here.

In the distance more columns of soldiers were marching forward into the trenches. At the rate they were taking ground now, the front line would soon move beyond the old earthworks, abandoned in the retreat. In the open the casualties would be far worse.

Joseph began his usual work of helping with more minor injuries. He was busy in the General Admissions tent when Whoopy Teversham came to the open flap, his face frightened and smeared with blood in the lantern light.

"Captain Reavley, you'd better come. There's two o' the men beating a prisoner pretty bad. If you don't stop 'em they're loike to kill 'im."

Joseph shouted for one of the orderlies to take over from him and fol-lowed Whoopy outside, almost treading on the man's heels. It took his eyes a moment to adjust to the dark; then he started running toward the pale outline of the Operating tent. The ground was rough, gouged into ruts and shallow craters by gun-carriage wheels and earlier shelling.

They were ahead of him, a group of half a dozen or so crowded to-gether—lightly wounded men on guard duty. Their voices were sharp and high-pitched. He saw them jostle closer, an arm swing in a punch, and someone stagger. A star shell went up and momentarily lit the sky, outlining them luridly for several seconds before it faded and fell. It gave him long enough to see the figure on the ground, half curled over with his face in the mud.

He reached them and spoke to the only man he had recognized in the brief light. "Corporal Clarke, what's going on here?"

The others froze, caught by surprise.

Clarke coughed, then straightened up. "German prisoner, sir. Seems to be hurt." His voice was uncertain, and Joseph could not see his face in the dark.

"Seems to be?" Joseph said scathingly. "Then what are you doing standing around shouting at each other and throwing punches? Does he need a stretcher?"

" 'E's a Jerry prisoner!" someone said angrily. "Best put him out of his misery. Bastards spent four years killing our boys, then think they can just put their hands up in the air, and suddenly we'll bust our guts bandaging 'em up and looking after 'em. Oi say the war's still on. Their brothers are over there"—he jerked an arm toward the gunfire—"still troying to kill us. Let's shoot back."

There was a measure of agreement in murmured angry voices.

"Very brave," Joseph said sarcastically. "Ten of you kick an unarmed prisoner to death while your comrades go into no-man's-land and face the Germans with guns."

"We found him loike that!" The sense of injustice was hot and instant. Others agreed vehemently.

" 'E was escaping!" someone explained. "Going off back to 'is own to tell 'em where we are, an' how many. We had to stop 'im!"

"Name?" Joseph demanded.

"Turner."

"Turner, sir!" Joseph snapped.

"Turner, sir," the man replied sullenly. " 'E was still escaping." The resentment in his voice was clear. Joseph was a chaplain, a noncombatant, and Turner obviously considered him inferior. Joseph had now compounded that attitude with his holy-Joe interference, interrupting natural justice.

"And it takes ten of you to stop him?" Joseph inquired, allowing his voice to rise with disbelief.

"Two of us," Turner replied. "Me an' Culshaw."

"Go and join your unit," Joseph ordered. "Teversham and I will get him to the dressing station."

Turner did not move. "He's German, sir—"

"So you said. We don't kill unarmed prisoners. If it's worth bothering, we question them; if not, we leave them alone."

Someone muttered a remark Joseph did not hear. There was a ripple of jerky laughter, then silence.

Whoopy Teversham leveled his bayonet and poked the man nearest him. Reluctantly the group moved aside, and Joseph bent to the figure on the ground. The man was still breathing, but he was obviously badly hurt. If they left him here much longer, he might die.

Slowly one of the other men stepped forward and helped lift the prisoner so Joseph could get his weight onto his shoulders and carry him at least as far as the Casualty Clearing Station. It might offer the man no more than a chance to die humanely.

The German was not heavy; perhaps hunger had taken its toll. Many people, both army and civilian, were starving. Even so he was awkward to carry, and the ground under Joseph's feet was uneven. He knew it must be painful for the wounded man, but there was nothing he could do to ease it.

He was almost at the Admissions tent again when an orderly ran out to meet him and helped them both inside. In the light Joseph was stunned to see the German's face. He was so badly beaten that his features were almost indistinguishable. His left arm was broken, and a deep wound in his thigh bled so heavily, it was impossible to tell if shrapnel or bayonet had caused it. His eyes were sunken with physical shock, staring in terror. Joseph could see now that he was very young.

"You're all right," he said to him in German. "We'll dress the wound in your leg and clean you up a bit, then get you back to the proper hospital."

"I surrender," the boy answered thickly, his words blurred by the torn and swollen flesh of his face. "I surrender."

"I know," Joseph assured him. "We have lots of you. When we've got you bandaged and your arm set, we'll put you with the others."

"You going to ask me questions?" The fear was still there in his eyes.

"No. Why? Do you have anything to tell me?"

"No. I surrender."

"That's what I thought. Now be quiet until the doctor comes."

Joseph left him with the medical orderlies and went back to assisting others, but the incident stayed in his mind.

It was many hours later when he finally found the opportunity to go forward to look for Bill Harrison, Culshaw and Turner's commanding officer. He had known Harrison since 1915, and liked him. He was a quiet man with a nice sense of humor who had earned his promotion from the ranks.

It was now gray dawn, with a thin east wind sending ragged clouds across the sky and ruffling the rainwater pools in the mud. Joseph had to pick his way past lifeless tree stumps, many of them scarred by fire, and around craters where rusted guns poked up through the oily surface. The bones of dead men and horses had been buried and uncovered by succeeding shellfire over the years. Attempts at interring them had become pointless. The stench was thick in his throat, but he was used to it. He found Harrison crouched in a small dugout in the side of the supply trench. He had made a cup of tea in a Dixie can and was sipping it. Joseph knew exactly how it would taste: like sour water and the residue of tinned Maconachie stew.

" 'Morning, Chaplain?" he said questioningly as Joseph crouched beside him. "What are you doing this far forward?" He searched Joseph's face, knowing there must be some kind of trouble to bring him this close to the firing. "We lost Henderson. I'd like to write to his family and tell them myself," he added, a note of apology in his voice.

Joseph had known he would. It was the sort of thing Harrison would not leave to others. Such news should always be broken by someone who had at least known the dead man. However good the regimental chaplain was, a letter from him was still in a sense impersonal.

"It's about Culshaw and Turner," Joseph told him.

Harrison frowned but waited for Joseph to continue.

"Caught a German prisoner trying to escape," Joseph said, making it as brief as possible. "Boy of around sixteen, thin as a scarecrow. Beat him almost to death. Whoopy Teversham caught them and stopped it."

Harrison stared at the ruined tree stump ahead of them, with the carcass of a horse beneath it. Joseph knew he loved horses. He even liked the stubborn, awkward regimental mules. "Hard to stop it," Harrison said after a while. "It just goes on and on, one death after another. Men get angry because they feel so helpless. There's nothing to hit out at. Culshaw's father was in the navy, and his elder brother."

"Was?" Joseph asked, although he knew what Harrison was going to say.

"Both went down last year," Harrison answered. "His sister lost her husband, too. No idea what he's going home to . . . if he makes it."

"Nobody does," Joseph said quietly. He thought of his own home, instinctively moving his hand toward his pocket, and then away again. He knew the letter was there. Hannah's husband, Archie, commanded a destroyer. Would he survive the last few weeks or months of war? Would any of them? Joseph was still unhurt, except for the dull ache in his bones that cold brought, reminding him of his smashed arm and the deep shrapnel wound in his leg that had invalided him home in the summer of 1916. He had been tempted to stay in Britain. At his age he could have. Not that he would have been happy. It would have been a betrayal of his men still out here, and of the women at home who loved them and trusted him to sit with the injured, not leave them to die alone.

"It can't ever be the same," he agreed aloud. "The England we fought for is gone anyway. We all know that."

"You used to teach theology in Cambridge, didn't you?" Harrison asked. "Will you go back to that?" His face was curious, surprisingly gentle.

Joseph smiled at the innocence of the question. He had gone to teach at the university as a form of escape. His wife, Eleanor, had died in childbirth, and their son with her. His bereavement had been insupportable, his faith too shallow to sustain him. The thought of ministering to the human needs of a congregation had overwhelmed him, so he ran and hid in the purely cerebral teaching of biblical languages.

"No," he said in answer to Harrison's question. "It's a little divorced from the reality of living." What a weight of intellectual dismissal that carried. When you cradled a man in your arms as he bled to death in the freezing mud, theory was nothing, however beautiful to the brain. Only being there counted, staying with him no matter what else happened, no matter if you were freezing and terrified also, and just as alone as he. That promise—"I will not leave you"—was the only one worth keeping.

Harrison looked sideways at him. The light was broader now, cold and white, and they could see each other's faces. He lit a cigarette, cupping the brief flame in his hands. "Everything's changed at home. Women do half the jobs we used to have. Couldn't help it, the men were away or dead. Or crippled, of course! But it's still different." He stared at the dregs of his tea. "God, that tastes foul! But how long will clean water and no more guns be enough for us, Chaplain? We'll be strangers, most of us. We're heroes at the moment, because we're still fighting, but what about in six months, or a year? One day we'll have to deal with the ordinary things. We'll get used to each other, stop being polite and careful. When I'm home on leave now people can't do enough for me. I'm given the best in the house."

Joseph said nothing. He knew exactly what Harrison meant, the intended kindness, the meaningless conversations, the silences they couldn't fill.

"I still have nightmares on leave," Harrison said softly, blowing out smoke. "I can hear the guns even when they aren't there. I think of the men who won't come back, and I see that terrible stare in the faces of too many who look as if they're whole, until you see their eyes. We're frightened we'll be killed in the last few weeks, and we're frightened of going home and being strangers and alone, because we don't fit in anymore."

He waited several minutes before answering. Everything Harrison said was true. Joseph tried not to think about the emptiness of going back. He was needed here, desperately needed, so much that the burden of it was sometimes crushing.

"I know," he said at last. "We're all afraid of the future, because we don't know what it will be. But we can't let men kick a German prisoner to death, whatever they feel. If we are no better than that, in God's name, what have ten million men died for?"

"I'll talk to them," Harrison promised. He pinched out his cigarette, then threw the dregs of his tea away. "It won't happen again."

The following day, October 12, Joseph was back in the Casualty Clearing Station as prisoners continued to come through the lines. Most were marched back into camps, where they would be held as the Allied army moved eastward over the old battlefields toward the borders of Germany. The few who were seriously wounded were kept in the clearing stations until they could be moved on without risking their lives.

There was sometimes information to be gained from them, but it was of little use now. The terrain had been fought over back and forth and was known intimately, every dugout, every trench. Only the craters changed as the guns fired ceaselessly, churning up old clay, old corpses, the wreckage of armor. The movement of regiments varied too often for yesterday's prisoners to tell what tomorrow's deployment would be.

Joseph spent much of his time translating between the prisoners and doctors. His German had been fluent even before the war. He had spent time there studying, and he cared for both the land and its people. Like any other Englishman, he'd found the idea of fighting Germany troubling and unnatural. He knew that the soldiers on the other side of the lines were too much like the men from his own village whom he talked with every day. It was the governments, the tide of history, that made one country different from the other.

He had been behind the lines last year and seen the suffering of the ordinary people, the hunger and fear. He remembered the German soldiers who had helped him. They had shared Schnapps and sung songs together. Hunger, fear, and wounds were the same in any language—and weariness, and the love of home.

Now he was standing in the Resuscitation tent, trying to reassure a prisoner with an amputated leg. Rain beat intermittently on the canvas. The man was not much more than twenty, his eyes sunken with pain and the shock of being suddenly mutilated, his country beaten, and himself among strangers. Nationality seemed an irrelevance.

Joseph knew that he should attend to the wounded of his own regiment, even though none of them were seriously ill, but the terror in this man's eyes haunted him. He looked like Hannah's oldest son, the color of his eyes and the way his hair grew off his brow. Busy with small jobs—fetching and carrying, running errands—Joseph kept returning to the man lying motionless in the sheets, the stump of his leg still oozing blood.

"When will your armies be in Germany?" the young man asked him shortly after midnight.

"I don't know," Joseph said frankly. "There's still a lot of hard fighting. The war may be over before we actually cross the border."

"But you will get there, tens of thousands of you—" He left the sentence hanging as if he did not know how to finish it. His face was sweating despite the cold, and his teeth were clamped together so the muscles of his jaw were tight, bulging under the gray-white skin.

Suddenly, with a sense of shame, Joseph knew that the man's fear was not for himself. The desperation of his fighting had come not from hate or the hunger for a German victory, but simply from the driving fear of what would happen to his family when enemy soldiers poured into the homeland of those who had killed their comrades, their friends and brothers, and revenge for it all lay open before them. Perhaps he knew what had happened to Belgium in 1914, and had been repeated over and over in every town and village. It might have appalled him as much as it did British soldiers to see the beaten and bereaved people, the burned-out farms, and the eyes of the women who had been raped.

If the tide had gone the other way—and there had been years when it had seemed inevitable that it would—then German troops would be marching through the little villages of Cambridgeshire: St. Giles, Haslingfield, Cherry Hinton, and all the others. The enemy would walk the cobbles of the familiar streets where Joseph had grown up. German soldiers would be sleeping under the thatched roofs, tearing up the gardens, perhaps killing the beasts to provide food, shooting those people who resisted. Women he had known all his life would be confused and humiliated, ashamed to smile or be seen to offer a kindness.

He saw the fear in the German's eyes now, and the bitter knowledge that he had failed to protect his women, perhaps his children. He would rather have died in battle. And yet what use was he to them dead? What use was he to anyone, a prisoner, and with only one leg?

Could Joseph tell him with any honesty that his women would not be violated, or his house burned? After four years of horror, inconceivable to those who had not endured it, and slaughter that numbed the mind, could he say the victors would not take payment for it in blood and pain? Some men retained their humanity even in the face of hell. He had seen it. He could name scores of them—living and dead. But not all the men had done so, not by a long way.

Should he comfort this young soldier lying ashen and broken-bodied in front of him by telling him lies? Or did he deserve the truth? A dubious honor.

What would he want himself? Would he want to think Hannah was safe, even if it were not true? And her children—the boys and Jenny? What about Lizzie Blaine, who had been such a friend to him when he was home wounded in 1916? The thought of her frightened and shamed by a German soldier was so hideous his stomach churned, and for a moment he was nearly sick.

He had not heard from her lately. He had tried not to count how long it was, but he knew: six weeks and two days. He had not expected it to hurt so much, but every mail call without a letter from her was like a blow to a place already aching.

The German was still watching him, uncertain now if he was going to answer at all.

"Where is your family?" Joseph asked him.

"Dortmund," the man answered.

Joseph smiled. "It'll be a long time before they get that far." He tried to sound confident. "The worst will have worn off by then. There'll be some discipline. They'll be regular troops. Most of the volunteers will have gone home. We're all tired of war. Vengeance has little flavor once the blood has cooled a bit."

The man blinked hard, the tears running down his cheeks. He was too weak to raise his hands to check them. "Thank you for not lying to me," he said quietly. "If you had said British soldiers don't do such things, I would not have believed you."

"Most of us don't," Joseph told him.

"I know. Most of us don't, either." There was defiance in his voice, and his eyes were hot with anger.

"We've all changed," Joseph said sadly. "Not much is as it used to be."

The German closed his eyes and retreated into some grief or pain too deep within himself for anyone else to guess at.

Joseph waited a moment longer, in case there was anything further the man wanted to say, then turned and walked away. It was raining harder; the canvas rumbled with it. He kept in the shelter of the walkway between the tents. The ground was wet, the light shining on pools of water.

His thoughts turned to Lizzie again. He could not think of going home without her filling his mind. He remembered how she had been his driver all the time he was there two years ago, too badly injured to handle a car himself. Despite her husband's murder, she had found the strength and the courage to help him look for the man who had so fearfully betrayed them all, and to confront him when at last they could no longer avoid the truth.

Joseph had begun by liking her, finding her company easy because she understood loss and never evaded it with trite words. She knew when to talk, and when to stay silent and allow the pain to take hold, then slowly absorb it and carry on.

And she could be fun. Her humor was quick and dry. She had an easy laugh; the light of it reached her eyes, which were very blue despite her dark hair. If ever she felt sorry for herself she fought it alone, without blaming others. And yet she was imperfect enough to be vulnerable, to make mistakes. She needed help now and then.

Why had she not written?

Did she sense the growing affection in him and know that she could not love again—at least not love a man who had seen four years in the trenches and was so immersed in the horror of it, he was changed forever? Weren't all men changed? Could any of them be whole enough again to make a woman happy? No woman wanted to grieve forever. Women created life, affirmed it, loved no matter what else happened. They needed to nurture, to begin again.

Perhaps only women like his sister Judith, who was here at the front, could understand and speak to soldiers as equals, could endure the nightmares and the ridiculous jokes, the miseries that seared the heart and would not be let go. To forget the dead would be to betray them, and was unforgivable. It would be to deny honor, to deny friendship, to make all the injury and the loss not real anymore.

Judith understood. She had been here since the beginning of the war, driving her ambulance with the wounded and the dead, fighting the hunger and cold, the disease, the horrific injuries, the despair and the hope, like the rest of them. It was ironic that he could talk to Judith . . . yet at the same time he didn't need to, because she knew it all just as he did.

The rain was soft and cold in his face as he crossed the mud back to the Admissions tent to see if there was anyone newly arrived who needed help.

Would he be able to offer anything of tenderness or honesty to any woman who had no experience of war? Or would the gulf between them be made uncrossable by the ghosts of too many friends lying dead in his arms, too many journeys across no-man's-land with terror and grief tearing him apart, too many long nights being deafened by the guns?

Lizzie, why don't you write? Don't you know what to say anymore? What horror could there be in the future as terrible as that we have already endured?

He stopped, his feet covered in mud. He was not ready to go into the tent yet. He needed a short break before finding the next man to talk to, to try to comfort, or if not that, then at least to help him to a drink of water or turn him onto his other side for a little ease.

He had not faced it until this moment that Lizzie meant so much to him, far more than friendship, more than laughter or comfort or someone to trust. The thought that she might not write again was a loneliness he was not equipped to endure. It was pointless to evade it, even if it were possible. He loved her.

Joseph's brother, Matthew Reavley, was sitting in a bare, impersonal London office opposite Calder Shearing, his superior in the Secret Intelligence Service.

"A month," Shearing said, pulling his mouth into a tight line. "Possibly a week or two longer, if the Germans hold out around Ypres, but not much more. Prisoners are pouring third repetition across the lines, sometimes ten thousand a day. There's still hard fighting in Menin, Courtrai—and Verdun, of course. Casualty figures are bad on both sides." He did not need to look at the names on the map. As Matthew was well aware, he knew them all better than the furniture of his own house or the neglected garden behind it.

"Talks by early November?" Matthew asked. "Cease-fire?"

"Probably," Shearing replied. "But we're not ready. We're still arguing with Wilson and the French."

His voice was raw with emotion and barely suppressed anger. This had been the most devastating war in history. It had spread to almost every corner of the world. Thirty-five million people were missing, dead, or injured; a continent spread with ruin. The balance of power was altered forever, the old rule swept away. The kaiser was toppled, the Austro-Hungarian Empire crumbling. In Russia a revolution had occurred, even more terrible than that which had swept the Bourbon monarchy from France. America had emerged as a new world power.

"Wilson's Fourteen Points," Matthew said grimly.

It was a vexed subject. President Woodrow Wilson of the United States was in effect the chief arbiter between the opposing forces, and as far back as January he had laid out his principles upon which peace should be negotiated.

Shearing's strong hand clenched on the desk between the two men. "Don't argue it, Reavley. Not now."

"He has no grasp of history," Matthew said yet again. "If we force his terms on Germany, it will lay the foundation for another war just as bloody as this!"

"I know!" Shearing snapped, the muscles of his face tightening. "We all know it, but the man doesn't listen to us. He has the mind of a country schoolmaster and the soul of an army mule. But what matters is that he has the power of a nation that didn't join the war until close to the end, when the rest of us were already on our knees. He rescued us, and, very politely, he doesn't intend to let us forget it."

"If it was a European country schoolmaster it wouldn't matter," Matthew said drily, leaning back in his chair. He had grown comfortable in Shearing's room only lately, now that he understood why there was nothing personal in it. "He would at least grasp the reasons for our ancient quarrels, and know that we can't be forced to get over them by common sense, especially an outsider's idea of what is sensible."

"I know!" Shearing repeated sharply. "Dermot Sandwell has tried pointing out that if we destroy Germany's heavy industry with punitive restrictions, we will cripple the economy of the whole continent. Germany in violent recession could create a vacuum, which would suck in all of us, in time. Five or six years from now we could have an economic depression unlike anything we've seen before."

"Is Sandwell right?" Matthew asked with a sudden chill.

"God knows," Shearing replied. "Probably. And yet if we don't prevent them from rearming we'll be back where we started, and deserve to be." He smiled. It was very brief, but there was warmth in it, even a momentary revelation of something very close to friendship. "I suppose you still don't know who your 'Peacemaker' is?"

Matthew took a deep breath, startled by the sense of defeat in himself. The failure hurt more deeply than he had expected. "No," he admitted.

"I'm sorry," Shearing said quietly. "I suppose if I could help, you would have said so?"

Shearing was an intense man who never spoke of himself. Matthew had learned from someone else of the tragic and heroic history of Shearing's family. Only then had he finally trusted Shearing and understood his fierce loyalty to his adopted country. Not a trace of his original accent remained. His English was not only correct—it was completely colloquial. Nothing except the darkness of his eyes and an occasional sadness in his smile gave him away. Many times before that, Matthew had feared Shearing himself was the Peacemaker. There was a gleam of humor in the man's eyes as he looked back at Matthew now. Perhaps he knew it, too, or guessed it.

"Yes. And if I think of anything, I still will," Matthew answered.

Shearing tidied the handwritten notes in front of him and locked them in his desk. It was an unnecessary measure since the room would be locked also, but it was his habit to be careful, even though the notes would not be decipherable to anyone else were they found. "Bring me more as soon as you have it."

"Yes, sir." Matthew stood up. "Good night, sir."

"Good night, Reavley."

Matthew returned to his office, locked away his own papers, and collected his mackintosh. Outside in the dark street, he turned left along the pavement and began to walk briskly. Getting home to his flat would take him about half an hour, by which time in the fine, cold drizzle he would be pretty wet. Still, it was better than looking for any kind of transport. Buses were crowded and irregular. Taxis were rare. Everyone was competing for the little petrol there was, and he could easily walk the distance. In fact, after sitting most of the day at a desk sifting information, he was glad of the strange sense of freedom the dark streets brought to him. They were crowded with other people also hurrying, their heads down, their collars high. The occasional gleam of car headlights shone on the wet surfaces: smooth tarmac or rough cobbles, the sharp edge of a curb.

He would have known the way blindfolded. He passed the tobacconist on the corner. The man's son had been killed at Gallipoli, and a younger son had lost an arm at Verdun. His daughter's husband had been blinded at Messines. The greengrocer's son was in the Royal Flying Corps. He was still fine, but his mother had been killed in a zeppelin raid here at home. And so it went. Everyone had lost someone, even if it was a lifelong friend rather than a relative.

He crossed the street, facing into the wind. The rain was heavier. The Peacemaker that Shearing had referred to was the code name Matthew and Joseph had given to the man who had conceived a wild plan to prevent the war entirely, back in the summer of 1914.

Matthew could remember walking across the sunlit cricket pitch that afternoon in Cambridge as if it were yesterday, and yet in a way it seemed like another lifetime. He could still see the cloudless sky and the white gleam of flannels and shirts. The women wore long, pale muslin dresses. Wide hats shaded their faces, and their long hair was elaborately dressed. It had been a golden afternoon that seemed as if it would go on forever.

And Matthew had shattered it, at least for his own family. He had come to tell Joseph that their parents, John and Alys Reavley, had been killed in a car crash on the Hauxton Road. That evening as they sat in the silent, strangely empty family home, the village constable had come to express his sympathy, mentioning quite casually the news that in Sarajevo the archduke and duchess of Austria had been assassinated by some Serbian madman.

John and Alys Reavley's deaths had proved to be murder also. John Reavley had found one of the two drafts of a proposed treaty between Kaiser Wilhelm and King Edward. It would allow Germany to invade England, France, and Belgium and absorb them into an expanding German Empire, and then in time take the rest of Europe as well. The kaiser's price was German help to regain the former British colony of the United States, and of course to keep the rest of the British Empire of India, Burma, Africa, Australasia, and various islands around the earth. It would in effect be an Anglo-German Empire greater than any the world had seen before. It might bring global peace, but at the cost of national honor and individual freedom.

John Reavley had been driving to London to tell Matthew about it; given his job, Matthew could bring it to the attention of the right people, making it impossible to carry through. And he had died because of it. But before he left Cambridge, he had hidden the treaty, and no matter how the Peacemaker's men had hunted for it, they had not found it. Matthew and Joseph had discovered it, on the eve of war. It was still in its hiding place in the barrel of the unused punt gun in their home in Selborne St. Giles. Without both copies, the Peacemaker could not present it to be signed by the king, and there was no time left to get the kaiser's signature on another.

Once war had begun the Peacemaker had turned his efforts—and those of his followers—toward making peace again as soon as possible. In the early years his intent had been to sabotage the British recruitment, which was all still voluntary then. Later he had sabotaged the scientific inventions that might have saved thousands of lives at sea, both in the merchant and Royal Navy, and tens of thousands of tons of vital supplies of both food and munitions.

Still later he had used propaganda again. The reports of failing morale, escalating casualties, the pointlessness of so many deaths for an ideal that had been flawed from the beginning were designed to undermine British resolve and productivity.

Matthew had wondered if the fearful explosion in Halifax, Nova Scotia, had somehow been the Peacemaker's doing. It had happened on December 6 of the previous year. The French Canadian ship *Mont-Blanc*, carrying more than two and a half thousand tons of high explosives destined for the war effort, had struck a Norwegian ship in the narrows at the harbor entrance. Abandoned by her crew, the *Mont-Blanc*, rather than blowing up immediately as everyone had expected, drifted into the harbor itself until she rested against one of the piers. Then she exploded so violently that her every shred of shattered and burning debris fell on churches, houses, schools, factories, docks, and other ships. More than twelve thousand houses were damaged. Far more importantly, well over four thousand people were killed or injured. It was the biggest man-made explosion that had ever occurred. The devastation was bitter and lasting.

But of course it was the murders of people he knew and loved that hurt Matthew most sharply—his parents, the man who had stolen the treaty and brought it to England, Augustus Tempany, Owen Cullingford, Theo Blaine. He knew that was foolish. No man or woman had more than one life to give, or to lose, but the death of someone whose face you know, whose voice is familiar, whose laughter and pain you have shared, wounds a different part of you, and reason doesn't help its healing. He remembered Shanley Corcoran with a unique stab of pain, because his end had been worse than merely death.

And of course he remembered Detta Hannassey, beautiful Detta who moved with such grace, and would now never walk with ease again. That was different, and perhaps the Peacemaker was not to blame, but that did not lessen the hurt.

Now, in October 1918, he still did not know who the Peacemaker was, and could only guess at what else he might have done that was outside their knowledge. There could be a hundred other schemes, a thousand.

He crossed the dark street. A taxi swept by, lights gleaming on black puddles, wheels spraying dirty water high. He leaped backward, hand up as if to ward it off, memory drenching him with sweat for those other times when the Peacemaker's men had twice so nearly killed him. Once had been in the street in what would have looked like an accident. He straightened his coat and went on, feeling foolish.

Of course he had spent more hours than he could count trying to find the Peacemaker's identity and stop him. He had suspected several people and one by one ruled them out, only to find his facts turned on their heads by contradictory information. Most painful, as well as most compromising, was that it could have been Calder Shearing. The evidence had piled up. It was only last year that Matthew finally knew his superior's innocence.

Matthew and Joseph had both believed it could be Aidan Thyer, master of St. John's College, Cambridge. They still had Thyer under suspicion, as well as senior cabinet minister Dermot Sandwell, close to the heart of government.

Now it looked as if the war was going to end and they would never know. That would mean victory, peace, and a very personal failure. He had let his father down. John Reavley had never wanted his son to enter the intelligence service, had never liked the deviousness, the secrecy and lies it involved, the manipulation and betrayal inherent in its methods of gathering information.

Soldiers who fight face-to-face have a certain honor. They also endure a kind of physical horror that comes as close to hell as a human being can conceive. The suffering, not only of body but perhaps even more of mind, belongs in a realm outside the imagination of sane men. Matthew had heard it discussed, but even the words of poets—some of the most powerful ever written in the English language—could barely evoke it.

Men who returned on leave did not speak of it, not even his own brother. John Reavley would have been proud of Joseph—silently, joyously proud of him. Joseph had kept his word to his men throughout, swallowing his own pain and going forward again and again.

What would John Reavley have said of Matthew? Would he have understood now what vital work the Secret Intelligence Service did? How many lives it saved, silently, unknown and unrecognized?

He was only a couple of hundred yards from home now. Soon he would be able to take off his wet clothes and make himself a hot cup of tea. He would like to have had whisky, but it was becoming harder to get, and he would save it for later. There were shortages of just about everything: food, petrol, coal, clothes, paper, soap, and candles.

Inside, the flat was cold. He put on the kettle and cut himself a couple of cheese sandwiches, piling on Hannah's homemade chutney brought back with him from his last visit to Cambridgeshire. She had wanted to give him more, offering him all sorts of things he knew she could not really spare.

She was lonely, with Archie at sea almost all the time. They had grown much closer since the summer of 1916, when she had seen so much loss, and forced him to tell her far more of the truth of his life as a destroyer commander in the North Atlantic. Before that she had been happy not even to imagine it in any realistic detail.

Matthew understood why, and he admired her for at last taking that great step forward. But she had hated most of the changes the war had brought. She had never wanted the rights—or the responsibilities that went with them—that so many women now were forced to accept, willingly or not. She was nothing like Judith, who had gone without hesitation to France to drive an ambulance. Hannah was happy with her children and the village. She had stepped into her mother's shoes, taking on the organization of village affairs, the knowledge of families' loyalties and needs, the constant small kindnesses that bind a community together and make it possible to survive shattering loss. The end of the war would be a blessing for Hannah. At last she would be able to sleep without nightmares about Archie, or about her eldest son joining up, as he was so keen to do before it was too late to fight for his country.

Matthew ate the sandwiches slowly. The cheese was a little stale, but the chutney masked it. He thought about having a whisky, and knew tea would be better. It was too easy to let one whisky become a second, and a third.

For Judith the end of the war would be quite different. Suddenly she would be purposeless again, a single woman nearly thirty, in a marriage market almost bereft of young men. Those there would want someone more comfortable to be with: less passionate than Judith, less demanding, possibly even less brave or clever. The nation was tired. Beauty, even like hers, was good to look at, but disturbing and exhausting to keep. What would she do with all that fire that burned inside her?

He was jerked out of his thoughts by the sound of the doorbell. It startled him, and it rang again before he stood up and walked into the hallway to answer. Even then he hesitated. He spent very little time in his flat. He worked long and irregular hours, and when he had a day or two off he went home to Cambridgeshire. It was most unusual to receive a visitor here.

He opened the door slowly, keeping his weight at least half behind it so he could force it shut hard if necessary.

"Major Reavley." It was a statement, not a question. The bland face of the man in front of him held no doubt at all. He was of average height, his hair dark but thinning, his brows colorless, his features unremarkable, except possibly for his eyes. They were steady and penetrating. He wore the drab suit and white dog collar of a man of the church.

"Yes?" Matthew answered without moving to allow him in.

The man smiled very slightly, more with his eyes than his mouth. "I have a message for you that might have very little meaning for anyone else, but if it fell into the wrong hands could cost me my life," he said quietly. "Very much more important, if it did not reach you, it could alter the peace that faces us. The outcome of the war is now inevitable, but what follows it is not. There is still much to play for." This time the smile reached his lips as well. "I daresay it is just as cold inside, but it will be more discreet."

For Matthew there was only one decision possible. "Come in," he offered, stepping back and allowing the man to pass him before closing the door again and making sure the lock was fast. "If you are cold, perhaps you would like tea, or whisky? How about a sandwich? It's only cheese and chutney, but the chutney is good."

"Thank you. I have little time. I do not dare wait here too long, but a sandwich would be welcome." The man had a very slight accent, as if German was his native tongue.

Matthew boiled the kettle again while he made a sandwich, and then took the plate and tea together. "What is your message?" he asked, sitting down opposite the man. In the light from the lamp it was clear that he was well into his forties, and there were lines of strain and weariness in his face, especially around his eyes and mouth. "Is there any point in asking your name?"

"Not really. I am only a messenger," the man replied, swallowing hungrily.

"Army chaplain, by your clothes," Matthew remarked. "Does that mean anything?"

"No. It's just a convenient way to travel. But like you, I have a brother who is, or was. He was killed on the Somme last year."

"I'm sorry." Matthew meant it. He could imagine losing a brother very easily. He always read casualty lists. He had nightmares about it.

The man finished the whole sandwich and drank the last of the tea before speaking again. "Thank you. I imagine you are still interested in knowing the identity of the Peacemaker, as I believe you have called him?"

Matthew felt the sweat stand out on his skin, and yet inside he was suddenly cold. No outsider could know the name they had given him. Who was this man? The silence in the room was so intense, he could hear the faint sounds of footsteps outside in the street.

"For the death of your parents," the man went on, watching Matthew's face. "But also because he will have a very great effect on Britain's demands at the peace negotiations, which cannot be more than weeks away now. I would estimate about the second week in November. If we make the wrong decision, we will pay for it in pain all over Europe, perhaps in a world far bloodier and more terrible than this one. Not only this generation will be lost, but our children's generation as well, with weapons we have not dreamed of yet."

"I know!" Matthew said harshly. His chest was hurting. It was hard to breathe. The weight of grief seemed almost crushing. He remembered his father so vividly that he could hear his voice and smell the faint, familiar aroma of pipe tobacco and Harris tweed. Fragments of a dozen rambling jokes filled his mind. He was conscious of the man in the other chair watching him, seeing his intolerable hurt, and he resented it.

"We must not let that happen," the man said softly. "And if you do not stop the Peacemaker, he will rebuild his plans to create an Anglo-German Empire out of the ashes of this war, and then there will be another war, because Europe will never let that happen. Britain at least will not. We know that now. Perhaps if we had been wiser, we would always have known it."

"The Peacemaker—who is he?" Matthew demanded.

"His name is no use to you without proof."

"Then what are you here for?" Matthew knew he was being unfair, but he had waited four long, bitter years for this and seen too many good friends die by the Peacemaker's hand. To be offered knowledge at last, only to grasp it and find it a mirage, was like being openly taunted.

"To tell you that his counterpart in Germany is willing to come through the lines and travel to England to expose him, at the cost of his own life if necessary, rather than see this holocaust descend on Europe again."

Matthew's mind raced. Could it be true? Or was it one more chimera, another trick to obtain a final chance at destruction?

"You have nothing to lose by bringing him through and listening to him," the man said with infinite weariness in his eyes. "We are beaten. Germany has lost more than a million and a half men on the battlefield alone. The people are starved and broken, the land devastated, the government in ruins. No one who loves Germany, and is sane, wants to see that again. Manfred will come through the lines, if you tell him where and when. But it must be soon; we have no time to debate, or to weigh and consider. If you meet him, give him safe conduct, he will come back to London and tell your prime minister of the entire plot from the beginning. You already know much of it yourself. I imagine you still have the original of the treaty, or at least you know where it is." Again it was not a question. He probably did not expect Matthew to answer.

"What is his name?" Matthew repeated. Should he hesitate? Was there anything else to ask, any answer he could check? He was used to the double cross, the triple cross—it was the nature of his business. If this man was setting up some trap, he would carry with him at least one fact that could be checked. Its accuracy meant little. Even an amateur used one truth to disguise his other lies.

The man hesitated.

Matthew smiled. There was an irony in their situation, an absurdity, at this last stage with seas of blood already spilled.

"Manfred von Schenckendorff," the man answered. "Where should he come through the lines?"

There was only one possible answer. Joseph was in Ypres, as he had been since the beginning. He had friends there, people he could trust. "Ypres," Matthew answered. "Wherever the Cambridgeshires are. It changes from day to day now."

"Of course. Your brother."

"You knew he was there?" Matthew was surprised, and slightly disconcerted. This man had too much knowledge to be simply a messenger. Was this a last chance at vengeance by the Peacemaker, because Matthew and Joseph had been responsible for too many of his failures? No, that was impossible! He must have had far more plans than they could ever imagine.

Countless people must have helped, or hindered. It was naïve to think Matthew and his family were high in the Peacemaker's mind, now of all times.

And yet it was John Reavley who had seen the original treaty and taken it, foiling the plot that would have betrayed France and prevented the war in the first place. Perhaps the Peacemaker would never forgive that.

The man was waiting for him, watching his face. "We planned carefully," he said at last. "We assumed it would be the Cambridgeshire lines at Ypres. But if you had preferred somewhere else, we would have made it so. It will be as soon as he can come. It is not easy. Two days, perhaps three. We cannot afford more." He rose to his feet and stood still for a moment, then offered his hand.

Matthew rose also and grasped it, holding it hard for a moment. He was tempted to ask who he was, and how he knew so much, but he was already certain he would receive no answer but the same tired, enigmatic smile. Then he let it go and walked the man to the door.

Afterward, alone again, he stood in his silent flat, looking at the familiar, rather worn furniture, his favorite painting of cows on the wall, his shelves of books. In a few days he would know the identity of the Peacemaker at last. This time he would not know it through deduction, with its potential for error; he would have certain knowledge. How fitting that in the end the Peacemaker should be betrayed by his own, a man choosing compromise rather than dominion, honor rather than power, a hard peace that might last.

Tomorrow morning Matthew would go to Shearing and tell him the news, then leave immediately for the Western Front and Ypres. He must be there when Schenckendorff came through. This really was the beginning of the end.

He thought of his mother and father driving along the Hauxton Road to tell him about the treaty nearly four and a half years ago, on that last golden summer when the world had seemed so unbreakably innocent. In spite of himself, his eyes filled with tears.

TWO

*A*cross London, in Marchmont Street, the man Matthew thought of as the Peacemaker was standing in his upstairs sitting room with the lights out and the curtains wide open, staring down at the street. There was very little he could see, even though his eyes had grown accustomed to the dark, really no more than the occasional gleam of hooded headlamps on the glistening wet road as now and then a car passed by.

It was nearly the end of the struggle. There was just one more big hand to play, and then it was over. Peace was inevitable now—of a kind, but nothing like the peace the world could have had if his plans had succeeded in 1914. He had seen the horror of the Boer War at the turn of the century. The slaughter, the waste, and the shame of it had never left him. He had sworn that such things would never happen again if there was anything he could do to prevent them—any price at all he could pay.

He had tried. God knew, he had done everything in his power, sacrificing the time and substance of his life for the cause. And yet war had still broken out, and continued for four long, ruinous years. He and his cousin Manfred von Schenckendorff had almost prevented it four and a half years ago. They had been days away from success when John Reavley, a retired Member of Parliament and sometime inventor from a Cambridgeshire village, had stumbled on the treaty and understood what it meant. In his narrow-minded patriotism, he had stolen it. The Peacemaker had learned what had happened and had him killed before he could show it to anyone, but despite all his efforts he had failed to retrieve the treaty. The one copy he had was insufficient to take to the king in the hope that he would sign it, and avoid the coming conflagration.

Then there had been the idiotic assassination in Sarajevo, and Europe had hurtled toward war. Estimates of the dead and lost—those crippled, maimed, or damaged in heart and mind—amounted to more than thirty-five million. The futile, blind idiocy of it boiled inside him with a rage so intense it caused him physical pain.

He had done everything he could, and failed. Now, if he did not succeed in forcing the Allied powers to create a just peace, it would all happen again. A handful of years and a new war would foment like a disease incubating in the body, and a new generation would be slaughtered just as this one had been.

He had tried persuasion, but was not listened to. President Wilson had no concept of European politics, and no understanding of history. He wanted to dismantle Germany's heavy industry, destroy her army and navy, shatter the heart of her people, and weigh them down with debt that could never be repaid. He could not see the damage that would do to all of Europe, perhaps to the whole world.

The torrent of his despair was interrupted by the sound of footsteps on the stairs. He knew Mason would have come on foot, but how had he not seen him in the street? He had been waiting for him all evening.

"Come in!" he said sharply in answer to the knock.

The door opened and the manservant announced Richard Mason.

The Peacemaker nodded, and the manservant stepped back to allow Mason in. They had conducted this ritual often enough over the last five years that it needed no words.

The Peacemaker went back to the window, closed the curtains, and then turned on the lamps near the two large chairs. The yellow light shone vividly on Mason's face. It was gold across his high cheekbones and broad mouth, making his nose look even stronger and his eyes darker, the lines around them accentuating his weariness. His hair was so thick and black that he barely looked English, although in fact he was born and bred in Yorkshire and loved its wild moors and dales and the storms along the coast as a man can love only the land where his roots burrow deep into the earth.

The Peacemaker had no need to ask the question that was in his mind. He and Mason had known each other since Boer War days. They had seen the same horrors and made the same covenants with the future, and both had failed.

"Three or four weeks at most." Mason was just back from the Western Front, where the Allied troops were now moving forward so rapidly it was hard to keep up with the numbers of prisoners or the land gained. The fighting line was always advancing, and the casualties were still high. Each report looked much like the last, except that the names of the towns were different.

The balance of hope and tragedy was especially poignant. As a journalist, Mason found it difficult to write without his own anger pouring through, and he did not want it to. The whole continent had suffered enough, and there would be far more pain and loss still to come than most people realized. The long, grueling aftermath of war would very rapidly overtake the first wild joy of the cease-fire. Unlike the Peacemaker sitting opposite him in this safe, elegant room, he had spent the last four years reporting from every battlefront in the world. He had lived in the violence and the fear, the cold, the hunger, and the stench of death. The war was not simply an idea and a set of emotions to him; it was a terrible, physical reality.

He looked at the Peacemaker's face in the lamplight, one-sided in shadow, as his own must be, and to him now the imbalance in it was disturbingly visible. In the lit side were the dreams and the compassion of the early years, the vision of healing; in the shadowed side toward the open room were the arrogance and the disregard for the curbs of morality, the refusal to see the dreams of others. The Peacemaker had argued over and over that the greater end justified the smaller ugliness of the means.

Joseph Reavley had said that the means were inextricably bound into and part of the end. Being a chaplain, he had put it in religious terms. He had said that if you picked up and used the devil's tools, you had already served his purpose, because using them had changed you, and that was all he wanted.

Mason had thought it fanciful, an easy sermon. Now, sitting in this quiet room, he knew it was true. The Peacemaker was no longer the man with whom Mason had planned such noble things five years ago. They had used means he despised, and still they had not achieved their ends of peace. They had fought a war inconceivable even a decade ago and brought ruin that seemed endless and irredeemable. Art, society, and faith had changed forever.

He remembered how the Peacemaker had envisioned the revolution in Russia as the birth of a new social order sweeping away the old tyranny and putting in its place justice for the ordinary man. Mason had been to Russia and seen the blood and the violence, and the same old weapons of oppression, secrecy, and deceit, no more skilled and certainly no more merciful.

Above all, he could see in the Peacemaker an imbalance of judgment, a hunger for glory that disturbed him. His visions ignored the passions and the vulnerabilities of men.

The Peacemaker, leaning forward, broke the silence between them. "We have to affect the terms of the armistice now!" he said urgently. "Before Wilson can force a punitive settlement on Germany and start an economic ruin that will draw into it the whole of Europe. Germany is the key, Mason. Never forget that! They'll rise again. Let it be as our friends— not as our enemies. Think of the future. Whatever you believe of the morality of any of it, the simple truth is that we cannot afford revenge. The ordinary German soldier is no different from the ordinary British soldier. How often have you told me that? The mothers and the widows in a German town are the same as those in London or Cambridge or anywhere. Think, Mason! Use your intelligence, not your sentimentality."

Mason's resolve had been firm, yet in one short speech the Peacemaker had moved the ground under it, and it wavered. Revenge was the last thing Mason wanted. There was nothing left to take, no one left to hurt any more terribly than they already had been. How could he have been so certain only a few moments ago?

"There is nothing I can do," he said aloud. It was an evasion, an escape from responsibility, and he knew it before the words were finished.

"For God's sake, man, you can try!" the Peacemaker snarled, fury suddenly twisting his features. Then with an effort so profound the strain of it was visible, he forced himself to lean back and lower his voice. "If we don't make a just peace—one on which we can build a new and united Europe—then economic chaos will ruin every chance we have of building up what is left of our civilization. We must repair the spirit of our people so they have a will to work, and a faith that it is to some purpose. Can't you see that?" His face was pale, his eyes glittering. "Do I have to explain to you what happens to a nation if we rob it of its identity, its means of regeneration, its faith in its own worth and destiny?" He flexed his long, thin hands. "If the Germans accept that the terms are just, we can be allies in the future. If they can't, then they will hate us. Secretly, violently, they will plan revenge, and it won't matter how long it takes—they will have it. Nothing good is built upon hatred."

Mason knew this was true, but the use of the word *allies* shivered through him with all the warnings he had not seen or understood the first time, before John and Alys Reavley were murdered—or Sebastian Allard, or Owen Cullingford, Augustus Tempany, or Theo Blaine—and every village in Britain bereaved of its youth.

He rose to his feet, surprised at how stiff he was.

The Peacemaker stared up at him. "What?" he demanded.

"I'll consider what there is to say that will cut across emotion and make them look at reason and reality in the future," Mason answered.

The Peacemaker stood also, an inch or two taller than Mason.

"There's no time to weigh and measure," he said grimly. "It sounds like the evasion of a moral coward who won't say no to a man's face."

At another time, even months ago, Mason's temper would have risen to such a charge. Now he was too weary, too clenched inside in his gut with the reality of death, to be stung by the wound of words. He smiled. "And that sounds like the attempt at manipulation of an armchair warrior who is used to shedding other people's blood," he answered. "I told you, I would consider what I think, and then act accordingly. I am just as aware as you of how little time there is." And without looking back to see if the Peacemaker's face was twisted with rage or pain, or simply blank with surprise, he walked to the door, down the steps, and finally into the dark, windy street.

By early afternoon the following day, Mason was back in Yorkshire, in the land he loved. He had booked a room at the village pub and, after a late lunch of homemade sausages—he did not ask what went into them in these times of hardship—he put on good walking shoes and set out in the evening light. He was high up, and the whole panorama of the dales spread out in front of him, valleys already shadowed, high slopes gold in the sun. The purple was fading from the heather, and the dark bronze bracken gave the color a sudden depth. The sky was ragged with clouds toward the west, and there was a chill in the air with the sweetness of great distances and clean winds.

The South had a gentleness with its great trees and richly harvested fields, its winding lanes and meal-drift autumn skies, but it never healed him as this land did. It was too soft, too comfortable. It forgave too much.

The North was different. The bones of the earth were naked here, and there was a beauty in it that spared nothing. You could stand on a narrow road like this and stare across the hills, fold after fold, wind-scoured, to the horizon. In a month's time, when at last there was peace in the world, there would be the first snows on the shaws, pale-gleaming. The air would smell of it. The wild birds would be flying in for the winter, long skeins of them across the sky, wings creaking. The reeds would spear upward in the rippled water of the tarns. Strangers would disappear, and only the men who loved them would walk these ways.

There was wood smoke rising below him. Over the hills he could see, perhaps five miles away, the roofs of the next village, the church spire high above them.

He turned and continued climbing. He would be tired by the time he got back to the pub, and probably cold, but he would not lose himself up here. There was only one road, and he was long familiar with it. He needed to be alone in the darkness with the wind and the stars.

He thought of Judith Reavley. The painful memory was something he should let go of. Their last parting a year ago had seemed final, and yet he kept turning it over and over. He could not change to please her. Her dreams, like Joseph's, had no foothold in reality. She fought battles she could not win, for ideals that were rooted in religion rather than the nature of men or of nations.

And yet her face haunted his mind. He found himself watching women who walked as she did, with the same ease, the stride that was a little too long for femininity yet filled with its own grace. He heard someone laugh and turned to find her, then disappointment cut deep when he realized it was a woman he had never seen before but who, for a moment, had sounded like her.

He wanted her ridiculous hopes to be attainable, and he was angry because they were not, and she would always be hurt. He was angry with Joseph Reavley for not having taught her better, protected her. And yet how could he? He was just as naïve himself. Perhaps Matthew, the second brother, was more of a realist. At least he was not a preacher, trying to create a belief in God in the trenches. That was a dreamer's errand if ever there was one.

He turned and walked back down the hill with the cold wind in his face. A blaze of stars swept above him from horizon to horizon, so low in the clear sky that he felt as if he should have been able to gather them with his hands.

The following morning he took the bus into Harrogate and had lunch in the Rat and Parrot with Robert Oldroyd, who had retired from teaching the year Mason had started secondary school, but Oldroyd's energy of mind and love of learning had infected Mason, as they had so many of the boys who had come to him raw and ready to be shaped. His former teacher was nearly ninety now, white-haired and bent but still interested in everything, as inquisitive and irascible in his opinions as always.

"Read your pieces," Oldroyd said, nodding slowly and staring at Mason. They were sitting opposite each other at a small table near the window. "You did well, boy. Don't want to get your head too big for your shoulders, but you have a nice turn of phrase. Say what you mean, no nonsense, no silly pretensions of making yourself immortal. Make us feel we're there with you." He reached a gnarled hand for his glass of cider and drank deeply before continuing. "Would like to have been with you, once or twice."

"Would you, sir?" Mason said doubtfully. He was grateful for the praise. He had admired Oldroyd intensely in his boyhood. A single word of praise from him then had been as precious as an accolade from anyone else. If Oldroyd acknowledged that you were alive, it made everything worthwhile. You became important, and your wildest dreams were possible. It was a lifetime ago, but the memory lingered with an innocence he thought he despised . . . but for some reason clung to. "It was pretty grim most of the time."

" 'Course it was," Oldroyd agreed, ignoring his lunch of bread and cheese. "Do you think I don't know that?" There was a challenge in his voice.

That was exactly what Mason had thought, and anger at the old men who stayed at home burned hot inside him. The delusions of glory and the ignorance of what real death was like in the mud and terror of the trenches were what made wars like this possible. "Where exactly would you like to have been?" he asked, and then wished he had not. The cruelty would serve nothing. Oldroyd belonged to the past. It was pointless to try to drag him into the harsher light of the present. He would die of old age soon, still understanding nothing.

"One place?" Oldroyd asked, thinking about it, his face pursed up, eyes almost lost in the folds of his skin. "I would like to have walked into Jerusalem last year with Allenby. I could just about imagine it from what you wrote, but you saw it, you were there. December 11. You didn't say much about his big cavalry victory at Megiddo last month. Reckon Aleppo and Damascus won't be long. But Jerusalem is different; it'll always be different. Went in as a man should, to the Holy City." He looked at Mason. "Jaffa Gate, wasn't it, with that big, square tower above it, and the crenellated walls? Crowded with people, you said. All looking down at one Englishman, alone and on foot."

"Did I say that?" Mason thought it sounded overemotional, sentimental, and he despised himself for it.

Oldroyd was watching him intently now, judging. "Yes, you did. Did you lie?"

Mason was too tired to be offended. He picked up his bread to eat it. "No. That's how it was. It just sounds . . . predictable."

"Shouldn't it?" Oldroyd asked. "Did you expect differently?"

"I don't think I expected it to happen at all." Mason was quite honest. "After so much dust and blood it all seemed ridiculously pedestrian, exhausted and aching men doing things we have become desperately used to. No trumpets, no drumrolls, just a bald, middle-aged Englishman in an army uniform. Apart from his badges of rank, he looked like anyone else." He bit into his bread and continued with his mouth full. "I was actually thinking about the future of the Middle East after the Turkish Empire is gone. Who will rule what, and how? Will the ordinary people be any better off, any freer from hunger or oppression?"

"Heroes are ordinary people, Mason," Oldroyd told him. "They're not ten feet tall. It's the inside that's different, not the outside. You could walk past Christ in the street if you weren't looking for Him." He sighed. "Come to think of it, most of us do."

"Maybe that's why we usually put Him on a cross," Mason said grimly. "At least that's different. Although I think it's peculiarly appropriate as a symbol of humiliation and pointless suffering. No wonder Europe worships Him. We see ourselves, our whole race, in one image of the ultimate defeat."

Oldroyd leaned forward, his hands clenched, his face so grave that his skin was tight across the sharp bones of his cheeks beneath his sunken eyes. "It's what a man fights for that defines who he is, boy! And a man who doesn't love anything enough to pay what it costs doesn't deserve to have it. Sometimes it costs pain and blood and terror. Sometimes it's years of quiet weeping. Sometimes it's waiting in the dark, without giving up." He blinked, as if seeing other times and people for an instant. "My grandfather fought Napoleon at Waterloo in 1815. My father and I fought in the Crimea, Battle of the Alma, 1854. I was twenty-three. Heard General Campbell tell us, 'There's no retreat from here, men. You must die where you stand.' He died in my arms. My son lost his legs in the Zulu Wars, 1879, at Rorke's Drift—hundred and thirty-nine of us against five thousand Zulus. My grandson fell at Passchendaele. Fifty thousand we lost in the first day."

Mason said nothing. In spite of himself, the ache in his throat was too tight and hard for him to swallow.

Oldroyd blinked. "Of course we lose sometimes. What has that to do with anything? It's not winning or losing that says who you are, it's the courage that makes you stand fast, with your eyes forward, and fight for what you love. Never let go of hope. Real victories happen one by one, and they're over the enemy inside. If I didn't teach you that, boy, then I didn't teach you anything."

Mason put his hand up and pushed the heavy hair off his forehead. "You sound like the chaplain in the Cambridgeshires at Ypres, and an ambulance driver I know."

"Woman driver?" Oldroyd asked him quietly.

"Yes." Mason was surprised. Judith's face was as clear in his mind as if they had parted only days ago rather than after the court-martial last year.

"Thought so." Oldroyd nodded. "Women are as brave as any man. They die to save their own without a second thought. But then that's love, isn't it? Loyalty. Women never give up, not when it's someone they love. Many a child wouldn't be here if they did." Oldroyd sipped his cider. "But a good woman'll fight for anyone that's hurt. It's someone's need that draws them, anything vulnerable."

That was just what Joseph Reavley would have said. Mason knew it as he sat there in the crowded tavern with the voices and the laughter around him, the smell of ale, the sawdust, the light gleaming on pewter tankards hanging above the bar and horse brasses on the wall. That passion was what Judith looked for in a man because she had seen it and understood it in her brother. She had felt it herself and had carried its burden for years.

Then quite suddenly he realized that for all its weight, that passion was far less crushing than the doubt and sorrow he carried himself. He was looking at what he had lost, not at what he had won. It was not only Judith he had lost; it was something of the best in himself. No matter how difficult it was, or what comfort of surrender it cost him, he must change himself. He must become who he wanted to be: a man he could look at in the mirror with some sense of respect, at least for his aspirations, if not his accomplishments.

"Yes, you're right," he said aloud.

Oldroyd blinked again. "Of course I'm right, boy," he said gently. "Except I was a bit above myself when I thought I could teach you, or anyone. You can tell people, that's all. Life teaches, or it doesn't. Be damn grateful you got the chance to try a bit harder. Where are you off to now?"

"Back to Ypres," Mason replied without hesitation. "I have things to do there, before the end. Would you like another cider?"

Oldroyd pushed his glass across. "Seems like a good idea. Don't mind if I do."

Matthew Reavley crossed the English Channel on the night of October 13. He had told Shearing only that he was pursuing information about a British collaborator with the Germans, which was part of his job anyway. It would be time enough to speak of the Peacemaker if Schenckendorff really did provide proof of his identity.

The weather was overcast with a sharp wind and a choppy sea, but the physical discomfort was small compared with the constant danger of torpedo attack. Even at this late stage when surrender was only weeks away, the war at sea continued. Ships still went down. He stood on the deck staring toward the dark coast of Belgium ahead and willed himself not to think of it.

They disembarked at Dunkirk near dawn. He waited in a cold railway station until the first train eastward to Ypres. It stopped several miles short, where bombing had destroyed the tracks. He was tired and cold and very hungry, but rations were short and he was grateful for a tin mug of hot tea given him by an army cook at the railhead.

He was in uniform but had removed his insignia of the rank of lieutenant colonel, a recent promotion, and substituted that of major. It was less conspicuous. They had learned in the past that the Peacemaker had allies in the least expected places. Any rank was sufficient to ask for a lift toward the lines. "Intelligence service," he said with a smile, to explain his absence of kit or weapons. "Trying to run down a traitor."

"Before it's too late, eh?" the young driver said with understanding. "Know where you want to be, sir? If I can help, I'll be happy to. Nothing filthier than a man who turns against his own."

"Gathering information—the man I need to see will be just behind the front lines." Matthew cranked the engine for him, then climbed into the front seat. They pulled away onto the early-morning road, crowded mostly with wounded coming back toward the hospitals.

"Looking for anyone in particular?" The driver swerved expertly to avoid a loose dog running after small groups of wounded men on foot.

"I'll start with the chaplain of the Cambridgeshires." There was no point in being secretive about seeing Joseph. He would have to ask people for directions in order to find his brother. Evasion had become a habit with him. He didn't like it—he found he was often evasive even when there was no need.

"Oh, Captain Reavley? You said your name was Reavley. He related to you, then?"

"My brother." He was proud to say that, especially here, so close to the fighting.

The young man nodded and concentrated on the road ahead. It was muddy and potholed at best, at worst gouged out by mortar fire and littered with debris. In the ditch there were broken wheels and shafts from wagons, old boxes half decayed, and sometimes even the carcasses of animals, mostly horses. That was something that sickened Matthew more than he had expected it to. They looked so vulnerable, having loyally gone to the slaughter to service men's rage and futility.

He could smell the front line long before they reached it. It was like nothing else he had ever known, thick and cloying. He gagged at the mixture of raw sewage and the sweet, stale odor of rotting flesh.

The driver glanced at him, then ahead again. "You'll get used to it," he said cheerfully. "I expect you'll be sick the first few times you step on a corpse thrust up by the mud, especially if it's been there for a year or two and you realize it's one of our own. But you'll get on with it." He sniffed. "And if they're right, it won't be for much longer anyway. If you're around in no-man's-land, watch for craters. Some of them are pretty deep, and God knows what else is floating in them. Not much gas left now, but it's heavy, sticks to the low bits, so stay higher an' you'll be all right. Don't need to tell you about the barbed wire, you can work that out for yourself."

Matthew studied him in the now-broad daylight. He was a lieutenant, and he looked by his build and the fine texture of his skin to be about eighteen or nineteen. But from the weariness in his eyes and the dry, painful humor of his voice he was an old man, long past his prime.

"Thank you," Matthew replied. "I'll probably just be speaking to people, prisoners coming through the lines. But I'll remember your advice."

"You'll have to find the prisoners before you speak to them," the driver pointed out. "Chaplain's back at the Casualty Clearing Station now and then, but mostly he's forward. I'll take you as far as I can."

Again Matthew thanked him.

They continued on in silence past columns of men walking slowly in the opposite direction. They moved as if half asleep, and their eyes seemed to see nothing. They put one foot before the other, shambling unevenly on the ruined road. Had they been lying down rather than standing, Matthew would have assumed them dead.

Suddenly he saw the human cost not in numbers of millions but individually, each an irretrievable loss. He was no longer aware of the stench, or the far distant noise of guns beyond the flat horizon as the armies moved inexorably forward, closing on the old battlegrounds and then at last moving toward Germany itself.

He had no wish to speak now, nor did he care if the young driver thought it was a squeamish stomach that held him silent. When they reached the field hospital, he thanked the driver, shook his hand, and jumped from the vehicle.

Inside, he asked an orderly if he had any idea where Captain Reavley was. When that man could not help, he went to the next person, and the next. Finally a mild, good-natured American first-aid volunteer called Wil Sloan told him and offered, if he would work his passage by helping carry stretchers, to give him a lift farther forward to the station where Joseph was most likely to be.

"Known the chaplain since the Christmas of '14," Wil said with a smile as they started out. "I drive with his sister most of the time. I guess she must be your sister, too, eh?"

Matthew swallowed hard. He could not think of Judith in this mud and rain, working day after day trying to do the impossible, seeing men die all around her. She had never spoken of it in the few times he had seen her at home on leave. Had she worked to forget? Or did she simply believe that he would never understand the reality, and that to allow anyone to believe less was a betrayal of the courage and the pain? If she had thought that, it would only have been the truth.

But then he never spoke of his work, either, because he was not allowed to. It was founded on lies and delusions: who could deceive the more efficiently and commit his own kind of betrayal.

Three times they got stuck in waterlogged craters, and Matthew had to climb out and help dig while Wil struggled with the steering wheel and the reluctant engine to get it started again. He was scratched, bruised, and splattered with mud by the time they finally reached the casualty dressing station where Joseph was. It was only a series of tents with some wooden duckboards to mark the walkways between. Even before locating his brother, however, he needed to fulfill his obligation to Wil and help load the stretchers into the ambulance.

He worked hard, slipping and staggering between the Evacuation tent and the parking area, trying desperately not to drop anyone. The loaded stretchers were not as heavy as he expected. Many of the wounded were only boys, light-boned, with no muscle on them yet. Their faces were hollow with shock. There seemed to be blood on everything.

He saw Joseph, knowing his outline from the angle of his shoulders and the way he stood, unconsciously favoring his right leg. Joseph gave no sign of having recognized him, but then he was not expecting to see Matthew here. He was absorbed in his work, seeming to know exactly where to be, what to say, and when he could help.

Matthew was awed by it. This was the older brother he had known all his life, and yet it was a stranger whose moral courage dwarfed his own. How could any man keep sane in this? There were broken bodies everywhere, ashen-faced, wounds hastily bound, the blood seeping through. He saw one soldier, not yet twenty, with a scarlet stump where his leg should have been.

Finally the rear door slammed shut and the ambulance jerked, stopped, then plunged forward, sending up sprays of mud. At last it picked up speed and disappeared into the rain. Matthew walked over to where Joseph was standing with the last of the walking wounded.

"Good afternoon, Chaplain," he said quietly.

Joseph stood motionless, then slowly turned. He stared with momentary disbelief, then, as Matthew smiled at him, dawning joy.

"Matthew!" He clasped his hand and wrung it so hard, he crushed his fingers.

It was all Matthew could do not to cry out. At home he would have hugged him, but here in the midst of this absurd mixture of chaos and discipline, it seemed the wrong thing to do. "Hello, Joe," he replied instead, grinning back.

"What are you doing here?" Joseph demanded. "The war's not over, surely?" He looked momentarily bewildered. "They're still fighting like hell ahead." He gestured slightly eastward toward the old battlefield of the Ypres Salient, and beyond it Passchendaele, which was on the verge of being retaken. The German border was still miles away.

"Not yet," Matthew answered. "Another three or four weeks at the most. That's not why I came." The excitement was sharp in his voice, and he could not control it.

Joseph looked at him, searching his eyes and finding no grief in them, no holding of darkness he needed to share. "The Peacemaker? You've found him?" His hand tightened again on Matthew's.

"Almost," Matthew answered. "In a day or two we'll know. Get these men back to help of some kind, and I'll tell you."

Joseph was puzzled. "Why have you come instead of writing? He can't be out here!"

"I'll tell you," Matthew replied. "Get your wounded to wherever they need to be." He was still standing in the mud, and the rain was getting harder.

Reluctantly Joseph obeyed, knowing which had the greater urgency. It was gathering dusk before they sat together in Joseph's bunker, shivering over a Dixie can of hot, muddy tea.

"Well?" Joseph demanded.

The rattle of guns was muted, far in the distance forward, but every now and then one of the big howitzers sent over a shell the weight of three grown men, which exploded close to them, shaking the ground and sending up massive gouts of earth.

"A messenger came to see me." Matthew swallowed and tried to conceal his distaste at the oily residue in the tea. At least the warmth of it eased the clenched muscles inside him. "A Swiss priest, or that was how he was dressed. He said the Peacemaker's ally in Germany, Manfred von Schenckendorff, is going to come through the lines at whatever point I would suggest. I said here, of course. He'll give himself up, so we can take him to London to expose the Peacemaker to the government. To Lloyd George personally."

"What?" Joseph stared at him, his face almost comical with disbelief in the yellow light of the lamp. "And you believed him? Matthew . . ."

Suddenly Matthew's elation vanished. Was he so hungry for justice, before it was too late, that all sense of reality had left him? "Think about it!" he said huskily, feeling the heat burn up his face. "Half of Europe is ruined. America has lost more than three hundred thousand men killed, wounded, or missing, but we've lost over three million! Germany's lost twice as many, and Austria-Hungary even more. The estimates we have altogether are beyond thirty-five million. God Almighty, Joe, what man with even a shred of sanity left could ever bear to imagine that happening again?"

Joseph closed his eyes, overwhelmed by the vision.

"The Peacemaker is planning to urge a settlement that will allow Germany to rise and begin it all over again," Matthew went on. "He hasn't forgotten his dream of dominion that would force peace on us all, but at the cost of strangling our spirits until we have no individuality left, only police to keep the law."

"And does this Schenckendorff believe he'll do that?" Joseph asked. "Why now? Why did he not see that years ago, or always?"

Matthew searched his mind and answered reluctantly. "Perhaps it was a dream with some nobility in the beginning. If I had ever seen war, real war like this, I might have done almost anything to prevent it happening again."

"Sold out your countrymen, without asking them if it was what they wanted?" Joseph's voice was quiet, his face bleak. "Or if they understood the price?"

"Nobody understands," Matthew replied. "You can't imagine . . . this!" He swung his arm around vaguely to indicate the battlefield beyond the clay walls of the dugout. "It's a human abattoir. I don't know if you believe in heaven anymore, but you must believe in hell!"

Joseph smiled faintly. "I believe in summer nights with the sky pale with stars, and in the poplars at sunset, and in spring the beech woods carpeted with bluebells so dense you can't put your foot down between them. I believe in clean water and a quiet bed, in laughter and gentleness. I believe that some men have the courage and the honor to face anything at all, and die without self-pity or complaint. I believe in the possibility of friendship, the love that never betrays. That's as close to heaven as I can grasp at the moment."

Matthew sighed. "Schenckendorff is coming through the lines here. He knows your name, naturally. You should hear what he has to say. I expect your German is better than mine, colloquial anyway. Mine's a little rusty. Don't get enough practice. And I might need your help with the mechanics of getting to him, and making certain I can get him out of here and back to London." He looked at Joseph gravely. "We're so close to it, it would be easy to forget that the Peacemaker might still think he has a chance to win, and take the chance to kill him—and us."

Joseph winced. "I suppose he could. Why should anyone think themselves safe here?"

Matthew started to laugh, then stopped.

"Nothing we can do except wait." Joseph finished his tea as if it were fit to drink.

Joseph had one of the better dugouts, and he made room for his brother in it. At least it was dry. But he slept badly that night, excited as always to have seen Matthew, wondering if he was sleeping or only pretending to. He was concerned for his welfare in the filth and danger he was unaccustomed to. Joseph lay in the dark of the familiar space, knowing where everything was, the rickety table, the one chair, the shelf with his books and the picture of Dante Alighieri, who had written so brilliantly about a different hell.

Joseph was the eldest of the four siblings. He was quite aware that worrying had become a habit with him, and had increased since his father's death. He was not ready for the responsibility of caring for the other three, foreseeing dangers, comforting loss, finding a reason and an answer for pain. There was no answer, but you did not tell that to people you loved, and who had learned to rely on you. He was the wrong man to have chosen the church as a calling, but there was no way out now.

What if this Schenckendorff was one more trick of the Peacemaker's? Matthew had looked so excited, so hopeful, all because some man had turned up on his doorstep in London and said he was a Swiss priest! Anyone could say that. Heaven help him, Joseph had said exactly that himself when he had been behind the German lines last year. He had been believed, too.

They wanted to find the Peacemaker so desperately, and time was running out. After the war was over, what chance would they have? Still, if he were honest, what chance had they ever had? Maybe their hunger for revenge was the Peacemaker's final act of destruction of the Reavley family?

He drifted into half sleep and confused dreams. Then without any warning it was daylight. Cold and stiff, moving as quietly as he could, he got up, shaved, and began the long routine of paperwork, letters of condolence, and helping the wounded. He tried to comfort, advise, assist with practical things like eating or drinking with bandaged hands, or none at all, dressing with a shattered arm or leg, simple tasks that had suddenly become monumental.

Matthew woke late and excused himself to find something to eat.

There was no word of any German prisoner asking to see either Joseph or Matthew, and there were so many coming through the lines in the general area of Ypres that it was impossible to check all the names. Joseph continued with his usual duties. More often than not he was far forward of the Casualty

Clearing Station, beyond even the old trench line, as the armies moved forward. British troops had just taken Messines and were advancing on Menin.

Matthew spent the days restlessly, trying to look as if he were collecting some kind of information that would justify his presence in the junior intelligence work he had told Colonel Hook he was engaged in. He spoke to German prisoners, but there was nothing of use they could tell him, and the pretense would soon wear thin.

It was the middle of the afternoon of the sixteenth when Snowy Nunn came to tell Joseph that Colonel Hook wanted to see him. "Roight now, Chaplain," he added, his fair face puckering up with apprehension. "It's another German prisoner. Oi don't know what anybody done to this one. Officer an' all, by his uniform, and the way he stands. He's got a foot all mangled up, so looks loike someone ran over it or something."

"Right." Joseph's heart sank. Another piece of random brutality, pointless but so very understandable. "I'll be there."

Snowy nodded, his eyes grave. "Whole lot more for the hospital, Oi reckon. Some o' the poor sods are knocked about pretty bad. Look loike hell, they do. Oi thought winning weren't much fun after all, an' we waited long enough for it. But Oi reckon losing's got to be a whole lot worse. Roight away, Chaplain, he said."

"I'm going," Joseph said impatiently. He resented Hook sending for him over some breach of discipline. There were going to be lots of instances of loss of self-control. He had known people to nurse loved ones over years to a painful death, never complaining. Then when it was all over and there was some ease at last, they were suddenly overwhelmed, letting slip the courage and the selfless endurance that had governed their lives throughout the sacrifice. He could sense now the same longing for peace and fear of change. They wanted to go home to what they had originally left, what this whole bloody war had been about saving, but it wasn't there anymore. The past never is. The England they had paid for with such a price no longer existed.

He walked quickly through the mud, used to keeping his balance in it, not avoiding the rain because he was already wet and there was no point.

He found Colonel Hook in the command bunker nearly a mile farther east. He looked tired and too thin.

"Ah, Reavley." He looked up from his maps spread out on top of a packing case. "Odd thing's come up." He looked puzzled rather than angry, and it was unusual that he had addressed Joseph by name rather than rank or calling.

Joseph stood to attention. "Yes, sir?"

"Got a German officer, says he's a colonel, but I think he might be more senior than that, although my German's not good enough to be certain. Know everyday language well enough, but not the differences of education and class. But he's asked to speak to you."

"Is he badly injured?" Joseph was surprised. Snowy Nunn had mentioned only a crushed foot.

"Not at all. Painful, no doubt, but he didn't even refer to it," Hook replied. "He didn't ask for a chaplain, he spoke of you by name—Reavley. Seemed to expect you to be here." The demand for explanation was clear in Hook's eyes.

Was this the Peacemaker's ally in Germany at last? "No idea, sir," Joseph said aloud, his voice husky. He cleared his throat. "I'll go and talk to him. Where is he?"

"Casualty Clearing Station," Hook replied. "His foot's a mess. Looks like someone pinned him to the ground with a bayonet." His face was pinched with disgust. "Damn stupid thing to do. If I thought I had a cat in hell's chance of catching the man who did it, I'd have him up on a charge."

"What's his name, sir?" Joseph's heart was pounding. Could they really be this close to the Peacemaker at last?

"No idea!" Hook said impatiently. "They've only got one colonel. Go back and bloody well ask!"

"Yes, sir." Joseph stood to attention, and then hesitated. He knew Hook wanted to say something more. Their eyes met for a moment. Joseph smiled.

Hook shrugged. "Get out," he said quietly. "Go and find out what the poor sod wants. No favors."

"Yes, sir."

"You mean *no, sir*," Hook corrected.

It was Joseph's turn to shrug. He went out without replying. It was raining hard again. The wet khaki had rubbed his skin raw at his neck and his feet were getting new blisters by the time he caught up with the ambulances. There were very few men around. Most of the troops had moved forward, beyond Ypres now. Joseph remembered the town well, the places where in 1914 and 1915 they had eaten quite decent food, drunk wine, even sung around the piano in one or two of the better estaminets. He wondered how many of the people were still alive after occupation. Or had most of them fled ahead of the German army, back somewhere into France? How many of the buildings were still standing after the incessant bombardment? He had heard that Passchendaele was in ruins, nothing left but scattered stone and burned wood.

He walked back the way he had come through the mud to the cratered road. Thirty minutes later, he was back in the Casualty Clearing Station, standing by the cot of a German officer whose foot was swathed in bloody bandages, his face white and mask-like with the effort of controlling his pain.

"Captain Reavley," Joseph said, introducing himself. "I believe you wanted to see me, Colonel?"

The man stared at Joseph's uniform as if trying to understand his insignia, and the Military Cross and Distinguished Service Medal. These were both front-line awards, and yet he was still a captain. "You have been demoted?" he said in German. He spoke very quietly, the subject being a delicate one, and there was sympathy in his eyes.

It was Schenckendorff, Joseph was sure of it. He thought he was speaking to Matthew, and had therefore expected a major. And certainly the chaplain's collar confused him. Only the name was what he had been told.

But he must be careful. "What is your name and rank?" Joseph asked. "Why did you send for me?"

The man was exhausted, and to surrender must be almost intolerable for him. His accent was discreet, highly educated. He probably spoke English, even if he chose not to now. But if he really was the German ally of the Peacemaker, then he would be the man who had obtained the kaiser's signature on the original treaty, and he would unquestionably be of the old aristocracy.

"Why did you ask for me?" Joseph repeated.

"I asked for Major Reavley," the man replied, drawing his breath in sharply as another wave of pain overtook him. "I did not know you were a man of the church. It does not seem to make sense."

"It makes excellent sense," Joseph told him, moving a little closer but remaining standing. You did not sit on the narrow cot of a wounded man; the sheer alteration of weight could hurt intensely. "I am chaplain of the Cambridgeshire regiment, the remnants of which are still here at Ypres. I refused promotion because I want to stay with the men, not move back to regimental headquarters."

Schenckendorff nodded fractionally, both understanding and respect in his eyes.

"I think it is my brother, Major Matthew Reavley, whom you want, Colonel Schenckendorff," Joseph went on.

The man's face tightened. It would have been impossible for him to have grown any paler. Joseph realized with a sudden, searing pity what his decision must have cost. He was a man who loved his country and had once believed passionately that it could dominate and govern in a lasting peace. Now he was coming through the lines to betray, in turn, the trust that had deceived him. The courage and the grief of it were overwhelming. For the first time Joseph saw with wrenching power the meaning of defeat, not just of a nation but of individual men and the dreams they had lived and died for. Perhaps heroism could only be truly measured in those who had lost, and faced the ultimate truth without flinching.

"Yes," Schenckendorff agreed at last. "I would be obliged if I could speak with him. It is . . . necessary."

"He is here," Joseph told him. "I'll bring him as soon as I can. But as you will be aware, we dare not tell anyone else who you are, or why you are so important."

Schenckendorff did not answer.

"You must tell no one," Joseph said urgently, lowering his voice even further. "Be as invisible as you can be, just like any other prisoner. We have no idea where the Peacemaker . . ." He hesitated. "Where your counterpart may have allies," he amended. It was brutal, but he could not afford to be unclear. "He may have guessed that you have come to us, and he will see it as a betrayal, one he cannot afford."

"I know," Schenckendorff said in no more than a whisper. "He will kill me. Perhaps he will do that eventually anyway. With him the cause was always first." He spoke with difficulty. "Perhaps that is the germ of his moral decay—he cannot see that some weapons destroy the men who wield them in a subtler and deeper way than the enemy they kill with their use. I will be extremely careful, Reverend Reavley." The shadow of a smile touched his lips. "I have to survive in order to tell your prime minister what my . . . ally . . . has done. He will not believe it from anyone else. Even I may have some difficulty. It will be necessary for you to be there, and to swear to the existence of the original treaty your father took. Do you still have it?"

Joseph smiled very slightly. "Who is the Peacemaker?" he asked.

Schenckendorff smiled back. It was a thin, painful gesture but not without both humor and comprehension. "The treaty would help," he said, evading the question. His voice was growing weaker, as if the pain of his broken foot, the shock to the bones, the extensive loss of blood, and no doubt several days of bitter deliberation before the struggle to get through the lines had exhausted his physical and mental strength. He had risked being shot as a deserter.

Joseph debated within himself whether to tell the doctor in charge here that Schenckendorff was of special importance and to take care that he did not die of neglect to his wound. That was possible in the vast crowd of German prisoners pouring through the lines now in their tens of thousands. Not all of them would be fed, treated, and cared for. And Allied soldiers must come first, always. But he could give no reason. The doctors were harried to exhaustion. Burdening them with secrets was foolish, especially one they would not understand. The risk was higher than any advantage. He decided against it.

"I'll have my brother here by this evening," he said instead. "Get as much rest as you can. Sleep if possible."

There was a flash of appreciation in Schenckendorff's eyes that he had not indulged in platitudes. "Good night, Chaplain."

Joseph managed to find Matthew and get the message through to him. He arrived back at the Casualty Clearing Station by sundown, but when he saw Schenckendorff, the German was feverish and in intense pain. The wound in his foot was messy, as if a bayonet rather than a bullet had caused it. He had lost a great deal of blood, and there was a fear of septicemia.

"You'd better start praying," Matthew said grimly when he found Joseph in the storage tent. He was sorting through supplies and trying to tidy them up after the night's casualties. "That foot looks pretty bad. Hope to hell they don't have to amputate it. It would make him hard to move. We won't convince anyone if we can't get him to London."

"Did he tell you who the Peacemaker is?" Joseph asked, turning from the table where bandages, linen, disinfectant, and suture thread were laid out.

Matthew looked back at him steadily. "No. Did he ask you if you still had the treaty Father took from the Peacemaker?"

"Yes. But I didn't answer him."

Matthew chewed his lip. "Joe, do you think that's what he really wants? Is he still on the Peacemaker's side and they need to get that treaty back before the armistice, just in case we expose it then?"

The thought had crossed Joseph's mind with a bitter disappointment, but he could not dismiss it. "Maybe," he said unhappily. "Perhaps we'd better not tell Judith anything until we know more. Damn it." He swallowed hard. "Damn it! I'd begun to hope we had him."

Matthew gripped Joseph's shoulder hard. "Maybe we have."

Joseph looked at him. "Have you thought what it would cost a man in Schenckendorff's position to turn against his own like that? I can hardly imagine the courage and the moral strength to face the fact that you had dedicated your life to a cause that was fatally flawed, then give yourself to the enemy to undo your own efforts and accept whatever they choose to do to you."

"Nor can I," Matthew agreed. "Which is part of why I dare not believe it yet. He's either a true hero or a very clever double dealer. Either way, he's a brave man." He sighed. "And he could die of that damn foot. What did it, Joseph?"

"Bayonet, by the look of it."

"God in heaven! For what? What's the point of that now?"

Joseph did not answer. For a man who had seen half the men he knew killed, the rage to commit such an act was easy to understand, and impossible to explain.

THREE

*I*t was another long night of casualties. More German prisoners coming through the lines voluntarily, or taken in desperate, failed battles. Joseph worked between the first-aid post and the Casualty Clearing Station. He finally got a break at almost half past three in the morning and lay down in his dugout. He was exhausted and filthy, but here it was at least dry. Matthew was curled up, sound asleep, and he took care not to disturb him.

He woke with a jolt to find Tiddly Wop Andrews bending over him. There was a thread of daylight coming down the steps. He could see that Tiddly Wop's handsome face was gaunt with weariness, and now also creased with new anxiety. "Chaplain!" Tiddly Wop said urgently. "Wake up! The colonel wants you roight away."

Joseph struggled to the surface of comprehension, his head pounding. "Why? What is it now?" His first fear was that Schenckendorff had died. Then he realized that Hook had no idea how much that would matter. He struggled to sit up. Every bone and muscle in his body hurt. "What's happened, Tiddly?"

Before the war Tiddly Wop's hair had been long, and when he was worried he brushed at his brow as if it still were. He did it now, unaware of the movement. "Oi don't know, Chaplain, but it's bad. Looks loike hell, he does. Something at the clearing station, that's all Oi know. You'd better go now. That's whoi Oi didn't even get you a mug of tea. No toime."

Joseph was suddenly ice-cold. "Have you seen Miss Reavley?" he demanded, his mouth dry. That was always his first thought.

"Yes, an' she's foine, sir. But you'd better go," Tiddly Wop urged.

Warmth flooded back into Joseph as if the blood had started pumping again. That was absurd. Judith had been here for four years, and usually he managed not to think about what she faced, or he would cease to function at all. It was the only way anyone could survive. Most men had family here, or at the very least lifelong friends. They all came from the same few villages. It was what bound them together, made the sharing and the loyalty complete, and the loss devastating.

He struggled to his feet and followed Tiddly Wop out into the pale, misty daylight. The rain had stopped; a watery sun was gleaming on the mud. Here and there it shone on a flat surface of a crater, making it look like polished steel.

It was a fifteen-minute hard walk to the colonel's command bunker. Joseph went down the concrete steps and parted the sacking over the entrance. He asked for permission to enter. When it was given he went in and stood to attention. This was farther forward than the Casualty Clearing Station. It was an old German bunker, and deeper than the British equivalent. The floor was dry, the walls lined with pretty decent wood.

"Sit down," Hook ordered, gesturing to an ammunition box turned on end. They must have taken the chairs when they retreated. Tiddly Wop was right: Hook looked dreadful. "I'm afraid there's been a death at the clearing station," he said grimly. "I've no choice but to call in the military police, but I want you to be there. You know how to keep your head and deal with these things."

Joseph was confused. There were deaths every day, in the trenches, in no-man's-land, in the ambulances, in the first-aid posts, in the clearing stations, in the fields, and on the sides of the roads, violent, desperate deaths all the time. A hospital was the best place to die, not the worst.

"One of the nurses," Hook added. "Sarah Price."

"I'm sorry," Joseph said automatically. "I'll write to her family. What happened?"

"For God's sake, Reavley!" Hook snapped, his voice near the edge of control. "I wouldn't have woken you up to tell you if it were an accident! The poor girl was hacked to death with a damn bayonet!"

For the second time since waking up, Joseph was stunned into complete immobility. He struggled to grasp what Hook had said, and yet the words were clear enough. A nurse had been brutally murdered. Of course the military police had been sent for; there was no other possible action. "Yes, sir," he said slowly.

"Be there, please," Hook asked. "The men are going to take it very badly. I don't want..." He looked for the right word. "I don't want revenge. I suppose it was one of the German prisoners, but we can't have them all massacred. Do what you can, Reavley."

"Yes, sir." Joseph stood up sharply. His mind was racing now to Schenckendorff. How would they get him out? He could not tell Hook that the man needed to leave. Perhaps they would find out what had happened quickly and it would all be settled in a day or two, then Schenckendorff's fever would have broken and he could travel. He would be in pain, but so were tens of thousands of men. War was about pain of one sort or another.

Hook drew in his breath as if to add something further, then let it go again in silence. Joseph excused himself and went to find Matthew before going to the station.

Matthew was standing with a group of other men around a small fire with a Dixie can of boiling water. He was about to make tea. Joseph greeted him. He turned around, regarding Joseph with some concern. He did not ask what was the matter, but it was clear that Schenckendorff was just as much on his mind.

"You'd better come," Joseph added simply.

Matthew thanked the men for the tea, leaving it behind as he fell into step with his brother single-file between the old craters. Only when they could move side by side did Joseph tell him what Hook had said.

"I suppose he's sure?" Matthew asked, hunching his coat collar up. "That's going to make it harder to get Schenckendorff out, isn't it? They'll be pretty unhappy about German prisoners, even injured ones. And I was worrying about him dying!" He pulled his mouth down in a hard line. "I suppose the only good thing is that he was too ill to be suspected. Filthy irony of it."

"He wasn't too ill to stand," Joseph replied. "Not early in the evening, anyway. You'd be amazed what a man can do, injured almost to death."

"Murdering a nurse?" Matthew's voice rose in disbelief. "What the devil for? He's on his way to London to give up his ally, and pretty certainly to be hanged!"

"No one in the Casualty Clearing Station knows that," Joseph pointed out. "At least, please God, no one does. Let's hope this Swiss priest of yours was careful."

Matthew hastened his stride toward the clearing station. All the men were moving forward in file toward the ever-shifting front line: the wagons of ammunition boxes, two tanks mired in mud and making heavy weather of churning it up on their huge tracks, and mule teams pulling guns forward on carriages.

Judith Reavley pulled her ambulance into the mud as close to the Casualty Clearing Station as she could and climbed out. She was tired and stiff from driving most of the night, and more than anything she wanted a hot drink to ease the chill inside her. First she must help unload the wounded, however, then when they were safe check her engine, which was misfiring. It was early daylight now. Mist hung over the craters, softening the harsh lines of the old supply trenches and for the moment making them look more like cart tracks than the gashes in the land that they were.

She stood, turning slowly, looking for someone to help. It was a two-man job to carry a stretcher. Someone must have seen her coming. A doctor hurried by fifty yards away, increasing his step to a run, but he took no notice of her. She started toward the Admissions tent. She was halfway there when another doctor came out whom she recognized immediately. It was Cavan, one of the best surgeons in the army, a man with whom she had worked through some of the worst nights during the battles of Ypres and Passchendaele, and in the long, desperate days since. His courage had merited him a Victoria Cross, and his rash loyalty had caused him to lose it.

He saw her and went back to the opening, shouting something inside. Two more men appeared and ran toward the ambulance. Cavan came to her, his face grave, his eyes smudged with shadows of exhaustion. She assumed he had lost many wounded through the night. There was no point in saying anything comforting to him. They had both seen this happen so many times, the understanding needed no words, and nothing helped anyway. Even if the task had been hopeless and the men too mutilated ever to survive, death was still death.

"Judith!" he said the moment they were out of the hearing of the wounded. "Something pretty awful has happened. Sarah Price has been killed." He took her arm and held it, closing his hand to grip her as if afraid she might sway and overbalance.

"I'm sorry," she said sincerely. Death was still death, but it was somehow worse that Sarah had made it this far . . . only to be killed in what had to be the final weeks of the war. By this time next month it could all be over. "What happened? There's not much falling this far back now."

"Not shelling," he said. "She was murdered." He was frowning, his face furrowed with distress. "It was brutal. She was cut about with a bayonet, in the pit of the stomach, and then left out where the hospital waste is put."

"You mean . . ." She stopped. She tried to picture Sarah Price lying in the mud behind the Operating tent where they disposed of blood-soaked bandages, old swabs, litter that could not possibly be reused, sodden clothes, and the mangled, amputated limbs of the worst injured. "Who did it?" She felt her stomach churn with horror, then a hot wave of fury. She had not particularly liked Sarah. She was trivial, made fun of things that were important, laughed too loudly, flirted in a silly way, showing off. But she was also kind, and generous, always willing to share any food she had, or pretend she had not heard a joke before and find it funny all over again. "Who did it?" Her voice rose sharply, and she pulled her arm away from his.

"We don't know," he replied. "One of the German prisoners, I expect."

"I suppose it has to be," she agreed. "Why aren't they keeping them guarded properly?" But even as she said it, she remembered odd moments of rage breaking through what looked like banter taken a little too far, ugly comments that stayed in the mind, petty cruelties that betrayed an underlying contempt. Please heaven it was a German, but she was not certain. "What are they doing about it?" she went on.

"Sending for the police, I suppose," he said with a slight shrug. "No one really knows. It must have happened sometime during the night. I hope no one gets it in the neck for not having guarded the prisoners. I reckon there are just too many of them for anyone to watch. And they came through the lines themselves, most of them. Poor devils are glad the war's over, at least for them." He gave a rueful gesture. "They might have thought we have more food than they do."

She, too, found it impossible to think of them as enemies any longer, although she was disturbed by her sense of pity. They looked so desperately like their own men. More than once her mind had turned to the Peacemaker, and she had wondered what he was like. She had even thought that if she had known him as a man rather than a power behind the murder of too many people she had loved, she might have liked him. At the very least she would have understood his dreams. Was that a disloyalty to her dead parents, and to Owen Cullingford, whom she had also loved? Every one of the dead was precious to someone. It was contemptible to imagine that those dear to you, woven into your life so that the loss of them tore it apart, were really more valuable than all the uncountable others. It was an arrogance amounting to blasphemy.

What had happened to Sarah Price? It could as easily have happened to Judith herself, or any of the other women here. Now a hot drink was trivial, almost forgotten. Her wet skirt flapping about her legs, cold and heavy, was no more than a discomfort. She gave Cavan a smile of thanks, then walked over toward the Admissions tent and the extended tents put up to shelter the wounded Germans, as well as their own.

She was barely inside when she saw Joseph. He turned at the sound of her footsteps on the boards. She felt a sudden pinch of anxiety at how tired he looked. He would have to deal with the grief of this new loss, and the fear and blame that followed.

"Judith!" He excused himself from the orderly he was talking to and came over to her quickly, almost pushing her into a corner away from earshot, so that she was pressed against a pile of boxes and stretchers stacked upright. "Sarah Price has been killed—" he began.

"I know," she said, cutting him off. "Cavan told me. Murdered with a bayonet." She swallowed hard, her throat tight. "It's horrible, but I suppose we shouldn't be surprised. Victory and defeat are too close to each other here, and both of them have their bitterness. War is probably the most hideous thing we do to each other, but we've become used to it. I don't know about you, but I'm scared sick of going home." She looked at him, searching his eyes and seeing understanding leap to them, and pain. They knew each other now in a way they could not have in a lifetime at home.

"That's not all, Judith," he said in little more than a whisper. "Matthew's here. I didn't have the chance to tell you before. The Peacemaker's German ally has come through the lines to give him up, before he can affect the terms of the armistice so the war starts up again within a few years."

"You know who he is?" She was amazed, excitement surging up inside her now, her heart suddenly pounding.

"Not yet." His hand tightened on her arm. "He's here, but he doesn't trust us enough to give us the name. He'll travel to London to tell Lloyd George. We've got to keep him safe until we can leave. He's got a badly wounded foot and was feverish the first night when I met him, but the orderly says he's better now."

"Are we going?" Without giving it even a thought she included herself. "He'll need an ambulance. Can we explain it to Colonel Hook?"

He hesitated only a moment. Before the war he would have evaded an answer, protecting her; now he knew her strength. "No. I think Schenckendorff's genuine, but we can't be sure," he said. "And even if he is, it's possible the Peacemaker knows he's crossed through, and there could only be one reason. He wouldn't take the risk."

"Murder him, too? His own . . ." She stopped, realizing what she was about to say, and bit her lip. "Schenckendorff?"

"Yes. Looks like someone already put a bayonet through his foot, more than once."

She drew in her breath to swear, then remembered his sensibilities and checked herself. "You said Matthew's here?"

"Two days ago Schenckendorff sent a message to him in London, asking where he should come through and if Matthew could be here."

A chill touched her more than the wet skirts around her legs. Now she understood why Joseph was afraid it was a trap, a last attempt at revenge on the Reavleys, who had thwarted him from the start.

He must have seen the fear in her. "We'll get him out," he assured her.

"It'll be over soon. It's wretched about Sarah Price's death, but it may be solved pretty quickly. We can't wait for it anyway. I'll explain it to Colonel Hook if I have to. Matthew's rank should make it pretty simple. At the moment he's pretending to be a major to avoid attention. He'll just have to take the chance and explain who he is."

She nodded. "I've got to see if I can fix my engine before I need it again. I'll be lucky if it lasts the war out. I really need some new parts."

"Good luck!" he said drily.

"Luck won't do it!" she retorted. "I need a light-fingered friend willing to liberate a few spark plugs and one or two other necessities of life."

He had stopped bothering to warn her to be careful. He gave a very slight smile and walked away.

Judith spent the next hour taking apart various pieces of her engine, cleaning them, and attempting to make them work again. Finally she resigned herself to the fact that without new spark plugs it was pointless. She abandoned it and went to find a mug of hot tea and something to eat, even if it was only a heel of bread and some tinned Maconachie stew.

The clearing station was unusually tense. She passed medical orderlies moving briskly over the duckboard paths from the tent for the walking wounded to that for the lying wounded, their heads averted as if they dare not look at her. They were embarrassed because she was an ambulance driver, not so very different from a nurse. It was as if she were somehow related to the victim. She opened her mouth to speak to one she knew well, but he had passed her without meeting her eyes, and it was too late.

She found nurses Allie Robinson and Moira Jessop in a supply tent. They were busy boiling a pot of water on a portable stove. The place was full of boxes stacked up and a half-open bale of sheets.

"Just came in?" Moira asked Judith. She was a Scottish girl with red-brown hair and wide eyes.

Judith shook her head. "Spark plugs are burned out," she said resignedly. "Got enough for tea?" She looked at the pot.

"Of course. I suppose you've heard about poor Sarah?" Moira asked.

Allie Robinson gave a little grunt. "What I want to know is what she was doing there at all! Everyone's been warned, as if we needed it. Did she think German prisoners were going to respect her and treat her like a lady?" She looked defensively at Judith, seeing her surprise. "Of course I'm sorry for her!" she snapped, the color rising in her fair skin. "Everyone is. But she flirted like mad with the Germans, led them on like a—" She stopped short of using the word that was obviously in her mind. "You have to take some sort of responsibility," she finished. "Now everybody's scared stiff, and all the men are going to be suspected until we can prove who it was."

"Why men?" Judith asked.

Allie and Moira glanced at each other, then away again.

"Because of how it was done," Moira answered. "Like rape, but with a bayonet."

Judith imagined it, and felt sick.

"Sorry," Moira apologized. "But she was pretty . . . loose. The last time anybody saw her she was with somebody, we just don't know who."

"Are you sure?" Judith was trying to deny it to herself, refusing to believe.

"Of course we're sure!" Allie snapped. "Stop being so naïve!"

Judith saw the fear and anger in her face, and knew with chilling familiarity that it was Allie's own fear speaking. She despised her facile criticism, as if any of it altered the tragedy, but she also understood it. If it were somehow Sarah's fault—if Sarah could have avoided it by behaving differently—the rest of them could find a way to be safe.

"No matter how silly she was, she didn't deserve that! She was used and thrown away like so much rubbish, Allie!" Moira said with disgust.

Allie looked away from her. "We're all used and thrown away," she said bitterly. "Just this time it's against the law, that's all. They're getting police in. Not that they'll find anything, but I suppose they have to try. Where do they even begin? Men are coming and going all the time, our own wounded, German prisoners, V.A.D. volunteers, doctors, people bringing supplies, even burial parties. Could have been anybody at all. Like Piccadilly Circus here."

"Well, obviously it was one of the German prisoners," Moira said impatiently. "It's just a matter of finding out which one. She flirted with all of them, stupid creature!" The pot boiled and she made three tin mugs of tea, passing one to Judith. "Sorry there's no sort of milk, but it's tea, more or less."

"Thank you." Judith took it and sipped tentatively. She had forgotten what real tea tasted like, and this was at least hot. "I don't suppose you know anyone who has decent spark plugs?"

"Good luck!" Moira said ruefully.

"You could try Toby Simmons," Allie suggested. "He has some imaginative ways of getting hold of things. At least that's one way you could phrase it." Her face pinched with distaste. "Gwen Williams says she thinks he's behind this. He was always making vulgar remarks, and Sarah wasn't above flirting with him. Too openly, if you ask me."

"Nobody did ask you," Moira told her.

"You didn't, because you like him!" Allie retorted. "You never thought there was anything wrong with what he did, even when he was caught in the empty theater with Erica Barton-Jones."

"Really?" Judith was surprised. Toby was handsome, and sometimes amusing, but Erica Barton-Jones was from a very good family and fully expected to marry into a title of some sort, or at the very least into money.

"That's rubbish," Moira said quickly, her face flushed. "That was just spread around by Sarah as a piece of spite."

"Why would she do that?" Allie asked.

"How do I know? Boredom, fear, loneliness, sheer stupidity," Moira snapped. "Why do we do any of the things we do? She was lonely, and she had nothing much to go home to. Not that many of us have."

Allie was silent, her face filled with a sudden, overwhelming grief.

Moira looked at Judith. "It's as if something has sort of . . . broken," she said quietly. "Yesterday we were all stiff upper lip, and today nobody knows what to say or do. I don't know how many of us actually liked Sarah, but she was one of us, and nobody at all should be used that way, and left . . . exposed like that." She put her arms around herself, holding them folded tight, protectively. "I feel . . . naked too, as if every man's looking at her but seeing me as well. I know that's idiotic, but I can't help it."

"It'll be better once they find out who did it," Judith said, trying to reassure her, although she feared it was a lie. Suspicions might be proved wrong, but did you ever forget that they had been there? Trust broken is not easy to mend; sometimes it is not even possible. "Thanks for the tea. I've got to see if I can find some spark plugs." She put the mug down and with a small wave of her hand went outside into the cold midmorning light.

In the empty Resuscitation tent Joseph reported to Captain Cavan to ask what he could do to help. He knew Cavan well and had an immense respect for him. After Major Northrup had been killed, it had been Joseph who had saved Cavan's life at the court-martial, although he could not save the Victoria Cross for which he had been recommended for his extraordinary courage under fire. Naturally they did not speak of it now; a gentleman did not mention such an obligation.

"Glad you came," Cavan said sincerely. He was sitting on an upturned box emptying stew out of a Dixie can, and there was a mug of tea on the makeshift table. His blood-splashed white coat was slung over the back of a hard chair. "Need all the help we can get to keep control of this." He was in his middle thirties, an angular man with fair hair and tired, heavy-lidded eyes over broad cheekbones. With long rest and regular food he would have been handsome.

There was no need for explanations; he knew Joseph understood. "Police are here already. Damn nuisance, because nobody can leave until they get this sorted out. Means we're piled up with German prisoners, and this fellow Jacobson won't even let our regular ambulance crews in and out, except the women, in case it's one of them." He looked exhausted and thoroughly fed up. He shook his head. "God, what a bloody stupid mess. Sorry, Reavley. See what you can do to help. Jacobson's in the first tent at the end."

"Yes, sir." Joseph was outside on the wooden pathway before he fully realized what Cavan had said—no one could leave. He, Matthew, and Schenckendorff were imprisoned here until this crime was solved. It would probably only be a couple of days, but it was already October 17. What if it took longer?

The air was cold, with a raw wind coming in from the east. He walked quickly, his boots pounding on the slats, but at least the planks were firm under his weight, not like the constantly rocking duckboards in the trenches, the best of them covered with chicken wire to help men avoid slipping when they were wet.

He reached the tent and knocked on the door frame. He heard the command to enter, and pushed it open. Inside, it had been cleared of most of its medical supplies, no doubt because they were needed as much as for the convenience of the police. The man sitting behind the bare, wooden table was plain-faced with dark hair brushed straight back and a short bristly mustache. He appeared to be of average height. Only the hands holding a pencil above a clean sheet of paper were in any way remarkable. They were slender, fine-boned, with particularly long fingers. His insignia said that he was a captain.

The other man in the tent was fairer, his nose a little crooked as if at some time it had been broken. He stood a little distance from Jacobson's chair and stared at Joseph with undisguised curiosity.

"Yes?" Jacobson inquired. He was very pale, his voice sharp. It was apparent that he was nervous, and Joseph guessed that he was probably a civilian policeman fairly recently drafted to the front. The stench of it would turn his stomach, and the scale of death everywhere must be something he had read of, but could never truly have imagined until now.

"Captain Reavley, sir," Joseph replied. "Chaplain. Dr. Cavan thought I might be able to help."

Jacobson's face relaxed; even the tightness of his shoulders eased a little. "Oh. Good. Yes, Captain. I'm obliged. This is a very ugly business, and there are only Sergeant Hampton and myself to deal with it." He indicated the other man briefly. "We need to question everyone: doctors, orderlies, nurses, and of course the patients . . . men . . . injured men." He did not seem certain what term to use. "I'd be grateful if you could help. You might know better how to deal with it, what to say. Colonel Hook says you're . . . experienced." He was obviously at a loss to understand what that might mean.

"Yes, of course. You'll have to give me some of the facts, or my questions won't be of much use," Joseph said. He had no intention of telling Jacobson about the other crimes he had solved.

Hampton shifted his weight from one foot to the other but did not interrupt, and Jacobson ignored his restlessness.

"Sarah Price," Jacobson said grimly. "Twenty-five-year-old nurse. Been here just over a year, according to my information, pleasant enough, and good at her job. Turner, the slightly wounded man on guard duty, found her at the back of the Operating tent, on the ground near where the . . . the waste is left for removal." He looked embarrassed because he could not think of any words that were decent to describe what he knew were amputated limbs from injured soldiers, parts of their bodies that could not be saved. He was shivering as he tried to control his feelings. "What . . ." He swallowed. "What do you do with it . . . the waste?"

"Bury it," Joseph replied. "As deep as possible."

"Never be found," Jacobson said with relief. "Maybe whoever killed her was hoping the same would happen to her. Could be why she was left there."

"Possibly," Joseph agreed, trying to save Jacobson's emotions. Then he realized how false that was. They could not afford to cater to squeamishness, even as a mercy. "Still, bodies come back to the surface here, sir, quite often," he continued. "New shell holes, craters, even new graves dug. He couldn't hope to conceal her. More likely he just left her there because that's where it happened."

Out of the corner of his vision Joseph saw Hampton nod. He looked as if he had been here at the front longer than Jacobson. Possibly he was not in the regular Criminal Investigation Department, merely seconded for this crime.

"What time was she found?" Joseph asked.

"Just after half past six this morning. You'd better come and see the body, and where she was found." Jacobson rose to his feet and motioned for Joseph to follow him. "Hampton will get on with investigating the physical facts." He did not bother to glance at his assistant as he led the way out.

Joseph had seen more dead men than he could think to count: whole ones, white and motionless. They did not look as if they were sleeping; it was profoundly obvious that the spirit that made them unique and alive was not there anymore. And he had seen men who had died in agony and terror, blown apart, half their bodies gone, soaked in blood, mutilated beyond recognition. Some of them had been men he had known in life, friends he had cared for and with whom he had shared deep and unforgettable emotions. Some he had held in his arms as their lives bled away. Still, he had not seen a body that shocked him as this one did.

No one had tried to make her decent, on purpose, so the sight of her would stir rage and pity, and leave whoever saw her so wrenched and violated of all decency that they would never forget or forgive what had happened. The most private parts of her womanhood were lacerated and exposed, as if whoever had done it had hated not only her but all that was female as well. It was grotesque, and Joseph stared at it as if every woman he had known and loved were torn apart on that wooden table, everything to do with the act of sex debased. She had in effect been raped with the blade of a bayonet, almost certainly still affixed to the rifle.

No wonder Jacobson looked sick. It wasn't just the stench of the latrines, or a hundred miles of corpses half rotted in the mud over the last four years; it was this desecration of the source of human life.

"Cover her up," Joseph said hoarsely. "God in heaven, she didn't have to be left like that!"

"Yes, she did, Chaplain," Jacobson said at his elbow. "I need your help. I don't want any feelings of mercy for your men, any loyalties to anyone, or pity for the living, or ideas of peace and forgiveness, to make you let this man go. You've seen fighting and I haven't, but a man who would do this to a woman has to be stopped. If we say this is all right and it doesn't matter, then I don't want to live in the England we just spent four years of hell to defend."

Joseph took off his jacket and laid it over the lower half of Sarah Price's body. He was shuddering with cold without it, but he did not even hesitate. Anything was better than leaving her like that. He wondered who Jacobson had lost: brothers, perhaps even a son. Many boy soldiers were as young as fourteen or fifteen. They hungered and died just like anyone else. Perhaps that was why the trenches shocked Jacobson so profoundly. He was thinking of someone in particular.

"What do you want me to do?" Joseph asked.

Jacobson sighed. "Dr. Cavan said you'd solved other murders out here. Didn't elaborate, he just said you had a way of finding the truth. Originally I was thinking of helping to keep control of things. Everyone's pretty upset. They've enough to deal with in ordinary war; they don't need this on top of it. But any other help would be good. We need this closed as soon as possible. Get back to some kind of sanity—as much as there's any kind of sanity out here."

"What are you going to look for?" Joseph asked. "There's a bayonet on the end of every rifle on the Western Front! And blood on all of them. And on most of us in a casualty station." He swallowed hard, as if there were something stuck in his throat. "There's nothing to say this was personal to her. It looks like hatred of all women. A madman." He thought as he said it that it was a shallow remark. Who could stay sane out here where all men's life expectancy could be counted in weeks? Life had a different meaning.

Jacobson did not reproach him for his words. Perhaps he saw the regret in Joseph's face as soon as the words were out.

"Opportunity, to begin with," he replied. "See who we can weed out with that. Eliminate any man who was accounted for all last night. Won't be so many, but perhaps more than in civilian life. For a start, I expect all the doctors were busy, and can prove it, and maybe some of the ambulance drivers, too? Orderlies? Understand you speak German pretty well?"

"Yes, well enough. Do you want me to start with the German prisoners?"

Jacobson debated with himself for a minute before replying. "Let's narrow it down a bit first. Can hardly expect them to tell us the truth anyway, can you? They'll try to blame us, and we'll try to blame them. It's natural."

"It'll be difficult," Joseph warned. "People come and go all night long in a station like this. Usually it's mostly wounded and drivers, but right now it's prisoners as well. It's not guarded, except the German prisoners, and that's only by men not wounded badly enough to go home, but not fit for the front line. Sometimes men bring in a friend or someone they found or rescued, or come to see someone too ill to be moved. Still . . . I'll see what I can learn."

Jacobson put his hand on Joseph's arm. "First speak to some of the nurses, Chaplain. They'll be pretty badly upset. They know you. They're used to seeing you around. Maybe they'll tell you things they won't tell me. See if you can find where people were. Find out what you can about this girl." He gestured toward Sarah Price on the table. "And take your coat, man. You'll freeze, and we need you. I'll see she's decently covered."

Joseph left the hut with his jacket back on again, cold from the dead body rather than warm from his own. The back was now stained with dark blood from where the cloth had touched her.

The wind outside was knife-edged, blowing hard and flat from the east so that it stung the skin. He walked slowly along the wooden boards, passing nurses who smiled at him nervously. One or two even stepped off into the mud to avoid being too close to him. He was a chaplain and a man they knew; what must they be feeling about others?

What lay behind the savagery that had swept over some man until he had lost everything within himself that made him decent, all gentleness, all respect for life or dignity or hope? Had war changed him, or had it merely stripped from him a veneer concealing the barbarism that had always been there, just hidden from view?

Did he know the man, and had he failed to see it? What manner of priest does not recognize hell when it is in front of him, face-to-face? A man so blunted by the sight and sound and smell of suffering that he has shut himself off from the pain of it, a man who refuses to, because seeing hurts? Seeing forces you to acknowledge that you must also act. The excuse of ignorance is stripped away, leaving you naked before the truth.

He stopped outside the Pre-operation tent. He was not ready to go around it to the Treatment tents yet, even though he was so cold his muscles were tight and his teeth clenched.

Who had done this? One man must answer for it. But was one man alone responsible, or were they all, because they had taken young men and taught them that fighting and killing are necessary for the nation to survive? And they were necessary! Surrender was not just a matter of ceasing to fight; it meant forfeiting all the freedoms that gave you the chance to make any choice about good and evil, for you and your children, and maybe even their children as well.

Perhaps it was how you fought that made the difference. Maybe some of the soldiers who lived on and went home were just as much casualties as the dead. What had war done to the man who had torn Sarah Price open that way? Could they ever heal him and make him something like whole again? Or must they simply execute him, for the sake of society? Whose was the guilt?

He would speak to the nurses one by one. He must get some sense of order into his mind, learn all he could about that night. Where had Sarah been working, and with whom? Could other people establish that beyond doubt? It was a busy place, men coming and going all the time, but with their attention on the injured and on their own jobs and the terrible urgency of them.

Still, if he could discover what time she had been killed, then it would be possible to eliminate most people, and it might begin to make sense. Of course he would learn as much as he could about Sarah herself, just in case there was any personal element to her death, but it could so easily have been no more than being alone in the dark at the wrong time.

First he walked around the Admissions tent into the wind and across the open space to where he found Judith in the lee of the supply tent, very carefully fitting new spark plugs into the engine of her ambulance.

"Don't ask me where I got them!" she warned. "Believe me, you would prefer not to know."

He'd had no intention of asking. He was a lot wiser now than he had been two years ago. Odd how your family was the last to realize that you had grown up, or had learned from your mistakes.

"Were you here last night?" he asked her.

She smiled at him. Her face was smeared with engine oil and more than a little mud, but she still had the same steady eyes, the high cheekbones, and the passionate and so very vulnerable mouth. What on earth was she going to do in St. Giles after the war? Marry some local worthy who would never begin to understand her? He repeated the question.

"Driving back from the front line, most of it," she answered. "I dropped wounded off here at about three, helped get them inside, had a cup of tea and something to eat. I cleaned the ambulance. I suppose I left again about half past four. I got lost somewhere about Polygon Wood, I think, but it could have been any other hill with tree stumps on it. I got back here about daylight."

"Are you sure of the times?"

She frowned. "I think so. Why? Was that when she was . . . killed?" She said it with difficulty, and he could hear the pain in her voice.

"I don't know yet," he answered. "How many wounded did you have?"

"Six, same as usual."

"Badly wounded?"

"Yes. Does all this matter?"

"I don't know yet. It was probably one of the German prisoners, but we have to be sure." Joseph sighed. "Was Wil Sloan with you?"

"Wil?" She was startled. "Yes, of course he was. You can't suspect him, for heaven's sake!"

"I need to place everyone, Judith, or I can't begin to make sense of it. Someone did a terrible thing to her."

She turned away. "I know! It must have been one of the German prisoners. I daresay they hate us all. Or at least some of them do. They look just like us, don't they, especially when they're hurt and covered with mud and blood. I hate this!"

He touched her arm gently. "It'll be over soon. Or this part of it will. But we've got to find out who did that to Sarah Price. Apart from justice, and stopping him from doing it again, Matthew and I need to get Schenckendorff back to London. They're not going to hold up the armistice negotiations because of this mess here."

"Can't you explain it to Colonel Hook and get away anyhow?" she asked.

"I don't think so. We don't know who the Peacemaker is, or what allies he might have here. He may know Schenckendorff has crossed over. It won't take a genius to guess that it could be here. He'll know Matthew's left London, and probably where he's come to."

Her eyes widened, fear sudden and gripping. "Joseph, be careful!"

"I am. Tell me about Sarah Price, honestly. We haven't time for blurring the edges with kindness."

She pursed her lips. "I didn't know her well; I don't think anybody really did. She was a bit flighty, enjoyed a laugh and a joke, even if it was pretty silly. Didn't seem to take anything very seriously, and that annoyed some people. She seemed awfully shallow." She looked away for a moment, toward the edge of the light from the lamps, then back at him, and spoke with painful honesty. "I think she stopped allowing herself to feel when her brothers were killed. She wasn't going to let herself feel that kind of loss again. She made light of pretty well everything, and she drank rather more than was good for her. She flirted and led a few people on, but most of us knew it was just the way she was. We all deal with loss and fear in different ways. That was hers."

One of the orderlies crossed over at the edge of their vision, and she waited until he was beyond earshot before continuing. "She didn't gossip and she didn't tell tales. And she was generous with things. I think she had stopped valuing anything, so it was easier for her to give it away. Almost as if she knew she might not make it home." Her lips tightened. "I'm not sure she had any home now. I remember her saying once that there was only her grandmother left. I don't know what happened to the others. Her mother died in the winter of 1916, and she lost both her brothers at the Somme."

She took in a shaky breath and let it out with a shiver. "Hell, Joseph, I think I might drink and flirt and behave like a fool if that were me. Catch the creature who did this to her!"

"I'll try. But we have to get Schenckendorff back to London."

"I know. At least we've got Matthew here to help."

He stayed with her a few minutes longer, then spoke to some of the nurses. They all said more or less the same as Judith had, although they were less frank with him than she had been, and some were less kind.

He walked into the last tent at the end of the row without hope of learning anything new, or even remotely helpful. There was just one nurse there, standing with her back to him, cleaning surgical instruments on a wooden table. Her dark hair was tied up and back, but the natural curl in it made it impossible to keep tidy. Her neck was slender, and there was grace in the line of her shoulders. It reminded him of something gentle and happy that he could not immediately place.

She must have heard his boots on the floorboards, because she turned.

Her blue eyes opened wide and the scalpel slid out of her fingers onto the floor with a clatter.

Joseph also stopped abruptly, his heart pounding. It was Lizzie Blaine. It was absurd. He was shaking and his hands were stiff and clammy, even in the cold.

"Hello . . . Chaplain," she said awkwardly.

"Lizzie . . . Nurse . . . Blaine." He found his tongue clumsy, words idiotic, banal. Of course she had said she might join up, after her husband had been murdered in 1916. He had thought she was just searching for something to do—ideas, not reality. "I . . ." He swallowed. "I thought you were going to be a driver." He remembered the miles she had driven him during that nightmare time when they were looking for a traitor. She had been the only good part of that summer.

She bent and picked up the scalpel, holding it carefully in her hand to keep it separate from the clean ones. "I started that way, but they needed nurses." She smiled. "I'm quite good on ordinary roads, but out here it's a different thing altogether, and I'm not so clever at the maintenance. I'm not inventive enough."

"Have you been in this section long?" How had he not seen her before, or at least known she was here?

"A few weeks. People are being moved around all the time, to fill in the gaps. Are you here because of Sarah Price and what happened to her?"

"Colonel Hook asked me to help, if I can. Did you see Sarah last night?"

"Yes, of course. We were both working in the Admissions tent and then the Operating tent. She was in Resuscitation for a while. She has—" Lizzie stopped and took a breath. "Had more experience than I do."

"Do you remember what time you last saw her?"

She flinched, understanding exactly why he asked. "Not really. I saw her coming and going up until we had a new lot of wounded in at about half past two, three o'clock. I went to Admissions." She looked down, avoiding his eyes. "I hate that. I feel so helpless and I'm never sure if I'm making the right decisions. Some of them die before any doctor even gets to them." She stopped abruptly, violent emotions naked in her face.

"I know," he said gently. He touched her, just fingers on her arm, but tender with the ache to comfort her that burned through him.

She looked up. "Yes, of course you do. You must spend hours there, doing what you can. I'm sorry. It's . . ." Clearly there was no way to finish.

"Did you know Sarah?" he asked. "Can you tell me anything about her?" He would value her common sense. She was older than many of the other nurses, and he already knew her wisdom from two summers ago, the steadiness she had shown in the midst of her own grief at her husband's death. She had even kept up a bleak, brave humor when she had been suspected of his murder herself. She had been afraid, but she had never sunk to anger or bitterness. How sweet that was now—like sudden sunlight on a winter landscape.

"Not very much," she answered. "She seemed a nice enough girl, a bit flighty." Her face was blank for a moment. "But then she was alone, with nothing in particular to go home to." She said the words with only the slightest tremor. "Her parents are dead, and her brothers; she had only a grandmother. I heard her say that, and for a moment I saw something more than the rather trivial person she seemed to be."

She looked away for a moment, and he saw that she was struggling with emotions. He wanted to say something wise and gentle that would comfort her. He wanted overwhelmingly to reach out and touch her, but it would be completely inappropriate. It would startle her, and she would be embarrassed; worse, it would be an abuse of the trust she needed to keep in him as chaplain. He put his hands behind his back, clasping them hard enough to hurt.

"Did she flirt, to lead anyone to suppose . . ." He did not know how to finish the sentence.

She gave a tight little smile, meeting his eyes. Then, seeing him color faintly, her smile widened. "Probably," she agreed. "But that's no excuse."

Of course she had not seen the body. The bestial intimacy of it flooded his mind with a revulsion so violent, it made him feel physically sick.

Lizzie saw it, and without hesitation moved forward to put her hand very lightly on his sleeve. "I'm sorry. Was it terrible?"

"Yes." She had seen her husband's body. She was a nurse. He should be able to trust her strength. "Yes, it was bad. Please be very careful." That was a ridiculously inadequate thing to say. The thought of anything happening to her was worse than it happening to himself. How had he not realized that she was so much more than a friend, even the best kind of friend to whom one could talk of the innermost things, or keep silence and still feel the warmth of trust? He had crossed a boundary within himself, and there was no way to retrace his steps, even if he wished to. Part of him did want that; he was afraid to care again so much. In fact, he was more afraid, because new places had been carved out inside him to a depth he had never touched before, an emotion that was not part of him, but all of him.

"We are all being careful," she said wryly. "None of us has gone anywhere alone today. It's all ridiculous and ugly. I find myself talking to someone quite naturally, a doctor or an orderly or driver, or a man wounded but not disabled by it. Then suddenly I remember, and I can see that he does, too, and neither of us knows what to say. I'm frightened of him, embarrassed, and he knows it and is sorry for me, or angry because I'm being unjust. It's all horrible."

He nodded. It was a situation he had never faced before, and he tried to imagine it. "It won't be long," he said aloud. "We'll be able to prove pretty soon that there were only a few people it could have been, then all the others will be cleared." Please God that was true. Apart from the other sordid and dangerous things, they had to solve the murder and be free to get Schenckendorff back to London. But he dare not tell Lizzie that, for her own safety.

"Is that what you are doing?" she asked. "Helping the police?"

"Yes. Can you account for any of the men last night, from three o'clock onward, or when you last saw Sarah?"

She thought hard before answering. "I was working with two of the orderlies for most of the couple of hours when the new cases came in. I don't think they were out of the Admissions tent for more than a few minutes at a time, and then it was to take them into the Pre-operation tent."

"Names?" he asked.

"Carter and Appleby. I think the surgeons were operating all the time, or with people in Resuscitation." She looked at him anxiously, searching his eyes. "I saw people after that, of course, but about five or six in the morning. You don't look at watches when you're trying to stop people from dying. And everyone was covered with blood. We always are."

He nodded. There was nothing to say. He took brief notes of all she told him, then reluctantly left her and started to speak to the injured British men who had been here last night. The first he saw was Major Morel. They had known each other since Morel had first come to Cambridge as Joseph's student in 1912, to learn biblical languages. He had been there when Sebastian Allard had died. That had been his first experience of the shock and emotional confusion of murder. They had served four years of war, seeing most of the same horror, enduring the grief for loss of men they both knew. Morel had been the leader of those who had come so close to mutiny last year, and together he and Joseph had gone east and through the lines into Germany to bring back the one man guilty of murder.

Morel had been injured in the shoulder last night, and was now among the wounded. Joseph found him propped up in a bed in one of the Treatment tents. He was very pale, his cheeks sunken, but that was the result not so much of the new injury as of the weariness and hunger of four years in the trenches. His dark eyes were red-rimmed and looked enormous.

"Hello, Reverend," he said with a twisted smile. "Have you come to do your holy duty, or to find out if I killed that poor woman? I hope to God it wasn't one of us. What a bloody miserable way to end the war."

"Do you think it might have been one of us?" Joseph asked him.

"Of course not!" Morel said in assumed horror. As always, he was struggling between intellect and dreams. He desperately did not want it to be one of his own men. For all his pretense at an armor of cynicism and his biting, irreverent wit, his care for his own men was deeper than any loyalty that duty could impose. They had journeyed through a kind of hell together, seen the deaths of half of those they loved, and it was not over yet. The ones who survived were weighed down by the ghosts of lost lives—joy and pain to carry for those who had forfeited their own chance to feel at all.

Joseph looked at him. His skin where his uniform usually protected it was clear and fine, apart from the scratches and louse bites they all had. The bones of his shoulders were still slender as a youth's, yet his eyes were those of an old man. Everyone was like that, but Joseph knew Morel, and that made it different.

"Do you mean not British, or not the Cambridgeshires?" he asked him.

Morel grimaced. "I'm a realist, Reverend. Not the Cambridgeshires. I know a lot of people are saying it had to be one of the Germans, and since they're not locked up because we've nowhere to put them, it's a nice thought. But it could have been pretty well anybody. I don't envy you your job of finding out who, and I suppose you have to. You would, anyway." He winced. "You never could leave well enough alone, even when nobody else knew there was even a problem."

"I've learned," Joseph said rather tartly.

Suddenly Morel's face softened and a sweet affection shone through. "I know." Then it vanished again. "But I hear there are a couple of policemen this time, so you won't be able to hide anything. Don't even try!"

"I have no intention of trying!" Joseph snapped. "There's nothing ambiguous about the morality of this." Even as he said it he knew that that might not be true. When was a crime ever utterly one-sided? Was the man who did this born violent—bestial? Or had they taught him how to hate, and that killing was the answer to rage? Had they created what he was now?

Morel rolled his eyes and did not bother to answer. Instead he recounted what he knew of men's comings and goings through the night from the time he had arrived, in pain but very definitely conscious and observant.

Joseph thanked him, asked what he could do to help, then moved on to the next man.

That evening Joseph joined Matthew in the dugout. There was no spare accommodation in the clearing station now that only the most seriously wounded could be moved on. Anyone able to stand remained, imprisoned by Jacobson's command. The Germans were herded together, but they had only the barest shelter, apart from those for whom exposure might mean death. Even the male members of the Voluntary Aid Detachment—Wil Sloan and two others—were not allowed to leave.

"It can't last," Matthew said grimly, trying to get a candle lit in a tin in order to create a makeshift stove to boil water. "Damn this thing! How the hell do you ever manage?"

Joseph did it for him with the ease of practice.

"Thank you," Matthew said drily. "I hope I leave here before I do enough of that to become as good as you are."

"I've had four years' experience," Joseph replied. "Although I usually managed to cadge from somebody else."

Matthew looked at him gravely. "You love these men, don't you, Joe." It was an observation; there was no question in his voice.

"Of course," Joseph answered without hesitation. "If you can pass through this with men and not care for them, then you aren't fit to call yourself human. It's a kind of friendship no number of years of safety could forge. There won't be anything like it again in our lives. We leave part of ourselves here with those who'll never come home: an obligation, a debt."

He swallowed hard, his eyes stinging. "We've got to get this solved, and get Schenckendorff back to London," he finally said. "His foot is a bit better today. His fever seems to be breaking."

"That's the least of our worries," Matthew answered grimly. "Somebody butchered that girl, which would be bad enough at any time, but as you know, out here nurses are viewed pretty well like angels. They're the one link with the women they love who represent home, and decency, and everything they're fighting for. For one or two I spoke to, it was as if something inside them had been violated, too."

Joseph stared, realizing suddenly that this was what he had seen in Morel and the others he had spoken to. They assumed it was rape, although the details of the crime had been kept quiet. That kind of violation, he realized, causes a deep internal injury to men also, all decent men.

Matthew gave a little shrug. "If we don't solve it soon, Joe, there's going to be a whole lot more violence, possibly toward the German prisoners. Our men want it to be one of them, not one of our own. I've heard some ugly things said. The veneer is thin; it won't take much to break it."

It was another hard night, but most of the casualties were taken to a clearing station five miles away, which was closer to the actual fighting as it moved eastward. Joseph arrived back to find Matthew waiting for him outside the tent for the walking wounded. His face was haggard and his uniform sodden wet in the rain. As soon as he saw Joseph he strode toward him, splashing through the mud with complete disregard.

"Joe, it's getting worse," he said abruptly. "There's been more violence. Several British soldiers, three or four at least, lit into half a dozen German prisoners and beat the hell out of them. The worst thing is that the officer in charge didn't do anything to stop it. He didn't even punish them for it after. What in God's name is this . . . this whole bloody slaughter for"— he swung his arm around violently to encompass the entire battlefield—"if we end up acting like barbarians ourselves? We might just as well have surrendered in the first place. We had nothing worth saving." He was so shaken that his hands were trembling. "We've got to get Schenckendorff out of here," he went on, deliberately lowering his voice. "If he still thinks we're worth saving?"

Joseph understood his anger. The sight and the stench of so much suffering, and so unaccountably many dead, had temporarily torn away his normal reserve. His brother was used to the intellectual tensions of waiting, of cat-and-mouse games of the mind, but the sheer physicality of the line was new to him. "Who were they, do you know?" he asked.

"Two of them were Black and Youngman. I don't know the others."

"Bill Harrison's men. I'll go and speak to him."

"The officer already knows!" Matthew said impatiently. "I told you, he didn't give a damn. He just let it go."

"I'll deal with it." Joseph turned and walked away.

He found Harrison surprisingly easily in the Casualty Clearing Station. Stan Tidyman, one of his men, had lost a leg; the officer had come to see if he was still alive and give whatever support he could.

Joseph looked at Stan's gray face and sunken eyes, and waited until Harrison was ready to leave him. Not that you were ever ready, but there came a time when it was necessary.

He waited outside and spoke to Harrison as he stepped onto the boards and into the wind. His face was tight and vulnerable with pity, and he looked relieved to see Joseph. "There's not much you can do right now, Chaplain," he said grimly. "But he'll be pleased to see you."

Joseph felt a stab of guilt. "Actually it is you I was looking for," he answered. "Four men beat more injured German prisoners last night. Two of them at least were from your unit, Black and Youngman. It's got to stop, Bill. Apparently the lieutenant on duty didn't do anything. That isn't good enough."

"I didn't know," Harrison said unhappily. "They're on guard duty, and they resent it. They're only slightly injured and they want to be pressing forward with the rest of the regiment." He gave a slight, rueful smile. "We've been telling them to go and kill Germans for the last four years, Chaplain. Some of them hated doing it so much they were almost paralyzed at the thought of deliberately blowing another man's body to pieces, even if he was German. They look just like us, walk and talk, have homes, parents, pet dogs, things they like to do."

He was obviously distressed, his disgust running deep, but he refused to evade the issue. "I've had to punish men because they couldn't pull the trigger, and I hated doing it. I've seen hundreds of men aim high, on purpose. And I've seen those who didn't, and the nightmares they've had afterward."

He shook his head. "We gave medals to the ones who could do it without flinching. They were ordinary men when they came here, bakers and blacksmiths, bank clerks, farm boys, bus drivers. A lot of them have lost brothers, friends, even parents at home from the bombings." His voice dropped. "Wives have been unfaithful over the long years alone, sweethearts have found someone else. It hurts. It doesn't seem fair to punish them now for being what we've made them into." His gray eyes looked steadily into Joseph's with an honesty that would not flinch or accommodate. "I'll speak to them, but I'm not going to punish them, sir."

Joseph admired his loyalty, stubborn though it was, and perhaps technically wrong. He could understand it, and he knew that from Bill Harrison he should even have expected it.

"What if it takes us awhile to find this man?" he asked aloud. "Closed up here like this, these incidents could get worse, especially since he got away with it this time. I know that what someone did to Sarah Price was bestial, but that isn't the reason for this, it's the excuse. Next time someone may be critically injured, or even killed. Then we will have to charge whoever did it with murder, because beating to death an injured and unarmed prisoner is murder, Bill. You know it, and so do they. So do the Germans, incidentally."

Harrison stood very stiffly, shoulders square. "I'll talk to the men, Chaplain. I won't let that happen."

"Good." Should he trust him? What if the violence did break out again, and this time Schenckendorff were killed? He dare not say anything. The Peacemaker had eyes and ears in all sorts of places, followers who were often good men, idealists whose dreams were more passionate than their understanding of human nature. They killed for another man's vision, and Joseph could not afford that. They were so close. This was the last hand to play against the Peacemaker, win or lose.

It was not Harrison's honor he didn't trust; it was his wisdom, his ability to see evil where he had a right to expect it would not be.

FOUR

*I*t was Judith's turn to be questioned by Jacobson. She had known it would come, and tried to prepare herself for it. He was speaking to all the women, asking them where they had been at the time of Sarah's death and which of the men they could account for. Had anyone seemed troubled recently, or had they noticed anyone behaving peculiarly? It was the obvious thing to do, but Judith was still uncomfortable when she was ordered to enter the tent that had been hastily put up for him. Someone had found a table, two chairs, and a box for him to keep his papers in. There was a duckboard floor, but it was bitterly cold.

Judith went in and closed the flap behind her. She stood to attention, not out of any particular respect, but because it marked her as part of the army and was a tacit statement of unity with the others. He was civilian, even if he was employed by the military police for this specific crime.

"Thank you for coming, Miss Reavley," he said without expression. He pointed to the wooden chair opposite the desk. "You may sit down."

She considered it for a moment. It would be more comfortable, but it would also instantly put her on a physical level with him and take away any resemblance she had to a soldier.

"Thank you, but I prefer to stand," she replied. She was also not going to call him *sir.* "I sit a great deal," she added. "I drive an ambulance."

"Yes, I know." He indicated a piece of paper in front of him on the table. "You've been here a long time."

"Since the beginning."

"Then you will know the other people here as well as anyone can. You will have known Sarah Price."

"Not much. I'm a driver, not a nurse," she pointed out.

"Don't you bring wounded men here to be treated?" he asked.

She thought he was a plain man, but in other circumstances he would not have been unpleasant. There was intelligence in his face. "Yes," she answered. "The orderlies help me unload them off the ambulance, then I turn around to go back for more."

He blinked. "Don't you tend them at all on the way?"

"I can't drive an ambulance through the mud and shellfire and tend to wounded at the same time!" she said tartly.

"Don't you have anyone to help you?" He looked at her with intent.

"Yes, most of the time."

"People trained to give medical help?"

"Of course. Otherwise they wouldn't be of any use." She was keeping her temper with difficulty. It was unfair to resent him—none of this was his fault—but he was still an outsider probing with a civilian's lack of understanding for the terror, the grief, and the loyalties of soldiers.

"Nurses?" he questioned. "Orderlies?"

"V.A.D.'s," she answered.

"What happens if your ambulance breaks down?"

"I mend it!" she said with her eyebrows raised.

"Yourself?"

"Of course. There's no one else."

"You must be extremely competent. Where do you do the regular maintenance work?"

At last she saw his point. "Usually here. But I don't often see many nurses. None of us has a lot of time to stand around."

"But you see a lot of orderlies, other drivers, doctors, soldiers?"

"Of course. But I have no idea who attacked Sarah Price. If I had, I would have told you."

"Would you, Miss Reavley?"

"Of course I would!" The anger burned through now. It was a stupid question, and offensive. "No decent person would defend a man who killed one of the nurses! Or any woman, for that matter." She stood even more stiffly. "We work together, Mr. Jacobson. We have done so in more hideous circumstances than you could imagine. You know nothing about it. I can see that in your face, even if I didn't know. We have a kind of loyalty to one another that peacetime couldn't create."

The ghost of a smile crossed his face, full of regret.

"I believe that, Miss Reavley, which is why I think that one of you could well be defending a man with whom you have shared danger and pain, perhaps who has even saved your life, because you cannot believe he would do what he has. You will have different judgments of right and wrong from mine, and debts of honor I couldn't understand."

With amazement like a slow-burning fire inside her, she realized what he was saying. "You think I would defend the man who did this?" she said incredulously. She could feel her temper slipping out of control. "I want him found and arrested even more than you do! The worst that can happen to you is that you fail!" Her voice was shaking now, and she was gulping for air. "I could be assaulted or murdered, or both. So could my friends! Of course I want him caught . . . and . . . and got rid of . . . like . . . sewage!"

"Even if he were, for example, your friend Wil Sloan?" Jacobson asked. "A man who would never hurt you, surely?"

"That's disgusting. Wil would never even think of doing something like that!"

"What kind of a man would, Miss Reavley? Do you know who would and who wouldn't?"

He had caught her, this ordinary civilian who knew nothing about the reality of war. She had walked straight into his verbal trap without seeing anything of it. She hesitated, unable to frame an answer. He was right: She was trying to protect those she cared for most, because they could not be guilty, not because she feared they were. But any such reply would sound ridiculous.

"Of course I don't," she said at last. "All I know is who couldn't have because they were somewhere else." How lame that sounded.

"And was Wil Sloan somewhere else?" he asked, almost casually.

Her mind raced. How could she say anything that was of value without making him suspicious? She did not even know when the murder had happened, or if he had already spoken to Wil. The only time she and Wil had been at the Casualty Clearing Station was roughly between three o'clock and half past four. If it were not then, would Jacobson even be asking?

"Miss Reavley?" he prompted.

She tried to look innocent. She must not seem too clever, or that in itself would make him distrustful of her. "We were both in the ambulance most of the night," she answered. "Miles away from here."

"But not all of it," he pointed out. "You brought the wounded back. Surely that was your entire purpose?"

"Yes, of course. We were here a couple of times, a little before midnight, and again at about three."

"And when did you leave again?" His face was almost expressionless.

"The first time about quarter to one, the second at half past four, roughly."

"So there were at least two and a half hours that you were both here," he pointed out.

She wanted to say something sarcastic, referring to their whole purpose, but swallowed her temper. "Yes. We have to get the wounded off and into the Admissions tent, then clean the ambulance and refuel it." She nearly added that it had needed maintenance, too, but since she'd mended it without Wil, it would be walking into another trap. Where had Wil been the second time? She did not know. But he could not have killed Sarah. No one who knew Wil would have had such an idea even enter their minds. He was hot-tempered on very rare occasions, but never toward women. He was generous to a fault, and idealistic; otherwise he would not even have been here. An American, he had come voluntarily in 1915, when his own country had had nothing to do with the war. Like many others, he had simply believed it was the right thing to do, and so he had done it. He was patient, funny, too honest, a little unsophisticated, and one of the kindest people she knew.

Again Jacobson prompted her, more abruptly this time. "Miss Reavley?"

She took a gamble. "I don't know where he was at midnight," she answered. "I was trying to think, but as far as I can remember, he went to the tent with the walking wounded. You'll have to ask him."

She saw the lack of interest in his face. So Sarah had been killed between three and half past four. The cold bit inside her like ice. She took the risk, certain beyond any doubt at all that Wil would have done the same for her. "The second time I had to clean the spark plugs in the ambulance. They often get dirty and then they don't work. It took us awhile to get the wounded in, and after that he got me some tea and a piece of bread and jam. Jam's rationed now, so that's not easy. Then he held the lamp for me. The engine was in a bit of a mess, and I needed two hands."

"I see." He was looking at her more closely, almost narrowly, as if he was trying to discern something about her. It made her uncomfortable. Did he know she was lying? Had Wil said something different?

"Ever had any trouble, Miss Reavley? Any unwanted attentions?" he asked.

"No!" she said, and knew she had answered too quickly.

His eyes widened. It was obvious that he did not believe her.

She felt her face color. "Nobody has behaved badly!" she said curtly. "I deal with wounded men on the battlefield, Mr. Jacobson. We all have one aim in common—to stop them from dying, and get them to the nearest medical help. Nobody has time or thought for much else." It was not his fault that he knew nothing about the front, and it was unfair that she was angry with him for it, but she was. And she was frightened, and guilty for lying, even though it was necessary. Her friends were in trouble, and he was an outsider who did not understand.

"That is clearly not true, Miss Reavley," he said steadily. "Or I would not need to be here. And while I haven't fought on the line, I've seen plenty of men under pressure. Emotions are close to the surface. It results in violence sometimes, and people close to death want to touch life and all the pleasures it offers, sometimes even the source of life." His voice dropped a little. "At those times it does not have to be someone you love; anybody will do. Please don't tell me you are unaware of that, or that it shocks you. You have seen four years of war. You cannot be blind to the realities of men's fears or needs, or the extremities of death."

Her face was blazing and she knew it. He had touched a nerve in her, and without knowing why, she felt a passionate need to defend the vulnerability she had seen so often. "Of course I'm not!" She was shouting at him, although she had not meant to. She heard herself and could not stop. "We are all . . ." Now she did not know what to say, and he was still staring at her.

"You do not want to betray anyone whose weakness you have seen and understood," he finished for her. "You protect one another. As well as showing loyalty, and honor to men on whose courage your life may depend, you cannot afford to antagonize them." There was gentleness in his face, even pity. "You will have to work with them in the future, and with the other women who may love them, or hate them. But I remind you, Miss Reavley, that you will also work with the other women who may become their victims in the future. I can see that you have a very terrible conflict as to where your duty lies."

"No, I don't!" she said hotly. "I don't know anything!"

He did not believe her. She could see it in his eyes, and in the slight smile touching his mouth. She must control herself or he would be even more certain that she was lying. She stood rigidly upright, her hands by her sides, touching the seam in her skirt, as a soldier would stand to attention. "If I should learn anything that would help you, Mr. Jacobson, I shall inform you of it immediately. Is that all? Because if it is, I would like to get back to my duties."

"For the moment, Miss Reavley. But please remain here. I will wish to speak to you again."

"Unless I am needed," she told him. And before he could protest, she turned and marched out. There were duties to do. Nurses were always shorthanded, and the men needed more care than they could give.

It was midmorning when she found Lizzie Blaine unpacking medical supplies. She did not know the woman well; Lizzie had moved into St. Giles with her husband after Judith had already left for France. She had heard of her from Joseph, and the one or two times they had met here she had liked her instinctively. Lizzie had a penetrating honesty that made Judith comfortable, because it not only was directed at others, but was also within herself. She made no excuses and never shifted blame, and neither her friendship nor her courage was ostentatious.

"Can I help?" Judith offered.

"Please." Lizzie pointed to an unopened box. "You'll have to check that everything is what it says. They get put in the wrong places sometimes." She glanced at Judith again, frowning a little. "You all right? You look a bit upset."

"Furious!" Judith said sharply as she bent to the box. "I've just been talking to Jacobson, the policeman. He misunderstood everything I said, and I wound up talking too much, and now he thinks I know more than I do."

"That's stupid." Lizzie turned back to the unpacking. "You'd hardly defend anyone you knew was guilty!"

"That's not what he thinks," Judith explained. "I suppose I could lie about a small incident that looked bad, but I hadn't believed it really was. The man just doesn't understand what friendship is out here, and it made me angry."

Lizzie smiled. "And then you felt guilty for that? I know what you mean."

"I suppose we all do." Judith started to unpack the box, looking at each item carefully. "But things like that don't happen out of the blue. Whoever it is must have bothered other people from time to time, even if it was only stupid remarks or being too free with his hands. Although we don't know whether he raped her or not. We're just thinking he did because rumor says it was that sort of killing."

"I suppose so." Lizzie kept her face averted. There was no emotion in her voice now.

"Everybody's stupid sometimes," Judith went on. "You just realize why, and if it isn't bad, you forget about it."

"Yes." Lizzie's fingers were tight on a box lid. It slipped from her grasp and scattered tablets on the bench top, half a dozen on the floor. She drew in her breath sharply, as if to swear, then bit it back.

Judith bent and picked them up. She regarded them for a moment, uncertain.

Lizzie held out her hand. "Think of the amount of dirt and mud we eat. These are too precious, even off the floor, to waste and have someone perhaps die without them." She examined the tablets, then put them separately in a small screw of paper and wrote on it what they were.

Judith looked at her more carefully. There was something remote about her, closed off and hurt, as if she was afraid. "Do you know somebody who's been bothered?" she asked as gently as she could.

"No," Lizzie said quickly, without looking up from what she was doing. "I don't know that I would recognize it if I did. Sarah used to flirt like mad, and I've no idea how far it went, but I'm not telling Jacobson that. There are enough people saying she deserved it." Her face was flushed and her knuckles white where she gripped the small box she was holding. Her voice was thick with anger when she spoke again. "It's a vicious and idiotic thing to say! What happened to her was not flirting gone too far, it was violent and brutal, a man who has no decency left in him. He has descended into something less than human. Please, let's talk about something else. I liked Sarah, silly as she was sometimes. She was only trying to survive."

"I'm sorry," Judith said immediately. She had forgotten for a moment that Lizzie had probably known Sarah quite well. Friendships could grow quickly out here—bad experiences shared, an act of kindness, and bonds were forged. "I'm talking too much because he made me angry and I behaved like a fool. And I'm afraid, too."

Lizzie looked at her with a sudden smile. "We all are," she admitted.

That evening Judith was back in her vehicle with another V.A.D. who had not been at the Casualty Clearing Station when Sarah was killed. They were driving toward the fighting, which was moving steadily farther ahead with each new assault, stretching the supply lines. She thought back to her exchange with Lizzie. Lizzie was frightened, and Judith had an increasing feeling that it was something more personal that troubled her—something she guarded not only from Jacobson but even from the other women. Was she afraid for someone in particular—a man she was fond of or, worse, who had threatened her? It was a hideous thought that there was someone here who either was guilty or looked it, and somebody else was carrying the burden of that knowledge. If so, then surely their lives could be in danger, too? They were all used to death; the place was saturated with it. It did not startle or horrify anymore.

The gunfire was growing heavier in the distance, over toward Courtrai. The roads were worse here. She could see huge craters in the intermittent light of the star shells.

Perhaps they were all pretending not to know anything for precisely that reason. How could Jacobson, or anyone else, protect a witness? There was no such thing here as safety of any sort. She wished Lizzie could have trusted her. She felt an acute awareness of failure. She should have tried harder, said different, gentler things, and been far less occupied with herself.

She was one of the fortunate ones in that she could leave the field hospital, even though Jacobson had told her not to and had refused to let Wil come with her. But the fighting was still going on, and there were more casualties that had to be brought back. The war plunged inexorably toward its last days. Individual lives had never mattered in these circumstances.

She drove eastward through the darkness toward the glare and the roar of guns.

German prisoners came through that night as well, some captured, several badly injured. More came willingly, with an air of desperate bewilderment. Most were passed on immediately without coming anywhere near the Casualty Clearing Station. They had been hastily bandaged, often lame or half blind, and then made to trudge on foot through the mud toward the railhead and the journey back into France. Only the wounded who could not be moved along without jeopardizing their lives were kept here.

It could not continue like this for many more days. Tension was mounting not only with overcrowding of men critically injured, and the growing expectation of peace, but above all with the endless questions by Jacobson stirring up suspicion and anger over all kinds of old loves and betrayals, fears of violation too deep to name or face. Beyond the question of who could have been guilty, the speculation of rape was more divisive than anyone had imagined.

Judith found that people she had known since the earliest years of the war, and beside whom she had fought illness, disaster, and grief, held views she could not accept. Even Cavan surprised her. She admired him intensely for his courage, both physical and moral. After the stand in the trenches for which he had been put up for the V.C., and then the murder of Major Northrup, she had risked the firing squad herself last year to help him escape. The other men involved in the crime had all gone, but Cavan had chosen to remain and face trial. That decision had infuriated her, yet he had refused to be swayed. She had known it was born of supreme honor to duty, and she never forgot it in him.

Now he stood at the operating table having just amputated a man's shattered foot. He was exhausted; there was blood on his white coat and up both his sleeves. It was even splattered on the pale skin of his face, which was hollowed about the eyes by exhaustion.

"Thank you," he told Bream, the orderly. He looked at Gwen Williams, the nurse who had assisted him. "Call me if he gets feverish, but I think that should be all right."

Judith had remained to help after bringing the man in. Cavan had already complimented her for getting him there alive. "I'll fetch you some water," she said, turning to go outside.

"Yer can't go alone!" Bream waved sharply as Judith reached the tent flap. "I'll get it, after I've taken 'im to Resuscitation." He gestured at the unconscious patient.

"It's only fifty yards away," Judith countered. "I'll be perfectly safe."

Bream opened his mouth to protest. He was about twenty. A London clerk before the war, he was too flat-footed to make the infantry.

"For goodness' sake!" Gwen cut across him. "Nothing's going to happen to her."

"It can 'appen to anyone!" Bream replied, his eyes wide. "Well, any woman. We've got a madman 'round 'ere, and no one knows 'oo 'e is."

"It won't happen to anyone," Gwen contradicted, shaking her head irritably. "Some women invite disaster of one sort or another. If you behave with sense, don't lead people on and behave like a—I'm sorry, like a tart—then people won't get the wrong idea."

"The right idea being what?" Judith asked with brittle civility. She had thought she liked Gwen. Suddenly she didn't. They were strangers in culture and belief, allies only by force of extraordinary circumstance.

Gwen stared as if she, too, was seeing the other woman clearly for the first time. "I'm surprised that the chaplain's sister should need anyone to tell her the right way to behave," she said coldly.

"We weren't talking about my behavior, or Sarah's," Judith pointed out. "We were talking about whoever it was who killed her—which, as you put it so pithily, was *the wrong idea.*"

"Judith, let it be," Cavan said wearily. "It's over. It's a tragedy that we can't undo, like pretty well every other bloody useless death here. Some wretched man forgot that you are only allowed to kill the enemy who's wearing a different uniform from you and carrying a gun at the time. An enemy who's wearing a dress and whose weapon is her tongue has to be treated differently. Someone forgot that, or simply stopped caring."

Judith stared at him. She had thought she knew him as well as it was possible to know almost anyone. She had seen his superb courage under fire, his tireless, selfless work, never giving up on anyone no matter how mutilated or ill. She had seen him share his food, sit up all night to watch and comfort men, seen him encourage young doctors afraid to try tasks that seemed impossible, or offer solace and refrain from blame when they failed. And yet he was speaking of this horror as if it were simply one more foreseeable tragedy. He even had some pity for the man.

He looked back at her very directly. His blue eyes did not waver in the slightest, but there was regret in them now, and a very faint color in his cheeks. "We can't teach a man to tear another man apart with a bayonet, then expect him to control his temper when he feels someone made a fool of him," he said grimly. "When fear has reduced you to nothing in your own eyes, the contempt for yourself doesn't heal just because someone says the war is over. Some of our men have a sanity so deep nothing can break it, but that's not true for all." He shook his head, his lips tight. "People can lose their belief in anything. When they see the good die hideously, some of them find they have nothing left to cling to. Let Bream get the water. Don't go out alone. It's arrogant to think your virtue will protect you." He turned to Gwen Williams. "Or you," he added coldly.

"You didn't know Sarah," Gwen retaliated, her cheeks pink. "She led men on. She flirted and she teased." Her voice grew sharper. "I'm not saying she deserved it—of course she didn't, no one does. But she did behave badly—stupidly. Nothing like this has ever happened before, or to anyone else, and that should tell you something."

Bream shuddered. "It tells me we didn't never 'ave German prisoners before," he said firmly. "Leastways, not so many we couldn't keep 'em locked up. Yer wrong, Doctor, it weren't any of our boys who did it to poor Miss Price. They may be a bit loud at times, even a bit free with their 'ands now an' then, but nothing more'n that. They're gettin' ready to go 'ome, an' no one knows who'll make it even now. This close, it's kind o' scary to think yer could still end up staying 'ere in the mud forever."

"Nobody stays in the mud forever, Bream," Judith told him gently. "At least . . ." She gave a sudden wide smile. "At least in a sense we all do, and when it comes to it, I don't see that Flanders mud is any better or worse than London mud, or Cambridgeshire mud, for that matter. The point is, the part of you that matters goes on to eternity anyway."

Bream was staring at her as if she had suddenly changed into a totally different animal in front of him.

Cavan smiled also, lighting his face with sudden warmth. "Chaplain's sister, Bream. You'll have to excuse her. She's probably been preached at since she was born. Prayers over the porridge, no doubt."

"Actually maths," she corrected him.

"Prayers over the maths?" Cavan asked in disbelief.

"Maths over the porridge!" she explained. "My father was a mathematician. Don't ask me where Joseph got religion from. I have no idea."

Gwen looked from one to the other of them with a sense of somehow having been made light of, but she knew there was no use pursuing it. She turned somberly to Judith. "You can mock all you like, but there is a very wicked man around here who was stirred to violence by something that Sarah Price was foolish enough to do, and she paid a fearful, terrible price for it. Whether he was German or British, he's still out there. But if you behave decently, you will be perfectly safe. I'll prove it. I'll go and fetch the water for Dr. Cavan." And without waiting for anyone to argue with her, she marched out of the tent and into the darkness beyond.

Judith did not hesitate. She went straight after her, catching up within half a dozen yards.

"You don't need to!" Gwen said loudly.

"I prefer to." Judith kept pace with her along the boards with difficulty, her feet slipping on the wet wood and clattering loudly. "Do you really think Sarah brought this on herself? Did you see anyone bother her before? I mean, was she having a romance with anyone?"

Gwen glanced sideways at her once, then kept on walking. "I have no idea. I know how she was generally rather loose in her manner, which is foolish as well as vulgar. I suppose I should have spoken to her about it, but I thought she'd just ignore me and get angry. I was wrong, wasn't I." There was a sharp acknowledgment of guilt in her voice.

Without warning Judith's anger evaporated and was replaced by pity. Gwen was not an easy person, always arguing; very few people actually liked her. Most treated her with tolerance and a general sharing, because that was what everyone did; it was a habit for survival. "No," she said gently, falling into step beside her. "She might easily have become worse just to spite you. Maybe we all should have said something."

"I saw her every day," Gwen argued. "It was more obvious to me." Her voice was so low, Judith could only just hear her above the squelch of the mud as they stepped beyond the boards onto the earth. They were now far enough from the fighting that the sound of guns was only a rumble in the distance. Curiously, as the battle moved ahead of them she felt not relief but a sense of being left behind, no longer of the most use she could be.

"Everyone could see how she behaved," she replied. "It's not your responsibility."

Gwen shot her a quick glance. Then they reached the water supply, and she began to fill the pail she had brought. "Not your brother's keeper? Your brother wouldn't agree with that," she said wryly. "Do me the kindness to be honest, Judith. Apart from the cruelty of it, lying won't work because I know what you really think. You don't often hide it."

Judith was chastened. She had not realized that her dislike of Gwen was so apparent, or that she was quite so free with her own opinions. A little tact, a little kindness would have been better. "I'm sorry," she said sincerely, and the moment after, wondered if that sounded dishonest, too. Then Gwen smiled at her, and she knew it was accepted, at least for now.

It was three days since the murder of Sarah Price and they did not appear to be any closer to knowing who had killed her. Suspicion grew, often absurdly. There were brief outbreaks of anger and violence, but no more

German prisoners had been seriously hurt. News of the fighting came every day. The British were advancing on Lille; the Belgians had occupied Zeebrugge and stormed Bruges. Someone said that the British forces in Syria had entered Homs and were headed for Aleppo. Everything was closing for a German surrender, but it hadn't happened yet. The hope itself was a kind of strange, exciting, disturbing thought, so very close and yet so many men were still dying every day, sometimes hundreds of them.

Judith heard many other arguments over Sarah Price, some like those in the operating theater, others quite different. Some young men, knowing their own innocence, were hurt when nurses were afraid of them.

The fighting was so heavy on the third night, all ambulance crews were needed. Judith and Wil Sloan drove beyond Menin to pick up badly wounded. It was cloudy, but there was no rain, and after a while the sky cleared, moonlight showing the devastated landscape and shattered buildings. Tree stumps were gaunt, motionless, but looking as if they writhed, pointing half-amputated limbs upward, reaching toward some help that never came. The lights showed rutted tracks swimming with water, glistening pale on the craters, punctuated by the black silhouettes of broken guns, wheels, even an occasional foundered tank, its giant caterpillar tracks high in the air. Judith knew there were also bodies drifting to the surface, but you could not tell their mud-caked outlines from the banks and paths.

"I guess even the Badlands are going to look good after this," Wil said with a half smile. "Main Street will be pretty wholesome."

"I'm sure it will," she agreed. " 'Specially on a sunny day."

He was silent for some time. She looked at him and in the light of the star shells saw a somberness in his face. When he had first come late in 1915 he had been very young, barely twenty. It was some time before he told her that he was actually running away from his hometown, even from America altogether, after an ugly incident in which he had lost his temper and beaten a man.

Now the world was different, and Wil himself looked so much older. He had not put on weight—no one did on army rations—but his leanness had turned to muscle, and there was a grave maturity in his face. He had not lost his midwestern accent, but he had picked up a great many very English expressions that he had begun using with humor. They were now so much a part of his nature, he no longer noticed them himself.

"I'll miss you," he said suddenly.

"For a little while," she conceded, not certain what else to say.

"Home won't be the same as when I left," he went on. He bit his lip.

"Some of that's good. Maybe they'll have other things to think about than what a fool I was."

"You still worried about it?" she asked with surprise. "Come on, Wil! That was years ago. The whole world's grown sadder and wiser since then."

"You don't know small-town people," he retorted. "They can hold a grudge for generations."

"Of course I know small-town people," she said with a laugh. "How big do you think Selborne St. Giles is? Everybody's related to everybody else, and has been for a thousand years! If you go into the shop in the morning they can probably tell you what you had for breakfast. They can certainly tell you who's quarreling with whom, and what about."

He smiled; it was a wide and unusually charming expression. "Perhaps I'll stay in England. Do you think I can?"

"Certainly, and welcome. But don't you want to go home?" She looked away from the road for a moment, then hit a deep rut and concentrated again. "Are you really that scared of it, Wil?"

"No!" He hesitated. "Well, maybe. I never got to go back and say anything, and now they've got real heroes, men who fought, even some who died. Not from our town, but not far away."

"Every town has someone who died," she answered.

"I guess you Brits have some for every street, eh? I'm sorry." His voice dropped. "I'm just not sure where I belong anymore."

"Nobody is." She realized how intensely she meant that. In St. Giles she had been something of a social misfit herself before the war, not content to marry suitably and become absorbed in home affairs as everyone else was. Well, that world no longer existed anyway. But what sort of world was it now? Women, old men, and children, with a million young men gone and near enough two million more injured or maimed who would need care. The jobs women had held over the last four years would, for the most part, have to be given back to the returning men. She would have to earn money. She couldn't possibly expect Joseph to keep her. Anyway, it would bore her to death not to do anything. Wil Sloan was certainly not the only one who had no idea what to expect.

"There's something vaguely comfortable about the place you are used to," she added aloud. "Even if it's plunging around in the mud being shot at."

"Only a Brit could say something like that." He stared straight ahead, his eyes very bright in the momentary headlights of an ambulance coming the other way. "And I will miss you," he repeated.

She could think of nothing that sounded right to say in return, or that would tell him the affection she felt for him. There were friendships to miss that nothing could replace. There would never be anything else like this again, thank God, but those who survived it would share dreams and nightmares that no one else could know.

Joseph was standing outside the Resuscitation tent when he heard a movement behind him and turned to see Lizzie in the entrance. Despite the anxiety in her face, he felt a quickening of pleasure. He drew in breath to ask if she was looking for him, and then realized that she was almost certainly seeking a doctor. One of the patients must be in trouble for her to have left him.

"Can I get someone for you?" he asked instead. "I know where Cavan is."

She looked disconcerted. "It's not really . . . ," she started, and then, as if annoyed with herself, she straightened her shoulders and met his eyes more coolly. "It's not really necessary," she replied. "He'll certainly be busy." She turned away, ready to go back into the tent again.

"Can I help?" he said quickly—not because he thought he could, but because he could not let her go without some response.

She hesitated, as though the decision was difficult for her. "Have you no one in greater need?" She seemed annoyed with herself, as if her question was foolish but amending it would only make the situation worse. "Private Fields is coming 'round. He isn't going to be able to feel his leg. It's still there, but he's going to be frightened . . ."

"I'll come," he said, moving forward immediately and catching up with her so he was on her heels as she went back in. It must have been him she was looking for in the first place, or perhaps someone who knew Fields. Joseph could not place the name.

There were several beds occupied, but Lizzie went straight to the farthest over by the canvas wall at the other end. The boy on it was fair-skinned, sixteen at the most, and his left leg was heavily swathed in bandages. There were also cuts on both his arms, blood already seeping through the gauze. Joseph met Lizzie's eyes questioningly. He had to know the truth, whatever he decided to say.

The gulf between them was no longer there. She understood as if they had spoken aloud everything they meant.

"Shrapnel through the flesh," she said quietly. "It will heal. But he was in a lot of pain. They had to give him morphine. I'm not sure he would believe me that it's still there." She did not add that he would believe Joseph, but it was there in her certainty. He felt self-conscious, his face flushing at the compliment, even if it was not meant as such. She was thinking of the boy, not of him.

Lizzie looked down as the boy stirred, breathing more heavily, and his eyelids fluttered open. A wave of fear came over him as he registered the pain, and her presence. He wanted to speak and clearly did not know what to say.

"Hurts like hell, doesn't it," Joseph said very quietly, moving a step closer to the bed. "I got shrapnel in my leg in 1916. But it healed. Hardly ever aches now, only if the weather's really cold and wet for a long time, and I get tired. I expect yours will be the same. Only you're a lot younger than I am, so you might do better."

"Chaplain?" Fields gasped, turning his head a little and trying to focus his eyes. "It's . . . it's still there? I thought . . ." He stopped, embarrassed. He desperately wanted to be brave.

Joseph nodded. "Our surgeons are pretty good. The bone's not damaged. Don't think that'll make it hurt any less."

Fields gave a weak smile. "As long as it's there . . ."

"It is . . . I give you my word."

". . . then I don't care."

"You will," Joseph said cheerfully. "I remember how mine hurt. I thought it would never stop. Actually it was only a few weeks, but I think I was a pretty good nuisance most of the time."

"I'll bet you weren't." Fields closed his eyes as another wave of agony passed through him. His skin was ashen white.

Joseph reached down and touched his hand lightly. "Don't bet anything you can't afford to lose. I'm not saying it to make you feel better. It's the truth."

Fields tried to smile, and nearly succeeded.

Lizzie pushed the damp hair off his forehead with her fingers. She had nothing she could give him to ease his pain. The small amount of morphine they had was saved for their most desperate cases. All she could do was come to him as often as she had time. Now she glanced at Joseph, her eyes bright and soft, and then moved to the next man.

Joseph stayed with Fields, a silent presence, simply being there, until he drifted off into either sleep or unconsciousness. Afraid it was the latter, he touched the pulse in the boy's wrist. It was not strong, but it was steady.

He should go back to the Admissions tent, but he must speak to Lizzie first. He wished to ask her why she had not answered his last letters, but if she had been training for this, in a hospital somewhere away from St. Giles, perhaps she had not received them. And then here in Flanders she certainly would not have. She might even have thought he had stopped writing, and she would not have pursued him. She would have thought it indelicate, afraid he read into her answers a warmth he did not welcome. How absolutely far that was from the truth!

Now he felt awkward, in case it was he who had presumed to go too quickly beyond simple friendship.

She heard him come and turned around from the medicine table quickly, concern in her eyes.

"He's asleep," he assured her. "His pulse is not strong, but it's regular, not fading or skipping. At least he's got a little while away from the worst of it. I must go back to the Admissions tent."

"I know. Thank you for coming. Not to be afraid helps—a bit."

He smiled. "Some of the time," he said. Then, abruptly: "Lizzie, why did you stop writing?" Instantly he wished he had not said it, but it would only make it worse to try taking it back, somehow explaining it away. He did not want to know the answer; it might be what he was afraid to hear.

"Because I was out here at last," she said very quietly. "To begin to realize what it was really like. I'd wanted to be a driver, like Judith, but they needed nurses. I started in Cambridge, actually quite a long time ago. I didn't tell you because it seemed so . . . mundane at the time. Safe at home. Then out here they kept moving me. I didn't know whether you were still writing to me or not. There was no one to forward anything."

"I was." Then in case it sounded like blame, he continued quickly, "It doesn't matter now." He wanted to add something else, something that would capture the old lightness, the ease they had had with each other in St. Giles, driving through the lanes, seeking a terrible truth, his leg aching like an abscessed tooth.

"Thank you for coming," she said in the moment's silence, fitting it in as if she was afraid what he might say if she allowed him. "It was what I hoped you would do. I know you have to go back to the Admissions tent. You'll be needed there, too." She looked at him an instant longer, then turned back to the medicines.

It was final, and there was nothing for him to do but go back as he had said he should, his heart bumping in his chest, a mixture of hope and confusion in his mind.

Richard Mason was sitting in Casualty Clearing Station to the east of Messines with a colleague named Harper, who was about to return to London. It was raining outside the Admissions tent, and even inside it was chilly.

"Bit unreal, isn't it," Harper said thoughtfully. "Used to think at one time that it would never end, and now we're nearly there. There's only one way it can go, and everybody knows it. Yet we go on shooting at everything in sight as if there were still something to fight about and it could all make a difference. It's as if we got so insanely into the habit of it that we can't stop."

"That's probably close to the truth," Mason remarked. "Have you ever thought how we are suddenly going to start enforcing the law and saying you can't shoot people anymore, or stick a bayonet into them, even if you think they thoroughly deserve it?"

"You talking about that bloody horrible business up with the Cambridgeshires near Ypres?" Harper asked, pulling a sour face, although it might have been the last of his tea that caused it.

Mason had avoided the sludge at the bottom by leaving the final couple of mouthfuls, but then he had been here many times before. "What are you talking about?" he asked absently.

"Haven't heard?" Harper winced again. "Some damn lunatic hacked a nurse to death in the clearing station nearest to Ypres. No idea who, or why. All pretty violent and disgusting. Killing any woman is bad, but one of our own V.A.D.'s is beyond the pale."

Mason's head swam. His mouth was dry, and there was suddenly a senseless roar in his ears, as if he were in the middle of a river. "V.A.D.?" His mouth could hardly form the letters.

"Yes. Nurse, or ambulance driver, or something," Harper answered. "As I said, pretty vile. I daresay they'll shoot the bastard when they find him. You were talking about the general difficulty of settling back into civvy life."

Mason swallowed, feeling as if he had a stone in his chest. "What was her name, the V.A.D.?" He felt bruised and sick.

"Don't know," Harper replied. "Don't think they said. Got to tell the poor girl's family first anyway. Pretty rotten way to be killed." He frowned. "You have family up there? I'm bloody sorry. I didn't know."

"No," Mason said with a feeling of being bereaved. Judith was not family. She should have been.

"Still pretty rotten," Harper responded. "Don't think you can make a decent story out of it, one that should be told right now. But of course I can't stop you going up there if you want to. Last throes of battle and all that."

Barely listening to him, Mason made a pointless remark, wished Harper well, and went outside to inquire for any sort of transport that would take him toward Ypres. He was prepared to set out and walk if necessary.

Impatiently he asked two or three people for a lift; he was refused because ambulances were full or staff cars were going in the wrong direction. As dusk was mantling the ruin of the fields and woods, he set out on foot, leaving the broken town, bombed out and abandoned, fire-blackened skeletons against a lowering sky.

He passed columns of walking wounded, the German prisoners

among them looking just as gaunt and shell-shocked as the British. It moved him to an intense pity, but he had no time for it to scorch his emotions. He must find Judith.

He moved from one first-aid post to another, using his press credentials. His name alone had earned a kind of respect, so people were more willing to help him. They wanted to talk, to ask what news he had and when he expected the war to end. Troop movements were no longer secret; they were reported in the newspapers, because it was one victory after another, as relentless as a tide coming in. He tried to answer the men who asked with the honesty they deserved, remembering that they had been here for long, desperate years and lost entire platoons of friends. Some were the last survivors of regiments raised from factories, neighborhoods, villages. They would go home to quiet streets and drawn blinds.

He did not tell them that he knew there was a strong German counterattack on the River Selle, or that Dunkirk was finally shelled by long-range guns. He did tell them that he had heard a rumor that there were peace demonstrations in Berlin.

Everywhere he asked if the ambulance crews included Judith Reavley. Many knew her, but events were moving too rapidly for certainty of anything anymore. A regiment that had been here a day or two ago was farther forward now, and ambulances went wherever they were needed.

"Could be in the Casualty Clearing Station that's closed off," one lance corporal told him grimly. "Been a murder there, so I heard. Don't know why the hell there's such a fuss. Been thirty million murders, last reckoning."

Mason was shivering. "Who was killed?"

"Half Europe," the lance corporal replied.

"In the Casualty Clearing Station?" Mason had no heart to banter. His chest was so tight, it was difficult to breathe. He thought of all the times he had seen Judith since their first encounter at the Savoy Hotel in London in 1915, at a meeting to help coordinate the women wanting to help the war effort, to sort the chaos into something useful. She was there because she was a V.A.D. on the Western Front and knew what they actually wanted. She had been wearing a blue satin dress that elegantly hugged the curves of her body. He could still see in his mind the way she had walked with the easy grace of one whose mind is so absorbed in her purpose, she cared not a jot what other people thought of her. She had barely glanced at him. Even then the passion in her face had captured him.

Later it was the vulnerability. Once he had found her slumped over the wheel of her ambulance, pulled in at the side of the road, only just behind the front line. He had been terrified that she was wounded, even dead. He was overwhelmed with relief to find her breathing. Then he saw her face, her eyes empty of the fire and the will that had always been there before. He had hauled her out of the driver's seat and forced her to walk with him along the road, talking to her, angry, fighting with her, anything to make her care again. When at last she did, he had held her in his arms and whirled her around for the sheer joy of having her back.

And then last year they had quarreled. It had not been violent, in a way that might be healed, but quiet, and with certainty. She still cared passionately for the same hopeless, naïve ideals she had started out with, and he had seen them for the delusions they were.

Except perhaps they were not. Perhaps Oldroyd was right, and faith, whether founded in dreams or in reality, was the only thing worth fighting or dying for. Or, more importantly, worth living for.

Still, he knew that if it were she who had been murdered in the casualty station, he would feel as if the light had gone out everywhere. There would be nothing left to win, or to lose.

The man, the lance corporal, did not know who had been killed; he could only say that it was a nurse. Mason moved on, mostly on foot. Always there was the smell of death and the knowledge of cold and pain, the sound of guns in the distance and squelching, struggling feet walking beside him.

He found her in the ambulance bay at the Casualty Clearing Station miles from the lines now, somewhere behind Ypres. She was bent over the engine, muttering to herself, an oily rag in her hands and her hair wet and falling forward over her face.

The relief was overwhelming. He wanted to laugh and shout and run over to her across the earth and stones, clasp hold of her, swing her around, kiss her so hard and so long she would fight for breath. Of course he could not. They had parted as enemies, at least ideologically. He had denied everything she had believed in, and her loyalty to her dreams was greater than to him. Perhaps that was the way to survive. Maybe she was one of the few who would come out of this something like whole?

He walked toward her, then stopped. She did not look up.

"Broken?" he asked. "Or are you just cleaning it?"

She froze, then very slowly turned and looked at him. Her eyes widened, and suddenly the disappointment and the hurt were there. His heart pinched. That was what he loved in her, the passion and the courage to care enough to be hurt and not grow bitter or run away.

She straightened up and took a deep breath. "Hello, Mason. Come to report on our murder? Or are you just passing through to the front? I think we're well beyond Menin now." She sounded nervous, even defensive.

He made himself smile, trying to look as if he were at ease. Would she believe such a pretense? Perhaps. She had no real idea how he felt. There was no certainty in her eyes, none of the confidence of a woman who knows she is loved.

"So I hear," he agreed. "I came about the murder. Actually . . ." Should he tell her the truth? It might not be wise, but there was no time to retreat from a lie. A couple of weeks and the war could be over. Would he find her after that?

She was waiting.

"Actually I heard about it near Messines, but they didn't know who it was, just a V.A.D. I was afraid it could be you."

Her face barely changed. In the reflected light from the lamps he could not see if she was blushing. "I'm all right," she said, looking away. "It's just rather rotten for everybody because we have no idea who did it, so we are all looking sideways at one another and misunderstanding half of what's said. You don't want to think it's anyone you know, but you can't help wondering." She stopped again, still keeping her face averted as if concentrating on the engine. "The worst thing is you realize that some people have very different ideas from the ones you thought they had. I am happier not knowing some of the beliefs they have about . . . assault." She straightened up and faced him, eyes hot and angry. "And if you write any of that down I'll not ever forgive you."

It was on the edge of his tongue to say that she had not forgiven him from last time, but he bit it back. He needed to begin again with no memories of failure. He was stunned by how overwhelmingly important it was to win her, and how hard it would be. He refused to face the possibility that he might not succeed.

It surprised Matthew to be called to see Jacobson, who was still questioning people, though with no success thus far. He had not told anyone of his true rank or position in the Secret Intelligence Service. With the Peacemaker's connections and his network of informants, he could not afford to trust even those of the most patent innocence. Far better Jacobson take him for the more junior officer he pretended to be.

Actually he had not told even Joseph that he had been promoted from major to lieutenant colonel. It could wait.

"Major Reavley," Jacobson began. "Sit down." He waved to the chair. Sergeant Hampton was standing behind him, his face almost expressionless. "You are not with the Cambridgeshires; in fact, you are not regular army at all. What are you doing here, sir?"

It was a blunter opening than Matthew had expected, and certainly more immediate. It left him no choice but to tell some version of the truth.

"I'm with the Secret Intelligence Service, Inspector. I can't discuss my reason for being here."

"Really?" Jacobson looked skeptical. "Can you prove that, Major?"

"I could, of course, but you would have to get in touch with Colonel Shearing in London, and you would have to do it in some secure way. Otherwise you could ask the chaplain. He would vouch for me."

"Isn't he your brother? Hardly an unbiased witness," Jacobson pointed out. "The fact that you are an intelligence officer of some sort doesn't automatically mean you couldn't have committed a crime."

Matthew was startled. Being suspected was a possibility he had not even considered. And yet what Jacobson said was true.

Silence fell as Jacobson waited. Behind him Hampton shifted from one foot to the other.

"I cannot tell you what I am here for," Matthew replied at last. "It would jeopardize my mission."

"Are you saying you distrust the inspector?" Hampton asked a little sharply.

"We make no exceptions," Matthew told him. "For anyone. I'm surprised you don't know that. I had never met or heard of Sarah Price before her death. I have no idea who killed her. If I had, I would already have told you. I am also unaware of the movements of anyone here that night. I was asleep in a dugout a mile or two away, so I cannot offer any information of use."

"Were you alone?" Jacobson asked.

"No. My brother was there." Even as Matthew said it, he realized that Joseph was used to the conditions and had slept for several hours without waking. He could not truthfully swear to Matthew's presence.

"Asleep or awake?" Hampton questioned.

He could be caught in a lie, especially if Joseph were asked without knowing the reason. He would answer honestly. "Asleep."

"All night?" Jacobson asked.

Matthew hesitated. He had gotten up twice, walked outside, and lit a cigarette. He knew the smoke would disturb Joseph, and even more he found the underground bunker claustrophobic. The second time he had gone some considerable distance along the old trench.

"All night, Major?" Jacobson repeated.

Someone might have seen him. "No," Matthew replied. "I got up a couple of times and went along the line a bit to smoke a cigarette. But I was the best part of a mile from the Casualty Clearing Station, and then I walked even farther away. I wasn't gone longer than fifteen minutes."

"Did anyone see you?"

Matthew tried to recall exactly what had happened. His mind had been on Schenckendorff and the possibility that this was one more trick of the Peacemaker's. Alternatively, if Schenckendorff *was* exactly what he said, how could Matthew make sure they got him back to London alive?

"Major Reavley!" Jacobson said impatiently. "Either you saw someone or you did not! Which is it?"

Matthew remembered one picture vividly, perhaps because he did not understand it. He had been tired, sickened by the stench, shivering with cold, but in the flare of star shells in the distance he had seen a man and a boy struggling. There had been a quick lunge, as if with a bayonet, then the boy had fallen, and the man had picked him up and carried him. He had seen the man's face for an instant, in profile. He had a large nose. It had made Matthew think for a moment, idiotically, of the cartoons of Mr. Punch.

"Yes," he said abruptly to Jacobson. "I saw a man with a profile like Mr. Punch, and a boy."

"Soldiers?" Jacobson said skeptically.

"Of course. Who else would be out there?"

"What were they doing? Did you speak to them?" Hampton put in.

"No. The boy was hurt. The man was carrying him," Matthew answered, still trying to make sense of it in his mind.

"Did you offer to help?" Hampton pressed.

"No. I don't have any medical training. He was going toward the Casualty Clearing Station anyway."

"What about helping to carry him?" Hampton, apparently, would not give up.

"He was only a boy!" Matthew protested. "It would have been more awkward for two of us than for one."

Hampton shrugged.

"I see." Jacobson nodded. "And you made a point of telling us that you did not know, nor had you ever heard of Miss Price, until the news of her death, is that right?"

"Yes."

"Are you certain of that, Major Reavley?" This time it was Hampton who spoke.

"Yes, of course I am," Matthew said somewhat tensely. "How would I know her? I haven't been to the front line before. Most of my work is in London." It seemed a stupid question.

"Indeed?" Jacobson raised his eyebrows. "But Miss Price has not been here long—in fact, less than a year. And she has been home on leave even during that time."

"Which she took in London," Hampton added.

"There are four or five million people in London," Matthew told him with a touch of sarcasm. "Curiously, so far as I know, my path and Miss Price's did not cross."

Hampton took a step forward. "That is not true, Major Reavley. In going through her effects I found not only a photograph of you and her together—taken; to judge by the clothes and the general surroundings, some time before the war—but also a note from you, undated. From the tone of them, it is quite clear that you had a relationship of some warmth, even intimacy. It must have been nice to find an old friend out here in this waste of mud and death. But she wasn't so friendly anymore. How did it happen, sir?"

Matthew was stunned. This was becoming grotesque. "I'd never even heard of her until after she was killed!" he protested.

Hampton moved a piece of paper on the table beside Jacobson and picked up a photograph, laying it where Matthew could see it. It showed a young woman, very pretty, with fair hair and a wide smile. She was facing the camera, and beside her was a handsome young man, posing a little self-consciously. He, too, was fair, with level blue eyes and a strong-featured face not very unlike Joseph's, and clearly recognizable as Matthew in his university days. He had on a cricketing pullover in Cambridge colors. His arm was around the girl. Sarah Gladwyn. He remembered her well. She had been courting a friend of his but found she preferred Matthew, and the courtship had ended. It had all been embarrassing, and he knew he himself had not behaved well.

"Sarah Gladwyn," he said aloud, his voice hoarse. He felt the heat burn up his face. "Her name wasn't Price. I . . . I never connected them. It was years ago!"

"Yes, Major, we can see that," Hampton agreed. "But you said you didn't know her at all."

"I didn't! Not by the name you told me!" Matthew protested.

"So you say." Disbelief was heavy in Hampton's voice. "But she was killed the night you arrived, and no one can account for your movements. The only person who can vouch for you at all is your own brother, the chaplain. If I may say so, he is a rather unworldly man, and obliged to think the best of people by his calling, not to mention by his relationship to you." Hampton took a couple of steps around the table. "I advise you not to make a fuss, Major. I am arresting you for the murder of Sarah Gladwyn Price. We will inform the chaplain so that he can make any arrangements you wish for your defense."

Matthew drew in his breath, then let it out again without saying anything. The whole thing was a nightmare. He felt the canvas walls of the tent sway around him and blur into unreality. And yet Hampton's hold on his arms was hard and very real indeed.

FIVE

*J*oseph was writing letters at the table in his bunker, catching up with condolences. There was a terrible grief in the senselessness of the slaughter this close to the end. Dusk was falling rapidly, and he found himself straining his eyes in the lamplight as the ink on the page blurred in front of him. He put the pen down for a moment, blinking. He was even more tired than usual. These last few weeks seemed to be the hardest. It was foolish. They should have been easier now that the cease-fire was in sight.

They would even know who the Peacemaker was. He had given up hope of that until Matthew had come, and then Schenckendorff had actually crossed through the lines. Fortunately his foot seemed to be healing. The swelling was reduced, and the infection they had feared had not materialized. As soon as Jacobson found out who had killed poor Sarah Price, Joseph and Matthew, and perhaps Judith, could leave and take Schenckendorff with them. It was the twenty-first of October. They probably had a couple of weeks left.

He was startled by the sound of boots on the step and someone banging loudly on the lintel. Even before he could reply, Barshey Gee pulled the sacking aside, his face smeared with mud. He was clearly very upset.

"What's happened?" Joseph rose to his feet in alarm.

Barshey came in, letting the sacking fall. "Chaplain, that daft policeman has gone and arrested Major Reavley for killing the nurse. He's got him locked up back in the hut next to where they have the German prisoners."

"That's absurd!" Joseph refused to believe it. Barshey must have it wrong. "Matthew's an intelligence officer. He isn't even stationed here. What the . . ." He started to push past but Barshey clasped his arm, holding him tightly.

"No, Chaplain. From what Oi hear, that other policeman, Hampton, was looking through Miss Proice's things, and he found a picture of Major Reavley and her, going back to before the war, and it looked loike they knew each other pretty well." Barshey appeared embarrassed. "But he says the major denoied it. And o' course he can't say where he was when she was killed . . . that is, he can, but there's only you would know it, and you were asleep. And seeing as you're his brother anyway, he doesn't put a lot of weight on your say-so, if you'll pardon me."

There was no point at all in being offended, and no time to waste. He had to prove to Jacobson that Matthew was innocent. He had no idea where to even begin, let alone to reach any conclusion. The idea was preposterous because he knew Matthew, but Jacobson obviously didn't.

His mind raced. Could he get in touch with Shearing in London and have him use some authority to persuade Jacobson? But Matthew had said Shearing did not know what he was here for. And did men in charge of intelligence units ever emerge from their secrecy to do such things? Would the police take notice of him anyway?

Joseph knew almost nothing about Matthew's work. No one did. By its very nature that was obligatory. There was no one to support them. They fought in secret, and there was no praise for them, except from their own.

If the police could not blame a German, then Matthew was an obvious scapegoat: a man in uniform who stayed safely at home in London, sleeping in his own bed every night. He never even got mud on his shoes, never mind shrapnel or a bayonet in his body.

"What are you going to do, sir?" Barshey asked, pulling himself to attention carefully to avoid cracking his head on the ceiling. He said it as if he was waiting for orders to help.

Joseph's mind was suddenly clear. "About the only way I can prove he didn't do it is to find out who did."

"Haven't you been troying?" Barshey asked with a frown.

"Not hard enough," Joseph answered grimly. "I left it to the police, and they've made a complete mess of it."

"What'd you loike me to do, sir?" Barshey offered.

Joseph was not even sure what he was going to do himself, let alone how anyone else could help, but he was loath to refuse even the slightest assistance. There was no one else he could turn to, apart from Judith. Even Barshey's trust was a kind of strength. "I have a pretty good idea about who couldn't have done it because they were all accounted for during the hour or so when it must have happened—" he started.

Barshey's eyes widened. "You know when it happened?"

"Only roughly. She was seen alive at three o'clock that morning, and the state of her body when she was found at about seven means it has to have been no later than around four." He did not need to explain how a dead person changes in the first few hours; they were all far too familiar with it.

"But they weren't all accounted for, were they?" Barshey observed. "Want me to work on that, sir?"

Joseph hesitated, torn. Barshey was loyal and willing. He knew she was dead; did he know how brutally and intimately she had been destroyed as well?

"I need to know more about Sarah Price," he said finally. "Maybe she was chosen at random, but maybe not. She might have had some liaison that was at least the start of this. I thought I knew most of the men, but it seems I don't. I half expected the violence toward the German prisoners, but nothing like this."

"Nobody wants to think that sort o' thing about anyone they know, Chaplain," Barshey said grimly. "And with respect, sir, most of us want to show a man loike you the best soide of ourselves. Men that'd swear a blue streak usually koind of keep a close lip when you're there."

"You're saying I don't see the real man?" Joseph shrugged. "I know that, Barshey. I make allowances."

Barshey did not look convinced, but he was too gentle to say so.

Joseph saw it in his eyes and understood. "All right, I'll tell you what you can do to help. Give me a more honest picture of the men you think I've judged too softly. Help me to see them as they are. Somebody killed that girl pretty obscenely. I saw her body. It was worse than you think."

Barshey was startled, then overwhelmingly disgusted.

"I'm not as otherworldly as you think," Joseph told him quietly. "I've heard some confessions that would surprise you, especially from men who knew they were dying. I just didn't think of anyone I know doing something like this. There was a hatred in it I hadn't imagined."

"Oi hope it's not someone from St. Giles." Barshey's face pinched as if he expected a blow. "Oi'll think about it, an' Oi'll ask."

"Don't think long, Barshey. It's going to be too late pretty quickly." It hurt even to say it aloud.

"Oi know that." Barshey did not offer any words of comfort. The belief in everything working out for good had long ago been swept away. You believed in honor, courage, and friendship, but not in any certainty of justice.

Joseph found Judith helping with nursing shifts in the tent for the walking wounded. It had been a quieter night than usual. The front line having moved farther east, the injured men were being taken to a clearing station closer by. There were half a dozen patients, two standing, and four sitting in various degrees of discomfort. Others had obviously received no more than first aid—a bandage to stop the worst of the bleeding, a sling for a broken bone. More were already treated and waiting to be told where to go next, their uniform sleeves cut away, bandages clean and white. There were two nurses in attendance, an orderly, and a young surgeon.

Judith looked at Joseph's face and excused herself from the man she was helping, leaving the job for the orderly to finish. She crossed the space between them in a few strides. "What is it?" she asked anxiously. "What's happened?"

Using as few words as possible, he told her, and saw her eyes widen with horror. "I'm sorry," he finished. "We have no more time to spare. Quite apart from getting Schenckendorff to London, we've got to find out who did it to save Matthew."

"They can't believe it was him!" she said desperately, struggling to find it absurd rather than serious. "Why on earth would he? He only arrived here a day before she was killed! It doesn't make any sense. Anyway, where would he get a bayonet?"

"Judith, there are weapons all over the place, rusted ones, broken ones, ones people have dropped or lost. And what does sense have to do with any of it?" he demanded, feeling panic rush up inside him. "Why would anyone do that to her? They need to blame somebody, open the station, and get on with ending the war. They want to get the men out of here and start operating it as normal again, probably even move it forward. We're too far behind the lines now. Above all, they want to say the matter is closed and forget all about it."

"Even if it isn't the right man? That's monstrous!" She waved her hands, refusing to believe it. She ignored the curious glances of the orderly and two of the wounded.

"Look around you!" Joseph said impatiently, keeping his voice low. "How many men are dead? What's one more if they can close this and say it's ended? They don't know Matthew; he isn't one of them."

"But somebody really did it! Somebody—"

"I know." He lowered his voice with an effort, breathing in and out deeply, trying to regain control of himself. "We have to find him, British or German, and we have to do it in the next two or three days, at the most. We need to begin by getting to know everything we can about Sarah Price. We agree that she didn't deserve it, nobody could, but she may have done something to provoke it—"

Her face tightened with anger. "And what does a person do, exactly, to *provoke* being hacked to death, Joseph?" she said savagely. "Funny how you never think your brother could be just like other men!"

"That's the point, Judith," he said with barely a flicker of change in his expression. "It's probably someone that nobody thinks of as having violent or uncontrollable passions, or having been so wounded in mind that at times he no longer behaves like ordinary sane people. But somebody knows him, has worked beside him, fought beside him, shared rations, letters from home, all the things we do and the ways we get to know people."

"Was that why you said it?" she demanded, her eyes wide and angry. "To make me think of that?"

"Not altogether," he admitted reluctantly. "I do think that she might have said or done something that infuriated someone. If it is entirely random, we don't have much chance of finding him, do we?"

Her face crumpled with regret. "I'm sorry. I suppose we don't." She took a deep breath and looked a little away from him. "I feel guilty because I didn't even take much notice of her. I thought she was trivial and empty-headed. Father always used to say I was too quick to judge. I thought I'd learned."

She bit her lip hard. "We've got to get Matthew to London with that German officer, whatever his name is, because we've got to expose the Peacemaker. My war won't finish until we have! I'll start finding out. At least I've plenty of time, compared with usually, and I have an excuse to be here. I suppose I even have an excuse to ask questions now. At least nobody can tell me it's not my business."

"We have to succeed—" he started.

"I know!" She didn't want to hear him say it, even though she had accepted that it was true.

She began with the other medical staff, knowing she had a better chance with them than Joseph did with the soldiers. None of them had been here very long: It was the nature of a Casualty Clearing Station for the wounded to move through it as quickly as possible.

"No more time for being charitable about it," she said briskly to Erica Barton-Jones as they were in the storage tent taking delivery of some clean blankets, having sent away those too torn or saturated in blood to use anymore.

"I thought they'd arrested someone," Erica replied, heaving the gray blankets up. She was not pretty, but there was a grace and strength of character in her face that was in a way more attractive. A highly practical woman, she held whatever grief she had experienced deep inside her.

"They have," Judith replied. "My brother."

Erica was incredulous. "The chaplain? That's idiotic!"

"No, Matthew. He's an intelligence officer." She had no compunction at all about shading the truth. "He's out here on some mission or other, which of course he can't tell us, and they don't believe him. He can't prove it because it's secret. That's what intelligence is about."

"So what are you going to do?" Erica's face was tense and anxious. "You could ask questions, of course, but what makes you think anyone will tell you something they haven't told the police? Not that I'm saying you shouldn't try." There was an uncharacteristic flash of sympathy in her eyes, perhaps because she thought Judith would not succeed.

Erica's pity only made it worse, and a flare of temper burned up in Judith. "Because I know what questions to ask," she snapped. "For example, before anything happened, who was Sarah nursing? Did she flirt with any of the doctors or orderlies?" She saw Erica's distaste. "And don't screw your face up and pretend it couldn't happen. We're all frightened and tired and sick with seeing people suffer, and we can't do much to help them. We don't get close to anyone for long because people are moved around all the time, lots of them die, but we still can't help the need for touching someone, emotionally or physically. Life can be too hard, too unbearably lonely without it. Friendship is almost the only lifeline to sanity and the things that are worth surviving for."

Erica stared at her, her eyes shadowed, her lips pulled tight. She looked as if her mind was racing and she wanted to speak, but the words eluded her.

"Well, who was she nursing?" Judith repeated. "Don't tell me you don't know, because you do! You are in charge and you never miss anything. You're the most efficient nurse on the whole Ypres Salient. Did she go anywhere near the German prisoners? I haven't seen the rosters, but we both know they don't mean anything. People go where they're needed. An emergency happens and everything changes."

"It's not on the roster," Erica said reluctantly. "But I'm pretty sure she did. We had a bit of a panic about one of the Germans who lost an arm. Thought he was going to bleed to death. Another one had a mangled foot, but he's recovering quite well. We lost a couple, but we never had much of a chance of saving them anyway. They were bad when they got here."

"Who? Did she quarrel with anyone—flirt too much? Was she careless?" Judith rattled off the questions, hearing the demand in her own voice and knowing the answers would prove nothing. "Did she go back again afterward?"

"I wish I could say she did, but she stayed pretty much with our own," Erica replied. She stood stiffly; her gray dress was soiled and very crumpled, but she carried herself with such a high head and ramrod back that on her it had a kind of style. "Mary Castalet did most of the nursing for the Germans," she continued. "There are only a few here, you know. About eight. Anyone fit to move got sent on. We need the beds. Some of them are on the floor anyway, poor creatures."

Her elegant face puckered in distress. "I imagine having fought for four years out here, losing the war, terrified that your wife and children will be treated pretty much the way you treated the Belgians, and then being wounded and lying on the floor of the enemy's field hospital! I wouldn't wish that on a dog."

Judith refused to let her mind picture it.

"How well are they guarded, really?" she asked.

Erica thought for a moment. "Not closely," she said, meeting Judith's eyes levelly. "Most of them came here voluntarily. They're wounded and they need treatment. Why would they escape and where would they go, assuming they were fit enough to go anywhere?"

Judith forced herself to ask the next question. "What about our men going in and hurting them? If that happened, couldn't they as easily get out?"

Erica's face hardened as her anger rose in reaction to the whole tragic, ridiculous turn of events. "Don't be stupid! You know the answer to that already—we can't spare extra men to guard Germans from our own soldiers."

"Then possibly a German prisoner, one not wounded too badly to walk, could have gotten out and gone looking for someone vulnerable, like one of the nurses?" Judith pointed out. "Maybe one who was childish enough to taunt them, or try flirting?"

"I suppose so. But the other prisoners would have seen it. They're in there like sardines in a tin."

Judith thought about it for several moments. Ideas raced through her mind. It would be easier for all of them if it had been one of the Germans. It was going to be bitterly painful to have to acknowledge that a British soldier could have done such a thing. Worse, it had to be someone they knew, because there wasn't anyone they didn't know, or had not fought beside, shared rations with, jokes, loneliness. They all wanted it to be a German.

But that might also be more difficult to prove. And might they want it enough to be tempted into making it look that way, whether they were sure of it or not? Nothing was clear enough. That was a sickening thought, but once it was in her mind she could not get rid of it.

"Describe Sarah to me," she said instead, picking up the blankets again and resuming folding them. They were rough to the touch and smelled stale. "What was she really like? I only saw her a few times when we were helping the wounded inside, and she came over to give a hand, or when she gave us tea or food."

Erica hesitated.

"Come on!" Judith said urgently, her patience slipping. "How was she in a crisis? What did she talk about if you had a really sick man and you had to sit up all night with him? What did she think was funny? What did she cry over? Was she saving money for anything? Did she write to anyone? Who did she like, or not? Who didn't like her?"

"What on earth can that have to do with who killed her?" Erica was making a clearly visible effort to keep her own patience. "Judith, for God's sake! Nobody's saying it, but everybody's thinking it! Some man went crazy and raped her!" She shuddered violently. "It wasn't just a quarrel where somebody slapped her too hard. You're talking as if it were all reasonable. It isn't!" Now her voice was growing uncontrollably louder. "Reasonable people fight sometimes. If they're men they might even hurt each other badly. But this wasn't human. There was blood everywhere. It was like a wild animal!"

"Foxes do that to chickens sometimes," Judith replied. "But animals don't kill for hate, and they don't indulge in years of organized slaughter of their own kind, leaving nothing but mud and ruins. This was very definitely human."

Erica put down the blankets she was holding. The lamplight flickered in the draft through the tent flap. It danced on her face, accentuating the lines of strain. "I'm only answering your questions because they've arrested your brother," she said, her voice shaking a little. "Sarah was all right in a crisis, pretty stupid the rest of the time. I never sat up all night with her. I took care to avoid it. According to Allie and Moira, she talked about men. And as to what she thought was funny, it was pretty juvenile: flirting, teasing, making people look silly. There was a cruel streak in her. I think it was partly because she wasn't respected very much, and she knew it." Erica turned away and her shoulders under the gray dress were stiff, as if she disliked herself for what she had said.

"Underneath the laughing and the flirting, she was pretty desperate," she went on quietly. "She didn't have a lot to go home to. She wasn't a bad nurse, but she didn't do it because she loved it. It was a job. What did she cry over? Nothing. I never saw her cry." Her face tightened, and she kept avoiding Judith's eyes. "Now that I think it over a bit harder, I think possibly she didn't dare to, in case she couldn't stop. Who did she like? Men, any men who would flirt with her. Who didn't like her? I didn't. She thought I was a stuck-up bitch, and said so, several times. Ask anyone, she wasn't discreet about it. Or about much else, either."

"In fact, she was rather common?" Judith concluded with a slight lift of her voice to make it a question. Then she remembered hearing that Erica's younger brother was an RFC squadron leader who had been burned to death when his plane crashed over Vimy Ridge, and wished she had been gentler. Matthew and Joseph were still alive, at least for now.

"If that's your conclusion, don't attribute it to me," Erica said sharply. "And don't say I said that she deserved what she got, because I didn't."

"I'm not trying to make trouble!" Judith exclaimed. "I've got more than enough already. I'm trying to find out who killed her!"

"You're trying to save your brother from being hanged," Erica corrected her, turning to face her squarely, eyes hot and full of pain.

Judith felt as if she had been slapped. It was perfectly true. Before Matthew had been accused she had cared very little who had killed Sarah Price. Her mind had been on Mason returning and stirring up feelings in her she had been determined to leave buried, as well as the amazement of finding someone who would identify the Peacemaker at last, and the passion to get him home to England in time. Sarah's death was horrible, but not personally wounding.

"At least you don't lie about that," Erica said with a bleak smile. "Good luck. You'll need it. Everyone has their own ideas about who did it, and whether they really want to know for certain, or not. Some of us don't."

Judith finished with the blankets, then went to find out who had been on duty guarding the German prisoners the night Sarah had been killed.

It had stopped raining outside, but the air was cold and it flapped her wet skirts around her ankles, making her legs and feet almost numb. The boards creaked when she stood on them. Wind rattled in the canvas and whined through cracks where it could not be tied down.

It took Judith some time and argument before she learned the names of both men who had been on guard duty. One was Lance Corporal Benbow, the other Private Eames. Both had recently been wounded themselves, and they were still insufficiently healed to be back on front-line duty. She found Eames first. He was in a dugout brewing up a cup of tea in a Dixie can over a flame, waiting patiently for it to come anywhere near boiling. He had fair hair and long, bony wrists that poked out of his uniform shirt. He moved stiffly, the wound in his shoulder clearly still causing him pain.

"We were there all night, miss," he said in answer to her question. "I'd an 'ole lot rather think it was one o' them Jerries 'oo done that to 'er, 'specially seein' as 'ow she were over that way toward the shed where they're kept. But Benbow were with me all the time, and no one came out o' the 'ut that I saw till about three in the morning, an' that were just ter stick 'is 'ead out and straight back in again."

"But you saw Sarah Price?" Judith said quickly. "Where? Who with? What was she doing?"

He shook his head, still watching and nursing the flame under his Dixie can. "She were alone, miss. Just walking along the boards wi' something in 'er 'and. Couldn't see what."

"What time?" She refused to let the faint glimmer of hope slip out of her grasp. "You were on guard duty, you must have an idea."

"About 'alf past two, near as I can remember. Or maybe three."

"Was there anyone else near her? Think! It could matter a lot."

It was clear that Eames was thinking. His brow furrowed, and he was deeply withdrawn into himself.

Judith waited.

"I don't know," he said at last. "I was thinking about the Germans."

"What about before that?" she asked. "Earlier in the evening?"

"She went to the Germans' shed," he replied. "But she came out and she were fine. I told 'er—" He stopped.

"What?" Judith demanded. "What did you tell her?"

He chewed his lip, eyes still concentrating on the candle flame. "I told 'er to give the poor sods a chance," he mumbled. "They aren't all bad, any more'n we're all good."

Judith breathed in and out slowly. "Why did you say that, Private Eames?" She did her best to sound patient.

He was silent for several moments.

"She was murdered, Private," she prompted him.

He looked away from the candle at last, his eyes grave.

"I know that, miss, an' I wouldn't 'ave that 'appen to anyone. Wot they did to 'er was 'orrible. But she did tempt them something rotten. Told 'em all sorts o' things as'd 'appen to their women when our boys got into Germany. I know she were just ignorant, miss, an' she lost some of 'er friends, like all of us." He looked across at her, the tea forgotten now. "But that in't the way ter treat people as can't fight back at yer." He was struggling to find the words to explain it to her. He understood his own laws of honor, but they had never been set out for him; they were simply learned by things he had seen other people do.

"It's all right, Private, I know it isn't." She felt a warmth in her stomach, as if she had swallowed the tea and it had blazed to life like a fire inside her. "Could it have been one of the Germans who got back at her?"

"I dunno, miss. I don't think so."

She thanked him, leaving him to brew his tea.

It was some time later that she found Benbow. He was a year or two younger, and quite clearly worried. She could draw nothing from him except an approximate agreement with what Eames had said. It surprised her.

He seemed a strong man, a good soldier. He was not much more than nineteen, but he had been promoted from the ranks and had an easy confidence. The question troubled him, but he did not hesitate in his answer. "I wouldn't like to say, miss, and perhaps be wrong."

She had to be content with that, which she told Joseph at dusk when they stood in line with forty others to receive their rations. It was a clear evening, banners of clouds shredded out and streaming across the north with a sharp wind carrying the sound of heavy gunfire in the distance.

Joseph looked unhappy. "I've come across the same thing," he said quietly. "No one wants to tell tales that could be misread, but they all want it to be over. I can't help wondering if I would be any different if it wasn't Matthew they were accusing. If it was somebody from London that I didn't know, somebody who had sat out the war at home, as far as I could see, would I care?"

"Don't say that!" she told him sharply. "Just because it—"

"I know," he interrupted. "But that's how some men see it. I was talking to Turner, who beat the German prisoner the other day. He's got a brother-in-law who has bad eyesight, or flat feet, or something, and has spent the entire war at home sleeping in his own bed every night and making a fortune on the black market. I think Turner would see him shot in a trice."

"We probably all would," Judith agreed as they shuffled forward a few steps. "But we could live with it only if he was guilty, if it was one of us and not a German. What happens to make somebody who looks just like the rest of us suddenly go barking mad and do something like this? Why?"

Joseph did not answer. Ahead of them someone laughed loudly, then suddenly bit it off. There was silence. The click of ladles against a metal can was loud.

"I'm not sure what madness is," Joseph said at last, keeping his voice so low that those next to them and behind could not hear. "Or maybe I mean that I don't know what sanity is, or exactly how you keep hold of it."

The remark frightened her: He had always been the one person who knew what he believed. But it was unfair to expect him to always hold up the light for everyone else. He must have his dark nights of the soul, too, moonless and starless like everyone else's, or what use was he? Without knowledge of despair, was hope real or only an untasted thought?

"You might lose sight of what's good," she said firmly. "You don't lose the memory of it or the certainty that it is what you want; that is sanity. You might have to kill, but you do it reluctantly, and without hate."

He put his arm around her in a quick, silent hug. Even in the chill of the wind, the warmth of it touched her mind if not her flesh.

"From what everyone says she wasn't a bad nurse," he went on, exploring the ideas. "I thought she might have made a mistake that turned out badly, or told tales, or anything else that was stupid, and might have caused somebody to get hurt, lose an arm or leg, even die. But I haven't found anything. She seems to have been perfectly competent—if anything better than some others. She flirted and occasionally, when the rations were decent, drank a bit too much and was silly, but only to laugh too loudly and be a bit of a nuisance. Some of the men thought it was quite funny. Nobody took advantage of her. She had a few romances, but short-lived, just while a particular man was here, usually too badly wounded to do much anyway."

They moved another step forward. "It was just . . . just grabbing at life while she could," he added very quietly. "She was frightened and lonely, like everyone else. According to one of the orderlies, all she really wanted was to marry and have children." He stopped. "At least that's what he thought."

She could barely see his face in the uncertain lamplight, but there was a deep understanding of loss in it, and a pity that hurt. She thought of his beloved Eleanor and the baby who had died at birth. Would Lizzie Blaine ever be able to take Eleanor's place, or at least make a new place where the old hopes could begin again? At that moment she wished more than anything else in the world, more than anything for herself, that it would happen.

It was not until he turned that she saw his eyes and realized that he was thinking not just of Sarah Price, but probably also of Mason, who had fallen so far below the courage and hope Judith needed to feed her heart. Suddenly her eyes filled with tears and she turned away. It was strangely painful to be known so well. It left her wounds exposed, too. And yet it meant she was not alone. As long as Joseph was alive, she never would be.

"We'll find who did it," she said, needing to say something practical, to stop looking at the things too delicate to touch. Times, places, who was where, who saw what—those were the things that mattered. But now they were at the head of the queue, and it was not until they had received their bread and stew that they were able to move into a quiet corner of a supply tent and resume talking.

"Let's be practical," she said firmly, taking a mouthful of stew and trying not to think what it tasted like. "After you've taken out all the people who couldn't have killed her because they were proved to be somewhere else, who's left?"

He gave a bleak smile, but there was a flash of humor in his eyes. "Sherlock Holmes? After you've eliminated all that is impossible, whatever is left, however unlikely, has to be the truth," he quoted roughly. "That's the trouble: Very little indeed is left. Most people are accounted for be-

cause it was a pretty busy night, but in the poor light and with people coming and going, there are still quite a few I'm not certain of." He ate another
couple of mouthfuls of stew before going on. "The trouble is, I think several people could be lying. I can understand it." He looked at her over the
top of the Dixie can. "No one wants to think it's someone they care about.
Perhaps they owe a debt to some friend, a pretty big one, and so they lie
to protect them, certain it doesn't matter because they would never do such
a thing anyway."

She looked down quickly, feeling the guilt burn in her face for her own
lie to protect Wil Sloan. It had been for exactly that reason. He could never
do such a thing. She knew him too well to even imagine it for an instant,
but others didn't, and he might be blamed. Jacobson didn't know anyone,
and didn't understand the men, any of them, let alone an American medical volunteer. Did Joseph know she had lied? She was not going to tell
him, not now, anyway.

"Yes, it's difficult," she agreed. At least her lie would not affect
Matthew, and owning up to it would hurt Wil without helping anyone else.
She bit into the bread and chewed it until she could swallow. Her throat
was tight. "We'll just have to work harder."

Judith could not tell Lizzie why Matthew had come here, but naturally she
knew he had been arrested. Everyone did. The sense of relief was palpable
for most of them. He had not actually been charged yet; Jacobson was still
gathering evidence, hoping for something more concrete, witnesses who
had seen something, heard something. But it was only a matter of time.

News was coming about the front line moving east, towns falling one
by one. The fighting was still bitter, with murderous losses on both sides,
but the end could not be much longer in coming.

Judith was in the Evacuation tent making room for more wounded to
be moved into it.

"I need to see one of the German prisoners," she said urgently to
Lizzie. "It's important. For Matthew." She was almost on the edge of
telling Lizzie why, but she remembered with a stab of pain still fresh the
consequences of a previous confidence she'd made, and she kept silent.

Lizzie must have heard the emotion in her voice. She did not argue or
ask for further explanation. "You'd better come with me," she said, looking away the moment after she had agreed. "I have a duty there as soon as
we've finished this, but I expect you know that."

Judith felt guilty. She was using Lizzie, who was a friend, but she
would have used anyone at all to help Matthew, and to get Schenckendorff
to tell them everything he knew about the Peacemaker. Her mind told her

that he must not be permitted to influence the terms of the armistice; her heart demanded that he answer for the deaths of her parents.

"Thank you," she said sincerely.

A flicker of a smile warmed Lizzie's face, then she led the way. There were two guards on duty, as usual, but they took no notice of nurses coming and going, and to them Judith in her V.A.D. gray was just the same. The thought flashed in her mind to wonder if nurses were always invisible to them. Had Sarah come and gone this way without being noticed?

Inside the hut eight men lay on narrow cots, close to one another. Dark blankets covered their bodies up to the chin; the white bandages that were visible were mostly stained with blood. Lizzie stopped at the first bed. Judith went on, looking for a man whose foot was bandaged.

She found him quickly, although he was not at all as she had expected. He looked leaner, more vulnerable, lying on the cot, his hair untidy from the rough pillow, his face tired and unshaven, etched with pain. She was aware of what Joseph had said about the courage it must have cost him to abandon his life's belief and promises because his moral loyalty was to a higher principle. How many people can ever do that? The loneliness must be almost beyond the imagination. Could she have left all that she knew and loved for any principle of right, however deep? Would not the accusation of betrayal, however false, bleed inside her forever?

Would he be able to go through with it, when the moment came?

The man stared straight ahead, not looking at her because he did not expect to be spoken to. She was anonymous, just another English nurse who was here only out of duty. The young man in the bed beyond him looked no more than sixteen or seventeen. There was barely down on the fair skin of his cheeks. He looked at her with fear.

"I'm not going to hurt you," she said in German. She wanted to add that nobody would, but she knew that might not be true.

Schenckendorff looked at her, woken from his thoughts. "It is not himself he is afraid for," he said in almost unaccented English. "He is afraid for his family. He comes from a village in the path of the army on its way to Berlin. They are alone there now. His father is dead and his sisters are only children, younger than he is. I apologize for him. He has heard stories."

"Of course he's afraid for them," she replied. "I understand that. My brother is in danger, and I'm afraid for him." She smiled at the boy, who stared at her, an answering smile touching his mouth and then vanishing. She looked back at Schenckendorff. "He has been blamed for something he didn't do. If we can't prove that he didn't, they'll shoot him."

There was no comprehension in Schenckendorff's eyes.

"One of our nurses was murdered," she said.

"I know," he answered. "It was not any of us, although I suppose it is inevitable that you should think it is. I cannot help you, Miss . . ."

She found her eyes filling with tears, and was furious with herself. "Reavley," she said in little more than a whisper.

His face was gray with exhaustion and pain, but he still managed to blush. "I'm sorry," he said so quietly that she saw his lips move more than heard the words.

She had no idea what to say. She wanted to accept what she thought was at least in part an apology as well as an expression of sympathy, but her father's face was so vivid in her mind that the absolution would not come. "Who is the Peacemaker?" she said instead.

He remained silent.

"They are accusing my brother Matthew of having killed that girl," she went on. She heard the rasping emotion in her voice and could not control it. "If we don't manage to prove that he didn't, they'll shoot him. Everybody just wants an end to it. We'd like it to be one of you, but it seems it couldn't be. The next best thing from them is if it was someone like him, who's only just arrived here. Anything is better than it being someone they know."

He frowned. "Why do they think it's him? Why would an intelligence officer from London, who's never seen her before, suddenly do such a thing?"

"Because he knew her before, and told them he didn't. It was a long time ago, and she wasn't married then. He knew her by her maiden name and he didn't associate the two."

"Don't they understand that?" he asked.

"They don't want to." She lifted her shoulders very slightly in dismissal of reason. "It's an answer. They can take him and the regiment will be happy. The police can pack up and go home, get away from the smell, the mud, and the hard rations." She stared at him, seeing a pain of disillusion far deeper than anything physical could be. "Who is the Peacemaker, Colonel von Schenckendorff?" She almost added that he owed them that much, then changed her mind. He knew it already, or he would not be here.

"That is dangerous knowledge, Miss Reavley."

"You think it is going to make Matthew's life any more dangerous than it is? They'll shoot him—or hang him perhaps." To say that was so painful, she faltered.

He closed his eyes. "Dermot Sandwell," he whispered.

She was stunned. Was that true? Could it be? She thought they had proved it could not be, years ago. Was this the Peacemaker's last, most daring trick of all, to blame someone else? Was Schenckendorff prepared to sacrifice his life to save the real Peacemaker and ruin Sandwell?

She realized he was looking at her, even smiling very faintly.

"You don't believe me," he observed. "That is why I have to go to England, whatever the cost. Knowing his name will give you nothing, Miss Reavley, except perhaps a bullet in the head. I must face him and prove it. I know dates and telegram texts, people, places. You must free your brother from this absurd charge, however you do it, and we must go to London. We have not much more time to waste. Please . . ."

She nodded. "Thank you. I'll do everything I can."

His smile grew a little. "You are still not certain, are you? You think it could be a double cross, a triple cross."

She nearly said she did believe, then something in his eyes made her feel that lying would be cheap, a thing unworthy of either of them. "I don't know," she admitted. "Can I do anything for you? I'm really an ambulance driver, but I can do basic nursing, emergency care, something to make you more comfortable." It was evasive, a moment's release from the tension that threatened to snap inside her, and yet part of her meant it. They were both trapped, and he was in a different kind of pain. She would have helped it if she could.

"Matthew Reavley?" Mason said in disbelief. "That's impossible!"

He had followed the Cambridgeshire regiment forward to get the stories that would justify his being here. The weather was gray, with a slicing wind and occasional bursts of sun, but they were beyond the old battleground with its trenches lacing through the wasteland. Here there was nothing to shelter them except a slight rise in the ground and a few scratched-out hollows for sleeping.

"Maybe," the other correspondent said drily, shifting his position to ease his cramped legs. The guns were too close for carelessness. Snipers could shoot a long way. "Nevertheless it's true," he went on. "Been a lot more convenient if it'd been one of the Germans, but apparently it wasn't. Just as well, or we could have had a bloodbath in reprisals. Anyway, who is this Reavley? Why is it impossible? That's a word I wouldn't expect to hear you use so casually."

"I know him." Mason's mind was racing. Judith would be desperate. He could barely imagine what she must be feeling. He should go back to the Casualty Clearing Station immediately and do something to help. The police must be idiots. Surely a word with whoever was in charge would unravel the mess they had made?

"And nobody you know could commit a crime?" the other correspondent said with mockery in his voice. "Come on, Mason! Whoever it is, somebody knows him! It's not like you to be stupidly sentimental."

Mason slithered down the hill until he was well below the ridge, then stood up. "I know him well, you damn fool!" he snapped. "I know his whole family. I have for years. He's based in London, for a start. He wouldn't even know the damn woman. You can have this." He waved his arm to encompass the entire region of the battle line. "I have to find out what's behind the . . . the foul-up at the clearing station."

"You can't . . . ," the other man began, but he was addressing Mason's back, and he gave up.

Mason started to walk—there was no other means of transport this far forward—and the sheer physical effort of it gave him some release from the fury of frustration inside him. Why was Matthew Reavley up here at the front line anyway? What had brought him to France or Belgium so close to the armistice? Why was he not in London doing all he could to influence events the way he would want them to go?

He passed a gun crew hauling a cannon up the incline until it was clear of the stream. He had no time to think of helping them.

He remembered vividly his last encounter in Marchmont Street, and how the Peacemaker had been at his wit's end to prevent a settlement on Germany punitive enough to create a vacuum in the economy of Europe that might end swallowing half the world. Could it be something to do with that? Or was he being fanciful to imagine that anything that any handful of men could do would seriously affect the tide of history? Was there not going to be chaos whatever they did?

They were firing behind him, the noise almost deafening. One blessing peace would bring would be silence. He trod on a patch of shifting ground and nearly lost his balance. There were shell craters all around, and a low mist rising off the wet earth. Some of it stank of old gas, and the clinging odor of decay was everywhere. He thought of the clean wind in the grass off the high fens, the scent of bracken, the silence that stretched to eternity, the blue hills beyond the hills, and the bright sky.

How ironically senseless that this policeman, whoever he was, should arrest Matthew Reavley of all men for a barbaric murder. Matthew had been the Peacemaker's most implacable enemy, even more than Joseph. But this was one thing the Peacemaker could not have accomplished, another absurd twist of fate. This final injustice to the Reavleys was sheer, blind chance.

And yet they had never given up. He could imagine their efforts now. They would be doing everything possible, at any cost, to prove that Matthew was innocent. They would be outraged, burning with the stupidity and fear of it, but not self-pitying, certainly not defeated.

He was passed by an ambulance taking wounded back to the nearest casualty clearing station, but it was not the one where Judith was. The tide of events had left that behind. It would be another two or three miles before he could hope to beg a lift on any vehicle.

His feet squelched in the mud. His legs ached with the effort of pulling himself out of it again and again.

The Peacemaker had begun with such high, clear ideals. They would broker peace, prevent the slaughter and ruin of war, at a relatively small price. Except that it was not a small price. They had not seen then that the lack of open war is not the same thing as peace. There are internal prices to pay that create a different kind of war, another sort of destruction. The Peacemaker had paid, principle by principle, until the crusader in him had become a tyrant, making choices for others that they would not have chosen for themselves.

Why had Mason joined him in the beginning? So that the atrocities he had seen in the Boer War would never happen again. He was heartsick at the suffering he had seen and would have made any sacrifice to prevent another single further human from enduring such loss. Nationality was irrelevant.

But it wasn't nationality that was the issue. It was the passion and the belief of the individual, the right to rule himself in the manner of his choice, the chance to be different, funny, inventive, to learn anything and everything, to question, to make mistakes and to start again. And to be bloody-minded and brave and kind, like half the ordinary soldiers he had seen. And like the crewman who had given his life on the way back from Gallipoli, to avoid betraying the people who trusted him. Mason would never forget him. He could still see his white face in the bottom of the boat, then in the water. In the moment of his death he had become Everyman, the ordinary British soldier, the one Joseph Reavley had said would never understand or accept the Peacemaker's world—not at the price it cost.

Without realizing it he had quickened his step, sloshing through the mud in what he hoped was the general direction of the station. He must help Judith; that was one thing about which there was no question or doubt. Where he stood or what else he believed could wait until later.

SIX

*M*atthew stared at the rough wooden walls of the inside of the hut in which he was locked. It had been a toolshed once, then used for supplies. Now it was the only place secure enough to keep a prisoner. He had been left a cot, two blankets, and a pail—that was all. He could hardly believe that Jacobson really considered him guilty of having murdered Sarah Gladwyn—Sarah Price, as she now was. He had not lied; he had never connected the present army nurse with the girl he had known at the university. "I haven't thought of her from that day to this!" he had protested with absolute honesty. It was preposterous that Jacobson stood there convinced he was lying, not a shadow of uncertainty in his face.

"Hard to believe, Major Reavley," he said almost without expression. "Pretty girl. Doesn't look in that picture as if you'd forget each other."

"Know lots of pretty girls, do you?" Sergeant Hampton had asked, his lip very slightly curled perhaps less from skepticism than a faint contempt, an unworded suggestion of moral callousness on Matthew's part.

"Yes," Matthew snapped. "Actually the university is full of them. Lots of them are pretty, and some are clever as well." Instantly he wished he had not said that. It was an arrogant remark, and in the circumstances extraordinarily stupid. It was just the sort of indifference to feelings that justified their suspicion of him. The truth was that it had been an uncomfortable episode. Sarah had been pretty and fun, in a superficial way, and he had certainly been flattered that she chose him. It had had a lot to do with beating the competition, which was not a pleasing thought, and far too close to what Jacobson assumed of him.

Sarah had been easy to like, undemanding, ready to laugh. He remembered now how pretty her hair had been, soft and always shining. Her features were no more than pleasant, but she had danced marvelously, following as if she read his thoughts in every step. He blushed now to think how much he had enjoyed that, the easy movement in unison, the way she had never been heavy in his arms, never tried to lead. Poor Sarah.

He had wanted to forget it because he had not behaved well. The flattery had turned his head, and he had not considered anyone else's feelings. It was one of the stupidities of youth he preferred not to recall, but that was a luxury he could not afford now.

"I behaved badly," he admitted, staring at Jacobson. "We were both young, and only flirting. It meant nothing in any lasting sense, just fun at the time. She moved on to somebody else, and so did I. *Sarah* is not an uncommon name. I didn't see her here, and I didn't connect the woman you spoke of with the girl I had known."

Jacobson had said nothing. Hampton's face expressed his total disbelief.

Matthew walked four paces, turned, and walked back again.

Jacobson had interviewed him again, briefly, but there was nothing to pursue. There was a soldier nicknamed Punch, but he had denied being anywhere near where Matthew had been. He had brought in a wounded soldier, a fifteen-year-old, but he'd come from the opposite direction, naturally, from where the fighting was.

Jacobson had pressed Matthew about his exact position in the intelligence service, and what he was here for. Matthew had considered telling him, but he had nothing with him to prove it, and he had left London telling Shearing only that he had gone to collect vital information—nothing as to what it was. If Shearing had read between the lines anything of the Peacemaker, he would not substantiate that to anyone, certainly not to a policeman he did not know. The Peacemaker's power was far too wide and deep to take sides like that.

Matthew's rescue depended on Joseph and Judith. The only answer was to find whoever had really killed Sarah. The huge and ugly thought always at the edge of his mind was that the whole trip here was the Peacemaker's last ploy before the defeat of Germany, and the end of at least this part of his plan.

Was Matthew in some way closer to him, more of a danger than he had supposed? Or was it no more than revenge for the trouble the Reavleys had caused him from the day John Reavley had found and taken the copy of the treaty, in 1914? If he had not found it, or not understood it, might there now be an Anglo-German Empire across the northern half of the world? Would there have been peace, at least on the surface, even if there were terror, betrayal, and suffocated lives underneath?

No, there would not have been peace. America would not have given in. It might have been crushed, with the combined weight of Europe against it, but not without fearful cost. The bloodshed would have been terrible, perhaps eventually even as all-consuming as it was now, just in a different place; the same protagonists, only on different sides. And the shame of England would have been irredeemable.

Now it was almost over. Matthew was locked up in a shed behind the front line in Belgium, and Jacobson thought he had murdered a woman. Or perhaps he knew perfectly well that he had not, but it suited the Peacemaker to have a final revenge?

If Joseph could not prove him innocent, Matthew would be tried and shot—or, more ignominiously, hanged. Or possibly the men who had cared for Sarah, had worked with her, and were sickened by the brutality of her death might come and drag him out and "accidentally" shoot him. Of course that was illegal, but what was the nicety of the law in the face of the carnage these men had seen in the last few years? Bodies of friends they had loved had been torn to pieces beside them, shattered to bloody pulp. Death was an everyday occurrence. If some of them could not bear that their brave, funny, kind friends were slaughtered while a bestial murderer was taken home to England without a scratch on him—well, that was not hard to understand.

He paced back and forth, four steps, turn, four steps. He must not panic, must not lose control. Come on, Joseph! Do something!

Judith woke alone in an old bunker and immediately felt almost suffocated by desperation. It was impossible that Matthew could have killed Sarah Price, and yet Jacobson had arrested him, probably so pressed by those senior to him to find a solution that he was grasping at one too easily. Whatever the reason, Matthew was locked in one of the few actual buildings still standing, and Jacobson and Hampton were busy collecting more evidence to close the case. There were days, at the very most, to prove Matthew innocent, possibly only hours.

Nobody else wanted to disturb the conclusion. The fear was melting away, suspicions dying, and the end of the war resuming its place as the most important subject.

Judith was close to panic. Apart from Joseph, the only person to whom she could turn for help was Lizzie Blaine. She both liked and trusted her, and, at the moment even more importantly than that, knew that Lizzie had the intelligence to weigh and measure answers and reason through the tangle of facts toward some truth.

She shivered and pulled her cape closer around her.

Thank goodness at least casualties were low for an hour or two. Joseph had gone forward into no-man's-land. He'd had no choice, and even if he had been able to stay here, they had run out of ideas about who else to question or even what to ask.

It was midmorning, and for once cold and dry. She was so tired her whole body ached, but there was no time to sleep. Two or three hours' worth would have to do.

She stood up slowly. She was stiff; her muscles ached. She had slept clenched up with fear and cold. Climbing up the steps and emerging into what was left of the old trench, the wind struck her. Lizzie was in another bunker about twenty yards along. It was better than sleeping in the open, and there was no room in the tents.

Judith hated waking her, but she could not afford to waste any more time, and there was no one else to turn to. At the second bunker she went down the steps; they were wet and slippery, surfaced with a thin layer of clay from disuse. She pulled the remnants of the sacking curtain open. There was silence inside, and not even a candle burning. It was a respite she knew Lizzie needed, but desperation won. She went in, allowing the daylight to fall through the narrow opening.

Lizzie was curled over on the bunk, her dark hair spread out on the hard pillow and the blanket drawn up around her. She looked as if she had gone to sleep cold, and Judith felt a deeper, sharper stab of guilt.

"Lizzie," she said quietly. When the woman did not stir, she touched her on the shoulder, gradually tightening her grip until Lizzie sat up, pushing her hair out of her eyes and answering in a level voice.

"Sorry," Judith said, and she meant it. "I can't afford to wait. Jacobson's looking for final evidence to send Matthew to trial. He doesn't seem to have any doubt. Apparently Matthew said he saw someone who looked like Punch Fuller fighting with somebody, but it was a couple of miles from where Punch says he was. I have to get to the bottom of it, and I need help. There's no one else I can trust, or who is willing to think Matthew could be innocent. Everyone else just wants it to be over."

Lizzie rubbed her eyes and drew the blanket around her shoulders. She was so tired that waking up fully took several moments. "Was Punch Fuller injured?" she asked. "I don't remember that. Badly?"

"No, he brought in a young soldier, about fifteen or sixteen, who was injured. Carried him." Judith spoke the next words with difficulty. "But he wouldn't pass anywhere near where Matthew was. That's at least a couple of miles from the way he'd come from the line to the clearing station." It sounded even worse aloud.

Lizzie was properly awake now. "Then there must be some other explanation," she said. "Assuming Matthew wouldn't lie, then perhaps he was mistaken—and since he doesn't know the men here, that has to be possible. Alternatively, maybe for some reason or other Punch Fuller is lying."

"Why would he?" Judith said miserably. "He brought in a wounded man, or boy in this case. What is there to lie about?"

"I don't know." Lizzie moved the blanket aside and climbed out of the bunk, shivering. She started to put on her outer clothes again and reach for the brush to untangle her hair and pin it up. "We can start by asking Cavan, and then see the boy. I can get to see him, even if you can't." She gave a very brief smile, then turned her attention back to her hair.

Judith felt a sense of gratitude that was almost like a physical warmth. All she could say was a simple "Thank you." She would have to find some way of telling Lizzie how much it meant later on.

"Hodges," Cavan answered. They were standing in the Pre-operation tent. He had just come on duty after a brief rest. In busy times the surgeons in casualty clearing stations worked eight hours on and four hours off. That way several of them could keep two or three operating tables working all the time. Cavan was freshly shaved and looked better than Judith had seen him for a few days. "He'll be all right. It was actually not nearly as bad as it looked. I think he was shocked more than anything."

"Punch Fuller brought him in?" Judith asked.

"Yes. He was in a pretty bad state." Cavan's face twisted with pity. "Poor little devil's only fifteen. Had his birthday a week ago. His best friend was just ripped to pieces by a shell. Couldn't find enough of him to bury." He said the words clearly, but his shoulders were tight, and the muscles of his neck stood out like cords. "Hodges was barely hurt, only a cut on his thigh," he went on. "Flesh wound, painful, but it'll heal."

Judith was just about to ask if she could speak to the boy, then caution stopped her. Cavan had to know Matthew was her brother, and that she would do anything she could to free him. She should be more oblique, possibly even leave it to Lizzie. "When was that?" she asked instead.

She saw the instant flash of understanding and sorrow in Cavan's face. "It won't help, Judith. Fuller got here just after four, and I know that time's right."

"Are you absolutely certain?" She was aware that it was futile even as she said it, but it was fear that drove her rather than reason. "How can you be? You were very busy. Do you watch the clock? It wasn't change of shift."

"No, of course I don't watch the clock. It wasn't change of my shift, but it was of the guards on the German prisoners, and they're pretty regular. It was just as Benbow and Eames came off and Turner and Culshaw went on."

"You saw all of them?"

He hesitated. "Actually I saw Eames over by the Resuscitation tent, and he made some remark about it being change of duty. I went back in a moment later and Punch Fuller arrived with Hodges. I know what your brother said, but Fuller couldn't have passed that way from the lines carrying a wounded man. I'm sorry."

Judith wanted to argue, at least offer some other reasonable explanation, but she could not think of one. In the end, she turned away without saying anything at all.

Punch Fuller had gone back up to the front, and she had to wait an hour before Benbow and Eames were on duty again. Every minute dragged by as she grew more and more frightened. She filled the time with petty errands, never sitting still. The wind blew up harder from the east, carrying rain with it, and the gray sky leached all color from the earth. There was nothing in sight except mud and withered tree stumps, the ungainly angles of tents and the irregular pools in old craters, pockmarked by the wind.

Finally the hour was over and she saw them coming on duty, changing places with Culshaw and Turner. As soon as the patrol was handed over, she went first to Eames. She had tried to work out some clever way of introducing the subject, but he would know why she was asking, whatever she said. Perhaps complete honesty was best. It would at least save time and the wasted energy of trying to lie.

They were standing in the lee of the Treatment tents, the wind rattling in the canvas. A nurse walked past them twenty feet away, her feet slithering in the mud.

"Do you remember coming off duty the night Sarah Price was killed?" Judith asked Eames after reminding him who she was.

He looked uncomfortable, but that was probably out of pity because he could not help. "Yes. I didn't see anything, Miss Reavley, least nothing that would be any 'elp. That policeman, Jacobson, already asked me."

"It's times I'm really looking for," she replied. "When you saw Captain Cavan as you were coming off duty, was that four o'clock exactly?"

"Well, I . . . I'm not sure, not for certain." His obvious discomfort increased.

"Don't you go off duty at four o'clock?"

"Yes, but there was a bit of a scuffle earlier, an' I waited to see what it was. There was a woman yelling an' I thought one of the nurses might be in trouble, so I went to see. Think that was when I saw Captain Cavan. I don't know what time that was, closer than fifteen or twenty minutes."

"Was it Miss Price yelling?" she asked immediately.

He shook his head. "No, it definitely weren't, because I saw 'er comin' away from the 'ut the Germans are in as I got back. She was fine, laughin' and actin' happy."

She was puzzled. "Then who was it?"

"Miss Robinson. She just tripped on a broken board."

"Was it long before you changed duty?"

"About . . . I don't know . . . awhile." Now he was so awkward, she was certain he was not being honest. She was not sure why. He shifted his weight from one foot to the other and turned his collar up against the wind. "But Miss Price was fine," he said earnestly. "So it doesn't matter, does it!"

"No, I suppose not," she conceded, and to his clear relief, she went to find Benbow.

He looked less nervous, standing to attention in the open as she asked him the same questions.

"Yes, I heard the woman shouting out," he agreed, looking at her gravely. "Eames went to see what it was. It did sound like someone hurt, but it turned out to be Miss Robinson, just because she slipped."

"You didn't go?" She was not sure why she was asking. It seemed pointless, but she wanted to sound thorough.

He shook his head slightly. "Didn't make any difference. Sarah Price went into the Germans' hut after that to see to them." His face was bleak, as if he was thinking of what had happened to her, and the anger at it was bright in his eyes.

"But she came out all right." That was a statement. Judith already knew the answer.

"Yes. One of the Germans came out, too," Benbow added. His expression flickered. She could not read it.

"But you watched him, of course?"

"Of course."

She could not think of anything else to ask, and finally turned to leave.

"That was the last time I saw her," Benbow added. "With the German. They were still there when I went off duty. She went back inside with him." He tried hard to keep the contempt out of his eyes and his voice, but it was too deep within him, and she could not help recognizing it.

"At about quarter past four?" she asked aloud.

He blinked, knowing what she had read in him, daring her to make an issue of it. "Yes."

She swallowed hard. She understood, and part of her agreed. Pity for any wounded man, British or German, was one thing. To flirt as if nothing stood between you, no years of slaughter, was different. Respect, yes, even honor—but not laughter and teasing, as if the dead did not matter.

She thanked him and left without meeting his eyes again.

She found Lizzie coming out of one of the Treatment tents. Her face was pale, and there was an urgency about her that made it plain that she had learned something.

"What is it?" Judith demanded. Then she realized that Lizzie was suffering some acute distress, struggling within herself to make a decision. "What is it?" she repeated more gently. "At least tell me!"

Lizzie took her arm, steering her away from the half-open flap and out into the wind. She walked some distance until they were clearly alone before she spoke.

"I know what happened, but I don't know what to do about it," she said almost under her breath, even though there was no one within fifty feet of them.

"Does it clear Matthew?" That was the only thing Judith cared about.

"Yes . . ."

"Then we'll tell Jacobson, and—"

"No," Lizzie cut across her. "And Punch Fuller isn't likely to ever change his story."

"Yes, he will! Joseph—"

"Be quiet and listen," Lizzie said firmly. There was a charge of emotion in her voice so intense, Judith stopped.

"Hodges's friend was blown to bits beside him," Lizzie went on. "He was only fourteen; Hodges is just fifteen. He was sort of an older brother to him. It must have been a howitzer." She gulped and swallowed. "Or something like that. Hodges lost control and ran in blind horror and panic. He went all the way from where they were, very near the front line, back to where Matthew saw Punch Fuller catch up with him. Punch knifed him himself, to make him a genuine injury, and then carried him into the Casualty Clearing Station as if he'd come from the front line."

Judith nodded. She understood profoundly.

"He'll stick to that story to save the boy's life," Lizzie went on quietly. "If the truth gets out he'll be shot as a coward. He's only a child, for heaven's sake. The other boy was his best friend, and he feels responsible, and guilty as hell for surviving, and now for running, too. He knows Punch saved his life, and he'll die rather than betray him as well. And he does look on himself as a traitor. He's terrified and so ashamed he's not sure if he even wants to survive."

Judith was numb. "How do you know all this?" she said hoarsely. "If Punch wouldn't tell you, and Hodges wouldn't betray him . . . ?"

"Some I guessed," Lizzie answered with a sigh. Her face was very white. "His wound is superficial. And it's obviously a bayonet. A German soldier would have stabbed him in the chest or the stomach, not the leg where it really does little harm. It's not self-inflicted, but it's not battle-inflicted, either. I worked it out, and then I asked him. I didn't let him lie, and I think in a way he didn't want to. His mother's probably not much older than I am. He shouldn't even be here!" There was a sudden fury in her voice so violent that her body was trembling. "If you tell that story they'll court-martial him, then shoot him. And if you don't, they'll hang Matthew, I know that!"

Judith drew in her breath and let it out again. "We have to do something. Perhaps Joseph can—"

"They won't believe him," Lizzie said reasonably. "He's Matthew's brother. They won't believe you, either. But if I go to Jacobson, he might believe me. I can't make Punch Fuller say anything, but if Jacobson wants to catch whoever really did it, he'll let Matthew go. This could prove it wasn't him."

Judith nodded. It was a risk, appalling, cruel, inescapable, but to do nothing was worse.

Jacobson agreed. Lizzie's story corresponded exactly to what Matthew had described, and he understood enough of the terror and the grief to see how it could have happened. Such things must have occurred many times before. He did not explain, he simply let Matthew go. He questioned Eames, Benbow, Cavan, and several others again. What little evidence he had pointed toward Schenckendorff. He had no choice but to arrest the man.

Joseph, Judith, and Matthew sat huddled together in Joseph's bunker. Outside, the rain fell steadily, dripping down the steps. The star shells were too far away to light the sky, and the flash of muzzles was invisible beyond the slight rise in the land.

"There's no point in going to London without Schenckendorff," Judith said quietly.

"There's no point in going at all until we can tell the prime minister who the Peacemaker is!" Matthew answered bitterly.

"I could tell him," Judith said.

Joseph stared at her, his face incredulous in the yellow candlelight. "How do you know? And without Schenckendorff, why on earth would anyone believe you?"

"I would go to him with Father's copy of the treaty, which has the kaiser's signature on it, and put it in front of him," she answered. "Then I would tell him that the Englishman who had planned it, with his German cousin, was Dermot Sandwell. Colonel Schenckendorff couldn't come himself because he died after being injured coming through the lines."

Matthew's face went blank with surprise for an instant. Then it changed to anger and disbelief, and the struggle to understand.

"Schenckendorff's alive, and getting better," Joseph pointed out. "Except that they'll hang him for murder. Or more likely shoot him."

"Lloyd George won't know that." Judith was practical.

"It can't be Sandwell," Matthew said at last, his voice rough. "We ruled him out. And Lloyd George certainly wouldn't believe you. I understand your frustration, Judith, but you can't fling accusations around like that."

"It's not an accusation!" she said vehemently. "Schenckendorff told me it was Sandwell. When we ruled him out, we were wrong. He fooled us."

"You asked Schenckendorff, and he told you?" Joseph's voice rose sharply in amazement.

"It wasn't exactly as bare as that," she explained. "I told him Matthew had been arrested for the murder. I think he felt guilty because Matthew wouldn't even have been here if he hadn't come to meet Schenckendorff, at his request."

"For God's sake, Judith!" Matthew's fists were clenched, his back rigid. "The man was prepared to tyrannize half of Europe! He's not going to feel guilty that I've been wrongly accused of a crime because I came over to get him back to London."

"Guilt is about shabbiness of behavior, hypocrisy, not the enormity of the sin," she answered him. "Isn't it, Joseph?"

Joseph put his hand up in dismissal. "I've no idea, and it doesn't matter. We don't know whether Schenckendorff is telling the truth or not. For that matter, we don't even know for certain if he is who he says he is. It's not beyond the Peacemaker's ability to get him a false identity. Not that much identity is needed by prisoners coming through the lines."

Judith frowned. "Do you think, this close to the armistice, that he really has time to bother with us, even to get revenge?"

"Maybe it isn't so much trouble." Matthew looked at her, his face pinched with a fear he was struggling to hide. "Just a single act by one German who may be desperate and have little to lose. It was our father who ruined the Peacemaker's plans in the beginning. He won't have forgotten that, and I don't think he's a man to forgive. If you're losing, revenge may be the only sweet taste left."

Joseph gazed steadily at the broken duckboards on the floor, and the single piece of old matting over them. "Or perhaps Schenckendorff is completely genuine, and his realization of what the Peacemaker has become, the slow corrosion that power has worked on the morality he started with, perhaps when they were younger, and knew each other well—"

"That wouldn't account for his killing poor Sarah," Matthew interrupted. "If he did that, he deserves to hang for it." His voice was rough with emotion.

Judith knew it was for his own treatment of Sarah also, for the whole, helpless destructive path of violence and blindness that had ended alone in the dark beside the amputated limbs and human refuse of a battlefield hospital. It was no one's fault, and everyone's. The world had changed, and much of the brutality of that had altered forever the role of women, not only for themselves but in others' eyes as well. Nothing was safe and reliable anymore. Nothing could be trusted to be as it was before.

"What I was going to say is that he may be exactly what he says he is," Joseph explained. "But it won't have happened suddenly. The Peacemaker could have sensed his change of heart awhile ago, and struck first."

Matthew stared at him. "You mean instead of just having Schenckendorff shot, he set up this elaborate plan and had him blamed for Sarah's murder?" His face tightened. "Then there's someone else here who's the Peacemaker's man! He did it, and is making it look like Schenckendorff. God Almighty! What a revenge. A German officer and aristocrat, to be hanged for murder, when really he came through the lines at hideous cost to himself to commit the final act of honor to his principles rather than his leader." He pushed his hand through his hair. He sighed and caught in his breath. "That's our Peacemaker! What are we going to do?"

Joseph looked from Matthew to Judith, and back again. "What we set out to do: to find out for certain, beyond any doubt, reasonable or otherwise, who killed Sarah Price. All we're working with now is people's stories of where they were, what they were doing, who else they saw or didn't see, and what kind of a person Sarah was."

He leaned forward a little, the candlelight gold on his cheek. "But all the time we're thinking of what we did to her."

Matthew turned toward him. "What do you know that we don't, Joe? There's a lot of talk about rape or mutilation, but if anyone knows, they aren't saying."

Judith winced. She had been refusing to think further. No one had imagined that the motive was anything other than sexual, but that was not the same as giving words to the act.

Joseph's eyes moved from one to the other of them gravely. "It's the violation of the inner person that is unbearable," he answered. "The complete loss of control of your own body and its passions and needs, the core of the way in which it belongs to you. In a woman it is if she is violated by someone else; in a man it is if his own body betrays him by degrading every decency he ought to hold and turning him into a creature outside the acceptance of his fellows. We're all afraid of it. We don't know how to stop it from touching the core of identity, of life. We run away from truth; we build lies that we can live with."

Judith stared at him. He was trying to say something bigger than she had even considered, a more painful idea. There was something in it that touched her own knowledge of passion and change, the freedom she had won here in slaughter, and was not sure how to deal with once her carefully outlined job was over. Without an ambulance ... a uniform ... who was she then?

"We need the truth," Joseph finished, his voice half an apology. "Whoever it hurts. It was somebody here. To find that we may also find a whole lot of other things we would very much rather not have known. Do you believe Schenckendorff's guilty?"

"I don't know," Matthew said.

"No." Judith had no hesitation. "I think somehow or other it's the Peacemaker."

Judith was not called out that night. She slept on a cot in one of the outer rooms of the hospital until four in the morning, when the first casualties came in. They were now some considerable distance from the fighting as it moved eastward toward the borders of Germany itself, and there were other casualty clearing stations far closer. This was just the excess that others could not treat.

She worked helping the orderlies, carrying stretchers, assisting those able to walk a little way the few steps from the ambulance to the waiting area, or from there into a theater.

By six o'clock the worst was over. She drank a hot mug of tea and ate a heel of bread, then she went to help the nurses. She had not their skill, but she could at least fetch and carry for them and do the simpler jobs. She was prepared to sit, with a calm face and a quiet voice, with those who were beyond all practical aid. She knew Joseph did it often enough. It was a small service, but no young man should face the final darkness alone, unnoticed, and with no one to say they cared.

By eight o'clock she was sharing rations with Lizzie and trying to think of what questions she could ask to strip bare the lies that were painting Schenckendorff as a murderer. She refused to accept that there were no loose ends anywhere, no one who knew something that would eventually unravel it all.

Moira Jessop joined them, sitting on an upturned empty box with her mug in both hands. "In a month's time we could all be home," she said cheerfully. "Eating proper food. Having a bath and sleeping in sheets. I'd love to be clean." She pulled an expression of complete disgust.

Lizzie gave a slight, bleak smile.

"What's the matter with you?" Moira asked cheerfully. "At least now we know it was a bloody Jerry who killed poor Sarah, and not one of us. We don't need to look sideways at each other anymore. Or walk around in fear, for that matter. And don't pretend half of us weren't!"

Lizzie swallowed hard, but with the dryness of the bread that was not surprising. "Half of us were afraid it would turn out to be someone we knew well, or really liked," she said, not looking at either of them.

"Were you?" Moira's eyes opened wider. "Who do you like, then?"

Lizzie shook her head. "I am speaking generally."

Judith looked at her, not just at her face but also the angle of her shoulders and body, the slightly awkward way she sat on the ammunition box, as if maintaining her balance with an effort. She didn't know that Schenckendorff was important; she probably hadn't even known his name before the evidence implicated him. Why was she not as relieved as everyone else? Surely she had not thought she knew something or suspected something about one of their own men? If so, how could she have allowed Matthew to be blamed, and said nothing? To whom could she possibly owe a loyalty like that?

Moira was still talking, rattling on about going home once all the wounded had been evacuated, what it would be like in peacetime again, which hospital she would find work at in England. Lizzie was obviously not listening to her.

Judith finished her tea and stood up. "Let's go and clean up the theater while there's a chance," she said to Lizzie. "I'll help you."

Lizzie rose a little stiffly. "Thanks, but don't you have to do maintenance or servicing on your ambulance?"

"Not yet," Judith said firmly. "The theater'll probably be needed first anyway." She led the way, and Lizzie caught up with her. It was a warm bright day with only a hint of chill in the air. At home, late October was one of Judith's favorite times of the year, with its rich, heart-aching beauty of wind-riven skies, stooks gold in the fields, wood smoke, blazing color in the leaves, bright berries. Here it was like a harvest aborted, the barren earth too full of blood to bear the fruits of summer.

The Operating tent was deserted, the surgeons and orderlies either with critical patients or taking a brief respite, snatching sleep or some kind of food.

As soon as the flap was closed, Judith turned to Lizzie. She had no time for subtlety. She liked Lizzie better and better each time she saw her, and she was perfectly sure that Joseph loved her, which mattered far more. Now she was also intensely grateful to her for her courage and decisiveness in going to Jacobson and getting Matthew released.

"What is it?" she asked bluntly. "Everyone else is thrilled that Jacobson has arrested a German, but you're not. Is there someone else you're afraid of?"

Lizzie lifted her chin and stared back in surprise and complete denial. "No! If I knew anything like that, don't you think I'd have told you when they were blaming Matthew? I'd have grasped at any other answer rather than tell him about Hodges."

"Yes, of course. I'm sorry," Judith said immediately. "But something is wrong. Everybody else is relieved, and you look as if it's worse. What is it?" She was aware the instant she had said it that she was being intrusive. Nothing gave her the right or excuse to demand answers to what might be a very private grief.

Lizzie turned away and began to tidy up the theater, moving soiled dishes and swabs, picking up bandages and pieces of bloody cloth cut away from a wound. All this would have to be done before they could even consider cleaning the blood off the floor. "Perhaps you'd fetch some water," she asked, head still averted, watching what she was doing. "If you can find anything fit to use. I'll have this ready by the time you get back."

It was dismissal. She was not going to discuss the subject. She kept on picking up, tidying, folding. She did not meet Judith's eyes at all.

Judith obeyed because she recognized that she was not going to receive an answer, and pressing any further would make an enemy where she wanted a friend. She went looking for water. It did not have to be especially clean—it would only be swilled around the worst of the blood and mud on the floor. Nothing dropped could possibly be used again without sterilizing anyway.

She walked along the boards deep in thought. Why would Lizzie not confide in her? They had spoken openly before. Even if briefly, it had been honestly. The only answer that came to her was the one she least wanted to believe. Had Lizzie realized how deep Joseph's feelings were for her, but she could not return them? Perhaps she was still grieving for her husband, who had been murdered in the summer of 1916, and she could not yet love anyone else. Theo Blaine had been brilliant, one of the finest scientists of his generation. How could Joseph equal him in her estimation?

It was a crushing thought Judith could not tolerate. Joseph had endured enough pain with the loss of Eleanor and their child. Lizzie knew that, and it would hurt her to have to reject him, but you could not accept someone out of pity; that would be the worst of all.

She filled the pail with cold water that was too stale to drink but good enough for a floor, then carried it back to the Operating tent. She opened the flap and banged the pail down. Lizzie looked up at her. Her dark hair was coming out of its pins, and her skin was almost drained of color. "Thank you," she said quietly.

Judith was pinched by the loneliness in Lizzie's face. She looked as if she was managing not to weep only by exercising the most rigid self-control. She opened her mouth to ask again, but Lizzie took the pail and turned away, and Judith felt clumsy.

"You'll need more," she said aloud. "As soon as you've used that, I'll fetch another one."

Lizzie did not answer, as if she could not trust herself to speak.

Judith spent the rest of the day on an ambulance run taking men who had arrived after the murder to the next hospital along the line. Wil Sloan rode with her. He, too, was unusually somber. There was no time for her to say much on the way south with the injured men, but on the way back he sat beside her as dusk mantled the fields and hid some of the scarring of the land. They moved in their own small, noisy world, their headlamps picking out only occasional ruined buildings, skeletons of walls and windows jagged and partial against the darkening sky.

"Are you still thinking about going home?" she asked him after a violent jolt on the road where she had hit an unexpected crater.

"Oh, probably. Sooner or later," he replied. "Longer I leave it, harder it'll be. I suppose."

She glanced sideways but could not see his face in the dim light. "I didn't mean will you go, I meant are you still worrying about it," she corrected. "Don't. They'll be proud of you. They'll have forgotten about your quarrel. It's history. The whole world's different now." She said it firmly, trying to think only of the positive, and convince him.

"You reckon?" He looked straight ahead.

"Of course! You were one of the first to come, long before the rest of America. You nailed your colors to the mast. You should remember that."

He frowned.

"Naval term," she explained, negotiating the next crater, but only at the last minute and throwing him off balance so that he grasped at the dashboard. "Means attaching them to the mast so you can't pull them down and surrender, no matter what."

He smiled. She heard the amusement in his voice. "I know that! Just because I came from the Midwest doesn't mean I know nothing about history, even if I'm a thousand miles from the sea."

"Sorry."

He rode in silence for a while, so obviously deep in thought she did not interrupt him.

"Do you reckon someone lost his temper with Sarah 'cause she flirted with him, then wouldn't come across?" he asked as they veered around a corner and straightened up again.

She realized the question was serious, deeper than she had thought. He had fled his hometown originally because of a stupid quarrel in which he had lashed out and hurt a man far more than he had intended to. He had stowed away in a railcar and gone east until he reached the coast, then taken a ship to England to join the ambulance service as a volunteer.

"Wil? Was your fight a lot worse than you're telling me? You said he was all right, just bruised and maybe a broken jaw."

"He was." Wil was still looking forward, as if his seeing the road would somehow make them safer. "I was lucky. I should stop kidding myself, Judith. I could have killed him. I lost my temper—I mean really lost it. I didn't know or care what I was doing. Maybe I would do it again?"

"What made you think of that now?" she said, puzzled by the intensity of his feelings. She had never heard that before. Was she so insensitive?

"Sarah," he replied after a moment. "I guess I never really thought about . . . that sort of thing before. And don't tell me he just killed her, as if being British was enough. Nobody said exactly what he really did to her, but I know there was a hell of a lot of blood. I can guess. He didn't choose a woman because she was weaker . . . lots of the men are wounded and couldn't have fought back." His face was flushed. She could see the dark color in the occasional flashes of light. "I can see now that all the women feel . . . embarrassed, threatened," he went on. "Some of them even blame her because it makes them feel that they can be safe by not doing whatever she did. Even if they are angry with all men, as if it were all our fault, when actually we're just as . . . No, I guess it's different." He was fumbling for words, awkwardly, trying to be honest. "We're scared of being blamed, not of it happening to us. But we're scared that it could happen to the women we like. I'm not in love with you or anything, but I'd want to kill anyone who hurt you!" He very carefully did not look at her, even for an instant.

"Thank you," she said gravely. She knew that he had been at least a little in love with her a year ago, but of course she did not ever want him to know that she had seen it in his eyes, his hesitation, the things he had not said. "I would like to think you'd hate them. But nothing's going to happen to me. Not that sort of thing, anyway."

"You reckon that German did it?"

She hated the thought of lying to him. "I don't know. I'm not totally sure. Do you think so?"

"Not really," he admitted. "War kind of uncovers lots of things you didn't know were there. Maybe whoever killed Sarah didn't have anyone to stop them, and they simply lost it . . . so bad that all the fury and the pain they'd ever felt just boiled up to the top, and by the time they got their wits back again it was too late."

She could not think of an answer. She turned the idea over and over in her mind.

"I've had men tell me about fear," he went on. "Men who wanted to be brave and charge over the trench wall and attack, but their legs just wouldn't move. They'd soil themselves from plain physical terror. They'd have died rather than do that, but they just couldn't control it. Their bodies betrayed them, not their minds or their hearts." He turned toward her. "Could rage or humiliation be like that, too, d'you reckon? Maybe if you felt so helpless, so . . . so put down, laughed at, not as good as the rest of the guys, that you just lashed out where you could. Anything to get back to where you were in control of something, that actually you didn't see that you'd lost it for real?"

They were within a couple of miles of the trenches. The sky had cleared; a thin moon shed light on the wet road.

"Do you know who did it, Wil?" she asked quietly. "I think you should tell the truth."

"No, I don't." There was no hesitation or wavering in his voice. "But I think quite a few of the men could have. The urge to have a woman can be pretty powerful, and Sarah didn't mind using how . . . how pretty she was. Put her down a bit, and she could get her own back by making you awful uncomfortable. I'm not saying that makes anything right, it doesn't," he added quickly. "But if you know you could die, or get so shot up you might as well be dead 'cause no woman's ever going to look at you, or maybe you've been injured so you can't anyway, then you might look at things differently."

"He didn't just rape her, Wil," she said softly. "He butchered her, and left her lying on the rubbish as if she were waste as well, along with the amputated limbs! That's more than even the worst frustration anyone can feel. It's hate."

He sat very still, letting out his breath slowly. "Jesus! I didn't know that . . ." He was breathing hard, and for a moment he sounded as if he was going to be sick.

"Wil?" As she turned to look at him, she veered wildly close to the edge of the road, sending the ambulance bucking and slewing across the craters. She pulled up sharply. "Sorry."

"I didn't do it, Judith!" he said haltingly. "I just know that everybody's scared, not only the women." He wiped the back of his hand across his mouth.

"Do you know if anyone is lying to protect someone else?" she asked him. "Maybe someone they owe a really big debt, like having pulled them off the wire or carried them back from no-man's-land? That would be something you'd pay for the rest of your life, wouldn't it!"

"Yes," he agreed. "That's why pretty well everyone's happy to think it's one of the Jerries."

"But what if it isn't?" she insisted. "We can't hang somebody who didn't do it because it's convenient. Surely to God we are better than that?"

"It isn't that easy," he replied. "Haven't you ever owed anybody something? Something so big you can hardly breathe for the weight of it. You have to pay debts like that. You have no choice."

"You know something, Wil!"

"I hear wounded men talk," he admitted. "You don't, because you're up here driving, but I spend a lot of time with some of them."

"What do you know? I'm not moving until you tell me."

"I can walk back from here better than you can."

"Wil!" she protested desperately.

"I know how some of the men feel," he answered. "That's all. I told you I don't know who did it. I don't. Hell, Judith, if I did I'd have said when they had your brother!"

"Yes. Yes, I know." She eased the engine into gear again and straightened the wheels on the rutted road. They still had more than a mile and a half to go.

When Judith pulled the ambulance in and parked it, Wil went to help the orderlies with the new wounded, and she began the usual maintenance of the vehicle. She was in the back tidying and cleaning the stretchers and sweeping the floor when she heard footsteps outside in the mud, and a moment later a shadow blocked the light at the door.

She looked up and saw a familiar silhouette that made her heart jolt and her stomach tighten far more than she wished. She wanted to be in control of her emotions, but as Wil had said, her body let her down. She was hot and cold at once, and her hands were clammy.

"Can I help you?" Mason asked.

"Not really, thank you. I'm just about finished," she said a trifle more coolly than she had intended. Although perhaps it was for the best. She did not want to hope, or imagine, that she could see in him a tenderness or a belief that was not there. "What's the news from the front? Where are we now?"

"About two miles from Tournai, the last I heard," he replied. "The fighting's still pretty heavy."

"Yes, I know. We're still getting quite a few of the casualties."

"I heard you found the man who murdered the nurse. It was one of the Germans."

She kept on looking at the ambulance stretchers even though there was nothing more to do to them. "They've arrested him, but they haven't collected all the evidence to charge him yet. He's under guard more to protect him, I think."

Mason was silent for a moment or two. She stepped out of the ambulance, taking his hand because he offered it, and it would have been pointed had she refused it. She found herself absurdly self-conscious. His physical nearness intruded on her concentration, and she was angry with herself for allowing it.

"But he did it?" he said at last as she closed the doors. They turned toward the tent where there was most likely to be hot tea. The night had closed in, and the wind was harder and colder from the east.

"I don't know." She knew the admission would leave questions he would be bound to ask, and answers that would betray more of her emotion than she wanted to share, but she refused to lie to him.

They were inside before he replied. "You don't think he did, do you?" That was a challenge. "Why? Because you're afraid it's what everybody wants?"

"No. I . . ." What could she say that made any sense, yet did not betray who Schenckendorff was? That she could not do, whatever lies it cost. She was already bitterly aware of Mason's dark view of war's futility and the senseless pain of it. The hurt of realizing that he did not share any of her faith—blind, admittedly—in some kind of inner victory was cut too deeply into her mind ever to forget, even for a moment. There was a shadow inside him that separated them, no matter how much she liked him, or even loved him. Joseph had said he would never make her happy. She had momentarily hated Joseph for that, probably because in the depths of her belief, the passion and the light that made her who she was, she already knew it was true.

Mason was waiting. There was an urgency and a gentleness in his eyes that she had not seen before. He was waiting for her to speak, wanting to understand.

"I talked to him quite a lot." She started with the truth. "I was helping one of the nurses. Before he was accused, of course. His foot was pretty badly injured, but apparently he could stand on it. I've seen men do extraordinary things when they were so terribly wounded you wouldn't have expected them to live, let alone crawl for miles or fight. There just . . . wasn't any anger in him. You must have to be terribly angry to rape and then kill."

He studied her face. She felt increasingly self-conscious but did not look away. She had to force emotion away from herself, crush the hope inside, in case he saw it and understood. Friendship was everything. She would give him that, but love was far too dangerous, too consuming of reason, judgment, the courage or purpose to go on after it was betrayed.

"What are you going to do about it?" he asked finally.

That was not at all what she had expected him to say. She had been waiting for an argument as to why she should leave the matter to the police. She looked for mockery in him, and saw none.

"Try to find out who is lying to protect someone else, before they take Schenckendorff away," she answered. "Everybody's afraid, and there are . . . loyalties, debts that seem bigger than blame for a crime. We all want to resolve it in whatever way is least painful to us." She thought of Wil as she said it. She was still aching with surprise at the depths of himself he had trusted her with. She had been blind to much of him beyond his easy, smiling face, his good humor, the way she could rely on him always being there. How many other people had she not bothered to understand?

"We've faced so much together, we think we know one another," she went on. "But we don't. We know the duties, the courage, and the personal habits. We probably wouldn't even recognize one another on the street in civilian life, when you can wear what you want, choose your work—or at least some of it—make whatever friends you like. Here friendship is the one sure sanity. Do you think it'll last, afterward?" The answer to that mattered more than almost anything else. She had not even dared ask it before. She should have asked Joseph or Wil, not Mason. What sort of answer did she expect? Perhaps the loneliness was what all of them were afraid of, after this was all over. And for her it was even worse than many others. She could never go back to the life she had once expected, to domestic happiness like her sister's or her mother's, no matter how much she loved anyone, even Mason. And would any man love the kind of woman she had become? War had released her. She was something better or worse, but forever different.

"Some friendships will always last." Mason did not waver from her gaze when he said it. "The good ones. Sometimes we'll want to forget all this, but at other times we'll need to remember, because we've seen things other people can't even imagine. Who else would we share it with? We can't tell anyone." She stared at him. "We'll need somebody who understands why we laugh and cry when we do," he went on. "Why we look at a tree in bloom and can't take our eyes off it. Why cruelty to a horse makes us want to beat the person who did it until they can't stand. And why we sometimes feel guilty to be alive and whole when so many of the best men we knew are here under the mud, and will never come home."

She nodded, aching with too much memory and sorrow to speak. She put out her hand and touched his face, then self-consciously snatched it away again.

He smiled slowly, and the hope in his eyes dazzled her.

The following day Judith drove more men south and west to larger hospitals. She was only just pulling in at the Casualty Clearing Station when Joseph came splashing across the mud toward her, his face drawn with anxiety.

She scrambled out. "What is it?"

"They're sending Schenckendorff out the day after tomorrow," he said desperately. "In roughly thirty-six hours. They'll try him immediately and he'll be hanged." He did not add all the other things that were racing through both their minds. Was he guilty or innocent? Was the Peacemaker really who he said he was? Was he telling the truth, and had the Peacemaker deliberately engineered this way of exacting revenge? Or was he lying, to make them all try to expose the wrong man, perhaps destroying him, and freeing the real Peacemaker? Or was it all coincidental, the ultimate farce of the whole affair?

SEVEN

*J*udith sat on the cot in her bunker and tried to think. Nothing made any sense that was absolute and unarguable. Every possibility they had thought of depended upon so many accounts that might be lies or mistakes, it dissolved the moment they tried to prove it.

Now it seemed Sarah must have been killed later than they had thought, if Benbow really had seen her after four o'clock. Yet from the state of the body, the blood, and her coldness when she was found at half past six, she had already been dead at least two hours. So she must have been killed between four and half past.

Were any of the guards telling less than the exact truth, intentionally or not? Any of them could have been alone for a while, if his partner had been called away by some alarm or emergency; and if both had, then it was at least possible that any of the wounded Germans who were able to walk, other than just Schenckendorff, could have come out of the hut and killed Sarah. If she had jeered at them about what would happen to their women, that could have been reason enough.

She shivered. Inside, the bunker was sheltered from the wind, but it was small, enclosed in the earth like a tomb, and the clay always seemed to carry the damp with it. It smelled stale and cold.

How long did it take a man to rape a woman and then slash at her with a bayonet? Judith had no experience with anything like this kind of behavior, and found it difficult even to guess. Surely it had to be ten minutes or a quarter of an hour at least? Joseph had seen the body but had refused to discuss it, which was ridiculous in a way. Judith was an ambulance driver; there was no kind of death or mutilation she had not seen. Except, of course, deliberate sexual violation of a woman.

She went over it in her mind. Between four and five o'clock most people were so thoroughly accounted for that they need not be considered. Tiddly Wop Andrews had been walking wounded, with a bad slash in his side, but once it was cleaned, stitched, and bound up—well before three o'clock—he had been in the Resuscitation tent. Cully Teversham had sworn to it. He had been in to see his brother, Whoopy, who had been struck by shrapnel in his leg and side. Allie Robinson had accounted for Cavan for all but a few minutes here and there—certainly not long enough to have found Sarah, raped her, and killed her. Not that Judith had ever imagined that Cavan could be guilty.

The guards Culshaw and Turner had accounted for each other, but that meant almost nothing. Snowy Nunn had been in because he had brought Stan Tidyman, who had lost his leg. Snowy had accounted for Barshey Gee, injured in his left shoulder and with the skin torn open on the side of his head, also walking wounded.

Except that was the heart of the problem. Barshey Gee had not been in the tent where Snowy said he was, not all the time, because Judith herself had seen him at quarter past four outside near the entrance to one of the old connecting trenches. He was a long way from where Sarah had been killed, but it meant Snowy was lying to protect him.

And she knew this because she had been there herself, not where she said she'd been when she'd lied to protect Wil Sloan.

How many other people were lying to protect someone they knew, trusted, and were convinced, beyond even the remotest question, was innocent? And one of them was wrong!

She sat motionless and cold, exhausted by the hopeless tangle of it. Matthew and Joseph had even talked of the possibility of Matthew racing back to London and trying to persuade Shearing to intervene, claim some sort of intelligence coup that would override even the needs of justice. But how could they persuade Shearing that Schenckendorff was legitimate, that Dermot Sandwell was the Peacemaker, and that he was on the brink of sabotaging the armistice agreement? They were not even sure themselves.

There was a sound of light footsteps outside, and the sacking moved. "May I come in?" It was Lizzie's voice, tight and weary.

Judith looked up. "Of course." Then instantly she regretted it. She liked Lizzie—everything about her was individual, strong and candid, quite often unexpectedly funny—but just now she had no patience for anyone else. Her mind was eaten up with endless, fruitless anxiety.

"What is it?" she asked as Lizzie came down the steps and let the sacking fall closed behind her. Judith stood up. In the light of the one lamp

Lizzie was white-faced, almost haggard. She sat down on the cot as if not certain her legs would support her much longer.

"They're saying that the German will be taken away in a day or so," she said hoarsely. "What will they do with him?"

"Try him, and then hang him," Judith replied. The words hurt to say; there was a despair in them that she had not fully acknowledged before.

"Hanged?" Lizzie whispered. She tried to swallow and could not. Her mouth was too dry. "But . . ."

"They believe he is guilty of a terrible crime," Judith said harshly. "Someone raped Sarah with a bayonet and hacked her to death. Nobody's saying that, because they're trying to keep it quiet—stop the panic, or the revenge. But it's true. Then they left her lying like a whore, legs wide, in among the refuse. Don't you think whoever did that deserves to hang?"

"If you hang someone, and then discover you were wrong . . ." Lizzie's voice faded away and she sat down suddenly, her eyes wide and hollow, as if she were looking inward at something unbearable.

Was it possible Joseph had broken his secrecy and told her about Schenckendorff and the Peacemaker? Judith sat on the other bunk and leaned forward. "Lizzie . . ."

It was as if Lizzie could not hear her.

"Lizzie," she repeated urgently, "did Joseph tell you that—" She stopped. At the mention of Joseph's name Lizzie had winced. The movement was almost too small to see, but it was as if the misery inside her had increased. Why would she feel such desperate pain if they exposed the Peacemaker, or if they failed? Did Lizzie know more of the truth than they did? Judith refused to believe that. Lizzie was exactly what she seemed to be. She must not allow the Peacemaker and the suspicions he awoke to poison everything.

Lizzie sat frozen, her knuckles white. Very gently Judith put her hand over Lizzie's without closing it. "I think you'd better tell me. Is Schenckendorff guilty?"

Lizzie shook her head so slightly it was barely a movement at all.

"Are you sure?" Judith asked.

"Yes." It was forced, as if her throat was raw.

"Who is?"

"I don't know." Lizzie met Judith's eyes at last. "I really don't. I have no idea. It just isn't Schenckendorff."

"If you don't know who it is, how can you know it isn't him?" Judith asked. "That doesn't make sense."

Lizzie did not answer.

Judith waited. The bunker was silent, nothing moved. Outside boots squelched in the ruts of mud and voices came from far away.

At last Lizzie took a deep, hollow breath and let it out very slowly, then another. "Because someone else was raped before Schenckendorff came through the lines."

"Someone else! Are you sure?" Then with a sudden shock, Judith realized what Lizzie had really said. She put her arms around Lizzie's shoulders and clung to her, longing to be able to comfort her and knowing it was impossible. What ease of any kind could there be? She had been violated beyond imagination. How must she have felt when Sarah's body was discovered, and she knew the man who had raped her had been capable of such a thing?

Moments ticked by. They seemed frozen. Then Lizzie pushed Judith away and put her hands up over her face, the heels of her palms pushing into her eyes. "That isn't the worst of it." Her voice broke. She was shaking so badly, her teeth chattered together. "I'm pregnant."

It was obscene. "You can't know!" Judith told her. "It's too soon! Maybe . . ."

"I am! It was over a month ago."

"Over . . . then it was before Matthew came here! You knew it couldn't have been him, either! Would you have let them hang him?"

"No . . . no, of course I wouldn't. If you hadn't been able to prove it wasn't him, I'd have told." Lizzie looked up, her eyes swimming with tears. "Do you have to tell Joseph? He . . . he'll never have me—not now."

Judith felt bruised inside by pity. It was like a great swelling pain that drowned out everything else. She understood perfectly. Had it been she who had been invaded, soiled, terrified in such an unforgettable way so that her very core was no longer secret and safe, no longer even her own, she would not have wanted the man she loved ever to know it. She would have nursed it herself, angry, confused, and terribly, desperately alone.

Then she was furious. Rage scalded up inside her that any woman should be so brutalized and made to feel ashamed, as if it were her fault, so that she dared not even report the crime. It was not only the things the men said—far from it. It was what the women said every bit as much. Fear for themselves made their blame ruthless.

If it had happened to her, she could have said she ran the ambulance off the road, or fell with a stretcher—anything to explain the cuts or bruises so no one ever knew what had happened inside her. In time they would have healed, and she might have forgotten—at least on the surface.

But what if she were pregnant? There would be no forgetting that! Unmarried, with child. Lizzie had not even any family. What was the use of winning the war here if a woman dared not report being raped, and was left to bear the rapist's child alone?

Jacobson was not a bad man, not crude or violent, and yet when he had questioned Judith he had accused her of lying. He had assumed her a victim who would not admit it, and she had been outraged by it, even though it was not true. What would he assume of Lizzie? Would he even begin to understand why she had hidden this?

She bent down and took Lizzie's hands, only lightly, just to touch, not imprison. "Don't tell anyone yet," she said gently. "We may find a better way. Don't do anything. I won't leave you alone in this, now or later."

Even as she said the words she had no idea what she was going to do. No one else would know now, but in another two or three months it would be obvious. What would she say to Joseph then? She remembered his grief over Eleanor's death, and that of their child. He had seemed to be numb with it, as if his heart were paralyzed. After all the other losses, how could he endure this? It had appeared that he and Lizzie were on the brink of happiness at last, and it had been snatched from them and broken into too many pieces even to find them, let alone mend it.

The grief was like watching someone you love fight for breath, struggle, and lose. She did not know what to do but kneel down and hold Lizzie close to her and let the moments pass by.

She did not even think how long it was before Lizzie finally pulled away and stood up. She said nothing. Her lips trembled, and her eyes filled with tears. Then she shook herself impatiently. There was no time for weeping now.

"Thank you," she said, her voice cracking. She turned and climbed up the steps past the sacking and into the cold air outside.

Judith knew that she had to tell Matthew alone. Joseph would need to know one day, but not yet, maybe not for a long time. Perhaps it would be better when they were all home, the Peacemaker was exposed, and the old wounds of loss were beginning to heal. Lizzie might not bear the child. With all the fears and the violence of war, the physical deprivations, she might miscarry. Most women did not consider themselves secure in a pregnancy until after the first two or three months. She might even have the luxury of not having to tell Joseph at all. Certainly it did not have to be now.

All this turned over in her mind as she searched for the opportunity to speak to Matthew when she could be certain they'd be alone and uninterrupted.

She found him asleep in the bunker, at a time when she knew Joseph had briefly gone forward toward the front line to help the stretcher-bearers. Despite the desperate need to prove Schenckendorff innocent, that was a duty he could not abandon. They were his men from the farms and villages around St. Giles. Some were critically wounded and might die. You could never tell; a man who appeared to have no more than a piece of shrapnel through the flesh might be so weak from exhaustion that the shock and loss of blood killed him, or the cold. Sometimes there were other wounds, masked by lesser injuries that had torn the skin and produced more obvious lacerated flesh.

She went down the steps into the dark. Knowing where the lamp was, she lit it with difficulty, then set it on the table Joseph used for writing letters of condolence, as well as love letters for those who found the words awkward or were clumsy with the pen, or too wounded to hold it at all.

Matthew was asleep, curled over uncomfortably on the narrow cot. He did not even stir. His fair hair was longer than a soldier's should be, but then he was used to a different kind of battle. This was not his arena. He had to outthink, outwit, and out-imagine, not struggle through the mud with rifle and bayonet, food, water, and ammunition on his back.

She touched him gently, and when he did not respond, more firmly. He grunted, still deeply asleep. But there was no time to allow him to rest. This would not wait on comfort, not even on need. "Matthew!"

He opened his eyes and focused with difficulty. He searched her face for grief. When he didn't see it, he breathed out slowly. He had been afraid she had come to say Joseph was hurt, or even killed. It was the fear all of them lived with, all the time. It was your first thought with every startled awakening.

"Sorry," she apologized. "I have to speak to you while I know Joseph is away."

"Why?" He sat up slowly, swinging his legs over the side. He was fully dressed, apart from his boots, as they all were. It was too cold for anything else. "What's happened? Do you know something?"

There was no point in trying to soften it. She sat on the one chair. "Schenckendorff can't be guilty," she told him. "There was at least one rape before he even got here. Apparently it was sufficiently like Sarah's that it pretty well had to be the same person. Less violent, of course, because she's still alive, just bruised pretty badly. Maybe Sarah fought more, which I suppose is stupid. Or perhaps he's just getting worse. The first was over a month ago."

He blinked. "Are you sure? It wasn't reported. Why is she speaking out now? It won't be to clear Schenckendorff; it could be to protect somebody else who might have come recently." His mouth pulled down at the corners. "Obviously not me. We've stirred up something of a hornet's nest by starting asking questions again. I've pushed one or two people pretty hard. So has Joe."

"It's the truth," she said softly. Even now, knowing the necessity, she hated having to tell him. If she could, she would have protected Lizzie against anyone at all knowing.

His eyes widened in sudden, chilling horror. "Judith?"

"No!" she said instantly. "Not me! For God's sake, Matthew! Do you think I'd have let you be blamed if it were?" She sighed, swallowing hard. "It's Lizzie Blaine."

His shoulders hunched. He put his hand up to push his hair back and rubbed his eyes hard, as if they hurt. He swore with deep, wrenching anger. "Does Joseph know?" he said at last, looking back up at her.

"No. That's why I'm telling you now, while he's away," she explained. "She doesn't want him to, in case . . . in case it's more than he can bear. She loves him, and she's terrified it will turn him from her, or that what was love will become pity . . . especially since she's discovered that she's pregnant."

He shook his head slowly.

"Judith, he's going to have to know! You can't . . . she's not going to lie about it, is she?" He tried to keep the emotion out of his voice, and failed.

"No, I don't think she'd do that, although I couldn't blame her if she did. How could she love the child, knowing how it was conceived? She's going to need a lot of help, Matthew." She stared at him, needing to see that he understood. "All that we can give her. I don't think she's got anyone else. First her husband is murdered, now this! And if she loses Joseph it's going to hurt like hell. But after Eleanor and the baby, then Mother and Father, and all the other friends since, can Joseph take this as well?" She wanted him to reassure her, tell her that Joseph would be all right, that he would accept it and be strong. Perhaps if he tried hard enough he could even make Lizzie believe it.

He sat still on the edge of the cot, struggling for the answer. Finally he sat up a little straighter. "I don't know," he admitted. "But we can't tell him, I'm certain of that. Not yet. She doesn't need his pain to deal with as well as her own. In fact, maybe she doesn't need to know that you've told me. Do whatever you think is right on that. Just let me know."

She nodded, uncertain what the answer would be, but glad to have the freedom to judge for herself.

"But we know for certain now that Schenckendorff's innocent," he went on. "Which doesn't mean he's everything he says he is regarding the Peacemaker, but there's no way we can prove it until we get to London. We have to assume he is and get him there. I'd rather make an almighty fool of myself by trying and being proved wrong than be a coward who could have caught the Peacemaker but hadn't the guts to put it to the test. What we'll lose as fools will be personal, and relatively little, compared with what Europe will lose if we were right and did nothing."

"And we need to find whoever did kill Sarah Price," she added. "He's still around."

"The police can do that," he replied.

She looked at him, frowning. "I don't think that's enough for Lizzie," she answered. "If it were me, I'd want to be sure he was put away. Not for revenge, but so I was absolutely positive he wouldn't ever come after me again."

He raised his eyes, wide with horror. "God Almighty! I never even thought of that. Poor Lizzie." He reached across suddenly and put his hand on Judith's. "We will find him, I promise you."

After Judith had gone, Matthew remained on the edge of the cot for several minutes. The oil lamp flickered on the table, lighting the earth walls boarded up to keep them from collapsing inward, the bookcase hastily knocked together out of packing cases and filled with Joseph's books, and the copy of Dante's portrait from his study at St. John's. How would he bear knowing that Lizzie had been another victim of the rapist? Matthew hugged the thought of it inside him like a wound too deep to let go, in case it bled away all the strength he had.

He and Judith could work all they liked, every hour, without sleep, but he knew they would find it hard to learn anything sufficient to stop Jacobson from shipping Schenckendorff out. Matthew had promised to do it because he wanted to, and to comfort her, not because he really believed it was possible. He could not tell Joseph anything. His brother would know he was being lied to, at least partially; he would work out some of the truth and then worry out the rest. They needed help other than his, but who else had the kind of mind that could detect and deduce, and was not bound by the loyalties or debts that crippled everyone else?

The answer was clear even before the question was complete in his mind. It had to be Richard Mason. Judith might immeasurably prefer that they did not involve him, but circumstances had left them no choice. He stood up slowly, his back stiff from the hard cot and the cold, and put on his boots. It was two o'clock in the morning, but he could not wait until dawn.

Mason was going back and forth from the front line to the Casualty Clearing Station, writing dispatches about the work saving men critically injured in the last few weeks of the war. There was an irony to serving right to the eve of peace, and then losing sight or limbs when victory was perhaps no more than days away. And yet he had found little bitterness. Again and again he was humbled by the courage of men, and infuriated that the whole insane horror had ever happened.

Most of the officers who had lived in these bunkers for so long were now either injured or dead, or had gone forward with the regiment over no-man's-land to the abandoned German trenches. He had seen them himself. Better than those of the British, they were deeper below the ground and drier, and many had electric lighting and something approaching comfort.

Of course the forward lines, covering the ground rapidly, had moved beyond them now as well, an army most often in the open, striving to keep rations and ammunitions circulating along the stretched supply lines.

He had gone to sleep forcing the fighting men out of his mind and thinking instead of Judith. He woke with a start to hear a man's voice speaking his name urgently. A moment later there was a hand on his shoulder. He opened his eyes to see the oil lamp on the table burning and Matthew Reavley sitting on the upturned ammunition box that served as a chair. There was stubble on his chin, and his eyes were red-rimmed, but he was very much awake.

Mason sat up slowly. "What is it?" he asked, fear fluttering inside him. "What's happened?" He did not bother to ask how Matthew had found him; many people knew where he was.

"We need your help," Matthew replied. "I need to explain why, so please just listen. If you don't know, you won't understand why we can't trust anyone else. I wouldn't trust you if I had any choice, but I don't. I've watched you with Judith, and I can see how you feel about her. We have a very short time and we can't do this alone."

Mason had no idea what he was talking about. "Do what?"

"Find out beyond doubt who killed Sarah Price."

"The German. Jacobson's almost ready to charge him," Mason responded, knowing even as he said it that there must be something far deeper that Matthew meant. "Is it an intelligence job?" Ironic if now that he had effectively left the Peacemaker's side and it was too late, he might at last be trusted with information deeper than the obvious.

"I suppose it is," Matthew answered. "But it's also personal. Schenckendorff is innocent, at least of killing Sarah Price. I can't tell you how I know, but I do. What I need you to know now is something quite different that started a long time ago."

Mason felt a chill of apprehension and dismissed it as absurd. It could not have anything to do with him. "Yes?"

Matthew seemed still to be having difficulty finding the words, and Mason became aware of the intensity of his feelings.

"In 1914," Matthew began, "my father found a copy of a treaty between England and Germany. It could have prevented the war, but at the cost of initially betraying France and Belgium, and eventually just about everybody."

Mason felt the semi-darkness of the bunker sway around him and blur as if he were going to faint. He knew with a hideous certainty what was coming next, but to hear it from Matthew himself, laden with his personal loss, gave it a reality it had never had for him before. For the first time he was face-to-face with what he had allowed to be done.

"It was signed by the kaiser, but not yet by the king," Matthew went on. "Father understood what it would mean, and he was bringing it to me in London when he and my mother were killed in a car crash. Joseph and I discovered quite quickly that it was actually murder. A young man, a student of Joseph's of high but blind ideals, had been persuaded to sabotage the road they were traveling on. It cost him his own life, and eventually his brother's as well."

Mason's mouth was dry, his throat tight. He could not have spoken even if he could have thought of anything to say.

"The man behind it," Matthew went on, "we called 'the Peacemaker,' because we had no idea of his identity. He continued to campaign against Britain and the Allies even though the war—"

Mason started to protest but bit the words off, ending as if he had choked on his own breath.

Matthew had no idea of the turmoil inside him. He continued, lost in his own anger and grief. "He was always trying to bring the war to an end while both sides were still strong enough to ally together in an Anglo-German Empire that could dominate most of the world. It would be peace, but without any passion or individuality, any freedom to think and question, to be different, to dare new ideas, to complain against stupidity or injustice, to question or work or laugh aloud. It would be the peace of death."

Again Mason drew breath to interrupt, but here in this bunker dug out of the Flanders earth where so many men had died hideously, all rational justification of such grandiose philosophical issues seemed not only vaguely obscene, but divorced from any kind of reality. It had once been the hope for a better, saner world, a way of avoiding all this wealth of loss. Now it looked like the arrogance of a lunatic, and as doomed as all madmen's dreams.

"The Peacemaker went on murdering," Matthew continued quietly. "General Cullingford; Augustus Tempany; indirectly Lizzie Blaine's husband, Theo, one of the best scientists we ever had. Perhaps even worse than murder was the corruption, and you could call that murder of the soul. Except, of course, we have to allow it ourselves before we can be corrupted. We collude in our own destruction there."

Mason still did not answer. Everything Matthew was describing was a world away from the high ideals with which he and the Peacemaker had begun, but Matthew had not seen South Africa in the Boer War: the slaughter of men; the caging of women and children in camps, starving and imprisoned. He'd had no conception before this of what total war was like.

Finally he looked up at Matthew's face in the lamplight. "If you had known, in 1914, what this would have been like, the sheer overwhelming horror of it, would you have tried to stop it?" he asked, then wished he had not. He sounded like an apologist for the Peacemaker, and he was frightened by how powerful the compulsion was within him to be honest, to cleanse himself from lies. But he had asked, and he had to wait for the answer.

Matthew looked surprised. "Maybe," he admitted. "I don't know. If I had, I hope it would have been openly, without betrayal. But it would have been futile. The balance of power was fatally flawed in Europe. We could never have bought peace without coercion and oppression. The Austro-Hungarian Empire was collapsing from within. So was Russia, in its own way. If you are asking me if I could see that at the time, no, of course not, not clearly enough to have done anything useful about it. Could you?"

"No. But I might have thought I could." Mason had already come closer to honesty than he should have. "What has this to do with finding out who murdered Sarah Price?"

"The Peacemaker hasn't given up yet," Matthew said with a jerky little laugh. "He's still in power, and there's the armistice and its terms to negotiate, and all the peace after that to fight for. If we get it wrong we could sow the seeds of another war just as terrible as this."

"Didn't you say he wanted peace?" Mason asked, remembering everything the Peacemaker had said about crushing German industry and creating a huge vacuum in the economy of Europe.

"Peace on his terms," Matthew amended. "He still hasn't learned that you can't force people without at the same time destroying them. He may well be an idealist, but that does not excuse the lies or betrayal of trust. It is the final arrogance to blind us so he can lead us whatever way he will, and we would have no power to resist. The fact that he believes he's right is irrelevant. We all believe we are right. Some of us even are."

Mason smiled very slightly, moving only his lips. "You want the right to go to hell in your own fashion?"

The shadow of humor touched Matthew's face as well, uncertainly. "If you like to put it that way, yes. The point is, one of the Peacemaker's allies in Germany has come through the lines. He's willing to come to London and identify him to Lloyd George."

Mason now saw with hideous clarity what Matthew was doing here in the front line, and why he cared so intensely that Schenckendorff not be executed for a crime he had apparently not committed. Possibly even if he had committed it, the price was too great, at least to the Reavleys. Mason wondered what Joseph thought of it.

Matthew mistook his silence. "I know it's not simple," he said earnestly. "Much that the Peacemaker wanted is right, and perhaps to begin with he was the most farsighted, the sanest of us all. But he usurped power to which he had no right. He is a man fatally flawed by the weakness to abuse it. Right or wrong in his vision, he can't be trusted not to betray, to kill, to corrupt in order to keep that power in his own hands. And once he has it, it's too late to change if you find you have no way to control him, or to take it back from him.

"Our war was worse than anything we could have imagined," Matthew went on, still watching Mason intently. "But what would his empire have been? And how long might it have lasted? I don't know. We didn't make the choice seeing all the way; no one ever does. We do it step by step, doing our best with each one, trying to see where it will lead. Sometimes we're wrong. But to decide for others, against their will, has to be an arrogance we can't allow. That kind of power is more than any man has the wisdom or the morality to handle."

Mason was desperately tempted to ease his hammering conscience by telling the truth of his own part. He longed to explain what he had seen in Africa and why he had tried so desperately to stop it from happening again; why he had seen the same vision as the Peacemaker, and believed in him. It would be a relief to speak honestly, justify at least his beliefs, however they had ended. But it was a luxury he could not afford, a selfishness to ease his own burden of guilt. It was an excuse too small for the cause, and the immeasurable sacrifice of others. Mere discomfort was so trivial it would be obscene to mention it.

He looked up at last and met Matthew's eyes. "So that's why you need to get Schenckendorff off this charge, and to London. What can I do to help?" He could have told them who the Peacemaker was, but he would have to tell them how he knew, and why should they believe him? It would appear entirely self-serving. The Peacemaker would deny it. Of course he would. Mason was stunned at his own gullibility; even now he had no proof. There was not and had never been anything in writing. The Peacemaker had always said it was for the protection of them both, above all of the cause, but perhaps primarily it was for his own safety. He trusted no one. It was oddly painful to understand now that that had always included Mason himself.

Nor would the Reavleys dare to trust him if they knew the part he had played. They would not know how totally Mason had at last understood what he had done, and seen it in its futility, its final ugliness.

He must tell them nothing, however badly the guilt twisted inside him and set him apart and alone.

"Help us find and prove who killed Sarah Price," Matthew told him. "Or at least demonstrate irrefutably that it wasn't Schenckendorff."

Mason's decision was without shadow. It was a long path back, one he might never complete, but he knew how to begin. "When do we start?"

Joseph returned from the front line with more wounded. As soon as he had seen them into the orderlies' care, he went to Matthew. They stood together in the evening light as it splashed red and pink over the puddles across what had been no-man's-land. It was one of the few places where they would be uninterrupted.

"It isn't Schenckendorff," Matthew said. "But we're not much closer to knowing who it is."

"I didn't think it was him," Joseph replied unhappily, staring across the now-gaudy mud. The sunset burned in the sky to the northwest. Perhaps it was foolish, but he had hoped for something more definite. He was weary, his body ached, and he had several gashes on his arms from old barbed wire still embedded in the clay. "Doesn't it help with proving who did it? How are you certain?" Then he asked the question to which he would rather not have had to know the answer. "Who lied?"

Matthew's face was almost invisible in the shadows, but his voice was pinched. "I know because one of the other women was violently raped almost a month before Schenckendorff came through the lines."

Joseph drew in his breath, only beginning to imagine the horror of it.

"Don't ask me who," Matthew said quickly. "I can't tell you. I believe it. That's all anyone needs to know."

"I see. Poor woman." Joseph could understand very easily why her only chance for healing might lie in anonymity, the certainty that none of her friends or colleagues was ever aware that it had happened, still less that she was the victim. "Can you help her?" He also understood why she had chosen Matthew, a relative stranger, to tell. She might find it too difficult, too humiliating, if it were a man she knew, even the chaplain.

"I'll try." Matthew seemed happy to dismiss the subject, at least for the present.

Joseph saw Lizzie very briefly during the long, busy night. More wounded men arrived, none of them critical. But then a junior officer of nineteen who lost a leg was brought in, and Cavan struggled all night to save his life. The shock of the amputation, and then the long journey in the ambulance, had left him in a bad state.

Joseph was so exhausted, he was shuddering with cold by the time he sat on the floor in the empty Resuscitation tent. Cully Teversham brought him a mug of tea and two slices of quite reasonable bread.

"You need that more than anyone, Chaplain," he said cheerfully. "Wish Oi could get you some hot Maconachie stew, but there's none left, not till the next lot comes." He frowned. "Is he going to make it?"

"Probably." Joseph spoke more from hope than expectation.

"If Oi can foind anything else fit to eat, Oi'll bring it," Cully said with a shrug.

"Thank you," Joseph said to acknowledge the kindness. He wanted to see Lizzie again. He wanted to hear her voice, see the smile in her eyes when she recognized him. He knew she would be too tired to talk, but they understood the same emotions too well to need more than a glance. He remembered vividly driving together in the Cambridgeshire lanes two summers ago. He had not needed to explain anything to her then. She had understood his confusion and how slowly he had been forced to face the truth of betrayal, and that it had hurt him almost more than he could face.

And here they had both spent the night fighting to save a young man's life, knowing the searing physical pain he must be feeling. But just as deep as that they could imagine the lifelong wound of being crippled, less than whole, limping when other men ran.

Was she also afraid of returning home to an emptiness after this hideous familiarity was over with: its horror and its companionship, its silly jokes, its physical deprivation, its desperate, heart-tearing loyalties? What purpose could possibly be consuming enough to take its place?

He saw her come into the tent and forced his aching legs to support him as he rose to his feet. He walked over to her, stopping just short of where she was, very careful not to crowd her or assume too much. But he wanted to be closer, even just to reach across and put his hand near hers. He saw that it was slender, bruised where she had carried a weight too heavy for her, the nails very short, one broken.

He had no idea what to say. Nothing was profound enough.

She turned and smiled at him. Despite her dark hair, her eyes were the bluest he had ever seen. What could he say that was comforting and not idiotic, so false as to be a denial of trust?

"I talked with Matthew," he told her. "He said that Schenckendorff couldn't be guilty. There's evidence that makes that certain. He couldn't tell me exactly what, and I couldn't repeat it if I knew."

She turned away quickly, looking hurt, as if she had read in his face something she did not want to see.

"I'm sorry," he said, puzzled. Who was she afraid for? Was she also terrified that someone she liked, or admired, someone she felt protective of, had killed Sarah? He could not believe it of her. He remembered vividly her clarity of thought during that terrible time when he had been so confused and led by his emotions. There had been anger, bewilderment, grief, but always that honesty, above all with herself.

There was a gulf widening between them now, and he did not understand it. The pain it caused him, the sense of loss, almost took his breath away, as if he were hollow inside. "Lizzie, I can't repeat things like that. How would anyone trust me if I did? I understand why Matthew has to keep silent—"

"I know," she said quickly, but she looked at him for only an instant, then away again. "I didn't ask you, Joseph. No one wants to talk about it, but you keep on asking. I'm . . . I'm so sorry for Sarah Price I don't think I could ever find words for how much I . . . feel for her. But I can't undo any of it. Nor have I any idea at all who did it." She was stacking bottles and dishes, and her fingers were clumsy. A dish slipped out of her hands. He lunged forward to catch it, but he was no more skilled than she, and actually knocked it farther away until it crashed on the floor and broke in half.

He felt ridiculous. "I'm sorry," he apologized.

She gasped, then blinked several times rapidly, tears in her eyes. Then she started to laugh. It was a sharp sound growing higher and more desperate until she couldn't stop.

He kicked the broken dish out of the way with his foot so no one would tread on it, then put both arms around her and held her as her laughter turned to weeping. Her whole body shook, her slender shoulders relaxing against him for several minutes. The softness of her hair touched his cheek. He would never forget the feel of her: the stiff cotton of her gray uniform dress, the smell of antiseptic and blood and soap.

Then she pulled away and sniffed, turning aside with sudden strength so as to keep her face from him. "I'm sorry. This is completely feeble. I won't do it again."

"We all need—" he began, not knowing how he was going to finish.

"Don't make excuses for me, Joseph!" she said huskily, reaching for a handkerchief and blowing her nose fiercely. "Pity doesn't help anyone. It's self-indulgent and a complete waste of the time in which we could be doing something useful. These men need nursing, not weeping over. There'll be plenty of time later . . . if there's any point then. I've taken twice as long cleaning this up as I should have anyway." She yanked her apron straight and turned away to continue working.

He had no idea why the distance was widening between them, as if the friendship that was so immeasurably precious had been tarnished by some act he could not remember committing. And it mattered. It was more a part of him than all the turmoil of these last days of war playing themselves out around them: the violence and fear, comradeship, hope of peace and dread of the unknown. They all spoke of going home, and yet all but the most naïve knew that the homes they had left no longer existed as they had known them.

Lizzie had been a friend: candid and funny and gentle, and yet always keeping her own honesty a clean and separate thing, brave enough to stand apart from him and generous enough to remain beside him, sharing the darkness as well as the light.

He knew now, watching her straight back as she walked out of the tent flap, that he had loved Eleanor because he had wanted to, promised to. But he had never liked her as he did Lizzie, and the best lovers were surely friends as well? He loved the women who stayed at home and preserved all that they treasured, whose sacrifice was in ways as great, but he could never explain to them what the front line had been like. No one could.

He must not let Lizzie go. He strode out of the tent into the darkness and saw her figure ahead of him, pale for a moment as she passed by the light of an open flap, and then dark again in the shadow. He ran to catch up with her. If she were angry or confused that he was so determined to clear Schenckendorff, he must explain to her why he had no choice.

"Lizzie!" he called, breaking into a run.

She slowed but did not stop.

He caught up with her. Without thinking he took her arm, then felt her stiffen. Even that slight pulling away hurt him. It created a distance he did not want. "Lizzie, it's far more than simply for justice that we have to prove Schenckendorff's innocence." He kept his voice low so that in the darkness it would not carry even to the closest tents, or anyone standing just outside in the shadows where he could not see. He had to tell her, explain the importance, the urgency.

"It doesn't—" she started.

"Yes, it does," he cut in. "To me. My parents were murdered just before the war."

"I know." Her voice was gentle. "In a car crash. That is, I didn't know it was murder. But—"

"It was. My father had discovered a plot to stop the war with an Anglo-German alliance to betray France, then form a new empire to divide up most of the world." There was no need, and no time, for details. He felt her stiffen with surprise. "It was led by a man whose identity we spent all the war trying to discover, because he never gave up plotting to make the plan still work, if he could only end the war, even if it was by Britain losing. He tried all sorts of ways. We know at least some of them—destroying morale, sabotage of our scientific inventions, which was why he had Theo killed—other ways of corruption and mutiny as well." Joseph stopped when he heard Lizzie gasp, then plunged on as he knew he must. "Many people were murdered, including General Cullingford, because he worked out this man's identity—we named him 'the Peacemaker.' Now he is trying to affect the terms of the armistice, and if we don't stop him, he could succeed. He has immense power."

She was turned toward him, and there was no doubt in her voice. "How can you? You said you don't even know who he is!"

"Schenckendorff does," he answered simply. "He has been his ally since the beginning, but now he realizes that the Peacemaker will try to enforce terms that will enable the whole thing to start again. Germany will rise from defeat in a short time, and a new Anglo-German Empire will become possible. He will never give up trying. Schenckendorff has seen the horror of this, and he will come to London with us—even if he is hanged for his part—rather than see his country dragged into such destruction again."

Her voice was thick with emotion, so intense she could barely force the words. "You have to get him there, Joseph, whatever it costs, absolutely anything, you must stop this . . . Peacemaker . . . from letting this happen again!"

"I know." Without thinking he put up his hand and touched the stray wisps of dark hair that crossed her brow. "We'll do everything we can. But Jacobson is convinced that Schenckendorff killed Sarah Price, and we haven't yet worked out any way to make him doubt it enough to let us take Schenckendorff out of here. Tomorrow, or the next day, Jacobson will charge him and send him back for trial. There's nothing you can do. I just needed you to know why it matters so much."

"I understand," she whispered. Then she pulled away from him and walked quickly to the nearest tent flap. She went in without looking back.

Judith was alone in one of the Treatment tents, watching the man whose leg had been amputated. She felt helpless, inadequate to ease his pain or offer any comfort that was real. How on earth did Joseph manage to do this day after day and not make things even worse by talking rubbish, promising hope that did not exist, saying it would get better when they all knew that nothing would heal the loss? Driving an ambulance was so much simpler. She had nothing to contend with but an inanimate machine, shortages of parts and fuel, filthy weather, cratered roads, the constant danger of being shot or blown apart. And of course, the knowledge that she might not get the injured men to help before it was too late.

Still, that was uncomplicated compared with trying to find faith and keep your own inner strength clean of lies to cover your despair, or the confusion that threatened to drown every shard of light. How did he manage to cling to any idea of a God who loved, whose plan made sense, and who had even the faintest idea what it was like to be human?

She heard the tent flap pull open with a surge of relief simply that there would be someone else there, a voice other than her own.

It was Lizzie. Her face was white, her dark hair pulled loose from half its pins and curling untidily. She closed the flap behind her and came over to Judith, glancing at the man in the bed moving restlessly in his pain.

"Can you help him?" Judith asked.

"No," Lizzie answered quickly. "He just has to get through it alone. I expect Joseph will come and sit with him again, if he has time. There are so many . . ." She bit the inside of her lip, avoiding Judith's eyes. "And he has to get Schenckendorff back to London."

Judith was startled, and then the moment after knew that she should not have been. Of course Joseph would trust Lizzie. He had no idea of the burden that it laid on her.

Lizzie rushed on, not allowing herself time to hesitate. "We don't seem to be having any success finding out who killed Sarah. I'm going to go to Jacobson in the morning and tell him the truth, all of it that I know." Her voice wavered and she swallowed. "But I have to tell Joseph myself first. He should hear it from me, not from someone else, gossip and half a story. I—"

"Not yet," Judith interrupted. "At least wait until tomorrow. We might still . . ."

Lizzie looked at her levelly, blue eyes bright with the grief burning inside her. "So you can find something in a day? We've been trying everything we know since it happened. I'll go as soon as I can find Joseph alone again. I'm only telling you because you'll have to help him . . . I think. He . . ." She could not bring herself to say it.

"He loves you, and he'll feel like hell," Judith finished for her. "Wait. Just another day. Please!"

Lizzie hesitated, hope fighting against reason.

"A day," Judith insisted. "There are no plans to send Schenckendorff out yet. Jacobson's still trying to find a witness who can tell a straight story. There have been so many lies; he has to find a clear thread. Please . . . then we'll tell Joseph, I promise. But don't, please don't until you have to."

"A day," Lizzie said wearily. "Then I must. I know what it means. What will anything that's left be worth if I don't?"

Judith admired her passionately. It was like looking at a man about to go over the top into the gunfire, and she was keeping him balanced on the parapet. But she could not let go of hope, not for a few hours more.

EIGHT

*E*ver since Matthew had told Mason about the Peacemaker from his family's point of view, from the murder of John and Alys Reavley right up through the struggle to get Schenckendorff back to London, Mason had been tormented by the weight of his lie to Judith, albeit by silence. He had hidden his own part in it because he had seen confession now as a self-indulgence for which there was no time or emotional energy. They needed his practical help, not his admission to a complicity that would render him useless in their estimation.

Now he was standing on the fire step behind one of the old parapets, staring across no-man's-land as the morning light picked out the ruts and pools in the gleaming mud, the paths between the old craters a tangled web between the wreckage. There was a faint mist over it, shining silver as the sun struck it. It hid most of the smaller mounds—bodies of men and horses churned up by the shifting pattern of shell holes and seeping water. At this hour it was possible to imagine that sometime far in the future, it could be beautiful again.

Judith was beside him. It was one of the few places they could be certain of not being overheard. She was more desperate than ever to find the truth of who had murdered Sarah Price, partly because she knew all these people in the regiment—and particularly in the Casualty Clearing Station—and felt the pain of suspicion tearing apart the few certainties they had after years of hardship and the loss of half the people they knew. Yet even more urgent was her need to clear Schenckendorff from suspicion so they could take him to London and expose the Peacemaker.

That was the burden that crushed him now.

He looked at Judith, her face calm and pale in the harsh light. He saw very clearly the weariness in her, the depth of emotion, the intense vulnerability in her eyes and mouth. And yet he knew her courage also. If he wished her ever to speak to him in the time ahead, whatever it held for them, then he could not build it on such a vast lie as silence over his alliance with the Peacemaker. He had already carried it almost too far to forgive. Once Schenckendorff was cleared and they left Ypres, it would be too late.

He had thought how he would do it, which words he could use to begin, but now that he was faced with it they all sounded trite and self-serving. They had talked about Schenckendorff, and a silence had settled between them that at least for her seemed comfortable. If he said nothing now it would become a lie, one from which he might never be able to return.

"Judith . . ."

She turned to look at him, waiting for him to speak.

There was no alternative to honesty; he would make it brief and perhaps brutal, like a quick knife thrust.

"I used to believe in the same ideals as Sandwell does, or did in the beginning," he told her.

It was a moment before she realized the meaning of what he had said. Then, very slowly, a light of astonished disbelief filled her face, and after it, pain. "You knew," she said, her voice husky. "When?" She swallowed. "Always?"

"Yes. I always knew it was Sandwell. I didn't know that he had killed. I should have. I could see that the power was taking him over, the desperation to stop the slaughter at any cost. What is one life here or there, quickly, when tens of thousands are dying slowly and hideously every day?" He waited for her answer as if it were a verdict on him—hope or despair.

He saw the flicker of uncertainty, as if, for a moment at least, she had understood.

She frowned. Her words came very slowly, with intense thought behind them. "If that is a serious question, I think the difference may be in small acts, one by one, when you can refuse to do the violent thing, the irreparable thing. But then that might also be cowardice, mightn't it? And to say that he should have asked us isn't really honest, either, because we couldn't have given an answer that had any meaning. Most of us had no idea what the alternatives were. We hadn't seen war. We wouldn't have known what we were being asked to choose."

"So what were we supposed to do?" he asked, surprised that she had addressed the problem with pity rather than rage. "Just let Europe stagger blindly into a holocaust rather than try everything possible to stop it?"

This time she did not hesitate. "Yes. Rather than sell our honor, yes, he should have argued, pleaded—perhaps uselessly—but not tried to sell us without our knowledge." She stared across the cratered land in the broadening light. Now the waste of it was easier to see. The mist no longer softened the outlines or hid the corpses. "It wouldn't have worked anyway. Trying to make a nation of Englishmen do what they don't want to is like trying to herd cats into a barn. You can't do it. There's always some awkward cuss who's going to go the other way, or stop and demand to know why. It isn't practical, Richard; it never was. Some of us might buy peace at that price, but you'd never get us all to."

He was watching the light on her face, not on the land. "I know," he admitted. "At least I do now. There'll always be someone like John Reavley, and Joseph, and perhaps tens of thousands of others just as willing to die for their dreams. I'm not sure how practical they are, but I'm beginning to believe that they hold the one hope we have of surviving into a future that is still worth keeping, worth having paid this much to have."

She turned to meet his eyes, searching, trying to read into the depth of his mind to see if the final honesty was there inside him.

He answered impulsively, and yet he was absolutely certain that the very best of himself meant it. "I'll come to London with you, and tell Lloyd George all I know, and that will back up everything Schenckendorff says. He will have to believe us."

She stiffened with instant fear. "You'd be admitting to treason," she said in a whisper. "Don't you know that?"

"Yes." Said aloud like that, it brought a chill he had not fully realized before, but it did not alter his certainty that this was what he had to do. It was a payment he owed, and it was the only way she would ever look at him with the shining honesty that she did now, with the possibility of the kind of love that he could not turn away from, even if his life were the price. He would be clean; he would have given all he could to pay for his mistake.

"Are you sure?" she asked.

He was sure. He did not know if he would still have the courage when he was alone, and knew that his name would go down in history not as Britain's greatest, bravest, and most articulate war correspondent, but as a man who had betrayed his own country for a flawed ideal. If he faltered later it would be because of fear crowding in; weakness, not a change in belief. "Yes, I am sure," he said firmly. "I love you. More than anything else I want to be the man who can live up to your dreams, and your courage to pay what they cost."

She gave a little nod. It was a very small, very certain gesture, and then she smiled. Then she touched his face and leaned forward and kissed him, long and tenderly. For those moments he felt an infinite happiness he thought it would be impossible ever to forget.

Later in the morning, when Judith found Joseph in his bunker having just finished more letters, she knew that he saw the happiness in her immediately, and that he also probably recognized it as what it was. But she had no intention of telling him that Mason had always known the Peacemaker, or—at this point—that he was willing to come to London with them and tell the prime minister so. They still needed Schenckendorff; otherwise they could not expect to be believed against a man as powerful as Dermot Sandwell. Alone, Mason might be written off as a lunatic, a man too shocked by his experiences at war to have retained his balance of mind.

And Schenckendorff had not brought any papers with him. It would have been impossible to keep them after capture, even if he had dared to take the risk of removing them from Berlin.

The only written proof was the treaty John Reavley had hidden in the house in St. Giles.

"We've got to think," she said to Joseph. "Have you made a list of all the people it still could be, so we can concentrate on them and eliminate them? It's the first of November. We can't have much longer or they'll have ended the war and we'll be too late anyway. Jacobson must be working on it all the time. He's out there like a dog worrying a bone. And Hampton is, too."

She sat down on the cot, and he turned himself around on the box to face her. He looked tired, and there was an unhappiness under the surface courage that twisted her inside to see. She knew it was because a gulf had opened between Lizzie and himself, and he could not understand it.

Judith ached to be able to reach out and help, tell him that it was because Lizzie loved him intensely, not because she didn't. But would he be able to bear the knowledge of what had happened to her, and that she was now carrying the rapist's child? She did not know. He had been so desperately hurt by Eleanor's death, and the scars had taken years to heal. Might this new blow even rock his faith? And wasn't that the foundation of his strength?

Staring out over no-man's-land, Lizzie thought that of course Joseph would have to know. Soon her pregnancy would become obvious. Then she would either have to tell him or walk out of his life forever, without explanation, and that would surely hurt him even more.

Mason had described to her how Joseph had been in Gallipoli when he had first met him. He had tried to capture his compassion, his tireless work for the wounded no matter how exhausted he was himself, his steadiness in the unspeakable horror of it. He had said the sea was red with human blood.

Then he had told her about his long argument with Joseph in the open boat on the channel, after the U-boat had sunk their steamer and left them to find their way back to England as best they could. The others had died, leaving only Joseph, Mason, and one injured crewman. Joseph had been willing to die, if that was what it cost to prevent Mason from writing his story on Gallipoli and sabotaging morale for the recruitment needed to prevent surrender. Yes, Joseph could take disappointment, betrayal, even defeat, and survive them all.

Her eyes had moistened with tears of pride, and of happiness that Mason believed so well of Joseph. Still, she wanted to protect both Joseph and Lizzie as long as she could—and perhaps all the others here as well, except the one man who was guilty. It was the very last resort of all to tell Jacobson about the earlier rape.

Joseph was holding out a piece of paper to her with names and times and places on it. She took it and read.

"An awful lot of this doesn't make sense," she said at last. "For a start, I really don't believe it could possibly have been Major Morel. I know he's a bit odd, and I think he really would have led a mutiny last year." She glanced at Joseph's wry expression. "All right, he did. But I don't believe he would rape anybody. He's a rebel in his own way, and he'd fight for any cause he believed in, but violence against women isn't a cause."

"And Tiddly Wop Andrews?" Joseph asked. "He said Moira Jessop saw him in the supply tent the only time he wasn't with the walking wounded, but she says she wasn't there. Why would she lie?"

"I suppose she was somewhere she shouldn't have been," Judith answered. "Or she's already lied to protect someone else, and she can't go back on it. But I can't believe it's Tiddly Wop. We've known him for years! He's good looking, but he's as shy as . . . as a choirboy."

"That's rubbish, Judith, and you know it," Joseph said gently. "He was shy at home. He's been on the battlefront for four years. He's not a boy anymore. He's twenty-six, and a soldier."

She was startled. "You don't believe it could be him, do you?"

His face was tight. "I don't want to, but we've all changed. The whole world's changed. Nobody is who they used to be." He looked at her earnestly. "It won't only be those of us who've been here who are changed, or on other fronts; it'll be the people at home, too. Read Hannah's letters between the lines. She hates some of what is new, but she knows she can't escape." He gave a slight shrug. "We don't look at anything the way we used to, socially or economically. The old rules of how to behave have been swept away. Distinctions in social class are blurred into each other more and more all the time. We've been forced to see the courage, intelligence, and moral value of men we used to barely even notice. They aren't going to go home and doff the cap anymore. We know, in a way we can never forget, that we are all equal when it comes to injury and death, human need, the will to live, above all the honor and the self-sacrifice to go over the top and give your life for your friends."

"I know," she said softly. "But I'm so afraid that once we've grown used to the silence and the comfort again, we'll sink back into the old bad things as well: the indifference, the malice, the inequalities, the stupid lies that we only believe because they're comfortable. Will we go back to ignorance of what real pain or real sorrow is, and complain about stupid little things again as if they mattered? Will we take offense over trivia, get greedy for more than we need, forget that we are more alike than any differences there are among us? Will we even remember to be grateful just to be alive and at home, able to see and hear and walk? Will we remember to look after those who can't see or hear? And those who are alone, and will always be alone?"

"I don't know. But I know what we'll deserve if we don't," he said softly. "If there is a God, a resurrection—and I have to believe there is—then when we meet those who paid, I want to be able to look in their faces and say that I honored their gift."

"So do I. If I can't, maybe that would be hell," she agreed. "And I still hope it wasn't Tiddly Wop, or Barshey Gee, or Major Morel."

"Or Cavan," he added. "There's something odd about his story. I don't know what yet, and I wish I didn't have to find out, but I do."

"Cavan would never have killed anyone!" she said aghast. "Even you can't imagine that!"

"I don't," he replied. "But he's lying. I need to know why, unless we can solve it first."

"I will!" she said, standing up. "I'll go to it right now."

"Be careful!" he said with quick fear, standing as well. "You're not safe just because you're an ambulance driver, Judith."

She swiveled to face him, one hand holding back the sacking. "I know!"

Joseph started to look for Tiddly Wop Andrews. They were all finding the enforced idleness a strain, especially since they were held here in a sense captive and away from the last of the fighting. Most were torn between relief that now they would get home uninjured, and the sense of having let down their friends by not being there at the very end. They felt useless. Hours dragged by in small jobs that were largely no more than filling in time. There was no point at all in shoring up trenches; they would never be used again. Rifles had not been fired, so they did not need cleaning. It was still done, but it was a waste of time. The only thing that actually had value was helping the injured, but there was only so much that an unskilled man could do.

Tiddly Wop had been mending duckboards. There was no point—they would not need them much longer—but it was better than idleness. He put down the hammer as Joseph's shadow fell across him.

"What can I do for you, Chaplain?" he asked. "I really don't know anything more."

"Yes, you do," Joseph answered, squatting down on a pile of sandbags opposite him. "Where were you the night Sarah Price was killed, Tiddly? The truth."

"I was in the Evacuation tent," Tiddly Wop said doggedly. "I already told you that."

"Yes, you did. And Cully Teversham told me so, too. But Moira Jessop said you weren't, the first time I asked her. And she said the same thing to Jacobson."

Tiddly Wop looked unhappy. "Don't know why she'd say that."

"No, neither do I," Joseph agreed. "She said later that you might have been; they were all so busy she couldn't be sure. But that's not true, either. The Evacuation tent was actually pretty quiet. Between half past three and half past four there was no one in there at all. And that's the time that counts."

Tiddly Wop blinked. "Is it? Is that when . . . when she was killed?"

"Yes. Didn't you know that?"

"No. I . . . I saw her earlier." Again he looked away. "She was pretty upset. I tried to make her feel a bit better." He mumbled the words as if he was embarrassed by them.

"What was she upset about?" Joseph persisted.

"Lots of things," Tiddly Wop answered, his voice thick with sadness.

"That's not an answer," Joseph told him. "This girl's dead, Tiddly. We need to know what happened to her, and why. Why may be the only way we catch the man who did it. I'm not going to repeat it if I don't have to. What was she upset about?"

"She was afraid of going home," Tiddly Wop said slowly, searching for the words he needed. "She knew things had changed. She'd only been out here a year or so, but she realized that it isn't ever going to be like it was before. So many young men are dead, and two or three times as many are injured, or crippled, or just different." He looked sad and puzzled. "And women aren't the way they used to be, either. She felt she wouldn't fit in anywhere, nobody would marry her, because even though she was pretty enough, she hadn't any . . . I don't know . . . she didn't think with all the women there are who are well bred, know how to behave, are charming and modest and good at domestic skills, that anybody'd choose her. And she'd got a bit of a reputation. She was nearly twenty-six. She flirted a good bit. She had a sort of a fling with Benbow, until he got too keen and she ended it. Then she . . . I don't know . . . made sure she could still attract men by flirting something rotten with the German prisoners. Safe, if you like. They can't do anything, poor sods. She just wanted to boost herself up a bit."

He looked earnestly at Joseph to see if he understood.

"I told her that was silly, but she knew that already. Makes people angry with her. She was pretty enough, more than most. I said to her not to sell herself cheap. I didn't go too far because I didn't want her to think I was after her, but I tried to get her to think well of herself." He searched Joseph's face anxiously.

Joseph saw the kindness in him, the sense of pity for a young woman afraid and foolish, probably like thousands of other women who saw what had once been an assured future disappearing as an army of young men melted into the earth and all the old patterns of behavior shifted.

"When was that?" Joseph asked.

"About midnight," Tiddly answered. "Maybe one o'clock."

"Then where were you between half past three and half past four?"

"In the Evacuation tent, like I said."

"With Cully Teversham?"

Tiddly Wop said nothing. His silence confirmed the truth.

Joseph waited. He would dearly like to have believed him, but he could not afford even a single lie, no matter how much it was better or easier than the truth.

Tiddly Wop sighed. "You aren't going to leave it, are you, Chaplain?"

"No. Where were you, Tiddly?"

"In the Evacuation tent! It's just that Cully weren't there. He said he was to cover for me."

"Why?"

Tiddly looked at Joseph, his eyes begging for a leniency, an understanding. " 'Cause I pulled him off the wire at Passchendaele an' he reckons he owes me something. I didn't ask him for that. Don't drop him in it, Chaplain, please?"

"Who else was in the Evacuation tent, Tiddly?"

"No one! I swear! But before you go blaming Cully, or thinking he did anything, he was with Snowy Nunn that time, but Snowy's gone back up to the front again. And that's the truth!"

Joseph believed him. He understood the debt of honor. Any man who owed his life to someone else never forgot it. Cully was like tens of thousands of others. Joseph had not known that Tiddly Wop had saved him. It was just one more piece of heroism done for its own sake, no recognition expected or wished for. It was what you did for friends.

"Yes," Joseph acknowledged. "Where was Moira Jessop?"

"I don't know. But she wasn't in the Evacuation tent."

Joseph thanked him and left him to go find Moira Jessop and question her again.

She was asleep, taking advantage of a brief respite. She had worked all night and he felt unkind disturbing her, but there was no time for such considerations. Added to which, of course, if she were called to an emergency he would not be able to speak to her anyway.

"What is it, Chaplain?" she said, fumbling to straighten her dress and collect her thoughts. She sat upright and scraped her hair back into something like neatness, even if it was unflatteringly tight.

"I need to talk to you about Sarah Price," he said, standing in front of her.

Her face clouded. "I don't know anything more than I've already told you. She flirted with the Germans." Her face pulled into lines of distaste, her lips tight. She was sitting more stiffly now, the gray fabric of her dress stretched a little over her shoulders. "Of course I wouldn't say she deserved it, but she certainly invited it in a way none of the rest of us would think of. She had no . . . modesty. It lowered all of us in the men's eyes."

"What did she do?" he asked. That was not what he had been going to say, but he was curious and disturbed by her comment.

"I told you," she replied. "She flirted with them. Far more than looked after them or attended to their wounds."

"Are you certain?"

She was angry now.

"If you doubt me, ask Allie Robinson," she challenged him. "She knows it was cheap and disgusting. For heaven's sake, these are the men who slaughtered our own boys, whose bodies are shattered by shrapnel, torn on the wires, riddled with bullets, frozen to death. Who in God's name does she think did it to them?" Her face was white, her voice sharp and rising out of control.

"I expect she knew that, even if she forgot it for the moment," he said gently. He could understand her anger and the fear of chaos that welled up inside her. You could become drowned in pain, desperate for any kind of right and wrong, anything at all that made sense of something too terrible to bear. The nurses dealt with the worst of it, endlessly, night after night, and they endured the same miserable rations, exhausting hours, and endless hunger, weariness, and cold as the men. Sometimes people forgot it simply because nurses were seldom shot at, and they did not have to shoot back. Their task was always one of mercy. None of them would lie awake in the night sweating with horror as the face of a dying man swam in front of them, and they knew they had killed him. Joseph had held men who wept with terror and guilt over that. The nightmares would never leave some of them.

But nurses had their own nightmares, their own drowning in helplessness. Had the women at home even the faintest idea of their courage, or strength, the steel of endurance that anchored their lives day and night?

"I don't know anything," Moira repeated stiffly. "I already told you."

"Yes, you do," he said firmly. "You know where you were, and it was not the Evacuation tent. It's time for the truth."

She looked startled, drawing in breath to deny it. Then she met his eyes, obviously realizing that he was not going to accept that. The resistance drained away. "I was with Private Eames," she said very quietly. She did not explain, but it was unnecessary; her implication was perfectly clear.

"Where?" He tried to keep judgment out of his voice.

"Does it really matter?" The challenge was back, as if he were asking from some prurient curiosity.

"Yes, it does matter," he replied. "The only hope we have of finding out where people actually were is to get as much of the truth as possible, and weed out the lies. Unfortunately you are far from the only one to say they were somewhere they weren't."

She blushed hotly. "I don't know who killed her!"

"Somebody does. Where were you?"

"On the far side of the water drums." It was almost an accusation in return, as if he were to blame for driving her to it. It was a muddy and miserable spot; they could not have been doing more than kissing at the most. Perhaps that was what she meant him to know.

"Out of sight of the Germans' hut," he observed aloud.

"Yes."

"For how long?"

"I don't know. Ten minutes, or fifteen."

He automatically assumed it could have been more. She would err on the side that excused her, and—perhaps of greater importance—that excused Eames, who had left his post.

"I won't report it this time, if I can avoid it," he said to her. "But if that time is crucial to Sarah's murder, then I might have to."

"I didn't have anything to do with it!" she said indignantly. "Nor did Private Eames."

"Yes, he did, Nurse Jessop. He was away from his duty, and so he cannot account for what happened around the German prisoners' hut. One of them may have come out. Also, of course, Sergeant Benbow cannot account for himself, either. And he lied, because he said they were together."

She was now very shaken. She had obviously not allowed her mind to travel so far. But she was angry, and she refused to apologize. He left her sitting on the cot, miserable and defensive.

He confirmed what she had said with Eames, then sought out Benbow and confronted him with his lie.

Benbow looked acutely uncomfortable, and a tide of guilt swept up his lean face. "He was having a bit of a fling with Nurse Jessop," he said, not looking directly at Joseph. "Didn't see that it mattered. He wasn't gone long."

"How long, do you know?"

Benbow hesitated.

"You don't know," Joseph said for him. "Which means you are not accounted for, either. It's time for the truth, Benbow. It would be better if you gave it to me honestly rather than my having to drag it out of others. Any lie is a form of guilt at this point, whatever you are lying to conceal: your error, or anyone else's."

Benbow looked wretched. "I don't know how long he was gone," he said in a low, hard voice. "I wasn't there, either, not when he came back. I think it was only a few minutes we were both gone."

"You think?" Joseph said softly. "Did you lie to cover Eames or yourself?"

"Both." Benbow hesitated again. "I was with Sarah Price, but only at the water. I helped her carry a bucket and stopped to talk to her for a few minutes. She was looking after some of the German wounded. I was angry with her for flirting with them. She seemed to prefer them to us." His hands were clenched, and the muscles were tight in his neck and jaw. "It was then that I realized why. She liked to tease them, flirt, bait them a bit. Fun, she called it. But the poor bastards couldn't do anything about it. Most of them were too badly shot up, and scared stiff of what would happen to them—even more, to their women at home—and she liked that."

"You're not painting a picture of a very pleasant young woman," Joseph observed.

Benbow glared at him, then gave a short bark of laughter. "It's a true one."

"I am assuming, Corporal, that you knew her fairly well?"

Benbow colored again. "She was around a lot."

Joseph said no more on the subject, but neither did he promise Benbow not to report it if it should become necessary. Instead he went to speak with the German prisoners, to see if any of them could corroborate how long Eames or Benbow was absent from duty.

He asked Schenckendorff first. He looked pale still, but his foot was less inflamed and his fever appeared to have gone. Now he faced the possibility of being tried for murder and hanged, and his eyes held a black humor at the irony of it, but he had summoned all the strength he possessed to mask his fear.

He corroborated Benbow's story, hope flaring up for an instant that somehow it would help prove his own innocence, then dying when Joseph did not say so.

"I'm closer to the truth," Joseph said quietly. "But I'm not there yet."

"I did not do it," Schenckendorff replied. "I stood outside on the earth for a little while, and felt the rain. I spoke to no one. The girl who was killed was the one who came in here and laughed and joked with our men? A very pretty girl, but shallow, I think, perhaps frightened, and cruel at times. It is terrible that she was killed. I'm sorry. Stupidity does not deserve such a fearful punishment. We are all stupid at times, led blindly by our hopes or fears. Too busy looking at what we are running away from to see what we are running into."

Joseph said nothing. Schenckendorff could have been speaking of a dozen different things, physical, emotional, or moral. In another time and place he could have liked the man, even been his friend. Now all that mattered was to clear him of blame so they could get him to London in time.

Joseph rose to leave, and as he was walking past the cots one of the prisoners spoke to him in excellent English, calling him by name. Joseph stopped. There was something familiar about the voice, but he could not place it.

"Chaplain?" the man repeated. He was lean and dark with prominent features, handsome in his own way.

"Do I know you?" Joseph asked, puzzled.

The man smiled. His head was bandaged, and there was still blood oozing over his right ear. There was also heavy padding on his right shoulder and arm. "Feldwebel Eisenmann," he answered. "We discussed English football in no-man's-land, 1915. I'm glad to see that you are all right. Can you tell me if my friend Corporal Goldstone is still alive, please?"

Joseph remembered the incident with a sudden glow of warmth. It had been terrifying one moment, overwhelmingly funny the next. They had discussed Arsenal's dismal defense against Chelsea, as if it actually mattered—a moment of beautiful sanity in the middle of hell. Two Jews and a Church of England chaplain lost in a waste of mud and corpses, talking about a football game, and parting as friends.

"Yes, he is, Feldwebel," Joseph replied. "He got a blighty one about a year ago. Lost his left foot, but he's adjusting well. I hear from him every so often. I'll write and tell him I saw you."

"Tell him I lost my right ear," Eisenmann said. "He'll see the joke in that. He always said I couldn't sing. By the way, I have a message for you." He smiled, a sweet, gentle look in his eyes. "From a man called Sam. Tall fellow, dark hair. Did some work in Germany and said he's going to stay there, at least for the time being. Asked you if you'd do him a favor and tell his brother the truth. Does that make sense? And he said, 'Be happy.' Tell a good joke and eat a chocolate biscuit for him."

Joseph felt the warmth flood through him. Of all the friends the war had taken from him, he missed Sam Wetherall, a fugitive for three years now, more than any other. "Yes, the most excellent sense," he replied. "Thank you, Feldwebel. I am much in your debt." He turned and left before emotion overtook him. He wanted to be alone outside, to walk in the rain along the old trenches, to recapture memory and the companionships that had been the best of it. He wanted to remember the voices, the laughter, the eyes of all those he knew so well who would stay here after the rest of them had gone home, when the good and bad of war had drifted into the past and become stories told to people who had no idea what it had really been like.

Judith also was working on everything she could. The increasingly clear picture of Sarah Price that emerged was easy to understand, and to pity, but less easy to like.

"Loose," Allie said pithily. "Heaven knows, anyone can understand falling in love. We're all lonely, frightened, and very much aware that what we lose the chance for now we may never have again. But Sarah didn't love. In a way you could say she was always lying, promising something she didn't even have, much less intend to give!" Her face was bleak with anger and a consuming pain. "By being what she was, cruel and vulgar, she betrayed us all."

"Betrayed us?" Judith repeated with confusion. She was not understanding.

Allie stared at her with frustration bordering on contempt. "The men who died out here, the wounded and broken, everyone they loved at home—we must be worthy of it. She wasn't! She mocked them. She had no loyalty." She looked away. There was a bitterness and a deep, harsh anger in her voice. "Over centuries men and women have given all they had to make the England we love. If we let ourselves become cheap and grubby now, we betray the dead not just of this war, but of all wars. Every sacrifice made in two thousand years is wasted. What irony if we beat the Germans, then let the prize slip out of our own hands into the mud to be trodden on."

"You can give it away for yourself," Judith said firmly. "You can't give it away for others."

Allie continued to glare at her. "Of course you can, you stupid woman! You can give it away for all the people who follow you! What are you going to teach your children? Are you going to teach them honor and chastity and how to care for others and be loyal and patient and decent? Or how to take everything you can for yourself, make sure you know all of your rights—and none of your duties?"

Judith opened her mouth to argue, then knew it was useless. And Allie had some justice on her side. A generation that forgets its beliefs cannot pass them on. It was the depth of Allie's emotion that startled her and made her a little afraid.

Only after she had walked hunched against the wind and was back in Joseph's bunker comparing her notes did she realize that Allie had said she was with Cavan working in the tent for the lying wounded at the same time that she had also said she was in the Resuscitation tent. And one of the orderlies had confirmed the second story.

Why would Allie say that if it were not true? And why had Cavan confirmed it? She sat on the edge of the cot and read through it all again, some in her own hand, some in Joseph's. Note by note, it was clear that Cavan and Allie were lying; the orderlies' stories fit in with everything else. She could not believe that Cavan, of all people, was guilty, even if, according to several people, he had known Sarah and at times laughed and joked with her, and perhaps a little bit more. She was easy to like—if you did not witness her cruelty—and she asked for nothing in return. She was not seeking any kind of commitment. That's what he had implied.

Dreading the answers, Judith forced herself to find Cavan and ask him. He was in the Operating tent, and she had to wait. Finally he came out into the Resuscitation tent, his arms still bloody and his hair wet where he had dashed water over his face to keep himself awake. Judith felt guilty for bothering him, but Schenckendorff had to be saved, and Lizzie's grief was far worse than any brief embarrassment Cavan might experience.

Cavan smiled. He looked pleased to see her.

"I've been talking to Allie," she said straightaway.

"She's a good nurse," he responded, but his attention was directed toward the man just brought in, who was not yet stirring from unconsciousness.

She looked at Cavan and decided it was best to speak bluntly. "Why did you let Allie lie to protect you at the time Sarah was killed?"

He stiffened and turned around slowly. His face was pale, and there was a very clear flare of anger in his heavy-lidded eyes. "Just who do you think you are, questioning people like this?" he said abruptly. "It's none of your business, Judith. I put up with a certain amount when your brother was accused, but now it's just some German, and you are overstepping yourself."

"Probably," she said tartly, stung by his coldness. "If you prefer me to go and tell Jacobson, I can. Allie lied, and you didn't say anything, so in effect you lied also. I understand lying. I do it myself to protect those I care for, especially if I believe absolutely in their innocence. But I won't see an innocent man hanged, German or British or anything else. Either tell me or tell Jacobson. The choice is yours."

He was angry, very angry. She had not seen it in him before and it startled her, but she refused to back down.

"Allie is protecting me," he said icily. "I was exhausted and took a few minutes outside alone to collect myself. I didn't say she lied because I was grateful, and I didn't want to get her into trouble. I don't know if your self-righteousness can understand that or have any pity."

The word *pity* struck a spark in her mind. Suddenly she understood something she should have seen before. Allie Robinson was in love with Cavan, and he did not feel the same for her. He knew it and was ashamed. Perhaps he had allowed her to misunderstand a word, a gesture, during long watches over the wounded or the dying. It was this guilt that made him so angry. This terrible need to not be alone, to reach out to some human comfort, was not the same as love, at least not love between a man and a woman. But the illusion of love could spring from it, and the aching, devouring hunger.

"I see," she said gently. "Yes, I understand. Thank you. Did anyone else know you were outside?"

His look softened. Something else showed in his eyes for a moment, a warmth that flared and died almost before she recognized it. "Not so far as I know."

The night was drawing in. It was long past the equinox, and by late afternoon an autumn sun burned orange across the northwest. Veils of rain smudged gray, driving in hard and cold. Matthew, Joseph, and Judith sat on the two cots. Judith had told them what she had learned.

Joseph chewed his lip. "So we have accounted for everyone except Cavan, Benbow, and Barshey Gee."

Judith was stunned. "Barshey Gee? Don't be ridiculous, Joseph. Barshey wouldn't do that to anyone." She felt the blood burning up her face. She had lied to protect Wil Sloan, saying that she'd been working on her ambulance and he'd been there with her. Actually she had finished it early and gone to sit inside, out of the wind and rain. Barshey had brought

her a mug of hot tea. She had watched him shorten the flame and wait until the water boiled. It had taken a long time. After that he had walked back
to the ambulance with her and they had talked.

"I don't believe he did it, either," Joseph said grimly. "But he lied,
Judith."

"Did he?" The words stuck on her tongue. "What did he say?"

"That he'd made you a mug of tea in the walking wounded tent, then
gone out with you to your ambulance. He said Wil Sloan wasn't there. You
said he was, and you didn't mention Barshey."

Matthew looked unhappy. "That's a stupid lie, Joe. Why would
Barshey say anything that could be disproved so easily? He had to know
we'd all talk together. Why Judith? Any other V.A.D. we might not have believed, but to say it was her was idiotic!"

Quick, ugly thoughts raced through Judith's mind: memories of how
frightened Wil had been, his words about men afraid of the violence
within themselves, the rage that betrayed their control. No, that was nonsense! She knew Wil too well to allow that, even as overtired imagination.

Joseph was staring at her. She had told others to tell the truth. She
had despised Allie for lying to protect Cavan, and seen his pity and guilt
for her.

She lifted her eyes to meet Joseph's. It had to be now. "Barshey didn't
lie. I did. I'm sorry." She swallowed. "I wanted to protect Wil because I
knew they would suspect him. He has a temper. Barshey made the tea inside, and then came out with me to the ambulance, just as he said." She saw
Joseph's face. "I know! I'm sorry!" She was tangled in lies as if in the arms
of an octopus. As soon as she freed herself from one she was gripped by
another. Now she had had to betray Wil when she had said she would not.

"And could it have been Wil?" Matthew said gravely. "This time the
truth, please?"

"We all have our debts, Matthew." Joseph shook his head. "We can't
choose when they come due." He touched Judith's arm in a moment's
warmth, then leaned away again.

"I suppose so," Judith whispered.

"So Cavan, Benbow, or Wil Sloan." Joseph looked from one to the
other of them questioningly.

"Benbow," Judith answered. "I refuse to believe it was Cavan or Wil.
So do you. We've known them for four years. Cavan has saved more lives
than any other doctor on this part of the front. He'd have had the V.C. if
it weren't for that idiot Northrup. Even then he put his man before himself and stayed behind to answer the charge."

"That doesn't mean he wouldn't rape a woman," Matthew pointed out.

"Of course it doesn't!" Judith shouted at him, her voice rising in a kind of desperate denial. "But it was Benbow. It has to have been."

"Probably," Joseph agreed. "But we haven't proved it."

Matthew's response was cut short by Mason banging on the makeshift lintel and pulling open the curtain.

"Come in," Joseph invited, although Mason was already down the first step. As he came into the full lamplight, they saw that his face was haggard, his wide mouth pulled into a tight line. He looked briefly from one to the other.

"It's a hell of a lot worse," he said without waiting for any of them to speak. "Someone above Hook has ordered Jacobson off the case and put a military policeman in charge. Hook's furious, but there's nothing he can do. This bloke's already arrived, fellow called Onslow. He's ordered all investigation to cease; Schenckendorff is to be shipped out tomorrow after all. He doesn't give a damn whether he's medically fit or not."

"The case is not proved," Matthew protested. "It's only a charge; there's far too little evidence to bring it to trial."

Judith looked at Joseph, and saw in his eyes that he was more accustomed to military police and the needs of war than his brother. There was no such hope in him, no trust of reason or law.

"We can't prove Schenckendorff is innocent," he said, looking from Matthew to Judith. "That's the only thing that would do now."

"There isn't any proof!" Mason's voice was tight with anger. "What a bloody irony!" He did not need to put it into words. They were all thinking the same thing. Blind chance, a chain of individual lies and debts, a military policeman ruled more by ambition than justice—and the Peacemaker had won again.

"What have we been fighting for?" Joseph said softly. "If in the end we hang an innocent man for our convenience, to save us the trouble of finding the truth and the discomfort of facing an answer we don't like? We could have saved the slaughter and simply surrendered in the first place."

Judith put her head in her hands and knew that she must go and speak to Lizzie. It would be a pain almost unendurable, but it was no longer possible for Lizzie to remain silent about her own rape.

NINE

*J*oseph spent a wretched night. It seemed that after all their efforts they were finally defeated. He had pleaded with Onslow, who was a lean, pale, hazel-eyed man with a fresh-clipped haircut. Onslow had listened with civility, then said he was sorry but the matter had dragged on too long. The crime was a hideous one, even by the standards of violence they had become tragically used to. Now at last they were looking forward to peace—it could come within days—and this matter must be settled. It was not only for the sake of justice, but for the men and women of this Casualty Clearing Station whose morale had suffered so profoundly.

Nothing Joseph could say about injustice, lack of evidence, even the possibility of someone else being guilty had altered Onslow's judgment in the slightest. Schenckendorff would be moved out sometime the following day, as soon as safe conduct could be arranged. He must be protected. For the sake of the men here, they must not be allowed to harm him. But his transportation would be early afternoon at the latest.

Joseph had lain sleepless, knowing that Matthew was awake in the other bunk, but neither of them could think of anything more to suggest, so each sought sleep fitfully and with little success.

In the morning Matthew went out early without saying what he intended to do, and Joseph wrote two condolence letters left over from the previous day. He had just finished them when there was a brief rap on the lintel. Without waiting for a reply, Lizzie came down the steps.

She was hollow-eyed and bereft of color. His first thought was death—Stan Tidyman, who had lost his leg? Had the amputation been too much of a shock to a body already exhausted?

"Who is it?" he said, offering her his chair and moving to sit on the bunk.

"No one," she replied, accepting the seat awkwardly, as if she would rather have remained standing. "That's not why I've come."

"What is it?" What else could have happened? He had not had time to tell her about Schenckendorff last night. She had been on duty and busy with the wounded.

In short, cutting words she told him, sparing herself no fact, however harsh. She did not once look up at him or offer any excuses or blame. It was simply an account of a sudden rape in which she was violated and left bruised in body and soul, hurting beyond anything she could have imagined, soiled forever. Something was damaged inside her that could never be repaired. And now she was carrying the man's child, as if she had been fused with him in one terrible act, and a living person had been created so she could never forget. She had no idea who the rapist was. Still she did not look up or meet Joseph's eyes.

"It happened before Schenckendorff ever came through the lines," she finished in a flat, tight voice. "He could not have been the one. I need to tell Onslow that, so he doesn't charge him and take him away."

Joseph was so shattered that he felt as if he, too, had been attacked deep inside himself, scorched by filth he could never be rid of. He would rather they had done this to him than to her. He had no idea what to say or do that would ever reach her pain, let alone comfort it. He was overwhelmed, robbed of everything except the throbbing red wound of it. Even rage had not come yet. It would. He would want to kill the man, beat him senseless, then castrate him when he was conscious and aware of every movement of the knife.

Would that help? Would it ease anything?

Lizzie was waiting for him to look at her, to say something. He realized with shock that she was not certain he believed her. Incredibly, she was afraid he could think it was a lie constructed to cover some moral lapse of her own.

What could he say? Words were so clumsy, inadequate to express any of the desperate emotion inside him. She needed to be believed. She could hardly care now that he loved her. The thought that the creature who had murdered Sarah Price had also been violently intimate with Lizzie, leaving his seed inside to grow and become her child, left him seared with horror. But he must think of her, not himself.

"Joseph?" Her voice was shaking. The terror in her was so consuming, he could feel it in the room. "Will you come with me to Onslow?"

He must say something, the right thing. There was only this one chance; he could never take back a mistake. He reached out and touched the tips of her fingers with his own. It was the lightest possible brush of skin on skin.

"We'll find another way to clear Schenckendorff . . . ," he began, and knew immediately that it was not true. There was no more time.

She shook her head, a tiny movement as if her muscles were locked. "I've waited as long as I can. I have to do it. You know it's right. Don't make it harder. I just had to tell you myself before I did it." She stood up; then her body swayed for a moment until she regained her balance. "I couldn't live with anything else, and neither could you." She turned very slowly and walked to the door.

Joseph was too late to stand up, but he was not sure that his legs would hold him anyway. He knew she was right; Schenckendorff had come through the lines to surrender himself and betray the Peacemaker, with all that that cost him, because his honor demanded it. If she allowed him to hang for a crime she knew he had not committed, it would poison the rest of her life—and Joseph's, too, if he colluded in such an act of cowardice.

And yet every part of him wanted to protect her. His mind screamed at him to find another way, any way, but not this. Please God, let there be something else they could do! But even as he prayed he knew there was not, and he was wasting time protesting while he allowed her to go to Onslow alone. He should be with her, beside her. What it cost him was irrelevant.

He stood up and parted the sacking, climbing the steps, his legs as heavy as if he were struggling through the thick mud of no-man's-land. He went outside and followed after her, knowing which way she would have gone. He caught up with her as she opened the door to the hut where Onslow had made his office, and they went in together.

Onslow was sitting behind a table with half a dozen sheets of paper on it. He looked surprised to see them, and somewhat irritated. He addressed Joseph first. "Yes, Chaplain. Please don't waste your time and mine asking me to delay charging the German, or with any more theories as to who else could be guilty. You are not serving your men, or your regiment's honor."

"Sir—" Joseph began.

"We need this wretched business to be over and put as far from our minds as possible," Onslow said tartly, cutting across him, his hand up as if to silence him physically. "You should write to the poor girl's family, if you have not done so already, then turn your attention to the living. There are more than enough wounded who need your help . . . your undivided help, Captain Reavley." He still had done no more than glance at Lizzie.

Now she stepped forward. Joseph could see something of what it cost her to stand so stiffly to attention, shoulders squared.

"Captain Reavley came only to support me in what I have to tell you,

Major Onslow," she said clearly. "He knew nothing of it until I felt obliged to inform him just now."

Onslow drew in his breath to interrupt her also, but something in her face and bearing stopped him. He made an attempt at patience, but it was brief.

Lizzie plunged on. "Unfortunately Sarah Price was not the only woman to be assaulted. There was an earlier rape, extremely unpleasant, but very much less violent—"

This time he did interrupt. "Nothing was reported, Miss—"

"Mrs. Blaine," she said. "I know it was not reported." Her voice dipped.

Joseph ached to be able to say it for her, explain, force Onslow to understand, but he knew he must not. It would rob Lizzie of the only dignity or control she had in the matter. He stood rigidly, his hands by his sides, clenched so his nails dug into his palms. The silence in the tent was oppressive, the air stale.

"It is very . . . difficult to report such a thing." Lizzie's voice sank despite her will to keep it strong.

Onslow's face darkened with anger. "Mrs. Blaine, rape is a very serious crime! Not to report it is completely irresponsible. I am very sorry that such a thing should have happened, and if you tell me who the woman is, we shall add that to the charge." He jerked his hands, as if freeing himself from some restraint. "Although of course I cannot unless the victim herself tells me. Please point out to her that it is her duty, and perhaps if she had had the courage to come forward at the time, we might have caught the man then, and Sarah Price would still be alive."

It cost Joseph such an effort of will to keep silent that he could feel the blood throbbing in his temples. He wanted to beat Onslow until he lay senseless.

Lizzie struggled to force the words through her lips. "I was the woman, sir. I have no idea who it was who raped me. Had I known, I would have reported it . . ."

Onslow looked taken aback, but it did not alter the anger in him. His face was red, his eyes bright and hard. "Then your accusation now is pointless, and too late, Mrs. Blaine." He stood up and walked around the table toward her, looking her up and down as though to see whether she was injured.

Joseph was trembling, the sweat hot and then cold on his skin.

"It has every point!" Lizzie's voice was choked with tears. "It happened more than a month ago, before Colonel Schenckendorff was anywhere near here. It could not possibly have been him."

It took a moment for the full import to strike Onslow. He froze. "You mean you have allowed us to accuse and imprison an innocent man while you said nothing?" he shouted at her.

"I . . . I hoped he would be proved innocent in some other way," she whispered. "I—"

"You hoped?" he demanded incredulously, his eyebrows arched high. "You hoped?" he repeated. "If you had spoken at the time we would have investigated then, when the trail was fresh. At the very least we would have known there was a rapist loose in the clearing station, and women would have taken the proper precautions for safety. Sarah Price would still be alive, and we would not have wasted weeks questioning and accusing and finally locking up the wrong man! Have you any concept of what you have—"

"Yes!" she cried out, tears running down her face. "Yes, of course I know. Why do you think I came to you now? But I don't know who it was—"

"You should have come—"

Joseph lunged forward and hit Onslow, hard, throwing all his weight behind the blow. The major staggered backward, crashing into the canvas, losing his balance and falling sideways onto the floor.

"Joseph! No!" Lizzie shouted, throwing herself at him and clinging to him so he could not strike again, and they both lurched to a standstill.

Onslow blinked and lay still for several seconds before raising himself onto an elbow. He drew in his breath and shook his head. Then very slowly he clambered to his feet, still half leaning against the wall.

Joseph was so angry that if Onslow had turned to Lizzie and spoken he would have hit him again, even though the realization was beginning to sink in that he had struck a superior officer and could find himself court-martialed—possibly even dishonorably discharged.

Onslow was staring at him. He might want to apologize, try to explain, but nothing could excuse what Onslow had done to Lizzie, and Joseph would not yield. He was a chaplain, not a career soldier, and Lizzie was more important to him than any calling. He stared back without wavering.

Lizzie, too, must have been desperate to think of something to say. She looked from one to the other, her face ashen.

Onslow straightened his tunic and brushed himself down. "I'm sorry, Mrs. Blaine," he said quietly. "I am quite sure you feel your omission more than sufficiently. I should not have mentioned it. I cannot imagine the suffering you have already endured, and the insensitivity of some people's remarks. I apologize that I added to them."

"You were right to blame me, sir," she said, her voice trembling. "I thought perhaps it might have been my own fault, that somehow I had unintentionally allowed someone to believe I held a regard for him that I didn't. We . . . we all tend to think that somehow we were stupid, careless . . . but I have no idea who it was. I've gone over and over it in my mind, and I don't know. It's too late now to say who was here then, I realize that. I was so ashamed . . . I wanted to pretend it hadn't happened. I'm sorry."

Joseph waited for Onslow to agree, but instead he turned to Joseph, his face already beginning to swell from the blow. "You should watch your temper, Chaplain. Not every senior officer may appreciate your remarkable service to the men here, or realize that to charge you with assault at such a time, when the morale of the whole unit is so fragile, would not be in the army's best interest. You are very fortunate that I do." He put his hand to his cheek and touched it gingerly. "If anyone inquires, I shall say that I fell. You would be wise to be quite unaware of the whole incident."

"Yes, sir." Joseph was suddenly embarrassed. Onslow was a better man than he had given him credit for—simply out of his depth with the subject of rape. And like most people, he disliked intensely having made a very public stand on an issue, and then being proved wrong. "Thank you," he added.

"Thank your record with the Cambridgeshires, Captain Reavley," Onslow replied. "You are loved by the men. I think if I were to charge you I would lose their support completely. I'm not fool enough for that."

There was a certain pain in his voice, a knowledge of having been a fool in other things. He stood awkwardly, beginning to realize that he had been hit very hard indeed. "Now I have to make certain that Schenckendorff is released from this accusation, and that everyone knows that he could not be guilty. I don't want him attacked—again."

He turned to Lizzie. "I regret that I shall have to tell them why, Mrs. Blaine, because if I do not, they may not believe me, and someone will take a private vengeance on him. I will not mention your name, but it is possible someone may guess. There is no alternative. I cannot allow the man to be murdered in an *accident*"—he emphasized the word—"because I am not believed."

"I understand," she said hoarsely. "That would be almost as bad as his being hanged. Thank you, sir."

Onslow nodded.

Joseph and Lizzie turned and went back out into the rain.

Later, Joseph walked alone around the old supply trench, remembering the men he had known who were gone, so many of them dead. He thought of them in the good times, the jokes, the sharing, the long stories about home, the letters, the dreams for the future. Had they loved him as much as Onslow thought? He had loved them, and watched them die. Had he been any help in this nightmare?

What help was he now to Lizzie, whom he loved? He thought he had learned to deal with death, even with mutilation, which was sometimes even harder. But there was an element in rape that was different, a violation not just of the body but of the inner core unique to a woman. If it had been somebody else, possibly even Judith, he would not feel so wounded within himself. There would not be the horror, the . . . he had been going to use the word *revulsion* in his mind. Part of him wanted to run away from all of it, the whole issue—even from Lizzie, as if she had been spoiled for him.

But she had done nothing wrong, and he knew that. She was a victim, brutalized by a violent man, randomly—unless there was something in her vitality, a moment's kindness misunderstood, possibly even something as stupid as a passing resemblance to someone else he knew, that had sparked his act? It could have been anything.

But even if she had allowed a moment's carelessness, or worse, she was still a victim. If he turned away from her because that man had touched her, known her, was it not totally selfish, nothing to do with anything but his own feelings, not love at all? He would make her a victim again, doubly so, by rejecting her as if she were unclean.

He knew with complete, sickening finality that to do so would not only devastate her, but also destroy the bedrock of the faith that had sustained him throughout the war. It had made endurable the endless boredom, the sudden blood-red agony, the nights in no-man's-land with men caught on the wires and torn apart by bullets, left hanging there, bleeding to death. He had sat cradling in his arms the broken bodies of those he had loved. He had seen them starving, freezing to death, drowned in mud, gagging and vomiting up their own lungs from poison gas, and he had not turned away, not said he could not bear it.

Was he now going to turn away from Lizzie because he wanted to spend the rest of his life with her, passionately, intimately, and he could not bear that she had been raped? If what had happened to her could kill his ability to love, then he had learned nothing, and there was no hope for any of the wounded, the damaged, the millions who would come home changed forever. And who was not damaged, in some way perhaps more hidden, more inward to the soul?

He must overcome it. To fail at this bitter test was to lose it all. He leaned against the trench wall, his clasped hands resting on the clay.

"Father, help me to do what I cannot do alone." In the silence of the wilderness and the miles of the dead, he asked again and again, until finally a kind of peace settled over him and a stillness blossomed inside, growing stronger than the pain.

"It doesn't happen without something starting him off," Matthew said a couple of hours later as he and Joseph sat on a pile of sandbags that had collapsed from an old parapet. It was one of the few places they could expect to be alone. Time was growing desperately short, not only to find the rapist before he struck again, but because the war news that poured in every day made it obvious that the armistice was no more than a couple of weeks away—perhaps not even that. If they were to unmask the Peacemaker in time to prevent his taking a primary part in the final negotiations, then they must begin the journey to the coast within a day or two.

Despite his resolve, Joseph's emotions were so raw, he was unsure how well he could control them. Subtlety was needed, not violence, even in words. A careless comment or accusation, an implied threat, could damage their investigation. He was sharply aware of it, but still he could feel the pain taking over inside him, and he was afraid it would slip out of his control.

Most likely to snap his frail mastery were the men he knew well but who were still lying to him, or to themselves, through old loyalties to those they had fought beside and whose most intimate griefs they knew, perhaps even shared.

He made an intense effort. He must make his mind dominate his emotions. Think! There were facts that remained unaltered by what Lizzie had told him. The only men who were not accounted for at the time Sarah had been killed were Cavan, Benbow, and Wil Sloan. Surely it must be Benbow. And yet the impossible did happen; people changed beyond imagination. Nothing could be assumed. It was not only illogical to do so, it was morally unjust.

"A man to whom something has happened that has changed his life," he said aloud.

"Or at least his pattern of behavior," Matthew replied. "The violence toward women has to have begun very recently, or he'd have been caught before."

"I suppose so," Joseph said slowly. "The change could come slowly, as it has for everyone, and perhaps the thought of going home has made him realize how deep it is."

Matthew looked puzzled.

"Take Judith, for example," Joseph tried to explain. "She isn't the only one, but can you imagine how an average man would feel faced with a wife like her?"

"I know she's my sister, but I always thought she was beautiful," Matthew replied. "And rather fun. Awkward—but you get used to that. Underneath it she's pretty decent, if you're being serious. And you are, aren't you?"

"Yes. Very. She's also bright and articulate, and she's got more courage than most men I know. She's a better driver, and can mend an engine with almost anything that comes to hand. She's steady under fire, can give first aid to the wounded or the dying. She'd probably shoot a man if she had to, and I can't imagine her fainting or having a fit of the vapors like our aunts and grandmothers."

"I know. We've all changed," Matthew agreed.

"Do you know it, really?" Joseph pressed. "I think I'm only beginning to see how much. Are we going to be able to deal with it with some courage and grace?"

Far over their heads a reconnaissance plane circled slowly and banked hard, swinging off to the east, looking like a dragonfly over an endless marsh of zigzag ditches in the mud. "It isn't that sudden, Joe," Matthew pointed out.

"He may not have had much chance until recently," Joseph reasoned. "If he were at the front line, and not injured, he wouldn't see anyone except the occasional ambulance driver. Maybe not even that."

"You mean this was his first opportunity?" Matthew asked. "Could be. Before then his violence was very properly turned toward the enemy." He winced.

Joseph knew what he was thinking, but there was no time now to dwell on the effect of war on young men. Certainly there was nothing they could do about it. "We have to find out what happened to someone that made his rage or sense of helplessness explode." His memory reached back over the distress he had seen even in the last few years, the letters men had received from home about the loss of other members of their family or close friends. The grief was hard and deep-scouring. But it was deceit that tore men apart, wounding irreparably: the sweetheart who could not or would not wait, the children they barely knew, the babies born whom they might never see. Worst by far were the wives who betrayed.

Matthew watched his brother's eyes squint narrowly in a sudden burst of sun, dazzling where it caught the water in a series of craters, rippled by the east wind till the light danced. "Don't you know, Chaplain, if you really think about it?" he asked quickly. "Who's been cheated and left by a woman he loved, and should have been able to trust? Who's been belittled or laughed at? Everyone's been changed by what they've seen out here, even more by what they've done. Nobody is going to go home the same as they were before. Who has a wife that can't accept that?"

Joseph thought of them, one after the other, hearing again in his mind the tight, quiet voices of men for whom the gulf had become too great, whose friends were now strangers to whom they could no longer explain themselves, no longer share the laughter or the pain of the things that lay deepest. Perhaps it was the ultimate price of war, the change to the living more than the loss of the dead.

"It's Dante again," he said aloud. "Rewarded not for what we do, but by it—and by what we see, and what we see others do?"

Matthew said nothing.

"The *Inferno*," Joseph explained unnecessarily, wondering if some of Dante's wasted landscape of hell might look a bit like this. Did the River Styx look like this slow-moving mud, filled with human remains from battles won and lost? That would symbolize despair very well. What about the forward lines now, all rage and noise, flame of gunfire and shattering destruction, the landscape of anger?

What about the uniquely human sins of corruption and betrayal? How would they look? Probably perfectly ordinary, like a smiling face, only the eyes would be empty.

"Everything we do changes us, becomes part of what we are," he said. "Do you think we'll ever get over this, Matthew? Will we recover and become human again, innocent enough to have hope, to value human life and believe in a God who loves us, one who has enough power to heal us, to affect anything that happens on earth? Or are we finally on the edge of the abyss, and falling?" The minute he had said it he wished he had not. It was selfish. Matthew was his younger brother, the one man above all others to whom he owed a better care than this, and some kind of protection from the darkness inside.

"Sorry," he said quickly. "I'll try to think who had bad news of some sort about a month ago. Whoever was closest to him will have noticed something. Trouble is, I'm the chaplain. If I know of it as a confidence, there's only a limited amount I can repeat." He pushed his hand over his forehead and back through his hair. "What a bloody mess."

Joseph sat in his bunker alone trying to remember every private and wounding grief he had heard some man stammer out to him, looking for any kind of comfort, any sense of justice in his pain. There were dozens of them. More often than not it wasn't the loss here—the friend crippled or killed—it was the betrayal of those at home, the wives or sweethearts who had grown tired of waiting. Would the women who had loved them accept what they had become, or would they be unable to cope with the memories? Would they even begin to understand the guilt of those who had survived when their friends had not?

Would the horror of killing an enemy soldier so much like a mirror image of yourself make any kind of sense? He was not there because he wanted to be, any more than you were. On a still night you could hear him talking with his friends, laughing, singing.

No wonder you could not sleep. It was easy to see the petty problems of home—a blocked drain, a disobedient child, a spilled jug of milk—as nothing at all. Life was what mattered. Friends, a whole body, someone to watch with you through the night.

Who had spoken of something bad enough to make him hate all women? He thought of the men betrayed or deserted and went through their names one by one, ticking off each as he remembered that they were dead, too badly injured, gone home already, or somewhere else far forward of here.

Turner was the first of those left who seemed possible. His wife had left him for Turner's own brother, who had escaped military service because of flat feet or something of the sort. Turner's rage had been almost uncontrollable. Joseph had thought it was against the war in general and the Germans in particular. But perhaps in time it had bent instead toward women.

And it seemed Culshaw was lying to protect him, again as one man did for his friend, perhaps not realizing there was anything more than a lapse of judgment and discipline.

"Of course he's bloody furious!" Culshaw had exploded. "His own brother! Flat feet or cross eyes or some damn thing! So he stays safe at home coining in the money on the black market while we're out here in the rats and the filth getting shot at. Sometimes I don't understand women at all. Have they got no honor, no sense of friendship, loyalty . . . anything?"

"Women are no more all alike than men are," Joseph had answered him. "Some men will sleep with anything that stays still long enough, and you know that as well as I do. Don't you think their wives feel just as used and betrayed?"

Culshaw had looked confused. "Are you saying it's the same, Chaplain?"

Joseph had sighed. "No," he said wearily. He was honest enough to admit that whatever reason or justice told him, it was not. His own reaction to Lizzie being raped forced him to acknowledge that reason had very little to do with the deepest passions, the intimacy of violation. "No, it's not the same, Culshaw. If a man is betrayed by a woman he loved, he doesn't forget it, and he doesn't heal easily. And if a woman is raped by a man, she doesn't forget that, either, or heal. Neither does any man who loved her. Have you considered that?"

Culshaw's face was very pale, the lines of exhaustion deep in his skin. "I never saw it like that."

"How did you see it?" Joseph had asked him.

Culshaw's eyes were wide. "He didn't do that!" he breathed out. "I swear! Jesus, do you think I'd have covered for him if he had? He skewered that German officer's foot, and he'd have beaten the hell out of any of the other prisoners, if we'd let him, but he never touched Sarah Price. You have to believe me!"

"I don't have to," Joseph told him, disgust filling his mind at the senseless violence toward men already beaten by violence and shame.

"But it's the truth!" Culshaw protested desperately.

"Yes," Joseph conceded. "I daresay it is."

Judith was thinking of the same things, but she at least faced the practical questions she had been wishing she could avoid. Material proof would have been so much easier, less viciously painful, but perhaps in the end it was always going to have come to this. She could not expect Joseph to do it, or Matthew, for that matter.

Now it could wait no longer. She told Wil she would be gone for a while but gave him no other explanation.

She found Lizzie helping Allie Robinson. They were preparing some of the more seriously wounded for evacuation. There was an almost euphoric sense of release now that the station was open again at least in part; and men could leave. It was as if a long paralysis were ended.

"Lizzie, I need to speak to you," she said quietly. "Sorry, but it's urgent."

Allie looked at her sharply. "When this is finished, Miss Reavley," she said with a certain coolness. There was a warning in her eyes and her manner. Judith was overstepping her authority.

"It's urgent," Judith repeated. "I'm sorry, but there's no time to wait."

Allie stiffened. "If you have wounded, Miss Reavley, then you need either an orderly to help you or a doctor. You do not need Mrs. Blaine, who is already occupied here."

Judith's emotions were raw with loathing of what she had to do. She felt guilty because of the pain she knew she was going to cause, and afraid Lizzie would hate her for it. Allie was a nuisance she had not foreseen, and the irritation of it scraped her raw, but if she lost her temper it would only make it all the more difficult, especially for Lizzie.

"I don't have wounded," she replied as civilly as she could, but her voice had an edge to it and she could hear it herself.

"I thought not." Allie smiled bleakly. "Then you will have to wait."

Judith took a deep breath and let it out slowly. "It can't wait, Allie. It's important."

Allie's eyebrows rose. "To whom, Miss Reavley? To you?" The use of her name was a rebuke, and her face had no warmth in it, no possibility of yielding.

"It's not your concern, Miss Robinson, but if you force the issue, then it is important to Major Onslow of the military police. It is a matter of information that obviously I cannot discuss." It was no more than half a lie.

Anger flared in Allie's eyes. "Then why did you not say so in the first place?" she asked angrily. "Just because you drive an ambulance around like a man does not give you the right to come in here giving orders. You forget yourself. You are going to find it extremely difficult after the war when you're not needed anymore. You would be wise to learn how to behave like a woman again. You're in danger of becoming a complete misfit, unwanted by men and an embarrassment to women."

Judith was stunned. The fury in Allie's manner had taken her completely by surprise. Was it her own fear speaking? Surely not. There were going to be years of skilled nursing ahead; peace would not affect that.

"Well, if it's so urgent, get on with it!" Allie snapped. "Experience your authority. You won't have it much longer."

Judith bit back her retaliation and turned to Lizzie. They went out together, Lizzie looking anxious and unhappy.

As soon as they were beyond the Evacuation tent and in the open, the day bright and cold with frost in the wind, Lizzie spoke again.

"Does Major Onslow really want to see me?"

"No," Judith said quickly. "I do. But in a way it's half true. Not here, however; your bunker or mine."

"Mine's closer. What is it?"

"I'm sorry," Judith said fiercely. "I really am. I wouldn't do this if there were any other way."

Lizzie walked in silence. It was a bad beginning. She was already afraid. They reached the bunker and went down the steps inside. It smelled of damp earth and enclosed space. The wooden slats on the floor were rotting but still better than the bare mud.

"What is it?" Lizzie demanded again. "Do they know something?" She did not sit down but remained standing, facing Judith in the gloom.

Judith could understand very easily how Lizzie might rather not know who had raped her, whose child she was carrying. Anonymity kept it one step further away. She wished with passion that she could leave it that way, or at least leave the choice to Lizzie.

"I'm sorry," she said again. "I am! They don't know, and all we can work out is that it had to be Cavan, Wil Sloan, or Benbow."

"How?" Lizzie's face was not clear in the faint light inside the bunker, but even in the shadows her disbelief was obvious. "It could have been anyone! I have no idea."

"It couldn't have been just anyone who killed Sarah. Everybody else is ruled out." It was brutal, but Lizzie had to know it was true. She had said so herself, to Onslow.

Lizzie sat down slowly on the bunk. Now she seemed unbearably tired, as if the strength inside her was used up. "I don't know," she said again. "I'd hate to think it was Cavan, or Wil Sloan, but I can't say it was Benbow because I don't know! It might not have been." She stared at Judith. "When it comes to it, even the people we like can have terrible secrets that we have no idea of. I'm not going to say it was Benbow just because Cavan and Wil are your friends. I'm sorry."

Judith was momentarily stunned. It was the last thing she had considered, at least consciously, but she could see how easily Lizzie must have thought of it.

"I don't want you to! That isn't what I meant at all. Of course I don't want it to be them, but if it is, then we must face it."

"What do you want?"

Now was the moment. "Onslow didn't ask you to go through it for him in detail, did he?"

"No!"

"Joseph wouldn't, or Matthew." That was really a statement rather than a question. She knew the answer.

"No." Lizzie's voice was quiet, but there was dread in it.

"Somebody must," Judith said as gently as she could. "You might remember something . . ."

"I don't! I don't know who it was! Just a man . . . a soldier. Judith, if I knew, don't you think I'd tell you?"

"Yes, of course you would. Just tell me anything. What time was it, roughly?"

"Sometime between midnight and three. I can't remember now. We were busy."

"What were you doing before it happened? Where were you?"

Lizzie hesitated. "In the Resuscitation tent. We'd just finished a bad one. We lost him."

"Who did the operation?"

"Cavan, Bream, Moira Jessop."

Judith felt cold. "Then what?"

"We had the body taken away. Joseph wasn't here, he was up in the lines. I don't know where everybody went. I felt dreadful. We'd fought really hard. Thought he was going to make it. He was . . . about seventeen." Her voice caught, and she struggled to keep control of it. "I went outside. I wanted to be alone and not have to look at anybody else's face. I . . ." She stopped, then started again. "I was standing outside in the dark, somewhere beyond the Evacuation tent, when I realized there was someone near me."

"How?" Judith interrupted. "How did you realize it? Did you see him?"

"No." Lizzie thought for a moment. "I heard his feet squelch in the mud. It wasn't so bad then, but it had rained earlier and there were a few places that never seem to get dry."

"Did he speak? Did you hear him breathing?"

"No, I don't think so. Does it matter now? I can't tell one person's breathing from another." Lizzie's voice was strained, tight in her throat as memory brought it back to her.

"It might," Judith insisted. "Then what? Were you frightened?"

"No, of course I wasn't! I didn't think there was anything to be frightened of. Then the next thing I knew he'd caught hold of me from behind, and . . . and twisted me around to face him. But before you ask, we were in shadow and it was cloudy. I didn't see his face at all. That's the truth."

"How tall was he?" Judith asked.

"What?"

"How tall was he?" she repeated. "A lot taller than you? A little?"

Lizzie shut her eyes. "It doesn't matter, Judith. Cavan, Wil, and Benbow are all much the same height, within an inch or two. They're all half a foot taller than I am."

"I know. But he kissed you?"

"Yes! I told you!" Lizzie's voice was ragged, her control slipping.

Judith felt brutal, but she did not stop. "Where were his hands?"

"Hands? I don't know! I . . ."

"Yes? What? Why didn't you twist away?"

"He held my face—"

"Smell," Judith said instantly. "What did his hands smell of?"

Lizzie froze, her eyes wide.

"Ether? Disinfectant? Blood?" Judith demanded.

"No . . . no, smoke, like cigarettes," Lizzie replied. "And oil?"

"What kind of oil?" Judith's voice was shaking now, too. "Think! Was it petrol, metallic oil, butter? What? Bring it back, exactly?"

"It wasn't Cavan, was it," Lizzie said with certainty. "He couldn't have gotten rid of the ether and disinfectant. Engine oil from Wil, gun oil from Benbow."

"Yes. What was it?"

The silence was intense, as if the clay walls behind the wood shoring them up was somehow absorbing the sound, even their breath.

"I'm not sure. Bitter," Lizzie said at last. "I couldn't smell petrol, just tobacco, cigarette smoke, and a tiny bit of metallic oil."

"No . . . he . . ." Lizzie stopped with a gasp.

"What? What?"

"I heard him put it down . . . ," Lizzie said with slow, gasping amazement. "I remember . . . I heard him put it down. It unbalanced and fell against the duckboards. It was Benbow! It had to have been! Wil and Cavan don't have guns. And his tunic was rough, khaki. Cavan was still in his white coat." She swallowed convulsively. "Why didn't I know that before?"

"You didn't want to remember it. Who would?" Judith said simply. "I'm sorry . . ."

Lizzie shook her head. "No. Don't be. What should I do? I suppose I have to tell Onslow?" Her fear was palpable in the closed room, even in the semi-darkness.

"Not yet," Judith replied. "I'll tell Joseph first." She heard Lizzie's sharp drawing in of breath, and understood. "He has to know sometime. Get it over. I'll do it. At least you won't be afraid of everyone now. But don't be alone . . . promise?"

Lizzie gave a very slight smile. "I promise."

"Come on then. Now! Come with me back to Allie. She's a pretty good bitch at times, but at least you know where you stand with her."

"Benbow? Are you sure?" Matthew asked.

Joseph repeated the essence of what Judith had told him. He tried to keep his emotion out of it, think of it as a string of facts, imprison his imagination so none of it was real.

"Sounds pretty solid," Matthew said gravely. "I'm glad it wasn't Cavan or Wil Sloan. I'm sorry, Joe. Do you want to face him, or would you rather not?"

"We'll have to go to Onslow anyway," Joseph pointed out. "I hit him. I should do that."

Matthew frowned. "Are you sure?"

"Yes. Come on, if I don't do that I'm going to fall long before the last fence." Joseph made himself smile. He was the eldest. He was the one who loved Lizzie. It was his responsibility. "I'll go now."

But it proved far harder than he had anticipated. Onslow accepted the evidence without argument, but when he had Benbow brought in it was a very different matter. He looked haggard, ashen-faced, and, standing feet away, Joseph could smell the fear in him.

"I didn't kill Sarah Price!" he protested, struggling uselessly against the manacles that held his hands tight behind his back. "I didn't, I swear to God! I never touched her!" He wrenched himself around to face Joseph. "Chaplain, I swear! All right, Moira Jessop played me around rotten, an' I took her, all right, an' I weren't none too gentle, fought like a wildcat, but that was a month ago, more. I never touched Sarah Price. Jesus! What do you think I am? She was sliced to bits!"

"You raped Moira Jessop?" Onslow said incredulously. He stared from Benbow to Joseph, and back again.

"Where?" Joseph demanded. "Exactly where? What time?"

Benbow looked stunned. "Out . . . outside the Evacuation tent," he stammered.

"Were you carrying a rifle?" Joseph asked.

"I never hurt her!" Benbow shouted. "I swear . . ."

"Did you drop it?"

"Yes! I don't know. I must 'ave. Why? I never used any kind of knife on 'er. I never even hit 'er. I just . . ." His face was gray, his eyes wild. "I didn't! She led me on, played . . . Oh God!"

"Did she see your face?" Onslow asked.

"She couldn't 'ave. It was dark," Benbow responded. "Could hardly see where you were going."

Onslow looked across at Joseph.

"How do you know it was Moira Jessop?" Joseph asked Benbow.

"I . . . I followed 'er out of the . . ." Suddenly Benbow surged and gulped air.

"It wasn't," Joseph said quietly. "You forced yourself on another woman, one who had never given you the slightest indication that she had any interest in you at all."

Benbow stood silently, blinking as if blinded.

"And Sarah Price?" Onslow asked again.

"I never touched 'er. I swear to God," Benbow replied hoarsely.

Joseph nodded slowly. There was no proof. He was not sure whether to believe it or not, but it was possible that the man who had raped Lizzie and the man who had murdered Sarah were not the same person.

Onslow looked profoundly unhappy. "That will be for a jury to decide," he said grimly. "Take him away."

After Benbow had been removed, Onslow faced Joseph. "I'm sorry," he emphasized. "Perhaps Mrs. Blaine will find some kind of relief, however small, in the knowledge that she was not the intended victim. I hope so."

"Do you think it is possible that he didn't kill Sarah Price?" Joseph said slowly, trying to work his way through the maze of facts, contradiction, and anger.

"Frankly, I have no idea," Onslow admitted. "If I had to stake anything on it, I think it is possible, yes."

"It has to be Benbow!" Matthew said savagely, staring at Joseph in disbelief. "You can't think we have two rapists loose here?"

"I don't know what I think," Joseph admitted. They were walking slowly along the rotting duckboards of the old supply trench, heading back to the bunkers.

"Did Benbow have blood on him?" Matthew asked. "Eames must have noticed."

Joseph bit his lip. "He was pretty wet and he had mud on his boots up to his knees. He says he slipped in one of the shallow craters. That could be true."

Matthew swore. "And I suppose Cavan was covered in blood from operating, and Wil Sloan from carrying in the wounded?"

"They would be," Joseph agreed.

They discussed it further, achieving nothing. Finally Joseph left and walked on past the bunkers toward the Admissions tent. The wind from the east was rising, and in the gathering dusk the clear sky promised a frost. The colors were fragile and muted, even over the ruined landscape to the west, where the dying light was a faint lilac-pink after the sun slipped below the horizon. The gunfire was too far away to hear except as a distant rumble.

They had to solve this obscene crime. It could not be allowed to slip into oblivion because the war was ending and bit by bit the weary, soul-bruised men would be allowed to go home to whatever love and passion and change awaited them.

Then a thought occurred to Joseph, so ridiculous he dismissed it. It must be Benbow, despite the lack of blood on him. Apart from anything else, he was carrying a rifle and bayonet. Every man on guard duty did. Neither Cavan nor Wil Sloan had such a weapon. Cavan could have a scalpel. But he still refused to believe that Cavan could be guilty. No evidence short of an eyewitness would make him accept that the man he knew had descended from the selfless courage of a year ago, unnoticed by anyone, into the pit of madness where he would rape a woman he knew and had worked beside, even cared for, not with his body but with the raw blade of a bayonet!

It would be like walking side by side with a friend and turning to discover a creature beside you who had the devil's soul looking out of his eyes.

But Cavan could not account for his time. Allie Robinson had lied to protect him, and he had allowed her to until Judith had caught him in it. He had said he had been in the Evacuation tent, but he hadn't.

Joseph was sick with misery, as if the evidence were closing in around him like an enemy in the dark. Any hour now it might strike the blow that could not be defended against, the proof that could not be denied. There was no point in asking Cavan himself, and he could keep Allie Robinson until last when she could no longer lie.

He began with Erica Barton-Jones. He found her with Stan Tidyman. The soldier was still gray-faced, his eyes hollow, but he was wrapped up with a pillow and a blanket rolled tight to support him. He managed a faint smile.

Joseph asked after him briefly, then took Erica to one side, over in the corner of the tent beside a table piled with old blankets, bandages, and other stores. They could hear the rain drumming on the canvas.

"The night Sarah was killed," he said without preamble. "Tell me what you can remember of where everyone was, just what you are certain of. From about midnight onward."

"It was a bad night," she said grimly. "I can't tell you times, only where I was."

"How many surgeons on duty?"

"Two—Captain Cavan and Captain Ellsworth—and there were anesthetists and orderlies, of course."

He did not tell her that he knew this already, or that all but Cavan were accounted for. "Tell me what you recall," he said.

She repeated what she had said from the beginning, every case, what was done and an estimate of the time. He stopped her, questioned, made her repeat and be as precise as possible, everything checked against what others had said.

"What is it you expect, Chaplain?" she demanded exasperatedly. "Going over and over it isn't going to help. I don't know who killed Sarah, or what snapped in somebody's head, or why it was her and not somebody else. Except that she was the one who flirted, but she certainly wasn't the only one who fell in love or had normal human feelings." Her face pinched, and she turned half away from him. "If you are looking for some unique sin in her that's going to make you feel there's any kind of justice in this, then you aren't going to find it. And quite frankly I think you are morally dishonest to try. There isn't any justice, and nobody with any . . . any courage . . . is going to believe there is."

He was startled. He had not even considered such a thing. "If life were always just, then there would be no courage necessary," he pointed out. "If being good automatically made you safe, then it wouldn't even be good, it would just be sensible: buying safety, buying your way out of pain or fail-ure, confusion, everything that hurts. Is that what you thought—that I was looking for sense in it?"

She stared at him, her face pale and tired in the half-light. "Aren't you? Aren't you longing to explain God so we won't stop believing in Him?"

"No. I gave that up years ago, even before the war, let alone since." He thought first for an instant how he had felt after Eleanor's death, the anger and confusion, the long retreat from emotion into the religion of the brain. That was over now, a kind of little death from which he had been awoken. "No," he said again. "I'm still looking for whoever killed Sarah because they have to be stopped. I'm not sure it's even anything to do with justice for her, or for them. It's a very practical matter of them being prevented from doing it again."

She blinked. "Sometimes I think you are so pointless, so divorced from the realities of life, well-meaning but essentially futile." She gave a sigh. "Then you come out with something that makes me feel that perhaps you are the only one who really is dealing with the truth, bigger than the little bits of reality we manage."

"Sometimes," he said with a slight smile.

She smiled back at him. "I still don't know who did it."

"Do you know if Cavan was in the Evacuation tent when he said he was?"

"No, I don't."

"Allie Robinson said he was, but she was lying, to cover for him," he told her.

"That was stupid," she said drily. "She can't have been there herself. I saw her at about four o'clock, or shortly after, and she'd been in the Admissions tent for some time."

"No, she was in Evacuation," he corrected her. "She was seen there by Benbow, and Eames as well."

She shook her head. "I saw her, and she was covered in blood. She must have been in Admissions. She was perfectly clean apart from a few spots on her skirt at about half past three, and by the time any of the wounded get to Evacuation they're bandaged and fit to go, or they wouldn't be there. You only get soaked in blood like that either in Admissions or in lying wounded, waiting for operations." Then suddenly her eyes widened and she stared at him, aghast.

He could not believe it. It was hideous, terrible, but he knew exactly what she was thinking. The images raced through his mind also, increasing, growing clearer and more real. The hatred was there, the sense of morality, and the belief that the meaning of life was falling apart. It was not only in violence and death on every side, but then finally at the core, the very fount of creation, the reason that redeemed all else and gave hope for newness, cleanness in the world again.

Men were dead or damaged everywhere, the flower of a generation. No one could count the number of women who would live alone, and childless. A new, harsher order had taken over, and it was terrifying. Women, the keepers of sanity, had themselves cast it aside. There was a way in which that was the ultimate betrayal, the end of hope itself.

That was why the bayonet had been used—woman punishing the suicide of womanhood. How had he not even guessed at it? Sarah's playing with Cavan and then flirting with the German prisoners was the final, unbearable offense, committed while British men were only yards away, bleeding to an agonizing death, awake and hideously aware of all of it.

Erica was still staring at him, but there was no struggle left in her eyes. She knew it was true. "I'm sorry," she said gravely. "I didn't see it, either, and I should have. I was so sure it was a man. I thought it was Benbow. I saw certain . . . certain things he did, a way he looked at some of the women, especially Moira Jessop. That isn't evidence, and I misjudged him. I even thought of warning her not to tease him. I would have wronged him, wouldn't I?" She gave a bleak grimace of self-criticism.

Joseph did not answer. It was all past, and it would not help. He needed to find Onslow, and Jacobson, too. Jacobson deserved to know. They would have to arrest Allie Robinson and release all the rest of the men kept here, sending the wounded home and the few able-bodied back to the fighting. The station itself would be moved forward to where it was still needed.

"A woman?" Onslow said slowly, as if the very word were a new concept to him, let alone the idea.

Patiently, allowing the horror to fill his words, Joseph explained to him the passion of betrayal that he believed Allie had seen: the ultimate obscenity of a woman like Sarah threatening to defile the very source of life, of nurture, of every hope to make everything clean and new.

"If there is no home to go back to, no one to love, to forgive and to start again, what was the pain all for?" he finished.

"Can we prove it?" Onslow asked, his voice hushed.

"Not easily, but I think so," Joseph answered. "We must certainly try."

Onslow wiped his hand over his brow. "Come on, then. We'd better go and find her." His hand went automatically to the revolver at his belt, reassuring himself that it was there.

Joseph did not tell him that it was unnecessary. He did not know.

Allie Robinson was in the Operating tent. Cavan was busy suturing a lacerated foot. He barely looked up.

Allie saw Joseph's face, and Onslow just behind him. She stiffened, her eyes wide.

Onslow walked forward slowly, moving a little toward the operating table so he cut her off from it, placing himself between her and the soldier whose foot was being stitched.

She saw the finality in his expression. She stepped back, closer to the table with the instruments on it, scalpel, forceps, needles, clamps.

"Don't do that," Onslow said quietly. "It's all over, Miss Robinson. Don't make it worse."

"Worse?" she said, as if he had asked her a question. "What could be worse? We've destroyed everything. What we haven't killed or maimed, we've defiled beyond help. There isn't anything left to win or lose. Our civilization is dead. Nothing is clean or modest or gentle as it used to be. It's all strident, dirty. We've forgotten who we are, and when you do that, there's nothing worth having at all. It's all dirt and blood." She took another step back.

"Miss Robinson!" Onslow said loudly, his voice high with alarm.

But it was too late. She swung around and grasped the scalpel, looked at him for an instant, then plunged it into her chest. She was a good nurse; she had seen lots of men torn open by shrapnel. She knew exactly where to strike. The blood gushed out scarlet. She crumpled to the floor and did not move again.

The soldier on the table fainted.

Cavan went as white as his coat and gagged, holding his hands over his mouth, the needle dangling by its thread.

Onslow sighed. "I'm so sorry," he said quietly. "I should have stopped that. Not that it would have helped, really."

Joseph bent and straightened her out, removing the scalpel. The blood was still pouring, but it would stop soon. She was already dead. He felt sad and helpless.

"Poor creature," he said quietly. "And it won't change anything. We'll still have to find a way to heal."

$\mathcal{N}$ ow they must race for the coast. There were only days to get Schenckendorff to London. Judith and Lizzie were volunteers, and could leave without difficulty. Mason could do as he chose. Matthew was due to return to London. Only Joseph was regular army, and for him to leave would be desertion.

"You have to," Matthew said simply.

"I'll tell Colonel Hook—" Joseph began.

"You can't!" Matthew's expression left no room for argument or negotiation. "We're this close, Joseph." He held up his hand, fingers and thumb half an inch apart. "The Peacemaker has eyes and ears everywhere. Hook has the power to stop us all. We can't take the chance."

"Colonel Hook!" Joseph was incredulous. They were all crammed into his bunker, which was so narrow they could not sit without touching one another. Only Schenckendorff was missing. Joseph looked at Mason, having to twist around to do it.

Mason's face was bleak. "Anyone," he said simply. "I don't know who else believes the Peacemaker, or I'd tell you. We have to just leave. Fill cans with as much petrol as we can get hold of, as much food, and go. We could still lose it all."

Joseph gave in. It was legally desertion, and it felt like it: no goodbyes, no explanation. But it was his men he cared about, and if Hook explained to them, news of it could reach the Peacemaker in hours.

He sighed and nodded.

Matthew resumed making plans.

* * *

Judith wanted to say goodbye to many people, particularly Cavan and, above all, Wil Sloan, but she, too, was aware of the danger. However she did it, or whatever she said, someone would notice and say something. Word would be passed around before they were more than a few miles away. For her, as for Joseph, any risk, however small, was too much. No one else could know how ruthless the Peacemaker was, or how far his knowledge and his alliances had spread.

So she said nothing and felt disloyal as, shivering in the dark, she drove the ambulance out of the Casualty Clearing Station onto the mud track to pick Joseph and Matthew up. They were supporting Schenckendorff between them, as he was still unable to put his weight on his injured foot. A few yards farther on they were joined by Lizzie and Mason, climbing in the back of the ambulance hastily and closing the doors as Judith accelerated and made for the road.

Mason came forward and sat beside her. He alone was of no immediate use in the back, where Lizzie was swallowing her occasional morning nausea and attending to Schenckendorff's injured foot. Joseph and Matthew were talking quietly about a route back through Belgium, and then across the channel. Time was short. It was already the third of November; a cease-fire could be declared within days. Matthew had a little money, but where to find further supplies was a far greater problem than paying for them. Food and petrol were too scarce to be had simply for the right price.

Judith drove steadily, with concentration. She worried not only about fuel but also about spare parts if they should have any sort of breakdown, not to mention accident. The ambulance was on its last legs anyway. Once away from the army lines with their supply stores, there would be nowhere to get oil or any of the parts she might need. She had had no compunction about taking with her all that she could, begging, borrowing, or removing without the owner's consent three new spark plugs. Had she been able to explain the urgency, she was quite sure they would have been given willingly.

Now they drove through the fine, dry night. The air became increasingly cold in the open front of the vehicle, and the wind from the north swirled around, creeping between folds of coats and scarves, numbing hands and whipping the blood in cheeks and brows.

Mason was used to it. He had spent the last four years in every kind of vehicle, on every battlefront from the deserts of Arabia to the arctic snows of Russia. As he sat here now moving along the ruined roads of

Belgium on the last journey of his own battle, he had a smile on his face and seemed almost relaxed.

Judith looked sideways at him once or twice and saw the change in him. She was almost frighteningly happy to think that it was his feeling for her that had caused it. She wanted it to be so much that she could neither believe nor disbelieve it. And she felt guilty, because it would cost him a high and terrible price. In exposing the Peacemaker he would be confessing to his own part in the treason. Only now was she realizing the meaning of that. There was peace ahead, and justice that would finally call Dermot Sandwell to account for the betrayal of his countrymen and the murders of all those who had stood in his way.

And there was honor for Matthew and for Schenckendorff. Perhaps for Mason there would be at least the acceptance of a faith in life that he had denied before, even fought against. But there would be no future for him with Judith. The only future he could await was execution. That thought hurt her with a finality she had not expected.

She stared into the darkness ahead. The road was nearly dry. At the sides were occasional poplars. Many of them were little more than stumps, but now and then a few had branches, leafless like broken bones. Clear patches in the sky let the moonlight gleam fitfully, showing a landscape of craters and stretches of mud, and now and then the jagged walls of a bombed-out building. They passed a canal, its walls breached, the flooded water flat and pale and irregularly shaped as it seeped away into the fields, sometimes lapping right up to the raised edges of the road.

She would not have changed Mason or had him sink back into the cynicism of before. She remembered their quarrel at the court-martial, the sense of futility that seemed to touch all his thoughts. It was not simply that he believed Joseph's efforts were pointless, but that he found them foolish, in a way even contemptible because they were rooted in a refusal to face reality. He had thought both she and Joseph were cowards, clinging to faith in a God who did not exist because they lacked the courage to live alone in the universe.

Why had he changed? Yes, he was in love with her. But so was she in love with him. No matter how much you loved someone, you could not alter who you were in order to be comfortable with them. If you loved the right person it should make you stronger, braver, gentler, perhaps eventually wiser. It should never make you deny your intelligence or forsake your integrity. What were you worth if you would do that?

She looked sideways at him again, trying to read his face in the few moments she could spare from watching the road. His eyes were wide and dark, staring ahead of him, and there was a deep sadness in the curve of his mouth.

He must have been aware of her—because he turned and smiled.

"It isn't for me, is it, that you're doing this?" She asked it with something close to certainty, willing it to be so.

"No," he said without hesitation. "Because of you, perhaps, you and Joseph, but because I have to to satisfy myself."

She felt something of the fear ease out of her, the knots loosen.

"Were you afraid it was for you?" he asked, and this time there was amusement in his voice. "That then you would owe me something?" He did not add that you cannot owe love; she knew he was thinking it, just as she was. She felt the heat in her face and was glad of the concealing darkness. There was only the occasional yellow glare of lamps as they passed some lone farmhouse still standing, or a group of people stopped temporarily and huddled around a fire, now and again car lights going the other way.

Perhaps at last they understood each other in the deepest things; the values that are woven into nature, the need to be at peace with who you are, together or alone.

As if the emotion were too strong, and the time too short, he moved away from it. "I know you've dressed Schenckendorff as a British V.A.D., but you'd better not let him speak. He still sounds German to me. I'll wager any Belgian in the country knows German when he hears it. They have five years' hate to avenge. They aren't going to forget it. Does Joseph really think they will?"

"No," she said simply. "Have you got a better idea?"

"No, I haven't. But we'd better be right. We're going to have to stop for fuel sometime. We won't make it all the way to the coast on what we have. One mistake will be the last."

"I know." It was what she had been dreading. Even the basic difficulty of finding fuel could be enough to delay their journey fatally, let alone if any part of the ambulance broke down and she could not find the parts to mend it, or had not the skill. Even any prolonged time in one place brought the danger of exposure. The very best they might be taken for was British deserters. Once anyone realized Schenckendorff was German, they might all be suspected.

"Judith?" Mason said quietly, his voice breaking through her thoughts.

"Yes?"

"We'll make it." He was smiling. "You, of all people, are not going to fall at the last fence."

"Why not? It can happen."

"There are three of you!" His smile was broader now, a kind of happiness in him.

"There are six of us," she corrected him, slightly puzzled.

"Three Reavleys! That should be enough to take on the world, let alone the odd corner of Belgium," he retorted.

She glanced at him and saw the laughter under the surface, and also the tenderness in his face, even in the pale, shifting reflections of light from the road. He was not mocking her; he wanted to mean it, wanted to hope.

The first stop came after about five hours. They were in flat country, farther from the fighting, but this land had been occupied by enemy troops, and the roads had been heavily bombed. One small river had spread wide, flooding the area behind the broken bridge and the scattered debris that had blocked it. There was nothing to do but go around the water-logged fields, which took them extra miles and cost precious time and petrol. That meant they now needed to get more fuel. They dare not run too low.

They stopped at the next village, and Judith made the request from a mechanic attempting to mend a battered van. She was in uniform and felt consumed with guilt when the few cans were given willingly. They had assumed that her passengers were wounded men being taken to the nearest port for passage to England. One man asked her if the railway line had been bombed—was that why they had come this way? He looked surprised that this sort of difficulty should crop up so late in the war.

"By zeppelin still?" he said questioningly. "Stupid! They'll lose now whatever they do. It's nearly over." His voice choked. He was elderly with a heavy, ugly face and gentle eyes.

"Very nearly," she agreed. She wanted to tell him the truth—he did not deserve any more lies—but she dared not. "No more bombs that I know of," she equivocated. "Just too many people, thousands of them everywhere. It's all clogged up, and we need to be quick."

"Badly wounded?" he asked sympathetically.

That lie might catch up with them. "Some wounded," she said, praying he would believe her. "Some pretty urgent dispatches. Kill two birds with one stone." Then suddenly she wondered if he was familiar with the phrase, or might wildly misunderstand her. "Two jobs in one," she explained.

He smiled, bringing sudden light to his heavy features. "I know. We say much the same. Good luck."

More broken bridges drove them farther north, where the Belgians had opened the dikes and let the sea fight the invader where they could not. The armies marching in had found a different kind of ruin, one they could hardly equal.

A gray dawn saw them creeping forward through shattered villages. The houses were gutted by fire and bomb blast, some little more than mounds of rubble scarred black, perhaps a chimney breast still standing, or here and there a door frame. The fields around them were barren, the men who would have worked them dead or too mutilated to labor anymore. The bones of animals shone pale, picked clean by scavengers.

They saw a group of buildings half in ruins. It had once been a thriving farm with barn, cow byre, pigsties, and henhouses.

They stopped and asked for breakfast, willing to pay for it.

An old woman came out of what was left of her house. She saw the two women in V.A.D. uniform and recognized it immediately, her gaunt, sagging face lightening.

"What you need?" she said in thickly accented English.

Judith smiled at her. She could see from her worn, broken-nailed hands, and the pallor of her skin under the weathering, that she had almost nothing, and yet for British soldiers she was willing to part with it.

"Water so we can make some tea," Judith replied. "And if you have bread of any kind." She was suddenly uncertain whether an offer of payment would be welcome or considered an insult.

The woman was waiting, as if she expected to be asked for more.

Joseph came up beside her. "We have a little jam," he said to the woman. "Army ration, not very good, but we would be happy if you would share it with us. Tea, bread, and jam. It could be worse."

"Yes, yes, yes!" the woman said happily, nodding. "Bread is not much good, either, but with jam, will be fine. Yes, yes."

"Thank you," Judith murmured to Joseph as the woman hurried off to fetch what bread she had.

"I liberated a few tins," he said. "With Barshey's help."

"You didn't tell him—"

"Just told him I needed it. He didn't ask why. Got me a couple of tins of Maconachie's as well. Won't last long, but it's something."

"You pinched army stores!" She rolled her eyes. "There's hope for you yet!"

He did not answer, and suddenly she wondered if she had hurt him. It was something she would have said before the war, before she knew him so very well, understanding what he did and why, knowing the hurt he did not show, the pity he knew better than to display because it did not help. She had always admired him but found him distant and a little intimidating. He was the eldest, she the youngest. He conformed, she rebelled. Except that was far too facile a judgment. He also rebelled, in his own way. Hannah was the only one who really conformed. And yet she was going to find the changes of war the hardest of all, because the old ways that she had loved and that had been natural to her were gone forever.

No one could conform now, or be comfortable: There was no standard left with which to conform.

"I'm sorry," she said aloud. She did not know how to retreat without making it worse.

He smiled at her. There was warmth in it, even amusement. "It's all right. You can't think of everything."

"What?" she was confused.

"Jam," he replied, laughing at her. "You liberated the petrol and the spark plugs—ever practical. I have the jam." And he turned and walked back to the ambulance. There was a very slight swagger in his step.

The meal was anything but easy. They ate in the farmhouse kitchen. It was the one room in the house the woman had taken the care and labor to repair. She had even found odd tiles from somewhere to replace the shattered ones in the floor. There was hot water, clean from the well in the yard, and it made the tea impossibly fragrant after the sour water they were used to. But the bread was coarse and nearly black, and without butter. It needed Joseph's tin of army jam to make it palatable at all. It did not go far among seven of them. Even so they saved the hardest and driest of the crusts for the scrawny dog that lay on the tiles watching them, eyes following every mouthful.

They all knew the story they had to tell. Mason was better being himself. It was always possible that his face might even be recognized. His reports were famous all over the world, occasionally with a picture of him at the top of his column in most of the newspapers. Matthew and Joseph were in uniform; Joseph in particular needed no explanation. Judith and Lizzie similarly—their purpose was universal. Schenckendorff was the difficulty. Matthew had found a V.A.D. uniform that fit him and simply taken it; to request it would have needed explaining, which would in turn have raised further questions he could not answer. But despite his injured foot, Schenckendorff's posture was that of an officer. He was born and bred to it, and he did not know how to abandon it in a few days. His accent was slight, but it was distinctive.

Far more than that, as Judith sat at the old wooden table eating the black bread and smelling the pure scent of the tea, she was aware of the dismay in him, perhaps even the guilt. There had once been men in this house. The evidence of them was still here in the carefully carved, slightly irregular wooden bowls on the dresser, which was itself handmade to fit exactly into the space available for it. There was a low nursing chair in the other corner, as a mother might use holding a baby when she had other children at her knees. There was a handmade wooden engine on one of the shelves. No doubt there were other artifacts outside where once men had milked cows, dug the earth, harvested.

She saw Schenckendorff's eyes take it all in as hers had, and the grief in his face. He was eating more and more slowly, as if to accept this gift of hospitality choked him. Was it pity, or the guilt of having deceived the farm woman? She would never have given it to him if she had known he was German. Still, Joseph had said often that Germany was every bit as devastated as Belgium or France. That had been true when he had gone through the lines last year. How much worse must it be now?

The old woman was talking to Mason, her attention momentarily absorbed.

"You must eat it," Judith whispered to Schenckendorff.

He turned a little to look at her. There were shadows around his eyes and a pallor to his skin that must have been caused by more than the pain of his foot, which Lizzie had assured her was improving. Was it because it had been his own people who had wasted this land, just as now the Allies would be wasting his, and the people he loved?

He swallowed with difficulty and took another mouthful.

She reached for the pot and poured him the last of the tea. He needed it more than the others. Everywhere around them was ruin and loss. More lay ahead, and he would see all of it: a land that smelled of death.

Was he thinking of the old treaty that had never been ratified? He and the Peacemaker had tried so hard to prevent all this. Would betrayal and dominion really have been so very much worse? Did this old woman who gave them black bread and tea made with clean water care who made the laws in Brussels, or who collected the taxes, if her husband and her sons were home and safe, and her land bore its harvest, her cattle their milk? No one had asked her what she thought or wanted.

Was that what was going through Schenckendorff's mind now: not guilt at the ruin but guilt that he and the Peacemaker had failed to prevent it all? When he looked at Matthew and Joseph, did he see the two men who, above all others, had foiled the treaty that might have arrested war? Were they heroes in his eyes? Or men whose patriotism was too small and too blind to allow them to see the whole of humanity and the future that could have saved them all?

She studied the slow way he ate, the courtesy in his manners, and the distance between the few words he said, brief communications only when necessary.

They finished as quickly as they could and thanked the woman, hurrying out with no time for extra words, all afraid in case something gave them away.

They pressed on westward, moving slowly because the roads were so badly cratered that they dare not go more than twenty or twenty-five miles an hour. It rained again, washing mud everywhere, soaking Judith and whoever sat beside her.

It grew dark about five o'clock. Heavier clouds rolled in from the north like gray smears across the sky, wind-drawn curtains of rain hiding the trees. Mason had gone back into the body of the ambulance; Joseph was beside his sister.

"How's Schenckendorff?" she asked him.

"His foot hurts, but I don't think it's any worse," he replied, hunching himself up a little and pulling his overcoat closer around him. "He's not feverish, but he looks miserable. It must hurt. Wounds to the feet do."

"Do you think that's why he looks so unhappy?" She swerved to avoid a pothole filled with water that she had noticed only just in time. "Sorry," she said automatically.

"Do you think he's dreading getting to London?" he asked. "He's bound to. In a way he's riding to his own execution, even if it is his own choice." His voice was low, muted with a kind of awe.

"I hadn't even gotten that far," she replied. "Although I suppose he has to be. Will they execute him, Joseph? He's done no more than fight for his country, as we all have. You shoot a man for that during the war, while he's armed, but you don't execute him for it afterward. There's no crime in it." She refused to think about Mason's situation. As the hours went by, that was becoming more and more difficult. It was not only that she loved him: his passion and subtlety; his energy of mind; the honesty that had driven him to act where so many others merely dreamed and bemoaned their own helplessness. As she at last faced the situation with a cool head, and the will to consider and believe other ideas, she realized that the moral issues were not so easy to sweep entirely to one side or the other.

She would still have fought, been blown to bits in Flanders, rather than live a life of guilt and regret under the domination of anyone else. But driving through the ruins of Belgium, passing graveyards filled with endless white crosses all the same, she could see that it was mistaken, but not monstrous, to have considered a different path.

Perhaps Joseph was also thinking about Mason, because he said nothing.

"I was wondering about guilt," she said aloud. "Did you watch his face as he ate the bread today? He looked at her farm, and it almost choked him. Don't you think he would have thought that it would still be standing if we hadn't found the treaty, and there'd been no war?"

"There would still have been a war," Joseph said quickly, staring ahead at the rain now beating on the windscreen in front of them. It was swishing around and blowing inside, bitterly cold. The headlamps shone yellow in the gathering gloom, shining on puddles on the rutted road, broken trees, and fallen debris at the sides. "It might have been months later, or even years, but it would have come."

"Do you think so?"

"The balance of power was too precarious to last." He spoke thoughtfully, feeling his way. "There were too many promises that could never have been kept, too many alliances weighing one against another. Germany might have conquered most of Europe in a military sense, but there would always be a resistance. Possibly it would gather strength in time. There'd be sabotage to anything vulnerable, such as railways, bridges, fuel supplies. They would need a vast occupying army and a network of secret informers and police for years, if not indefinitely. And there would be all the other ugly sides of oppression and government by force: betrayals, large-scale imprisonment, censorship of all communications, and probably limitation of travel, curfew after dark, suppression of all artistic or literary opinion that questioned anything.

"In Britain I daresay it would be even worse. It might descend to civil war before there was any kind of order. The death toll would be appalling. It would make our troubles in Ireland look small. Canada might accept British rule, but America never would. Whatever armies anyone sent, they'd fight to the end."

He shook his head. "And the rise of socialism internationally was going to create revolution if we hadn't each had to unite our own country against an enemy outside. The revolution in Russia was probably inevitable. Austria-Hungary was falling apart. Hungary would have demanded its independence sooner or later. If Princip hadn't shot the archduke and duchess, something else would have sparked it off."

"Do you suppose he sees it that way?" she said doubtfully. "He believed he could succeed, in the beginning."

"Of course. We're wiser now, and I daresay sadder." He swiveled sideways to look at her. "Are you afraid Schenckendorff will change his mind when he gets to London?"

"Haven't you thought of it?" she responded.

He hesitated.

She felt a surge of guilt. In her awareness of Schenckendorff's feelings, and the threat he posed to them in Belgium, she had temporarily forgotten about Lizzie. She wondered how Joseph must be feeling watching her struggle to hide the nausea she suffered, especially in the mornings, and the emotions that both of them must be feeling. Confronting Allie Robinson had changed nothing about Lizzie's rape or the reality of its effects. Of course they knew now that the rapist was not the person who had killed Sarah, but the relief of that can only have been short-lived. Everything else was just as it had been before.

"I'm sorry," she said, meaning it intensely. "It's only a small part of everything, isn't it." That was not a question; it was an admission of truth. She was trying not to think of personal things, above all not about love, or the time after this was over and they could start living in peace, picking up daily routines again, and choice—and loneliness. There would be very few men left for anyone to marry, and those there were would not find her such an attractive prospect any more than she would them. It had been hard enough before when she was in her early twenties. Now, four and a half years later, it was going to be impossible.

Apart from the scarcity of available men, she would compare them all with Mason. At first they would bore her to tears; then she would begin to hate them, because they were there and alive, and he was not. They would be so flat and tame next to him.

It was easier to concentrate on getting Schenckendorff back to London to expose the Peacemaker, than to worry about food and petrol and how to mend the ambulance if it broke down, and how to make sure the Belgians didn't guess who they were.

They drove on through the darkness. She was growing very tired. She was used to long hours driving, more often at night than during the day, and always in difficult conditions. However, her eyes felt gritty, and her head ached as if she were wearing a helmet that was heavy and too tight. They would have to stop soon or she would risk losing control, which could be lethal.

Within half an hour they found a ruined farmhouse. It was too badly shelled to live in, but a sheltered place within the old dairy was dry and out of the wind, and the men could make themselves places to rest. They had a meal of Maconachie's and some army ration biscuits washed down with tea. It was all prepared by Joseph, since he was the only one used to such chores. Mason had seen army cooking done, of course, as had Schenckendorff, but neither had actually boiled water in a Dixie can over a flame, all balanced in a tin. It was more difficult than it looked and required a lot of patience.

Judith considered working on the engine, but knew she was exhausted enough to make mistakes. If something slipped from her clumsy fingers, was replaced crookedly, or was not tightened far enough, they could break down.

She was asleep within moments of lying down in the back of the ambulance, but she woke stiff and uncomfortable while it was still dark. She could hear Lizzie moving slightly on the other side, a couple of feet away, but she did not know if she was awake, too, or just stretching or turning in restlessness, dreaming of fear or loss.

There had been no time for the two of them to talk, and she did not know what to say anyhow. She did not even know if Lizzie wanted to keep the baby, or if she would be relieved to lose it. Perhaps both were true, at different times. One thing she was certain about; she had seen it in Lizzie's face, in a dozen small actions even in the short times they had all been together: She loved Joseph. And—perhaps in a more lasting way, the thing that would carry them over the pain, the doubt, the times of failure—she liked him. She was not looking for a solution to her own need, or an answer to any difficulty; she liked him for himself. It was there in the quick, rueful laughter, a brief moment of teasing, the acceptance of help and criticism. Underneath the present fear and the knowledge of future pain, she was comfortable with him.

Judith lay on her back on the hard surface and stared up into the complete darkness of the ambulance, letting the near silence wrap around her. It was almost like being at home again after a long and violent journey. There was no sound but the rain on the roof, and that was intermittent now. Perhaps by morning it would have stopped altogether.

That comfort was the kind of feeling she had about Mason also—at least most of the time. And when she looked at his face, she saw certainty in him, as if he had found at last something he had been looking for, and for longer than he knew.

But he must be afraid underneath the courage. He could not imagine that the prime minister would accept his unmasking of the Peacemaker— with all his own involvement in the plot, and his knowledge that it intended to bring about the surrender of Britain—and then simply allow him to walk away. The fact that he had believed that it was for the purpose of a greater world peace was immaterial. Just the knowledge of such plans, in wartime, was treason, and the punishment for treason had always been death. She closed her eyes tightly, even though she could see nothing in the dark anyway. Death by hanging. These few days of exhaustion in the rain and the ruin of Belgium, the channel crossing, and then the drive to London, were all the time they had left together.

But then, for how many women was that true? She was only one more who would lose the man she loved. It was selfish and cowardly to cry as if she were the only one. She was one of millions, all over Europe, all over the world. It was the price of the battle she had never doubted they should fight. Yet that did nothing to lessen the pain. Every man she looked at, she would wish were him: every man with thick, dark hair, or who stood very straight and turned with grace, or who spoke of wild open spaces as if they were antechambers of heaven.

Would he change his mind about surrendering himself when he got to London and the final moment closed in on them, irreversible at last? Perhaps past loyalties and old dreams would overtake his present sense of duty, and he would find that he could not say the words that would hang the Peacemaker.

But it was equally imaginable that he was going with them to turn at the last moment, betraying them and saving Sandwell so he could help create a peace that would allow Germany to rise again, soon, and resurrect the old plan for dominion.

That was a wild and useless thought, and she would be better asleep. Before they set off she must work on the ambulance engine, then drive all day again. Whatever any of them did, it must be what conscience demanded. Nothing else would bring happiness of any sort, or peace of heart, or the ability to love or trust anything.

In the morning it was clear and colder. They breakfasted on tea and the last of the bread they had brought with them, with plum jam. The bread was hard and stale, but no one complained. Uppermost in Judith's mind was the fact that they would have to buy or beg everything from now on, and that could be another two days, if they had any problems. Time was pressing urgently. It was already the fifth of November—Guy Fawkes Day at home, when they lit bonfires and set off fireworks to celebrate the fact that the plot to blow up Parliament, and kill all its members, had been foiled. A celebration of freedom and the defeat of treason and murder. Did they still remember what it was about? Or was it just an excuse to have fun?

The ambulance would not start. She cleaned the spark plugs, and it made no difference. It was hard to quell the panic inside her. It felt like a fluttering in her stomach and a tightening of her throat so that it was difficult to breathe. No one else had any idea how to help, but she had expected that from the beginning. Mason could observe, assess, write brilliantly. Matthew could plan, judge men, think ahead, unravel truth and lies, and he was a good driver, but he never mended his own cars. Schenckendorff was at least a colonel. Colonels did not maintain their own cars. Lizzie was a nurse and a pretty good driver, too, according to Joseph, who was more than a little biased. And Joseph himself was good at medical emergencies, a fair army cook—at least with a candle and a tin—and a better soldier than he knew. But mechanics of any sort were a closed book to him.

She worked quietly, steadying her hands with an effort of will. At least it was light, and not raining. She changed the plugs. It was sooner than she would have wished. Now they had nothing in reserve.

Joseph was watching her.

"Perhaps you should say a prayer for it," she said ruefully. "Otherwise we shall have to descend to stealing. Highway robbery."

"Do you know what parts we need?" he asked, his face puckered with doubt.

She saw the comical side of it. "I was thinking of a trade," she replied, picking up the crank handle ready to attempt starting the engine.

"Trade?" He was puzzled. "Still doesn't help if we don't know what we need."

"Their vehicle for ours," she replied. "I told you, highway robbery." She passed him the crank handle. "Please?"

On the third attempt it sputtered into life. They looked at each other, laughing, drenched with relief, and clambered in.

After they had gone forty-five miles west, they found the roads more crowded with other vehicles and people on foot. It began to look as if the country closer to Dunkirk was making something of a recovery as well.

They managed to find a roadside café at which to buy a meal. It was meager—no eggs, no meat, only dumplings seasoned with herbs—but it was sufficient to sustain them. They spoke little and listened to the conversation around them. There had been other victories. Judith watched Schenckendorff's face as one group talked about Allied troops pressing forward rapidly now, with terrible loss of German life. She saw the sudden flash of pain in him, and then the effort to hide it and pretend to feel pleasure, like the people around them. A few people around them started cheering, as if each death or mutilation were some kind of victory in itself, a payment for all the loss over the last years: the dead they would never even find, let alone bury.

Then the conversation shifted. There was other news that was more frightening. Spanish influenza had struck, and thousands of people were dying. No one could count how many, and the disease was spreading. Paris was particularly hard hit.

They left the café with a new sense of darkness on the horizon, unknown and closing in. Joseph walked closer to Lizzie. Mason touched Judith's arm and stood beside her as if to help her up into the driver's seat, although he knew better than to do so. Instead he went to the front and cranked the engine.

Inside the ambulance as it set off again, Joseph sat with Lizzie, absorbed in quiet conversation. Matthew sat opposite Schenckendorff, clearly searching for something to say, but all conversation seemed trivial compared with the enormity of the truth.

At lunchtime they stopped for necessities and to eat some of their rations. They had pulled in at the side of the road, leaving the engine running in case it was reluctant to start again. All of them were aware of its frailty. They looked for clean water to drink, and found nothing. There was no time to light a candle and heat any. Thirst would have to wait.

Matthew and Schenckendorff walked back together from the semi-privacy of a clump of trees, picking their way through rough grass. The land was flat, cut by canals where once there had been straight lines of trees. It was more orderly than England; it looked man-made. Someone had created these avenues and dikes, these farmhouses with their stone walls dipping down into water. In Cambridgeshire, even in the fen country where there was water everywhere and it was as flat as a table, the paths were winding and the rivers seeped in all directions, as though taking as long as possible to reach the sea. Invaders had been lost there since the last stand of the Saxons against the Normans in 1066. They were a people who fought to the last ditch and dike, to the last island and quicksand, the final stand.

Schenckendorff was limping badly. He should not have been walking on that foot. It must hurt like hell, but he had never complained. Matthew found himself hoping intensely that it would not be damaged permanently. He waited for him to catch up so they could walk side by side.

"Where are you from?" he asked conversationally.

"Heidelberg," Schenckendorff replied. "It's a very old city, steep, over-looking the Rhine." He smiled slightly. "It's nothing like this." He left the wealth of comparison unsaid, but Matthew guessed at what might be racing through his mind.

Schenckendorff glanced at him and saw it in his eyes. "And you are from Cambridgeshire," he said as if it were all some easy exchange—two men passing the time of day. "Flat like this, but far more eccentric, more full of individual oddities that go back to your Domesday Book and before. Nobody has ever forced you to change them. You are very stubborn." He gave a little shrug. "It used to annoy me. Now I have changed my mind. I think perhaps it is good. We found some kind of identity in being different, something to stand on and believe it worth paying the greatest price to save. If you give up the right to be different, maybe sooner or later you give up the right to think at all, and then perhaps you are dead anyway. You haven't had your life taken from you, you gave it up yourself—for nothing."

Matthew stopped in the rough grass by the edge of the road, staring at him.

Schenckendorff smiled. "You were wondering if I would change my mind when I got to London. I know. You all are. You would be foolish if it had not at least crossed your mind. You must take every possibility into account. I won't change. The cost of the peace I thought of is too high, and I am not sure now that it is peace at all." His face shadowed. "I think it might be the beginning of a slow death. Life, real, growing, passionate life, is not peaceful. Learning hurts, and has costs. My onetime friend Sandwell misunderstood that, and he lost sight of the purpose of it all."

Matthew waited.

"Individuals matter," Schenckendorff said quietly. "Moments of joy, a man's victory over the darkness within himself, a perception of beauty, whether it is of the eye or the mind. I think we had better get back into the ambulance. Your remarkable sister is waiting to leave."

Some of these same thoughts crossed Joseph's mind, but he was preoccupied with Lizzie. As a child he had watched his mother endure the same distress, but she had been in her own home, secure and deeply loved, and the children she was carrying were wanted.

For Lizzie it was in every way different. She was alone, facing an unknown future and a child she must dread. Would she think of the violence, assault, degradation every time she looked at its face? Could she possibly learn to love it, to be tender, to laugh, to find joy in its growth, its achievements? *It.* Would it be harder if it was a boy?

Now she was sick again, desperate for privacy, and surrounded by men, two of whom she barely knew. They were always in a hurry, feeling the urgency all the time, the need to move, the knowledge that if they made even one slip they could be stopped, imprisoned, even executed summarily. The hunger for revenge was in the air like the smell of decay.

How could he help her? She was walking back over the grass a little shakily. Her face was bleached of all color, and her hair was straggling out of its pins. He ached to comfort her, but might he be making promises he could not keep? Could he love that child as if it were his own, and never even for a moment look at it and hate it because Benbow was its father?

He remembered how he had felt as a child: the certainty of his father's interest, his time and attention. He thought of countless hours shared: in listening to his father's long, rambling funny stories; in pottering in the garden feeling he was helping, learning weeds from flowers. Later there had been more complicated discoveries about the first thoughts in philosophy, feeling his way toward wisdom. He remembered long walks in comfortable silence, always certain that he was not only loved but liked, valued, believed in, a necessary part in the greater happiness. Arguments meant nothing; the security was always there underneath, like a deep ocean with an inexhaustible current.

A warmth opened inside him, a steadiness that had been absent for some time—he could not remember how long. It was back again now, a bedrock on which every good thing could be built. Lizzie's child deserved that. Everyone did. Nothing less was enough.

He walked toward Lizzie and took her arm, lending her his strength. She looked up at him quickly, and he met her gaze without wavering.

She saw the knowledge of something new in him, a complete absence of fear. She took a deep breath and smiled at him, hope flaring up.

* * *

By evening the rain had returned, steady and hard. They were grateful to be offered both food and shelter at what before the war must have been an excellent café. During the occupation it had housed German soldiers. Now the original owners had taken it back and were trying to salvage all they could of the past.

"Broken!" Madame said furiously, picking up a blue-and-white china platter to arrange the food on. It had been cracked across the center and carefully glued together again. "Everything is tired and dusty and broken. I'd kill every last one of them if I could."

Joseph struggled for something to say. She clearly wanted justice, some answering pain to compensate for all that had been taken from her and from all the others she had known and loved.

"I know," he answered her. "There's not much left."

She grunted and regarded his chaplain's uniform with contempt. "Aren't you going to tell me to have faith in God?" she demanded. "Or at least remind me that we should be grateful to you British for fighting for us? That's what my husband tells me."

"You don't do what you think is right for other people's sake," he said. "You do it for yourself."

She was surprised. It robbed her momentarily of the response she had been going to give. "I suppose you'd like something decent to eat?"

"Wouldn't we all? But we'll be grateful for anything," he replied.

"Don't be grateful!" she snapped. "I'm not giving it to you."

But when the meal came it was prepared not only with care but with imagination and skill as well. Dark bread was set out on the mended blue-and-white platter, made to look inviting with a few leaves of parsley and red radishes. There were small dishes of something that resembled Brussels pâté, and others of pickled fish to add taste, and the suggestion of meat. They were all sitting around one long table, and she placed them in the middle with a baleful glare, daring them to make any remark.

They thanked her and shared the meal in equal portions, although Lizzie gave half of hers to the others.

Monsieur came and stood in the doorway smoking a clay pipe with something dark and pungent in it. It might have been half tobacco, but it smelled as if it were at least half dung.

"So what are you doing away from the fighting, then?" His English was thickly accented, but he had some confidence in the language. "Isn't over yet, you know. Still some men out there being killed."

They had expected this, and were prepared.

"Taking information back to London," Matthew replied. "It's urgent, and secret. Can't trust it to letters."

"All six of you?" Monsieur clearly did not believe them. He looked at Mason. "You're not a soldier. Why not? You look fit enough. Flat feet, have you? Shortsighted? Know what I tell people who are shortsighted? Get closer to the enemy. You'll see him all right when he's a bayonet length away."

Madame mumbled something unintelligible at him.

He ignored her and glared at Mason, waiting for an answer.

"War correspondent," Mason said truthfully. "Miss Reavley is an ambulance driver and Mrs. Blaine is a nurse. Major Reavley is an intelligence officer." He indicated Schenckendorff. "And Major Sherman is also. He's been behind the lines and, as you can see, been injured."

Monsieur was mollified, but not happy. He looked at Schenckendorff doubtfully. "What's any use behind the lines now?" he asked. "Kill them, I say. Same as they killed us."

Everyone stiffened. Joseph drew in his breath sharply, afraid of what Schenckendorff would answer. He loathed what the Belgian was saying, but perhaps—if this had been his land and his people—he might have felt much the same.

Monsieur was waiting, a challenge in his eyes.

"Exactly," Judith said, swallowing her mouthful of food with a gulp. "We are not so different from them."

Monsieur's face flushed hot red. "Speak for yourself, woman! We are nothing like them. They are animals, pigs! They steal and they rape and they kill."

Lizzie's spoon slid out of her hand, spilling gravy on the table.

Joseph searched frantically for something to say or do to cover it. Nothing came to his mind but fury.

Judith looked at the man. "Yes, of course. I only see the enemy who have been wounded. I forget: The ones who are able to be are violent. We are not like that. We don't steal, we don't hurt women, and we don't kill the unarmed."

Mason bent his head to conceal his expression.

Madame glared at Schenckendorff, challenging him to argue.

The silence grew.

"The hunger for revenge is natural," he responded uncomfortably at last. "Especially after so many years of being helpless."

Monsieur glared at him. "We're not helpless! Where do you come from? You have a funny accent. You don't sound English at all."

Joseph's throat tightened. He dared not look at Matthew. He reached under the shelter of the tabletop and took Lizzie's hand, and felt her fingers grasp his.

"I'm not," Schenckendorff said calmly. "I'm Scots. From the Western Isles. We spoke Gaelic when I was young."

Joseph prayed silently that no one in the room had the faintest idea what Gaelic sounded like. Actually, he had none himself.

Monsieur seemed satisfied. "Really? Western Isles, eh? Rains a lot, doesn't it?"

"Yes, I suppose so," Schenckendorff went on, turning to the woman. "You can make the most ordinary ingredients taste good. That is an art."

"There's no more," she said ungraciously, but there was a flush of pleasure in her cheeks and she very nearly smiled at him.

Joseph slept well. It was the first time he'd had a real bed in more than half a year, since he had been at home on his last leave in the spring. He was woken violently by a banging on the door. Even before he could sit up, it burst open and a large Belgian policeman stood just inside the room, a German pistol in his hand, pointing it at Joseph.

"Get up," he ordered. "Slowly. Don't touch your uniform!"

"I can't get up without my clothes," Joseph pointed out. "Who are you, and what's wrong? We're British army officers and volunteers, going back to London with important information." He was sick at the thought that perhaps he had actually been posted as a deserter, and Hook had sent out his information. Surely not so soon?

"Maybe. Maybe not." The man moved toward Joseph cautiously and, with one hand, picked up his uniform shirt off the back of the chair where Joseph had left it. He shook it hard. Papers fell out of one of the pockets. He dropped the jacket and picked up the trousers, shaking them also.

"I'm not armed," Joseph said patiently, controlling himself with difficulty. "If you look at the collar, and the insignia, you'll see that I'm a chaplain. I don't carry weapons."

"How do I know the uniform's yours?" the man demanded. "Anyone could wear it."

There was no reasonable argument to that. It was true. Going through the lines last year Joseph had worn a Swiss chaplain's uniform to which he had had no right. "They could," he conceded. "But why bother? What is it you think I am? An army deserter, with a war correspondent, two army officers, a nurse, and an ambulance driver?" He tried to convey the absurdity of it in his voice.

"No, I think you're a collaborator trying to get a German occupying commander out of Belgium before we can catch him and hang him, like he deserves," the man replied quite calmly. "We'll give you over to the families of those he murdered."

Joseph looked at his face and saw the years of suffering burned into his heart, the deaths he was helpless to prevent, and, more bitter than that, the corruption of fear and loneliness and greed that had destroyed what had once been clean. He had found weakness and disappointment that peace would never have revealed. He did not want to forgive.

Joseph felt real fear, hot and sick inside him. Lizzie would be hurt, and Judith. They did not spare women. He and Matthew would be killed. They would never catch the Peacemaker now. Bitter, terrible irony—the Reavleys would never exact their own vengeance.

Would John Reavley have wanted vengeance? Probably not. When Joseph thought about it, after four years of mutilation and death, he felt that his father would definitely not have. It ended nothing. The Peacemaker must be stopped because of the damage he could still do; no more than that.

"There may be such people, I don't know," he said quietly. How much of the truth should he tell? One lie, if caught, could kill them all. But they must all tell the same story, true or false.

"Let me get dressed, and we can all answer your questions. I presume you do not wish to imprison British army officers on military duty. Or perhaps you do? Maybe it's you who are helping the occupiers to escape, and you think we will discover that, and—"

The policeman lifted the gun and swung his arm around. Joseph only just managed to fend off the blow, but he did it hard, with his weight behind it, and the gun clattered to the floor. He thought for an instant of diving to get it first, and realized he would be just too late. He forced himself to stand still.

The policeman watched him, eyes hard and angry, then bent and retrieved the gun, pointing its muzzle at Joseph's stomach. "Wise," he said between his teeth. "Very wise. I'd have shot you."

"I can see that," Joseph answered. "You would have had a lot of explaining to do to the British army as to why you'd shot an unarmed priest in his bed, but it would have been a bit late to help me."

"You say you're a priest. I say you're a collaborator."

"By then it would be obvious that you didn't care. You just wanted to shoot someone, and you didn't have the guts to pick anyone who could fight back," Joseph said with contempt. He was frightened, especially for Lizzie and Judith, but he was beginning to be angry as well. "For heaven's sake, think about it! We're in British army uniforms. The ambulance is pretty obviously a real one; you can see the state of it. There's years of blood on its boards, it's splintered with shot, and any fool can see it's at least four years old."

"Oh, it's real enough," the man agreed. "I don't doubt you stole it from a real British hospital. But we got reliable information that you have a German officer with you who's one of those that led the invasion and occupation of our country. To collaborate with the enemy makes you one of them. Worse, you betrayed your own." He said it with total conviction, the contempt in him scalding like acid. "Put your clothes on, priest. You're going to answer to the Belgian people. Unless you want to come as you are?"

Ten minutes later they were all downstairs in the gray early-morning light, shivering and silent. There were three more policemen, all with guns. Madame and Monsieur were there, too, bristling with anger because they had been made fools of, their hospitality abused. Madame, her puffy face gray, her hair in a thin braid over her shoulder, glared at Joseph in particular and spat, her loathing too deep for words.

The man who seemed to be in charge, who was narrow-shouldered and tall, assumed that Joseph was the leader, since he appeared to be the oldest in uniform. Mason he disregarded, and Schenckendorff was the focus of his suspicion.

"You say you are taking information back to London. That's absurd. Doesn't take six of you, and women, to do that. And if it's urgent, as you say, you wouldn't go in an ambulance that's old and ready to fall to bits. You've got no papers of authority, no money, no supplies, no extra fuel. If you were on genuine army business, you would be properly equipped. Now tell me the truth and we might believe you."

Joseph looked across at Matthew. At least nothing had been said about desertion. They might have one chance left, but it would be only one.

Judith was next to Lizzie, so close as to be almost supporting her. Joseph could only guess how ill Lizzie must feel at this hour.

Schenckendorff moved his weight from one foot to the other to ease the pain. He looked as if he was trying to decide whether to speak or not.

Mason smiled as if the whole thing was faintly ridiculous. But under the bravado his shoulders were stiff, and the graceful posture was only half convincing.

"What on earth is it you think we're doing?" he asked, eyebrows raised. "Last week of the war, and after four years here we're deserting now? We'd still be shot, you know. As lunatics, if nothing else."

Joseph winced at mention of deserting. Was it a piece of bravado too far?

"We know what you're doing!" the narrow-shouldered man replied. "You've captured a German commandant and you want him for yourselves. He's plundered our works of art, paintings, reliquaries, ornamental weapons, and if you spare his life he'll give them to you. Well, we've caught you, and after we've tried you and you've told us where you've hidden our material treasures, we'll execute you as thieves, and him as the murderer he is."

Matthew looked at Joseph, then at Schenckendorff. A single thought had occurred to them all.

"There may be such a man," Matthew said in a voice that was very nearly level. Only Joseph, who had known him all his life, heard the fear in it. "It is not Colonel Schenckendorff, who I admit is German. But he is a senior officer in Berlin, and at no time was part of the occupation of Belgium. I am Major Reavley of British Secret Intelligence Service, and I am bringing him back to London, where he can expose certain collaborators we have of our own. We are doing it this way, in an ambulance and without papers of authority, because the collaborators concerned have spies in many places, and are attempting to stop us naming them even now. If you attempt to prevent us, I can only assume that you are in league with these collaborators yourselves. Perhaps you owe your own people a more detailed account of your part in the occupation of your country than you have given them so far?"

The narrow-shouldered man was startled. A counterattack was the last thing he had expected. He was thrown off balance.

"By all means try us," Matthew pressed his advantage. "We shall try each other!"

The Belgians looked confused.

"Don't listen to them!" Madame said bitterly. "They'll talk their way out of it." She looked at the leader. "Aren't both of your sons dead?" She turned to another of them. "Isn't your sister a widow? You used to be rich. Where's your house? A pile of rubble. Wasn't your daughter raped before she killed herself? What do those people know of what war is really like? It's over, and they're going home again. Where are our homes, eh?" She swung her arm violently and only just missed knocking a chipped candlestick off the mantel to the floor.

"Lock them up," the leader ordered. "We'll find the people who say this is the German commandant. Someone must know."

Before anyone could move to obey him there was a knock on the door. Almost immediately it opened, and Sergeant Hampton came in. He glanced around the faces and stopped when he recognized Joseph. " 'Morning, Chaplain. You seem to be in a spot of bother."

Joseph was weak with relief and astonishment. "Yes," he gulped, drawing in air as if he had suddenly come to the surface from being close to drowning. "We are finding it hard to prove we are who we say." Then, like sudden nausea, he realized that Hampton might have come to arrest him for desertion. At least the others could go on!

"Really?" Hampton looked at the Belgians. "Captain Reavley is chaplain with the Cambridgeshires at Ypres," he said solemnly. "Major Reavley there is with the Secret Intelligence Service. Mr. Mason is one of our most distinguished war correspondents. Miss Reavley is an ambulance driver, and Mrs. Blaine is a nurse. I can swear to this because I have been conducting an investigation in which they were of assistance. Fortunately it is all cleared up now." He fished in his pocket and brought out his police identification. "Sergeant Hampton of the British military police." He displayed it but kept it in his hand.

"And him?" the narrow-shouldered man asked, looking at Schenckendorff. "Can you swear for him, too?"

"Of course. He is Colonel Schenckendorff, whom they are escorting to London. I would not like to have to insist that you permit them to go on their way unhindered, but I shall have to become unpleasant about it if you do not." He had a revolver in his hand and was holding it with the muzzle pointing up, a little toward the middle of the man's chest. The shot would undoubtedly have killed him. "Let us part amicably," he said with a chilly smile. "This would be an ugly end to a war that we entered originally on your behalf, in order to keep a rather rash promise we made to you, before . . . all this."

The Belgians looked at one another, uncertain now, and embarrassed.

Hampton did not wait. "I suggest you go outside and get back into your ambulance," he said to Matthew. "I shall follow you, when I am certain there will be no . . . ill-considered behavior."

Matthew did not hesitate. He led the way, and the others went after them, Hampton bringing up the rear.

Lizzie looked ill. Judith put an arm around her, half holding her up. Matthew went to the front. "I'll drive," he said, giving Judith no chance to argue.

Mason cranked the engine, then, as it fired, got in beside Matthew.

Joseph helped Schenckendorff, who was limping badly. Hampton was the last to get into the back, slamming the door behind him.

They jerked forward, then picked up speed, bouncing and lurching over the potholes in the road and slithering where the surface was wet and covered with mud.

Joseph looked at Lizzie. She smiled at him, eyes bright with relief.

"Thank you," Schenckendorff said sincerely to Hampton.

"How did you know where to find us?" Joseph asked him.

Hampton gave a slight grimace. "Deduction," he replied. "And a few discreet questions. You've chosen the best route. I did the same." A ghost of warmth crossed his face, enigmatic rather than friendly. "You have friends." He said something deeply uncomplimentary about the Belgians they had just left behind. "Won't happen again," he added, tapping his gun, which was now in the holster on his belt.

Joseph wondered if Hampton was actually part of some intelligence service rather than merely a military policeman seconded to Jacobson. If not, why had he bothered to come after them to be helpful rather than to arrest Joseph for desertion, and possibly Judith for taking the ambulance? More than that, how had he known that Schenckendorff would be with them? Had they been far more careless than they thought? No one had seen them leave.

Did Matthew know that he could be trusted, and had he told him the story? But if Hampton had known Matthew, he would never have allowed Jacobson to suspect him of having killed Sarah Price.

He couldn't ask Matthew; he was in front at the wheel, separated from them by the back of the cab.

He glanced at Judith, next to the front wall, on the seat beyond Hampton.

She stared back, eyes wide.

Schenckendorff and Lizzie were on the opposite side.

Schenckendorff must have picked up some look, some motion of anxiety in Joseph, perhaps in Judith also. Maybe he, too, was wondering how Hampton knew him.

Then suddenly it was obvious—he was an accomplice of the Peacemaker!

Hampton saw it and understood. His hand went to his belt and the gun appeared, leveled at Joseph.

"You are a good detective, Chaplain, but not good enough. Shortsighted as always. A man with a small vision, loyalty to a little idea, in fact parochial. For a man who claims to serve God, you should think of the whole world, not just your own, narrow few. I cannot allow Schenckendorff to betray the greater cause." He lifted the gun a little higher and moved it from Joseph to Schenckendorff.

At that moment Judith stood up behind him and hit him as hard as she could over the head with the first-aid box.

He slumped forward, the gun slipping out of his fingers. But he was only stunned.

Lizzie dived for the gun, and her hand closed over it inches before he reached it.

"You won't!" Hampton said with a sneer.

She pulled the trigger and the bullet struck him cleanly between the eyes. Then she dropped the gun on the floor and was sick.

*L*izzie was deeply shocked. Joseph took off his own jacket and put it around her. Still she sat shivering and white-faced. She did not say anything at all, but Joseph knew what must be racing through her mind. He had seen young soldiers like this after they had shot their first enemy, even though it had been in battle and all those around them had been doing exactly the same thing. This was different. Hampton was a man she had known, spoken to civilly over many days. He was as English as she was, and wearing a British uniform. She had stood less than a yard from him, looked in his face, and killed him.

"Thank you," he said softly. "You've saved all of us, and I know it has been at great cost."

"Schenckendorff," she murmured, even though she knew that Schenckendorff himself, sitting in the back of the ambulance only a couple of feet away from her, had to hear all she said. "Not the rest of us."

Judith was outside. She had found some water, albeit muddy, and cleared up the mess where Lizzie had been sick. Matthew and Mason had taken Hampton's body, and Joseph had not even asked them what they intended to do with it.

It was Schenckendorff who answered Lizzie. "If he had shot me, as he apparently intended to, he would not have allowed you to remain alive. He would have killed all of you, then very probably have made it look as if the ambulance had gone off the road. He might have set fire to it, rather than have it obvious that you were shot. Your courage saved the lives of all of us."

Lizzie blinked and frowned at him. "I suppose so. I hadn't thought of it, but you are right." She smiled very slightly. "That does make me feel less . . . brutal."

A slight amusement touched Schenckendorff's face, softening the lines around his eyes. The instant after, it was followed by intense sadness.

She looked away, not to be intrusive.

Judith came back into the ambulance. She looked anxious. "Matthew and Richard aren't back yet," she said, turning from Lizzie to Joseph. "They don't need to bury him! You didn't tell them to, did you?"

"No, of course I didn't." Joseph stood up awkwardly in the narrow space. "I said to hide the body, that's all. Better he isn't found. We don't need any more trouble than we have. He may have spoken to the authorities about us, and they'll follow up on him. We don't want them to find him. I'll go and see what they're doing."

But he had barely straightened up outside in the road when he saw Matthew and Mason a dozen yards away walking briskly across the rough grass toward him. They were both mud-stained, and Mason's jacket sleeve was torn.

"Finished," Matthew said as they reached the ambulance. "Took his identification and insignia of rank off him and burned them. That's what took the time. Hard to get wet cloth to ignite, but we can't afford to be caught with it . . . if he's got allies. Is Judith all right to drive, or shall I? That engine sounds very rough."

"Then she'd better," Joseph replied. "She knows it. If anyone can nurse it along, she can."

"Right." Matthew opened the back doors and climbed inside.

"I'll ride with her." Mason made it a statement, not an offer.

A few minutes later the engine was cranked again. It sputtered to life and they lurched uncertainly forward, then stalled. It took four attempts before they were finally on their way, moving at about twenty-five miles an hour in the cold morning sunlight.

"I think we have to face the fact that the Peacemaker knows Schenckendorff has crossed sides," Mason said after five minutes of silence as they wound their way with difficulty through a small village. The streets were crowded with carts and people walking: some soldiers, some refugees returning to stare in dismay at once-familiar houses now crumbled to stained and ugly ruin.

"Do you think he'll send someone else after us?" Judith asked.

"We can't afford to take it for granted that Hampton was the only one," Mason replied. "It's a toss-up which is better: speed on the better and more obvious roads, or discretion in taking byways, perhaps even having to ford the odd stream and follow a few farm tracks."

"Wouldn't an ambulance on a farm track draw attention?" she asked.

She was worried now. This road was bad enough, and the engine was misfiring. She had no more spark plugs, and much could go wrong now that would be beyond her ability to mend. "And we'll need more fuel in another fifteen miles." She smiled grimly. "We might be better to fight, if we have to, than to try running. The poor old thing's not got it in her anymore."

"We need to make the coast by tomorrow night, if we can," Mason answered, a sudden sadness in his voice. "We've still got to make it from Dover to London, or from wherever we land."

"Did you like Dermot Sandwell?" she asked as quietly as she could and still be heard over the noise of the engine. They were through the town and onto open, flat road again. "I met him once," she added, thinking back to 1915 and a brief leave in London. "He was different, powerful, as if he had a brilliant mind. I remember his eyes: pale blue and very bright."

Mason thought for a moment or two before he answered. "I don't think *like* is the right word," he said finally. "I admired him. I thought he had a greater vision than the rest of us, and the courage to do what he believed was right for all mankind, not just a narrow few. Other politicians were always so partisan, playing to the crowd. Sandwell was above that. He didn't really care if he was liked or not, or even if the majority understood him or saw his vision."

She drove with difficulty for half a mile, veering right and left to avoid all the rubble in the road, and potholes deep enough to break an axle. She was thinking about Mason, and how the disillusion must hurt him. It had been a great dream, selfless. At least that was how he had seen it at the outset.

"How did you know him?" she asked when the road was less dangerous and she could increase speed a little.

"After Africa," he answered. "We were both involved in the Boer War, although we didn't meet then. At that time it seemed terrible."

She looked sideways at him and saw pity and self-mockery in his face. He must have been aware of her gaze, because he turned to meet her eyes and smiled. The tenderness in them was overwhelming, the pain for all that was impossible, and that he longed for.

It caught her breath, and tears blinded her eyes. She veered sideways and hit a pothole, jarring the ambulance. She swore, partly in fury with herself.

He started to laugh, the emotion in him too powerful to contain.

She laughed with him, and managed to stop it from turning into weeping. They had today and tomorrow, and they were infinitely precious. They must not be spoiled with a word, a look, an instant of self-pity or blame that they would afterward regret. Above all there must be no cowardice.

"No, I don't think I did like him," he said at last. "But I loved the dream. Now it's time to wake up." He put his hand over her shoulder and she felt the warmth of it through her. "I hate to admit it," he added. "But I rather like Schenckendorff. There's nothing manipulative about him."

She smiled, steering around a chicken in the road. "So do I. And I admire his quiet courage. He never complains."

In the early afternoon they came to a village that seemed unusually deserted on the outskirts. But as they reached the square in the center, they found at least thirty people gathered. Most of them were watching while half a dozen crowded close, pushing and jostling, arms raised, flailing against one person who cowered beneath the blows, unable to resist.

Judith jerked the ambulance to a stop and Mason jumped out. A moment later the back door opened and Joseph and Matthew scrambled out.

Joseph started straight toward the crowd, most of whom were shouting and snarling at the figure now fallen to the ground and being kicked. They parted to allow him through, thinking he wanted to join them.

"You lost someone? You deserve to help her die!" a heavy-boned woman cried out. "Kick her for me! Kick her for my son!" Her voice became choked in a racking sob.

Another woman let out an animal cry of hate, wordless and raw with pain.

Joseph found himself pushed to the front, only feet away from the figure huddled on the ground. Her head was shaven, and her few remnants of clothes torn and covered with blood.

Joseph stared at her. She was no more than thirty, and slight. Barefooted, she looked as if she had been dragged along the ground.

Joseph was sick with revulsion at the violence. He stared around him at the people, their faces gloating, vivid with hate.

"What in God's name are you doing?" he demanded in French.

The man nearest him spat one word. "Collaborator!"

Others took up the cry, adding taunts and curses. It was the worst accusation of all, worse than *enemy*, even than *spy*. It was the lowest form of human life, the final betrayal. Still Joseph was horrified that they could do this to her. Without thinking of the danger of attracting their anger, he bent and lifted the woman off the ground, pulling first at her shoulder, gently, to turn her so she could rise.

Her face was beaten; her nose broken and bloody, her eyes swollen half shut, her teeth chipped and lips torn. Even so he recognized her, because the one time he had seen her had been so powerfully engraved in his memory. It had been last year, in Paris, when he had needed to get evidence for the court-martial. Sam Wetherall had asked her to help. Her name was Monique, and she worked for the French, spying against the Germans in the heart of their command, risking her life every day.

"Monique . . . ," he said softly. "Monique . . ."

She blinked once, her eyes focusing with difficulty. "Did you find him?" she whispered, her words distorted by her shattered face.

"Yes, I found him. Thank you . . ." She knew him. There could be no doubt it was her.

He cradled her in his arms, trying to think what he could do for any of her injuries. How bad were they? She was covered in blood and it was still oozing through her thin dress, but—far more urgent than that—how bad was the bruising, what bones were broken?

"Collaborator!" A man spat on the ground. "Get out of the way, Monsieur, I am going to hang her. You, too, if you stand in the path of justice."

"She worked for the Germans," a woman said harshly. She looked no more than thirty herself. "Pig! Filth!" She aimed a kick but was too far away to reach.

Another man lashed out, and he was closer. His boot caught Monique in the chest, and she gasped and cried out. She slipped from Joseph's arms onto the cobbles. Her eyes rolled back and she stopped moving, blood running from her mouth.

The man regained his balance and lifted his foot to do it again.

Joseph shot to his feet and hit the man as hard as he could with his fist, all his weight behind it. "She's not a collaborator, you fool!" he shouted. "She's part of the resistance!" He hit the man again and again, feeling his fist strike bone, then soft flesh: yielding, sagging deadweight. Still he didn't stop. "She was braver and better than any of you, you cowards!"

The man staggered and fell backward onto the stones himself, but Joseph didn't stop. He lunged after him and hauled him to his feet, then hit him again, one fist and then the other. His own hands were bleeding, but he didn't care. Another man came at him, and he hit him, too, full in the face, sending him reeling backward, then again, knocking him to the ground. He was bending over him, ready to strike, when he felt arms holding him, stopping him from moving, sending him off balance.

He heaved himself away and spun around to lash out, and saw with surprise that it was Matthew. Then Mason caught him from behind and pinned his arms to his sides.

Judith was on the ground by Monique. The crowd was staring at them, shocked into silence.

Judith laid Monique down gently. "It's too late," she said, looking at Joseph. "She's dead."

Joseph stiffened.

Mason held him more tightly.

Lizzie and Schenckendorff were standing on the edge of the crowd, their faces white.

"You know her?" Matthew asked, looking at Joseph with concern.

"Yes. I met her in Paris last year. She worked for our intelligence there. She risked her life to help her country, and these stupid animals have murdered her." He was finding it difficult to breathe, as if there were a great weight tightening around his chest, crushing him. The distance blurred in his vision, figures becoming fuzzy and distorted.

"Not a collaborator?" someone asked quietly.

"We didn't know," someone else offered.

"No, you didn't!" Joseph grated the words between clenched teeth. "And you didn't care. You murdered her anyway."

"But we didn't . . . we thought . . ." His words trailed off in the withering blaze of Joseph's eyes.

"Tell her that!" Joseph said bitterly.

"Joseph, she's dead." Matthew's voice was gentle, insistent.

"I know!" Joseph shouted, ending in a sob. He struggled for breath. They were all dead: his mother and father, Sebastian Allard, the man who had brought the treaty from Germany in the first place, Owen Cullingford, Charlie Gee, that damn reporter in his arrogance, Theo Blaine, Shanley Corcoran, Tucky Nunn, half the men of the Cambridgeshire regiment that he had grown up with, the young men from St. John's College, half the armies of Europe torn and blinded and choked in their own blood. Now Monique: stupidly, senselessly murdered after all she had done for her own people. It was unbearable.

He was too late to save her, or to save those stupid, ugly people from their own fate. They could not undo what they had done. Had he really helped anyone? Those who believed, or those who didn't? The sick, the frightened, the hopeless, anyone at all?

He had kept a grip on all the despair that threatened him like a towering, consuming darkness all the years of war. He had not wept for his own pain, but now it could not be denied. It tore through him like a storm, sweeping reason, self-mastery, and consciousness of others away like a tidal wave. He wept for all of them: every lost and terrified soul of the last dreadful years. Matthew held him, and the crowd swirled around, confused and ashamed, frightened by the power of what they had done. Suddenly they understood that it was irretrievable, and one by one they also saw that it was undeniable. Ignorance did not pardon them.

Matthew took Joseph back to the ambulance. Someone brought him a stiff jolt of cognac. It burned his throat and set a deep fire in his stomach. He was aware of people coming and going.

Matthew left, and it was Lizzie who sat beside him. She said nothing, simply held his hands. He had no idea where anyone else was, or what they were doing.

Finally his mind cleared and the vision of Monique's bleeding, disfigured face faded from his vision. He began to think, to remember other people, other losses that were also what he grieved for, young men whose deaths would always be woven into his mind and his memory.

He had wanted to serve, to lessen the suffering, to give people the hope and the love of God in the darkest places they would pass through. He would have given his own life had it been asked, but it had not. He was barely even injured, except the once in 1916.

He had promised God in the beginning that he would keep faith, but he would not attempt to feel everyone's grief. That he could not bear. It was too much to ask of anyone.

But in Gethsemane, that was exactly what Christ had asked—"Watch with me." It was what He asked of everyone.

Joseph remembered all the men he had sat with in their pain, their fear, their loneliness, their acceptance of death. He had cared intensely. So often all he could do was simply be there. He could not ease their agony, take away their terror of mutilation, of failure, of the last unknown step of death. He could not promise victory, or offer any reasons for the horror of it, or explain why God allowed such hell to be.

He had crouched in the mud of no-man's-land, freezing and sodden wet, smelled the stink of decaying flesh, of gas, of death, and all he could do was promise "I will not leave you."

And in that moment it came to him with absolute certainty that what he wanted, needed, was to stay with Lizzie. He could do it, and love the child because it was hers, and because it needed to be loved, as everyone needs to be. He could give it the love his father had given him: wholeheartedly, generously, because he wanted to. He—or she—would never for an instant imagine that it was the product of violence or pain. The child would not be unwanted, so it would never feel pain more deeply than the growing pains all humans know, the finding of identity in the world.

He turned to Lizzie and smiled, then pulled his hands from hers, wincing as his lacerated skin was touched, then took hers again and held them gently, more firmly. "When we get home," he said, "there'll be a lot to do, a lot of people who'll need help, and more courage than they may think they have now. There are those wounded not only in body, but in heart and hope as well. There'll be disappointments, changes that are very difficult to accept. I expect there will be injustices and a great deal of lone-liness. The bad things of war will be gone, but so will the good things: the friendships, the purpose, the knowledge of who you are and what you are doing, and that it matters."

"I know," she answered him. "I had planned to go on nursing . . . un-til . . ." She stopped, a slow color working up her cheeks. She was afraid of pity, and he saw it in her eyes.

How could he ask her to marry him without her fearing, even for an instant, that that was what it was—pity, not love?

"I would very much rather that you helped me," he told her. "I am not sure that I can do it without you, and I am perfectly certain that I don't wish to. But with you, and the child, I might make a reasonably good job of it. I've learned something about what a real ministry is."

She looked at him, searching his eyes slowly, very carefully.

He smiled, knowing there was nothing in him that he needed to hide from her. She knew his weaknesses already, as he knew hers, and he knew that in the end they would bind them together, not apart.

"I think that would be a good idea," she said at last. "We might make quite a passable job of it."

Happiness opened up inside him like a great dawning light. He leaned forward and kissed her, and realized with surprise how long he had wanted to do that, and how sweet it was.

He had only just let her go when Matthew opened the door.

"Are you all right?" Matthew asked, then decided that the question was unnecessary.

"Yes . . . thank you," Joseph replied. "We should go. We can't be far from the coast now, but there isn't much time."

"We've got a lot more help," Matthew told him. "Food, petrol, and someone to show us the best roads. We could make it tonight."

Joseph was startled. "How did you do that?"

"Guilt," Matthew answered simply. "They felt like hell."

Joseph was embarrassed. For the first time in years he had completely lost control of himself. He had wanted to kill the man who had kicked Monique. He might have, if Matthew had not stopped him. That was a frightening thought. He had had no idea that there was so much rage in-side him, or bottled-up pain.

"The man I . . . hit. Is he all right?"

Matthew rolled his eyes. "He'll live, but you broke his nose and jaw and two or three ribs. Good thing he's fairly heavily built, or you might have done worse. You took him totally by surprise. He didn't imagine that the priest would try to kill him, or you might not have come out of it so well."

"You don't need to belabor the point," Joseph said a little tartly. "His behavior was unforgivable."

"That rather is the point, Joe." Matthew looked at him steadily, not moving from the spot where he stood. "You can't leave them like this. You've pretty well consigned them to hell and left them in no doubt that you meant it. That isn't how you'd like it to stay." He said it with certainty, no shadow in his eyes.

Joseph did not want to go back and face them again. It was deeply embarrassing, and he did not forgive them for what they had done to Monique. He could not tell them it was excusable. It would betray his own beliefs, and no one with an ounce of sense would believe him anyway.

"I can't offer them any forgiveness," he said aloud. "There's no penance I know of that's going to heal what they just did. To say there is would be a lie."

"There's always a way back, Joe, from anywhere," Matthew replied. "You told me that. If you can't help them, what hope is there for any of us?"

"It's time to begin," Lizzie said, touching Joseph's hand lightly. "You don't have to lie to them. Tell them how hard it will be, just don't say it's impossible."

He climbed out of the ambulance, standing a little unsteadily at first, then turned and thanked her. Matthew was waiting. He followed him to where the villagers were gathered together with a pile of food in boxes and three cans of petrol. They were the most precious things they had; perhaps a week's supply. There were also spark plugs and a small tin of oil. They looked frightened, and hopeful.

Suddenly Joseph wanted to tell them they were forgiven, but that would be weariness, gratitude, and pity speaking, the desire to escape, and none of those made it the right thing to do. It would be facile, an escape for himself.

"Thank you," he said to them, looking at the pile. "We know what a great gift all of this is, and how much it represents of what you have. I would like to say that it will redeem you from what you did to Monique, but that would not be true. You don't deserve that. Like all of us, you need honesty. The way back from such a sin is longer and far harder than that, which you know as well as I do. But never forget that the way does exist, and you can walk it if you wish to enough. I can't tell you how to find it, because I don't know. But your chance to pay the price will come, if you want it enough to look for it, and accept it."

They stared at him, shifting awkwardly from foot to foot. No one spoke. Hope sprang to life in one or two faces. In others it died. They had been expecting something easier.

"I apologize for standing in judgment of you," Joseph went on. "I have no right to. That is something you will have to do for yourselves. You know what you did, and why, and what drove you. And you know she didn't deserve it. Begin by not lying to yourselves. What I say is true, for you, for me, for everyone."

One of the older men nodded. Then he turned to others, and they signaled agreement also. They said their goodbyes formally, and seemed relieved to see the ambulance begin its journey to the coast, with one young woman of the village in the cab beside Judith to guide them for the next ten miles. No one asked how she would get back.

They reached the harbor a little after sundown. The salt wind off the sea smelled clean and felt bitterly cold, but there was an excitement to the taste of it, an energy in the wind and tide.

It took considerable bargaining, and ultimately a threat on Matthew's part, but by midnight they were on their way across the channel. Most of them attempted to sleep, but Matthew paced the deck looking out over the dark water. The foam rose and fell, patterns shifting on the surface. He remembered standing like this on the deck of the *Cormorant*, before the Battle of Jutland, knowing that any moment it could erupt in white water, then flame and inconceivable noise. There would be twisted metal, screams, the smell of burning corticine, and juddering, pitching decks as the ship reeled. Always at the end lay the threat of being swallowed by that black sea and sucked down, never to be released.

There were only days to go until the end, and yet ships were still being sunk, all hands lost. It was a kind of wild madness he did not understand. What was there left to win or lose now? Only hate, the most pointless of all passions.

He kept looking ahead, trying to discern the dark outline of land. They were making for Harwich, not Dover, so there would be no familiar cliffs to see, but they had been grateful to take the first transport that would take them and the ambulance, too. They couldn't have simply abandoned the vehicle. It would be an added difficulty to try to get rail transport with as little money as they had been able to gather, and on a crowded train it might be impossible to conceal the fact that Schenckendorff was German.

It was still before dawn when at last he saw the low, black line of land ahead. An hour later they were on the windswept quay with the ambulance—which, to their intense relief, had started after the third attempt.

"We should be in London by early afternoon, unless we run into major difficulties," Matthew said, shivering as the wind blew spray up off the water. They were all tired, and the cold bit into them. It was now his responsibility to make certain that they persuaded Shearing, and then the prime minister, of Sandwell's guilt. They would have only one chance, and Sandwell already knew they were coming. The danger was far from over; in fact, this could be the worst part. Victory was so close that emotions that had been held in check for years were now boiling to the surface. There was hope and a desperate fragility almost perceptible in the air.

Would Sandwell try again? Of course. But how? Overt violence would be harder now that they were in England. Anything he did would have to look like an accident. Was it possible that Sandwell did not yet know that Hampton had failed? Probably not. He would have some prearranged signal, a time to contact each other. Hampton's silence would be answer enough.

"We need to get to London as soon as we can," he said aloud. "Thank heaven we don't need to use trains, or risk getting separated or lost in a crowd, where we'd be far more vulnerable."

He saw Lizzie start, and realized she had thought they were already safe. She was standing next to Joseph, and unconsciously she moved closer to him.

"Sorry," Matthew said briefly. "He'll assume we are home, and he knows what for. He'll have worked out by now that Hampton failed. We need to keep close together and on our guard. I've still got Hampton's gun, but I don't imagine any attack will be as obvious as that." He turned to Mason. "You know him. What's your best guess as to what he'll do now?"

Mason thought for several moments. "He might try to stop us between here and London. It would be too good a chance to miss, unless he has no one he can trust . . ."

"We can't rely on that," Joseph said instantly.

"Agreed," Matthew replied. "Then maybe we'd better travel separately. Finding three or four men to reach us would be very much harder. And since we've traveled together so far, he won't be expecting it."

"That's not all," Mason went on. "There's only one thing we can do in the end, which is accuse him openly. He'll be expecting that. It's the last throw of the dice left, so to speak. He'll be prepared for it. I don't know whether he'll try to say the Peacemaker is someone else." He smiled with bitter amusement. "Possibly even me. He might do it well enough to confuse events for a while. Or he might deny that there was ever such a conspiracy at all. That's why we need to have the original treaty that your father took in 1914." He turned to Joseph. "You still have it in Cambridgeshire, don't you?"

Matthew felt a moment of alarm. They were so close to the Peacemaker at last, but was it possible that there was a final twist and it was not

Sandwell—and Mason's slight, almost halfhearted jest was the truth? Was Mason himself the leader, and perhaps Sandwell and Schenckendorff followers? No, that was ridiculous. Mason was in love with Judith, deeply in love. He was not attempting to hide it now: This was the last time they would have together.

He looked at Joseph, wanting to know his thoughts, wishing he could speak to him alone.

Mason was waiting.

"Joe—" Matthew started.

"Yes," Joseph cut in. "I know where it is."

Too late. They were committed. Had Joseph thought of Mason's possible complicity, or was his religious naïveté still too powerful for him to consider that the man Judith loved could yet betray them?

"Better not tell us where," Matthew said aloud. "That way we can't accidentally reveal it."

Mason smiled. "Understood," he said wryly. "Joseph should get the treaty and we'll all meet somewhere in London. Perhaps Judith and I should travel together, and Matthew with Schenckendorff, and Lizzie with them to see to Schenckendorff's foot. You take the ambulance. You can drive it, can't you?" The last question was directed toward Matthew.

Matthew hesitated. He did not want Mason to direct what they did, and yet he could not think of a better alternative. If they stayed together, they were one target. They could not hope to convince Lloyd George without Schenckendorff, Mason, and the treaty. It had to be either he or Joseph who went to St. Giles to get the treaty from the gunroom. Judith didn't know one end of a gun from the other, and the last thing he would allow was for Mason to go with her.

"Right," he said decisively. "I'll take the ambulance with Lizzie and Schenckendorff and I'll meet you at my flat. Judith and Mason go by train to London. Joseph, take the train to Cambridge and then to St. Giles. We'll wait for you in London. Telephone me, but not from St. Giles."

Goodbyes were brief as they pulled up outside the railway station. Judith and Mason went to wait for the first train to London, Joseph to Cambridge.

As Joseph sat by the window—given a seat willingly because of his uniform—he watched the countryside slip past him. For a moment he could delude himself that nothing had changed. The soft slopes of the land rolled away to the horizon, dotted with occasional copses of trees. The late-harvest fields were stubble gold, one or two plowed ready for a winter crop, the earth dark and shining, black soil rich. The villages looked as they always had: many roofs steeply thatched; square church towers, Saxon solid; little streets winding. Here and there he saw the flash of light on a duck pond in the center of a green. The leaves were bronze where they remained. Most were already shed in copper-colored drifts on the ground.

He ached with a love for the ancient, familiar beauty of it. To come and go as he wished, here in these lanes and across this land, was what they had fought and died for. It was far from perfect, because people made mistakes, but there was a freedom here that had been learned and paid for over the centuries. It was the right—not only in law but also in practice—to disagree, to be different, inventive, sometimes to be wrong, and still be a part of the fabric that was treasured. There was honor and tolerance throughout all the errors and wrongs of history, and that must be saved, whatever the cost.

They pulled into Cambridge station, and he asked about the next train to St. Giles. It was too long to wait for. It would take him hours to get there and back. Nor did he have sufficient money. Even as it was, he was going to have to borrow the return fare, Cambridge to London, from Hannah. He would not even entertain the thought that she might not be home.

His mind raced. Who could he ask to drive him, with precious petrol, first to St. Giles, and then back to Cambridge? Who did he know?

St. John's. That was the only answer. There must be somebody there he still knew. The question was, would they have a car, and petrol to put in it? Aidan Thyer, the master of St. John's, would be his best chance, and there was no time to waste starting with others he might prefer. He remembered ruefully that Thyer was one of those he had suspected of being the Peacemaker. He had never been ruled out. The only thing he could do now was trust that Schenckendorff was telling the truth, and Mason also. Good men could lie, if the cause was great enough; he knew and understood that, but it was too late to hedge his bet.

He walked rapidly through the ancient streets, past the colleges he had known and loved so long. Most of them were centuries old, built of towering stone, carved, bearing their coats of arms proudly. Behind them the green grass of the Backs sloped down to the river where four summers ago young men had pushed flat-bottomed boats along the quiet waters. Pretty girls had sat in the sterns trailing their fingers in the stream, muslin dresses stirred by the breeze, hats shading their faces. Now there were no young men in sight, and girls had short hair, and skirts not far below their knees, and they were working on buses, in factories, and on the land. How short a time it had taken for the world to change utterly.

The Master's House at St. John's looked exactly as it always had, probably for at least three hundred years. The quad was silent. There were no leaves on the trees.

He knocked on the door. If Aidan and Connie were in, they would answer it themselves, since nobody had servants anymore. The silence closed in around him. Would they still even have a car? If they did, would Aidan be willing to help Joseph? Would he just drop everything, ask no questions, and give up his day to drive Joseph to St. Giles, wait, then bring him back?

What if he was one of those who sympathized with the Peacemaker? Victory could slip out of their hands at any moment up to the very last.

The door opened. It was Aidan Thyer himself. He still looked elegant and faintly mystified, as if he had sustained some unexpected wound and was wondering how to deal with it. Was it still because he loved Connie more than she could ever love him? Or was it the loss of so many of his young men before they had fulfilled the promise or the hope of their lives?

"Joseph?" he said in amazement. "Joseph Reavley! My dear fellow, come in." He stepped back, holding the door wide. The light shone on his pale hair and the subtle lines of his face. "What can I do for you? Is it acceptable to ask what you are doing home so soon before the end? I hope it is not bad news of your family?" Sudden deep concern shadowed his eyes.

"No, thank you." Joseph followed him inside. "We are all fine, so far as I know. But I have an urgent errand. I need to get to St. Giles as soon as I can, and then back to the station to London. It is very urgent indeed, and I need help." There was no time to waste in prevarication, and he would not have known how to do that anyway. "Can you drive me, please? Or if you can't, do you know someone who would?"

Thyer regarded him with concern. "Of course I will. Are you sure you are all right?"

"Yes." Then suddenly it occurred to him that Thyer might wonder if one of the Cambridge students he knew was in trouble. "It's not personal business at all," he added. "It's something I have to collect and get to London today."

Thyer nodded. "Would you like anything to eat first, or even to drink? You look as if you have been up all night."

"Yes, I daresay I do," Joseph agreed with a smile. "But I haven't time. Perhaps after."

"I'll get the keys and tell Connie. She'll be glad to hear that you at least are all right."

Thyer returned a few moments later, accompanied by his wife. As always, Connie was delighted to see Joseph, but she understood that it could be no more than hello and goodbye. She had made a quick sandwich for him and offered it to him now, wrapped in a piece of paper.

"Only bread and what I would like to call pâté, but it's really meat paste," she apologized.

He thanked her and suddenly realized he was ravenously hungry.

She watched him, smiling, and handed him a glass of lemonade, knowing that anything hot to drink would take possibly more time than he was willing to afford.

Standing just inside the Master's House, looking at Connie, gave Joseph a startling sense of timelessness. She was still beautiful in her own warm, generous way. And there was still the restlessness in her eyes, although the edge of it had softened, and she looked toward Thyer more often than he remembered her doing before.

It was as if only months had passed since he had stood here in the summer of 1914, speaking of war and peace with such innocence. No one had imagined that the world could change so much in so short a time. The past they had known was gone forever. He knew that here in its fullness for the first time. In this quiet hallway looking into the quad where nothing changed, he realized the enormity of the change in everything else.

"Joseph?" Thyer asked. "Are you ready?"

"Yes . . . thank you." Joseph gave the empty glass back to Connie and bid her goodbye. He followed Thyer across the first quad and then the second into the street to where the car was parked.

The drive to St. Giles was swift. Not once did Thyer ask him what the purpose was of his sudden and urgent journey; nor did they talk of those they knew who were dead. Instead he discussed politics, in particular the character of Lloyd George, and the new ideas of widening the political franchise to include all men, property owners or not, and even many women.

"Times are changing at an extraordinary pace," he said with a slight frown. "I hope we can keep up with them without too many casualties. The men coming home aren't going to recognize the land they left behind, and may possibly not like it entirely. Women have all kinds of jobs, and we need them to keep doing them. We can't now send them back to the kitchen." He shook his head slightly. "A great number of them will not marry because there is no one for them to have. They have no choice but to earn their own way. We cannot make that impossible for them."

Joseph did not reply.

"And very few places for servants. We've learned to do without them," Thyer went on. "Jack's as good as his master. We discovered that in the trenches. There are an awful lot of 'Jacks' to whom we owe our lives. I daresay you know that better than I do."

Joseph smiled and agreed. They were racing through the November countryside at a far higher speed than Joseph would have expected from the master. He had always thought of him as a trifle staid, a scholar with little action in him. Perhaps he had been wrong.

They passed the quiet fields of the farm where Charlie and Barshey Gee had grown up, then that of Snowy and Tucky Nunn. The blacksmith's forge was open, Plugger Arnold's father bent over the anvil. It was all desperately familiar, and Joseph would have given all he possessed if the men he had known and loved could have come home again with him.

The street was quiet. There were half a dozen women in it, coats closed tight against the wind. The green was deserted, the duck pond flat and bright in the momentary sun.

They pulled up outside the house where Joseph had grown up, from which John and Alys Reavley had left that morning the world had changed, when Gavrilo Princip had fired a shot in Sarajevo that had ended history and begun the present.

"I won't be long," Joseph said briefly. "One day I'll tell you exactly what all this is about." He climbed out, walked a little shakily to the door, and knocked. He had already made up his mind that, if Hannah was not home, he would break in and leave her a note to explain what he had done.

He had raised his hand to knock again when the door opened. She stood inside. She looked so like their mother that for a moment Joseph was stunned, just as taken aback as she was. Then she threw herself into his arms and hugged him, and he held her hard and close.

"It's all right," he said, still holding her. "I've come for the treaty. We know who the Peacemaker is, and we have to prove it to Lloyd George, and then it will be over. I have dozens of things to tell you, but Matthew and Judith are waiting for me in London, and there's no time now."

She pulled back and stared at him. "Who is it?"

"Dermot Sandwell."

"The minister? It can't be!"

"Now you see why I have to prove it."

She did not argue. She could see the certainty in his face, and simply stood back and followed him through the house to the gunroom at the back. The door was locked, as it had been since 1914. He opened it, took down his father's old punt gun and broke it, then very carefully eased out the rolled-up piece of paper from inside the barrel.

"Has that been there all the time?" she asked in amazement.

"Yes. That's where Father hid it. We thought it the safest place, since they had searched the house during the funeral, remember?"

"You didn't tell me!"

"Safer for you not to know." He smiled briefly. "Give my love to Tom and Luke and Jenny. It'll all be over in a matter of days now. Then we can begin to build again and help the people who've been hurt more than they know how to bear."

"A ministry again?" There was light in her face.

"Yes. I'm going to marry Lizzie Blaine."

She smiled. "Good. Very good. I thought you might."

He kissed her quickly on the cheek, then put the treaty into the inside of his tunic and strode back to the car.

One day he would tell Aidan Thyer at least some of the truth, but not now. At the station he thanked him again, then went immediately to the platform to catch the next Cambridge-to-London train. The journey still held the vestige of a sense of escape, of which he was ashamed. He should not have suspected Thyer, and yet he had a definite sense of relief to be alone again, anonymous among the other uniforms scattered here and there. Around him were men on leave and men wounded, some too seriously to ever return to battle. It could be months, or even years, before the last stragglers returned. And of course so many would not.

When the train pulled into London, he alit. He paid for the extravagance of a taxi, which earned a few black looks, since he was obviously able-bodied and apparently didn't need it.

The city looked weary, and even in the fitful sunlight there was a grayness to it. There were hardly any men in the streets except the old and the very young. There were women in all sorts of places that a couple of years ago would have been unthinkable: driving buses and lorries, even in police uniform. They looked busy, competent. The few who were fashionable had changed beyond recognition. The feminine glamour that was designed for idleness was utterly gone. Now beauty was subdued and extremely practical—short skirts, quiet colors.

The air seemed charged with emotion. A kind of expectancy lay behind the simplest exchange: a request for directions, the purchase of a newspaper. He felt a moment of terrible pity for them, a fear that nothing was going to live up to the dream of what peace would be like when it came at last.

Very soon, when armistice was announced, he expected the womenfolk to experience an almost unbearable excitement, anticipating welcoming home their men. Then, as they settled into a new life, they would have to rise to the challenge of redefining their roles as men and women, and their positions in society.

There was nothing in his life sweeter and more precious than the hope that Lizzie would be with him, sharing the work of rebuilding individual lives, communities again, helping people come to terms with change and loss.

The taxi stopped a block away from Calder Shearing's office, where

Matthew had told him to go. He paid and got out, thanking the man, then turned and walked as swiftly as he could, grateful that the taxi had pulled away from the curb. He went to the entrance and was admitted as soon as he identified himself.

He was kept waiting in the outer room only moments before Matthew appeared, his face filled with relief. "Got it?" he asked.

"Of course. Is everyone here?"

"Yes. No trouble?"

"None at all. You?"

Matthew smiled. "Nothing that matters now."

"What happened?" Joseph demanded.

"Difficulty getting petrol," Matthew replied. "Once we were stopped by police, and I was terrified it was another attempt by the Peacemaker, but it was just because I was going too fast. Come upstairs and we'll show Shearing the treaty." He turned and led the way.

Inside Shearing's office Judith, Lizzie, Mason, and Schenckendorff were already waiting. Calder Shearing stood behind his desk, his face dark and tense, his eyes bright.

Wordlessly, Joseph handed him the treaty between the kaiser of Germany and the king of England with which the Peacemaker had proposed to create an Anglo-German empire to dominate the world, and to achieve peace by betraying France and the Low Countries to Germany, with Britain taking back all the old empire, including the Americas.

Shearing read it, his face filling first with quiet, bitter amazement, and then with fury. He picked up his telephone and placed a call to No. 10, Downing Street. When he was finished he looked at them one by one. "Are you ready, gentlemen?" he asked, although his glance included Judith and Lizzie. "The prime minister will see us."

TWELVE

*I*n deference to Schenckendorff's injured foot—which was still severely painful—they traveled in two cars. Alighting outside No. 10, Downing Street, they were shown in immediately.

David Lloyd George was not a tall man, but he had a dynamism of character and a music in his voice that commanded attention. His inner energy, even after the terrible years of struggle, filled and dominated the room. He looked from one to the other of them. His main interest fell first on Mason, then on Schenckendorff, but he did not fail to notice the women, especially Judith. He had never in his life failed to perceive the beauty of a woman, and far too seldom had he failed to enjoy it as fully as opportunity allowed.

"Well?" he asked Shearing. "This had better be quick, and it had better be damn good! Which of you is going to explain to me what the devil you are talking about?"

Shearing indicated Matthew. "Lieutenant Colonel Matthew Reavley, one of my men." He did not bother to introduce the others yet. They could be mentioned as their parts in the story arose.

Matthew stepped forward. "Sir—"

"Speak, man!" Lloyd George commanded, waving his hand to order the rest of them to sit—or as many of them as there were chairs for. "Forget the niceties. What is this tale of yours?"

Matthew began. "On the night of June 27, 1914, my father, John Reavley, telephoned me from St. Giles in Cambridgeshire to say that he had found a document that could change the history of the world, and shame Britain forever, if it were put into effect. He said he would bring it to me the following day."

Lloyd George blinked. "Twenty-seventh of June, 1914?"

"Yes, sir. My mother and father set out the next day, and were murdered on the way, in a car accident. That was, as you know, the same day as the assassination of the archduke and duchess in Sarajevo. After much difficulty and more tragic murders, my brother, Joseph, and I found where my father hid the document. We read it and replaced it where it was."

"Why in God's name—" After a glance at Shearing's face, Lloyd George stopped abruptly. "What was it, and why does it matter now?"

Wordlessly Joseph took the treaty out of his inner pocket and spread it on the table before the prime minister.

Lloyd George read it. The blood drained from his face, leaving it as white as his hair. "God Almighty!" he said in a shaking voice. He swallowed and looked up at Joseph, still standing in front of him. "You had this throughout the war?"

"Yes, sir. We had no idea who was behind it, only that he had great power and was willing to murder to put this plan into effect. He tried all through the war to bring about an Allied surrender so that this empire of his could still come about. We code-named him 'the Peacemaker' because we believed that the avoidance of war was his purpose, even if it meant robbing us of both freedom and honor to do so. We now know that he wishes to influence the terms of the armistice so that Germany can rise again quickly and rebuild its armies, and the plan still be carried through."

"Never!" Lloyd George said instantly. "We must find out who he is and hang him as a traitor."

Matthew resumed the story. "We have tried all through the war to do that, sir. Only now have we succeeded, and only because some of the men who believed in peace and were unaware of the true extent of the price he was prepared to pay for it have finally seen what he is, and are willing to come forward to unmask him, regardless of the cost to themselves."

Lloyd George turned instantly to Schenckendorff, the one man in the room about whom he knew nothing. He wore a British volunteer uniform, but the command in his bearing, and the obviously painful injury to his foot, which was still heavily bandaged, marked him as other than he seemed.

Schenckendorff stood up, without the slightest wince even as he put his weight on his foot, and bowed. His face was tight and pale. "Manfred von Schenckendorff, sir. It was I who obtained the kaiser's signature to the treaty. At the time I believed it was for the peace of Europe and so that we might rule without war for all the years to come. Now I know that that dream was never possible. I have seen both your country and my own lose the best men of a generation, and wash the earth in blood. I have come through the lines to where Chaplain Reavley fought in Ypres, in order to expose my cousin, my former British ally, so this never happens again. Because if he is not stopped, he will engineer a peace that is only a hiatus between this war and the next."

"Your cousin?" Lloyd George asked tensely.

"Dermot Sandwell. His mother and mine were sisters," Schenckendorff replied. Then, seeing the disbelief in Lloyd George's face, he added, "Beautiful women, Irish, not English or German."

"For God's sake!" Lloyd George exploded. "Sandwell's one of the best, most loyal men we have! That's preposterous." He looked at Shearing with increasing anger. "What possessed you to believe this poppycock, man? Have you no more sense—"

Mason stepped forward, freeing himself from Judith's arm. He stood to the right of Schenckendorff, facing the prime minister. His voice shook as he began to speak, then gathered emotion and strength.

"My name is Richard Mason, sir, war correspondent. As a young man I reported on the Boer War and was horrified beyond my power or ability ever to forget by the brutality and waste of life I saw there. So was Dermot Sandwell. I met him shortly afterward, and we both swore that such slaughter should never happen again. I believed that there must be a better way, even if it had to be brought about by deceit and a conspiracy of men who had more power than our soldiers or politicians. I was prepared to give my life to that cause. All through the war I reported to Sandwell to help at least part of his activities, in an attempt to bring the carnage to an end, and create a peace that would last."

Lloyd George stared at him in incredulity and something close to dismay.

"What Colonel Schenckendorff says is true, sir," Mason continued. "I could give you chapter and verse of it, were there time, but there isn't. Colonel Schenckendorff and I are willing to give our lives to pay the price of our delusion. Matthew, Joseph, and Judith Reavley have followed in the steps of their father to lay this open and show that we fight our wars, we do not appease. Their passion and belief have showed now that it can and must be done. I will face Sandwell. He cannot deny me; I know far too much."

Lloyd George sighed, his face masked with a deep grief. It was clear that he no longer denied it to himself.

There was a deferential but insistent knocking on the door.

"What is it?" he demanded.

A man put his head around it. "Mr. Sandwell is here, sir."

"Good! Just the man I want. Send him in," Lloyd George ordered. "And have the policeman at the door come inside."

The man looked startled.

"Do it!" Lloyd George shouted at him.

A moment later the door opened again and Dermot Sandwell came into the room. He was tall and startlingly elegant. His fair hair was polished smooth, his eyes a curious, pale, brilliant blue. He looked first at the prime minister, then at Mason and Schenckendorff. The others he ignored. His face, already lean, seemed to tighten and fade to a pallor so bleached he looked about to faint, but he stood rigidly straight.

The door behind him closed with a sharp snick.

It was Schenckendorff who spoke. His pronunciation was precise, his English so perfect it was almost without accent. Only the pain thickened his voice. "It is over, Dermot. The slaughter of nations and the murder of individuals has come to an end, and those of us who tried to force on them a peace without honor must pay the price. I saw the same vision as you did, in the beginning, but now it is finished. We cannot do this again; we must not. If you will not stop yourself, then I will stop you."

Sandwell stared at him, the shock in his face turning to scalding contempt. "Coward," he said simply. "I trusted you with a vision of Europe without war, and you have betrayed me. If we had succeeded, if that idiot John Reavley had had a larger mind unfettered by the petty prejudices of nationalism, we could have saved the lives of thirty million men who now lie dead or mutilated across the world. Think of that, Manfred, when you weep for Germany. We were betrayed in the beginning by lesser men, too blinded by what they thought was patriotism to see the whole of humanity. Now it seems I stand alone. That does not make me any the less right."

He turned to face the prime minister, then caught sight of Mason. "And it seems you have turned out to be no more than a Little Englander after all, despite the horror and the death that you have seen. In the end you ran back to your own small square of the earth, blind to the rest of it." He looked at Joseph. "Of you I expected no better. You are your father's son. We might have hoped that a man who professes a Christian religion would have a larger view, but we hoped in vain."

Lloyd George rose to his feet. "I trusted you, Dermot. It pains me to find you a traitor of such monumental proportions. You will hang for this."

Sandwell gave a bark of laughter. "Don't be absurd! You dare not prosecute me. What will you say? That I tried to save the world from this ... this charnel house of blood and ruin, but I failed because of the shortsightedness of a few men who thought more of England than they did of humanity? And now that you have won, and we are up to our knees in the corpses of our own men, you are going to kill me, too, because I would have saved them? How long do you think an exhausted and bereaved country will thank you for that?"

"Your proposed treaty was iniquitous," Lloyd George said bitterly. "It would have been a peace without honor."

Sandwell's eyebrows rose high over his brilliant eyes. "Tell that to the millions of women with fathers, uncles, brothers, husbands, and sons whose broken bodies lie buried in the fields of France and Belgium. See if they agree with you."

Lloyd George's hands closed over the piece of paper, which had rolled back upon itself after four and a half years inside the barrel of the punt gun.

Sandwell stared at it as he finally realized what it was. He made a movement toward it, then froze. Very slowly he turned to Matthew.

"Yes," Matthew replied, staring back at him. "We had it all the time. My father hid it where all your searches failed to find it."

"Then the blood of millions is on your hands," Sandwell replied between his teeth. "The best and the bravest of the nations of the earth lie crushed beneath the weight of your stupidity."

"You are wrong," Joseph answered him with absolute conviction. "I do not believe our king would have signed it, but if he had, it would not have bound us, not all of us. There would always have been some who would pay for the freedom for us to make our own laws, speak our differences aloud, follow the faith we choose, make our own mistakes, laugh at ourselves and try again. If we pay with our lives, then so be it. We will not pay with the slow death of our minds or the withering of our souls."

"You patronizing idiot!" Sandwell spat at him. "Do you think anybody cares for that kind of empty sermon now? Death is real! It's broken bodies, men blinded, crippled, choked on their own blood! It's corpses riddled with bullets, frozen to death. It's not high-minded valor, you fool! Look at reality! Say that to the mutilated, the blind if you dare!"

"I dare," Joseph replied unflinchingly. "I know them as you never will, or you would not have misjudged them so completely. Again and again you were wrong. You did not understand their courage, their loyalty, their friendship, their love of the right to come and go as they like, to keep their ancient customs, the little ways that make life sweet. Men and nations will always seek the right to make their own choices, whatever the cost. You can guide, but you cannot rule. You misjudged humanity in general, and Britain in particular.

"But worse than that, and far worse, you confused the ends with the means until they became one in your mind. You destroyed the very spark of life that you wanted to give us. Without the freedom to be right or wrong, to choose your own way rather than the way forced upon you, there is no virtue, no courage, no honor or laughter or love worth having. Men with far less intellect than yours know this in their blood and their bones, and they will die rather than sell it to you and your dreams of dominion. And that is what they have become—dreams. It is not the wisdom or the intent of power that corrupts, it is the totality of power that can no longer be curbed."

Sandwell stared at Joseph with a hatred so violent, his whole slender body trembled with it, then he quickly stepped toward him and hit him as hard as he could.

Joseph staggered backward, overbalanced, and fell, his head striking the floor with a crack. He lay still.

Judith went ashen. Lizzie drew in her breath with a sob and started forward, but Matthew blocked her way.

Sandwell moved forward to hit Joseph again. Matthew suddenly saw in Joseph's motionless body all the dead men he had loved: his father, Sebastian Allard, Owen Cullingford, and all the others once full of passion and dreams, who had talked and laughed and cared so much. He struck Sandwell in the middle of the back and, as the man swayed, caught him and spun him around. He hit him with the blow he had been taught and never expected to use, hard under the nose, driving the bone into his brain.

Sandwell slithered to the floor, and when Matthew bent over him he was not breathing. Without rising to his feet Matthew turned to his brother. Lizzie was beside him. Joseph was coughing, struggling to get his breath and to sit up. He looked dazed and unsteady, but unquestionably alive.

Matthew was overcome by a wave of relief so intense he felt dizzy with it himself. He realized that for an instant he had thought Joseph was dead. The crack of bone on the hard wooden floor had filled him with a fear just like the terrible grief he had felt for his father.

"Joe?" he said huskily.

Joseph groaned and put a hand to his head, then stared beyond Matthew to the Peacemaker lying on the floor. "You hit him," he observed. "Thank you. I think I really angered him. He wanted to kill me."

Matthew looked at the figure almost at his feet, sprawled out, one leg under the other. He seemed smaller than when standing up. His brilliant eyes were open and staring sightlessly.

"He is dead," Schenckendorff said quietly. "I think perhaps that is a good thing." He looked at Joseph as he was being helped into a chair by Lizzie and Matthew. "I hope you are not badly hurt. You are quite right: You angered him, because what you said is true. Great men use power as little as possible. It takes supreme humility to allow others to disagree and to make their own mistakes. The right to be wrong is worth dying to protect, because without it all our virtues are empty. What we have not paid for slips through our fingers, because we do not value it enough to do what is necessary to keep it." He held out his hand to Joseph.

Joseph reached up to take it, and clasped it tightly.

Schenckendorff stood to attention and faced Lloyd George.

"I am at your service, sir," he said stiffly.

Lloyd George was still standing, pale-faced. "Thank you," he said simply. "You are a prisoner of war. You will be treated accordingly, and in time repatriated. I am mindful of how much we owe you, and it will not be forgotten." He walked to the door and spoke to the man outside.

Minutes later Schenckendorff said goodbye to them. Matthew and Joseph saluted him. Two more men came to take the body of the Peacemaker.

"Heart attack," the prime minister told them, even though it was patently untrue. No one argued or made the slightest movement to intervene as the men carried the body out. The door closed behind them, and those left in the room faced the prime minister.

Joseph's head ached appallingly, but his vision had cleared. All he could think of was Judith, and how she would bear it when Mason was arrested. Since she was no blood relation of Mason's, she might not even see him again. Were he in her place, and it was Lizzie who would be taken away to face trial and execution, he would not know how to endure it. And yet there was nothing he could do to help. Mason was as alone as if there were no one else in the building.

Mason stared at Lloyd George, waiting, his face white, eyes steady.

Lloyd George chewed his lip and very slowly shook his head. "This grieves me," he said softly. "You were the bravest and the best of all our war correspondents. You went to every field of conflict. Your words framed the way we at home saw and felt the pain of our men, and their valor. Through your experience we have shared what our men endured, and the spirit they carried with them. You were the voice of those who could not and now never will speak for themselves."

Mason swayed a little. Joseph held Judith's arm to prevent her from going to him.

"We are weary of war," Lloyd George went on. "We are heartsick, bereaved, and frightened of a future that is stranger and more complex and difficult than ever we have faced before. We do not need to know that one of the voices that comforted us and led us through our darkest hours was that of a traitor. I shall hide that—not for your sake, but for the sake of my country. You will never speak of it again. No one in this room will."

He looked from one to the other of them, and saw agreement in their silence.

"Your punishment," he went on, addressing Mason, "is that you will leave these shores and never return. You are no longer an Englishman."

Mason drew his breath in with a gasp, as if he had been struck a blow that took the breath from his body, but he did not complain.

Judith was clinging to Joseph so hard her fingers hurt his arm, but he was aware only of what Mason must be feeling: the absolute and final rejection. He would never again walk the moors and see the wind-riven skies, hear the curlews call, return to the cobbled streets and the familiar speech, take ale with his friends in the village pub.

The silence was thick with the knowledge of what it was to be alone.

Judith let go of Joseph's arm and stepped forward. She touched Mason, and at last he looked at her. She had never seen greater pain.

"I'm coming with you," she said, having made the decision without even questioning it.

"You can't—"

"I'm not asking you," she replied. "I'm telling you. We'll go to America. Start again. There'll be work to do there, too."

He drew in his breath to argue, and changed his mind, and in any case was too overwhelmed to speak. He nodded, gripping her hand so hard she momentarily pulled away. Then he realized what he was doing and was suddenly, passionately gentle. "Thank you" was all he said.

Lloyd George nodded. "Wait outside," he instructed, his voice hoarse with emotion.

When they were gone, he turned to Matthew. "You have done a good job, Reavley. I knew your father. He was a fine man, and honest. He loathed the secret services, but he would have been proud of you. Your country will never know what you have done, or what it may have cost you, but we are in your debt." He held out his hand.

Matthew took it. "Thank you, sir. I hope he would."

Lloyd George nodded. "Don't doubt it. We are in a new age, and those who wield secrets are as necessary to us as those who wield swords." He turned to Lizzie. "Or those who heal, and try to make the best of the damage we have done."

Finally he turned to Joseph. "And you, sir, have kept the faith. You have helped us heal the wounds of the soul. Without that, the rest is pointless. But it is not the end. This is only the middle."

"I know, sir," Joseph replied. "There is a long ministry ahead. But first I must go back to my men in Flanders, before the end."

"Of course you must," Lloyd George agreed. "Be with your regiment."

Outside, in the November dusk, it was time for goodbyes. There was nothing to say. They were used to parting, but nothing ever eased the hurt of it or made the pulling away less like a tearing of the heart. Judith clung long to Matthew, and even longer to Joseph, but still the moment had to come. She walked away beside Mason, her head high. The streetlight caught the bones of her cheeks and the wide, vulnerable mouth, smiling, lips trembling. Then the shadows took them both.

Lizzie kissed Joseph and then moved away, taking Matthew's arm. "We'll see you soon," she said firmly, smiling at Joseph.

Matthew saluted. Joseph returned it, then walked toward the railway station for Dover, and the crossing back to France.

On the morning of November the eleventh Joseph crouched in a new, hastily constructed dugout. It was little more than a foxhole. He stared across the stretch of no-man's-land, far to the east of the old one at Ypres. The guns were still firing. Heavy artillery shells gouged up the earth. Snipers picked off the odd, careless soldier who raised his head too high.

Morel was twenty yards along to the right, Tiddly Wop behind him. The sun caught Snowy Nunn's fair hair.

"Knew you'd come back, Chaplain," Barshey Gee said beside Joseph.

Joseph turned to look at him.

Gunfire roared again, obliterating Barshey's words.

Joseph shook his head to indicate that he had not heard.

"You wouldn't leave us," Barshey repeated in the sudden stillness.

Joseph looked at his watch. It was eleven o'clock.

The silence went on. There was no answering fire. All along the line was silence—everywhere.

Slowly men stood up, tentatively at first, then more and more, until there were tens of thousands of them, as far as the eye could see, in every direction. Someone cheered, and another, and another, until there was a roar that filled the air and echoed across Europe from the mountains to the sea.

About the Author

ANNE PERRY is the bestselling author of the World War I novels *No Graves As Yet, Shoulder the Sky,* and *Angels in the Gloom;* as well as four holiday novels: *A Christmas Journey, A Christmas Visitor, A Christmas Guest,* and *A Christmas Secret.* She is also the creator of two acclaimed series set in Victorian England. Her William Monk novels include *Dark Assassin, The Shifting Tide,* and *Death of a Stranger.* The popular novels featuring Thomas and Charlotte Pitt include *Long Spoon Lane, Seven Dials,* and *Southampton Row.* Anne Perry lives in Scotland. Visit her website at www.anneperry.net.

About the Type

This book was set in Centaur, a typeface designed by the American typographer Bruce Rogers in 1929. Rogers adapted Centaur from the fifteenth-century type of Nicolas Jenson and modified it in 1948 for a cutting by the Monotype Corporation.